D0403388

PALOVERDE

By Jacqueline Briskin

CALIFORNIA GENERATION
AFTERLOVE
RICH FRIENDS
PALOVERDE

PALOVERDE

a novel by
JACQUELINE BRISKIN

McGraw-Hill Book Company
New York · St. Louis · San Francisco
Toronto · Mexico · Düsseldorf

Copyright © 1978 by Jacqueline Briskin.

All rights reserved.
Printed in the United States of America.
No part of this publication may be reproduced, stored in a retrieval system, or
transmitted, in any form or by any means, electronic, mechanical, photocopying,
recording, or otherwise, without the prior written permission of the publisher.

1234567890DODO78321098

LIBRARY OF CONGRESS CATALOGING IN PUBLICATION DATA
Briskin, Jacqueline.
    Paloverde: a novel.
    I. Title.
PZ4.B8587Pal   [PS3552.R49]   813'.5'4   78-15955
ISBN 0-07-007915-3

Book design by Lynn Braswell

For Bert

Long before the house was built, the ledge had been a holy place to Southern California Indians. Perhaps three acres, covered with saffron grasses, stretched between the thighs of hills, and here the peaceable Shoshonean tribes gathered to look down on their gigantic, fertile valley that slipped abruptly into the Pacific. Then a handful of Spaniards strode up and down the western side of the continent, claiming it for their king. Don Tomás García was rewarded by the crown with a carelessly drawn map granting him much of the valley—more miles than many a European princedom. He chose the sacred ledge for his hacienda. He called it Paloverde and his recreation was to stand outside the four-foot-thick adobe walls gazing down on the rich flatland that was now his. In spring, when the tall mustard came up, it covered the heads of his cattle so they could be marked only by movements of the golden flowers. As was customary, Don Tomás slaughtered his herds for tallow and hide, leaving the flesh to the buzzards. He prospered. He added more and more rooms to his hacienda until Paloverde's wideflung wings embraced the plateau. So many coats of lime daubed the long adobe walls that in summer their blazing whiteness hurt the eyes.

After California was gathered into the Union, the American newcomers weighted the tax structure in their own favor. What Don Tomás's son Vincente didn't gamble away, he paid in ruinous taxation. Within ten years the huge rancho was divided up. The family moved into the nearby town, retaining only the hills straddling the homesite. Empty, Paloverde fell into disrepair. Sections of red roof tiles caved, winter downpours washed lime from earthen bricks, and the hacienda began melting back into the ledge.

BOOK 1

The Railroad: 1884

If there is money to be made in Los Angeles, I mean the company to make it.

—Colonel Thaddeus Deane,
Los Angeles General Manager
of the Southern Pacific
Railroad

CHAPTER 1

· I ·

On that September noon in 1884, the fierce white sun trapped the town in quiescent immobility.

The khaki-colored foothills rising to the north were creased with unwavering black. No lizards scurried in the broad, sandy riverbed, no dragonflies hovered above the irrigation ditches that most long-time residents persisted in calling *zanjas*. The new frame houses of the Americans enticed the heat while the older places, with their thick adobe walls, retained none of their normal coolness. The Southern Pacific tracks shone orange as though they were melting. The short business blocks were deserted. No teams were hitched on Main or Spring streets, no customers moved on the wooden sidewalks, though shopkeepers kept them shaded. (On Spring Street, the awnings of Van Vliet's Grocery and Van Vliet's Hardware touched one another in cousinly camaraderie.) Against the Plaza fountain leaned a few Sonorans; in their big sombreros they appeared as rooted to the earth as the wilting pepper trees.

The sunstruck town mingled raw Western ugliness with older, softer Hispanic influences. A little over a hundred years earlier, the eleven founding *pobladores* had grandiosely christened their new home El Pueblo de Nuestra Señora la Reina de Los Angeles de Porcunciula. Under Spanish and Mexican rule the name had been abbreviated to *El Pueblo*—the town. Americans had chosen another part of the long name, and in 1884 the fourteen thousand inhabitants, of whom only half spoke English, universally called it Los Angeles. The gringo mispronunciation was Loss Anjuh-less.

· 2 ·

That blinding afternoon the only activity in town centered around Rosedale Cemetery. There, near an open grave, perhaps three hundred people were gathered, the women shaded by parasols, fanning themselves, the men mopping bared foreheads. This hot spell had lasted well over a week. By now, under normal conditions, Angelenos would have remained limp and exhausted inside their homes or businesses. To draw such a crowd, the presumption would be that the man in the massive bronze coffin was either beloved or greatly respected—or, most likely, both.

Yet the crowd remained ominously clustered to the south of the gaping yellow trench. Many had mounted a low hillock for a better view. None wore black armbands or black satin rosettes in their lapels. Heat-flushed faces gazed with the avidity seen at a public execution. As though fearing contamination, they had hitched their buggies, surreys, Studebaker farm wagons, and phaetons well apart from the black-fringed hearse with its black-plumed horses and the lone mourners' carriage. The pair of fine bays that drew this carriage were also black-plumed; the bridles and harnesses had been adorned with black tassels and black satin draped the windows.

There were no flowers other than the blanket of wilting red roses that draped the coffin of Colonel Thaddeus Deane. A shabby Episcopal priest, his gaunt face dripping with sweat, mumbled rapidly from *The Book of Common Prayer*. Those Episcopal communicants present didn't recognize the man, for he had been brought in after their regular minister had declared himself too heat-stricken to conduct the service.

The crowd had ranged itself to get the best view of the three black-clad female mourners who stood by the grave. The widow— Madame Deane, she called herself—was tall, slender. Though her bonnet's thick black chiffon veiling hid her face, only a young woman secure in her charms would have worn the braided black silk gown with its elaborately draped bustle and carried the fringed black parasol at so becoming an angle. From time to time Madame

Deane's narrow, black-gloved hand reached a black-bordered handkerchief under her veil so she might dab at her eyes.

To her left, a stout old lady quivered and shook with sobs. She was Mademoiselle Koestler, the governess, and she wore the impenetrable, full-length mourning veil of her native Alsace.

To Madame Deane's right stood her daughter, a very erect girl still in short skirts. Amélie Deane was barely fifteen, so the short veil drifting from her black leghorn hat was thin. Most people, therefore, directed their curiosity at her. The sheer veil accentuated rather than hid her pale, delicate features, which were so pinched that it was impossible to tell whether she was a pretty child. Grief was all that showed, grief and a fiercely proud determination to keep her grief in check lest the spectators see her weep.

Halfway between the mourners at the graveside and the curious crowd stood four people, obviously a family group: a man, his wife, and their two grown sons. Neighbors to the deceased, they were the Van Vliets.

Doña Esperanza Van Vliet, a large, stately woman, wore black silk cut in the full-skirted fashion of an earlier decade although the dress was new. Doña Esperanza always wore this outmoded style. Above her serenely high forehead she wore a peculiar bonnet that, like her other clothing, ignored current styles: a ruffle of black tulle attached to a band that tied with black satin streamers under her full, rounded chin. The bonnet showed a smooth sweep of graying hair fastened with a tall silver comb. She looked regally foreign. She was, in fact, less foreign than anyone there. Doña Esperanza was a García, and it was the Garcías who had once owned Paloverde, the great rancho that curled along the Los Angeles basin from the river toward the Pacific Ocean.

Her husband, Hendryk Van Vliet, sweating into his high wing collar and alpaca frock coat, was a stout, choleric Dutchman whose fair head reached only to her ears. He held his high silk hat awkwardly, with the thumb and little finger of his right hand. The other three fingers had been lost to a poisonous snake when he crossed Panama in 1858. Hendryk's face was drawn into lines of ponderous gravity, and it was to his credit that there was not even a glint of satisfaction in his blue eyes. For this was the funeral of the man who, eight years earlier, had almost ruined him.

The two sons were far apart in age.

The elder, Hendryk Junior, whom everybody called Bud, was twenty-four, and everything about him underlined his cockiness, which was the pleasant cockiness of a young, self-made man. Vitality showed in his compact, muscular body as well as in the unusual contrast between his deep tan and his vivid blue eyes and shining blond hair. He had inherited his father's stubborn, strong nose. Bud looked, and was, a man of many drives, including the sexual. Though not handsome in the accepted sense, he was the most sighed-after, shivered-over young man in Los Angeles. Parents knew that he was a frequent visitor to the better class of whorehouse; still, there was never a whisper about him and any "nice" girl, so he was invited to every party and sociable. His short-coated business suit was cut a shade too narrow, and his black cravat was tied in a flashy knot.

Another story entirely, the younger son. Vincent Van Vliet had been named after his grandfather, Don Vincente García, but he was seldom called anything but 3 Vee. At seventeen, he was six feet tall, and he held the new length of his slender body awkwardly. He resembled his mother, with his soft black hair waving back from a high forehead, his oval face, and black eyebrows. He was crimson with the heat. His heavy broadcloth suit was part of the wardrobe he was taking back east for his first year at Harvard. His narrow black mustache obviously was new, too, for he fingered it continually as he gazed toward the young girl who stood by her father's grave. His soft brown eyes glowed with sympathy. He wanted to comfort her. Amélie never let herself look at 3 Vee—or anyone else.

"We therefore commit his body to the ground," the minister mumbled. "Earth to earth, ashes to ashes, dust to dust: in sure and certain hope of the Resurrection to eternal life."

There were no pallbearers. The crowd murmured at this, for Los Angeles was a neighborly town, and not even the lowest pauper was buried with strangers to perform this last melancholy duty. Four old men shuffled from the dubious shade of a black obelisk. They were the elderly Gabrielino Indian gravediggers. Squirming in their unaccustomed, ill-fitting frock coats, they ranged themselves two on a side of the bronze coffin, grasping silver handles, grunting in their effort. They raised the coffin, took a step, and one man stumbled on the iron railing that surrounded a family plot. He lost his grip, the coffin lurched and its floral blanket slithered off. From inside came a shifting sound. Heavy. Evocative.

7

The young girl's slight body flinched as if she had felt a lash between her shoulderblades. Through the thin veil one could see her eyes squeeze shut and the full, soft mouth contort.

3Vee swallowed convulsively.

Again the Indians lifted the coffin, and again the body shifted. The child clenched her hands together below her chin, an immemorial gesture of grief.

An appreciative murmur passed through the heat. The crowd pushed forward, descending the hillock, shoving and stumbling around gravestones, muttering, sweating, craning for a view.

"About time she showed something," a woman said loudly.

"Maybe she's not so fond of her pa any more."

"Shouldn't be. He went against God's will."

Amélie Deane's slight body returned to its proud posture and she lifted her head, gazing through her veil at the blinding sky.

The four old men, streaming with sweat, used a wide sash to lower the coffin into the open ditch. Again the body was heard to move. The coffin dropped with a series of thuds. Yellow dust rose. The undertaker's assistants wiped dusty gloves across brown wrinkled faces before lifting their shovels. This task they knew. Dry clods of adobe struck the coffin with hollow slaps. Dust rose in clouds. Madame Deane held her parasol to protect herself. The old governess turned aside. Amélie didn't move.

It was over.

The three mourners started toward the black-decorated carriage. The minister didn't accompany them. They were alone. Madame Deane tilted her black parasol between herself and the crowd; the girl held her shoulders too squarely, and the old governess, still sobbing, reached to take her charge's arm. Amélie must have said something, for the old lady dropped her hand.

3Vee glanced at his parents and older brother as though searching to see which of them would accompany him to the carriage. Yet he remained rooted between his parents when Bud stepped forward.

Moving in his graceful yet masculine lope, Bud braved the hundreds of eyes focused on him. He had the true generosity of the strong. It wasn't Madame Deane's charms that drew him forward any more than he was held back by her being the widow of his enemy, his father's enemy. Had she been old and ugly he would have gone to her. Women were frail creatures, and God knows Madame Deane needed his help.

"Madame Deane," he spoke respectfully into the carriage window. "I'm Bud Van Vliet, your next-door neighbor, and I'd like to offer my condolences and those of my parents and my brother on your bereavement. This is a sad time, I know, and we want to help you through it. If any of us can be of the least assistance, please call on us. It doesn't matter the hour. 3 Vee's leaving tomorrow, early. But Mama or Papa or I will come."

"How kind you are, Mr. Van Vliet," Madame Deane replied in her French accent.

"We're neighbors," Bud said, "and we want to help."

"Is this not kind of the Van Vliets, *ma chère?*" Madame Deane asked her daughter.

And the girl, not yet in the carriage, kicked a polite little curtsey. "Yes, Mama. Mr. Van Vliet, thank you." Her voice wasn't muffled as he had expected it might be, by her grief. It was clear, pretty. She had no accent, but in Los Angeles, where one heard every kind of regional speech, her precise intonation made her voice seem somehow foreign.

The black-plumed horses drew the lacquered carriage from Rosedale Cemetery. And the crowd slowly dispersed in heat-slowed steps, again becoming clusters of friendly folk. For, despite all recent evidence to the contrary, Los Angeles was a friendly town.

· 3 ·

The friendliness came from so many people being newcomers.

Eight years earlier, in 1876, when the Southern Pacific's twin steel lines had arrived to connect Los Angeles to the rest of the country, the town had less than half its current population. The railroad had played troubador, luring people west with exhibitions, pamphlets, brochures, magazine articles, even novels aimed toward filling the Southern Pacific's wooden cars with settlers to buy Southern Pacific lands. And the settlers had come, well-to-do family folk, blowing westward like the warm Santa Ana winds, and just as easily they had been absorbed into the fabric of the town.

Colonel Deane, from the beginning, had run the local branch of the railroad in all details. Everybody believed him to have taken the late Mark Hopkins's place as one of the Southern Pacific's Big Four, along with Charlie Crocker, Leland Stanford, and Collis P. Huntington. The Colonel never denied the rumor. A powerfully built man running to fat with brown hair and a well-trimmed red beard, he had managed his office with an owner's avarice. Mercilessly he had carried out the railroad's dictum to gouge anyone who needed to move freight. The red-bearded Colonel had bankrupted farmers and businessmen and had pushed many, like Van Vliet's Hardware, to the brink.

Madame Deane defied convention by living seven or eight months of the year in Paris, apart from her husband. Each May the Colonel went to New York to bring his wife and daughter west in Collis P. Huntington's private railroad car. The Colonel's inordinate fondness for the little girl made him human—almost. Neither Madame Deane nor the child invited guests to the elaborate mansion that the Colonel had built at the southern edge of town. They rarely emerged from the lavish gardens.

The spite shown at Rosedale Cemetery was not vengeance against the Colonel's hard business practices; Angelenos, like the rest of the country, accepted the pursuit of money as a worthy occupation. What had drawn so large a crowd into the awesome heat was a need to penetrate the mystery surrounding the Colonel's death.

·4·

Hendryk Van Vliet reined in Pollie and the brougham jolted to a halt on Spring Street in the business part of town. Bud and 3Vee, who were in back, jumped down, and 3Vee climbed in front, squeezing past his mother. The desert lavender sachet that clung to Doña Esperanza's clothing was strong in today's heat.

Hendryk handed the reins to his younger son. "Hold on tight now," he instructed. "Don't let Pollie get lathered. Be careful of that pothole when you cross Fourth. Tell Juan to make sure Pollie has two buckets of water." Heat irritated the stout little Dutchman unbearably, and his tone was dictatorial.

3Vee, already depressed beyond reason, sighed. "Yes, Papa."

"Remember that pothole. Don't go into one of your daydreams and forget!"

3Vee's shoulders, under the heavy jacket, slumped more. "I won't, Papa."

Hendryk climbed down and stood for a moment staring at the building before him. It was divided into two commodious shops, Cousin Franz Van Vliet's grocery and Hendryk's own hardware store. Above were two floors of cathedral-windowed offices, and over the top rose an ornately scalloped false front. The central scallop was engraved:

VAN VLIET BLOCK
1874

Ownership of a block was the local gauge of a man's success. Hendryk had built this block and then been forced to sell it. Last year Bud had arranged for him to buy it back. Hendryk's shop sign had recently been painted:

VAN VLIET'S HARDWARE

but if you looked very carefully, beneath the bright green lettering, you could make out the words

AND OIL DRILLING SUPPLIES

No matter how often Hendryk had the sign repainted, the old words seeped through, a ghostly reminder of failure.

Hendryk glanced at the clock above Di Franco's Dry Goods. "Time, my dear," he said. As he tipped his high silk hat in farewell to his wife, he wore a look of uxorious pride. Hendryk's keen eye for quality was famed in town. Even at eighteen he had seen that this tall, childless Californio widow, four years his senior, was a very great lady. He was a poor, recently arrived clerk. Yet, stubbornly, he set out to woo her. In the intervening quarter century, he never got over his amazement that Doña Esperanza had agreed to be his wife. He treated her with vast respect at all times, even in their large, high bed.

"It's so hot, Mr. Van Vliet," Doña Esperanza said. "Why don't you come home early?"

"A man must work, a man must work. But you—" A pause. "Lie down, my dear."

"I'll try my best," she agreed.

They both knew she never rested in the afternoon.

3 Vee touched the reins to Pollie's broad back, iron wheels grated on adobe and yellow dust rose in sheets, engulfing them. The dryness grated in 3 Vee's nostrils and his eyes. His new broadcloth suit itched and the heat prickled sweat from every part of his body. He was grateful for his physical discomfort. It took his mind— slightly—from his internal agitation.

"Is it so bad, 3 Vee?" Doña Esperanza looked at her son, her luminous brown eyes filled with concern.

"How could I not have gone to them?"

She sighed.

"Bud went," 3 Vee said bitterly.

"Vincente, Vincente." Often, when they were alone, Doña Esperanza called her younger son by the Spanish version of his name. She never called her elder son by his given name. "Bud's a man."

"I am, too. Supposedly!"

"You are, of course. I keep forgetting." There was no amusement in her low, grave voice.

"Why should you remember if I don't act like one?"

"Bud offered our family's help. Tomorrow morning you leave for Harvard College." A note of pleasure crept into her soothing gravity. "Bud will be here, as Papa and I will be, and the three of us will assist Madame Deane in any way we can."

"Bud's never met them, even. Amélie's *my* friend."

Doña Esperanza took a handkerchief from her jet-beaded reticule and dabbed her forehead. The brougham lurched and she had to hold out her gloved hand to steady herself. 3 Vee had let Pollie guide them into a pair of deep narrow ruts, the imprints of wagon wheels baked hard by the sun. Hendryk had not thought to warn his son against so routine a hazard.

A trolley, pulled by a bobtail horse, was heading north to the Southern Pacific depot. The driver clanged for 3 Vee to get out of the way. 3 Vee chucked the reins. Pollie slowed. Gingerly he used the red-handled whip. Pollie dropped her head, took one more step, and stopped. The trolley bell clanged, insistent. 3 Vee was forced to apply the whip firmly. The old mare strained, extricating the brougham from the narrow ruts. 3 Vee was sweating even more profusely. He took the handkerchief his mother extended. Neither of them even considered that he should remove his hat or his heavy wool jacket.

They passed the cavernous depth of Jake's Livery Stable, with its buzz of flies and overpowering aroma of horse. Homes began mingling with businesses. In the still gardens, trees were dusty, vines hung limp, and grass was yellow.

"I'm not going tomorrow," 3 Vee said abruptly. "She—Amélie—has no other friend here."

His mother turned, her fine eyes alarmed. 3 Vee was a García, and Garcías made grand gestures, throwing away all.

"3 Vee," she said, unconsciously lapsing into his nickname. "This isn't Amélie and Madame Deane's true home. Soon they will return to Paris."

"I'll stay until they leave."

"Amélie is a little girl. It wouldn't be proper for you to act so. She would be compromised."

"Madame Deane needn't know why I'm staying. Nobody need know."

"Amélie would know. And she's far too young to be placed in that position."

3 Vee said nothing. His jaw tensed and he showed a resemblance to his stubborn father.

They had reached what remained of Wolfskill's orange grove. As they turned toward Fort Street, both 3 Vee and Doña Esperanza glanced back in the direction they had come. From here they had a view of the uncompromisingly sun-etched town, its flatness cupped by brown hills. For the most part they remained empty, although Poundcake Hill was crowned by the clock-towered high school from which 3 Vee had just graduated. They moved into the shade. Wolfskill's grove had been watered from the *zanja* and the evaporating moisture, which gave off a sweet citrus odor, lowered the temperature. 3 Vee let the horse amble more slowly.

He turned to his mother. "It was like she—I mean Amélie and Madame Deane and Mademoiselle Koestler were being guillotined. But guillotining's faster and therefore more merciful."

Doña Esperanza sighed. She, too, had been profoundly affected by Amélie's fragility.

"You were there, 3 Vee. She—they—saw you. Your presence gave comfort. And comfort is all one can hope to give at the time of grief."

Doña Esperanza understood grief. Her first husband, a middle-aged Scottish doctor, had diagnosed his own illness as terminal, leaving her after three years of marriage to return to die in his native Edinburgh. She was not a woman to love in the carnal fashion, but she had cared deeply for him. And in the first year of her marriage to Hendryk, her beloved father, Don Vincente, had died. She had borne three daughters between Bud, her first child, and 3 Vee, her last. None of the three had been stillborn, but each little girl, before her sixth birthday, had died of one of the childhood diseases. It was a normal loss, yet Doña Esperanza's maternal grief had been terrible. She reached out to pat 3 Vee's knee. The bond between Doña Esperanza and this son went deep and strong. Her stately way hid shyness, and the new, busy, crowded Los Angeles terrified her. 3 Vee, her true García, seemed to her a link with the gracious Californio past. He was the person she loved most deeply on this earth, and it was a tribute to her that neither Hendryk nor Bud suspected.

3 Vee sighed. "She's a very unusual person, Amélie. She has more honor than anyone I've ever met."

"That's why you mustn't even consider putting her under your obligation."

"She was very attached to her father. I don't mean in a simpy, sticky way, like the Poundcake Hill girls." He meant his sentimental female classmates. He used his whip to flick a horsefly that Pollie's tail couldn't reach. "I know Papa doesn't like our friendship."

"That has nothing to do with Amélie. It concerns the way the Colonel treated him."

"Everyone hated the Colonel. But Papa didn't have his revenge today."

"Of course not. These new people, they have no idea what real behavior is." This, 3 Vee, knew, was as close as Doña Esperanza ever came to criticizing the Californio's American supplanters.

"Amélie's only a little girl, of course. Still, she's the only girl in town worth talking to. Mama, she goes to the opera all the time in Paris, she and her governess use the Lamballe family box. She's seen Monsieur Gounod conduct his *Faust*, and heard Madame Galli-Marié sing *Carmen*. She speaks French and German with no accent. She knows Greek and Latin. Imagine! Yet she has a wonderful sense of humor about it all. And poetry. Well, she reads the *real* poets, like Swinburne." 3 Vee turned even redder, for Swinburne was considered a decadent poet, and while his mother didn't know this, he didn't care to expose Amélie to the charge of being permitted to read decadence—even if the charge *was* true. "She, well, she has the finest mind of anyone I've ever met. Mama, remember that book I was telling you about? Mr. James's *The Portrait of a Lady?* Well, Amélie's only a child, of course, yet, well, there's a line that describes her perfectly. It goes something like this." He gazed ahead as if his soft brown eyes were focused on a page. "'It had been her fortune to possess a finer mind than most of the people among whom her lot was cast, and to have a larger perception.' Isn't that fine? Even in Paris I would imagine that Amélie is superior."

Doña Esperanza, who rarely smiled, succumbed. She turned so 3 Vee wouldn't see.

3 Vee, however, was extremely sensitive, and he realized his mother's amusement.

"For a child she's very unusual," he added.

Of course he didn't think of Amélie as a child. He thought of her with the heavily veiled respect with which he thought of all nice girls—he hadn't yet approached the other kind—that is, as the object of noncarnal desire. Los Angeles universally accepted as pretty those girls with full bodies, pink cheeks, and curly hair. Amélie was very slender, and her complexion a clear, pearly color. Her thick, long hair, which was an unusual topaz and extended below her waist, alas, had no curl. The only exoneration 3 Vee could show to public opinion was her magnificent carriage. His mind, however, rarely was influenced by public opinion. He bucked the mass. He knew that Amélie was possessed of exceptional character, intelligence, and wit. She might not fit in with current ideas of beauty, yet she had something far rarer than beauty: the lively force of charm.

"I mean it about staying. You see, I failed her once before." His voice went low with misery. "She knew the Colonel was in some sort of trouble, and she thought maybe his problem had to do with business. She asked me some questions. You know me. Business is a mystery to me. I wasn't any help. And she needed help badly."

"The Colonel was beyond help from Amélie. Or you. 3 Vee, stop blaming yourself."

They had reached their red-shingled house. Deep verandas surrounded both stories, with pink and red oleanders shading the lower porches. Now other houses extended beyond this and the Deane place, but a few years ago, Fort Street had ended here, at cheesebush and sandy dirt.

3Vee, reining in Pollie at the stone carriage block, put two fingers in his mouth, whistling. Juan emerged from the back, pulling down his loose white shirt. He was one of what the family called "Mama's people," an Indian who had lived on Paloverde. Under Spanish and Mexican rule, Indians had been slaves, yet not in the usual sense, for they weren't bought and sold as individuals. For countless centuries they had lived and died peaceably in their own small worlds, and those who had survived the Spaniards' conversion, measles, and venereal diseases remained as unpaid servants within their old boundaries. In effect, whoever owned their land owned them. Don Vincente García, though a kind enough master, was an indifferent cattle rancher and an even worse euchre player. The grant he had inherited was ten leagues, almost 45,000 acres, roughly resembling a long cat with its tail in the Los Angeles River and its tongue lapping toward the Pacific Ocean. About a third of this land was uninhabitable chaparral of the Santa Monica Mountains. The flatland, however, rich with alfilerilla and other grasses as well as small game and acorn-bearing oaks, had supported several Shoshonean tribes. This fertile acreage Don Vincente lost for taxes and gambling debts.

The gringos who took it over knew nothing of the old ways. They nailed up no-trespassing signs and used their Sharp's rifles on every Indian. After Don Vincente's death, the men and women who once had inhabited Paloverde came on bare brown feet to the Van Vliets's back door, requesting Doña Esperanza's medical help (she was a skilled nurse and midwife), or money to buy corn, or money to buy masses for their souls, or very often they wanted a little quiet talk, no more. These bewildered and elderly people never considered her the descendant of their enslavers. To them, Doña Esperanza was their only support in the hard new American land. Juan, who had been born on the *corredor* of the wideflung adobe house, was of the Yang Na, the tribe whose village had been where the heart of Los Angeles now lay. He handed Doña Esperanza from the brougham.

"Doña Esperanza, welcome back. Was it hot for you?"

"Not too, thank you, Juan. But indeed I am glad to be home."

They spoke in Spanish, Juan's only language. Juan led Pollie around to the carriage house. 3Vee and Doña Esperanza went inside.

The front rooms, dimmed by oleanders and drawn yellow

16

shades, were furnished with massive, rough-hewn pine and natural-colored rugs made in Paloverde. The sagging horsehair chairs and sofas had come around the Horn decades earlier. As a small boy 3 Vee had considered the furnishings from once-great Paloverde as romantic as a page from a Sir Walter Scott novel, yet at the same time he had been embarrassed that his home was so different from the fussy, knickknacked houses of his schoolmates. In this one area, 3 Vee's shyness and romanticism both had melted. Now he simply accepted his home as a comfortable place.

Doña Esperanza started upstairs immediately to take off her good dress. Tall and stately, she paused at the oval of colored light that fell from the stained-glass window at the landing. She looked down. "You will go tomorrow," she said. "There's nothing for you to do here. Nothing."

·5·

3 Vee went through the kitchen to the back porch.

Maria knelt at a hollowed-out stone metate, her body moving back and forth rhythmically as she ground corn with a stone roller. Small grunts escaped her each time she pressed forward. Maria also had belonged to Paloverde. Nobody, including Maria herself, knew her exact age, but she had been a grown woman when Doña Esperanza was born. Maria's white hair was drawn back around an oddly unwrinkled face. The umber flesh had sunk around her toothless mouth; her high cheekbones were intensely prominent so that in repose her face resembled a darkened skull. On her loose black blouse hung a large pierced-tin cross. Under this blouse, between her sagging breasts, she wore a rabbit-hide pouch that contained a carving of abalone shell, a bit of green polished jade, an eagle's feather, a salamander skin, a strand of hummingbird's claws. Amulets. Maria was considered to have inherited those magical powers for which, before the Spaniards came, the local tribes had been famed.

She watched 3 Vee take down the *olla*. She waited while he gulped cold water directly from the sweating clay gourd.

"So you went to the funeral?" she asked. Like Juan, Maria spoke only Spanish.

"You know I did," 3 Vee replied, also in Spanish.

"And?"

He dribbled water on his forehead.

"Did the mourners suffer?" Maria asked.

"Yes."

"And the new people enjoyed this?"

"Very much."

"The child didn't cry," Maria stated.

3 Vee looked at her. Sometimes he actually believed she *was* a witch.

"You are surprised I know this?" Maria sifted corn through her fingers. "She has a proud spirit. Noble and very proud."

"Oh stuff it! You've never even met her!" 3 Vee snapped in English. He hung the *olla* back in the shade. "I'm sorry, Maria," he sighed in Spanish. "I just don't wish to talk about Miss Deane."

"Your lives are connected."

Again he was annoyed. "She's just fifteen!" For Amélie's birthday last week he had given her a tissue-wrapped copy of *Idylls of the King*. "We're neighbors. And I'm sick and tired of being teased about her!"

"Who teases?"

"Everybody. Papa's angry. Bud says I'm robbing the cradle."

"Your brother thinks he knows all about women. He knows nothing."

She spoke factually, yet with respect. All of the Paloverde Indians considered Bud heir to Don Vincente. This annoyed 3 Vee, for he knew he was a Californio, and it was apparent that Bud was a typical American.

"He has them falling all over him."

"He kisses the pretty ones and sleeps with the whores. This, he considers, makes him knowledgeable." Maria gave her quivering laugh. "He will learn, don't you worry, he will learn about one woman."

"You always talk about the future as if you see it!"

"Maybe I can. You believe I can. That's what matters. And listen to me. You must not think your brother is truly one of them. Or that you are not. All blood is mingled." Her face grew grave and the toothless lips sucked inward. "Far better for you and for him if that house"—she nodded in the direction of the Deane mansion—"had never been built. But there it is. And there lies the future."

The small hairs on 3 Vee's shoulders prickled.

"The two houses have a line between them," Maria said, "and this line is drawn with the blood of your family. You will suffer, your brother will suffer, and there is nothing anyone can do to halt the trouble."

"What trouble?"

"I have said too much."

"Oh, I should know better than to stand around talking to you," 3 Vee snapped at the old woman.

"Go take off that hot suit," Maria said calmly. "It is irritating you." And again she knelt over the metate.

·6·

All week Doña Esperanza had been packing for 3 Vee. His small room was crowded by an old steamer trunk, a portmanteau, and a cavernous calfskin grip. The grip remained open, awaiting his last-minute things. It was to be with him in the Pullman car on the eight-day journey to Massachusetts. As 3 Vee stared at the baggage, his expression turned bleak. Staying is the only way I can prove my friendship, he thought. He threw his heavy, damp jacket on the bed, took off his broadcloth vest and, struggling with the buttons of his stiff collar, looked out his window.

The unusual stillness took on a malevolent quality at the Deane place. Every curtain in the house was drawn. No horses could be seen moving through the open doors of the carriage house. The two Sonoran gardeners who puttered eternally in the beautiful grounds were gone. An evil sorcerer might have raised his hand, killing off every form of life. Empty sunshine glanced off the tips of the iron spear fence and touched the giltwork of the closed gates. Fenced gardens were rare in Los Angeles and gates even more so. This barrier further set apart the mansion with its fretted gables and pointed turrets roofed with slate. The most elaborate residence in town, the Colonel had called his place a "simple country chalet," probably to differentiate it from his yet more magnificent home on Nob Hill in San Francisco.

As 3 Vee stared at the Deane place he was thinking of the storm of gossip that surrounded the Colonel's death. He resented every word. Madame Deane came from the aristocratic Lamballe family, and 3 Vee could see Amélie's resemblance to the lovely and fragile ladies of the *ancien régime*. (His reference to the guillotine had been no accident.) He loathed the thought of crude Angelenos prying into her solitary grief.

Yet he, too, found himself wondering about the mystery. Why *had* the Colonel shot himself? Amélie believed a financial matter had bedeviled her father. But didn't the Colonel own a fourth of the Southern Pacific Railroad Company, the most powerful force in the West? Without the railroad, Los Angeles would have remained a hamlet, its inhabitants glued to these few miles. The Southern Pacific remained the only line that linked Southern California with the rest of the country. The Colonel set the freight rates on all grain, meat, agricultural products, machinery, and oil that came and left the area. He had power so vast as to be incalculable. The power of life and death. How like a god, 3 Vee thought. Does a god put an ivory-handled dueling pistol in his mouth and pull the trigger?

Amélie adored her father.

From this window, 3 Vee had watched her, a tiny girl with long pale hair, jumping her fat pony over bars for the red-bearded Colonel, or sitting in his lap. Later, he had seen her, a small, erect figure in exquisite white frocks, talking with animation and clutching the Colonel's meaty arm as they wove in and out of green shadows.

Until this summer 3 Vee had never said a word to her.

In June he ran into her and the governess at C. C. Burham's Bookshop and Rental Library. She asked what he was borrowing. *Atalanta at Calydon*, he replied, flushing. But it turned out that she was permitted to read Swinburne. They chattered as they walked home. And after that he was permitted to visit the Deane place twice a week. Naturally Mademoiselle Koestler was always present. But she was a kindly old woman whose presence was marked only by the occasional grumblings of her dyspeptic stomach.

For 3 Vee, the summer was strung on those green afternoons.

He was sensitive and perceptive. He had the solitary nature that goes with a creative mind. In Los Angeles, an open, friendly little town on the bumptious western rim of the continent, his finest qualities were suspect. Amélie was the first person, other than Doña Esperanza, with whom he was able to talk freely. Amélie, a Parisian through and through, with a lively perception, grasped his every idea, however incoherently voiced, and argued every point, arching her finely etched brows and moving her delicate shoulders and small hands gracefully.

About a month ago something in Amélie had changed. Alert to mood, 3 Vee was disturbed that he was unable to analyze the difference. Her pretty laughter rang as often. Her quick arguments and sharp humor were the same. The very elusiveness of the change added to 3 Vee's sense of unease.

One afternoon she inquired about bonds and notes. Her questioning wasn't intense, yet the casual tone of her voice slipped a little, as the resonance alters when a crystal goblet is struck at a different spot.

"A bond and a note are both loans," he said.

"There is a difference, though," Amélie said. "A bond is a public debt and a note is a private indebtedness. But what else?"

She already knew more than he. Embarrassed by his ignorance, 3 Vee replied in a slightly superior tone, "I've never been good at business. Why not ask the Colonel?"

"My father is the one person I cannot ask," she replied, turning away too quickly.

And after that she never intruded her worries on him again.

The morning 3 Vee heard of the Colonel's suicide, he experienced terrible guilt. And there was no way out. He hadn't been able to apologize. The Van Vliet family, the four of them together, had gone next door to offer their condolences as if the Deanes were normal Angelenos. Mademoiselle Koestler had talked to them. A quivering mass of stomach disturbances, she had said that Miss Deane and Madame Deane were prostrated with grief. The only time since the Colonel's suicide that 3 Vee had seen Amélie was this afternoon, at the funeral. He might have made it up a little (to himself, anyway) had he stepped forward. He hadn't.

A sparrow darted toward the iron fence, then turned away, as if it sensed death. 3 Vee sighed. Only Bud went to the carriage, he thought.

To 3 Vee, Bud's stepping forward was an annihilating fact. His one-sided fraternal rivalry went back further than he could remember. Always, or so it seemed to him, he had loved, admired, and bitterly resented his brother. Bud teased him mercilessly, and 3 Vee eternally rose to the bait. Bud was popular. Bud was a man of action. Bud never delved into his own soul in this stupid, futile way. All Los Angeles respected Bud's business acumen, Bud's hunting skill, and Bud's grace on waxed canvas dance floors. Bud had protected him during the bad times. Bud still stepped between him and their father's worst irritation. He was the biggest cross any younger brother could be forced to carry: a protective, teasing older sibling whose footsteps are impossible to follow.

3 Vee, in light of Bud's actions this afternoon, saw too clearly his own weaknesses. It was impossible to console himself with the thought that nobody else in town had the courage and decency to walk the short distance to the Deane's carriage. Bud had done it.

3 Vee began to weep in hoarse gulps that were filled with despair. He wept from his own helplessness and cowardice. He leaned his cheek against the window ledge, which was gritty, pressing hard against the bone in an effort to relieve the ache in his throat.

· 7 ·

Because it was 3 Vee's last evening at home, Doña Esperanza had planned an elaborate supper. 3 Vee heard his father and Bud when they returned from the store. But he didn't go down. He stayed in his room, lying on the bed.

Around seven a knock sounded at his door. "It's me, kid," Bud said.

"I'm not hungry."

"Start working up an appetite, then. Supper's on in ten minutes."

"Tell Mama for me."

"Tell her yourself, when you come down." Bud's easy tenor voice was amused. "You have a note from the little girl next door."

3 Vee sat up. "She has a name, dammit!"

"What? Baby?"

"She's Amélie Deane," 3 Vee said, and his throat clogged.

"Kid, kid. You've got to get over taking every damn thing to heart."

A second later a note slid under the door.

There was no envelope. The paper, embossed with the Lamballe coat of arms, was folded once. Inside, two sentences:

> Thank you for being there. Mama has given her permission
> for me to write to you at Harvard.
>
> *A*

3 Vee sat on his bed, thinking he would cry, but no tears came. He was still miserably unhappy, yet as he rubbed his forefinger

over the embossing, he was soothed. She intended that, he thought. He held the letter to his chest, realizing the unique grace of a girl barely fifteen years old who, on the worst day of her life, had managed to find the words that would give him absolution. And finally he permitted himself to think of the word *love*. I love her, he thought, and didn't feel stupid. If only she was old enough to tell.

Sighing, he went into the big, square bathroom, splashing water on his face, combing more water through his thick black hair. Back in his room, he put on his collar, his tie, his vest, his coat. He went downstairs.

Doña Esperanza ladled steaming bowls of thick chicken soup. Then Maria's niece handed around stewed chicken, a flat dish of olive-topped enchiladas, a bowl of green tamales wrapped in cornhusks, mashed potatoes, creamed onions, peas, fresh tortillas, and beaten biscuits. On the table were glass dishes of beet salad, salsa, and sauerkraut. Dessert was a fudge cake dolloped with whipped cream. The enchiladas and tamales, 3 Vee's favorites, were the special feature. Otherwise it was the usual supper. Midday dinner, even in this heat, was larger, including a platter of cold ham, somersausage, and lacy, thin slices of bologna. Hendryk, like every other local husband, would have considered lighter meals proof that his wife cared nothing for his welfare.

3 Vee ate little. He pushed food around various plates, not talking, mentally composing the letters he would write to Amélie.

Before he went up to bed, Doña Esperanza asked with a grave, worried glance, "Are you ready?"

"Yes, Mama. I'm ready."

At night, as usual, the temperature dropped. Coolness and the sound of crickets came through the open windows. 3 Vee lay awake a long time, his thoughts centered around Amélie. As soon as she is sixteen, I can tell her I love her, he thought as he drifted off to sleep.

The next morning, the sun blazed oppressively. 3 Vee, again sweating profusely in his new suit, left Los Angeles aboard a Southern Pacific Pullman car.

CHAPTER 2

· I ·

The week following 3 Vee's departure, the door knocker sounded during supper. Maria was frying apple fritters for dessert, her niece was clearing the dishes. Bud put down his napkin and went to answer. Neighbors and friends often dropped by at this hour with an invitation to spend the evening. Two years earlier the telephone had come to Los Angeles, but as yet only ninety-one had been installed; most people, Hendryk included, believed that the instrument damaged hearing. The Deanes's black manservant stood at the door and held out a note addressed to Mr. Hendryk Van Vliet. Bud took the note back to the table, and Hendryk slit it open with his fruit knife. Madame Deane requested: *An hour of your time this evening to assist me in a matter of business.*

Hendryk gave a small cough. The temperature had dropped sharply, fog banked in every night, and he was nursing a sore throat. He coughed again.

Doña Esperanza gave her husband a worried glance.

Bud said, "Want me to go, Papa?"

Hendryk, secretly pleased to have an excuse not to enter the lair of his old nemesis, handed the crested stationery to his son. "You're Hendryk Van Vliet, too."

Later, as Bud straightened his tie in front of the octagonal mirrored inset of the hall hatrack, there was a sensual expression around his wide, humorous mouth. He was thinking of the well-known laxity of Frenchwomen. At the funeral he had offered Madame Deane his help, and so now he would be setting out even if she had been a crone. But she was not much older than he; and, tilting his derby on his pomaded, sun-streaked hair, he thought that going to help a charming, young (and French) widow made neighborly duty infinitely more pleasant. I've never had a woman I didn't pay, he thought. Except Rose. And his pleasant face turned hard, haunted.

Madame Deane received him in the drawing room, a room solemn with dark oil paintings, a huge rosewood piano that Amélie played, red-flocked wallpaper, and upholstery in every shade of red. Bud thought the room opulent—*very smart* were the words in his mind.

And the widow, well, she was very, *very* smart.

He preferred full-bodied women. Still, Madame Deane was quite something. A black velvet necklet rode high on her slender white neck, her perfectly fitted black silk gown was cut into a deep ruffled V at the bosom, and from her narrow waist dangled a lacy black fan. Though her mourning was unrelieved, the black was far from harsh. It added to her look of helpless femininity, and combined with her thin, aristocratic features and prominent brown eyes to give her an air of being high-strung and vulnerable. She was neither high-strung nor vulnerable nor helpless.

As Bud entered, her large eyes widened. "Ah, Mr. Van Vliet. How kind of you to be so prompt." The French accent revealed none of her surprise.

"I didn't want to keep you waiting," Bud said. "Besides, it's not far to come."

"It is still most generous. Please sit here."

"Your home is magnificent. It suits you."

She smiled "Do you like it? The Colonel arranged everything. Poor man, he so enjoyed planning houses for me."

"I don't blame him," Bud said, leaning forward in his chair.

The door opened and the child came in. Bud, annoyed at being interrupted just as he was getting to know this handsome Frenchwoman, stood negligently.

"Mr. Van Vliet, you met my daughter at . . . but permit me to introduce her properly. This is Amélie."

The girl, too, was in black: tucked, lightly fitted lawn that ended in a small ruffle at her slender calves. Her white petticoats, edged with tatted black lace, showed briefly as she bobbed a polite curtsey. A black satin bow tied her hair. She was very pale, and her pallor, combined with the deep mourning, turned her unusual topaz-colored hair into a long, shimmering ornament.

"Mama," she said, "I thought that you wrote to the senior Mr. Van Vliet."

"Amélie! Mr. Van Vliet, please do pardon my daughter."

"I understand," Bud replied, but he thought that his brother was sure running true to form, wasting his afternoons with this nasty little girl. "My father has the grippe," he said. "But I promise you, Amélie, that I'm not as stupid as I look. In fact, I'm pretty good at business matters."

Bud had learned to be good. At fifteen, during Hendryk's bad time, he alone had protected his dazed father from bankruptcy and the town's laughter. He had taken on the responsibility of the family and "Mama's people." It was a huge weight for a boy's unhardened shoulders. Bud had never had 3 Vee's sensitivity; his was a wild, reckless, sweet nature, and much of that had been lost forever. His business capabilities, however, had been enhanced. Like an arm-wrestler, he knew in any negotiation when to let up in order to throw his opponent off balance. He knew the precise moment to pin him down. He battled good-naturedly with his brilliant smile and easy, flat Western voice. But when necessary, his tone grew steely and his eyes turned the flat blue of a noon sky. At first, winning had been a necessity. Later, the imperative gone, the urge remained. He had to win—he had to. This drive saddened him. Yet any loss, however minor, made Bud feel as if his family would starve, as if his bones were crumbling, as if he were experiencing death.

He added, "Reasonably good, anyway."

Amélie's delicate shoulders rose in a tiny Gallic shrug of acceptance. "3 Vee said you were."

Bud's stomach tensed with anger. Who was this nasty little girl to judge him? He gave her an avuncular smile. "That, Amélie, isn't proof of anything. Arithmetic is 3 Vee's worst subject." He turned back to the charming widow. "Now. Tell me, Madame Deane, how can I help you?"

"As you know, we are here alone. My brothers, alas, are in France. I need a gentleman to explain how I may best carry out my late husband's wishes."

"Possibly a lawyer?" Bud asked.

"Our attorney, Mr. O'Hara, will be in Los Angeles tomorrow morning."

"Mama, if Mr. Van Vliet is to help us, he has to know the truth."

Bud heard the girl's clear voice, but he refused to glance at her. "Mr. O'Hara does not represent us, Mr. Van Vliet. He is counsel for the Southern Pacific."

"He was your papa's attorney and friend, *ma chère*," said Madame Deane. "I merely need another gentleman who can talk to him."

"That's me, then," Bud said. "Another gentleman. Before tomorrow I better figure out your legal circumstances."

"You cannot know how much your kindness means," said Madame Deane, sinking gracefully into the depth of her chair, raising a lacy scrap of handkerchief to her eyes, which were dry. "Amélie, *ma chère*, will you show Mr. Van Vliet Papa's documents."

"They are in the library, Mr. Van Vliet," Amélie said.

· 2 ·

In the book-lined room, she pulled the gasolier. She didn't close the door. Glancing into the marble-squared hall, Bud saw a dark, heavy figure sit down on a straight gilt chair. The governess. What does the old lady think I'll do, he thought, rape this nasty infant?

A large desk and a heavy oak library table were covered with neatly stacked papers.

"Everything is here," Amélie said.

"Then I'll manage."

"Mama inherits everything—except the house in San Francisco. Papa left that to me." The last sentence was spoken wistfully.

"I'll read the will." It was a dismissal.

"Mostly he owned stock in the Southern Pacific. He had twenty thousand shares—at least that is the amount on the certificates."

"I can figure it out as soon as I see the papers."

"Everything is not in the papers, Mr. Van Vliet. Mr. O'Hara has already been here."

Bud picked up a folded document, untying red string. Another dismissal.

"Papa paid off his shares."

"Then I'll find his canceled note."

"It is important that you understand—"

"I will, in a minute."

"—that Papa was not the real owner."

Irritation finally overcame Bud. No female could understand

legal technicalities. "Did your papa train you to help him, Amélie?" he asked. "Were you his clerk?" He spoke with a pleasant, teasing drawl, but his intent was clear. To put her in her place.

She took a deep breath and the fine-woven black cotton of her dress tightened, revealing delicate young breasts. Not such a child, Bud thought, and was ashamed. She moved to a shelf as though searching for a book. Her back was to him. Bud, like everyone else in Los Angeles, knew how close the Colonel and his daughter had been.

"Honey, I'm sorry," he said, and took a step toward her.

She turned. With an effort he couldn't yet imagine, she was dry-eyed. "I did not mean to lecture you, Mr. Van Vliet. But there are so many papers and so little time. And I thought—"

"You thought I'm like my brother."

"I know you are not."

"Is that good or bad?"

She glanced at the papers neatly arranged on the desk and table. "In this case, good," she said, giving him a tiny, conspiratorial smile. Then her face saddened. "You have been kind and brave," she said.

"Brave?"

"You offered us your condolences. You were the only person who..." Abruptly she ran from the room.

Bud listened to light footsteps on marble, fading up the stairs. Amélie's reluctance to weep in front of him he considered one more unfortunate trait. He liked girls who wept openly, without mottling their pretty pink cheeks. When 3 Vee comes home next summer, I'll have to find him a proper girl. Yet as Bud thought this, he had a sharp vision of the child weeping in proud, private grief someplace over his head.

· 3 ·

He closed the library door—the governess was gone—and sat at the Colonel's desk. Either Colonel Deane had kept his papers in immaculate order or Madame Deane had arranged them. No, Bud thought. More likely the girl. A large black-lacquered tin box with a key stood directly in front of him. He unlocked it. He saw a jumble of letters all addressed to the Colonel in the same firm, angular hand. No point, Bud thought. He set the lacquered black box on the Kashan rug.

There was a silver tray on the desk with a decanter of brandy and a single glass. Nursing a small tot of brandy, Bud read the will.

The Colonel had left the house on Nob Hill, as Amélie had said, to her. Madame Deane got everything else. The major portion of her inheritance was a large block of Southern Pacific shares. Bud picked up a canceled note of indebtedness. Studying it, he frowned. Six years ago, the Colonel had been given the opportunity to purchase twenty thousand shares of restricted Southern Pacific stock at far below market value. In return he had signed a note for $150,000. He had paid off the note this past July. What did the child mean when she said the Colonel was not the real owner?

Bud read through more papers. Madame Deane owned a few utility stocks and this house, no more. Still, the Southern Pacific shares she *had* inherited were worth a fortune, many times their cost. When Mark Hopkins, one of the original Big Four, died, the *Los Angeles Times* had printed an impartial court appraisal of the true worth of an identical railroad issue. I'll look it up, Bud thought, jotting down numbers.

It was almost midnight when he emerged. Madame Deane was in the red parlor sipping tea. She poured him a cup.

"How generous you are to take such time," she said. "You are most kind."

"When do you expect Mr. O'Hara?"

"At half past ten. This is not too inconvenient?"

"Not at all," he reassured her.

Fortunately, it was long past the child's bedtime, Bud thought as he chatted with Madame Deane over a second cup of tea. When he said good night, the black servant, stifling a yawn, handed him his derby and he trotted down the steps and through the iron gates toward the mist-hazed glow of the gas lamp on his own front porch. He was whistling.

·4·

Amélie was awake. She heard the swift crunch of footsteps on gravel and Bud's tuneful whistling. He is the only person in this terrible town who said he was sorry that Papa is dead, she thought. Even 3 Vee could not say it. Mr. Van Vliet is not sorry, either, but he is brave and generous enough to say the words, and in front of all those monstrous people.

Her thoughts mingled a woman's unrelenting grief with a child's bewilderment at the injustices of life. Amélie mourned her father with an adult intensity that so far had precluded eating or sleeping. Since his funeral she had hated everything and everybody in Los Angeles with the absolute and blind filial loyalty of the very young. This is such a spiteful, ugly little town, she thought. I am glad I have no friends here. And she soothed herself with a brief vision of the Bois de Boulogne. Amélie guessed that Madame Deane would sell this house and the one in San Francisco, where Amélie had many friends, and remain permanently in Paris—there, too, everyone thought Amélie witty and delightful. Her high spirits drew people wherever she went. For until the Colonel's death she had been a lively, happy girl, somewhat spoiled, perhaps a trifle too conscious of her maternal ancestry, but also proud, loyal, and fiercely honorable.

The whistling had faded and a distant door slammed. Amélie clasped her slender bare arms. She had often teased 3 Vee about his older brother. *What a funny name, Bud*, she would say. *Why not Sprout?* Now she saw Bud as Mr. Van Vliet, a grown man. I annoyed him, she thought. He did not like me at all. She was surprised that this should make the nerves across her chest ache.

And with an unhappy, childish defiance, she thought, I am glad he does not like me. Mama is right. Nobody in Los Angeles is worth a bean.

· 5 ·

Bud returned to the Deane mansion from his office in the Van Vliet Block at ten-thirty, promptly. Madame Deane led him to the library. The papers remained piled as he had left them, although the black tin box had been put away.

A lanky figure stood staring out at the gardens. He was Liam O'Hara, the Southern Pacific's chief counsel, a tall, cadaverous bachelor who lived monastically, dedicating the hours and years of his life to the railroad. He believed he served the god of Progress, thus permitting himself in good conscience to lie, steal, ruin. Colonel Deane had done the same, but with the minor saving grace of knowing he was ambitious and that ambition led men—and railroad companies—down a dark path.

As Madame Deane introduced Bud, Liam O'Hara's somber eyes rested on him so intently that Bud felt like a badly laid piece of track. This bony man represented the greatest power in the western United States. Bud's mind went cold. I must win, he thought. Not only for Madame Deane. For me.

She left them. Both men stared at the closed door.

"A lady," said Liam O'Hara. "For her late husband's great service to your town my employers wish to be generous with her."

"Generous? She owns a big piece of their company." He went to the desk, found the canceled note, and held it out.

Liam O'Hara did not take it. He opened the Colonel's silver humidor, taking out a cigar to sniff. "Havana. Thaddeus certainly enjoyed his luxuries." He replaced the cigar. "Have you considered yet, Mr. Van Vliet, how that"—he glanced at the vellum paper in Bud's hand— "was paid off?"

"With cash."

"Whose cash?"

"Colonel Deane's."

"Mr. Van Vliet. I've never been a man to waste words. So I'll put the facts before you. Thaddeus Deane was paid ten thousand dollars in annual salary. A handsome sum, very, but my employers believed him worthy of it. When he came to work for them, he had a few minor investments. Madame Deane's family is titled, true, but there is little money. Thaddeus lived well." The attorney gave an eloquent glance at the shelves filled with leather-bound volumes, the bronze statues, the pair of velvet-draped windows with their tree-lined vista. "How do you suppose he paid off a note for a hundred and fifty thousand dollars?"

Bud lost his breath. Yet he wasn't surprised. It was as if he had fallen into a gulley he knew was there yet had forgotten. *It is important for you to know that Papa was not the real owner,* Amélie had said. The odd irritation that the child roused in him had gotten the better of his intelligence. He had neglected to consider her words. Now he did. So the Colonel was an employee. To make him give his utmost, he had been granted an option, a dangling carrot. He was permitted to buy shares for which—it was assumed—he could never pay. Paper rustled as Bud dropped the canceled note back onto the desk. Of course, of course, he thought. Why else would a ruthless man like Colonel Deane blow his brains out?

He had been caught with his hand in the till.

As if following Bud's thought processes, Liam O'Hara said somberly, "He paid for his shares with the company's own funds."

"That's a plenty serious charge," Bud said, stalling.

"My employers suspected he might have been falsifying the books. But Thaddeus Deane, aside from being a valued, trusted servant to the railroad, was their friend. So they kept quiet—until now. I spent several days last week in our local offices. My carriage is here. If you'd care to accompany me, we can go over the books."

This time Bud didn't hesitate. He wasn't stubbornly tenacious, like his father. He knew when to cut his losses. The Colonel embezzled, Bud thought. All right, let's go on from there. "I believe you," he said.

Liam O'Hara stretched his long, bony fingers, pulling the knuckles until they cracked. "Our late friend spent a good deal more than he earned," he said in his somber way. "This house, the one in San Francisco—"

"Mr. O'Hara," Bud interrupted. "I believe you about the books. And you must believe me on this. Los Angeles is a neighborly town. Warm, sentimental. It wouldn't look good for the Southern Pacific to leave a widow and child homeless, penniless." His normally pleasant, husky voice had a sharp, steely timbre. "You and your employers should consider public opinion here. Next year —or the next—the Atcheson, Topeka and Santa Fe line will be here. My family and my friends would rather patronize the line that my father helped bring to Los Angeles. Still..."

The two men looked at one another. They both understood the deal Bud offered. Assuming he could convince Madame Deane to forget her shares, the railroad must forget the past. They must let her keep her houses, her other assets. In exchange, Bud, when the rival railroad came to town, would support the Southern Pacific.

Liam O'Hara again cracked his knuckles. "Mr. Van Vliet," he said, "you are an able young man. Frankly, I never expected to find so keen a business mind here in the Cow Counties. Providing Madame Deane is reasonable, we have no wish to press her."

I've managed the Southern Pacific, Bud thought, exhilarated. It'll be duck soup now, convincing a woman.

·6·

After Liam O'Hara's carriage left, Madame Deane, Amélie, and Bud went into the solarium that bulged like a faceted crystal bowl from the side of the Deane mansion. There was a moist, fresh smell of palms and potted plants.

Bud sat on a low wicker chair opposite Madame Deane, explaining that she had not inherited any part of the Southern Pacific Railroad Company. Amélie stood at a small distance, a fern shadowing her pale, luminous cheek. "Mr. Van Vliet?" she said.

Bud glanced at her, his blue eyes showing a hint of annoyance.

"There is a letter of indebtedness for some Southern Pacific shares—is that called a note?" she said. "It was stamped canceled. Does that not mean Papa had paid for his shares?"

"*Ma chère*, you must not interrupt," said Madame Deane. "I am sorry, Mr. Van Vliet. Do continue."

"What Amélie says is true. There is a paid-up note for twenty thousand shares. But Mr. O'Hara claims there are irregularities in the books that the Colonel kept for the company."

"My poor husband! He worked day and night. How could he be perfect? And with the inferior help in this desert—ah, forgive me, Mr. Van Vliet. I do not mean to insult your home."

Amélie moved to where they sat. Her slightly tilted eyes were the spring color of chaparral, Bud decided, not green or brown but a complex mixture of the two. "Mr. O'Hara accuses Papa of cheating the railroad?" The clear voice didn't falter.

"Yes. He says your father paid for his shares with the company's own money."

Her thick lashes lowered as if to hide her pain from him. He expected the arguments, the refutations, to come from her.

It was Madame Deane who cried, "But that is ridiculous! My poor husband lived for the railroad! And Senator Stanford, Mr.

Huntington, and Mr. Crocker, they were his dearest friends. And now that he is dead, they try to get out of their obligation! Ah, such a sordid world!"

"Mama . . . if they are right?"

"They are not!"

"But if?"

"They are lying, *ma chère*. And that is that."

"Please, Mama, please listen. Papa spent so much. He built two houses, he kept us in Paris. He spent, we spent. How could he have paid off such a lot of money besides?"

Bud's eyebrows went up. She's been thinking about this before, he thought. She understands. He felt pity for the child. Yet her sharply analytical honesty disturbed him. Females weren't meant to look on the truth. The nakedness of truth wasn't decent. Females were meant to accept the subterfuges and euphemisms men presented to them.

"*Ma chère*, this is a business matter," said Madame Deane firmly. "No lady understands business."

"Mr. O'Hara is bargaining, Mama. If we give up our claim of owning part of the railroad, they will keep silent about Papa." She gave Bud a desperate, questioning glance.

He lowered his chin in assent. He was amazed at how quickly she had grasped this essential point.

Madame Deane said, "Your papa did own part of the Southern Pacific Railroad Company. It was his dying wish that we inherit this."

"We cannot inherit what was not his."

"We have the document, do we not?"

"Mama, you know Mr. Huntington and the others. They will stop at nothing. They will take Papa's good name."

"That is impossible."

"They will show him to be an embezzler."

"Amélie!"

"They will make him small and petty. Mama, please, please. I cannot bear it if Papa becomes small. Mama, I implore you, I beg you—" Amélie stopped abruptly. She seemed to shrink into herself, to become younger. She drew a trembling breath. "Excuse me, Mama, Mr. Van Vliet," she said in a colorless yet clear voice. She walked across the bricked floor, but as soon as the door closed after her, light footsteps pattered, fading quickly up the stairs.

Madame Deane sighed. "The poor child." There was genuine concern in her face. "She is so distraught. Mr. Van Vliet, do pardon her. She grieves so for her father. Normally she is a most delightful little girl."

Delightful was the last word Bud would use to describe Amélie. However, the child's obvious grief touched him, and he said, "I understand, Madame Deane, truly I do."

"Now, where were we?"

Bud leaned forward in the wicker chair, explaining to the charming French lady that if she persisted in claiming her shares of the railroad she would find herself in litigation with the most powerful entity in the West. And her little girl was right. All that would be accomplished was the destruction of the Colonel's good name.

"What are the shares worth?" Madame Deane inquired.

"Two million."

"So much?"

"Or thereabouts."

"I had no idea."

"There's not a chance of keeping them," Bud said.

For an hour he went over and over this same ground. But again and again Madame Deane gazed at him with her large brown eyes, repeating, "How can I deny my husband's last wishes?"

·7·

Bud left her at five to one. Dinner at home was at one, and Hendryk insisted meals be on time. Bud walked briskly along the gravel drive, but the muscles of his thighs had gone rubbery and his stomach twitched. Pushing up his hat, he wiped a palm along his hairline, which was sweating. This was the weakness that came over him after a loss. No matter how trivial his defeat, it was invariably followed by these symptoms of debilitation. I handled Madame Deane all wrong, he thought. She and the girl will end up with nothing. He had failed.

He found his father in the dining room sitting alone at the food-laden table. Doña Esperanza, he said, was over in Sonora Town, where old Ignacio's daughter was having a baby. "Can't they find another midwife?" he demanded, his buttery chins bobbling. He needed to show annoyance in order to hide his own humbleness about the Californio lady, his wife.

Maria's niece carried in Bud's *albondigas* soup. As he ate the meatballs and spooned up the thin, spicy broth, he told his father about the meeting with Liam O'Hara.

"So the Colonel was cheating *them?*" Hendryk asked.

Bud nodded.

Hendryk, never a vindictive man, gave a brief laugh and no more at his old enemies' confusion. "Well, why look so gloomy?" he demanded. "Under the circumstance you did fairly well." His highest compliment. "Keeping her houses and utility bonds won't be too bad."

Bud said nothing, for he was again experiencing the sensations of defeat.

"A very pretty woman," Hendryk said, glancing at his son. But Bud, in the past hour, had lost every carnal inclination toward Madame Deane. He shrugged.

"So you will continue to help her?" Hendryk asked.

"How can I? She's dead serious about those shares. She insists they're hers. She doesn't need me, Papa, she needs the best lawyers in the country."

·8·

To fight her battle, Madame Deane chose the best.

Mayhew Coppard, her attorney, was a New Yorker with excellent connections in Washington. He was silver-haired, florid. And a widower. Before he agreed to take this case, he was aware that the charges of embezzlement were true, and that in California the Southern Pacific had never lost a case. On the other hand, Madame Deane held a paid note for two million dollars worth of shares. He weighed all possibilities on his scales, which were not necessarily the scales of justice. The pretty widow and two million dollars won. He claimed, on behalf of his client, twenty thousand shares of stock from the Southern Pacific.

At the preliminary hearing, Liam O'Hara, his voice ringing with somber righteousness, accused Colonel Thaddeus Deane of embezzlement and moral turpitude.

The longest, most sensational trial in Los Angeles history had opened. The cheaper top-floor rooms of the Pico House and Remi Nadeau's hotel were crowded with reporters. Readers are always titillated by the doings of the rich, and in this case they were able to look both up at and down upon Colonel Deane. They could both condemn and enjoy his extravagances. They were fascinated by the cost of his wine cellar, what he had spent on rose bushes alone. Clothes—one week of court time was devoted to the testimony of a Savile Row tailor whose fare from London had been paid by the Southern Pacific.

Whenever Mayhew Coppard suggested their presence would be helpful, Madame Deane took Amélie to the packed courtroom: a dainty girl sitting at the side of a tall, helpless widow. Angelenos had always considered them different—foreign. The women stared and whispered. Tobacco-chewing men and reporters from everywhere kept an even more merciless watch, openly discussing the two.

Madame Deane had no great feelings for her late husband's memory. She conferred incessantly with her lawyer, the urbane Mayhew Coppard. She had two million dollars at stake. Let reporters scribble. Let Los Angeles talk. Who pays attention to the lowing of cattle?

Amélie felt every eye upon her, and each revelation of her father's character brought on a kind of dizzying nausea. Yet that oddly vulnerable pride kept her from altering her expression. She looked, as men said within her hearing, a fine little French snot. They also snickered obscenities that she couldn't comprehend. The idea of revenge, when it finally, inevitably, came, was not directed at her own tormentors. No. Her vengeance would be to exonerate her father.

CHAPTER 3

The Deane Trial had been in progress for two weeks on that December Saturday when the first rain of the season slashed down. A stream raced through the center of the broad, hitherto-dry bed of the Los Angeles River. Rills cut this way and that in the washes. Thick black clouds hid the Santa Monica Mountains. The hills in town turned that indefinable shade of yellow which precedes their brief transformations to green. As usual the downpour kept everyone inside, and merchants were delighted that this necessary evil had come on a Saturday, when businesses closed at one anyway.

Around two the rain let up to a soft, misty drizzle. Adobe streets had softened and Bud's buggy plowed through the light mud of Fort Street.

"Mr. Van Vliet!" A slight figure in black moved under the pepper trees.

It was the Deane child. He reined in his bay. Girl's boots stepped daintily over yellow ruts to the buggy wheel.

"Amélie Deane. Where's your dragon?"

"Kindly dragons sometimes sleep," she said. A smile lifted one corner of her mouth. "May I talk to you?"

"Sure thing," he said. As he swung out to hand her into the buggy, she was climbing up. "Haven't they taught you man's use on earth?" he joked with a hint of annoyance. "It's handing ladies into buggies."

"Obviously, then, you have a higher purpose."

"I sure do," he grinned.

Droplets of rain clung to her hat and the black fur of her collar. A faint pink glowed in her cheeks. Her eyes sparkled. She must be over the worst of it, Bud decided.

"Mr. Van Vliet, even in winter you stay brown as an Indian brave."

She meant this, he knew, as a form of compliment. But her idea that any Angeleno could be complimented by being compared to a lowly Digger Indian was so foreign and naïve that it amused Bud.

"Maybe I am one," he said. "I enjoy hunting. The hunting does it." The buggy lurched and he leaned forward to quiet the impatient bay.

"Mr. Van Vliet, you said you would help us in any way you could. Does that help mean me? Just me?"

Bud always had difficulty turning down an appeal for help, but he had already decided not to reinvolve himself in the Deanes's messy affairs. Besides, the girl was too quick, too clever. She irritated him in a way he couldn't remember being irritated, and his irritation held a soft core of pity that she, even more irritatingly, refused to accept. He was about to turn her down. Then he saw how tightly her small, gloved hands were clenched on her purse.

"What can I do for you?" he asked.

"First you must read these." She opened the needle-point purse and took out five envelopes tied with a narrow ribbon. "There are more," she said.

"What are they?"

"You will find out when you read them," she said. "I like brown men."

Bud turned to look at her. "Amélie Deane, are you flirting with me?"

She laughed, a clear, pretty sound. Again before he could give her his hand, she climbed down and ran under dripping pepper trees.

That evening Bud spread the envelopes on his desk. The first letter he pulled out had *DESTROY* scrawled in huge letters above the date. It was addressed to *Friend Thaddeus* and signed *Your employer, C. P. Huntington*. C. P. Huntington had written his friend and employee that he must ingratiate himself with *a senator of extreme importance to our cause*. The senator had a taste for women who wore very sharp, very high heels.

Bud gazed out his window. Soft rain shimmered the lights in the

Deanes's windows. When the girl had read of women with very sharp, very high heels, did questions flash through her mind? Absently, he pulled another letter from its envelope. He was wondering which room was hers.

· 2 ·

It was on the side facing his. Amélie, too, was at her desk. She wrote :

Dear 3 Vee,

The trial is worse than I imagined. In court they poke into Papa's very soul, careful not to miss a poor, venial strand. It is like a medieval disemboweling.

Outside the courthouse the world is made of voices. Everywhere, everywhere, people talk about us. When Mademoiselle Koestler and I are forced to shop or the like, we speak only in French, both smiling vivaciously, pretending to see no one but each other. Your brother is the only one who greets us. The others watch, avidly, and talk. The worst words, the vile ones, I do not understand. And these they wish me most to hear.

Every day they walk outside our fence as if at a circus, loudly discussing how much Papa paid for this and this. Mama is magnificent. She ignores them all. I honestly believe she does not hear. She confers, she plans. She has Mr. Coppard.

I, of course, have Mademoiselle Koestler, but she is so kind that I worry I will break down in front of her. Once I break, something terrible will happen. 3 Vee, I do not know what this terrible thing is, but it frightens me. I have never been afraid before, not really. Fear is ugly. Degrading. Fear alters you.

It is raining now. The rain makes the ground like the chewing tobacco they spit near us.

This town is the cruelest place. I hate its ugliness, its spite, its unpaved streets. There is no music here, no cleverness, the women are fat, frumpy and have spiteful

eyes. I hate everything about it here. If only Papa were
still alive, I could bear—

She was sobbing. She ripped the letter in half, and the tearing
linen paper made a sound like the roar of a distant animal. She
dropped the pieces in her fire, using the poker to move a last
scrap that refused to burn. As it blazed, she took another sheet.
Drying her eyes, she wrote :

Dear 3 Vee,

Your letter of November 27 arrived. First I corrected
your syntax. Then I followed your advice. I am reading
The Idiot. You are right about the Russians. Their novels
are either deeper or wider than ours. To me Dostoyevsky
is of the deeper ilk. Is the ilk related to the elk?

This was her habit. She would write one letter to destroy, a second light, amusing letter to mail. She filled several pages with her
delicately spiked handwriting.

·3·

The rain fell softly all night, finally letting up on Sunday afternoon.
Monday was warm. Bud, at the warehouse, took off his jacket and
rolled up his starched, clean white cuffs. The golden tangle of hair
on his lower arms glinted in the sunlight cutting through the open
door.

Originally, the flat-roofed building had housed Van Vliet's Oil
Supplies. It lay a little to the west of the town's two main business
streets, in the cluster of cheap commercial structures, mostly tan-
neries and stables, at the foot of Bunker Hill. The hill itself was
empty, its grade too steep for streetcar horses. Coyotes and deer
came down to forage, and once Bud had killed a rattler coiled inside
a corrugated bucket.

As a boy, Bud had thrilled to work here. The oil men had exuded
an almost sexual excitement as they talked endlessly about oil
strikes and rumors of oil strikes. Their eyes glittered as they
selected the finest equipment to bring their dreams to reality. The

merchandise was vast, masculine, inspiring: room-size steam engines, man-high drilling bits, great spools of the finest Manila hemp, long slim fishing tools.

In 1876, when the railroad had come to Southern California, Hendryk had conceived this, his only speculative idea: Van Vliet's would cater to the area's growing oil industry. It would have been feasible—if Colonel Deane had not set prohibitively high freight rates on Hendryk's heavy machinery. His business failed, and ever since Hendryk had considered anything connected with oil-drilling a fool's venture. He wanted to blot out memory of his part in it. He came here as infrequently as possible.

The stored merchandise now was drab and domestic: black iron stoves, brooms, rakes, saws, barrels of screws, kegs of nails, paints, varnishes, window glass, lanterns, corrugated tin buckets.

Bud was checking the bill of lading for a shipment of crockery when again he heard that clear feminine voice. "Mr. Van Vliet?" He went to the sunlit entry, knowing it was Amélie.

"You shouldn't have come here," he said.

"I apologize," she said.

He took her into a small wooden enclosure where his father once had worked out the prices on his drilling supplies. He closed the door as she drew another ribbon-tied stack of envelopes from her purse.

"I take it you've read these letters," he said. "Amélie, what've you got in mind for me to do? Blackmail the Southern Pacific into paying your mother for her shares?"

Shocked, she stared at him.

"What else, then?" he asked.

She hesitated. "Mr. Van Vliet, have you ever needed to vindicate someone?"

Bud was about to reply No, of course not. Vindication is a waste of time. Then his mind went reeling back to Bud Van Vliet, fifteen and drunk in this very building, shouting that he would never fail. He would be a success always.

His browned face contorted, and the past drenched him like a cold rain. It was all there, the first year he had dropped out of the high school on Poundcake Hill to work full time in Van Vliet's Hardware, clerking by day, returning here by night for the hard physical labor of the warehouse. He had worked even harder every

Sunday up in the Newhall oilfield, twelve hours of work for a boy already tired, so that nobody in Los Angeles could say that Hendryk Van Vliet took the bread of charity from his cousin the grocer. For his father's pride, too, he didn't want people to know that he was supporting the family. Yet he had been. That year, and the following year, Hendryk had worn an expression as amorphous as a cloud, and it was Bud who paid the debts, Bud who pulled the customers, Bud who worried over daybooks, Bud who felt the bone-melting fear of bankruptcy that came with each decision—they were that near the edge.

It had been a very bad two years. But Hendryk had recovered, Van Vliet's Hardware had prospered, and Bud had made himself a tidy sum in the real estate boom of '82. Yet even now he continued to push his father's business for all he was worth. Why haven't I gone out on my own? I don't even like this tame shopkeeping, he thought. Bud was not one to examine his motivations. But in this moment of chill he recognized that, loving his father deeply, he wanted Hendryk Van Vliet's failure buried under a mountain of success. He, of all people, understood the filial need to vindicate. He fingered the desktop. It was old, warped.

"You must read all the letters," Amélie said. "They tell Papa how to control a congressman, buy a judge, sway an election. How to run Los Angeles. Rule Southern California."

"Well?" Bud spoke with an effort.

"Of every vice of which Mr. O'Hara accuses Papa they are a thousand times more guilty," she said. "The letters prove my father did only as they told him."

"Amélie, believe me, that won't gain you anything."

"The world will know that Papa's accusers are far more brutal, crafty, ruthless than he ever dreamed of being, and his misdeeds will be forgotten under theirs." She clutched the letters. Her lips had gone white.

"Honey, are you sick?"

"The only things wrong with me are my age and sex. I cannot do this myself."

"I'm not your man," Bud said as gently as he could.

For a long second they gazed at one another, and it seemed to Bud that those slightly tilted hazel eyes penetrated his flesh and she could see that fifteen-year-old boy who still dwelled in his bones.

Too, he decided, there must be something sexual in her look and he felt awkward, ashamed of his own thoughts. She was only a child. A child!

Amélie dropped the pack of letters. They thumped on the warped wood of the desk. She opened the door and left without a goodbye. Through the dust-streaked window Bud saw slender legs flash beneath black mourning. He didn't move for a long time.

· 4 ·

That night after supper Bud had Juan saddle his new roan, Kipper, and he rode southwest through town toward Agricultural Park. The lights of houses dwindled amid the dark fields. Night odors of recent rain were intensely sweet. After a long, dark stretch, he was at Carlotta's.

When Hendryk arrived in '58, Los Angeles was a raw, wild little village with few decent women. Adobe brothels lined Nigger Alley, off the Plaza. Nowadays every sectarian minister insisted that his program of Scripture reading, bouncy hymn singing, and church suppers had conquered sin—the euphemism for prostitution. These preachers ignored two basic facts. First, Los Angeles had become family terrain, and a wife and mortgage take a man out of his animal self. Second, amid the piety and the orange blossoms, a great many whorehouses still flourished.

Bud and his crowd favored Carlotta's. A handsome, motherly woman who drank creamed chicory coffee, cooling some on her saucer for her little pug dog, Carlotta ran a clean place with clean girls. Exciting enough, yet you never got into difficulty at Carlotta's.

Holding the reins loosely, Bud stared across the yard to a dim light on the veranda. A muted guitar plunked, a woman laughed. Bud ran his tongue over his lips. But then he suddenly gave Kipper a jab with his boot and rode home.

In the carriage house, he shouted, "Juan!" Juan didn't appear. He rarely appeared after suppertime. Bud unsaddled Kipper, watered him, led him to his stall, and poured rolled oats into the manger.

"Mr. Van Vliet?"

Somehow he had expected the clear voice. He closed the stall and raised a lantern to illuminate the slender figure standing in the doorway. "I can't help you, Amélie. They'll flatten me, the railroad, like they did my father. And your father."

"You are stronger and more determined than either of them, Mr. Van Vliet."

"So character reading is among your many accomplishments." His smile gleamed in the lantern light. "How old are you?"

"Fifteen."

"All of that?"

Unlike other girls, she had no embarrassment about her youth. She stood there, looking at him gravely. He could smell her flower cologne. Fifteen-year-olds don't use cologne, he thought, but then this one's half French. She wore no hat, and her long hair was confined in the furred collar of her coat.

He set down the lantern and with both hands drew out skeins of soft hair, spreading it over her shoulders. "I used to do that to the girls when I was in school," he said. He felt a tremor go through her. Stop it, he told himself, yet his fingers remained in the cool hair.

"Bud," she murmured. It was the first time she had used his Christian name.

"My brother says you call me Sprout. What do you two do together?"

"Talk."

"About what?"

"Books . . . poetry."

"Does he kiss you?"

She shook her head.

"Has any boy?"

"Nobody," she whispered.

He felt the trembling of her breath rather than heard her voice. His hands cupped her shoulders. Through the wool coat he could feel her fragile bone structure.

"A strange lack in a woman as knowing as you."

To kiss a schoolgirl was perverse, he thought. To kiss her was as crazy as knowing that he intended to help her in her vendetta against the Southern Pacific. He meant the kiss to be light. He never kissed nice girls any other way. A semi-teasing kiss flutters the feminine heart without involving a man in hurt feelings or expectations of marriage proposals. A young girl's first kiss, he excused himself; where's the harm?

His mouth met hers with a violence that took him by surprise. Her lips opened, her arms circled his waist, and she pressed herself against him. He was conscious of her pounding heart, a wild beat he could feel through layers of clothing, a heart covered by new, small breasts. He preferred ample, womanly mounds, yet surely these must be sweet. Without willing it, his hands moved up her sides, his thumbs cheating at the roots of her breasts, rubbing at the firm softness, and his forefinger gently touched over the nipple. Oh God, he thought. Jesus, what am I doing?

Abruptly he stepped away from her.

Horrified by his actions and by the raw, aching desire in his groin, he tried to joke away the intensity of his response. "You really are a woman of the world," he said, letting out a shaking breath. "Nice girls don't kiss that way."

She looked up at him and he saw tears in her eyes.

Instantly contrite, he said, "Honey, it's my fault. I shouldn't have said that. You *are* a nice girl. Sometimes I need to get the best of people. Don't cry. Please don't cry."

"I'm not crying," she said, her voice low.

He swallowed. "I'll walk you round to the front."

"Thank you, but no," she said, smoothing her hair. "I left a side door open. If Mama found out I had left, Mademoiselle Koestler would get into trouble. I do not wish that. Mr. Van Vliet, do I sound noble?"

"Very. I never cared for noble females."

"Alas for me." She was smiling.

Everything was all right again, he thought, and was grateful. He picked up the lantern. "About the letters," he said. "I'll help you."

"Thank you." The lantern showed happiness blazing on her face.

"But I think it's best to wait awhile," he said. "Later, when the trial drags, they'll get more attention."

"That is what I think, too."

"No more of this sneaking in barns, though."

"I am too seductive?"

"For your age."

"And that is why you needed to get the best of me?"

"You've got me down pat, sugar."

She laughed, a young, delightful sound, and he felt he was on safe ground again. Bud Van Vliet teasing a schoolgirl. He was smiling as she ran across gravel and disappeared into the black shadows of the Deane place.

· 5 ·

The next evening Mademoiselle Koestler puffed over to the Van Vliets with a black tin box. Bud recognized it immediately. It was the box he had given barely a glance as he went through Colonel Deane's papers. If he had realized then what it held, he wouldn't have hesitated to use the letters to make a deal with Liam O'Hara and the Southern Pacific. He would have had an unqualified victory, he was certain, and there would have been no Deane Trial. Was that why Amélie had put the box squarely on the desk, his first item for consideration? He wasn't sure.

"Miss Deane says this belongs to you, Mr. Van Vliet."

"Yes. Thank you. Please thank her for returning it."

He dressed in his boiled shirt and new swallowtail and danced at Mary Di Franco's birthday party. Afterward, he and some of the fellows visited Carlotta's. The others kept nudging him about the new girl from San Francisco; very accomplished, they said. To Bud these accomplishments were stale and mechanical. The woman was old and her breasts sagged.

He left Carlotta's as edgy as when he had arrived.

CHAPTER 4

· I ·

It was early March when Amélie's strain turned inside out. One damp, chill day she was in the courtroom while a druggist testified that Colonel Deane had worn a hernia truss, the point of his testimony being the extravagance of the silk linings. Judge Morado rapped his cherrywood gavel continuously, halting quips and laughter. Amélie sat in the front row, arrogance lifting her chin as she tried to conceal her inner turmoil. Time had neither numbed nor clouded her grief. She had dropped from cozy upstairs nurseries into a world where vulgar women and sloppily dressed men stared at her and joked loudly about her father. Each new burst of laughter at his pharmaceutical necessities echoed dizzily in Amélie's mind.

At home, alone in her bedroom, she fainted. She came to in warm, wet underwear. I lost control, she thought. If this happens in front of them . . . if . . . it will be one more disgrace for Papa. And I shall die. She fumbled, untying her lace-edged, knee-length drawers.

She told nobody of the incident.

Twice again that week, in her room, she fainted. And on Sunday, as she played the piano for Mayhew Coppard and her mother in the red drawing room, the dizziness began again. Amélie bit her inner cheek viciously, yet there she was, a Mozart chord abruptly ending as she toppled from the piano stool. Madame Deane, a cold woman preoccupied with the major drama of her life, was nonetheless genuinely fond of her daughter. Worried, she sent for Dr. Widney.

The doctor examined the girl. She trembled, closing her eyes as if seeking escape. The doctor remembered her grief at her father's deathbed, he thought how appallingly public her life had become. He was a very kind man.

"It's nerves," he said to Madame Deane. "She needs exercise. Do you ride, Amélie?"

From her narrow, canopied bed, Amélie nodded.

"In Paris, of course she does," said Madame Deane.

The doctor smiled down at Amélie. His graying beard was fluffed from recent washing. "This young lady will be quite safe around here. We can't have her sinking into nervous melancholia, can we? My prescription is to let her ride."

· 2 ·

Bud galloped into the dust-clouded, dangerous herd of bellowing cattle and bawling calves. His thighs clamped to his borrowed horse, he leaned sideways and with one liquid movement whirled his *reata*, bringing down a red-and-white heifer. Dismounting, he swiftly secured her hooves with the rope. The *marcador* lifted his iron. Decades earlier, the brand would have been a flourished *G*, García. Now, the burning letter was a plain American *S*.

Like all the vaqueros, Bud wore a kerchief protecting his nose and mouth from dust. Like the vaqueros, his hat was wide-brimmed and flat-topped. Like theirs, his trousers were made by Levi Strauss in San Francisco, the blue denim faded and dust-engrained to a flat colorlessness. Like them, he owned the traditional black suit, tight and adazzle with silver. Unlike them, he wore it as a costume to parties designated as fiestas. The vaqueros wore theirs to jangle from one roundup to the next. Born on Paloverde land, part of a life which no longer existed, they had been forced to become itinerant laborers.

Red-hot iron seared the calf's rump, and the animal struggled wildly, forcing Bud to strain every muscle to hold her down. Then the odors of singed hide and burned flesh were stronger and the *marcador* pasted the brand with curative lime. Bud loosed his *reata*. The little heifer rushed blindly into the lumbering, noisy herd.

Bud remounted, swerving into what appeared to be a meaningless mass of cattle and men on horseback. The dust, the smells, the pounding hooves, the deafening bellows of the herd were part of him. He gave a shout. Barely touching the reins, in one swift movement he came between a bull calf and its mother.

The sun was high when he left the roundup and returned his borrowed horse to the *remuda*. He thrust his head into a barrel of water. Snorting lustily, he washed his face, arms, chest, and pale, sun-streaked hair. He went to the cookwagon and helped himself to a tin plate of beans and tortillas. Then he mounted his own horse, Kipper, and started back to Los Angeles.

It had been a wet winter and the live oaks were lush. Elderberry bushes flowered in great, flat, lemon-colored bursts. The chemiso, driest and most flammable of all bushes, bore many leaves on its death-gray branches. Hillsides blazed with poppies. A wren tit sang, its ecstatic trill coming faster and faster like a train speeding up. Bud pushed off his flat, wide-brimmed hat and it flapped against his back as he rode. The morning's exercise had relaxed him and he was able to see the beauty of the day. He felt none of his usual prodding urgency. Whistling an imitation of the wren tit's joyous call, he wound eastward through the part of the Santa Monica Mountains that had once belonged to his forebears.

· 3 ·

The Santa Monicas erupt between the flatness of the San Fernando Valley and the equally flat Los Angeles basin. The range rises steeply and passes are few. Even on the sunniest days, a secret darkness falls on its meandering canyons. Always, the Santa Monicas have beckoned to those who wish to hide.

Her mare grazing nearby, Amélie knelt. Tiny beige flowerlets had fallen into a close-spun web, the work of a funnel spider, and Amélie was reminded of an embroidered sheer tulle scarf her father had given her. She heard hoofbeats in the distance. At the approach of another human being, her usual response was to gallop into a protective canyon. But when she looked up, she saw Bud Van Vliet trotting in her direction.

She hadn't talked to Bud since that night three months earlier when he had kissed her. She had thought a lot about that kiss, dwelling on her numerous and bewildering physical reactions. However, she was not infatuated with Bud. Amélie was part European, brought up in the hothouse snobbery of Madame Deane's world. She felt superior to Bud. Hadn't he been working at the warehouse in his shirtsleeves? Hadn't 3Vee told her that his brother had hired out? Yet he was the only one who had offered sympathy at her father's funeral. And he had agreed to help her avenge her father. He had treated her as a child until the night he kissed her. But even then there was kindness in his touch. Now she thought of him as a friend.

He reined in his horse. "Why, Amélie Deane, hello! What's so interesting down there?"

"A spider web that curls and curves."

"That's made by a funnel spider, honey."

Standing, she brushed at her habit, then made her small, polite curtsey. "Mr. Van Vliet," she said.

He had knotted the red kerchief around his neck. Sun glinted on his bright, tousled hair as he smiled down at her.

"Have you been hunting grizzlies?" she asked.

"Rounding up cattle."

"3Vee said you hired out." Her tone was condescending.

You snobby little girl, Bud thought with amusement. "No, sugar, that was in the oilfields. I was a roustabout. Today I was helping round up cattle. But all I earned was a few refried beans because I had to leave early. An appointment."

"For business?"

"Hardly. I'm escorting Mary Di Franco to the Cotillion."

"Is she your fiancée?"

"Mary? No. Just one of my harem."

At this Amélie's reserved expression melted. She laughed for the first time in many weeks. "Do you keep a large harem, Mr. Van Vliet?"

"Moderate-size."

"Where do you seclude the ladies?"

"Paloverde. Ever see Paloverde?"

"No. But 3Vee told me about it. It was your mother's family's chateau—hacienda."

"That's right. If your friendly dragon isn't snorting fire, I'll show you."

"I am permitted to ride alone, Mr. Van Vliet." She mounted her little mare easily, hooking a knee over the pommel.

He spurred Kipper into a gallop and headed up a slope. To his surprise she followed him without difficulty. He kicked his stallion again, and they began to race up a hillside covered with lupin. From a distance the flowers appeared a dusty purple. Close, they were a vibrant blue. Bud knew that this floral blanket hid rocks and gopher holes, and though Amélie kept up with him for almost a quarter of a mile he began to worry that she would be thrown from her sidesaddle.

"I give up," he shouted.

They reined in their horses.

"Honey, you're a good rider. Maybe I'll let you join my harem."

"I must decline your generous offer." Her skin glowed. The hazel eyes shone. "My second goal in life is to leave Los Angeles."

"And the first?"

"To deal with the Southern Pacific."

"There I'm to help you."

"Yes. And after that I go home to Paris." She was still panting a little, and her lips were open, lips that Bud remembered as soft and yielding.

"And you'll live happily ever after?"

"Mama says with the magnificent *dot* she will give, I shall make a great match." They trotted into a dry wash. "Of course she will lose her case and there will be no dowry. But I do not wish to marry some very fat, very ancient bourgeois, so—"

"You'll take the veil?"

"I will become a *grande courtisane*, like the Lady of the Camellias."

He laughed so violently that Kipper bucked. Controlling the horse, he said, "An interesting vocation."

"Paris is full of writers, artists, musicians, people with interesting ideas. They will all come to my salon. The conversation will be so witty and brilliant that nobody will ever go home to bed."

He repressed a smile. She so transparently didn't understand how the lady earned her camellias.

"And you, Mr. Van Vliet, what do you want?"

"Just to stay here, sweetheart, and be with my friends."

"It sounds far less adventurous than you are."

Until now he had been bantering in the flirtatious tone he used with girls. Now his voice became deeper. "I belong here," he said. "See this bush, the one with the polished-looking red whorly wood? It's called manzanita. It's native to Southern California. It belongs here. I belong here." He pointed. "There's Paloverde just ahead."

On a plateau between two gently sloping hills stretched a long ruin. The red roof tiles had tumbled in patches and were gone entirely from the east wing: here, the dun-colored walls had fallen unevenly. Built of adobe earth, Paloverde was returning to earth.

"But I have passed it often."

"You sound disappointed."

"3 Vee described it as, well, a kind of palace."

"That's 3 Vee for you," Bud said, smiling.

"It *is* large."

"Sugar, no need to be polite with me. It's a tumbledown ranchhouse."

"Who owns it now?"

"I own it. Land is one of my sidelines. Maybe I'm your fat, ancient bourgeois."

"I never could live in Los Angeles," Amélie said without smiling.

Loose dirt had mounded by the massive closed door, grass grew like green hair from roof tiles, and straw poked from weathergnawed adobe bricks. Circling the east wing, they rode around the overgrown orchard and dismounted in the U-shape patio. The grape arbor, vegetables, and rosebushes that once had grown here were long dead, but the heavy winter rains had caused great clumps of poppies and lupin to spring up.

"It is lovely and deserted," Amélie said. "Why does your mother not own it? Why you?"

"When my father had business reverses, we had to sell it. Last year I bought it back." He had paid more money than it was worth, and he was not sure what he wanted with a tumbledown ruin and useless hillside acreage five miles out of town. Yet he had to have it.

"Then you are the very one to give a guided tour of the ancestral home of the Garcías."

He looped their horses' reins around a *corredor* staypole and pointed up to where the wood joined the exposed rafter. "See? Tied with rawhide straps. On Paloverde they made their own nails, but even those were too expensive. This was tied when the strap was wet, and the leather tightened to steel when the straps dried. And those roof tiles came from the kilns of San Fernando Mission, on the other side of these mountains."

He reached out a hand to help her onto the *corredor*. They were an odd pair, he decided, she in a trim broadcloth habit with a high, tilted little top hat, he in the dusty and wrinkled clothes of a vaquero.

In the first room they entered the roof had fallen in and the windows were gone. Only the four-foot-thick walls of adobe brick remained. "This was the dining room, the *comedor*," Bud said. "It was the original room. As they needed more space, they just had the Indians build on. Oh, no! I forgot. They had this room at the beginning, too." They moved to the next room, which was as deep, but narrower than the first, and on the short wall facing them was the remnant of an arched oven. A rusted hook still hung over it. "They had to have a *cocina*, a kitchen. There were no chairs because the cooks were Indians. But see that?" He pointed to a ruined wooden stool. "A woman sat on that fanning the fire with a hawk's-wing fan. One woman had this same job for almost forty years."

"How terrible. So hot. And so boring."

"She was an Indian. And this slit here is the pantry. See, no windows. It was kept locked and my mother had the keys with her all the time. And this room—can you guess what it is?"

She raised up on the toes of her riding boots, peering beyond jagged broken glass. "That square hole looks like a miniature Roman bath."

"Very good. It *is* the bath."

They walked along the *corredor*'s eroded floor, looking into other rooms. He showed her the chapel, the priest's room, the music room. As they crossed the empty space, the house finches that nested in the eaves burst out noisily across the patio. Amélie jumped. "It's only birds," Bud said, taking her gloved hand.

He kept her hand and did not release it when he stopped to explain the hospitable old rancho ways. He kept remembering that kiss. She's a child, he told himself, a child. So why can't I think of her as a child?

"And here's the *sala*," he said. He had to let her go, for he needed both hands to push open the heavy door. "The parlor."

"What is that?" she asked, pointing to a faded heap in one corner.

"*Fazardas*—blankets. I leave them here for the vaqueros. They camp in here because it's the only room where the roof doesn't leak. Can you see the painting on the beams?"

She went inside, looking up. "Fleur-de-lis," she said.

He followed her. "You speak French like a native, sugar," he said. The room hollowed his voice.

"I like your Spanish."

"I like your hair," he said, touching the thick fall behind her riding hat. "I've met a few courtesans, but the *grande*"—he gave the French pronunciation, as she had— "makes it high-class, sweetheart, like you."

"Are all your harem called sweetheart and honey?"

"Some are, sugar."

"I prefer sweetheart."

"It's reserved for you, then," he said, his voice lowered. He cupped her shoulders and felt her quiver. I mustn't, he thought. Not again.

This time it was her mouth that touched his. He heard a peculiar roar in his inner ear.

"No," he said, his mouth next to hers.

"You do not want us to kiss?"

"I explained. Too much."

Tracing his jaw and neck with her hand, she kissed him again. Her kiss and her slow, wandering touch had a gentleness that he had never experienced, not with the local virgins who held their corseted bodies rigid as if to ward off possible invasion, not from the whores who got right down to business, not even with Rose, his first girl. Amélie's kisses were tender, yearning. They were the kisses of a child.

"Bud, I want us to . . . I want whatever people do."

He pushed the door closed. Rusty, handmade hinges creaked, dust whirled. He put both hands on the arch of her back and kissed her open mouth.

I want, too, he thought. Just once in my life let the act be without victim and victor, let there be only this sweet sadness I feel for her and for me. "Yes," he whispered as he began to undo the buttons of her habit. He struggled with the tiny, difficult gold stickpin and, still kissing her, he undid the pearls of her shirtwaist. Narrow embroidered ribbon threaded her camisole. Beneath it, he saw, she was naked. Swallowing, he said, "Sweetheart, I want you, more than I ever wanted anyone. But it's not right. You're meant to stop a man. Amélie, please stop me."

She looked up at him, her hazel eyes wet. Not tears, she'd told him. He pushed at the ribbon-laced straps, revealing a slim body unarmored by the abundant flesh that most men considered desirable. Yet the vulnerability of her slender shoulders, the delicacy of her breasts touched him profoundly.

Soon they were surrounded by his rough clothes and a froth of scented, convent-made underwear. They were both shaking violently. He pulled her down with him on the heaped blankets.

This moment was far more difficult for Bud than for Amélie. He was taking a risk that had been deeply ingrained in him: a whore you pay with cash, a nice girl you pay with the rest of your life. Momentarily he remembered the way Rose's mouth had contorted as she shouted *I'm not going to have your greaser bastard*. Stop, he thought, stop.

But he could not stop. "I don't mean to hurt you." And she gasped, holding him closer. "You're beautiful, so very beautiful," she whispered. Her eyes were squeezed shut and she was tracing the muscles of his shoulders and back, touching parts of him that he hadn't believed could be touched with tenderness. His hands moved over her body, and there was no struggle in the *sala*, only the sounds of their breathing. Then all at once she was crying out, "Oh, Bud... Bud Bud Bud Bud Bud Bud Bud." And all around him the world quivered and shook.

His heart still racing, he looked down at her. Her face was slack. Oh Jesus, he thought, I've killed her. I've gone and killed a little girl.

Her eyes opened and shyly, wonderingly, she touched his lips.

Bud knew everything about women. Women could not experience orgasm. It was scientific fact. Modern doctors confirmed it. Whores, of course, pretended orgasm, but the pretense was convention, and Bud accepted it as such. Yet Amélie had experienced the same release through his body as he had through hers.

His warmth toward her chilled and he turned his head away. He didn't mean to be cold or unkind. He couldn't help himself. She had wanted him as much as he had wanted her. She had found the same pleasure in him as he had found in her. The implications of their equality were too much for him. I must give myself to her as she gives herself to me, he thought. Threatened, he retreated to the reassuring beliefs of sexual order. A woman cannot be equal. The

ridges. Two pigs rolled noisily in the puddles. Mary Di Franco came into Van Vliet's Hardware, clamoring brightly to Bud that she could never, never cross to the Di Franco Block without his assistance.

Boards had been placed like steppingstones across Spring Street, and as Bud surveyed the safest route, he saw Mademoiselle Koestler and Amélie emerge from C. C. Burham's Book Shop and Rental Library. "Mademoiselle Koestler," he said, raising his derby. "And Amélie Deane, hello there."

Amélie dropped her well-bred girl's curtsey. "Good afternoon, Mr. Van Vliet."

"Not a riding day?" he asked.

"Monday I go again," she replied.

He introduced them both to Mary.

"Miss Di Franco," Amélie said with another curtsey.

Mary, staring at the younger girl, wrinkled her forehead and puckered her mouth, looking as if she were sucking a lemon phosphate through a straw.

"I am sorry, Miss Di Franco, Mr. Van Vliet," Amélie said, turning from one to the other with that amused little smile. "We are late."

Mary continued to stare as the girl, chattering in French to her governess, hurried along the covered wood sidewalk. "Stuck-up little thing," she said.

"Honey, how astute of you to see through her after one hello," Bud teased.

"Everybody in Los Angeles says it. I agree."

·6·

The little mare was tethered in the patio, a handful of grass nearby. Bud smiled. It was the sort of thing a child does, giving a horse something to eat while it waits. Amélie sat on the edge of the *corredor*, reading. As he dismounted, she marked her place and closed the book.

"Why, Amélie Deane!" He held his hat over his heart, bowing. "Fancy meeting you here."

"I am equally surprised, Mr. Van Vliet." She stood, and as he looped Kipper's reins around the staypole, she stroked the horse's nose. "Bud," she said, "before we go inside, I have to explain. For me, in my situation, it is necessary that our meeting here be apart from everything else. You can understand, surely. So if you want this, us, to continue—and I do, very, very much—it will have to be as private as time spent on the surface of the moon." She spoke too quickly, as if she had been rehearsing.

Her anxiety caught Bud short. Her normal voice was that of a woman, a sophisticated young woman. But she really is a little girl, he thought, and once more his guilt was roused.

"Amélie, are you sure you realize what we did?"

"I was here," she said.

Her pertness irritated him. "Then you're so far away, up on the moon, that you don't worry we could've made a baby?"

Her kid-gloved fingers stroked Kipper's nose.

"You didn't know?" he asked.

She shook her head.

Again he was reminded that she was only a child, but this time he was filled with protective, masculine tenderness. With Amélie his emotions seemed to veer like a broken weathervane.

"Bud, how do you tell?"

"You miss your monthly cycle." He had never spoken of menstruation to any female, even a whore. He reddened.

So did she, but she looked directly at him. "I had it right after."

"Good, sweetheart. After this I'll take care nothing happens."

"Which means you *do* want us to meet?"

"Sure I do."

She gave him a blinding, happy smile.

"Aren't we both here for the same thing?" he asked, reaching for her.

She stepped back, looking at him. "I do not think so," she said finally. "I want more."

He frowned. "More?"

"I would like you to be my friend."

"What?"

"A friend. Since 3 Vee left, I have none in Los Angeles."

Her scrupulous attention to the points of honor touched him. "Sweetheart," he said gently, "I'm your friend already."

"You are?"

"For sure."

Again that lively, blazing smile. "Bud, thank you."

"*De nada*," he said, lifting her slight weight onto the *corredor*, not taking his hands from her narrow waist.

"Just here," she said.

"I understand. And you, you won't expect anything, well, permanent?"

"Permanent?" Shock tensed her delicate jaw. "I am leaving Los Angeles the minute this trial ends! How could there be anything permanent between us?"

· 7 ·

They met at Paloverde three afternoons a week. If she stayed more than an hour and forty-five minutes, suspicions might be roused, so Bud propped his gold watch on the *sala*'s deep, dusty lintel. While it ticked away the afternoon, emotions buried inside Bud began to poke up, as tentative and shy as burrowing little night animals.

"Bud, what is it?"

"What's what?"

"You seem sad."

They had been meeting a little over a month, and now they were side by side, naked, lying on the blankets.

"I have a lot of other friends," he said, "and none of *them* keeps asking how I feel. I'm always cheerful. Very even-natured."

"I am sorry," she said stiffly. "I do not mean to pry."

He shifted so they were no longer touching, and folded his hands under his neck.

"I was thinking about a girl," he said. "Her name was Rose."

Amélie made a small, questioning noise in her throat but said nothing.

"Rose was my first real girl." Bud paused. "I don't guess 3 Vee ever told you that your father almost destroyed our father?"

"No," Amélie replied quietly and without surprise.

"It happened in seventy-six, right after the railroad came. My father went into the oil-supply business. There's no oil in Los Angeles, but my father figured the town was the natural center for Southern California. It was a gamble, of course. Oil's always a gamble. But my father didn't think of it like that. He sees himself a tower of good common sense. He thought his idea was a good, sound business proposition. And the funny part of it is, he was right. Or he would've been right, if it hadn't been for the Colonel."

Bud paused again. He didn't want to hurt Amélie—yet, having begun this story, he was impelled to finish, and the Colonel was part of it. "Machinery's expensive. My father didn't have enough capital. He convinced his cousin Franz and one of Mama's García connections, Eugene Gold, to go in as silent partners. There was a big whoop-de-do in town when Papa went back East to Pennsylvania. He bought top quality. Like I said, he should've succeeded. Except the Colonel pushed local freight rates for heavy machines sky-high. To ship a boiler from Los Angeles to Newhall, which is thirty miles north of here, cost more than the sea rate around the Horn. Naturally my father had never figured on *that*. He lost money on every item he bought and inside of three months we were flattened. We both wanted to repay Cousin Franz and Eugene Gold, though they'd gone in with us as partners. So we were in the hole. I quit school and clerked full-time."

But even that wasn't enough. Bud had to work Sundays. He found a job in the Newhall oilfield as a tool-dresser, sharpening bits on the forge, doing whatever else the driller, his boss, told him. He wasn't able to afford the train fare up to Newhall, so he waited just out of town to hop on one of the freight cars of the last Saturday-night train, and at dawn on Mondays he came home the same perilous way.

"Rose was my boss's daughter. I was fifteen, and she was a couple of years older. Naturally I lied about my age. Oh, Rose was a pretty girl, curved in all the right places. The other men hung around her, but she seemed to prefer me. After I got off my job, I'd go walking with her. To make a long story short, well, she let me." Bud paused, remembering the joyous gratitude he had felt for Rose's surrender. "I was one wild kid then, and having a girl like Rose, not a whore but a nice type, let me do it to her would've given me plenty of swagger back home in Los Angeles. And I sure needed *some*thing at that time. I didn't tell anyone, though. I haven't told anyone, ever. Until now."

Amélie said nothing and in the silence he heard the ticking watch.

"Then one Sunday night Rose told me she was going to have a baby. Remember, we Van Vliets were at the bottom. I wasn't quite

sixteen. I didn't know how I felt about Rose, beyond lust and gratitude. But the idea of the baby tickled me. I don't know why, it just
did. I wanted that baby. I figured if I was working to keep my
whole family, I could manage this, too. Rose and me would be
married, she'd move into my room at home, and we'd put up the old
cradle. I mean, I wanted it. Oh Jesus! How could anybody be so
young and stupid? I told Rose the whole thing was fine with me.
And she . . ." Bud swallowed convulsively. "She said she didn't want
any greaser bastard."

"Greaser?"

"Greaser means you're Indian. Or part. I'm neither, for sure.
Garcías are Spanish all the way back. But this was Rose's way of
telling me I was nothing to her."

Then, of course, he hadn't taken her remark so calmly. He had
been beside himself with the pain. Greaser, especially to anyone
with Californio forebears, was the final insult. In the old days, cattle
had been raised for their hides and tallow, and the task of skinning
and cutting off what fat there was on the bony, verminous animals
had fallen to the Indians. If an Indian forever stunk of grease, who
cared? Greaser meant you were a Digger. Or part Digger. And Dig-
gers were at the very bottom of the heap. Bud had forgotten he
loved Maria and Juan. To him—and his friends—the epithet *greaser* signified that you were a bastard coyote—a lazy, filthy, stupid,
dishonest degenerate.

"Oh, Rose, she made it plenty clear she didn't want me. Or the
baby. She said to get her money for an abortion. But that's a very
dangerous operation. I argued. Rose insisted. So I managed to borrow the money. From Chaw Di Franco." It had cost Bud's pride
dear to ask Chaw for an unspecified loan. "The next week I gave
Rose the money and she took it."

Bud's skin went cold with the memory. "For a whole week I was
frantic about Rose. So when I got to Newhall, I ran to her cabin.
The place was empty. My boss was gone. Rose was gone. I raced
over to the saloon. It was late Saturday night and everybody was
pretty drunk. I asked a man about Rose. He was a big, fat old roustabout. 'You mean that pretty little tramp?' he said, squinting at me.
'She got herself in a fix. Know what I mean? Yeah, sure you do. It
was your turn, wasn't it? I'll say this for our Rose. She only took on
one at a time. So it was your kid, was it, sonny? Well, you paid for
our Rose's last operation. Bled to death, she did. After that, her Pa

took off. So you're out of a job, too.'" Bud inhaled sharply. "Rose was dead. The child was dead." His lungs compressed at the memory. "And if I looked sad, that's what I was thinking about."

"I hate her," Amélie said softly. "For wanting to kill your baby."

To his surprise, Bud realized that her fierce loyalty was the one response he had wanted to hear. He rolled toward her, pulling her fragile body to his, and the light touch of her fingers between his shoulders comforted him in his long-delayed mourning for his aborted child.

CHAPTER 5

· I ·

The train clanked its grimy, cindery way toward Los Angeles. 3 Vee sat in the wooden coach with a stove at one end and a water closet at the other. It was June and his first year at Harvard had ended. His forehead was pressed, jostling, against the gritty double window. Around him, newcomers to Southern California chattered about "real oranges growing on real trees" while they gathered food hampers and valises from overhead racks.

3 Vee, like most of the other passengers, had made the full eight-day trip from the Eastern seaboard, and like them, he was glazed with weariness. At a speed of twenty-two miles per hour, even the most magnificent landscapes become tedious.

To relieve their boredom, the passengers had talked. And most of the talk was about the Deane Trial. As soon as 3 Vee established that he was a neighbor of the Deanes, he was no longer considered a Harvard snob. He became a celebrity. When passengers alighted for their meals, 3 Vee was proudly pointed out to those in less fortunate carriages as a specialist on the Deane Trial.

That month, the newspaper reporting had turned feverish.

A San Francisco woman—Mrs. Sophie Belle Deane, she called herself—alleged that *she* was the Colonel's widow, and that her two daughters were his rightful heirs. It was news to 3 Vee. Amélie had never mentioned them; her light, charming letters never referred to the Deane Trial. But 3 Vee asserted to his fellow passengers that there was only one Madame Deane, an aristocratic French lady, as they doubtless knew. And Miss Amélie Deane was the Colonel's only child. That is, 3 Vee added with sophistication, his only legitimate child.

The months apart from Amélie had not changed his feelings for her. As the train passed the first shacks on the outskirts of town, he considered the idea of revealing his love to her before she turned sixteen. *She* might be young, he thought, but I'm older. 3 Vee had bought a new, stylishly close-fitted alpaca suit. His mustache had taken proper shape. Harvard had broadened the scale of his mind. Of course he couldn't mention to Amélie the somewhat skinny milliner and the five interludes on her creaking bed. Still, such relationships, he hoped, gave a man visible *savoir-faire*.

He knew that his thoughts were immature. His love, however, was real and tender. I'll tell her, he thought, smiling a little. Yes, why not?

The whistle screamed, the porter went through the car shouting "Los Angeles! Los Angeles!" And the train puffed into the mustard-yellow depot.

· 2 ·

He saw his family waving on the crowded platform. His parents looked smaller and older than he remembered. Bud looked more vigorous, stronger than he had let himself remember.

3 Vee forgot his new worldliness and let Doña Esperanza clasp him to her full body. She smelled, as always, of desert lavender. He bent, avoiding her high, tiny bonnet, to kiss her. "Oh Mama, Mama. How I missed you." Hendryk grasped 3 Vee's hands, for once gazing up at him with proud blue eyes. And Bud shook his hand heartily. "Welcome home, kid. Welcome back to Los Angeles." 3 Vee noticed that Bud was less formally dressed than any Eastern businessman. He was unmistakably a Southern Californian.

They left Juan to manage the trunks. Bud held the reins of the new brougham and 3 Vee sat up front with him. "Now we're just family," Bud said. "So you can take off the gloves."

"Everybody wears gloves."

"Not on the nicest day in June they don't."

Bud was teasing, the prerogative, 3 Vee knew, of older brothers.

But he still rose to the bait. "Gentlemen wear them the year round in the East. Los Angeles is a hick town."

Bud grinned. "Tell me about it."

It *is* a hick town, 3 Vee thought rebelliously. They were climbing up to Temple Street; these few blocks were the heart of Los Angeles, and right there was vacant land with grazing cows. Bud was still grinning at him. 3 Vee tugged off his mouse-gray gloves.

3 Vee's return was toasted with red wine and celebrated with a huge dinner that included tamales and enchiladas. After dinner, Hendryk went to nap on the sunroom sofa, Bud returned to the Van Vliet Block, and 3 Vee relaxed in the claw-footed bathtub. Then he put on his new suit, which Maria had pressed, pomaded his thick black hair, combed his mustache, and went whistling downstairs.

Doña Esperanza was darning socks on the front porch. "Vincente," she said. "We haven't had a chance to talk about your college."

"Mama, I'll tell you all about it at supper. Then Bud and Papa can hear, too."

He kissed her smooth graying hair. And her eyes followed him as he sauntered down the steps, adjusting his gloves, and turned toward the dagger-tipped fence of the Deane place.

· 3 ·

He might never have been gone.

"Thomas Hardy?" Amélie said. "You had a conversation with Thomas Hardy? Did you discuss *Far from the Madding Crowd?*"

"We didn't exactly talk together," said 3 Vee, who had just claimed the opposite.

"He gave a lecture?"

"Uh, yes. In Faneuil Hall," he said, reddening.

They sat near one another on the low wicker chairs of the solarium while Mademoiselle Koestler embroidered in the far corner. Amélie gave 3 Vee her lively smile.

His embarrassment faded. "Let's go outside," he said. "The weather's the only thing Los Angeles has."

"We cannot," Amélie said. He followed her glance through the windows of the solarium. Several couples were strolling along the walk in front of the house, gazing avidly into the Deane gardens.

"I have suggested to Mama that she buy some camels and an elephant," Amélie said. Her voice was scornful.

"Then it's always like this?"

"In Los Angeles we outshine Mr. Barnum and Mr. Bailey." Amélie's delicate nostrils flared in contempt.

What if she were to look at me like that, 3 Vee thought. He saw her clenched hands, the small nails cutting into the flesh of her palms. And he understood the ugly curiosity surrounding her. The people of Los Angeles were not monsters. They had merely mistaken her pride for arrogance. Amélie was young, fragile, appealing. If she had exposed only a little of her grief, her vulnerability (or if, as 3 Vee knew Amélie would think of it, she had pandered herself for pity), she could have easily won their sympathy. Yet 3 Vee would not have changed her in any way.

"They shouldn't be allowed to annoy you," he said.

"Mama is right. They are peasants." Her expression changed. Color left her cheeks. She looked ill. "This woman, this other woman and her daughters, that annoys me. It is such a terrible lie!"

"The Southern Pacific will stop at nothing," 3 Vee agreed. His was not a unique opinion. A good many people, and newspapers too, were against the railroad and assumed the new "widow" and her "daughters" were a put-up job.

"She begins her testimony on Thursday, and then we shall see precisely how far they are willing to go."

"But your mother cannot let you be exposed to *that!*"

"Mama does not wish us to be there. But Mr. Coppard, her chief attorney, says it will be best if we are."

"Your mother is right."

"No. If we are not there, how will Judge Morado see Papa's real family?" Amélie lifted her shoulders in a wry little shrug.

He ached to help her. Yet what could he do? Go to that important New York attorney, Mayhew Coppard? Insist that Amélie not be in the courtroom? Mayhew Coppard would reply, properly, that it was no concern of his. Besides, Amélie had decided that her presence would somehow exonerate the Colonel of these new charges. 3 Vee sighed. He had set out this afternoon to impress Amélie, and all he'd had done was uncover her misery and his own helplessness.

At least I can tell her what I feel for her, he thought. As soon as there's the opportunity I will.

Mademoiselle Koestler was gathering skeins of silk into a black velvet bag. *"Ma chère,* remember the time."

"Oh, 3 Vee. I am sorry. Mademoiselle Koestler will not let me forget my dental appointment."

It was the governess who led 3 Vee to the front door. "It is good to have you home, Mr. Van Vliet." 3 Vee could hear the rumbles of the kind old woman's stomach. "Miss Deane welcomes your company. It has been a most difficult winter for her."

As 3 Vee emerged from the house, two rotund matrons peered through the fence at him. He tried to ignore their gaze, yet his walk became mechanical and he heard his shoes crunch on the gravel. By the time he opened the side gate the fat pair had lumbered across the street. Thursday, he thought. What will happen on Thursday? In each human being there exists a unique and mysterious precipice beyond which he cannot be pushed. Amélie was approaching the edge of that dangerous precipice.

·4·

Bud strolled along Spring Street with Lucetta Woods.

Lucetta's father had moved here from Baltimore for his health. The Southern Pacific, as part of its promotion of the area, had touted Southern California into one huge health resort. The elderly came because they were convinced the climate was rejuvenating, arthritics and rheumatics came to sun their aches and pains, sufferers from asthma rejoiced in instant cures, and so many tuberculars had settled on verandas in the clear-aired eastern foothills that Los Angeles was being referred to as a one-lung town. Mr. Woods had inherited a weak chest and a large sum of money, and so Lucetta was viewed as an imminent heiress. Her Southern voice drawled daring remarks, her brown lashes fluttered. In no time at all she had become quite a belle. A few minutes earlier, meeting Bud at the Farmers & Merchants Bank, she had vowed she was on her way to Van Vliet's Hardware to buy some of their new iced-tea glasses for her mother.

Lucetta and Bud were nearing the Van Vliet Block when the

Deane carriage pulled up to the covered walk. Bud raised his brightly ribboned straw boater to Mademoiselle Koestler and Amélie as they stepped down from the carriage. Passersby stopped to look at them.

"Why, Amélie Deane, hello," he said, grinning at Amélie.

Sweetheart, yes that, ah, do that.

"Mr. Van Vliet." Amélie dropped her polite child's curtsey.

Bud Bud Bud Bud Bud Bud now Bud.

He presented them to Miss Lucetta Woods. Lucetta's thick lashes ceased fluttering. She stared at the younger girl openly. Amélie did not curtsey. She stood, hands at her sides, her face expressionless. Hastily Mademoiselle Koestler took her arm. "Come, Amélie," she said in her guttural Alsatian voice. She turned to Bud. "You must excuse us. We are late for an appointment."

"Have I just met the illegitimate daughter?" Lucetta drawled.

"Honey, what do you know about those things?" Bud spoke as pleasantly as ever, but his eyes were flat and angry.

"Well, every single soul in Los Angeles is talking about it. She's a cool little thing, isn't she? You must know all about her. She's your neighbor. Do tell! All."

"I have to get back to work," Bud said. With an absent tilt of his boater and no goodbye, he left her standing outside the store.

·5·

The next afternoon, Wednesday, Bud arrived first at Paloverde. Dusting off a cracked tile on the edge of the *corredor*, he waited, eyes fixed on the path through the dead orchard, his left boot scuffling a cloud of dust. Patience wasn't one of his virtues. Hurry up, he thought. Hurry up, Amélie Deane.

Teasing, he often used both her names. Yet the Deane eluded him. He rarely considered that she was the red-bearded railroad man's daughter, barely remembered that she was part of the biggest scandal to hit the West. He ignored her every connection with the great Los Angeles circus known as the Deane Trial.

If this was quite a sleight-of-mind trick for a practical man, it was done simply. To Bud the tumbledown hacienda had become a world with a population of two, and Amélie so dominated this world that he couldn't bring himself to acknowledge that she existed elsewhere. Like the real world, the Paloverde they shared had its own history, language, jokes, battles, loyalties, rites, festivities. He had taught her the Californio dances, the *jota* and the *fandango*. She mimicked his pet phrases until he had to laugh. After he had told her about Rose, he found himself telling her other stories about himself, and she listened gravely. And when they made love, her skin had a taste to it and she had a sharp, delicate odor, like sugarbush flowers.

But it was becoming more difficult to isolate her in the world they had created at Paloverde. Thoughts of her followed him everywhere, into Van Vliet's Hardware, into his bed at night, and yesterday into the streets of the town. For a brief instant, before the stares of Lucetta and curious passersby, she had been utterly defenseless, a small young girl dressed in the color of dark smoke. They're looking at Amélie, he thought, Amélie. *My* Amélie. Instinctively he started to lift a hand to take her arm, to protect her from the abusive eyes. But before he could move, the old governess whisked her away. Lucetta spoke, he replied, words and more words, and he turned to see the legs below short mourning, slim legs that he often kissed as he pulled down black silk stockings.

And in that moment after the Deanes's carriage door opened, Bud Van Vliet's worlds merged irrevocably. Amélie dominated them both.

A horned toad skittered from the shadows and Bud heard approaching hoofbeats. He hurried to the front of the rancho. Amélie's cheeks were smudged. Obviously she had been crying. He lifted her from the saddle, bitterly ashamed. How could he not have realized what she was going through?

Amélie held herself taut, but as his hands comforted her, she relaxed against him and began to weep. He wanted to cry, too, for the blind part of him that hadn't understood how cleverly this brave, proud, funny, irritating girl had concealed her sorrow even from him—this girl who, for one hour and forty-five minutes three afternoons a week, had made him whole, the only times in his entire flawed adult life.

He kept one arm around her as he tethered the mare and they went into the *sala*. Closing the door behind them, he sat on the *fazardas*, pulling her onto his lap. She blew her nose. He took the initialed scrap and wiped the smudges on her cheeks.

"There. That's better," he said. "Sweetheart, what's wrong?"

"Tomorrow."

"Tomorrow?"

"I will be at the performance."

"The trial," he said. The woman who called herself Mrs. Sophie Belle Deane would testify.

"As if they have not raked Papa over enough! Even his illnesses."

"I never realized how rotten this has been for you."

"The facts are fair, Bud. Even if they have no real bearing on whether Mama owns the shares. But why should they invent lies?"

Bud knew men like the Colonel often have unofficial families. He said nothing.

Amélie persisted. "What can their point be?"

He kept silent.

"Bud?"

"I figure," he said quietly, "it's the same as you wanting the letters read into evidence. You want to discredit them. They want to discredit him."

"But they already have. Thoroughly. If they want to hang him, let them go through the ledgers. That, at least, is honest. Bringing in false witnesses, this woman and the two girls, can only destroy all Mama and I have left." She paused. "He always told me that I was his only child. He never lied to me. He would just keep silent. He never lied. We were much closer than most fathers and daughters. He said it was because I was his only chick. What a silly phrase. Bud, I miss him so!"

He pressed his cheek against hers. "We should've talked about it before."

She shook her head.

"I told you my feelings. Shouldn't you have told me yours?"

"Yes, but..." She sighed. "This has been the only place I can forget. I cannot really explain. But when I come up this hill I feel as if Papa is still alive. In Paloverde, the world seems safe."

"With me you are safe."

She didn't seem to hear him. "Tomorrow I have to face that woman and those girls. Oh, they are so vile, the imposters!" She gave him a small, painfully apologetic smile. Then the smile was gone. "Bud, what if I faint?"

"Faint?" Bud was surprised. He thought she was telling him,

obliquely, that his method of contraception had failed. His throat filled with a joy so great that he couldn't swallow. The child would be his and hers; he would live the rest of his life with Amélie. "Why would you faint, sweetheart?"

"I did, several times. Then Dr. Widney said I needed exercise and fresh air. He understood that I must get away from all the staring and whispering. He is very kind. Have you never wondered that Mama lets me ride alone?"

"I've been grateful, that's all."

"It is nothing like swooning in novels. It is horrible. Your bladder goes all loose. If that happens, I will die."

He took off her left riding glove and held her palm to his cheek. "I love you," he said. He had told her this often, but always when he was inside her. She had never said the words. "Amélie, I love you so much. I need to be with you all the time. Forever. I promise, things will be very different for you the minute everyone understands we're going to be married."

"Married?" Her hand jerked from his grasp. "Married? I live for the day I leave this spiteful town!"

"Amélie—"

"They say I am stuck up. How *should* I behave? Do they want me to grovel? Is that what they want, proof of how much they have hurt me? Oh, what horrors they are! My friends at home would never talk about a three-legged dog the way these—these creatures talk about my father!"

He stroked back her hair. "Sweetheart, you're right, and it's my fault. I should have stopped them from being so ugly in front of you. I don't know how I let it go on. I guess, like you, I set Paloverde apart. There are things about myself I don't understand. But I love you so much. Why can't we be married right away?"

When Amélie spoke, her clear voice was muffled. "I have been so confused. Here I am me, but other places my mind refuses to work. The stupidest little things seem impossible. I could not decide whether to curtsey to Miss Woods. Her eyes were so cold. The eyes are all cold. Last night I had trouble deciding if I wanted the soufflé, and finally Mademoiselle Koestler had to put some on my plate. If I cannot make up my mind about things like that, how can I know how I feel about anyone?"

Bud didn't really believe her refusal, yet it hurt him deeply. His muscles tightened. "Anyone?" he asked.

"Not you. You mean a great deal to me. But I cannot live in Los Angeles. I cannot!" Her voice was too high. "I never should have come here to meet you. Please, it is I who am at fault. Not you. Not you. And I could not bear it if I made you unhappy. That would be a dishonorable way to repay your friendship.... Am I saying this all wrong? Bud, I should not be able to hurt you. Please. I thought ... you are a grown man and I am just a girl ... too young ... Bud, how can I have hurt you? Please, please, I cannot live here."

She was gasping in small gulps of air. Her eyes were blank. He had never seen her like this. Even earlier, weeping, even in passion, in yesterday's bewilderment, he had never seen her stripped of pride, without her delicate sense of self. Again he was ashamed. My God, what I am doing? She has already been pushed enough. Why can't I take my time to convince the girl I love—and have already taken—to marry me? He picked up her ungloved hand, biting it gently on the index finger. "There," he said. "I've hurt you back. Now we're quits."

She blinked uncomprehendingly.

"We're friends, Amélie," he said. "No. You wouldn't pick a friend who does this sort of thing with a child." He toppled them so they lay on the faded, striped blankets. Her wet eyes had a tiny spark—or perhaps it was a trick of the dim light. "You are an aggravating little girl, and you should be in Paris playing jacks or whatever game they play there. Yet if that's so, if you're a baby, how are you so clever?" He was tracing the delineation of her mouth. "Tell me how you're so clever. And brave. What little girl takes on the entire Southern Pacific Railroad? And if you're such a baby, why didn't you cry before? Did I ever tell you how sweet these are, like firm summer peaches? Do you really want to be friends with a grown man depraved enough to say that to a little girl? There! Now you *are* smiling. You're meant to laugh. I say stupid things to make you laugh, do you know that? It's the prettiest sound, like crystal. Everything about you is pretty and dainty. Here, let me undo this. I want to take these down. Yes, do that. I love it when you do that to me ... ahh, sweetheart, you're so perfect and I belong in here."

For a while the *sala* was quiet. The first time Bud had feared her response. But since then her unfettered sensuality had brought him deeper pleasure than he had believed possible. He could not imagine a life without her. She began quivering, shaking, calling his name, and he thrust farther and faster, filling her with his dreams, his hopes, his love, every part of himself. At the final moment he gave a shout of exultation. The house finches scattered from the eaves.

For a long time they didn't move. They lay together, his lips pressed to her warm cheek, her eyes closed, his open.

He had brought some Riverside seedless oranges and he peeled one with his penknife. Juice squirted between her breasts, and he wiped away the drops, holding up his fingers for her to lick.

"Tomorrow," he said, "I'll go with you and your mother to court."

She shook her head.

"If I'm there, I'll be able to stop some of the talk."

"I cannot let you," she said with sad yet determined finality. "It is unfair."

"Why?"

"It would be taking advantage of your feelings."

"This is apart from that, entirely. We *are* friends." He pulled the orange apart and gave her half, as if to prove his point. "And with any other friend I'd have been there from the beginning. No strings."

It was true. For an act of friendship Bud expected no reward, no tit-for-tat, not even a thank you. Her eyes questioned him.

"For a friend there's never any strings," he said. "Now quit being so proud and honorable. You need someone to hand you the smelling salts. I'll be there whether you like it or not."

She lifted an orange segment to her mouth and surprised him with her delightful lopsided smile.

·6·

The breeze rattled chaparral in that endless, empty sound that 3 Vee had forgotten. Knowing that Amélie, too, was riding, he had been letting his horse amble, hoping he would bump into her. We would be alone for once, he thought. I could tell her that I love her. He was moving westward, in the direction of Paloverde. He hadn't been there in almost a year, and the rancho called to him.

Bud had bought Paloverde, but 3 Vee thought of himself as the owner. After all, wasn't he the real García?

There, on the narrow ledge between the hills, the adobe walls stretched in welcome, and from roof tiles a burst of house finches fluttered upward like a veil flung in greeting.

3 Vee dismounted under the sycamore that shadowed the front portal. The massive doors to the *zaguán* were shut, earth mounding against them. He moved around the left wing and saw that two horses were tethered in the patio: Bud's stallion, Kipper, new since 3 Vee had left for Harvard, and a pretty little sidesaddled mare. At first he thought of calling out, then decided against it. Bud would be furious. After all, he was here with a girl.

Which girl? Lucetta Woods? Mary Di Franco? It could be any of the town's dozen prettiest. The little mare's a thoroughbred, 3 Vee thought, the saddle's beautiful, so she's from a well-fixed family. Yet, would Bud bring a nice girl here? He never fools with nice girls. It could be an outsider. No, it's not a Los Angeles girl.

3 Vee, rubbing his small black mustache, gazed at the closed *sala* door. They're inside, he thought. His hands were clammy. He didn't want to know who the girl was, yet he moved silently on the balls of his feet across the weed-filled patio. He remembered a roundup from long ago when he had seen Bud galloping into a dangerous swirl of cattle. He couldn't have been twelve, but to 3 Vee he had seemed a full-grown man, his big brother, bright sun-streaked hair flying, exuberantly brave in the welter of huge beasts. Bud doing what 3 Vee had longed to do.

He halted, listening. He heard the wind, a horse nickering. No voices. The thick adobe brick would cut off all sound. Grasping a termite-rotted staypole, he hauled himself onto the porch. *In flagrante delicto*, he thought, and didn't want to move any farther. Yet there he was peering through window glass that had come from Europe, an old, convex pane that gave him the sense of looking through a magic spyglass into a remote land.

She lay on her back, one hand under her neck, while Bud, cross-legged next to her, peeled an orange. A domestic scene that said far more of their intimacy than any groping tangle of limbs. In that first benumbed instant, 3 Vee thought: how beautiful they are.

Bud's deep tan became ivory where his neck joined his torso. His shoulders were wider than they appeared in clothes, and a line of crisp gold hairs divided the strong musculature of his chest and flat stomach.

Then 3 Vee looked only at Amélie. He had never seen a woman naked. The Cambridge milliner always wore her nightgown. Amélie's white body drew light from the dimness as an opal does. She was all delicate, star-pale curves. Bud touched between her breasts, held his finger to her lips, and spoke to her in words that 3 Vee could not hear.

He drew back from the window and rested his cheek on deep-set adobe. Coarse straw cut his face. *A finer mind, larger perception*, he thought. And there she is with Bud, Bud who's never heard of Henry James, Bud who never voluntarily read a book in his life, and who thinks this is all a woman is for. Oh God, she's no fictional portrait of a lady, she's a sweating, monthly bleeding, thigh-opening female. And Papa is right. I'm a fuzz-minded idiot. Talking to her about books, waiting until she's older to mention the word *love*. Bud is unhampered by my stupid sensitivities. Bud doesn't talk. He acts.

Swinish, both of them, he told himself, knowing he couldn't condemn them. He envied them. He wanted to hate them. But he thought of Amélie's letters in his top drawer, beginning with that two-sentence absolution written on the afternoon of the Colonel's funeral. He thought of Bud at fifteen, astride a chair, telling him that he would have his own friends see that 3 Vee wasn't teased too fiercely in school. Bud forced into manhood yet taking on the job of protecting a younger brother.

How could he hate them?

Instead, he thought, I'll show them. The thought came in great, violent gusts. I'll show them, I'll show them. He found himself riding west, riding away from town. Below him, flat to the palisades of the Pacific, stretched the Los Angeles basin with its vineyards, beanfields, dusky citrus groves, wild yellow mustard. Above him, covering the hillside, the chaparral's tough, bushlike little trees—manzanita, buckthorn, greasewood—were green from the wet winter. Yucca thrust up their creamy, man-high blossoms. Quail called. A deer scampered. How is it I have never noticed how beautiful it all is? he wondered. Am I doomed to beauty at second remove, books, music, paintings? Beauty wearing clothes?

And I am banished. Forever.

3 Vee dismounted at the Cahuenga Pass, that wide break in the

Santa Monicas where, in 1847, Colonel John C. Frémont, conqueror, and General Andrés Pico, conquered, had signed the Treaty of Cahuenga, ending the dreamy order of the Californios, starting the reign of the Americans. 3 Vee, stiff from so much riding, walked a small circle, counting the money in his pocket. Seven dollars and thirty cents, less than he was given to keep himself for a week at Harvard. Not enough to start a life.

It has to be, he thought, as he hauled himself into his saddle and rode into the afternoon-shadowed Cahuenga Pass away from Los Angeles.

· 7 ·

The hall case clock chimed, marking the quarter hour.

"Fifteen past eight," Doña Esperanza said.

"Mama," Bud said, "remember how often I was late. All night sometimes. And I was younger than 3 Vee."

"I never stopped taking my belt to you," said Hendryk.

They were in the sunroom. In the adjacent dining room, Maria and her niece chattered as they cleared supper dishes from the table.

"Bud, you're not 3 Vee," Doña Esperanza said. Below her fine eyes there were dark, wrinkled shadows.

"3 Vee has been at Harvard College for a year," said Hendryk. "He's a man now. My dear, you must learn to let him be."

Bud stood, buttoning his jacket. "I'm going next door for a few minutes. I thought maybe Madame Deane would appreciate an escort tomorrow."

"Oh yes," Hendryk said. "The other woman appears."

"The child..." Doña Esperanza hesitated. "Do you suppose 3 Vee is with the girl?"

"The Deane child?" Hendryk asked. "My dear, it's not like you to be foolish. That girl is top-grade merchandise. Madame Deane and the old dueña watch over her like hawks. They might let 3 Vee talk of an afternoon to her, but no more, no more. She'll be a countess, that little one, and our 3 Vee will be home within the hour, you mark my words."

Bud said, "I better get there before Mr. Coppard leaves."

They heard the front door open and close.

"She's a pretty woman, Madame Deane," Hendryk remarked.

"The girl . . ." Doña Esperanza fell silent. She had never gossiped or speculated with her husbands. Her question, therefore, remained unasked. Yet hadn't there been a flicker of Bud's eyes when Hendryk said the girl was top-grade merchandise? Almost as if he hadn't realized it before. Bud, she thought, hadn't inherited his father's eye for quality. Why should that matter? I *am* being foolish, she thought. The girl is too young, even for my 3Vee.

Doña Esperanza struck a lucifer and lit a narrow brown cigarillo. Neither Bud nor 3Vee had ever seen her smoke, for she knew that young American men looked down on the pleasant Californio custom of a lady ending a meal in this manner. She inhaled the rich tobacco smoke, her head tilting with each sound outside.

Hendryk, on the horsehair sofa, was hidden by the *Los Angeles Herald*. Reading in English had never become natural for him, yet each evening he stubbornly waded through the papers. There was a full column about the Deane Trial.

· 8 ·

Originally, the Los Angeles Courthouse had been built as a market. It was undistinguished by square or statue, and on its only ornament, a clock tower, a pair of chickens roosted.

Reporters and spectators were moving inside. No lady, naturally, would enter a courtroom, yet this morning quite a few well-off matrons were strolling on Temple Street past the courthouse. Bud lifted his straw hat to Mrs. Di Franco, who felt compelled to remark that she and Mrs. Woods were out shopping. The men made no such pretense. "Hey, Bud, should be interesting today. Want me to save you a seat?" "So you're finally taking off work to see the show, too, Bud?" Nodding curtly to his friends, he waited for the Deane carriage to arrive.

When it drew up in front of the courthouse, Mayhew Coppard descended first, and the two men handed Amélie and Madame Deane down the narrow steps of the carriage block.

"Hello there, Amélie Deane," Bud said, suddenly loathing this uncle-niece charade.

"Good morning, Mr. Van Vliet." Amélie's clear voice and her well-bred curtsey.

Madame Deane put a light hand on Bud's arm and the crowd parted. "That's a new outfit on the Deane girl," one woman said. "Must want to be pretty for her sisters." "Think them two widows'll compare a few personal notes?" another woman remarked. Madame Deane ignored them. "A lovely day, is it not, Mr. Van Vliet?" she said to Bud.

Cigar smoke already grayed the courtroom. Just ahead of them a stream of yellow tobacco juice rang against the side of a spittoon. "Mr. Van Vliet, you shall sit between Amélie and me," Madame Deane said, as if arranging a supper party. At the counsel table, Mayhew Coppard and his junior partner were opening leather cases.

There was a sudden stir.

Into the courtroom strode the Southern Pacific's chief counsel. Liam O'Hara's tall angularity emphasized the rotund figure of the woman at his side. Stout, tightly corseted, her hair swept up under a bonnet with egret plumes that tilted too far forward, the woman in no way physically resembled Madame Deane. Yet the mourning and coiffure were overstated copies of Madame Deane's Parisian elegance. Behind her bounced two fat, reddish-haired girls of twelve and fourteen, stuffed into gray poplin jumpers. The elder girl was very erect, a cruel and clumsy parody of Amélie's graceful carriage.

Madame Deane raised her lorgnon, examining the three as if they belonged to some species of worm new to her. Steel-tipped drawing pens scratched. Audible comparisons were made. Everyone in the courtroom had turned except Amélie. She gazed rigidly at the judicial bench.

Bud leaned toward her. "You look very pretty today," he whispered.

She nodded, her eyes fixed ahead.

Behind them, a rasping male voice was saying, "Given the choice of any woman, nine times out of ten a man'll grab ahold of the same general type."

"This one's generally plumper."

Laughter.

"The girls're generally stouter, too."

Bud turned. The men were reporters. The raspy-voiced one, a newcomer to town, worked on the *Herald*. Thin-chested, with a small goatee, he was called George Something-or-other, a decent enough fellow. "George, why not keep your opinions to yourself?" Bud asked pleasantly.

George glanced at the back of Madame Deane's head. "Sure thing, Bud."

The sheriff rapped his gavel, everyone rose, and Judge Morado entered. He was a short man visibly deformed under his robes. One shoulder was higher than the other and he walked with a limp. To counteract this physical weakness, he scorned moral flaccidity. Since the opening of the Deane Trial, he had withstood tremendous pressure from politicians and his colleagues, anyone the railroad could buy or ruin. Judge Morado was a completely honest man.

He sat. Noisily, the packed courtroom followed suit.

"*Much* stouter than our Deane daughter." Bud heard the whispered remark and he turned again. "George, one more word and your paper will never get another line of Van Vliet advertising, either from our hardwares or my cousin's grocery. Your boss is going to ask why." His voice was low and hard. A command. "Bud, honest to God, I never meant..." Bud cut short the apology with a smile. He never pushed too hard—unless he had to.

Liam O'Hara rose and said the words everyone was waiting to hear. "I call Mrs. Sophie Belle Deane to the stand."

Mayhew Coppard half stood, leaning on the table. "Objection," drawled the urbane New York voice.

"To what, Mr. Coppard?" asked Judge Morado.

"If it please the court, the lady is not Mrs. Deane."

It took over an hour for a decision to be reached. The defense witness would be addressed as Mrs. Sophie Belle Marchand.

The witness stepped foward, a plump, common woman who may—or may not—have once been handsome. Amélie, forced to look at her, swallowed audibly.

Bud leaned toward her. "Think of something else," he whispered.

She bit her inner cheek, giving no indication that she had heard him. Her gloved hands were clenched.

A crosscurrent of desires swept over Bud. He saw himself taking aim with his Winchester at her enemies—his friends—the spectators. He saw himself grabbing her small hand and pulling her from the courthouse, holding her his willing captive in Paloverde. I have to do something, he thought repeatedly. He despised inaction. Yet hadn't he promised her to be here as a friend, no more?

Baffled anger glittered in his eyes.

·9·

There were two dining rooms at the Pico House, one for hotel residents, the other for the public. Local businessmen ate at home, so those dining in the big, many-windowed public room were prosperous ranchers, or professional men and merchants from the nearby little communities that developers (Bud included) were busily carving from local ranchos. Some of these men had Californio wives or mothers and were related to Bud through Doña Esperanza. Most were his friends. They said, "Hello there, Bud," and refrained from glancing too avidly at Madame Deane and Amélie.

"We seem to be in the midst of your people, Mr. Van Vliet," Mayhew Coppard remarked as they took their seats.

"A García—that's my mother's maiden name—was on the original Portola expedition that discovered this area."

"May we assume your ancestor kept going?" Amélie asked with an amused little smile. These were the first words she had uttered since "Good morning, Mr. Van Vliet."

He smiled back. "He sure did. His son, though, my great-grandfather, returned with a *diseño*—a map—granting him this land."

"Why did they banish him? For what terrible crime?"

"Amélie!" Madame Deane cried. "*Ma chère!* You owe Mr. Van Vliet an apology."

"It's me, Madame Deane, who should do the apologizing, for my town's lack of courtesy."

A whisper swept through the well-appointed dining room.

On the red Brussels carpet of the entry stood Liam O'Hara. And next to him was the woman who called herself Mrs. Sophie Belle Deane. Her two daughters were poking their heads into the dining room, staring around.

Amélie continued to smile a faintly malicious yet pretty smile at

Bud, but she had turned pale. He let his calf touch hers. Through layers of clothing he could feel her quivering.

"Excuse me a moment," he said, and still holding his starched linen napkin, he moved swiftly around tables to the chief waiter. "Arturo," he said, "every place is taken." He turned to Liam O'Hara. "Mr. O'Hara, the food at the Hotel Nadeau is excellent."

Mrs. Sophie Belle Deane pointed. "That table there, in the corner, isn't it empty?"

"It's reserved," Bud said. "My father and a group from the Turnverein are discussing a banquet to be held here."

At his lie, Arturo nodded. The chief waiter knew where his tips came from.

Bud turned again to the railroad attorney. "The last time we met, Mr. O'Hara, you assured me of your desire to help. I realize this can't extend into the courtroom, however..."

Liam O'Hara bent his skull-like head in acknowledgment. "Come, Mrs. Deane," he said. "We shall try the Nadeau." And, somber as a funeral attendant, he ushered the crimson-faced, arguing woman and the two fat, twittering girls through the hall separating public and private dining rooms.

Bud returned to the table, pressing his leg to Amélie's. The trembling had worsened.

"Amélie," he asked, "are you all right?"

"I would rather rest than eat," she said.

"I'll see you home."

"Mama, with your permission?"

"Dear child," said Mayhew Coppard, benign, "we need your presence in court this afternoon."

"Is it the dizziness, *ma chère?*"

"Mama, please?"

Her large brown eyes worried, Madame Deane turned to Bud. "It is not too much trouble, Mr. Van Vliet?"

"None at all. I'll be in court at two-thirty."

"You will go directly to your room, *ma chère?*"

"Yes, Mama."

Outside, Bud sent the doorman across the Plaza to get the Deanes's black servant from the Mexican cafeteria. A fat woman was climbing Fort Moore Hill, where flower-vined shacks were strung together by rickety staircases. She disappeared behind a mound of sweet alyssum, geraniums, and purple bougainvillea.

Amélie murmured, "Bud, I have to sit down."

He lifted his hand. A cab moved forward. He called, "The Deane place on Fort Street," and helped her in.

· 10 ·

She sank into her corner of the airless hack, closing her eyes. Bud pressed his palm to her trembling thigh. Yesterday, when he had promised no strings, he had meant it. Friendship draws boundaries. Love, however, has none. Today, his impotence to help her had been unbearable. The fantasies he had conjured up, the kidnapping, the rifle aimed at noisy spectators, were more rational to him than this pretense that she was a child and he a full-grown man. He felt as young as Amélie, as miserable.

"All right, sweetheart?" he asked in a low voice.

She nodded. He kept his hand on her leg, pressing down harder as the cab lurched to a stop. The Main Street Line trolley was stalled. A common occurrence, stalling, when a new trolley horse was being broken in and the untrained animal kept pulling the car off the tracks.

Amélie opened her eyes. "Bud, what did you think of them? The girls?"

He understood her question. He knew that it was life and death to Amélie that she be the Colonel's only child. "Just girls dolled up to look like you," he said.

"What about their reddish hair?"

"Fat and ugly," he said firmly. "Nothing like you."

"I did not think so, either. But everybody found comparisons. They were sizing us up like horses."

"Amélie," he said. "I can't stop the damn railroad from producing witnesses. But there's one thing I can do. The people around here aren't boors. I can stop them from acting as if they were."

"And so you did," she murmured.

"You think that's all I wanted to do? They're my friends—and I wanted to kill them all off!"

She drew a sharp breath. "I never should have let you be there."

The trolley, back on the tracks, clanged, moving, and the hansom eased forward.

"We will stop meeting at Paloverde," she said.

"What are you saying?"

"You must not make this more difficult. Bud, please?"

"For God's sake, you told me it's the only place you're safe."

"Therefore we both know I would be using your affection."

"That's insane. It's the man, sweetheart, who pays the woman for her affections."

"Bud, forget all of that."

"Can you?"

She glanced down at his hand, which still rested on her thigh, and shook her head miserably.

"So we'll keep on," he said.

"No."

"Tell me why not."

"I have tried to."

"I'm not very quick on the subtleties."

She sighed. "Meeting you would be using you."

He looked into her white face and tried to comprehend what she was telling him. She wants me, she knows I'm necessary for her survival, yet she won't use me. She could lead me down the garden path, pretending she'll marry me, then drop me when the Deane Trial ends. But not my Amélie. She's foolish, honorable, and completely dear. And suddenly he was shaken by the intensity of his love for her.

A few months back he would have had a good laugh if anyone had suggested that he—the catch of the Cow Counties—would plead on bended, public knee for any girl. But here he was, shifting from the leather seat to jounce in the narrow space in front of Amélie. The back of his neck was tight and by each ear there was a small lump where his jaw muscles were knotted.

"Know what I did last night?" he asked. "I sat on the porch staring at your window. I waited and waited. Your light stayed on. I didn't sleep either. Amélie, I've never been much on soul-searching, especially other people's souls. But while I sat there, looking at your window, I thought about you. It's never been all on my side. You came after me with those letters. You flirted with me. You wanted me to be your friend. You laugh with me, joke. And when we make love—sweetheart, women aren't like you are with me. They don't enjoy making love. Maybe you don't love me. It doesn't matter." Oh my God, he thought, it matters, it matters so much. "But you care something for me, I know. You'll be happy with me, I promise."

The brakes ground as they descended the incline to Fifth Street. He still knelt in front of her, but he couldn't make himself look into her face. Her chest barely moved. It was then that a destroying thought occurred to him. He was perilously close to tears. "Or is it as you said? Used? Have you, all along, in every way, been using me? The letters, the things we do at Paloverde, our laughter and jokes, have they all been just using on your part?"

He saw the tremulous intake of her breath. "I cannot think so," she whispered. "It . . . I cannot . . . Bud, talk to Mama this evening."

"You mean that?"

"Tell her I have given you my word." Her voice sounded very far away.

"Amélie, it means you'll always live here."

"Tell Mama I have given you my word."

"Thank you. Sweetheart, I love you so much." He leaned forward and briefly rested his lips on her breast. He could feel her heartbeat, smell the light cologne. He got up and sat next to her, his arm around her shoulders. By the time they neared home, his breathing had calmed.

The driver swung past the Van Vliets's red shingle house. Bud rapped on the glass. "Here," he shouted.

He tipped the man generously, saying, "Tell Arturo to explain to my party that I have urgent business and won't be able to return. Can you remember that?"

"Yes sir, Mr. Van Vliet."

"See?" Bud whispered to Amélie. "Already I'm luring you into my den of iniquity."

His teasing was a way of getting back to normal. He expected a clever retort. Under the drooping pepper tree she turned to him. It was like yesterday. Her expression, unbearably naked, was that of a child whipped so long and viciously that it can no longer comprehend what is happening.

CHAPTER 6

· I ·

Doña Esperanza, in her bedroom, heard the front door open and close. She didn't look up from the sheet of paper. A ragged Mexican boy had delivered this penciled note a half hour earlier, and she had learned the words by heart.

Dearest Mama,

I am writing this to you because Papa never in a million years would understand. I am sick of Harvard, sick of Los Angeles, sick of being a child. I must grow up. And the only way a man can grow up is to be on his own.

Papa would say I am a fool, throwing away my home, my chance at an education, everything. Yet what is life about? Is it a purse to be hoarded and cleverly spent?

There comes a time when one must risk all, and for me that time is now. I am going to explore the West. Maybe I will prospect for silver and gold. Don't be saddened by my decision, you will be very proud of me someday.

I love you very much. I always will be your,

Vincente (not 3Vee)

"Vincente," she whispered. "Why?"

She sat in an old chair that had been made by a Paloverde carpenter, a strong, clumsy piece of furniture with the seat woven of hide thongs from Paloverde cattle. As she stared at the letter of self-banishment that her younger son, her beloved son, had written, there were lines of bewilderment between her heavy brows. Why? she thought.

· 2 ·

An hour later Doña Esperanza came downstairs, slowly, leaning on the banister. In summer heat her ankles swelled. From the kitchen came a rhythmic chopping sound as Maria prepared supper, a job that no personal grief could halt Doña Esperanza from oversee-ing. She always made sure that the vegetables were as Hendryk liked, seasoned with sweet butter, not the olive oil that Maria doted on, and that his side dishes were properly cooked.

As Doña Esperanza passed through the dining room, she froze. The Deane girl slept in the sunroom, her knees drawn up on the horsehair sofa, one hand under her cheek. Bud's jacket covered her. The black hairbow had come untied and her loosened hair shone on his striped alpaca. Bud sat in a chair drawn near to her.

So there is something between them, Doña Esperanza thought. And that's why 3 Vee left.

A blackness came over her. A gentle, shy woman, she had never before experienced anything like this hot, dark retaliatory fury. Her swollen ankles turned weak. Spots formed in front of her eyes, blur-ring her vision.

Bud glanced up. Seeing her, he raised a finger to his lips.

It could be innocent, Doña Esperanza thought, trying to breathe. Bud always helps people. It is the strength in him, and I admire it. The chopping sounds from the kitchen were growing faster, more erratic.

The girl stirred, her eyes opening in bewilderment. Features rosy from sleep, her long topaz hair spilling over her shoulders, she was far lovelier than Doña Esperanza had realized. She's like one of those Sèvres figurines that American ladies cherish on their what-nots, breakable porcelain that's trouble to dust, Doña Esperanza thought in her unique venom. Buttons clicked on the hardwood floor as Bud's jacket fell. The girl, reaching to pick it up, saw Doña

Esperanza. The expression of bewilderment altered to fear. Bud moved swiftly to the girl and Doña Esperanza's inner rage diverted to her son. She is 3 Vee's, Doña Esperanza thought. And Bud knows it! She couldn't repress a prayer for God to punish this successful blond man, her son.

He was clasping the back of the sofa, making a circle around the girl. Doña Esperanza could not see his face, just the protective curve of shoulders. "It's my mother, Amélie," he murmured, bending until his forehead touched her hair. "Sweetheart, everything's all right."

After a moment the girl nodded.

He picked up his jacket, shrugging it on, facing Doña Esperanza. She had never seen this pleading expression. Even as a small boy he had never asked for favors or *pan dolces*. He had been a sturdy, independent child. "Amélie felt ill," he said. "Mama, she's so young for all this. The trial."

The chopping ceased. Bud was staring at her with that odd pleading look. Doña Esperanza took a deep breath. 3 Vee, she thought, and a bone-deep pain sliced her chest.

Then the years of gracious Californio hospitality took over and Doña Esperanza Van Vliet y García stepped into her sunroom. "Would you care for some tea, Amélie?" she asked. "Why don't we have a cup of China tea?"

"That's a fine idea," Bud said. His voice shook. "*Gracias*, Mama."

· 3 ·

"In this heathen town they marry infants!" Madame Deane cried.

She was in her drawing room with Mayhew Coppard. Forty minutes earlier, after Bud Van Vliet had concluded his talk with her, she had sent for the attorney. She was still white and shaken. She was fonder of her daughter than she had been of anyone in her life. She took proprietary joy in Amélie's hair, her complexion, her narrow wrists and ankles, her skill at the piano, her cleverness, her wit, her posture, even in the child's annoying and willful code of honor. *Très gentille*, Madame Deane would think. And if a good marriage—a title and/or money in France—had presented itself, she would have forgotten Amélie's age. She was not about to be separated, however, from her rarest and most valuable possession by a hardware clerk in this desolate Western outpost.

"She's a baby!" Madame Deane added.

Mayhew Coppard, too, thought of Amélie as a delightful if pert addendum clinging to the fragrant skirts of Madame Deane. He had considered Bud his own rival. The attorney's worldly expression showed none of his shock, surprise, and pleasure. "My dear, calm yourself, calm yourself. This is merely an impetuous young man. I'll speak to him."

"How good you are. Whatever would we do without you?" Madame Deane dabbed her eyes. "I have just talked to Amélie. She believes that having given her word to Mr. Van Vliet, she must marry him."

"Then she is infatuated?"

Madame Deane rustled to the fireplace, resting a slender arm on the mantel. While not an intelligent woman, she had a firm grasp on the relationships between men and women. "Here is the strangest thing, Mr. Coppard. She does not seem sure."

"Then, my dear, my advice is simple. Send her away."

Madame Deane had already decided this. "You think I must?" she asked.

"It's the only course."

"Amélie is a Lamballe," Madame Deane sighed. "She insists that she is committed. I know her. She will never leave here. Never. Unless . . . " She let her voice fade.

"Unless what?"

"She knows the truth."

The pretty widow and the sophisticated attorney stared at one another in silence. He knew what she meant. The Colonel had confessed to his wife that he had entered into a liaison with Sophie Belle Marchand and had fathered her two daughters. Madame Deane had obliquely conveyed this information to Mayhew Coppard and, forewarned, he had sought out evidence. His investigators found none. For once the red-bearded Colonel had covered his tracks. The only witnesses were Sophie Belle Marchand and her daughters. It was their suspect word against Mayhew Coppard's legal prowess.

He finally broke the long silence. "Until this morning I never fully realized the child's devotion to her father's memory. You were right, my dear. She should never have been in the court-room."

Madame Deane sighed. "Mr. Coppard, this decision has been most difficult. Most. But when Amélie sees how wrong she is about her father, then she will realize how ignorant she is of life." What Madame Deane really meant was that her daughter must be broken to the point of obedience. She gave another sigh, deep and honest. Amélie's spirit delighted her.

"My dear, loving her father as she does, will she believe?"

"She will ... if ... if *you* tell her."

"I?" Mayhew Coppard was shocked. "A stranger, practically."

Madame Deane lowered her face into her handkerchief. "Ah, it is most terrible to be alone."

"You are not alone, my dear," Mayhew Coppard said, walking heavily across the room to pull the bell cord.

·4·

There was a knock on the bedroom door. "Madame Deane and Mr. Coppard wish us in the drawing room." Mademoiselle Koestler's voice slanted around the door, frighteningly gentle.

"Thank you, Mademoiselle," Amélie called. "I will be ready in a minute."

They are not Papa's, she thought. No. Never. And the question is closed. To ask is to be disloyal. Closed.

She peered in the mirror. Was her hair right? She picked up the comb. Embossed silver roses held tortoise-shell teeth. She put it down and moved aimlessly to the pier mirror, then back to the dressing table. She picked up the comb again and it slipped from her hand. Should she pick it up? Why? She sat on the stool, covering her face with her icy hands.

Behind closed lids, she saw Bud. She had long ago forgotten her reservations about working in shirtsleeves and flashy checkered vests. Bud was Bud. He has a line of crisp, pale hairs curling toward the center of his chest and firm stomach, and a bump on the end of his nose that I wiggle with my finger, so. His teeth are very straight except for the left front one, which turns slightly, and this tooth makes his smile easy and very beautiful. He wants to win every argument and game, and usually does in a way that teeters between insensitivity and humor. He has a kind of sweet, hard strength. Even his sweat smells strong and tastes like salt. And that other, like runny egg white, and as it came into my mouth I trembled all over and he cried out sweetheart, sweetheart, and afterward he asked, "How did you know to do that?" and I replied, "In Paloverde I know everything," and we smiled at one another.

Do I care for him? Love him? If I cannot decide whether to comb my hair, how can I know what I feel?

And what does it matter? Everything was settled in the cab when he kissed my bleeding, terrified heart. If I go back on my word, I truly will not be me. Just as if those girls belonged to Papa, I would not be me.

She picked up the comb and quickly smoothed back her hair, tying it with a fresh ribbon. She bit the inside of her cheek to make the dizziness go away.

Mademoiselle Koestler was waiting on the landing.

· 5 ·

The governess sat in a remote corner of the drawing room, not sewing, her needle merely hovering above her embroidery hoop. Mayhew Coppard leaned his elegant bulk against the fireplace. Amélie stood by a gilt chair facing her mother.

"*Ma chère*," said Madame Deane, "you must realize that I do not act lightly. We may lose our case because of this, for your presence here has been most helpful." She paused to look at her daughter. "You and Mademoiselle Koestler will go to Uncle Raoul and Aunt Thérèse." It was an astute choice. She knew that Amélie dearly loved her widower uncle and his sister, her jovial spinster aunt, who kept his shabby households in Normandy and the Rue St. Honoré.

"You are getting forgetful, Mama." Amélie forced a smile. "Soon you will be a *belle mère*."

"Mr. Van Vliet has nothing to do with my decision."

"Why then, Mama?"

Madame Deane turned her great, helpless brown eyes on her attorney.

"My child," Mayhew Coppard said, using the deep tone with which he might inform a client of a death sentence. "My dearest child. I fear this trial will become more and more oppressive. There will be testimony that your mother wishes you shielded from, and rightly so."

Amélie gripped the rung of the gilt chair.

"Believe me, this journey to France is best."

"I . . . Mr. Coppard . . . what testimony?"

"Your mother and I have kept unpleasantness from you."

"They cannot be his daughters!" Pain rang in the clear, pretty voice.

Madame Deane winced, and the embroidery fell from Mademoiselle Koestler's plump hands.

"He admitted so. To his own wife," Mayhew Coppard said.

Amélie turned to her mother. Madame Deane hesitated, then nodded.

Amélie's eyes widened. "No!" she said. "It cannot be true."

"It isn't on the birth certificates," Mayhew Coppard admitted. "But it is true."

"The railroad is paying them! Mr. Coppard, everybody says the railroad is paying them!"

"Dear child, I wish it were not so."

Amélie gripped the chair rung. With a small, snapping noise, an ornamental shell broke away. She looked into her palm, staring at the curve of splintered wood. "Mama, I am so very sorry."

"It can be repaired. *Ma chère*, did you hurt yourself?"

"Is that why you did not wish to be in court today?"

Madame Deane's expression hardened. "Your father lived with that woman as his paramour for many years. No. Why should I wish to see a coarse, common woman smirking at me? Did you enjoy seeing those two fat, simpering girls, the sisters he gave you?" This was a painful matter for Madame Deane too, and she forgave herself her spite. "He was devoted enough to those two ugly girls. He visited them whenever he was in San Francisco. He spent much time with them. He sat them on his lap and told them the same stories he told you. He bought them the same presents he bought for you. He played Parcheesi with them, and he kissed them good night, too. They were part of his life. His beloved children."

"No," Amélie whispered.

"He kept all this secret from you. You never once guessed their existence. Now. Do you understand that you do not yet know enough about men to make your own decisions?"

Amélie was turning the gilt shell in her hand as if she didn't know what it was. Mademoiselle Koestler, a stout figure in rusty black, moved to take it from her. "It is all right, all right," she said, and turned to Madame Deane. "You could have been kinder."

"And you have betrayed your trust," replied Madame Deane in French. "You have failed to watch over my daughter. As soon as you give her over to Baron de Lamballe's care, you are no longer in my employ."

"Mama, please, please. None of this is Mademoiselle Koestler's fault."

"How can I keep a governess who does not guard you properly, *ma chère?*"

"I will obey her in everything."

"As long as you do," Madame Deane said, "she may remain."

"Thank you." Amélie swallowed convulsively.

Madame Deane sighed. "It is best you take tomorrow's early train."

"Bud—"

"Mr. Coppard will tell Mr. Van Vliet. After you have left."

Amélie shook her head.

"Someone must, *ma chère.*"

"I," Amélie whispered.

"You!" Madame Deane exclaimed.

"Dear child," Mayhew Coppard said, "I won't be unkind. I promise you. And Mr. Van Vliet surely must understand you're too young for any entanglement."

Amélie shook her head again.

"This is a matter for gentlemen," Madame Deane said firmly.

Amélie's face tensed. She moved to the couch where her mother sat. "It is terrible enough to break one's word. Must I also become a coward?"

The remark was uttered with hauteur, a tone that Madame Deane had heard used by her own circle. She felt an immense pride in her daughter. She was more determined than ever not to let the girl waste herself.

"You may tell him," she said.

·6·

Bud followed the Deanes's black servant across the hall. The hired carriage outside told him that behind the double doors of the drawing room Mayhew Coppard waited with objections, rejections. Mentally, Bud phrased his rebuttals : "I care deeply for her." "Even without my father's business I am not a poor man. She'll never want for anything." "She's young, I know, but she needs masculine protection." "I'll live for her happiness." A suitor's anxiety was so alien to Bud that he was amused. Yet his expression was intent. Losing never occurred to him. Until last night, when his father had remarked on the quality of the merchandise he loved, Bud had never considered that Madame Deane could look down on him. Forewarned is forearmed. If Mayhew Coppard brought *that* up, he would counter with the Garcías. He had never thought his maternal ancestors more than cattle ranchers, and unsuccessful ones at that; still, "Land Grant" conjured up past glory. He would say anything he had to say.

The servant opened the drawing-room doors with both hands. The kind of energy that precedes battle surged through Bud. He stepped into the room and saw that Mayhew Coppard was not alone. Shock drained him. Across from the attorney, on the loveseat, Madame Deane posed gracefully. Shadows swallowed the fat old governess. Amélie sat on the maroon ottoman, her spine erect, her face pale. Nodding to the others, he went to her.

"Miss Deane has something she wishes to tell you," said Mayhew Coppard, and Bud noted the formality. *Miss Deane.*

"I am going away," Amélie said, her clear voice toneless, as if she were speaking a language she didn't comprehend.

"Where?" Bud asked.

"France."

"Paris?"

"To be with my uncle and aunt," she replied.

"You're being sent away like a package?"

"I am being mailed home." The small joke was without inflection. A chill settled between his shoulders. "Amélie, what is it?"

She didn't reply.

"But this is your home," he said. "You were born here in California."

"I had to tell you myself," she said.

"How long will you be gone?"

She looked down at her hands.

"Miss Deane is trying to explain," Mayhew Coppard said, "that she will not return."

"Is that true, Amélie?"

"Yes."

"What about your promise?"

"I have never broken my word before," she said.

Over, he thought. Finished? He didn't believe it. He couldn't. Yet his fear widened, and this fear, as usual, emerged as anger. "That's nice of you, making me number one!"

She tilted her head, and the glow of the red-fringed lamp touched her forehead. There was no quiver, no life, in her normally mobile face. Concerned, Bud reverted to tenderness. "Forget I said that." He spoke quietly. "I pushed you today. We have no promises, sweetheart, so you've broken none."

"Mr. Van Vliet." Mayhew Coppard's voice. "You may not talk to Miss Deane like that."

"Amélie, what's wrong?" Bud said.

"Miss Deane is leaving tomorrow morning." The attorney lowered his voice to speak to Amélie. "Dear child, there's no reason to prolong this interview. Any further discussion belongs between Mr. Van Vliet and myself."

Obediently, Amélie started out of the room, the nervous old governess opening the double doors for her.

Bud moved swiftly, halting Amélie at the doorway. "Please don't leave," he said. "We'll go back to the way we were. Less, if that's what you want."

"This has nothing to do with you," she said.

"Leaving Los Angeles," he said, "is leaving me."

She edged around him and crossed the hall. He followed. He heard Mayhew Coppard and Madame Deane call his name. He didn't care. He was beyond caring. As she reached the staircase, he took her arm.

She looked up at him, her eyes expressionless.

It was as if they gazed at one another across a frozen arctic distance, blindingly empty, where nothing moved. His anger returned and without conscious thought Bud raised his hand. He tried to stop himself, yet he struck her and the sound rang through the hall. It was a sound that proclaimed physical intimacy. The slap was a confession of those afternoons when dim light had filtered through old glass to paint their naked, glowing bodies.

Her cheek drained of blood, then slowly on the whiteness a blotched red appeared. She raised her hand to cover the mark.

And with that gesture, Bud decided he understood. She's embarrassed, he thought. That's all. Embarrassed she's going back on her word. Leaving.

"All right, honey," he said savagely. "You've done your bit fine. Now go to Paris! Or Peru! Or wherever the hell you want!"

He turned from her, walked the length of the hall, and slammed the heavy oak door behind him. He trotted down the four stone steps, his heart—which he could neither control nor understand— pounding furiously. He heard the door open. Hope flashing, he looked back. It was the black manservant. "You forgot this, sir," he said, holding out Bud's hat.

·7·

Without thought, without purpose, Bud let his boots propel him up Fort Street, over Courthouse Hill and across the Plaza to the disreputable red light district that everyone called Sonora Town. Here, amid hovels and lean-tos, remained several of the rambling one-story Californio adobes. As brothels they shimmered in the mist, perverted ghosts of their gracious and hospitable past. Hungry-cheeked whores strolled past Bud, dark eyes inviting him. Yet many of the people on the streets were simply the poor. Many Chinese lived here, and from one window drifted the sickly sweetness of opium, while from another came the sizzle of wok cookery. In a dark doorway, a group of drunken Indians pushed at one another. Here Doña Esperanza nursed her people.

Bud almost tripped over a tiny boy. An Indian, naked under a short, ragged dress. Why was a child pissing in the dirt on a cold night? Oh yes. The mother sat, knees up, dirt-engrained hand out. Automatically Bud reached into his pocket and dropped silver and copper coins into the woman's palm.

Then he peered at the child.

And it was at that moment of total despair that a buried ugliness crawled out. As he stared at the Indian child, there came a flickering memory long submerged in his earliest childhood. Maria-the-servant, Maria-the-*bruja*, Maria-the-Indian, Maria holding little Bud in her warm lap, her wine-sour mouth telling a story that he had guessed was a secret shame, for he had never repeated it. Don Tomás García and Doña Gertrudis for years had been childless, Maria said, and then they had gone with Doña Gertrudis's Indian maid to pray at the shrine of Guadalupe in Mexico City. A year later they returned with a baby, very plump and dark and yet resembling Don Tomás. The dark child was his grandfather. Don Vincente, proud loser of cattle and land. The story had burrowed deep in the recesses of Bud's mind, surfacing only now.

Rose saw it somehow, Bud thought. She knew me for what I am. A greaser, a *cholo*.

He walked away from the half-naked Indian boy, cutting across the Southern Pacific tracks, turning into a narrower alley that smelled of urine. Another turn and he faced a shabby two-story structure with a flat *brea* roof. He had never been inside, but he knew of this house. Here sin was not cozy like at Carlotta's. Behind these dingy walls men bought a child or watched women copulate with animals, whipped or were whipped, burned and were burned, acted out every secret and perverse desire.

She kissed me everywhere and I kissed her, Bud thought. "Oh God, never to see her again," he said aloud.

The plank across the *zanja* shook under his boots. He hit at ruined paint of the door, bringing his fist down again and again. It opened. Dark silk swallowed him.

He had passed out between two whores when the morning train left Los Angeles. Mademoiselle Koestler and Amélie were aboard.

· 8 ·

Again and again he returned to the vicious Sonora Town whorehouse.

After one of these bouts he went home and climbed to the attic where Maria slept. It was past two and he was at that stage of drunkenness where the senses fade and then return with preternatural clarity. The attic had no gas. A kerosene lamp formed a hollow cavern of light and here Maria sat with her amulets in her lap.

"Tell me about Don Vincente," he asked without preface.

She did not appear surprised to see him, or to hear his question. "You know about your grandfather. He owned Paloverde and ruled over us. As masters go, he was good and generous."

Bud stepped unsteadily into the circle of light. "You once told me a story about him." His voice had a cold, demanding tone.

Maria watched him as she replaced her magic in the rabbit-hide pouch. "You drink too much," she said.

"What I do is nobody's goddam affair. Tell me about Doña Gertrudis not being his mother."

"I, too, drink much."

"What about the maid?"

"Maid?"

"You know who I mean."

Maria held the abalone-shell carving close to her eyes. "She was of the Yang Na, an old woman when I knew her. And I was a girl. Often the old tell stories to impress the young."

"That's the story, the impressive one."

Maria rubbed a wrinkled finger over the shell, tracing an ancient symbol. "We were kneeling together at our metates, grinding corn. It was after your great-grandmother died. Don Vincente had wept much for his mother and lit many candles. And now he had two men with him who were going to decorate the chapel in her name. They walked by and the old woman said to me, 'He pretends she was his mother, but he knows the truth. Doña Gertrudis gave me to Don Tomás to make them a child. Oh, I was a pretty girl, light-skinned as a fish, and young. We went to the great city in Mexico, and I bore their son, a fine healthy baby, and as a reward they let me be his nurse. They never told him, but I told him. He knows, Don Vincente, that he is one of us.'"

"Her story surprised you?" Bud asked.

"I am never surprised. And, too, I had heard it from others. Doubly I was not surprised. A year later, in the spring, the old woman died, and Don Vincente buried her in the plot below the orchard. Only the family was buried there. It was most peculiar. He explained that she had been his nurse, and he wanted his nurse by him when he died."

The land below the orchard had been sold long before Bud was born, and the bones of the Garcías removed to the walled enclave of Calvary Cemetery on North Fort Street. *Is she there?* Bud lifted the kerosene lantern. Shadows swayed. He was not mystical, the words *greaser* and *cholo* repelled him, yet it seemed to him that he and Maria-the-*bruja* were in some sort of moving pattern beyond time and civilization, together, of the same blood, the blood of the people who once had lived on this land, now a city, without thought of possession or ownership. He, she, the city were one. I'm very drunk, he thought.

"Does Mama know?"

For the first time the old woman showed alarm. "This is talk! Idle talk. The talk of old women! Señor Bud, you must never repeat this to Doña Esperanza. Never!"

Maria loved his mother more than anyone. Bud set down the lantern.

"Tell Mama? Can't you see I'm too drunk to remember?"

"There is no need for you to drink," Maria said. "You misjudge the girl, but—"

"Close your mouth!"

"—she knows your courage and generosity," Maria went on calmly. "You will be far greater than any of the other Garcías. It is you she wants, not Vincente."

"3Vee?" Bud's eyebrows jerked up. The old woman was talking nonsense. "They're friends. Nothing more. They talked about books, that's all."

"He left because of her."

3Vee had mailed notes from all over Nevada to his mother. He was prospecting for silver, he wrote. At the time the big Nevada lodes were considered played out, but still it was common for a young man to explore the West in the guise of prospecting. These men, some college students from good families, set out on their own, picking up the bare rudiments of geology, learning to fish and trap small game. They avoided towns and rarely stayed in one place more than a couple of days. Very few ever staked a claim. This was their rite of passage, their coming of age, and usually they were back home in less than a year, tougher, browner and willing (if not content) to take up whatever reins life had handed them. The knowledge of this kept the Van Vliets hopeful.

"He went into a trance about prospecting!" Bud snapped. "That's why he left!"

Maria hung the rabbit-hide pouch around her neck. "Time enough," she said, "before he takes his place in the tragedy."

"I came up to hear about my grandfather and you talk some madness about 3 Vee," Bud growled. He charged drunkenly down rough-finished stairs that exuded the odor of pine. *Cholo*, he thought, forgetting the rest of the conversation. Greaser.

·9·

The thick envelope was on the hall table with his other mail. The stamp and return address were French, a town he had never heard of, Honfleur. She had never mentioned Honfleur. The writing wasn't hers. He carried the letter upstairs to his room and slit the envelope. There were several sheets of thin paper inside and another envelope, this one addressed with only his name, Hendryk Van Vliet II, in her spiky, delicate handwriting. She left in June, he thought, and now it's September. Three months and she's finally managed the time.

> Bud,
>
> Mama asked me not to write without her knowledge, so I enclose this in her letter and she will have it delivered. I am not sure you wish to hear from me. What a way to have to begin a letter.

Puzzled, Bud paused, looked at the first envelope, and reassured himself that it carried French postage. Then he continued reading.

> Mademoiselle Koestler and I left on the *Normandie* from the Morton Street Pier in New York. Nine days later we were met in Le Havre by Uncle Raoul. Did I ever mention that I have twenty-two first cousins? All from Mama's side. Uncle Raoul, assisted by his late wife, propagated nine of these. Aunt Thérèse, Mama's oldest sister, tends the brood.

I am staying with them in the country. My room overlooks the court. The room's width is the same as the corridor and not coincidentally. Once it *was* the corridor. A huge bulbous lead-glass window makes the grounds and woods seem underwater. Or maybe this oceanic view is due to rain? It hasn't stopped since we got here. I can hear the hush of rain on old cobbles.

I would adore to give the impression that this is one of your grander chateaux. Unfortunately my ancestral home is a French equivalent of Paloverde, smaller, but in slightly better repair. My window has only five cracked panes, and the stones of the fireplace are all there, if chipped. You can see I am lodged in splendor.

My oldest cousin, Jean—he is heir to this magnificence—argues constantly with me so my wits may remain sharp. My youngest cousin, Linette, likes to be cuddled and to have someone (anyone) read to her. Only four and already she has a taste for Mr. Thackeray. Since I translate to French as I read, Mr. Thackeray would have problems recognizing *Vanity Fair*. Uncle Raoul is stout and absent-minded, always shouting for someone to find his spectacles. Aunt Thérèse looks like him, but lacks a mustache. She spends much time conferring with the cook.

They do not sound much like Mama, do they?

Oh, here comes Mademoiselle Koestler. She has a pot of hot chocolate made with cream. She force-feeds me.

I am a Strasbourg goose

A

Who gives a damn about her room? And how many cousins she has? She must have written a letter to one of her school friends and copied it word for word to send to me. No. There's that stupid opening paragraph. She thinks she owes me a letter. To hell with her! He ripped the linen paper in half and dropped the pieces on the floor.

He got a bottle of bourbon from his drawer, poured himself a large drink, and opened his other mail. Isobella (Betty) Bostwick desired his presence at a Mandolin Plucking. He owed $2.35

monthly dues to the Los Angeles Athletic Club he and a bunch of friends had started five years ago. Lucetta Woods wanted the pleasure of his company at a Fiesta.

To hell with her, he thought again. And then he remembered the other sheets of paper in the envelope. He unfolded them and began to read.

My dear Mr. Van Vliet,

Miss Deane requested that I enclose her letter to you inside a letter addressed to her mother. However, Madame Deane has told me that Miss Deane would not be allowed to communicate with you. You must, therefore, realize that I have mailed her letter directly to you to ensure that you receive it. In doing so I betray my employer's trust as well as risk my position. But the past months have made me conclude there are matters beyond positions and even trust.

Naturally I have not read Miss Deane's letter. I am positive, however, that she did not burden you with her illness. On the train journey to New York she was listless, moving rarely, speaking less. In short, completely unlike herself. In New York I telegraphed Madame Deane. By this unsatisfactory means of communication she decided that the ocean air might improve her daughter's spirits.

Alas, such was not the case. As soon as the *Normandie* sailed, she became feverish. Within a day her fever had risen alarmingly, and at times she lapsed into a coma. The ship's surgeon diagnosed her illness as brain fever. I have my own opinion.

Miss Deane's rare delicacy prevents her from inflicting distress upon another. I do not have to tell you she misses the Colonel. Probably you are unaware, however, that the trial with its vicious revelations have become a cross almost too heavy for her to bear.

Madame Deane, wishing her daughter to leave Los Angeles for reasons that we both understand, considered it necessary to tell Miss Deane the truth about the Colonel and his relationship to that woman who called herself his wife. It is my belief that Miss Deane, who in truth is but a child, could not cope with this final knowledge.

I have digressed. At sea her fever remained high. The fifth day out she lost consciousness for twenty-four hours. The surgeon gave her up. He was a cynical man, a disbeliever, yet he knelt with me to beg the Merciful One to save her. By the time we docked she had regained consciousness. The Baron de Lamballe has a home near Le Havre, and it is to this country seat that we brought her.

She is a favorite with her relations, and I cannot tell you the care that everyone has lavished upon her. Yet in my heart I know that human endeavors are as naught. God Himself could not bear to destroy His unique and shining creation.

Her fever abated slowly. She is still in great discomfort. Unlike most convalescents she has not become pettish or demanding. For the past two weeks she has requested pen and paper, and that is all. This is the first day that the doctor has permitted her to sit up long enough to write.

Mr. Van Vliet, I cannot know what is in your heart. If, on one hand, you think of coming here, I beg you not to. She must recover in body and in her own soul before facing any decision. If, on the other hand, you have no desire to continue the friendship, I can only beg you to be as charitable as He. She is so very frail. A letter, however brief, will cheer her.

I trust I have not intruded.

Your respectful servant
Matilde Koestler

P.S. Should you choose to write, I trust you will not mention this letter or its contents.

Normally Bud would have smiled at the old lady's pious sentimentality. But his teeth were clenched as he picked up Amélie's letter and fitted the two halves together on his desk. What had seemed schoolgirl cleverness he now read as courage. In spots, he saw, her handwriting wobbled. That last night she knew, he thought. Oh, my God! Not embarrassed, but mortally stricken. And his own words came back to him. "Now go to Paris! Or Peru! Or wherever the hell you want!" Ah, Amélie.

He went to his window and stood for several minutes looking at the Deane place. The curtains were drawn in Amélie's room, as they had been ever since she left. He returned to his desk and searched for paper.

Sweetheart,

First of all, what makes you think I might not want a letter from you? Is it because at our last get-together I hit you? That was a favor to a friend. The way I looked at it, you probably never had been hit, and it was high time.

You sound like you have landed in a very soft place, all those handsome, feisty cousins, fat jolly aunts and uncles, and Mademoiselle Koestler bringing you whipped cream. No wonder you prefer France.

What else is there to say? Oh yes. How much I miss having someone to boss me around and [Here he changed to pencil.] The nib broke. I was pressing down too hard, trying to be funny. I never wrote letters, except to 3 Vee. Everyone that matters to me is in Los Angeles, except him and you.

Amélie, since you left I've been a madman. I have no friends left. I got into a fight with Ollie Grant for talking about the trial. He's been just about my best friend ever since we were two years old, and I knocked him out and enjoyed doing it. I never meant to hit you. Sweetheart, I wanted to help you and protect you. But you hurt me. I needed to get back. I'm not a nice person. You know I always have to win. Now I have lost so much. I have lost you. I care. I care very much. I never imagined I was capable of caring about a woman so much. By care I mean love. Usually I am clever at getting people to do what I want them to. But there seems to be two people I can't control. You and me.

I remember one particular afternoon. I was telling you that every night the family, the hangers-on, and the Indians used to file into the *sala* at Paloverde to kiss my grandfather's amethyst ring. And you kissed my knuckle. It was cold and windy outside, and the *fazardas* were over us. I remember a lot of things. Like the little mole on your left shoulder, and your scent, like sugarbush flowers, and how small and fine your bones felt, and the way your eyes sparkled when I told you about the old cattle farmer. I remember what we did before and after. Yet it is that one moment I want back. I would give anything to be under the *fazardas* with dead grapevines knocking at the windows and you kissing my knuckle.

I won't even read this through. I don't think it makes any sense, yet it's exactly how I feel.

He didn't sign his name.

· 10 ·

Bud,

Two letters arrived today. One from you and one from Mama. She has given us permission to correspond. She has conditions, however. Each of us may write one letter a week. These letters must be read by someone else. I hope you will agree since (1) she is my mother and (2) I want very much to hear from you. Very, very much.

Mademoiselle Koestler is the someone who reads our letters. She should not have given me this one unopened, but she did. Bud, I am not ashamed of meeting you at Paloverde, but we cannot discuss it. We would only embarrass Mademoiselle Koestler, and then she would have to return the letter. Otherwise she would lose her position and it would be my fault.

I had a little fever and they cut off my hair. I look like a boy. If you keep that in mind perhaps your next letter will not be quite so personal.

There were many more pages, and in the last paragraph she wrote:

You must not forget that Mademoiselle Koestler is honor-bound to return any too private or too frequent letters.

CHAPTER 7

· I ·

He never went to bed without writing to her.

He wrote of wildflowers, of the song of birds in the chaparral, of vaqueros, of the slow blue banks of mist riding in from the Pacific, anything that might jog her memory toward Paloverde. Whatever he wrote, the paper came between him and the question: Are you coming back? One night he poured out his doubts. It was his habit to bundle the week's papers together and take the fat envelope to the post office. This particular sheaf, all of it, was returned without comment.

At best transatlantic mail took eighteen days, and often letters jammed up. If a week passed without one from her, an itch possessed him and he would scratch even in his sleep. Dr. Widney prescribed sulfur.

She too wrote a sort of nightly journal, amusing descriptions of Paris and the old house on the Rue St. Honoré where the Lamballes wintered; she wrote of books, musicians, and painters unknown to him.

From her activities he knew she had recovered.

Therefore without guilt he could be aggravated by her. Why couldn't she sneak him one reassuringly personal letter? He knew that having given her mother her word, she was bound. Her inviolability betrayed him. He wanted her bound not to honor but to him.

Neither of them wrote of the Deane Trial. The woman who

called herself Mrs. Sophie Belle Deane had long ago finished her testimony, leaving behind titillating unanswered questions. After Christmas recess, on January 3, 1886, there began a procession of accountants with evidence of doubly kept ledgers. Mayhew Coppard cross-questioned, Liam O' Hara objected for his defense witnesses. And, bookkeepers being dull stuff, the public lost interest.

· 2 ·

On a rainy morning in February, Bud leaned his wet umbrella with the others inside the courtroom. An elderly bespectacled witness listened while Mayhew Coppard read a long question. Bud took off his hat, walking down the side aisle, nodding to his friends, seating himself in the front row next to Madame Deane.

"Madame Deane," he whispered.

She inclined her elegant, black-feathered hat. "Mr. Van Vliet."

Both of them gazed up at the witness.

Since Amélie's departure, each day that Madame Deane graced the courtroom, Bud had come for an hour or so to sit near her. He had stopped most of the outspoken rudeness. At first his hurt and humiliation had made it difficult to look at her, and after Mademoiselle Koestler's letter, it became almost impossible.

They never spoke beyond the routine greetings and farewells. Even so, people might have linked them in gossip had not Bud occasionally been accompanied by his father. Hendryk would thrust out his round belly and tell anyone who asked—and some who didn't—that he and his son were in court offering their masculine protection to their neighbor.

A long wrangle had started between Liam O'Hara and Mayhew Coppard.

Madame Deane turned to Bud. "Mr. Van Vliet," she asked in a low voice, "do you honestly imagine that I write to my daughter of your presence here?"

"I figure you never mention my name," he said. "I don't tell her either."

"I do not understand you. Why do you come?"

He answered truthfully, "I promised Amélie that whatever happened between us, I'd stop the talk."

Madame Deane's large, somewhat protruding eyes inspected him. He wondered that he had ever thought her charming.

"From the beginning," she said, "you were the only one to offer help. Well, you are most kind. But it alters nothing. Amélie does not care for you." Her tone was rather sad, and this confused Bud. "She never will care."

He gave her a confident smile. But he did not feel confident. He sat back on the wooden bench thinking that he must go to Paris. He conjured up a huge, French brass bed and himself curled around Amélie's white body. *That* would settle it, he thought. It was a frequent thought, and now, as always, a wrinkled Indian face came sharply into his mind. Greaser.

I can't go to Paris. I have to get her here. But how? How? And then he remembered the letters in the black tin box.

· 3 ·

Bud had one of the Van Vliet Block's corner offices. The walls were varnished pine; his huge rolltop had as many intricate cubbyholes as the desks in a Wells Fargo office. He faced his visitors across a dropleaf table. He had all the trappings considered locally to be part of a successful businessman: a Smyrna rug, dark oil copies of famous paintings. Bud had selected the three he thought most smart, "A Stag at Bay," "The Drove at the Ford," and "Pharaoh's Horses."

A few days after his conversation with Madame Deane, sunlight came through narrow cathedral windows to glint on the silver-and-crystal tantalus from which Bud was pouring brandy. Mayhew Coppard sat in the visitor's chair.

"How is the case going?" Bud asked. A rhetorical question. He knew precisely how it went.

"To be frank, Mr. Van Vliet, badly. Quite badly."

"A shame for Madame Deane."

Mayhew Coppard appreciatively sniffed brandy. Both men knew it was a double shame. Mayhew Coppard's interest in the French widow had waned in direct proportion to the trial's ebb. Still, he harbored kindly thoughts for her. "I don't burden the lady with these matters."

"What if you come up with new evidence?"

"There is none."

Bud opened the tin box. He held out a yellowed envelope with rusty pen marks. "Take a look," he said.

"We've read enough letters into evidence."

"None like this."

Mayhew Coppard, warming the bowl of his snifter with his right palm, shook open a letter and glanced at it. "Mr. Huntington calls Colonel Deane 'Friend Thaddeus.' What does that prove?"

"That they were close as thieves." Bud took the letter. "Listen to this. 'Friend Thaddeus, I have been talking to our boys here in Washington. All are eager to help our cause, except one. Victor Clark from somewhere down in your Cow Counties seems to mis-understand the situation. See what you can do with the stubborn cuss.'" Bud picked out another envelope and removed a sheet of paper. "This one's dated a year later, when the Texas and Pacific was trying to get Federal support. 'All the Californians in Congress are doing a first-rate job except this Clark. He seems to think we need two rail routes to California. He is a stupid mule. I want him fixed.'"

"Nothing would please me more," said Mayhew Coppard smoothly, "than to agree that revealing this kind of chicanery would win our case."

"There are two hundred and forty-one letters in this box," Bud said. "Mostly about politicians bribed, ruined, and promoted. You have prices here, down to the penny. If a man can't be bought, and there were a few, there are the expenses for ruining him."

"Unfortunately what I must prove is that the Colonel wasn't an embezzler."

"This evidence is important."

"True. But pointless to my case."

"You will read these letters."

"Mr. Van Vliet." Mayhew Coppard set down his glass and stood. "I don't need to point out that you are not my client."

Bud, too, rose. "I'll be forced to give them to my reporter friends."

"Oh?"

"It won't look well."

"Spare me the knowledge that your family is entrenched in Los Angeles."

"It's not just this town. The state—hell, the whole country and the world will be figuring you're in the pay of the railroad."

Insult stiffened Mayhew Coppard's florid cheeks. "Madame Deane is my sole client!"

"That's not how it will look."

The two men stared across the table at one another. Mayhew Coppard turned away first. "You'll lie?"

"Do you think I need to?" Bud said. "If I have to give the letters to the press, won't people come up with their own interpretation?"

In the distance the Plaza church bells rang. Mayhew Coppard sat down. Sighing, he helped himself to more brandy. "You're a different man than I thought."

"It's this Los Angeles hayseed in my hair." Bud was smiling. "Frankly, the letters didn't impress me much until Amélie made me read them through. She was right. The total effect is damning."

At this, Mayhew Coppard smiled, too. Who was this man after all? A good-looking young rube who was trying to impress a chit of a girl. "This, then, is for Miss Deane?"

Bud, replacing envelopes in the tin box, didn't answer.

·4·

The drab bookkeepers had emptied Judge Morado's courtroom. On Tuesday, March 2, reporters sat chewing tobacco and doodling. They glanced up as Bud entered. By now they accepted him as a fixture. They went back to their pursuits.

Mayhew Coppard rose. "May it please the court, I have some correspondence I wish read into the record."

"Is it pertinent, Mr. Coppard?"

"It is, Your Honor."

"Proceed."

Mayhew Coppard adjusted his eyeglass. " 'Friend Thaddeus—' "

"Objection!" Liam O'Hara was on his feet. "Objection!"

"On what grounds, Counselor?" Judge Morado asked.

"The letter has no relevance to the case."

"The Court will gauge that, Counselor."

Liam O'Hara turned to whisper anxiously to a legal acolyte, and the young man hurried outside as Liam O'Hara replied, "If it please the Court..."

That afternoon the courtroom was packed. Word had gone around that something big was about to pop. Legal wrangling continued until just after three when Judge Morado, that unique specimen, a California judge who had somehow escaped the railroad's tentacles, ruled that the letters bore the same relevance to the plaintiff's case that Sophie Belle Marchand had to the defense's. If this were a matter of Colonel Deane's moral fiber against that of the owners of the Southern Pacific Railroad Company, then both sides must be heard.

At five after three, March 2, 1886, sixteen months after the trial had opened, Mayhew Coppard stood to read the first of the letters.

The Deane Letters became one of those scandals that erupt from time to time like hot lava in American politics. Over the next seven weeks they were printed in their entirety in every Los Angeles paper as well as the *San Francisco Chronicle* and the *New York World*. They were excerpted in the smallest American hamlets as well as in the European press. The letters, meant only for the eyes of Friend Thaddeus, had a level of candor rarely approached in business correspondence. People talked of little else but the vices and venalities of duly elected senators, congressmen, judges, and sheriffs. It was the railroad, however, in taking advantage of human frailty, by coldly calculating the price of a man, that drew public hatred. People were always ready to hate the railroad.

But in the end, Mayhew Coppard would be proven right. The Deane Letters, for all their revelations, had no bearing on his client's case. The dull accountants had convinced Judge Morado when, three months later, he handed down his decision. Colonel Deane had paid off his note with embezzled money. Madame Deane owned no part of the Southern Pacific Railroad Company. She had lost two million dollars and a new husband.

For the railroad the decision was a Pyrrhic victory. Its loss was far greater than the French lady's. In years to come every Southern Pacific attempt to put through legislation favorable to the line was thwarted by a journalistic rattle of the Deane Letters. No politician could afford the scandal-muddied touch of the railroad. The hold of the greatest power in the West had been broken.

Amélie had won her own little war. Unlocking the black tin box in front of the world had, in a peculiar way, exonerated the red-bearded Colonel. To the future he would be known only by that one railroad-damning phrase : The Deane Letters.

· 5 ·

3 Vee, reading excerpts of the Deane Letters, saw in a nearby column headed TRIAL TRIVIA: *Miss Amélie Deane no longer resides in Los Angeles.* Maybe this snippet enabled him to address the postcard not just to his mother but to the family.

He was visiting Silver City, New Mexico, he wrote, about four days by mule from where he had staked a claim. He had found secondary minerals and was sure to discover high-grade argentite—at least he hoped to. He had learned more in the last few months, he felt, than in his entire schooling, and that included Harvard. 3 Vee's bravado was punctured by his natural lack of dogmatism. His few lines read true. He was intuitive enough to accept that fate, in taking away Amélie and his home, had given him his life's work. He was beginning to realize, not without pain, that his creativity had nothing to do with writing poetry or novels but with uncovering the earth's wealth. He was finding himself.

The postcard was the kind made from a photograph. 3 Vee stood, both thumbs hooked into his low-slung belt, his trousers confined in high double-soled, waterproof cowhide boots. His body was broader. His black mustache had grown long and fierce. He would have looked a tough young prospector—if the chemical imprint hadn't forever caught the look of exile in his deep-set dreaming eyes.

Doña Esperanza put the card in a brass frame and kept it on her bedside commode. Each time she looked at it she felt a chill and thought, he's never coming home.

· 6 ·

Mayhew Coppard boomed, "'Friend Thaddeus—'" a hush fell, the court recorder's pen scratched, reporters scribbled, and the two hundred forty-first letter, the final letter, went into history. Bud edged past the close-packed spectators and quietly left the court-room.

Outside, buggies, saddle horses, two Studebaker farm wagons, surreys, a creamy basket phaeton were hitched to the gnarled railing. Bud turned left on Spring Street, walking briskly in the shade of shop awnings. Ladies out for the sunny afternoon spoke to him. Smiling a reply, he tipped his derby. What if she doesn't come, he thought repeatedly, what then? Would I have been better off without those spring afternoons at Paloverde? What would I have done if she had died? I never used to ask myself unanswerable questions.

What if she doesn't come to me?

He jogged up the wooden staircase to his office. The vestibule's green shaded lamp was on, and the chief hardware clerk, Milford, sat on the stool, obviously waiting for him.

"Bud, there's two ladies for you."

"Mr. Van Vliet." Mademoiselle Koestler rose from the bench, dark, heavy, yet as insubstantial to Bud as the black cloud of a train's smokestack. He peered at her.

"Amélie?" he asked.

"She is in your office."

"Madame Deane never said—"

"She knows that we are coming, but not that we arrived on the midday train."

The dusty odor of the vestibule filled his lungs and his mouth was too dry to thank the kind old woman.

Amélie rose from the chair behind the dropleaf table. Sun blazed through the windows and for a moment he couldn't see her. His hand fell from the brass knob. The door closed, setting up a draft that rattled loose papers on the open rolltop desk.

He stared at her. In his mind she had been either naked or in young girl's mourning. This was a chic Parisian. Her white silk frock, embroidered with pale blue sprays, was neatly fitted to her slender curves, and the gracefully draped skirt reached the narrowest white kid slippers. Even in his numbed state Bud for once achieved his father's eye for quality. Here was finer, more delicate goods than the local girls.

A streamered leghorn hat lay on his table. And when he saw that, he looked at her hair, a thick curve reaching only to her earlobes. The hair was a reminder of her mortality.

"I wrote that it had been cropped," she said.

"Like a boy, you said."

He had thought too much and too long about getting her here, never what would happen once she arrived. Years ago he and Chaw Di Franco had packed into the Sierras. After they struggled to the top of the first peak, Bud had stood a long time, breathing heavily and viewing an endless chain of even higher mountains. That was how he felt now. Faced with an impossible and natural barrier. *She was of the Yang Na*, he thought.

Her hazel eyes were searching his face. "It disturbs you?"

"You're no boy. Too pretty."

She smiled, relieved. "Thank you."

"*De nada.*"

"Did you have difficulty," she asked, "making Mr. Coppard present the letters?"

He shook his head.

"I thought you might have."

"He saw the light," Bud said. His facial muscles were stiff. "He says it won't affect the outcome."

"I do not care. Now people know what sort of men accused Papa."

"That's for sure," he replied, thinking to tell her about the courtroom objections of Liam O'Hara, finding he couldn't speak.

Amélie was looking around the office. "My imagination is very poor."

"What?"

"I had so many versions of this scene. Yet never once did I consider that we would face one another across a desk." She examined "A Stag at Bay." "Bud, I do appreciate your forcing Mr. Coppard."

"Is that what you're in town for? To thank me?" It was honest yet clumsy. He wanted more than her gratitude.

"I expected you to visit *me*," she said coolly.

"Then why didn't you invite me? You knew exactly how I felt." He put it in the past tense. "As far as I know you hate Los Angeles and don't truly care for me."

"Bud . . ." Her voice faltered. "I wrote to you."

"Never once."

"Every night."

"You wrote to Mademoiselle Koestler."

"I promised my mother."

"You had promised *me*."

"My behavior was unforgivable," she said, resting both hands on the edge of the table. "Bud, as soon as I was on the train I wanted to explain what had happened. I wanted to so much, but I had given Mama my word. If I wrote to you, Mama would discharge Mademoiselle Koestler. We had a Pullman drawing room. I wrote on the window, I wrote your name, I wrote that I am so very guilty, I wrote my explanations on that window. The moving finger writes and having writ moves on to the next station." She glanced at him to see if he understood that she had made a small joke. "As we crossed the Great Desert—I cannot really describe this —my mind got smooth. Like ice. Thoughts slid off me. I was not confused or unhappy. It all slipped away. Everything that had happened in Los Angeles, the wrong I had done you, even ordinary thoughts. I no longer wrote on the window. I ate what Mademoiselle Koestler ordered, looked at the sights she pointed out, I undressed when she said the berth was made up. And on the *Normandie*—I told you I was ill when I wrote about this?" She shook her head and glossy hair spun, one wisp catching at her temple.

"Yes," he said. "I knew you were ill." He ached to touch her hair.

"Our stateroom was over the main screw with its vibrations. I never noticed." Her cheeks grew flushed and her voice faltered. "Before we left here, I learned the truth about my father and that woman. Papa was not always ethical with others, and I accepted that. But he was so good to me, and I believed in him with all my heart. After he died—Bud, you know how I kept on worshiping him. And to find out that he had kept part of his life from me, told me lies. I would not bear it." She shrugged apologetically. "I am being melodramatic, I know, but I want you to understand why I became ill. I let myself drift. It was easy. So easy . . ."

She paused, her eyes lowered. "One day the sea was very rough. Waves covered the portholes. I think the doctor was there. Mademoiselle Koestler was weeping. She said your name. She believed me dying. And then I thought, I will never see Bud again, never in this world. For some odd reason that was unbearable." Another painful smile. "I forced myself to wake up. Everything hurt. My skull was clamped into a vise, my bones ached, and I was very seasick. But I stayed awake. Afterward, Mademoiselle Koestler talked a lot about the power of prayer. Prayer had nothing to do with this. I wanted to see you again."

Trapped in currents of shame, tenderness, love, relief, Bud thought of touching her, of kissing her. She would be his wife, and later, in bed, when nothing else mattered, he would tell her. Holding her in his arms, he would tell her the story Maria had told him. No, I won't tell her, he thought. It's only an old woman's tale.

He said quietly, "I couldn't have stood a world without you."

"Then you feel as you did before?"

"No."

"No?"

"Worse."

She smiled. "Then why did you stay away? Each day I expected you to knock down Uncle Raoul's door and sling me over your shoulder. I hoped you would carry me away. Bud, your not coming to Paris has terrified me. It is so unlike you."

"I got you here, didn't I?"

"Yes, the letters," she said. "When they came out in *Figaro*, I knew—I thought I knew—that you were doing as you had promised. A knight gallant."

"Very gallant."

"I told Uncle Raoul that I must come back to Los Angeles, and he coughed and replied"—her voice was a gruff imitation—"'Are you going to your Mama?' And I said, 'No, Uncle, I am going to Mr. Van Vliet.' And he said, 'Let the young man declare himself again. Forward girls trip and break their noses.' At this Aunt Thérèse put in, 'Raoul, the others fall backward on their anatomies. Niece, I will manage the fares.' So here I am, across the table, selling myself to you."

"That, in case you don't know, is the buyer's seat you've planted your pretty anatomy in."

She laughed.

He knew he could not wait. Abruptly, he asked, "How much would you feel for me if I were a *cholo*?"

"A ch— what?"

"A greaser. Part Indian."

Her nostrils dilated with hauteur. "You are confusing me with that poor, stupid dead girl."

"Would it matter to you?"

"Are you telling me your parents discovered a blond Indian

foundling? With a nose like your father's and eyebrows shaped like Doña Esperanza's?"

"Mama doesn't know. She must never know. Her father was half Indian. Don Vincente, the one 3Vee's named after."

"The one with the amethyst ring?"

"Yes. His mother couldn't have her own children. For that she required the service of her Indian maid."

"So much illegitimacy in our families." The smile was sad. "Does 3Vee know?"

Bud shook his head. "I don't think so. I heard the story years ago and never told anyone. I even forgot it myself until you went away. I just found out for sure a few months ago."

"How? Who told you?"

"Maria."

"You believe her?"

"She's a genuine witch. My guess is the servants all know. How do you feel about it?"

"Those paintings," she said, glancing at the elaborately framed pictures on the walls. "Did someone force them on you?"

"They cost me a lot," he said defensively, then realized she hadn't answered his question. "I asked you something important," he said.

"And I answered. Your being part local is nothing to me. Less. But your taste—oh, Bud!"

"Local? Local! Around here having Digger Indian blood is worse than being a mulatto in the South. Far, far worse!"

"I never considered you a bigot."

"You didn't grow up here," he said. "People with Spanish surnames are all suspect. In school I was forever being ragged about Mama's side. 3Vee was, too. Once, I guess I was being obnoxious and my friends wanted to put me in my place. Five of them held me down, pantsed me, stripped me, smeared me. 'Now you've got the right greaser odor,' they said. I smelled of bacon fat for weeks."

"Oh, Bud..."

"The final insult," he said, mockingly bitter, "was the truth."

Her eyes were sad. "And it is still important to you?"

"The more I've thought about it, the less it does matter—except where it concerns you. Hell, I'm no lump of adobe. I make my own life. I'm as good as any man."

"You are so much better than the others. Stronger. More giving. They huddle around you for warmth and protection."

"Rot," he said, smiling with pleasure.

"And this has kept you from Paris?"

"Yes."

"It is so stupid. And one of the best things about you is that you never question yourself. You are too confident."

"I used to be reasonably sure of myself. But you can see what love has done to me."

"Love," she said, inhaling sharply. "Love is why I must live here!"

Love had drawn her back to a town that had savaged her, a town that had pilloried her father; love had forced her from the most cultivated city on earth. She must consider love — as he had those first months of her absence—as the enemy.

"You're too honorable and I'm a driving *cholo* bastard, so we're going to fight," Bud said. "But not all the time, and not yet, not yet." His tone hoarsened. "Sweetheart, this is the first minute since I slammed your mother's door that I've been at peace."

Her eyes were filling with tears, a sign he knew well. Above the iron clang of a passing trolley, he could hear the Plaza Church bells, old and bronze and very sweet in the sunlit afternoon. "Your hair's still very pretty," he heard himself say. Then he heard only the roar inside his ears. When he reached across the table to touch her hair, his hand was shaking.

BOOK 2
Oil: 1891

*The discovery of oil forced
a ruinous if exhilarating
change on the town. Derricks
blackened the western side of
Los Angeles, and teams of
steel-shod mules dragged heavy
drilling equipment across
once carefully irrigated
green gardens.*

C. K. VAN VLIET
*(The Founders: A
History of Paloverde
Oil)*

Five years later as you rode up to Paloverde the changes weren't apparent. Only a sharp eye would catch the repair of earth-colored adobe, the deeper red of the new roof. Always, though, the outer walls had been a shell curled around Paloverde's meaning. And it was the interior that had changed. The encircling *corredor* had been floored with Mexican tiles, and the rotted oak of the staypoles replaced with indestructible sequoia wood. The east wing had been completely renovated, and in back, a circle of quick-growing Australian gum trees hid the water tower that provided indoor plumbing, an unheard-of luxury in a weekend cottage. And that is what Paloverde had become to the increasingly prosperous Bud Van Vliets. Their friends agreed that while retaining the casual charm of the old rancho, the couple had made it as modern and up-to-the-minute as any Los Angeles home.

CHAPTER 8

· I ·

By 1891, Los Angeles had passed through the Great Boom. On November 19, 1885, the first Atcheson, Topeka and Santa Fe locomotive, draped in flowers and bunting, had entered town. Until then passenger rates from the Mississippi Valley had been $125, but the Southern Pacific vowed that no line would undercut them. A declaration of war. Both railroads bloodied prices until, for a few hours on March 6, 1887, a ticket to Los Angeles cost one dollar.

Armistice was signed around forty dollars.

Settlers poured in, and with them land speculation reached wild proportions. Towns were staked out on cheesebush-covered desert. An ox would be barbecued, local wine sampled, then the promoter would climb on a wagon and give a speech. Visions of a hundred thriving, sunny communities were pulled like rabbits from these pitchmen's high silk hats.

By 1889, when the Great Boom sputtered out, a few nearby towns had taken root. Glendale, Azusa (everything from A to Z in the USA), Burbank, and the like would grow, sprawl, eventually converge, giving Los Angeles its atmosphere of an endless village. Elsewhere, white stakes that marked homesites blew away, and the false fronts of never-occupied hotels collapsed.

Southern California staggered. The lucky men like Bud Van Vliet, blessed with a sense of timing, got out. Others were bankrupts, even suicides. Still, the population of Los Angeles had tripled to fifty thousand. Fecund, the town drowsed amid orange groves and vineyards, awaiting the hard thrust of industry.

· 2 ·

On a cool, sunny October Tuesday in 1891, 3 Vee stepped down from the train into the Southern Pacific's New Arcade depot.

3 Vee had prospected for silver, then had tried for gold. In the six and a half years, he had become a bear of a man. His muscles, like a bear's, were strong yet appeared soft. His shabby corduroy suit fitted loosely. His collar rose, starched torture, cutting his neck where the curly black beard started. His brown eyes, though, had not changed. The dreamy eyes of a poet, inventor, saint. The soft, glowing intelligence of a man who profited not himself.

He handed down a sturdy, shawled woman from the train. Utah Kingdon Van Vliet. They had been married four days. She was three months pregnant.

"I ain't made of glass," Utah said, peering anxiously around the crowded platform. Light fell in a great dusty curve from the overhead arch of windows, and the odors of grease, metallic steam, and fresh paint were strong. "3 Vee, see to them bags afore someone grabs 'em."

"I'll get a porter."

"What do we want with a porter?"

"For the baggage."

"We managed fine until now, thank you!" Utah, circles from her round head with its brown pompadour to her full-breasted torso encased in an iron-ribbed corset, had a temper as warm and curving as her person. "How much cash've we got to waste?"

3 Vee apologized, "You're right. I'm rotten about money."

It was true. Like most prospectors who sought wealth in its natural state, 3 Vee had no real idea of the uses of money. Money embarrassed him. Yet in a black mine shaft, by the flickering carbide flame on his helmet, he could see, actually see, the glint of a wide vein of ore. His vision made no sense. And all the sense in the world. For 3 Vee understood that he lived in the eternal moment when a human sacrifice is made; he knew he was tossing away his life to prove himself worthy. A big strike will show them, he would think.

And by *them* he meant Bud and Amélie, whom he still remembered naked in the *sala*. This endless sexual jealousy amazed him. The act wasn't that urgent with him. Maybe four times a year he would ride off for an ugly, drunken debauch in one of the Mother Lode country's wild little mining towns.

He was shy of women, even the slatterns he bought. Utah had the warmth of a kitchen stove on a cold night. He had met her in a cheap rooming house, where she was a chambermaid. A prospector's widow, she had lost her husband and baby, but she didn't gloom. She bustled, scolded, coddled. And a few months ago when 3 Vee had convinced her to move into his remote cabin, it was as much for the rich burned sugar of the pies she baked for him as for the large, firm body under its flannel nightgown.

Ten days ago Doña Esperanza had sent him a carton of books. Between pages of the Oscar Wilde was a clipping :

VAN VLIETS TO MAKE GRAND TOUR

That ever popular couple, Mr. and Mrs. Hendryk Van Vliet Junior, have been enjoying a veritable whirl of festivities to speed them on their way to Europe. Mr. and Mrs. Van Vliet plan to spend four months in Paris, France, to visit with Mrs. Van Vliet's mother, the Countess Mercier, whom longtime residents will remember as Mrs. Thaddeus Deane. Then the couple will enjoy the Jungfrau, Florence, Rome, Venice, London and Stockholm. Bon voyage, oh, happy pair.

3 Vee had stared thoughtfully at the newsprint. His mother, having intuited his reason for flight, was letting him know he could return. I can see my parents again, he thought, and a yearning joy burst through him. He blew out the candle stub and crawled into the wide, built-in bunk. "Utah," he said, "I'm visiting Los Angeles. I'll only be gone a week or so, that's all. Then I'll be back."

Utah had broken her news, adding with a trace too much defiance, "I'm having it right and proper, like the other one."

So here he was, a married man, weaving around groups at the station, a little unnerved by the presence of so many people, a satchel under his left arm, a heavy carpet bag balanced on his right shoulder, his bride following with string-tied bedding. Though they were to be gone less than two weeks, she worried for her possessions.

Outside, he paused, blinking in the sun, then led the way to the line of hacks.

Utah pointed to the double-carred electric trolley. "What's wrong with that?"

"Too much baggage," he said, forcing credibility into his voice.

He had never brought himself to tell her about his family. Each time he had tried, his voice would catch in his throat. Saying *My family's well-to-do* would sound as if he were rubbing in *chambermaid*. Even now his overgrown delicacy prevented him from telling her. Easiest, he thought, when she sees the new Van Vliet Block.

As he hefted their baggage next to the wrinkled driver, he said, "Take us up Spring as far as Temple, then back down Fort Street."

"It is a most long way," replied the old man with liquid Spanish intonations.

"That is true," 3 Vee said courteously and in Spanish. "Are you familiar with the house of the Van Vliets?"

"Doña Esperanza's?"

"Yes. On Fort Street."

"Fort Street," said the old man softly, "is now called Broadway. Nothing, nothing, señor, is as it was."

Nothing was.

The electric streetcars were powered by great arms that extended from tall wooden poles, giving the streets a look of being lined by gallows. As far as Courthouse Hill, the streets were paved. There were no vacant lots, no cows grazing amid business blocks. Elaborate emporiums presented a united front. To the west, steep Bunker Hill, in whose empty shadow the old warehouse had once huddled, was crowned with large new homes, and through their spill of semitropical gardens, a cablecar slowly shoved its muzzle upward. In the east, across the autumn-dry river, towered a vast gas works. Around it, factories poured soot into the clear October afternoon.

Men and women hurried in dark city clothes. Buggies, carts, drays clattered, and a swift-moving street sweeper cleared horse apples. The sleepy little half-Californio town was gone. An American city shoved and grated.

3 Vee leaned back in the cab. Letters had left him unprepared.

Los Angeles had altered beyond recognition, yet his memory, like tracing paper, kept the old outlines. Typically he thought of a poem: *Here he lies where he longed to be:/ Home is the sailor, home from the sea./ And the hunter home from the hill.*

"Van Vliet's?" Utah asked. "Any connection?"

They were between Third and Fourth on Spring. When he had left there had been no business blocks this far out. Now tall buildings crowded one another. 3 Vee leaned out the cab window, examining stucco bulges and ells. Bud owned this new block. Under three stories of offices, a vastly bigger Van Vliet's Hardware sparkled with plate glass and green paint.

"You got a rich uncle?" Utah asked.

"My father," 3 Vee mumbled.

"Father?"

"The hardware is Papa's."

"It can't be," she said almost angrily. "Not that whole huge shop!"

"It's over twice as large as it used to be. They moved here three years ago, during the Great Boom."

"You're pulling my leg." Now her strident voice was low with anxiety. "3 Vee, tell me it ain't true?"

"It's true," he sighed.

"Why din't you tell me you were a millionaire?"

"I'm worth nineteen dollars," he said.

"3 Vee," she said, red and earnest, as if she were struggling to lift a heavy water bucket, "3 Vee, have the Mex stop at a rooming house. No need to tell them about me."

Her shawl concealed too-bright purple sateen bought long ago with some fortunate proceed of her first husband's pick. The gaudy trimming of her hat was battered. To 3 Vee, her clothing (and his own shabby workingman's corduroy suit) symbolized his every failure.

"They're not ogres," he said gently. "Utah, they'll like you. And so would Bud."

"Bud?"

"My older brother."

"Does he live with them, your folks?"

"No. He's married."

"I should of guessed you were a gentleman. All that reading." Her voice grew very small. "3 Vee, I just ain't up to meeting them.

They don't know about me—they don't even know you're coming. So just drop me off. And don't tell them nothing."

For a brief and ugly moment she tempted him.

"Utah, stop being silly. We're married. I'll be with you. Now stop worrying."

"Your brother and his wife . . ." She faltered. "Do I have to meet them, too?"

"You won't ever have to do that," he said. "They're in Paris."

"France?"

"Yes. They're visiting Amélie's mother. She lives there. She's French."

"So this Amélie, she's French?"

"Half."

"Humph," Utah snorted. She was Catholic and her aggressive faith was not a gentle religion but a clashing battle against the forces that the ignorant priest of her girlhood had considered sinful. France was tainted with sin. She had here, therefore, a moral edge, his pregnant bride. 3 Vee didn't condemn her. She needed all the help available.

"You're my wife and that's what counts," he said, taking her hand reassuringly.

· 3 ·

Fort Street—no, Broadway—had been widened and the pepper trees sacrificed. The Deane place had been shorn of its gardens. Flanked by swart Gothic Revival houses, it had acquired a shabby look and was too big for its lot. No cypresses, no palms, no young topaz-haired girl in a white summer frock weaving in and out of green shade.

3 Vee closed his eyes before looking at his own home.

The red shingles were freshly painted. Oleanders still crowded the deep veranda, the sanctuary of his overliterate boyhood, and 3 Vee knew the front rooms would be bathed in watery dimness. As he lifted the dolphin knocker, he could scarcely breathe.

Maria opened the door. An ancient brown woman with an umber

skullface that showed no surprise. "Ah," she said quietly. "It is time for the story to unfold." And with this her toothless mouth stretched into a smile, and she opened her arms, clasping him down into an olive oil scented embrace.

"Mrs. Van Vliet?" Utah asked.

"This is Maria," he said, and started a bilingual introduction, then stopped.

Doña Esperanza was descending the stairs, the colored light from the stained-glass window falling so that 3 Vee couldn't properly see her face. Even so, the missing years burst at him. The hair smoothed under a high tortoise-shell comb was totally white. The slow, gracious walk had become labored. Halting, she stared down, one hand on the banister, the other clutching the black ruffle at her throat.

"Vincente?" she whispered.

"Mama," he said softly. And took the steps three at a time. On the landing, she clasped him with her full, soft arms, holding him away, hugging him again. "Ah, my 3 Vee, my Vincente. How like my father you have grown." The slow, quiet voice, the sharpness of California lavender brought back his childhood.

"Mama, Mama, how sweet it is to see you."

Blue and red beams slanted from the stained glass. His arm around her waist, they moved awkwardly down the narrow steps.

At the bottom of the stairwell Utah waited, her hands clenched over her shiny skirt.

Doña Esperanza glanced questioningly at her son.

"Mama, this is Utah. My wife."

"Wife?" Doña Esperanza whispered, her fingers biting into 3 Vee's corduroy sleeve.

"We were married Saturday," 3 Vee said.

"Utah?"

"Like the state, ma'am," Utah said. "Uh, Mrs. Van Vliet, if it ain't right for you now, I'll come back in a while."

Doña Esperanza's fingers remained clamped to 3 Vee, yet her voice was welcoming, serene. "This is your home," she said. "And Utah, child, call me Mama or Doña Esperanza, whichever comes easier to you. Amélie, my other daughter, calls me Doña Esperanza."

They sat around the supper table. 3 Vee and Doña Esperanza reminisced about the pepper trees. Utah peeled a piece of fruit with a knife, her round upper arms tensing with effort—she who so easily carried great water buckets and chopped loads of firewood.

Hendryk cut a generous wedge of Gouda. He distrusted surprises. However, since his first shock at hearing 3 Vee's voice, flattened and distorted by the telephone (now commonplace in well-to-do Los Angeles homes), he had been overjoyed. The stubborn knob of his nose was pink, his eyes glistened. "Here, 3 Vee, try this. It is better than Holland." To Hendryk's mind, transplanting to Los Angeles enhanced every potential. "A dairyman in Anaheim makes it especially for Van Vliet's."

"Thank you, Papa," said 3 Vee.

"Our cousin Franz and his sons have a grocery business," Hendryk explained to his new daughter-in-law.

Looking up, she said, "Oh," in an impressed murmur, then went back to peeling her pear. Utah had spoken little today. She had stared with round greenish eyes at the Van Vliet magnificence.

She's not so bad at that, Hendryk thought. Big, a good full body and a round cat face. The dress, though! Here his well-known eye for quality rebelled. Strident purple fit so tight in the bodice that the seams were stretched into puckers. A small slit showed under her tensed right arm, and a spray of crude diamanté paste didn't properly hide a mismatched button at her throat. Hendryk looked away, thinking of Amélie. Light colors floated around her small, graceful figure, and her sparkle came not from the jewelry that Bud kept giving her but from her eyes and laughter. How could two brothers choose such different women? Hendryk stifled the question. He was a rigidly decent man. This Utah, too, was his daughter-in-law. He carved at the red wheel and with a fork pushed the wedge from the cheesecutter onto her plate.

"There, Utah," he said. "Well, how does Los Angeles strike you?"

"The grandest place. Like heaven."

"3 Vee," Hendryk demanded, "did you hear that?"

"We're only on a visit," 3 Vee replied.

"Visit?" Hendryk asked. "What does that mean, visit?"

"Next week we're going home," 3Vee said.

Doña Esperanza asked, "So little time?"

"A sort of honeymoon, that's all, Mama."

Hendryk said, "You're no longer a boy. It's time you settled down. Someday there will be children. And children need schools, a place to belong."

And Doña Esperanza, out of her own modesty, decided her new daughter-in-law's flush came from the word *children*. Children hinted at the marital act. "3Vee must give you a longer holiday," she said.

"This," Hendryk persisted, "is the only place to raise a family." Doña Esperanza glanced at her husband. "When the time comes, of course," he added.

Utah, setting down the pearl-handled knife, breathed in rapidly. "It's time now," she said, and her words were garbled. "3Vee and me, we're making you grandparents."

In the sudden hush the tall case clock chimed once, the quarter hour. Why, thought 3Vee, why? He had never intended to shame her by telling his parents—at least not until it was inevitable and could be wired from the nearest station : MOTHER, SON/DAUGHTER DOING WELL. And for Utah to tell them! Utah, to whom sin was sin and flames eternal a reality. Oddly, it had never seemed a contradiction to him that she had shared his unsanctified bunk, for Utah's natural warmth erupted as a force stronger than her religion. But now sweat broke out on his forehead as he stared questioningly at his wife. She refused to catch his eye.

Doña Esperanza's fruit knife dropped with a muted thump onto the old Paloverde-woven rug. She didn't bend to retrieve it.

Hendryk unconsciously yanked his napkin from its tether between the two top buttons of his waistcoat. "Well, Utah, this is good news," he said. "A surprise, but good news indeed."

"Yes, very good," Doña Esperanza echoed. The finely wrinkled shadows under her eyes were almost black.

Hendryk said, "So you see, 3Vee, I am right."

"A child doesn't alter the situation," 3Vee said.

"Of course it does. You have to live in Los Angeles and that's that. 3Vee—"

"No—" 3 Vee tried to interrupt.

Hendryk kept on talking. "—a man has responsibilities once he's a father."

And at these words, Hendryk's smooth, heavy face grew eager. He shed years, weight, the small pomposities that were considered part of his age and station. Out of love of Bud and fondness for Amélie, he had never permitted himself to dwell on his lack of grandchildren, but always it was there, a dangling rope, an unfinished sentence, an uncompleted story. He had come to this wide land with dreams of founding a family. A man is not meant to be bordered only by his sons.

"My dear, just think," he said, leaning across the table toward Doña Esperanza, his smile that of the excited, stubborn boy who had come to this land almost forty years earlier. "Our first grandchild!"

"Yes," Doña Esperanza whispered, for the idea had occurred to her, too. "Yes."

3 Vee kept looking at Utah. She still refused to meet his questioning gaze.

· 5 ·

They were in his room. Bud's old iron bedstead had been dragged in for Utah. 3 Vee, turning down the light, felt his familiar way around the calfhide rug. The mattress of his own bed rolled him into the sag.

"Why did you tell them?" he asked in the dark.

"Why're you here?" Utah countered.

"To visit my parents."

"You ain't been home in almost seven years."

After a pause, 3 Vee said, "My brother's not here."

"What's he got to do with it?"

"I told you. He owns that block you saw, and who knows what else." 3 Vee knew that Bud owned Amélie. The thought jabbed pain into him, and he rolled onto his side. "Here, I'm always younger, always trying to catch up."

"You hate him?"

"No. I love him."

"Then you're jealous." Utah's pronouncement was sympathetic, for she herself battled against the very human sin of envy.

"Yes," he admitted.

"Is he jealous of you?"

"Bud? He wouldn't know the meaning of the word. He goes out and gets what he wants."

"I'll bet you're smarter!" Utah's voice was fierce. Her love for 3 Vee was protective and intensely partisan. "You'd do way better than him in those hardwares."

"How I'd do is beside the point. We're not staying in Los Angeles."

"You heard your pa, 3 Vee. He wants you here." Her voice was earnest. "Listen to me. There's not a need in the world for you to worry about this Bud. He ain't so special. The building, he probably wangled it out of your pa. And that French wife of his, she's a thin little thing." Utah had pored through the red velvet family album that stood with gilded feet on the parlor table. "No wonder she ain't got children."

A profound relief to 3 Vee. In her barren state, Amélie remained aloof, inviolable, without Bud's mark upon her. She remained his—as long as he didn't have to see her with his brother.

"Utah," he said firmly, "Save your breath. We're going home next week, and that's that."

"This Bud you're jealous of—3 Vee, didn't you see the way your pa lit up about the baby? Now *you're* the one. The son and heir."

"Me? The heir?" 3 Vee snorted. "Bud *built* Van Vliet's. There was a time when we were almost bankrupt. He worked night and day when he was fifteen. Sundays, too. He left school..." 3 Vee's voice faded. How do you tell a woman with less than a year of schooling that your brother had to sacrifice his education? All is relative. And to Utah this must seem like paradise. He sighed and said, "You married a prospector. I'm sorry if seeing the house has made you unhappy. But you're stuck with me the way I am. A pick-and-shovel man. Utah, one day, I promise you, you'll have far, far more than this."

A team clopped slowly along Broadway, horsebells jingling in the night.

When Utah spoke, her voice was subdued. "We'd been in California three months. We was broke, no cash for a stake. My husband got work in the Independence mine." 3 Vee had heard this story before. "We moved into one of the cabins, and as soon as I got the cracks caulked, the snow started. The baby took sick. He'd never been weakly, but now he was burning up. I sponged snow over his little body. It should of brought down the fever, but it didn't help. He had the runs and his little belly swelled up. He was such a good boy, he didn't cry. He lay there, red with the fever, and after three days his eyes turned so the white showed. Maybe a doctor would of saved him. Maybe . . . but what's the good of guessing? The doctor was in Columbia, twenty miles from us. There wasn't no money to send for him. The other miners was all Chinks. And, well, they pay Chinks less, so they had nothing. My baby gave a little sigh, one little sigh. And he was dead. I held him until he turned stiff. He would of been two the next month."

"Utah—"

"My husband got drunk. I dug the grave myself. Everything was froze, and the shovel made a clank as if the ground was rock. I'll never forget that sound. There weren't no priest, nothing. And three weeks after that, the bottom level of the Independence caved in. My husband was took. So don't think I'm blaming him or something . . . "

3 Vee got out of his bed, tripping on the calfhide rug. Springs creaked as he half fell onto the iron bed where his wife was. Lying outside the quilt, he patted Utah's firm shoulder.

"I've been married to a prospector," she said. "Everything is promises. Someday. Someday he'll find gold in the next pocket. Someday you'll be living in a palace, someday you'll wear velvet and furs. And your baby dies without a doctor and is buried without a priest."

"I promise you that'll never happen. Never."

"You've been at it seven years. You've got less'n twenty dollars," she said, sighing. "3 Vee, it ain't just the baby. Today was the first time I ever rode in a hack, the first time I ever used a fruit knife. I never been in a house like this, not even to do the wash. It's me, too."

3 Vee rubbed his fingers over the worn, balled flannel of her nightgown. "Utah, it's all right. I understand."

"How can you understand?" she said in a whisper, pressing her hot, wet cheek against his neck. "You ain't been a nobody all your life."

The next morning 3 Vee and Hendryk set off to have their midday meal at the Arcadia Hotel on the beach at Santa Monica. Train tracks ran direct from the Los Angeles depot to the new hotel's grounds. The trip took half an hour. Hendryk, however, wished this day to have substance: the return of the prodigal son. Driving to the Arcadia Hotel would fatten the day by a couple of hours.

Hendryk held the surrey reins in his good hand, and as they passed by an orange grove, wind stirring the dusty sweetness, he observed, "Riversides." Signs warned TRESPASSERS WILL BE SHOT and a huge mongrel watchdog attacked the surrey, snarling at the wheels.

When they had left the barking, angry dog behind, Hendryk said, "During the Great Boom people were prophesying there wouldn't be any oranges left." He chuckled, waving at the grove. "Imagine! They said all this would be houses and shops. And they call *me* a booster! People were saying Los Angeles would have a population of a million. I tell you, everybody in town went crazy!"

3 Vee was staring at the trees. "They look like pampered dowagers hung with big jewels." He turned to his father. "Last night Utah and I were talking. She thinks a lot of Los Angeles."

"To live, you mean?"

"We'll stay a few months," 3 Vee said, his shoulders slumping. He was trapped between his intense sympathy for Utah and his own imperatives. How can I be here with Amélie—and Bud—he thought.

"What will you do?"

"I haven't decided yet."

"There's a place in Van Vliet's for you."

"Thank you, Papa. But that's one thing I do know. I'm not going into the business. I wouldn't be any good at it."

"Did you discuss work with your wife?"

"Utah thinks, well, like you . . . Van Vliet's."

"She's a good, sensible girl, and in a wife, believe you me, common sense is what counts. Mama and I are delighted about the child." Hendryk, eyes brimming, stared beyond the grove, beyond the approaching outline of Santa Monica rooftops to where the Pacific Ocean drew a grave blue line. The moment 3 Vee said he would stay in Los Angeles, Hendryk saw a future for the boy in the business. It didn't matter what 3 Vee thought. The boy was a García and didn't know what was best for himself. But where to put him? Clucking at the horse, he pondered the matter.

The Arcadia Hotel, set in impressive grounds, had rooms for more than two hundred guests. Flags whipped on the octagonal lookout tower, gulls swooped about the fresh-painted dormers, a white-clad couple bounded on the tennis court, and a gust of wind sprayed the fountain's rainbow into a line of palm trees. This was one of the area's many new resort hotels, resorts that were luring wealthy Easterners to winter in Southern California rather than the spas of Europe. Hendryk gazed down, his expression mingling awe and skepticism. To him, the Arcadia Hotel might have been set down by a djinn. And, in truth, its opulence, set against the gangling little beach town of Santa Monica, was unreal.

Dinner, called luncheon on the menu, consisted of six large courses. In addition, Hendryk ordered an avocado pear *en salade;* it was the Angeleno equivalent of a fatted calf. A string trio played Viennese waltzes. Bubbles of Piper Heidsieck rose. Gaudy sunlight bounced from the roofs of the bathhouses below. The bay held glittering stripes of ocean. Hendryk kept darting glances of paternal pleasure at 3 Vee. He was pondering his son's future. 3 Vee was thinking how much he had missed his stubborn Dutch father.

To walk off the large meal, they strolled along the windswept observation veranda. Hendryk took out his cigar case, turning into the protection of the building. The plump hand with the missing fingers struck a sulfur match. The flame went out. Again he struck. This time 3 Vee cupped his hands protectively, and Hendryk touched his son's arm in gratitude. They smiled at one another and resumed their walk. Short, stout Hendryk in his frock coat, puffing on his Havana cigar. Tall, dark-bearded 3 Vee in worn corduroy. So different. Yet the walk was the same. Duckfooted. Heavy.

"I've been thinking of a spot in Van Vliet's for you," Hendryk said.

"Papa, I told you. The store's out."

"Your wife wants you to," Hendryk said. "Besides, where else should my son work?"

"I've been alone for a long time now. I prefer it."

"Of course I know that. And in this spot, you'll be alone." Hendryk paused triumphantly. "You went to Harvard College. You're educated. And we need someone to keep the books."

A bookkeeper! It was so ludicrous that 3Vee almost laughed. "I always had to be tutored in arithmetic. Remember? Anyway, doesn't Bud do the books?"

"He's not here. He doesn't have the time any more. And you need a job."

It was a paternal reminder. Utah was right now learning to make guava jelly and trying to get her new mother-in-law to forget a precipitate marriage. Utah and the child were his responsibility.

Hendryk again touched 3Vee's arm. "I want you near me." The salty sea air made his eyes shine. "I need you, 3Vee."

3Vee had never experienced the full strength of his father's love. Since his earliest memory, a faint irritation had always seemed to corset Hendryk's warmth toward him. The bookkeeping idea was preposterous. 3Vee exchanged nuggets and pouches of gold powder for cash, he spent cash, he never kept a single record. Sums, to him, were dead and inert as stones. Only his dreams were alive.

Yet that shining warmth in his father's eyes.

I'm soft, he thought, gripping his father's hand. "I never wrote how much I missed you, Papa," he said.

CHAPTER 9

· I ·

The door of Van Vliet's Hardware was outsize, the top half a glass diaphonie with interlocking green V's, the lower half intricately carved oak. As 3 Vee pushed open this impressive portal, a bell jangled and half a dozen clerks in green jackets looked up. An early afternoon lull lay upon the shop, and the only customer was a stout cabinetmaker. 3 Vee, with an uncertain and encompassing smile, inhaled. The sharpest odor was turpentine, which was sold from corrugated drums, but the other odors were there, paint, varnish, stove-blacking. 3 Vee had no great respect for the mercantile, yet as soon as he stepped inside the store he was everywhere faced with what was obviously a raw commercial talent. Bud's talent.

Bud, in planning his Block, had designed this store. With the town's burst of growth its character had changed. People wanted the sophistication of a city. Van Vliet's was more luxurious and better stocked than any other hardware store in the West. The walls were lined with innumerable bins of nails, screws, bolts, and plumbing supplies, and above these bins were shelves of tools and building materials. At regular intervals hung long, hooked poles to retrieve buckets and other light items from the upper shelves. 3 Vee walked down an aisle formed by a stepped display case that contained every brand and variety of kerosene heater. No Los Angeles home had a furnace and few were equipped with fireplaces, so in winter these squat little heaters were the ubiquitous source of warmth.

3 Vee passed through the newest and most unusual section of the store. A hanging sign proclaimed FINEST HOUSEWARES, and shelves and long display-case counters were crowded with steel and silver cutlery, glassware, and crockery of every grade from cheap, bright Mexican bowls to the finest English bone china. This department had been Bud's idea and Hendryk had protested. "Who ever heard of a hardware store selling bone china?" he demanded. But soon after, he was pointing out with pride that Housewares was more profitable than all the other departments of the store combined.

Hendryk enjoyed overseeing his little world, so Bud had glassed off a rear corner for his father's office. 3 Vee, entering this clear-walled room, removed his hat and jacket, put on a billed cap, and snapped on celluloid cuffs. He opened a clothbound ledger inked in Bud's large, decisive (and boyish) hand: *HOUSEWARES*. 3 Vee used his pencil on a slip of paper to check a column he had added up this morning. He reached a sum three cents less than his earlier total.

Sighing, he glanced up and saw Mrs. Di Franco and her daughter Mary Di Franco Townsend in the Housewares section. Mary was blond and pretty and Bud used to beau her. She waved a gloved hand to 3 Vee, and Mrs. Di Franco bowed. 3 Vee returned their mimed greetings. His skin crawled as if with ants. He shifted in his chair so he couldn't see into the store. But the clerks and customers could still see him.

His third try at addition came two cents over his original. He muttered, "My God, to waste a day over a nickel." Abruptly he yanked off the green cap and celluloid cuffs, strode out of the store, and at Pioneer Livery arranged for a pinto.

· 2 ·

He rode west from the crowded business section, moving around Bunker Hill on Colton Street, which was two blocks north of Water Avenue. He and Utah had rented a cheap little clapboard bungalow on Water Avenue, but 3 Vee was not going home. He needed to be free of buildings and streets; he needed to be where there were no people.

The fuzzy expression he wore in public was gone. Brooding intelligence drew his thick black brows together. As he clopped along the wide, quiet, unpaved residential street, he looked as if he were in considerable pain. He rubbed a hand over his hip pocket, feeling the slight bulge of a letter he had received last week from Bud. *We're in London now,* Bud had written. *Some cold, wet city! We'll be back in the sunshine on May 16. And we're sure looking forward to seeing you, meeting Utah, and that new Van Vliet she's busy producing.*

They would be home two months from now, and 3 Vee would still be in Los Angeles. His parents, Utah, and the baby due in April had all conspired to keep him here. In two months Bud and Amélie would have to be faced. He dreaded seeing them. They were forever tainted by his one glimpse of them in the *sala* at Paloverde. He could never think of Amélie without a prickle of lust, or of Bud without a wave of sexual jealousy.

And how will they view me? he thought. In the light of my great accomplishment, taking a few ounces of gold from the reluctant earth? Or will they see me as an animal in a glass cage, adding columns of figures that refuse to balance?

Colton Street wound through low hills. He had reached a cuplike dip where an acquisitive builder had put up sixteen small houses. Five had FOR SALE signs. The tiny patches of weedy grass around each house were sunburned, dry leaves mounded on their porches, and dust streaked their windows. They had the sad look of wallflowers who are beginning to suspect they aren't going to be asked to dance. Colton Street trailed into a path where a sign proclaimed:

LOTS FOR SALE
RYAN REALTORS
BROADWAY AT ORD

They'll never sell, 3 Vee thought, not with this smell of tar. Then, suddenly, he was dismounting. To his left was a pool of tar about a foot across. He dropped the pinto's reins, staring.

To a native Southern Californian, dusty black tar seeps weren't unusual. Yet 3 Vee gazed, hypnotized. A thick bubble forced its way upward, capturing light and space like a lens into one point until it burst.

Local Indians had called tar *chapopote,* caulking their woven canoes with it and riding to the Channel Islands through rough waters more swiftly than the white men now moved in their sailing vessels and steamships. The Spanish word for tar is *brea*, and Californios had spread it on their flat roofs to keep dry during the rainy season. Americans knew that tar was the residue of petroleum, and petroleum meant money. But there never had been an oil-producing well in Los Angeles.

3 Vee, who had been very young when Van Vliet's Oil Supplies came a cropper, had none of Bud's vivid recollections of the excitement of oil men. In fact, 3 Vee was only dimly aware that Bud had spent twelve hours every Sunday working in the Newhall field. What 3 Vee knew of oil came to him secondhand, but his knowledge was great. The earth's wealth fascinated him. He had learned about petroleum wherever he could, from other miners, from books and journals he ordered from the East. He devoured their turgid vocabulary and fine print with the same pleasure that he did novels. He also read the popular accounts of the great oil strikes in the East. But Southern California was a new land, geologically speaking, with rocks and formations jumbled and tilted. A man could drill down through the maze of rocks and end up with no bit, no rope, a dry well. Again 3 Vee thought: There's never been an oil-producing well in Los Angeles.

He looked around him, taking in the configurations of the land. Once arroyos swept down here, he thought, knowing therefore that he stood on layers of deep alluvial earth. The oil is above the rock strata, available, he thought. He had no savings, for he handed over his salary, a generous hundred dollars a month, to Utah. And the cheapest drilling rig cost around fifteen hundred dollars. But 3 Vee's mind always moved in great, often erratic leaps, jumping over difficulties, thereby obliterating them.

Pulling a marker stake from the ground, he squatted to prod the black tar. Another slow bubble formed, and with it his mind seemed to grow and expand. Oil, he thought, and it's not too far down. I don't need a rig. I could dig an ordinary well. He dropped the stake, and remounting, cantered briskly back to town, dig for oil, dig for oil, dig for oil ringing through his head in time with the clip of hooves.

Hendryk hadn't yet returned to his office. 3 Vee, never pausing to consider his father's hatred of all matters connected to the oil business, knelt by the battered Tilton and McFarland safe, counting out his month's salary. He licked his thumb and counted again. He had one bill too many. He replaced it in the stack, snapping on the rubber band, closing the safe.

At Ryan Realtors he didn't bargain. He never bargained. His hundred dollars bought one skimpy residential lot. The lot with the pool of *brea*.

· 3 ·

"I din't quite hear you," Utah said. "A man could what?"

"Use a pick and shovel."

"You drill for oil," Utah said. "You don't dig for it."

"The Senecas considered oil a cure for rheumatism—they dug at seeps."

"Indians," Utah reproved mildly. "What can you expect?"

That same afternoon, winter's early dark had fallen and the kitchen light was on. Utah was feeding chunks of wood into the Glenwood stove, which she had blacked that morning. She kept her little house immaculate. Every day, happily, she scrubbed, mopped, and polished the dining room, which was still unfurnished, the parlor, and the two bedrooms in the rear. She invariably hummed as she cleaned the small, square bathroom and the kitchen; to her, these two rooms were the grandest. Never before had she lived—or worked—in a place with indoor plumbing.

She prodded the fire with the stove handle, then used her apron to lift the lid from a pot. The smell of lamb stew spread through the kitchen.

Utah was in her last month. A large, tall woman, pregnancy made her enormous. Her huge weight gain pleased her, for it meant a good, large child. A boy. The Van Vliet heir.

She replaced the lid, turning to 3 Vee, who sat with his arms crossed on the table's red-checked oilcloth.

"You was saying?" she asked. "About the oil?"

Her expression was fond. She didn't yet know he was serious. Her countering arguments were routine and maternal. Two years older than 3 Vee, she thought of him as very young. His encyclopedic knowledge she saw as a kind of dangerous toy; she sometimes believed God had brought her to him so she could protect him from his feckless mental processes.

"Digging's feasible," 3 Vee said.

"What's that mean?"

"The oil's above the rock strata. I'll stake my life on it. The earth's very deep there. Two rivers once joined, and that means layers and layers of soil came down from the mountains. You can see the topography clearly at the end of Colton Street."

"Two blocks over?"

He nodded. "That's where my lot is."

"Your what?"

"That lot with the *brea* seep, I bought it."

"*Brea?*"

"Tar. That's what I'm explaining." 3 Vee's brown eyes shone with excitement. "The tar's how I know there's oil."

"What did you pay with?" Utah demanded.

"The salary due me."

"This month's earnings?" Red marks, like smudges of rouge, appeared on Utah's round cheeks. She was staring around the cozy little kitchen as if it might suddenly disappear. "3 Vee," she snapped, "tomorrow we go and tell that salesman you ain't going through with it."

"We won't do that," he said, the excitement in his eyes gone. "I start digging tomorrow."

"When? Early morning? After work?"

"I'm leaving Van Vliet's. Utah, this is our big chance."

Her hands at her hips, she asked, "What for? To starve?"

"No. Don't you see? I need to work full time at the digging. I want the well to come in before..." His voice faded.

Utah, however, knew what he had been about to say: before *they* come home. After that first night in Los Angeles, 3 Vee had never mentioned his feelings about Bud. He didn't have to. Anyone who has a jealous streak recognizes the symptoms in others. And Utah was immensely jealous of both Bud and Amélie. Her in-laws were generous and kind to her. Indeed, she and Doña Esperanza had become close, for, despite their overt differences, they had much in common. Both had been widowed early, then married men their junior; both took pride in setting a good table and enjoyed their rich, heavy meals; both were devout Catholics, and both cherished 3 Vee. Yet each time Hendryk praised Bud, Utah had to bite back the words *3 Vee's your son, too! 3 Vee's clever, too! And he's the one who's making you a grandpa!* And as for Amélie, well, both Van Vliets talked about her as if she were some kind of princess. But fortunately, Amélie had a crucial failing for a princess. Infertility.

Utah said, "I understand how you feel about getting ahead. Honest I do. But you ain't making sense in the way you're going at it. Your only chance is to stay with hardware."

"I hate the business," 3 Vee said in a low, unhappy voice. "I'm rotten at it. I have no feeling for it. I'm cooped up. I've never seen any purpose to it."

"Working and making a living, that's purpose."

"I've earned my own way since I left here," 3 Vee said quietly.

"It ain't just us. Someday this boy"—she curved a hand to her stomach—"will get everything from your pa."

"Van Vliet's belongs to Bud," 3 Vee said. "Bud helped my father build it. No. He did more than help. He built it himself."

Each time she heard this remark, Utah panicked. It seemed inevitable to her that Bud would push 3 Vee out—if 3 Vee didn't walk out on his own. And then where would they be? "I've heard once too often about that brother of yours! What a great, clever man he is! And what a wonder in Paris gowns that Amélie is!" Fright increased Utah's anger. She took a deep breath, trying to control herself. "3 Vee, I ain't going to say nothing against your brother. Maybe he is clever. But one thing I do know. Your pa's told me time and time again as soon as you get the knack, you'll be a very fine businessman."

"He knows I'll never be that."

"Why'd he say it, then?"

"Papa's famous for hanging on to lost causes."

"I don't want to get mad!" Her voice rose. "3 Vee, don't make me lose my temper."

Utah hated losing her temper. Afterward, she felt nauseated and sinful, as if she had disobeyed one of God's laws. Blessed are the meek. . . . Yet, wasn't this home, hers and 3 Vee's, being threatened? And wasn't the baby about to be disinherited by 3 Vee's foolishness about digging in tar? Surely God never intended meekness at such a time.

"Utah," 3 Vee said quietly, pressing his fingers on the checkered oilcloth. "I've made up my mind."

"3 Vee—"

"I gave in to you before," he interrupted, calm, precise. "Staying in Los Angeles was a mistake. Working at Van Vliet's compounded the mistake. You know I've been miserable. Don't bother to argue about it. You've asked me often enough why I'm laying crepe. Well, that's over with. I'm keeping the lot. I'm working full time on sinking a shaft. Now, let's not argue."

"I ain't arguing!" she shouted.

"And we're going to be rich."

She could feel her anger growing, bubbling. "And just how do you intend to make us rich? Oh, I forgot! Digging up tar like those dead Indians, is that it?"

"Yes."

"And while you're out there digging, making this fortune, how're me and the baby meant to eat?"

"You and the baby will have everything you need, always. I've already promised that."

"And I heard promises before!"

"I've never let you down, have I?"

"And we ain't been married six months yet, have we?"

"Utah, please don't fight me. I was never meant to be cooped up doing books. I'm like Mama's family. The Garcías never were shop people." He gazed up at her, a pleading gentleness on his bearded face.

Finally, it was his gentleness that did it. Utah's first husband, when she argued with him, had hit her with his large, red-haired fists. But of her two husbands' responses, Utah found 3 Vee's infinitely more battering. In her mind, his sweet gentleness was the quality that summed up an aristocrat. And while she fervently admired aristocrats, she looked down on them with bafflingly equal fervor. They were superior creatures who at the same time were a coddled and stupid form of creation. They threw away their own birthrights and those of their children. Yes, Utah thought, he's throwing away a fortune that belongs to the baby, too. At that thought, a red wave of anger engulfed her.

She stepped heavily to the stove. "You—ain't—leaving—them—hardwares!" she shrieked. With unprotected hands, she grasped the heavy cast-iron stewpot. She raised it above her head and stood for a furious instant like some avenging goddess.

3 Vee got up out of the chair, holding a hand toward her. With a convulsive gesture, she hurled the pot to the linoleum.

Steam burst up. Lamb, beans, carrots, potatoes, onions flew. Pale, rich gravy splattered her skirt. The cast-iron lid, Van Vliet's best-quality merchandise, spun in circles like a wheel before clattering down.

Utah jumped back. She would have fallen if 3 Vee hadn't grasped her shoulders. He pulled her swollen breasts and stomach against him. "Are you all right?" he asked.

She gasped for breath. The blood was draining from her lips. He held her a bit away, examining her.

"Come on, honey, you need to lie down." And putting a strong, supportive arm about her waist, he drew her along the narrow brown hall. Their heavy footsteps echoed on uncarpeted wood. He helped her onto their double bed.

She tried to push up.

"Rest," he said.

"I got to clean up," she whispered.

"Stay. I'll do it."

When he returned to the dim bedroom, she lay stretched out on the bed, one hand gripping a damp washrag, her blue serge skirt sponged clean, her high button shoes splayed on a piece of newspaper that protected the quilt. Without lifting her head from the bolster, she said, "I try so hard on my temper, 3 Vee, so hard."

He sat on the edge of the bed. "You wasted a pot of stew, that's all."

"It's sinful to get that angry."

"You're sure you didn't hurt yourself?"

"Only in here," she said, holding a hand to her left breast.

He misunderstood. "The child?" he asked, alarmed.

She shook her head. "Inside my heart. I only want to stop you doing the wrong thing. I didn't mean to blow up. Every time I blow up, I worry you're going to run off."

"I won't ever leave you," he said with a sigh. "Would you like a cup of tea?"

"Later." She reached for his hand. Her fingers were hot. "3 Vee, you're going back to Van Vliet's, ain't you?"

"Try to understand me, Utah. Some men must go to sea, others have to climb mountains, explore. Or paint, or write. I have this compulsion to uncover what nobody's ever seen. I've *got* to try that well."

Her fingers tightened. "What if there ain't no oil? Then what?"

Vitality drained from his tall, bulky body. The light left his face. He said nothing.

"Stop hanging crepe," Utah said briskly. "You got about two months to find it."

"Two months?"

"There's no more'n that put aside."

"You've saved money?"

"I ain't been married to two prospectors for nothing. Seventy-one dollars and some change."

His bearded face was alive again, his eyes glowing and warm. "Wife," he said, bending to kiss her. "Wife."

· 4 ·

"Madness!" Hendryk barked.

"It's down there. Believe me, I know geology."

They were in Hendryk's office, and the glass walls were rattling. Hendryk was stamping up and down on his short, heavy legs. "So then geology is another word for madness!"

"Papa, Colonel Deane squeezed you out. That doesn't mean there isn't a fortune in petroleum."

"Nobody makes money from oil," said Hendryk flatly.

"A lot of men have. Rockefeller has."

"You don't see Mr. Rockefeller drilling in California, do you? And even in the Eastern states, he'll soon fail, you mark my words." Hendryk inhaled. "If only your brother were already home! Bud would talk sense into you."

Anger hardened 3 Vee's expression. "Would you like me to finish out the month?"

Hendryk stopped marching. He sat at his desk, and his smooth, heavy cheeks waggled as he tried for control. "I'll give you a raise," he said. "You've been improving."

"You double-check the figures every night."

"You're wrong for accounting, that's all. Mind you, I'm not say-ing you couldn't be good if you'd set your head to it. But that's beside the point. I've been thinking of putting you in charge of Housewares." Hendryk glanced out at the crowd of early-morning shoppers at the rear counter. "We carry the finest merchandise in Los Angeles, and you've always had an artistic bent."

"I can't stand being locked up."

To Hendryk's anger was added the hurt of having his cherished hardware store, the finest west of the Rocky Mountains, likened to a prison. "All right," he snapped. "You've always been a García! You throw away everything. You threw away Harvard College, and now you throw this away. I wash my hands of you!"

"We can see one another often," 3Vee said, pulling up a chair to his father's side. "Utah's very fond of you and Mama. We both want you to share the baby with us."

"Don't expect any help from me. Or Mama."

At times during 3Vee's prospecting years he had been hungry. But never had he written to either of his parents for money. "All I ask is that you take me seriously."

"Who," countered stubborn Hendryk, "can take anyone in oil seriously?"

· 5 ·

Later that morning, 3Vee walked from his house on Water Avenue to his lot on Colton Street carrying a pick and a shovel. He was within one mile of the Van Vliet Block. He could see the houses on top of Bunker Hill, where Bud had built a delicately spooled white Queen Anne "cottage" for Amélie. He could raise his voice and Utah, two blocks away in their ugly clapboard bungalow, would hear his shout.

He had changed to faded denim coveralls and a worn plaid shirt. He strode to within three feet of the *brea* pool and dropped the shovel. With both hands he raised the pick, burying it in weed-covered earth.

As he pulled out the pick, he said aloud, "Spudding in"—the col-loquial term for the start of an oil drilling venture.

He threw back his bearded head and laughed. A joyous sound, it bore no connection to his need to accomplish greatness in the brief time before Bud and Amélie's return, no connection with the amassing of wealth. 3 Vee laughed because he was doing as his nature intended. He was uncovering what no man had yet laid bare, discovering the unknown. He was beginning the act of creation.

·6·

A grasshopper rain, as Angelenos called soft, intermittent spring showers, fell on the morning of April 5, when the child was born. As both parents had determined, he was a boy. A few weeks premature, he weighed well over eight pounds. Utah's labor, like her anger, was violent and brief. She screamed, sweated, tore at the velvet ropes Doña Esperanza had tied to the foot of the bed. She gave one animal howl. Doña Esperanza, who had delivered so many children, received her first grandchild into her hands.

Long of limb, he had a thatch of black hair, eyes of indeterminate darkness, baby-fine black brows. "He looks like 3 Vee," Doña Esperanza announced, her normally grave face suffused with smiles.

Hendryk, first ordering a bonus for every Van Vliet employee, hurried through the light rain to the little house to stand proudly at the foot of the cradle. The newborn infant was swaddled in six layers of clothing that his grandmother and mother had stitched from the finest Canton flannel. Despite this impediment, he managed wild, jerky kicks of his arms and legs.

"He's strong," 3 Vee said.

"A fine boy," Hendryk agreed. He turned to his own son. "Now you understand what I've been trying to tell you. It's time to forget foolishness and start back to work."

Almost every night since 3 Vee had left Van Vliet's, Hendryk had driven over in his buggy. He missed 3 Vee. This weakness he couldn't admit, so he pretended his visits were solely to express his disapproval of the oil venture.

"Papa, let's not argue today."

Hendryk couldn't let it go without extending a plump, two-fingered hand toward the baby. "What about your duty to him?"

"Who do you think he resembles?"

Hendryk struggled with his irritation at 3 Vee and his pleasure with his first grandchild. Pleasure won. "He's the image of your mother," he said, beaming. From his vest pocket he took an envelope, handing it to 3 Vee. "One hundred for the boy," he said. "One hundred for the parents."

"Papa, thank you. But it's too much."

"Let Utah handle it. She knows the meaning of money."

The baby's face contorted with redness, and under the swaddling, his body tensed. He gave a sharp wail, then another.

Alarmed, 3 Vee asked, "What's wrong with him?"

"Your son is telling us he's hungry," Doña Esperanza said. She bent to pick up the newborn infant.

After a while she emerged from Utah's room. "Now you may visit," she said.

The baby slept in Utah's arms.

"What name have you decided on?" Hendryk wanted to know.

"Charley Kingdon," Utah replied.

3 Vee jerked with surprise. They had decided on Thomas, after Don Tomás García, whom a careless king had gifted with Paloverde.

Utah pressed the tiny, capped head against her big, round breast, then looked up at 3 Vee. "It was my first boy's name," she said, and her eyes held a plea.

3 Vee said, "Charley. I like it. A good, strong name."

· 7 ·

During Charley's first week of life, Doña Esperanza slept with him in his tiny bedroom. Utah, who had been up firing the stove for breakfast two hours after the birth of the original Charley, reveled in this time of her recovery. During the second week Maria slept with Charley.

Utah was uncomfortable around the skeletal old woman. She didn't trust Indians. Maria spoke only Mex and smelled of strange, unknown herbs. Maria padded on bare, high-arched feet around the house. Maria's rheumy, sunken eyes never looked directly at Utah.

Worst of all, with Maria about, Utah felt uncomfortable in her own home. She had never had a servant. Yet having been a servant herself, her standards were impossibly high.

"She douses everything in that olive oil," Utah complained to 3Vee as they sat at the kitchen table eating a dinner Maria had cooked. "She don't boil the cabbage long enough. And as often as I've shown her how, she ain't learned to scrub the sink proper."

3Vee glanced at Maria, who stood at the stove with her back to them. The baby began to cry. Maria left the kitchen.

"Ask her where she thinks she's going," Utah demanded.

"To see what's wrong with the baby, what else?"

"She's spoiling Charley Kingdon."

"She was our nurse," 3Vee said. "Maria's famous for her ability to soothe babies. Listen."

The crying had ended.

"She's teaching him to howl every time he wants to be picked up, that's all," Utah said. They finished their pork chops. "I better go see what she's doing," Utah said.

3Vee heard her vigorous step in the hall, heard the bedroom door open.

"3Vee!" Her shriek echoed through the little wooden house.

He bolted down the narrow hall. Utah was clutching Charley. The baby, enveloped in a blanket, began to give piercing cries.

"What is it?" 3Vee asked. "What's wrong?"

"She had him all naked! She was shoving some filthy old stuff at him!"

By the dim light through drawn shades, 3Vee saw the cradle was piled with infant clothing topped by an assortment of tiny objects. He recognized Maria's fetishes. A little apart lay the ancient and ruffled feather.

"The child is uncomfortable trussed up like that," Maria observed in Spanish. "That one needs to be free."

"What were you doing to him?"

"Showing him the ways of life and death. Once, we showed this to all our children when they were born."

3Vee put his arm around Utah's waist. She was shaking all over. "He's not one of yours," he said.

Maria ignored his remark. "He chose the eagle. In all my days I have never seen a child choose this way. The feather is too difficult for an infant to grasp." Her deep-set eyes looked up at 3Vee. "It is impossible, your son's choice. The eagle means it is his fate to soar above the earth."

"What's she gibbering about?" Utah asked.

"Nothing."

Utah clutched the child tighter and his screams became more vehement. "Just tell the filthy old Mex she ain't never to come near him again."

Maria, who couldn't speak English, understood it reasonably well. "I will go home," she said.

"Maria, I'm sorry," 3Vee mumbled.

"There is nothing I can do here anyway," she said, and her tone implied that the baffling threads of the infant's future were already woven. Our *bruja*, 3Vee thought as she gathered up her sacred things, hanging the rabbit-hide pouch around her neck. Utah had taken the baby in the other room to dress. Maria put her veined, wrinkled hand on 3Vee's arm, but said nothing.

·8·

Utah pinned the broad swaddling band tight over the little stomach, which was heaving with sobs. She folded the diaper around him, pulled on his undershirt. As she replaced the layers of garments, her terror eased. Charley Kingdon is all right, she thought.

Even in her own mind she called the baby his two names. It had something to do with her sin. She had been Utah Kingdon, widow, when this squirming, sobbing baby was conceived, and for this she couldn't forgive herself—or Charley Kingdon. Until she had met 3Vee, she had never given in to her carnal warmth, and now she felt a quiver of guilt each time she looked upon the visible results. Tears squeezed from Charley Kingdon's closed eyes, running down his tiny red face. He had been fed an hour earlier, so she knew he wasn't hungry. He had been frightened, and he wanted to be held, that was all. Utah's milk-laden breasts throbbed with the desire to cuddle him. But as she tied the blue ribbons of his nightshirt, she thought: He'll have to cry it out.

She knew she must be strict with Charley Kingdon. For his own good I don't want him spoiled, she thought. This child, to her mind, born out of her illicit heat, had concupiscence bred into him, and when she thought I don't want him spoiled, she meant he must not learn the comforts of the flesh.

The baby quieted to small, pitiable gulps and Utah put him back in his cradle, gently covering him with the crocheted blanket. She closed the bedroom door.

Maria had left the dinner dishes stacked. 3 Vee had gone back to his digging. Utah, humming, began to clean up her kitchen. She was delighted to have the place to herself.

After a while Charley Kingdon was silent.

He was an active infant, what Utah described as a "bad sleeper." Later that night 3 Vee was wakened by the movements in the cradle at the foot of their bed. He got up without disturbing Utah, took his son from the cradle and tiptoed down the hall to the parlor. The room was arranged with Paloverde furnishings that Doña Esperanza had given them, comfortable old things that Utah longed to replace. 3 Vee sat in a thong-seated chair, the baby on his lap. He began to change him, and remembering Maria's words, left the dry clothing loose. Then he held Charley to his heavy chest, and the baby grasped at his beard. 3 Vee smiled down at the baby until he finally fell asleep.

·9·

At first, after the months over ledgers, each swing of the pick had been agony. Even after six weeks of digging, he was still conscious of a tenderness between his shoulders. He had taken off his shirt and sweat glued his long-sleeved underwear to his body. Sweat beaded his forehead. A handkerchief protected the lower half of his face. At sixteen feet down, the *brea* fumes were oppressive. This was the lowest, brute-slave kind of work. Yet 3 Vee, who had never enjoyed physical activity for its own sake, was perversely content. No wonder Utah feared his intellect. 3 Vee himself was surprised that his inclination toward dreamy inertia was forever being overcome by the prodding of his inventive brain.

Leaning the pick against the shaft wall, he shoveled tar-drenched earth into a pair of large buckets. The walls of the four-by-six shaft were planked with redwood, and this shoring made a crude ladder. Reaching for a bucket, he grunted. As he lifted the dead weight, his arm quivered. I need to eat, he thought. The fumes numbed his appetite and generally he had to remind himself of hunger. He climbed upward, halting to grasp the bucket with both hands. Thighs and stomach muscles tensed with effort, he braced himself to raise the weight to ground level.

Tanned, clean hands gripped at either side of his filthy ones. The bucket turned weightless, and he was looking into Bud's blue eyes.

3 Vee's thoughts raced and jumped. Bud? It's only May 1. They're not due for two weeks. I meant to have struck oil before they got back. His hair's getting thin on top. And that suit was obviously tailored in London. The last time I saw him he was sitting naked, peeling an orange.

"Let loose," Bud said.

3 Vee released his grasp on the bucket. The tendons in Bud's hands stood out like wires. He swung the bucket easily onto the ground, and 3 Vee climbed up.

Disregarding the tar on 3 Vee's coveralls, Bud hugged his brother. There was masculine awkwardness in the embrace, yet moist affection welled in Bud's eyes. 3 Vee forgot his rivalries, his jealousies, forgot his plans of greeting his older brother with an oil-producing well on his own doorstep. Seven years, 3 Vee thought, seven years. Grasping Bud's shoulders, he returned the embrace. For this moment of reunion, 3 Vee's love was pure and untainted.

"You weren't due until two weeks Friday," 3 Vee said when they released one another.

"We took an earlier boat. We were in a rush to see Charley Kingdon. That's some boy you've got there."

"He is, isn't he?"

"That's for sure."

"When'd you get in?"

"The morning train. We came right over."

"Then Amélie," 3 Vee said slowly, a faint sting marring his pleasure, "is with Utah?"

"And your son. I gather it's dinner time. Old Charley Kingdon began howling, and the three of them disappeared. So I came to see the site."

Bud stepped over piled, tar-black soil and climbed down the

shoring. His voice came upward. "You're a damn mole, 3 Vee." He rose from the shaft, hauling 3 Vee's other bucket. "Here," he said. "Haven't you heard about this new thing? It's called a drilling rig."

Bud's jesting voice thrust 3 Vee back into his boyhood. Some of his warmth melted, and he regretted the loss. "The oil's not much further down," he said.

Bud sat on piled boards, opening 3 Vee's dinner pail. "What've you got in here?"

"Just some bread and cheese."

"I like bread and cheese. Swap you some for a drink." Bud pulled a silver flask from his pocket, unscrewing the top. "Bonded Scotch," he said. "Here's to Charley Kingdon Van Vliet." He took a long swallow and extended the flask.

"To Charley," 3 Vee said, drinking smooth liquor that was warmed to his brother's temperature.

Bud broke off some cheese, handing the bigger piece to 3 Vee, and helped himself to a slab of Utah's fresh wheat bread. "What makes you so sure there's oil around here, kid?" The tone was amused, yet Bud's face was intent, serious.

Nobody, not even Utah, had asked this of 3 Vee.

He munched his cheese reflectively. "In the last seven years I've learned more than I did the rest of my life. Geology, mostly. You know the kind of thing. How mountains and rivers and valleys were formed. The layers of the earth, and how they came into being. Mineral deposits, coal and oil. Do you know what oil is, Bud?"

"'I get the feeling I'm about to learn."

"Where we are right now didn't used to be land," 3 Vee said. "Millions upon millions of years ago, the continents had already formed, but their outlines were very different. The Pacific covered all this." His gesture was meant to include the entire Los Angeles Basin.

"Are you speculating?" Bud asked. "How do you know for sure?"

3 Vee had placed a few dirt-encrusted objects on a piece of newspaper. He held up a fossilized shell. "Today I found this. About fifteen feet down." His finger, as dirty as the fossil, pointed out the embedded marks. "See? It's a limpet. This limpet lived and died before man walked upright. That's what oil is. The little marine creatures that lived and died by the billions, then sank to the ocean floor to mingle with mud and silt."

"Why've there been only dry wells in the Los Angeles area?" Bud asked, and 3 Vee remembered that his pragmatic brother always aimed for the utilitarian heart of every question.

"I don't know. Probably nobody's drilled at the right spot."

"Maybe digging by hand'll do the trick." Bud's jesting tone had returned.

"The earth goes very deep here," 3 Vee said stiffly, avoiding mention of the fact that he couldn't afford a rig. "The pool is straight down, above the igneous strata."

"Besides, you enjoy healthy exercise."

3 Vee reddened, biting back his anger, which was childish. "What've you been doing?" He couldn't keep a faint aggrievement from his voice.

Bud was grinning. "Well, 3 Vee, it's like this. I've been on the first real vacation I've ever taken. And Papa's been writing me daily to put my mind to work. I'm meant to come up with ideas to bring you back to sanity."

"There's nothing you could say or do."

"You asked about me. It's me we're talking about. Papa overlooked two important facts about me. I've always enjoyed gambling—except with me nothing's ever really a gamble. I'm a rotten loser. It scares the hell out of me to lose. So I win. I have to win. And the other matter Papa forgot is that oil gets in your blood. And I'm an old oil man."

"That's right. I'd forgotten. You did work up in the Newhall field." 3 Vee flushed with embarrassment. How pompous he must have sounded, explaining oil to Bud, who had been in the business. "I really am an ass, aren't I, playing college professor?"

"That's one more thing about me. I'm willing to learn. 3 Vee, quit feeling bad. I used to clerk in Van Vliet's Oil Supplies, remember? I never stopped listening to the drillers. But I never heard anyone mention the Los Angeles Basin once was ocean. When I worked up in Newhall, sure I learned fossils might mean oil. But nobody ever could explain why to me." He kicked a polished shoe at the mound of tar-drenched soil. "*Brea*'s the best sign. So you have here an oil man who's willing to gamble with you. What's say we buy us a rig?"

3 Vee felt his jaw open. A rig! he thought. Us?

"You need a partner," Bud said. "I know you can't afford to drill."

In this first moment, 3 Vee felt a vindicatory triumph that Bud, practical Bud, believed in him, took him seriously. For it wasn't only Hendryk who considered him mad. People in the neighborhood would stroll over to the end of Colton Street, and 3 Vee often heard chuckles drifting across the vacant lots. He had never been able to shrug off laughter. That Bud, his successful older brother, believed in him revived his fraternal warmth. But in the next moment 3 Vee thought of Amélie. And knew he could never accept Bud's offer. How can I become partners with the man who debauched the girl I loved, a girl I thought too young even to speak of such emotions? The man for whom I feel a profound envy, and over whom I must prove my own superiority?

"Thank you for the confidence, but—"

"Come on, 3 Vee. I'm serious."

"So am I. I need to manage this on my own."

Bud, picking up the silver flask, stared at 3 Vee, a long testing glance. Then he dropped the flask into the lunch pail and as silver rang on tin, 3 Vee glanced down and saw that it was engraved with his initials, three Vs. "I didn't realize it was for me," he said. "Thank you."

"De nada."

"Bud, you're the only person who's believed in me. And that means a good deal."

"We're going to be partners," Bud said easily. "You can count on it." He stood, brushing breadcrumbs from his well-tailored suit. "My nephew must be finished with his dinner. Let's head on back to the house."

Amélie, 3 Vee thought, and swallowed hard. Seeing Amélie at any time would be painful. How could he face her like this, caked with tar, filthy, a failure, a laughingstock? Next week, when I hit oil, I'll be able to see her, but he knew that thought was a childish compound of hope and trying to avert the inevitable.

"I've got to get back to work," he said. "There's not many daylight hours left."

"Cut the horse apples," Bud said in a low, harsh voice.

"What?"

"I don't know the hell what. You tell me what. Why can't you come back to the house? Is it too much effort? Are you too damn busy digging to take off a half hour to say hello to my wife?"

3 Vee winced. Never had he realized how much it would hurt to hear Bud say those proprietary words. My wife.

Bud's feet were slightly apart, his elbows were flexed, his fingers curled into his palms. His stance was a belligerent one that never had been directed at 3 Vee. As a boy 3 Vee had known his brother as a strong, if infuriating, source of protection. Now he saw Bud as a very dangerous man to cross. Yet he didn't give in to him out of fear. It was because of those words *my wife*. Amélie belonged to Bud, and that was that. Maybe it was best to have her see him at his worst, so there would be no danger in this yearning he felt for her. Slowly he pulled on his faded wool shirt.

Bud set a brisk pace along Colton Street with its vacant houses, and walked swiftly up the grade of Patton Street. Two pinafored girls playing jacks nudged one another, giggling as 3 Vee passed. As they turned on Water Avenue, Bud took his brother's arm. "I'm going to tell you this once," he said in a low, cruel voice. "So listen and listen carefully. My wife went through a very bad time in Los Angeles, and I made a promise to her, and to myself, that if anyone hurt her or said anything against her, they would have me as an enemy."

I cared for her before you knew she was alive, 3 Vee wanted to say. His tongue seemed to swell. He couldn't speak.

The front door of the little clapboard house burst open. Utah, holding Charley in the crook of her arm, came onto the porch. "We been waiting for you!" she called, her voice loud with excitement. "I got coffee on. 3 Vee, hurry up! You got to see the presents. Such fine things. And Amélie 'n' me, we been getting to be the best of friends."

The smile on her round face was warm and genuine.

· IO ·

The two women had been in the parlor. Paper was strewn on the floor; the plain, rough tables and chairs were covered with open boxes.

Amélie stood by the window. She had removed her suit jacket, and her gauzy white shirtwaist was as delicately tucked as her girlhood summer dresses. She was as fragile as ever, as erect, as delicate. Her hair no longer fell to her waist the way he remembered. The topaz mass, not ratted into the rigid pompadours favored by local matrons, was swept up loosely, with a few tendrils escaping around her high forehead. She's the same, 3 Vee thought with relief. She hasn't been coarsened. What had he feared would coarsen her? Dry Los Angeles air? Bud?

"3 Vee?"

"Welcome home, Amélie," he said.

"It *is* you. The beard changes you completely." There was no scorn in her hazel eyes, only that quick, smiling pleasure. "3 Vee, you are a man."

"Time does that," he said, pausing. "Your letters always seemed to catch up with me too late to answer. I'm sorry."

She had written to him before and after her marriage. Doña Esperanza had forwarded her letters. He had been unable to force himself to reply.

"Oh, you are still the same," she said with that pretty laughter. "3 Vee, you are blushing."

Bud had come to stand at her side. "I kissed my new sister," he said easily. "Now it's your turn to be a brother."

"Amélie doesn't want tar all over her," 3 Vee answered.

Bud shot him a hard, blue stare.

3 Vee had never kissed her or held her hand. Positive that Bud's command would emasculate all pleasure, he bent to Amélie's cheek, careful to touch her only with his lips. Yet as he pressed against her smooth warm skin, inhaling the scent of flowers that were evasively, tantalizingly familiar, he experienced a jolt. A shock. And for a moment *he* was the man in the *sala* with a luminous, naked girl. His response was instantaneous. He pulled away quickly.

He heard Utah's fond, maternal voice. "3 Vee, go wash up."

He soaped his face and arms with a new bar of red Lifebuoy, scrubbing long and futilely at his nails. He searched through his collar box, found a new white one, and put on his good broadcloth suit, bought for working at Van Vliet's. He brushed his wet black hair and beard. He was no longer drowning.

The rich odor of coffee drifted from the kitchen. The three of them were laughing around the table when he entered.

Amélie smiled up at him. "3 Vee, remember you told me about fandangos? We have given two at Paloverde." She turned to her husband. "Bud? We could have one for Utah and 3 Vee."

"What's a fandango?" Utah said.

"It is an old-fashioned Californio dancing party," Amélie explained. "With this *Ramona* craze, people have dances they call fandangos, but Doña Esperanza showed me how to arrange the real thing. We barbecue a steer, Maria and the others make all the old foods. We break *cascarones*, dance the old dances."

3 Vee, listening to the eager tumble of words, found it difficult to categorize his emotions. He felt the vivid force of her personality that had captured him before, yet at the same time he wondered if this could be the same proud girl who had hated everything about Los Angeles.

Now she was saying, "Utah, has 3 Vee showed you Paloverde? Bud and I have restored parts of it, and it is perfect spot for a fandango. We can all wear the old clothes. Doña Esperanza has so many in her boxroom, the high-waisted dresses and silver-button suits. I am positive some will fit you and 3 Vee, and she has lovely shawls and lace mantillas. We could invite all 3 Vee's old friends. Chaw and Lucetta Di Franco, Bader and Mary Townsend, Ora Lee and Tim, the Bostwicks. Everybody. 3 Vee, Utah can meet all your old friends in one fell swoop."

Of course they weren't his old friends. They were Bud's friends. Yet 3 Vee realized that Amélie, wishing to give a party to introduce her new sister-in-law, had hit upon a generous means. No expensive new clothes, no worrisome formality.

"You haven't had a chance to unpack yet," he said uncertainly.

And Bud added, "Or noticed that Utah's got her hands pretty full."

"Utah," Amélie said in a conspiratorial whisper, "now you see how stodgy the Van Vliet brothers really are."

Utah gave her short laugh. The two women smiled at one another. They've hit it off, 3 Vee thought with relieved amazement.

"It sounds grand to me," Utah said. "If I can bring Charley Kingdon?"

"What do you think the main point of the fandango will be?" Amélie said. "To show off Charley. He is such a beautiful baby." For a brief flicker, her expression was wistful, then she smiled again. "So it is settled. We will have a three-generation Van Vliet party."

· I I ·

"I been dreading meeting them," Utah confessed after Bud and Amélie had left and she was energetically cleaning the kitchen table. "I figured she'd be out to high-hat me. Him too. But there they was, friendly as can be."

"I told you they were friendly."

"Bud, he's got the devil's own charm, don't he? He takes over. Bossy, but in a nice way." Plates clattered into the enamel dishpan, followed by the spoons and forks that were part of the massive set of sterling flatware that Bud and Amélie had bought in London, a wedding gift. (I never sent them anything, 3 Vee thought, least of all my good wishes.) "And her, she's a little thing. You'd think with all that money she'd dress better'n a plain old shoe. But when you're with her you forget all that. She's, well, she's like gold. Know what I mean? A small bit of it shows up. She never once bragged about their trip or their fancy new house. We talked mostly about Charley Kingdon. Did you see how she fell in love with Charley Kingdon?" Utah turned to 3Vee. "I could tell she misses having a baby something fierce. Poor thing. They been married over six years and it don't look like she'll ever have one."

Utah's pity rang counterfeit, yet there was no malice in her voice. She turned back to her soapy water.

So, 3 Vee thought, Amélie's barren state makes it possible for Utah to accept her sister-in-law's social position, her wealth, her personal charm. As long as Utah retains her position as the sole provider of Van Vliet heirs, all is well. He examined his tar-blackened fingernails. Am I any better? Amélie's private misery enables me to believe she doesn't truly belong to Bud.

"Know something, 3 Vee? I never had a woman friend. And I always wanted one." Utah spoke with gruff shyness. "I think me 'n' Amélie are going to be real good friends."

Abruptly, 3 Vee said, "Bud asked to invest with me."

Utah turned, her mouth a circle of surprise, her soapy hand clenching a cup that dripped water on the linoleum. "In the well? You mean he believes in it? That there's oil down there?" Her tone made it apparent that she never had believed.

"He seems to."

Impressed, she raised her brows. She had heard too often from Hendryk what an astute businessman Bud was. "How much?" she asked.

"Enough to buy a rig," 3Vee said. "I told him no."

"Good," Utah said. "We don't want his money!"

Utah, like him, wanted their success to be against Bud, not with him. 3 Vee felt a pang of comradeship for his wife.

"Don't give him more than ten percent, if you do take him in."

"I turned him down and that's that."

"You done the right thing."

3 Vee went to a cabinet, squatting to get the bottle of bourbon he kept there.

"Ain't you going back?"

"No."

3 Vee carried the bottle outside and sat on the back steps. It was late afternoon, and the low sun shone through a row of tall gum trees, eucalyptus that farmers had imported from Australia to act as windbreaks. With a quick jerk of his wrist, he downed a jolt. During his years as a prospector, he had gone on sporadic drunks, howling binges that had been unsuccessful attempts to drown his bodily urges.

He didn't consider whether Bud and Amélie loved one another. The Bud he had known as a young man was incapable of love. It would be too painful to wonder if Amélie—his honorable, clever, proud, delicate Amélie—could feel love for a man so forcefully careless of deep emotion.

He was thinking of his own reaction to the touch of his lips on her cheek. He had been surprised as well as embarrassed. He and Utah had resumed the marital relationship that had been interrupted by Charley's birth. Yet the desire he had felt for Amélie had the urgency that comes after lengthy abstinence mingled with a sharpness, an infinite sweetness, that he had never before experienced.

The gray mist rolled in, and with it, twilight. 3 Vee finished the bottle, gazing into the gloom, thinking of making love to his brother's wife. When he finally came inside, Utah helped him through the kitchen, down the hall and onto their bed. She folded a towel on the bolster under his face and took off his boots. He was soddenly drunk.

CHAPTER 10

· I ·

During May, night mist rolls in from the sea and the dawn is overcast. On Saturday, May 7, the sun burned through late. By two-thirty, however, a clear yellow light bathed the open carriages that crowded a wide street on the northwest corner of town.

Bud had arranged for the sprinkling cart, so there were no clouds of dust from horses as the male guests rode up to greet the ladies who waited in their carriages. Since this was a family affair, girls who hadn't yet had coming-out parties sat excited and giggling under ruffled parasols. Their older sisters flirted with the younger men on horseback. Doña Esperanza's stout Californio kin and friends wore their usual black gowns. The American-born ladies wore a wild variety of costumes: high-waisted, calico frocks, embroidered blouses with full skirts, fitted lace that exploded below the hips into ruffles, Carmen-style skirts that daringly exposed a pretty ankle. There was a homespun dress that looked as if it had crossed the continent in a covered wagon, white Sonora dresses, hoop skirts, black-lace mantillas, gaily embroidered silk shawls. Most of the women wore high Spanish combs behind their pompadours.

The men were dressed in vaquero costumes: short embroidered jackets studded with silver buttons, tight riding trousers, vicuña hats that were low-crowned and wide-brimmed. Spurs jingled. Voices called out, "Hah, Don Benito!" "Greetings there, Don

Enrique." "Hello there, Doña Amélia. We're expecting a mighty fine day at your hacienda." Other than the elderly black-clad ladies, very few of the Van Vliets' guests had Californio blood—the Van Vliets themselves, the very dark Bostwicks, the Gold boys, and a few others. No one had a Spanish surname.

The men made their way on horseback to Amélie's brougham, greeting her warmly. She introduced them to Utah, and Doña Esperanza proudly held up Charley. Women rose in their carriages, calling out admiration for the dark-haired baby, warmly welcoming Amélie home.

3Vee, in Don Vincente's silver-laden suit, sat a hired bay watching the affection that surrounded Amélie. Again he found it impossible to believe that she had been the victim of mass cruelty less than seven years earlier. Yet he knew Los Angeles. It was a quality of the town, with its eternal flood of newcomers, never to look back but always forward. The past rarely stained. And sometimes after a great scandal had ended, a hint of fame was all that was left, glossing its participants as varnish enhances a fine portrait. So it was with Amélie Van Vliet.

While the noisy gathering waited for the last arrivals, someone strummed a guitar and two of Maria's nephews served the men cold beer and carried tinkling glasses of iced lemonade to the ladies' carriages.

Bud, in his silver-studded vaquero outfit, his narrow waist circled by a crimson sash, rode with Chaw Di Franco to the head carriage. "Utah," he said, "let me present a ruffian friend of mine, Chaw— pardon me—Don Chaw Di Franco. And that on Mama's lap is our young Charley. Don Carlos."

"Doña Esperanza, that's a mighty fine grandson you have there," Chaw said.

Radiant, Utah wore the turquoise silk that Doña Esperanza had been given forty years earlier by her first husband, the elderly Scotch physician. The dress, trimmed with black braiding, had a hoop skirt and puff sleeves that showed Utah's plump round arms. Before today, Utah had met only Doña Esperanza's elderly friends. This party was a new world, one for which she had yearned. She was meeting the illustrious names immortalized on business Blocks and in columns of the papers, and not one had high-hatted her. Her round cheeks burned with joy.

The last two vehicles expected, a surrey and a landau, rolled up. Bud raised his flat-brimmed hat. *"Vamanos, señores, señoras y señoritas,"* he shouted over the tumult of voices. "Let's go, everybody."

The men spurred their horses, carriages formed a ragged line, raising a sheet of dust as they moved from the watered-down street onto the narrow, rutted path. Wild mustard blazed. A dry ranch sprouted soft green barley. In a celery field Chinese laborers watched from under flat coolie hats as the procession wound by.

A group of men rode first. 3 Vee lagged apart from them. Pausing, he raised his new silver flask and took a long drink. He wished he were anyplace else but on his way with this festive group to Paloverde. The men kept glancing at him, then at one another, with amusedly raised brows. 3 Vee had become, if not a laughing-stock, at least a smilingstock. He hadn't hit oil, but the tar fumes had become so heavy that he had been forced out of his shaft. So he had figured out a way of boring with a pointed eucalyptus log. Standing high in the shaft, he rotated the log until the earth below was churned, then he climbed down fifty feet to haul up buckets full of noxious, gummy earth. He was trying to sink an oil well without a rig, and in Los Angeles where everybody knew there was no oil. That, by God, was funny.

Bud dropped back and rode alongside his brother. "Something you probably haven't noticed, kid. This isn't a funeral, it's a fandango."

"I'm not much at parties," 3 Vee replied. "You must remember that."

"Let's try to forget then, and maybe you'll surprise us and enjoy yourself." Bud was grinning. "Come on ahead a minute."

The last thing 3 Vee wanted was a conversation with Bud. There was, however, no escaping. They spurred their horses. Bud said nothing until the sounds of laughter, horses, and the guitar were muted by distance.

"The rig," he asked. "Been thinking about it?"

"I work best by myself."

"Come on, 3 Vee, I'm not a deaf, blind idiot. I know you've been breaking your ass down there." He paused. "You borrowed to buy more lumber."

"Who told you that?"

"Isaachar Klein. One time when I was in his bank, he had me into the inner sanctum. He asked if I'd guarantee your note. I said, of course."

3 Vee thought he had convinced the banker with his geological explanations. The hired horse stumbled, and 3 Vee, slipping in the saddle, had to grab the pommel. "Why didn't you say something about it?"

"Hell, I know you'll pay him back. Besides, aren't you my kid brother?"

"I'm not your kid brother any more," 3 Vee snapped. "I'm a grown man. And I don't take charity."

"All right, all right! How about a straight business deal? Grown-up brother, let's sink this well together."

"Why?" Into 3 Vee's consciousness was sinking the annihilating stupidity of it all. Bud, the very man to whom he had set out to prove his worth, had signed his note, had in actuality therefore given him the money. Bud was still protecting him. He knew how infantile his anger was, yet he couldn't halt himself from snapping, "So you can rag me while you help me out of my little problems?"

"Calm down, 3 Vee, calm down."

"Tell me one thing, then. What's in it for you?"

Bud looked ahead, frowning as if he were trying to comprehend either the question or the answer. He said, "I explained. Oil's in my blood. You believe it's down there. So do I."

The path was shaded by the canyon. 3 Vee wiped his forehead and took the flask from his pocket.

"Why not wait for the party to begin?" Bud asked.

3 Vee bit back an annoyed response and drank deeply. A fold in the hills had cut off all sound of the procession behind them. After a minute he said in lieu of an apology, "Bud, I appreciate the party. Utah's loving every minute. And thank you for signing the note."

"But you still don't want me as a partner, is that it?"

"I prefer being on my own, that's all."

They reined in, waiting for the others to catch up. Bud was silent. 3 Vee, glancing at his brother, saw a sadness around the wide, good-natured mouth. He had never seen Bud sad, and accordingly decided he must have misread his expression.

This was the first time he had been to Paloverde since that long-ago day he had bolted. Knowing Bud had demeaned the old hacienda into a weekend place made it yet harder to face. He had emptied the flask before they arrived.

Above the tiled roof of the rancho hung savory smoke; a whole steer had been roasting in the barbecue pit all night. Amélie and her servants—Liu the cook and his fat wife, Juanita, and Bridget the downstairs maid—had worked for two days decorating the patio. The eaves were festooned with wild lilac branches that had withered a little from the sun, ivy twined the *corredor* staypoles, and palm fronds made shadowy bowers where matrons could chatter and young couples could flirt. The tall, handwrought Mexican candelabra that Amélie had borrowed from Doña Esperanza were decorated with spring flowers from Amélie's own garden.

Under the right side of the *corredor* dangled piñatas, animal forms made of brightly colored ruffled paper that, when broken, would spill presents. Waxed canvas was stretched on the patio for the dancing later, and near this square stood the guitar player and two violinists. They wore loose white clothing, as musicians had in Mission days. The padres had lured and wooed converts with music, then inflicted on all Indians these shapeless, coarse white garments.

Long trestle tables were covered with Doña Esperanza's and Amélie's best linen. The servants passed red wine and more lemonade. 3Vee stationed himself near the table with the *aguardiente*, local brandy. He drank because he was a failure, he drank because people were smirking at him. He drank because Amélie wore a white lace dress that bared her luminous shoulders and clung to her delicate body. He drank because as she introduced him to people he didn't know, she smiled at him. He downed a glass because she rested her hand on his sleeve, the silver-braided sleeve that had been his grandfather's pride. He drank because the guests, male and female, laughed and called him Don Vincente, and several asked how his digging was going. He drank because it was Bud who owned Paloverde.

Yet he wasn't drunk. A routine amount of liquor always

brought those red streaks to his eyes and blurred the edge of his vision. Certainly he wasn't drunk when he sat next to Utah on one of the backless benches to eat the smoky barbecued beef. If he were drunk how could he have explained to his wife the preparation of the traditional foods: the great platters of enchiladas verdes bubbling with melted cheese and soured cream, the tamales—choice bits of pork with hot pepper sauce enclosed in velvety corn masa, then tied into corn husks and boiled? If he were drunk how could he have been so coherent?

Maria ladled out refried beans with an iron spoon that, she told everyone in her toothless Spanish, had belonged to her grandmother when Paloverde was built. Bud translated the old woman's words, and Maria's Spanish and Bud's laughter combined in 3 Vee's mind. It's a farce, he thought. And once this hacienda was peopled with our ancestors, his and mine.

Maria bent over him with her garlic-and-cheese-odored dish. "Don Vincente, *frijoles?*"

"*Nada mas, gracias.*"

"You are seeing ghosts," Maria said.

"Yes, ghosts. Maria, it's me who's the ghost."

"It is important to remember that you and these others are equally real. Yes, tonight I think is the night when you need most to remember," Maria said, and her faded, sunken eyes swam before him.

"You ain't eating a bite, and you're going at that brandy heavy," Utah said.

"It's a party," he replied, wondering when darkness had fallen, when the flickering candles and fuzzy yellow lanterns had been lit.

"3 Vee, you've gone and gotten drunk," Utah said.

Across the patio, the younger guests had stopped all pretense at adult dignity. Laughing and shoving in an uneven line, they waited their turn for Amélie's blindfolding so they could swing a broomstick in the attempt to break a piñata for its shower of gifts. At the tables, their elders watched, smiling indulgently, cracking almonds, sipping the last of their wine.

At some point *cascarones* must have been distributed, for 3 Vee held one in his hand. *Cascarones* are blown eggshells packed with confetti; at Californio celebrations the trick had been to break one over the head of the member of the opposite sex that you cared about, without that person knowing. A shy old ritual of courtship. 3 Vee crushed the fragile shell, watching confetti stream through his tar-blacked fingers.

Doña Esperanza came over to him. He fumbled with a chair for her, and she sat heavily. "Vincente, what is wrong?"

"They're making fun of our past."

"Don't be silly," she said. "Amélie has worked so hard to make this party a success, and she wants only to please you and Utah." And then he wasn't positive if his mother said, or if he only imagined she said, "You must not stare that way at her."

Time blurred. Doña Esperanza was saying, "The dress is very becoming on Utah. The color suits her."

Among other bright-colored gowns, he saw the gleam of turquoise silk. "Where's Charley?" he asked.

"Don't you remember? You watched Amélie put him to bed in the cottage."

Chaw Di Franco was leaning over him. "Well, 3 Vee, old friend, when's that oil going to gush?"

"How the hell should I know?"

Chaw's fleshy face drifted away. "Just wanted to show interest."

The delicate figure in white lace was pulling at Utah. Utah shook her head, Amélie insisted, laughing. Even over the sounds of boisterous revelry, 3 Vee could hear the pretty sound of her laughter. The big, tightly corseted woman followed the small, graceful one to a bench by the waxed canvas dance floor. Three young girls already sat there. Amélie moved lightly among the younger women. Once she had moved so in the green shadows of the Deane garden...

Hendryk mounted a chair, clapping his good and bad hands until the guests quieted.

"Ladies and gentlemen!" he announced. "Ladies and gentlemen, our first dance will be *El Son*. In older days the fandango always started with *El Son*, for this was the way lovely Spanish belles were introduced. Each señorita showed off her best steps. And that is what our ladies will do tonight. Bud will act as the *tecolario*, the introducer."

The young women on the bench snapped open their fans. The three white-clad musicians began fingering and bowing their strings.

Bud didn't move to the bench, as everyone expected he would.

In small, graceful tapping steps, he clicked across the brightly lit patio to the *corredor* where the group of black-clad Californio ladies sat. Dancing in place, smiling, he held out his hand to his mother. She shook her head. He kept dancing, and there were calls of "Come on, Doña Esperanza, show us how." Doña Esperanza stood, holding out her shawl, tilting her head with its smooth white hair and high comb, dancing a slow, stately circle on cracked tile. All the time Bud's boots tapped on the adobe below her and he continued to hold out his hand. A well-built man with thinning, sun-streaked blond hair who somehow completely belonged in the black suit of a vaquero, a man who looked like his Dutch father yet with his dark eyebrows and high cheekbones bore a startling resemblance to the tall, gracious lady slowly rotating on the *corredor* above him. 3 Vee leaned back against the staypole thinking, he does everything well, my golden successful brother. He owns this place that truly belongs to me; he owns Amélie, who should be mine.

Doña Esperanza sat amid applause. Bud danced across the patio and bowed to Utah. She stood and whirled energetically in a sturdy dance that resembled a polka. More applause.

Bud held out his hand to Amélie. People leaned forward. "Best dancers in the Cow Counties," a woman said. Confetti clung to topaz hair, silk heels pressed hard to drum a wild rhythm on canvas. Bud's boots moved faster, adjusting to her tempo. Never touching, they whirled, turned, twisted, smiling at one another, their eyes never losing contact. Lanternlight gilded sweat on their foreheads.

The meaning of their dance was clear, very clear, to 3 Vee. *El Son*, he remembered viciously, had left decent homes half a century ago, moving to brothels, where the customers tossed hats to the whores whose dancing excited them.

Swaying a little, he made his way around the *corredor* to the *zaguán*. He pushed the heavy oak door, using both hands, stumbling as it swung open.

Out here it was quiet. Crickets chirped, an owl hooted, and he could hear laughter from the water tower where the coachmen were having their own party. Below him, horses nickered. In front loomed the shadows of carriages and buggies. He stumbled toward them, searching for someplace to sit by himself. He paused to look up at the misty sky. But if it was misty, why was the moon shining like a gold coin?

· 3 ·

He heard the light footsteps, but he didn't turn.

"Come back to the party," Amélie said. "Have some coffee with me."

"Nice out here," he said. "Hear the quiet?"

"We order the coffee from New Orleans."

"Fine party. Wonderful. Utah's loving it."

"It is strong and black. It will make you feel better."

"Utah's loving it," he repeated.

"I know she is, and it makes me happy. 3Vee, I do like her very much. Did I ever tell you how glad I am to have her for a sister-in-law?"

"A chambermaid?" he asked, his voice sullen and hateful. "Is that what delights you to have as a sister-in-law?"

"Utah is warm, enthusiastic, and why do you believe I am a snob?" Amélie's voice was clipped. "Please have some coffee. You need it."

"I'm not drunk," he said. "Amazing, how perfectly you've adjusted. Amélie, who belongs in Paris, happy where there's no wit, no culture, no music, in the town where she was crucified."

"As you see, I climbed off the cross," she said, "and learned the local customs."

"And you're happy sniffing orange blossoms and reading *Ramona?*"

"Yes. If you want the truth, I am very happy with Bud. Since you are so sensitive to my feelings, surely you can see that I am happy with your brother."

"I see a diamond among pebbles, that's what I see."

She said something more about coffee, but her words made no sense. In the moonlight, her face swam before his eyes, lovely, proud, cold. He couldn't bear for her to look at him that way. "Amélie, I'm sorry. Didn't mean to hurt your feelings. I . . . 'the world hath really neither joy, nor love, nor light, nor certitude, nor peace, nor help from pain.'"

"Why are you so sad, 3Vee? Will it help to talk about it?" she said, and her voice was gentle.

They were standing by a landau, and she reached up to open the door. He was too slow to help her. With quick grace she managed the big step. He hauled himself up and sat opposite her. Her hands were folded on white lace, and her round Tiffany-set engagement emerald glinted. The smell of her perfume was intensified by her dancing.

"Remember, 3 Vee, how we used to sit for hours arguing about books and poetry? Those involved arguments on the literary merits of Thackeray and Swinburne and Matthew Arnold and Jane Austen and Henry James."

"It was the happiest summer of my life," he said. "What happened to Mademoiselle Koestler?"

"Bud gave her a small pension, and she lives with her sister in Colmar. We visited her this winter. Poor Mademoiselle Koestler. Her eyes have become too dim for embroidery." Amélie sighed. "But failing sight or no, she is once and always a governess. She had a decidedly guilty expression, letting us return to the hotel unchaperoned."

"That was the happiest summer of my life. I'm repeating myself."

"Why are you unhappy now?"

"Everybody's laughing at me. Every man here has come up to ask how the digging's going." He drew a breath. "They know how the digging is going, and they think I'm a damn fool, burrowing into the ground like a gopher. They want to tell me I'm crazy, that's what they want to tell me. They're informing me I'm a stupid failure. A public spectacle, a laughingstock." His voice cracked. He wasn't drunk, yet in another moment he would be weeping as if he were drunk.

"I am sorry, 3 Vee. So very sorry. We meant to please you with this day. Not hurt you." She leaned toward him, resting her small hand on his. Her face was very close, and he could feel the warmth of her breath, see the delicate curve of her breasts above white lace. His body stiffened with desire.

"It's Bud, too. Bud even more than the others," he said.

"Bud laughing at you? He wants to be your part—"

"Why?" 3 Vee interrupted. "Can't figure why. He has everything he could want. He owns the Block, he owns Papa, he owns money, he owns Paloverde. So he has every right to do what he wants here. He can mock the past, cheapen all the dead Garcías any way he wants. His right to do what he wants. His right to bring you here and lie naked with you in the *sala*—" He stopped. My God, he thought, I am drunk. Very drunk.

She pulled back. Her face was utterly still and her eyes were fixed on the carpet of the landau. "You saw us?" she asked.

"Yes, I saw you."

She gave a low, tremulous sigh.

"Why d'you think I ran off'n left my happy home? Why I fled down the nights and down the days and down the arches of the years?"

"I must get back," she said, standing between the seats.

"No. Want to ask you some questions while I'm this drunk." He grasped her slender waist with both hands and held her until she sat back down. He moved his hands to cup her face. His heart pounded, and he thought, I must stop this. Yet the idea of releasing her was unbearable. Utah's flesh was solid; Amélie's flesh was soft and smooth, and as luminous as an opal.

"I cared for you," he said. "Did you for me?"

"You were my friend, the only friend I had in Los Angeles." She tried ineffectually to push his large, strong hands away from her face. "3 Vee, you did not care for me that way until you saw . . . me and Bud." Her voice was cold.

"I cared for you, yes I cared. I cared enough to wait until you were older to tell you how I felt."

"Let go." It was hauteur-edged command.

Her pride, he remembered, was her sole weapon. She is so very vulnerable, he thought, and his lust grew.

His palms pressed harder against her face. "What if I, not Bud, had stepped forward at your father's funeral? What if I'd stayed with you in Los Angeles? Been with you, gone to the trial with you, taken you in your loneliness and misery?"

"You *are* ugly when you drink."

"Answer me!"

"You did not speak to me at Papa's funeral. You would not have gone to the trial with me, either. Bud was a man, a generous and strong man. You were a sweet, gentle boy, pretending to be above Los Angeles, yet afraid of what the town thought of you. You were afraid of *me*."

He scarcely heard. He saw only her face before him and a hitherto unimagined violence raced through his body. He made an incoherent sound and kissed the soft mouth imprisoned by his hands. She neither fought nor responded in any manner; she retreated into stillness as if by freezing she could become safe, inviolable. Half kneeling, he pulled her to him. She was as fine-boned and delicate as he had imagined, but her skin was more silken, her body more sensual. Shadows reeling about him, he rained kisses on her face and neck. His embrace grew more frantic and unpredictable, like the jerkings of a creature thrust into an alien element. He was horrified at himself, yet he couldn't stop. His fingers reached under the lace bodice.

A convulsive shudder passed through her, and she came to life, hitting at his shoulders and face. He pushed himself onto her side of the landau, springs of the leather seat squealing as he fell with her under him. She was sobbing, kicking, slapping. He was conscious only of the inevitable act he must perform.

He pulled up her skirts. She struggled harder, calling out words he didn't hear, hitting him with her clenched fists. She was small and fragile.

He was a large man, strong-muscled from wielding a pick and shovel. He was very drunk. And he was filled with an overwhelming lust that would transport them both to a place where there were no divisions between them, where there was no success or failure, where minds and bodies joined, where the past was the present and the future, and he owned it all.

Her struggles ceased. And he was plundering the riches of the earth.

·4·

The only sound was his own loud breathing.

His drunken haze cleared instantly. His sight became vivid. In the blanching moonlight, he gazed down at her. Her eyes were closed. A thin line of blood trickled from her mouth.

He couldn't believe what he saw. He couldn't believe what he had done. He fingered away the blood and she didn't open her eyes. Shifting from her, he saw her bare, slender thighs. She didn't move to cover herself. Taking his handkerchief, he wiped her with infinite tenderness and covered her with her skirts. Her eyes remained closed. Cold fear prickled him, and he thought he would be sick.

"Amélie, are you all right?"

He held his breath. Slowly, she shook her head.

"I love you. I never meant to . . . never this."

"Bud gave up his boyhood to support you." Her tone was leaden, flat, and she didn't open her eyes. "He protected you. He has never taken anything from you. Why?"

"It has nothing to do with Bud. I've always loved you."

"You wanted me because you saw me with him."

He stroked back her hair. He took her hand. It was icy, limp, as if she were unconscious.

"Amélie, darling, what can I say to make it right?"

"Do not call me that," she said dully.

"There must be something."

"Later you will want to confess. It would hurt Bud too much. He cares very deeply for you."

"I won't tell him," 3Vee said, and at that moment it seemed the easiest promise he had ever made.

She began slowly to adjust her clothing. Her movements were stiff. As she descended from the landau she was forced to take his hand, but she immediately moved apart from him. He pushed open the heavy door. Light, voices, music hit him like blows. He remained in the shadows. She crossed the patio, her hurried step a parody of her usual rapid grace.

Nobody noticed their absence or their return except Maria. The umber face was filled with an unreadable sadness as the old woman watched Amélie enter the house and close the door of the bedroom where Charley slept.

· 5 ·

A dance had just ended. Bud was returning Mary Di Franco Townsend to her seat, the two of them laughing in their old flirtation. Mary's buxom blond prettiness was overflowing into matronly form. She requested something, Bud nodded, heading toward the linen-draped refreshment table.

Bud gave up his boyhood to support you, Amélie had said. *He cares very deeply for you.* 3 Vee clenched his fists. He went over to Bud. "I've been thinking about your offer," he said quietly. "Is it still good?"

Bud took the glass of lemonade from Juan's hand, thanking the old man before turning to 3 Vee. "Sure thing."

"Can we go someplace and talk?"

"Enjoy the fandango. Come by the office Monday morning." He put his arm over 3 Vee's shoulder, smiling. "I'm glad we're partners."

·6·

At seven-thirty Monday morning, 3 Vee sat opposite Bud, reading script from a typewriting machine. Farsighted, he held the sheet at arm's length.

> The name of the partnership is PALOVERDE OIL... the character of the business is that of developing Southern California mineral lands for the purpose of producing petroleum... names of the two general partners are Vincent Van Vliet and Hendryk Van Vliet II... each of the two General Partners is to receive fifty percent (50%) ownership in the partnership.

How much had Utah said? Ten percent. That was ridiculous. Fifty percent was high for capitalization but not unfair. However it gave Bud, supposedly the silent partner, equal control. 3 Vee looked down at the typewriting and felt even more guilty that he was mentally quibbling over so inadequate an atonement. He reached for a pen and dipped the nib in gummy ink.

Bud signed the contract briskly, and with a broad smile extended his hand. "Partner," he said. After they shook hands, he poured two shots of whiskey from his tantalus. "Like the name, Paloverde Oil?"

Mute, 3 Vee nodded. For too-numerous reasons, the last name on earth that he would have chosen was **Paloverde Oil**.

·7·

On the drilling platform Bud, 3 Vee, and the burly Xavier strained to turn the bullwheel.

The wheel, taller than 3 Vee, was connected to its mate by an iron axle. As the three men pushed, Manila hemp spooled. The rope went over the crown beam, forty feet above them, descending to a large fishhook bit that they were edging upward. When it was overhead, Bud and Xavier—the son of one of "Mama's people"—stepped back. 3 Vee adjusted the temper screw so the bit remained precisely over the well. He tripped the catch. With a whoosh, iron plunged, trailing loosened rope. They listened. A hundred fifty feet below there was a clean, grinding sound. 3 Vee let out a sigh, grateful that he hadn't heard the screech of iron hitting crooked. He had already had to replace three expensive bits.

Again the three strained to turn the bullwheel. The tar-blackened bit rose.

This time 3 Vee didn't trip the catch. Instead, Xavier lowered the baler to clean out debris while 3 Vee and Bud, mopping their foreheads, sat on the splintery boards of the drilling platform: 3 Vee, a bearded wildcatter, Bud, his starched white sleeves rolled up over his strong forearms. He opened a gold cigarette case.

"How do you and Xavier manage when I'm not around?"

"Sweat more," 3 Vee replied.

"Then why not get the steam engine?"

"No more cash outlay until the well comes in."

Bud struck a match on his thumbnail. "Funny, I never thought of you as a worker."

"How did you think of me?"

"A serious little kid who needed his nose jolted out of his books."

They both laughed. 3 Vee leaned back, inhaling the odors of his brother's Sweet Caporal, pomade, bay rum, sweat. He was conscious of the almost palpable quality of Bud's ease, his uncomplicated strength.

What 3 Vee had committed on Amélie's body six weeks earlier had proved, strangely, to be a kind of watershed in his fraternal relationship. From earliest childhood, 3 Vee had battled every encroachment of Bud's warm, thoughtless domination. It was a black obstinacy. But now the wrong he had done somehow forced him to accept his brother. And 3 Vee found the simple masculine closeness unexpectedly sweet.

He had no other reasons for happiness.

First, there was Amélie. Always Amélie. She had been ill for ten days after the fandango. Bud, like Utah and everyone else in town, attributed her illness to overworking on the party that had introduced Utah to Los Angeles. When she recovered, she had continued to befriend Utah, shepherding her sister-in-law through the relaxed socials of the summer. She treated 3 Vee in public with her usual lively amusement. But she went out of her way never to be alone with him. He was desperate to question her. Did she hate him? How could she not hate him? How ill had she been? He wanted to tell her of this hair shirt of guilt that constantly tortured him. He longed to apologize again.

Second, there was Utah. Since the fandango his marriage had bubbled into incessant small quarrels. Utah, anxious about her tenuous social position, blew up each time he arrived home late to accompany her to a refreshment party. Fearful of the opinions of her new acquaintances, she decried the *brea* caked into his hands, and for this same reason demanded a hired girl—though she dreaded having one. The only matter that pleased her was the salary that Bud insisted 3 Vee draw, but he had avoided telling her that his partnership with Bud was equal.

Then there was Paloverde Oil itself. Other than Bud's daily trips to the site, there was not a thing to cheer about. 3 Vee had been wrong about the depth of the sand and earth. They were drilling through rock as hard as steel. 3 Vee could look forward, no matter how careful he was, to more broken bits. Worse. He had lost that intuitive feel of an underground sea of oil and begun to believe that everyone was right. There was no oil. They were still laughing at him, and now at Bud, too. On Sundays after Utah and Doña Esperanza returned from Mass at the Plaza church and the Van Vliet family gathered for dinner at the red-shingled house on Broadway, Hendryk glared at those renegade oil-drillers, his sons. Doña Esperanza looked at 3 Vee with worried, shadowed eyes.

The clink of the baler had ceased. A kick reverberated on the drilling platform. Xavier was telling his employers that he was ready.

Bud stood, stretching. "One more time, then I have to get back to hardwares." Carefully he stubbed out his cigarette with his toe.

In 3 Vee's strip log:

> At 176 feet we got water flowing over the top. Tubed the
> well, pumped for three days, getting lots of water and two

barrels of crude per day. Pulled the tubing and dug again. Side caved badly. Rope broke. Fished for tools. Couldn't recover them and after three days gave up. LA out of bits. Had to take the train up to Santa Paula to Union Oil Supply to get another. Rope broke on July 1.

In the *Los Angeles Times*, July 3, 1892:

> Yesterday 3 Vee Van Vliet was seen in Los Angeles Oil Supplies buying Manila hemp. Does this mean the Van Vliet brothers are at the end of their rope?

Bud laughed and bought extra copies. 3 Vee, with a visionary's lack of humor, was furious.

Every night Utah scrubbed his back. These minutes were never invaded by acrimony. As her fingers worked the soap over his tense shoulders, 3 Vee's uncertainties would fade. One night he kissed her soapy red hand.

"What's that for?" she asked.

"Not laughing at me."

"What's funny about you?" she demanded fiercely.

CHAPTER 11

· I ·

Amélie sipped her breakfast *café au lait* while Liu, who wore loose blue clothing and oiled his pigtail, padded about serving Bud first salted oatmeal with a pitcher of thick cream, then a ham steak topped with scrambled eggs and a side dish of Dutch browned potatoes. Bud helped himself to golden-topped biscuits dripping with butter and bowls of lemon marmalade and Doña Esperanza's guava jelly.

When the clock chimed seven, Bud looked up from his paper. "What do you think, sweetheart?" he asked. "Are you?"

"Am I what?" replied Amélie, bemused. Rosy with sleep, she had been gazing dreamily out the window, seeing nothing. For her, breakfast was a continuation of bed, and it was for this reason that she insisted their places be set close, side by side, at the breakfast room table.

"I've already explained the signs to you," he said.

She set down her cup, looking at him. She had never become accustomed to his early-morning energy and appetites, other than the conjugal one.

"Remember? After you lured me to Paloverde a second time, I had to explain our pleasant activity could have lasting results."

"How long have I missed?"

"That, Amélie, is a very unusual question for a woman to ask."

Not really, she thought. After their marriage, they had never tried to stop a child, and for Amélie each month had brought the inconsolable mourning that has none of the finality of death yet is an end of hoped-for life. She had wept privately at the onset of each cycle. About two years ago, however, she realized that tears were in vain, and she tried to ignore as best she could nature's profound rejection. She no longer kept track of dates, although she still yearned with the hunger of an exile for a child.

Her barren state hurt her even more on Bud's behalf. Amélie's love didn't prevent her from seeing her husband from all angles. Despite his jaunty good looks, his ostentatiously well-tailored clothes, his easy humor, Bud was a patriarchal man. At one with this sunlit country he was building, he needed children. His imperative was to found a dynasty, and if that was a rather strong way of looking at it, Amélie, with her feudal streak, respected her husband's views.

"You missed last month," he said. "And you're late again. Ten days."

He put his hand on her flat stomach, rubbing his fingers on white silk. She leaned toward him, kissing his mouth, pulling away as Liu came in with more hot biscuits.

"What do you think?" he said after the Chinese servant left.

"Well, let me see. Your breakfast has been smelling stronger lately."

"And?"

"I have been going back to bed, and you know I never do that."

"Well?"

"I shall consult with an expert."

"Who?" he asked. "Dr. Widney?"

"You."

"Me?"

"Who else explains to me all the signs and auguries?"

"Oh."

"How could I not have noticed?" she asked. "Bud, how?"

"Well, it's like this. Amélie Van Vliet, you're just a little girl with very pretty hair." He paused, swallowing. "You really think so?"

She nodded.

They smiled at one another with a great and shared joy.

At the front door, as was their habit, they kissed goodbye, the kiss lasting longer than usual, and then, according to their ritual, Amélie went through the blue-and-white-papered hall, opened French windows and walked out onto the wide veranda. She breathed deeply. Her faint nausea passed, quelled by odors of the dewy foliage that spilled down Bunker Hill.

The Van Vliets's cottage, Queen Anne, one of the smallest of the new houses that crowned Bunker Hill, was also one of the loveliest. The architect had designed the veranda encircling it as the major ornament; a carpenter was hired in Vienna to carry out his intent. Amélie leaned against the delicately carved railing. Below her, on Grand Avenue, Bud came into view, moving down the steep grade with his brisk yet easy stride. He turned, as always, to lift his hat to her. She waved. Suddenly he broke into a jig, spontaneous, exultant. She curtsied. He bowed and then replaced his bowler, turning once again into a businessman on his way to the town below.

All at once Amélie's smile faded. She crossed her arms over her stomach, bending over. "Oh my God," she whispered, and made her way into the house, going into the library, closing the door behind her. The fireplace, lit last night, hadn't yet been cleaned; blackened bones of wood lay on ashes. She sat at her secretary.

There was no doubt in her mind that she was pregnant.

The fandango had been May 7, and this was July 13.

Her face drained of its color.

3 Vee, she thought, 3 Vee. The cold sweat of fear broke out on her face and body. With the memory of the fandango always came this fear, and she loathed it. For Amélie the absolute debasement of the act had been her own terror. 3 Vee, the shyly awkward boy who once looked at her with shining brown eyes and talked of writers and composers and poetry, had been transformed not into an animal, for an animal would have responded to her cries and struggles, but into a brutal, insensate force.

There had been large bruises on her pelvis and a muscle in her left thigh had been pulled. The bruises had faded to a greenish yellow, and after a week or so in bed, the pain disappeared. Her fear remained; and with the realization that she was pregnant, it engulfed her.

3 Vee? 3 Vee, she thought. 3 Vee?

Burying her face in her hands, she shook her head from side to side.

She heard the telephone, and a moment later Liu rapped on the door.

"Yes?" she murmured.

He came in. "Mrs. Utah is on the line." Liu, born in Los Angeles, had a flat Western accent that sounded strange coming from a man in blue pajamas with a pigtail.

Amélie stared at him blankly.

That she and Utah were friends had never struck Amélie as peculiar. Although normally she had contempt for social climbers, she was touched by Utah's eager yearnings to be "a somebody." Without envy herself, she did not consider the possibility that Utah's friendship might be tainted by jealousy.

"Mrs. Van Vliet?"

"Oh. Yes. Please ask if I may call her back."

After he closed the door, Amélie didn't move. She sat very erect, her hands clenched on the silver-cornered blotter.

At first her mind was clear. I am not positive that 3Vee fathered the child, she thought, but then neither am I positive that he did not. I simply am not sure. Still, there is a doubt, a very strong doubt, that cannot be ignored. How can I pretend the child is Bud's if I am not sure? It is the ultimate deceit that a woman can play on a man. Her code of honor refused to permit her to consider even for a moment that she might be able to get away with the deceit. He is my husband, she thought, and even if I did not love him so very much, I still would owe him my every loyalty.

I cannot have this baby.

How does one not have a baby?

She had always shrunk from this kind of feminine discussion. The women she knew seemed to get an acrid odor as they whispered about such matters. Still, she remembered overhearing snippets about knitting needles, crochet hooks, and glasses of castor oil. Yet hadn't Bud once told her of a girl? Rose? Yes, that was her name. Rose had bled to death having an abortion. Bud, even then, had wanted a child, and not once, not by a single word or glance, had he ever reproached her for being barren.

Amélie gave a long, shuddering sigh.

Who would perform such an operation? Certainly not Dr. Widney. He would never do it. Doctors do not kill.

Kill?

She put her hands over her eyes, longing to cry, yet no tears came. She thought that whoever had fathered this child, it lay in *her* womb, part of *her*, wholly dependent on *her*. Bud or 3Vee? Seven years or a few seconds? Love or terror? How can I kill my own child?

In the distance, she heard the vegetable wagon creaking uphill, heard the cry, "Veg-ball, flesh veg-ball." The kitchen door opened and closed, Liu hailed the vendor in Chinese. Two men conversed in a singsong language that was no less comprehensible to Amélie than her own thoughts.

What shall I do?

The telephone sounded again. Three short rings. Their signal. Liu was outside bargaining. Juanita, Liu's fat and shapeless wife, fearing the instrument, refused to touch it. Bridget, the pert, frizzy-haired Irish girl, would not arrive until nine. Amélie went into the cubbyhole near the front door. Flowered paper covered the walls and a small table with notepad and pencil stood below the wooden telephone box attached to the wall.

"Van Vliet," she said.

"One more thing," Bud said. "If we produce a girl, she's not to go riding by herself."

"Bud—"

"Don't argue with me about it."

"I—"

"No unchaperoned riding, and that's for sure." His voice went husky. "Amélie, sweetheart, I thought it would never happen to us. As soon as you finish at Dr. Widney's, come by the store."

"Bud—"

The phone had gone dead.

Standing there she began, finally, to weep. There was nothing she could do. She could not kill her child, whoever the father was. And she could not tell Bud what 3 Vee had done to her. The ties between the brothers went deep. A fight was inevitable. Bud would be ruthless. At the very least he would refuse to see 3 Vee again, and murder was not impossible. *I cannot risk it.*

Huge sobs wracked her body, coming from a place beyond consciousness, the grief of an unalterable and crushing misery. At last she managed to stop crying and stood, arms pressed to her sides, breathing unevenly. When she had forced herself to calmness, she spun the metal crank of the telephone and asked the operator—it was Netta—to get her fifty-nine, Dr. Widney's number.

· **2** ·

On the afternoon of July 25, one of those parades that advertise the opening of a new subdivision moved slowly along Spring Street. A brass band tootled, three elephants and a mangy camel left over from the Camel Brigade plodded, a cage with a recumbent lioness crunched over the paved street, clowns capered and two men on stilts carried a streamer:

EDEN VALLEY
Choice Lots to be Auctioned

Onlookers jammed the sidewalk. Amélie, who was out shopping, waited in Hendryk's office until the crowd dispersed. Hendryk's flat-top desk was covered with plans for enlarging the store. Bud and his father stood arguing over them, Bud jokingly, Hendryk with annoyed determination.

Hendryk was saying, "No hardware store in town carries furniture, Bud!" As always when his irritation was great, his Dutch accent grew more pronounced.

"They didn't carry fine crockery, either, until we started to."

"It's ridiculous!"

"Not ridiculous," Bud chuckled. "Just profitable."

Hendryk's good hand slapped down loudly on the plans. "Oh, what can I expect? Your mind is too full of this oil nonsense to see reason!"

Amélie's eyes sparkled with amusement as she watched father and son. Dr. Widney had confirmed her pregnancy. Bud was overjoyed, and when they were together, Amélie shared his joy. Often when she was alone, she wept. Looking up, she saw someone throw open the door from the street and enter the store. It was 3 Vee. His face was smeared with grotesque daubs, and this same dark filth drenched his hatless hair, his beard, his clothing. Everyone pulled back as he made his way down the crowded aisle, stumbling like a man fleeing some disaster of nature.

Amélie's hand tightened on the handle of her furled parasol. Something terrible has happened, she thought. Utah? Charley? Doña Esperanza? She tried to say something to Hendryk and Bud, who continued their involved argument over the plans. She couldn't speak.

3 Vee flung open the glass door of the office, standing with both blackened hands gripping the jamb, his long, heavy legs wide apart. From the street came the blare of the brass band. 3 Vee stared at Amélie, his jaw working. No words came.

"3 Vee . . . ?" she whispered.

"What is it?" Hendryk demanded.

"What's happened?" Bud said, and the question had the ring of command. "Is there an accident at the site?"

"Charley?" Hendryk asked anxiously.

3Vee gazed at Amélie. "The well came in," he said.

For a moment, Bud's body tensed. Then with a whoop of exultation, he threw himself at his larger, younger brother, hugging him around the chest. "Oh Jesus! 3Vee! You did it, you did it for sure! Everybody else said there was no damn oil in Los Angeles County. Not a goddam drop! And you, you found it, you clever, brooding bastard!"

3Vee made no move to return his brother's embrace. He was staring at Amélie. "Please?" he asked. "Please?"

Bud turned toward his wife, puzzled.

Hendryk said, "Oil?" His tone was almost irritated.

Amélie went to the brothers, putting one arm around Bud and the other around 3Vee.

"It's all right, then?" 3Vee asked.

"Yes," she said, as if the word was pulled from her. "Yes."

And then they were hugging one another, 3Vee's oil-soaked beard resting on topaz hair, Bud's hand pounding his brother's back. When they pulled apart, oil smeared Amélie's white lawn shirtwaist, oil marked Bud's alpaca summer suit.

Hendryk, struggling to keep his plump dignity, shook 3Vee's hand, then Bud's. "This is a great day for Los Angeles," he pronounced, his voice unsteady. His hatred of oil and everything connected with it battled with his paternal pride. Fatherly affection won.

He moved past his sons and daughter-in-law. Raising his voice, he addressed everyone in the large store. "My son, Vincent Van Vliet, has just discovered oil within our city limits. He and my other son, Hendryk Van Vliet, Junior, have brought in the first oil well in Los Angeles. Today is one of the great landmarks in the history of our city. To commemorate the occasion I wish to present each of our customers with a small gift, a *pilon*, as we used to say in the old days. Then, if you will excuse us, we at Van Vliet's will take the rest of the afternoon off."

Painted clowns leaped and cartwheeled along Spring Street. Children and a few bonneted farmwives watched. The rest of the throng clustered around those emerging from Van Vliet's.

Oil!

A crowd followed Bud and 3 Vee as they strode rapidly through the town to the end of Colton Street. Now and then a man would quicken his pace, keeping up long enough to shake 3 Vee's oil-smeared hand and congratulate him. 3 Vee, who had squirmed under the laughter, took no pleasure in his vindication. As they came within sight of the rig, Bud started to run, leaving 3 Vee behind.

Caged within the derrick, black oil howled and flumed. 3 Vee's bit had broken through the crust of ancient protective rock, and the earth's blood flowed, driven upward by the fury of compressed natural gas. An hour earlier the rig had started to shake, the bullwheel turned wildly, and Manila rope spewed back onto the drilling platform. 3 Vee and Xavier jumped. But 3 Vee hadn't run. He stood there letting the geyser of crude oil drench him. In that minute he felt a joy throb through his body—a lust as overtly sexual as when he'd taken Amélie.

Now, however, he walked toward the gushing well almost reluctantly. He had long known the kind of man he was. For him, the dream was infinitely more important than its realization. The search was everything. A goal accomplished was a step toward death. At least she has forgiven me, he thought as he moved slowly through the crowd that gathered around the derrick.

Utah was there, holding Charley. In her excitement, she had forgotten to take off her huck apron, and her shirtsleeves were still rolled. Her round cheeks shone. This gusher was a heavenly finger blessing her. Her mind was bursting with visions of purple satin dresses, ostrich-plumed hats, sable pelisses, furniture, carriages and liveried coachmen, pearls by the rope, diamond tiaras, a house five times—ten times—bigger than Amélie's.

She tramped through oil-blackened weeds, crying, "3 Vee, 3 Vee, you done it!" His gaze was so bleak that she shifted Charley in her arms and touched her husband's forehead. "Are you all right?" she asked anxiously. "Did the walking beam fall on you or something?"

"I'm fine."

"Then make a big smile. Ain't you a hero, with this gusher? You're the town's big oil man!"

"In a couple of months there'll be a thousand wells in Los Angeles."

"What do you mean? Anybody can steal your oil?"

"This is an oil field. Whoever owns the mineral rights can punch a hole on the property."

The pleasure left her face. Her mouth pursed. "Well, ain't it time to do something about what's wasting?" she asked.

"Not yet. By tomorrow, though, the pressure should be down enough to cap it off."

In financial matters, Utah rightfully considered him an innocent. About technical knowledge she respected him. "Then get on home and change them filthy clothes," she ordered. Charley Kingdon began thrashing in her arms. Patting the baby's back, she said, "We'll be along in a few minutes."

Bud stood staring at the caged oil, hypnotized. Then he stepped closer until the spray covered his suit and Panama hat. The stink overwhelmed him, the roar deafened him, and he was exhilarated.

This is it, he thought. This is what I've been waiting for. I never wanted the store. I built it up for Papa, to show his success. But it's too tame for me. Without the land deals I would have gone crazy. This is me. This excitement, this promise, this is what I've been waiting for. Ever since I listened to men talk oil in Van Vliet's Oil Supplies, ever since I worked the Sunday tour up in the Newhall field, this is what I've been waiting for.

He crossed his arms over his chest, his eyes fixed on the tower of oil. He was thinking of his ancestors, the secret ones, the Yang Na who had lived here, of the Garcías who had earned and lost this land—Paloverde. This was their legacy to him and 3 Vee, to Charley and the tiny creature curled in his wife's sweet belly.

More and more people were converging on the narrow lot. Hendryk drove up in the buggy with Amélie and Doña Esperanza. Amélie picked her way through the crowd toward her husband. Bud backed her away, but not before her fresh white blouse and gored skirt, her streamered hat were dotted with oil.

"It is awesome," she said.

"All my life I've been waiting for this," he said. "Do you understand? Ever since I was a fool kid I've dreamed of gushers." He paused. "Amélie, I'm going to take a big gamble."

"You appear to have won already."

"No. I'm going to put in a lot more money. Real money. All I can raise. Listen, I know some about drilling and equipment, but not enough. I'm going to pick every damn brain from the roustabouts to the chemists up at the Union Oil laboratory. And 3 Vee and me are going to sink more and more wells. We're going to build an empire."

Her eyes were fixed on his face. She was smiling.

"You look like you think I'm stupid," he said.

"No."

"Why are you smiling, then?"

"I have always known you would say those exact words someday. Other men have done it. You could be a Huntington, a Gould. A Rockefeller. You are as shrewd, as able, hardworking, ambitious."

"You make me sound ruthless."

"That, too. I never have cared for soft men."

"I plan to spend all my time at it."

"Bud, how terrible it will be for Papa Hendryk, your leaving Van Vliet's."

"He can manage. And 3 Vee's not practical. He'd let our chance slip through his fingers. He's always off on a tangent. No. He always has his eyes on the next thing and never pays attention to what's happening right now—isn't that a pretty fair definition of a visionary?"

She did not answer his question.

"Amélie, if I can't be with you—"

"This is something a woman does on her own," Amélie interrupted. "And this"—she nodded toward the fluming, roaring oil—"is what you will do."

He put his hand around her still slender waist, his fingers touching the front of her skirt band. In her ear, he said, "My prince or princess."

Amélie's expression altered to subtle misery. Bud, again watching the derrick, didn't notice.

Doña Esperanza moved slowly on her puffed ankles as Hendryk guided her around the piles of tar-soaked earth, explaining everything in a proprietary tone, as if he hadn't fought this well with every ounce of his strength. "The pressure of natural gas forces the oil up through the narrow piping, and that's why it is blowing so fiercely. My dear, this oil will be as important to Los Angeles as the railroad. Oil is a serious business, much more serious than oranges and tourists. Now we have a real industry. You mark my words, Los Angeles is going to be as important as San Francisco with this oil."

"And my 3 Vee discovered it," Doña Esperanza replied. "Where is he, Utah?" Her daughter-in-law had come up to them, cradling Charley in her arms.

"Washing up," Utah replied.

"Good," Hendryk said. "Now we'll all go to your home. Neighbors will wish to offer their congratulations."

"But I ain't got enough food in the house."

"Mr. Van Vliet and I will make the celebration," said Doña Esperanza. "Cousin Franz will send a grocery cart with all we need. It is a holdover from the old days, child. Here in Los Angeles we have a custom of sharing our good fortune."

·4·

In the *Los Angeles Times*, July 26, 1892:

OIL

Vincent Van Vliet and partner, H. Van Vliet II, have sunk a well at the end of Colton Street and discovered the first oil in this city.

The morning after the well came in, Bud explained to Hendryk that he was leaving Van Vliet's Hardware. It was a sad confrontation. Hendryk sat at his desk, clenching and unclenching his good hand, too dispirited to respond. Bud, buoyed by his own excitement, had neglected to take into account the depth of paternal emotions. Hendryk relied on Bud's business sense, and over the years his proximity to his son had given him security, comradeship, the greatest pleasure.

After a long silence, Hendryk managed to say, "Madness. You've gone mad. You're a real García." There was no certainty in his voice. His stout chest slumped into his round belly, his eyes were almost as lost as many years earlier, during the bad times.

His father's expression wrenched at Bud. "Papa, I never meant to give this up entirely," he lied. "You don't think I'm that crazy, do you? Besides, how can I let someone else make hash of the books."

"You'll do the accounting?"

"For sure."

At this Hendryk straightened his shoulders a little. "I'll have to adjust your salary down."

Bud's salary, they both knew, was a minuscule part of his income. His money came from rentals in the Block—including Van Vliet's Hardware—and his other investments. Nevertheless, he put on an abashed face and said, "Whatever you decide, Papa."

Hendryk still looked dejected, and Bud started to tell him about the baby, then stopped. He and Amélie had decided not to tell anyone until the fourth month, when it was safe.

Bud didn't consult 3 Vee about his decision to put everything he owned into Paloverde Oil. He simply showed up that afternoon at the well with deeds to eight nearby lots. "I'm taking the late train up to Santa Paula to arrange about hiring us some drilling crews," he told 3 Vee.

"We better wait until—"

"Until what?" Bud interrupted. "Everybody and his sister is drilling?"

3 Vee said nothing.

He was furious at Bud for taking over; he was furious at himself for letting Bud dominate him. His guilt prevented him from arguing. Walking around the new sites with Bud, he picked up clumps of earth, sniffing for tar.

· 5 ·

In the *Los Angeles Herald*, July 30, 1892:

NEVER BEFORE WAS THERE SUCH
A BOOM ON OIL PROPERTIES

The city has gone mad. A feeling of speculation and unrest is abroad, extending the length and breadth of Los Angeles County. In many ways this time resembles that of the recent Great Boom in real estate. Mineral lands are being bought at a rapid rate and speculation is rife. Lots that went begging at $75 now sell for $1000 and upward. Men who have made a study of the pumping of petroleum admit that they have never seen anything like this before. Operators just in from Santa Paula say a large number of people in Los Angeles appear to be actually oil crazed.

Oil-crazed they were. Men—and women, too—who knew nothing about oil knelt to feel and smell earth, then paid out their life's savings for a skimpy plot. Anyone who could afford it sunk a well. And the earth gave up its dark, ancient blood.

One afternoon in mid-August, three weeks after the strike, Bud sat on the ladderlike driller's stool between the temper screw and the big, square headache post. The day was very hot, well over a hundred, and he wore no vest, his shirt was drenched, sweat darkened his red elastic galluses. From time to time he lifted his leather helmet to mop his forehead.

The small houses remained with their spindly palm trees. Otherwise it would have been impossible to recognize Colton Street. Crews shouted to one another as they hammered up tall, skeletal pyramids. Drilling bosses bawled orders to roustabouts. On a nearby derrick a shirtless, sunburned tool-dresser stood at his forge, his anvil ringing. A team of six mules struggled up the grade with a load of lumber, the muleteer's whip cracking as iron-shod hooves kicked up what had been a lovingly tended velvet square of grass.

Bud enjoyed the work and deafening racket. Physically, he was experiencing the same pleasure he had riding with the vaqueros. Mentally, he was delighted that Paloverde Oil was punching down wells faster than anyone else.

He looked up as 3 Vee opened the crude gate with the slapdash sign, PALOVERDE OIL. Barbed wire surrounded their land. 3 Vee held the hot iron post gingerly as he replaced the rope that held the gate closed.

Unlike Bud, 3 Vee loathed the hubbub and clamor. By day and night it penetrated his being, for the sounds reached his house on Water Avenue. Whenever possible, he would hike into the Santa Monicas, and as soon as a crease of the foothills blocked the noise, he would sit under a live oak, a journal propped on his thighs. He read about petroleum. Despite his hatred of the activity around him, he was as obsessed with oil as he had ever been.

As he climbed onto the rig, Bud shouted, "Eaten yet?"

"Utah's having the girl bring me a supper pail," 3 Vee said.

"It's time for me to head on over to the store to pick up those damn daybooks," Bud said. "Joe," he shouted. The clatter drowned him out. He shouted again. The squat tool-dresser came to take his place at the temper screw. "Come on, 3 Vee. Let's relax a minute," Bud said.

Next to the headache post was a six-inch-wide trough known as the medicine box because here the crews stashed their bottles of snakebite cure. Bud took out the pint of bourbon with BUD inked on the label. The brothers climbed from the platform, sitting side by side in its shade. Bud handed 3 Vee the bottle.

3 Vee took a gulp of warm liquor. "There's a new use for gasoline," he said.

Bud, who was about to take his drink, lowered the bottle to look at his brother.

California crude, unfortunately, was high in gasoline content. Gasoline was a waste product, extremely volatile and therefore difficult to dispose of. Other than cleaning fluid, there was no use for gasoline.

"Well?" Bud asked. "What is it?"

"There's two Germans I've been reading about. Gottlieb Daimler and Carl Benz."

Bud's mouth tightened with disappointment, and he tilted his head, drinking. "I've heard about them," he said, wiping his mouth. "They've got some crazy idea about a horseless buggy."

"They've built one. The engine uses gasoline."

"Come on, 3 Vee. The whole idea's a pipe dream."

"Why?" 3 Vee asked. "Imagine the freedom they'll give a man. Imagine never having to hitch up the horses, never having to worry about stopping to rest and water horses. Why, you could go wherever you wanted, at your own convenience. There'd be no need for a city man to live tethered to a trolley line, or for a farmer to stay out in the country. These buggies'll be almost as great an advance as the railroad, especially out here in the West, where the distances are so great."

"Fine. Good. I grant you these Germans have quite some idea. But God alone knows when its day will come. Not in our lifetime, 3 Vee. Maybe in the year twenty-four hundred. And in the meantime we need uses for all this crude." Bud glanced at the furious activity around them. "Know of anything practical that's fueled with local crude?" He didn't mean the rudimentary engine that now, rather than 3Vee's sweat, turned the bullwheel. Bud knew, of course, that they powered it with their petroleum.

3Vee thought a minute. "Remember that tanker, the *W. L. Hardison?*"

"That's the ticket," Bud said. "The *Hardison* went up in smoke. Still, maybe we can learn something from it."

"I have a lot of clippings about it at home. Want me to bring them over tonight?"

"The damn hardware books should be done by nine," Bud said. "Drop by then."

<h1 style="text-align:center">·6·</h1>

That evening remained hot, a rarity in Los Angeles. 3Vee sweated as he climbed Bunker Hill. Below him, the business area slept in the hard blue glare of seven tall electric arc lights. In his pocket were the clippings he had saved about the *W. L. Hardison.* He remembered the story. In 1889 the Southern Pacific had jumped its freight rates on oil to a monstrous dollar a barrel, and Lyman Stewart and W. L. Hardison, who would form the Union Oil Company in 1890, had the revolutionary idea of moving petroleum in a boat with steel tanks. They then had conceived the even more innovative idea of fueling this steamer not with coal but with oil. That the *W. L. Hardison* had burned to a total loss disenchanted 3Vee not a whit. It was the idea, the idea. The story was all here, on yellowing newsprint. 3Vee, however, considered the fragile strips of old paper a passport to visit Amélie.

Since she had made her peace with him, his mind was no longer filled with the urgency to apologize. His guilt was still great, but he could look at her again. What he saw disturbed him. Her laughter was as clear and bright as ever, but when she thought nobody was watching, delicate shadows gathered around her eyes, and the light in her pupils receded. She looked ill. Worse. Her expression reminded him of that other hot August in 1884, just prior to Colonel Deane's suicide. She was in trouble. He ached to help her—and didn't know how.

As he approached the cottage, 3 Vee saw Bud on the veranda. He sat in a pool of yellow gaslight drinking with Dr. Widney. Seeing the doctor alarmed 3 Vee. However, he reminded himself that Bud and Amélie, a gregarious couple, encouraged neighbors to drop by and Dr. Widney's new house was only a few doors away.

"Hello, Bud," he called.

"3 Vee?" Bud half stood. "Oh yes. You were coming over, weren't you?"

Bud was never forgetful. 3 Vee's anxiety returned. He climbed swiftly up the stairs to the veranda and shook hands with the doctor. "Good evening, Dr. Widney. What brings you here?"

"Good evening, oil magnate," Dr. Widney said, chuckling into the warm night. "My professional capacity."

"What is it? Amélie...?"

"She's fine," Bud said. His words held a tentative note foreign to his voice.

"They're both fine," Dr. Widney said and turned to Bud. "Make her stay in bed. You know how lively she is. She needs to rest. A week at least, hear?"

The sweat chilled on 3 Vee. He gazed stupidly from the gray-bearded doctor to Bud. Bud refilled his own glass and handed it to 3 Vee. "Here," he said.

"What for?"

"Hell, 3 Vee, you're a grown man," Bud said. "You don't need it spelled out."

"Amélie?"

"For sure, Amélie. She's having us a baby."

"No..." 3 Vee whispered. "No."

"Yes."

"But..."

"Now don't you start worrying, too." Dr. Widney said. "3 Vee, if my brother had just given me such news, I'd drink a toast."

"Everything is all right?" Bud asked.

"I've told you already. She's narrow, but that makes for a difficult labor, not problems in carrying." Dr. Widney coughed delicately. "Still, remember what I told you about being careful with her."

Bud's wide shoulders were slumped. "We'll do anything you say, Dr. Widney."

"Bud, this happens to a lot of women in their third, fourth month. Nothing to worry about."

"You're sure?"

"As sure as I can be of anything. It isn't even proper staining. Now stop acting like your wife's the first woman to have a baby." The doctor turned to 3 Vee. "You're a father, 3 Vee. Tell the man it's not such an ordeal."

3 Vee couldn't speak. Forgetting he still clutched his drink, forgetting the clippings in his pocket, he bolted down the steps, moving blindly. My God, he thought, my God! So that's what's wrong with her. He realized he held the glass. He hurled it into a dark bush.

He was positive the child was his.

· 7 ·

Amélie lay in the wide rosewood bed she shared with Bud. A fringed lamp threw weird shadows into the corners of the large room. A hot night, the windows were open. She had thrown off her covers and her hands were clasped over her nightgown as if she were holding the child in her womb.

The small, dark stain she had discovered that morning on the bedclothes, the hint of a miscarriage, had thrust her into a place she had never been before. Motherhood. She remained tormented, obsessed with the question: Whose child? Yet the question, she now saw clearly, did not alter the necessity of giving birth to the child. She had no choice. She could not have gone through with an operation. The child was part of her, blood of her blood. Her obligation to her child went deeper than any other obligation. How could she, with her sense of honor, have forgotten this most primary debt? She was a mother. A mother owes her child tenderness, love, life.

Amélie stirred, moving cautiously, her hands still on her abdomen. She heard men talking below. The words weren't audible, but along with Bud and Dr. Widney she recognized 3 Vee's deep voice. She pressed her cheek into the pillow. She lay like this until Bud came upstairs to sit beside the bed holding her hand.

He stayed with her in their bedroom much of that week. As soon as she was up, he went back to Paloverde Oil.

·8·

Bud had wanted a child for so many years that the wanting had become part of him, ignored like the beating of his heart. But now that the actuality was upon him, he was rent by familiar pressures. Amélie had seen the dynastic impulses in him.

His remark to her that his child would be a prince or a princess was figurative, yet he had meant it. He saw the child as something he must build for. That old necessity for success gnawed at him more strongly than ever, and Paloverde Oil would be his means.

He bought more mineral lands, he bought the finest drilling equipment. He spent his available cash and then mortagaged the Van Vliet Block. Isaachar Klein, the banker who took the mortgage, told Bud, "You're crazy. Oil-mad like the rest of Los Angeles. I never expected it of you."

"If I'm doing it, Mr. Klein, then how can it be crazy?" Bud asked, smiling. He knew he was crazy, yet he was driven.

Before long Paloverde Oil had six wells, each producing a hundred barrels a day. Bud bought a revolving eccentric wheel that powered all six pumps with attached cables, an expensive piece of machinery. Once more he borrowed, this time on land he owned near the new University of Southern California.

Each day he stopped by Van Vliet's, listening to Hendryk lecture on his insanity while he picked up the books. He rose at four and still there wasn't time. So Amélie sat at the secretary, her stomach gently mounding her crisply ironed wrappers, her back never touching the leather chair. In schoolroom days she had been good at arithmetic. Bud was amazed at how quickly she picked up his routine. "If you expected me to lose my mental powers with my shape, you were mistaken," she said tartly.

She made the remark soon after Dr. Widney had banned intercourse and Bud dutifully slept across the hall. They were often sharp with one another. But after a few weeks, Amélie convinced her husband that the good doctor had meant what he had said, intercourse, not the other sweet pleasures they shared. Bud moved back into the big bed, and fell asleep holding her so he could feel the movements of his unborn child. I mustn't fail, he would think. I will not fail.

Failure, Bud was positive, would come not from too little oil but too much. Each hour he spent at what was now called the Los

Angeles City Oil Field, he was reminded by the increasing number of black derricks all around him that California crude would soon be a glut on the market.

One rainy morning just before Christmas he and 3 Vee stood together in the wire enclosure. For them to be at the Paloverde Oil site together was unusual. Lately, 3 Vee never showed up when he was around. Both brothers wore yellow slickers. Silent, they watched oil being pumped from a huge wooden vat into a tubular horse-drawn wagon.

Bud said, "The price per barrel's dropped again."

"I heard."

"Well?" Bud asked. "Thought of any more uses for the stuff?"

"Fuel's the obvious one," said 3 Vee, avoiding Bud's eyes.

The idea, Bud thought, is typical 3 Vee. Oil as a fuel is tantalizing—and impractical. "If it's so obvious," he said, "why does everybody use coal?" There was no coal in the far West. It came all the way from the British Isles or Australia, ballast in the holds of sailing ships on their way to pick up California wheat and redwood. Coal prices were high in Los Angeles.

"You asked me if I had any thoughts," 3 Vee muttered.

Bud wiped rain from his face. "Illuminants, that's how people use oil. Think in that direction."

"If you know how to think, why ask me?"

"Calm down, calm down. Any more ideas? And don't tell me about horseless buggies or flammable ships."

"A locomotive," 3 Vee said, his hair and beard wet with rain.

"What?"

"We use our own crude to power that." He waved toward the eccentric wheel. "Why not a locomotive?"

"That engine's far simpler and you know it." Bud paused. "Think it could work?"

3 Vee shrugged.

"What's wrong with you?" Bud asked quietly.

"Nothing."

"Trouble at home?"

"Nothing's the matter!"

"Just wondering if you need a little more salary."

"You aren't taking any. Why do I deserve more?"

"Listen, I've had it! For months you've gotten a bee up your ass every time you see me!"

A voice shouted. A whip cracked. Four horses strained through thick mud, hauling the oil wagon.

"I'm sorry, Bud," 3 Vee mumbled. "I've been working hard. Just forget I blew up."

His guilts swallowed him. He had to speak privately with Amélie, yet he knew it was impossible. He could not look his brother in the eye.

The only refuge from his tormented thoughts was in the world of ideas, his dreams. The concept of an oil-burning locomotive, which he had picked out of the rain-filled air that afternoon, stayed with him, and after supper that evening he remained in the dining room, which was now crowded with thick-legged furniture, waiting impatiently as the hired girl limped slowly back and forth clearing dishes. Finally, she replaced the linen cloth with the green baize that protected the ugly whorled veneer of the tabletop.

3 Vee hunched over, sketching. He had no idea of how much time had passed until Utah, yawning in her nightgown, opened the door. "It's long after bedtime," she said maternally.

After that, every free night he had, 3 Vee sat at the baize-covered table, sketching his ideas, discarding paper after paper. Frustrated by his lack of drafting skill, angry with his mechanical ineptitude, he checked out books on these subjects from the public library in the new city hall. He drew a hundred plans and threw most of them away, shoving his rejects deep into the big galvanized trash can. The rare uncrumpled sheet that he saved, he locked in his bottom drawer. He had always been embarrassed by his ideas.

In January he thought of a very simple one: spraying oil mixed with steam into the firebox of a locomotive.

As soon as his drawings were as good as he could make them, he decided to show them to Bud. He might have taken them to the site. Instead he chose to drop them by the house on Bunker Hill at an hour when he knew Amélie would be alone.

CHAPTER 12

· I ·

The Santa Ana wind howls in from the oven of the Sonora Desert.
It whips, hot and angry, through canyons and across flatlands, drying chaparral and citrus orchards, burning the grasses until each
blade is crisp and yellow. The skies are scoured to a painful blue
and the air is sharpened to such a vicious clarity that distances are
impossible to gauge. Trees topple, telegraph and telephone lines go
down, tiles blow from rooftops. The parched earth rises up in
amorphous shapes, attacking eyes and nerves.

Utah called the Santa Ana the devil wind, and when the heat
howled and wailed in from the desert, her temper exploded in ways
that surprised even her.

On this particular January morning she stepped down from the
trolley in front of the Plaza church. Hiring the lame servant to care
for Charley Kingdon gave her the freedom to attend Mass almost
every day. Despite the Santa Ana she was wearing her new plush
winter suit, the most expensive clothes she had ever owned.
Besides, she thought, wasn't this January? Winter? Now her face
was crimson. She stepped into the protection of the vestibule,
repinning her hat before dipping her fingers in the cool water of
the font. She genuflected, moved down the aisle, genuflected again,
then sank into the front pew that she usually occupied with Doña
Esperanza. The stained glass of the windows absorbed the glare,

and the howl of the wind outside was remote. Her heat flush faded as she relaxed, her beads loose in her fingers.

Utah sat there but did not pray. Inside a church she felt at peace, somehow released from the punitive quality that to her enveloped religion. She could think of Charley Kingdon without the memory of her carnal guilt. He's a good healthy boy, she thought, a fond smile curving her lips. He's got six teeth and he can pull himself to stand.

The Mass began and she gave it her devout attention.

She left the church composed and serene, climbing Main Street toward Di Franco's Dry Goods. She needed huck towels. But a blast of hot wind attacked her and sweat was soon trickling under her tight corset cover. She visualized a quiet room and lemonade tinkling with ice. Before shopping I'll drop in on Amélie, she thought, and her discomfort eased.

With Amélie she had none of the awkwardness that enveloped her when she was with the other young matrons of the town. Utah, despite 3 Vee's success, the lame hired girl, her new furniture, retained her old insecurity. She consulted Amélie about even minor social details. In return, she advised Amélie on pregnancy and motherhood. They shared a sisterly warmth—and much of the time Utah, to her credit, managed to overcome her corrosive jealousy. That her richer, more popular, aristocratic sister-in-law had proved equally fertile was a bitter draught to swallow.

The cable car took Utah up the almost-vertical grade of Bunker Hill. She alighted. Sweating, she climbed yet higher. An hour earlier, the watering cart had wetted down the street, but the moisture had already evaporated and fine sand whirled in spasmodic eddies. Utah leaned forward into the wind, yearning for coolness. She passed the Widneys' stone retaining wall. From there she could see the side of Amélie's veranda.

They stood protected from the wind, 3 Vee gazing down at Amélie, Amélie leaning against the spoolwork railing. Her crisp, ruffled wrapper didn't hide the great mound of her pregnancy. 3 Vee said something. She looked up at him. 3 Vee spoke again.

The serenity Utah had achieved in church left her. She's carrying badly, she thought, stopping. Why do they all say she's pretty? What's 3 Vee doing here at this hour? Why're they standing there, for all the world like they were lovers? Why's she talking to my husband like that?

Amélie said, "You are never to refer to that again."

"It's got to be said, Amélie, and—"

"I forbid it. You came here to bring Bud some plans. They are delivered."

"This is the first chance I've had to talk to you. Amélie, nobody can forbid the past. And the fandango—"

"I have forgiven you for that. But on the condition that you never mention it."

"You were never one to evade the truth."

"The truth? 3 Vee, there is no truth beyond your guilt."

"Do you know what I want to say every time I see him?"

She turned white. "Of course I know."

"Then you believe as I do?"

She looked at her hand, which was clenched on the veranda railing. "I do not know what to believe," she whispered.

3 Vee replied, "I love my brother. I will never forgive myself. And yet, never for a minute, not one minute have I been sorry that . . . that I was with you. Do you understand how much I love you, then?"

She put her hand on his arm. "3 Vee, there is no point, none at all. I . . . it meant nothing beyond fear to me."

"You're having my baby."

With a quick, unconscious motion, she struck 3 Vee across the mouth.

A small streak of blood showed at his lip. It trickled into his beard before he wiped at it with the back of his hand.

"I'm sorry," he said.

"I am too," she said. "My God. 3 Vee, I am sorry." Neither was quite certain what their apologies meant.

· 3 ·

Hot wind whirled their words across the garden.

". . . having my baby . . ."

Amélie's hand went back, and there was a sharp retort as she struck 3 Vee.

"I'm sorry . . ."

Utah stood, her plush skirt blowing about her ankles, her reticule dangling from the arm with which she held her hat. Gone forever, the affection she bore Amélie. Gone, momentarily, the deep love she felt for 3Vee. At this second all she felt was an anguish of jealousy so intense that she saw a bright redness before her eyes. She had never fainted, but now she thought she would faint.

Her brain whirled as if blown by the Santa Ana. Men are weak, she thought. She's to blame, the princess! She has to have everything! Money! Family! Jewels! My husband! She has to have him in her drawers. French. Yes, foreigners are like that and he's part Mex. They're roused easy. Utah's prejudices bubbled, then withdrew, leaving her with one devastating fact.

Her husband had fathered Amélie's child.

There was no doubt in her mind that this was the subject of their conversation. None at all. She was sharply practical. The few words, the slap had told everything. They had been together and made a baby.

Utah's intake of breath was sharp. Her sexual jealousy dissipated, and her body shook with another envy that, to her, was more absolute. Her husband, in fathering that bitch's child, had destroyed her one superiority. That child would eventually disinherit her own child, her children. Utah's breathing grew strident. He had destroyed her only hope for the future. Utah's knee bent, her booted foot raised as if to kick Amélie's pregnant body until the child was a bloody, never-to-be-born pulp.

There was neither sanity nor mercy in Utah. The wound had penetrated swift and deep. Turning, she started down Grand Avenue, her round, set face jolting with each step. She was no longer conscious of whalebone jabbing into her body or the hot, infuriating wind-blown sand. Her face crimson, she marched downhill.

She had no real plan until she reached Spring Street. Then she understood how to ease her frantic misery.

·4·

She found Bud in his glass-walled office in the Van Vliet Block.

"Why, Utah, honey, what a pleasant surprise." Bud was on his feet.

Utah closed the door to the office. Under the Czarina Purple feathers, her pompadour was windblown. Two red dots shone high on her cheeks. She was breathing rapidly.

"What is it?" he asked, pulling out a chair for her.

She sank down.

"Come in to escape the Santa Ana?" he asked.

"Yes. That's why. Ain't it the end, the way it blows so hot?"

One of the clerks put his head in the door. "Bud, the Santa Paula train leaves in thirty-five minutes."

"Sure. I know. *Gracias.*" The door closed. Bud smiled at Utah. "He's letting you know, tactfully, that I don't have much time. Did 3 Vee tell you I'm talking to a petroleum chemist up in Santa Paula?"

"You're sleeping there?" She had noticed the pigskin valise.

"One night, yes."

Utah's lips tightened. "Ain't it lonely for Amélie, you working so much?"

"She's never complained. I guess pretty soon I'll have to stay close to home."

"She ain't *never* complained?"

"Amélie's as involved in Paloverde Oil as the rest of us."

"What's she do while you're gone?"

The wind rattled the windowpanes of the office. "You know as well as I," Bud said. "She reads, practices her piano, she has visitors." He omitted her accounting work; they had told nobody that Amélie did the Van Vliet's Hardware books. "She sees Mama and you and Charley."

"Ain't it grand and ladylike, her visiting with her poor relations, me and Charley Kingdon!"

Bud looked at her narrowly. "I wouldn't say any more, Utah." The warmth had drained from his voice. "She likes you very much."

"Generous of her."

"The Santa Ana's hard on people who aren't born in Los Angeles. Go home, take a bath, lie down. You'll feel better."

"You best go home, too. Forget your trip. See what 3 Vee's doin' at your place."

The blue of Bud's eyes darkened. "My wife and 3 Vee have been friends since before I knew her."

"Friends? Hah!"

"Honey, I know you're jealous of her." Bud had long perceived what Amélie had not; from the first day he had met Utah he understood how very much she envied his wife. "Don't let it run you. Go home before you say something you'll regret."

Utah was breathing in audible gasps. "It's up to you to do the talking, Bud. You ask your wife how come she's havin' a baby after all these years. It's like a miracle, ain't it? Ask her how she turned the trick. Ask her about her good friend—"

"Get out," Bud said in a low, harsh voice. He was standing. "Get the hell out of this office. This building, too. It's mine."

"The kid ain't!" Utah's voice howled like the wind. "It's 3 Vee's!"

The twin red dots on her cheeks were brighter and her eyes glinted wildly. Purple skirts whirled. She slammed the door behind her.

Bud remained on his feet, staring out the window. Wind snapped at flags, bending the poles. Slowly he walked to the rack, reaching automatically for his hat. He left his pigskin valise on the floor.

· 5 ·

He let himself in. The front door wasn't locked. Nobody in Los Angeles locked up until bedtime, and even then a surprising number of people didn't bother. He took off his hat and paused to smooth down his hair. From behind the parlor doors came the sound of Amélie's piano. The music was unfamiliar. It rose and fell in sad and discordant notes. For him she played Victor Herbert, Offenbach, Broadway show tunes.

As he opened the parlor door, the music stopped. She looked up, surprised. "I didn't hear you come in," she said.

"3 Vee left?"

"Almost half an hour ago," she said. "Bud, what about Santa Paula?"

"So he *was* here."

"He brought some sketches of an oil-burning engine he said you once talked about." She closed the keyboard.

A chilling sadness swept over Bud for all the things he could never enjoy with her: the kind of music she had been playing, the books and poetry she cherished. 3 Vee shares her pleasures, he thought. What other pleasures have they shared? he wondered, clenching his hands in his pockets. What the hell's the matter with me? I've convicted her. Why am I taking the word of a fat chambermaid against the most honorable person I've ever known?

"Utah dropped by the office," he said slowly. "The Santa Ana's got her crazy." He shook his head. "Amélie, sweetheart, she's a very ugly person. Jealous of you, and everything you have."

As he spoke, he glanced around the room. Bud considered a smart parlor one that was furnished in dark velvets and darker brocades, and this was all blue and white and bright landscape paintings, like the rooms he had seen in southern France. Light and airy, it suited her, as the house suited her. Had he ever influenced her at all? Had he ever put any imprint on her?

Amélie rose from the piano bench. "What did Utah say?"

"It was too ugly . . . Jesus."

"You are not on the train to Santa Paula. You must have thought something of what she said."

"I swear I didn't."

"Then why, Bud, are you here?" Amélie's voice shook.

"Tell me I shouldn't believe her. It's impossible. You and 3 Vee?"

Amélie inhaled. Her shoulders squared, she moved slowly to a window, looking out at wind-tossed shrubbery.

"Sweetheart, I know you have books and music with him, things I can't share."

"Never, never think I do not share far, far more with you than with anyone else." Her voice was fierce. "Bud, how can you believe that?"

"Then she did lie?"

A wilder gust rattled the shrubbery; a drift of heated air came through an open window to rustle the sheets of music on the piano.

Amélie turned to face him. "The night of the fandango," she said in a low, clear voice, "that night 3 Vee imagined himself a failure. He was digging that well, and he thought everyone was laughing at him. He thought the day a parody of your past. He has moods of hopelessness."

"I know him. Remember? He's my brother." He shuddered involuntarily. Steady, he thought, steady. Don't judge yet. Hear her out. Suddenly he remembered Rose and his baby dead, and himself lying on night-damped weeds behind the Newhall saloon, retching out his grief and anger. He stared at his wife. "Go on," he said.

"He drank too much. He went outside. I followed him. He—I . . ."

Momentarily the breath was knocked out of Bud. He heard his own sharp exhalation. "So Utah's an honest woman," he said, and his loud, ironic tone startled him. "You've been having a go-round with my brother."

"I . . . it was that once. Please, Bud—"

"Please? For sure, sweetheart. I'm delighted you're such a loyal family woman."

"He was very drunk. He . . . I was not willing."

"3 Vee raped you?" Bud gave a dissonant laugh. "You're telling me that 3 Vee raped you? 3 Vee? Jesus! My guess is he has problems getting it up under the best of conditions. What prize horse's ass do you take me for? 3 Vee raped you! Honey, it's enough, what you just told me, without gilding it up. You fucked my brother."

Her open mouth trembled. He had never used obscenity in front of her, and he doubted if she knew the word.

"I never meant to tell you this," she said.

"And you so honest?"

"I thought if you knew, you would harm him."

"Sugar, I'd *rather* we keep it honest. So let's not drag your famed nobility of character into this, all right? You fucked him, fine. Then, like any sensible woman, you kept your mouth shut. Well, why should I be so upset? Obviously my stupid, eager cock needed help."

"Bud, please do not talk like that."

"One thing I can do is figure. I know when the fandango was, and when you're due, you stupid cunt!"

She winced, bewildered.

"Honey, if you're going to play the game, it's time you learned the lingo. You're a cunt. Do you know what that means? Would you like me to spell it for you? And that thing inside you is a bastard—but that word you already know from your papa's activities."

She turned a white so absolute that he, thinking she might faint, took a quick step toward her. He knew that she had never reconciled herself to her father's other family.

"The child . . ." She said in a soft whisper, "I am almost certain it is yours."

"I promise you, my darling, that *I'll* never think of it that way."

As he said the words, they became true. Some matters, he understood now, *were* irreconcilable. And he had many battle scars to prove it. Rose screaming at him, and the knowledge that she did not want his child, seven years with Amélie of hoping and even praying, then the joyous elation of the past months. And now this.

Amélie raised her knuckles to her trembling mouth. "What do you mean?"

"It's simple enough. I think of your load as my brother's bastard. Or have you any further revelations? Should I consider it as a niece or nephew, or just a friend's kid?"

"Why cannot you think of it as your own?"

"I suppose there's odds on that. Almost seven years, though. The odds aren't too good. So there was just 3 Vee?"

She looked at him, and her expression was icy.

"Thank you, then, for being thoughtful enough to keep the blood lines straight. Were you doing it with him when you were a little girl?"

"You know I was not."

"Do I? I know nothing, nothing about you. Except your father almost destroyed my father. Your father was a corrupt man." Good, Bud thought, good, there are tears in her eyes. "And you've been screwing with my brother. Honey, you're a bitch by heredity and action. It'd be easiest all round if you got rid of your little bastard."

Her hands clenched over her loose, ruffled gown, an instinctive gesture of protection, as if he intended physical harm to the child. He blinked, remembering her asleep in his arms, and the pleasure he had taken each time he felt that odd stirring against his own body.

"This is my child, whether you believe it is yours or not." Her expression was disdainful. "My responsibility."

"Whatever you want."

"Thank you," she said coldly.

"*De nada.* Just keep it the hell out of my way. I don't want to look at it or have it come near me."

Her coldness melted. "Bud, you cannot mean that."

"You've known me long enough, honey, to realize I'm not a very sweet man. You know I hate to lose. Well, think about the hand you've dealt me. Do you believe I'm giving you this straight?"

"Yes," she whispered, "I do."

"I'll provide for it. You can spend any necessary money, but no frills. I intend to keep tabs on that. As for the time you spend with it, that's up to you. So long as you don't neglect your household duties." My God, he thought, is this me, Bud Van Vliet, speaking to my love? "You'll stay away from it while I'm in the house. And you'll keep it away from me. On my side, I'll house it, give it clothes." His voice was hard and level, as if he were forcing a business deal. He wanted to weep and beg her forgiveness, yet he meant what he was saying. "Am I making myself clear?"

"Yes."

"Doctors and dentists, but no special lessons, no college. And one thing more. I don't want to be bothered hearing about its problems or bellyaches. It'll have my name, and that's more than most men would give."

"You mean to punish me." She spoke quietly, but in her eyes was the pleading look of an injured animal. "I cannot blame you for being angry."

"Angry, sure. But, Amélie, I've never lied to you. From the beginning I've told you all about myself. I'm not going to start lying now. The child in there is something I despise. I'll never hide my revulsion. Do you believe me?"

"Yes, Bud, I believe you."

The luminosity behind her skin was gone, and in the spare, ashen face, the shadows below her eyes were dark, her cheeks hollow. He looked at her, a small woman huge with child. He had never loved her more, never wanted more to hurt her. He was trapped between the inexorable pincers of love and hate, of victory and defeat, of joy and dispair, of trust and betrayal. His body was weak with loss.

He opened the parlor doors. "People, if they knew, would consider me generous, accepting the child."

"Bud, always remember this." Her voice was a low, choking whisper. "I love you."

"Well, right now I could happily kill you. So I'll get my ass up to Santa Paula for a few days until the urge passes."

The plans for 3 Vee's oil-burning locomotive lay on the hall table. He did not even look at them. Picking up his hat, he turned and saw that she had followed him into the hall. With one final cruelty he said, "I'll always see it as a monster."

She nodded. She seemed to have withdrawn into a place where he couldn't reach her.

Driven to make certain she was as destroyed as he, he repeated, "I'll always see it as a monster."

·6·

For several minutes after he left, she didn't move. The fanlight slanted yellow sunshine into the hall. The Santa Ana, with a sudden moan, hurled leaves and twigs against the door. Amélie shook her head. Slowly she went upstairs. The child was large, swelling her small body, so that each step was awkward and painful. She balanced her weight on the banister.

She closed the bedroom door and sat at her dressing table, opening the top drawer, removing a large, flat jeweler's box. The leather of the lid was inlaid with a small gold square engraved in cursive script: *Mrs. Hendryk Van Vliet II.* She pressed the catch. The lid sprang open. In grooves of black velvet lay a set of matched jewelry. A high collar of pearls with a clasp of round diamonds, two gold bangles set with pearls and diamonds, five small, crescent brooches, and a pair of earrings from which dangled strands of seed pearls and diamonds. The central diamond of the clasp of the necklace was more than a carat, the stones of the bangles slightly less. Bud had bought her this set in Paris, and she had worn it only once in Los Angeles, to the Woods' thirtieth anniversary ball. Everyone had eyed the jewelry for its value rather than its beauty. Now, for the first time, Amélie assessed the pieces in the same way. She picked up the smallest of the brooches. Diamonds glinted in sunlight. When Bud had given her the set, he had pinned this particular crescent, the one with the most delicate design, over her heart. She replaced the piece, her eyes desolate.

I'll always see it as a monster.

She bent her face into her hands, then straightened. "Stop it," she said aloud. "It is far too late for tears."

She moved heavily to her bureau, taking out three sets of underwear, three pairs of white, hand-embroidered stockings, two nightgowns. After a moment, she returned for a third. She stacked them on the bed along with a pale, knitted shawl. She went to the armoire, selecting one loose white wrapper, three smocks, a cream wool cape with a high collar, and two skirts that had been let out with gussets. She bent awkwardly for a pair of brown leather walking shoes and a black patent pair with beige velvet spats. She went down the hall to the windowless boxroom and found the small valise that had been hers as a girl. She returned to her room and began to pack the clothes. Normally she would have had a wry smile for taking as few and as plain things as possible—except for the most expensive jewelry she owned. But there was no glint of humor in her eyes. Carefully she took the set from its case, wrapping each piece in a different handkerchief. She removed her emerald engagement ring, holding it in her palm a moment before she put it in the case and closed the cover. She left on her plain gold wedding band.

She changed from the ruffled lawn into a loose dark jacket and skirt. She pinned on her hat, adjusting the fine veiling before the mirror, and as she did, she saw her ill, white face.

She sat at her small desk and wrote:

Bud,

I understand your doubts and cannot blame you for being unable to accept my child. My hope is that you will grant me the same understanding. The child is tied to me, part of me, we share the most unbreakable bond there is in life. Or are the ties of the blood stronger in me than in other women?

My father, whatever his mortal frailties, cared deeply for me, as my mother in her own way cares.

I am part of them as I am part of my child.

My decision to leave is not a sudden one. In the last months I have thought constantly about what I would do if you, on learning the ambiguities of the situation, put me to a decision. I love you with all my heart—you are everything to me. Yet I am everything to this small, utterly helpless creature. I cannot expose my child to scorn and hatred.

Before signing her name, she read the letter. To her it seemed cold, accusatory. He will understand without this, she thought. He will remember and my actions will be clear to him. She went into the big bathroom and, sitting on the couch that was covered in Turkish carpet, tore the letter into small pieces and flushed them down the toilet.

In the bedroom she pressed the service bell. There was no answer. It was midafternoon, she remembered; Liu and Juanita would be in their quarters over the carriage house. The Irish girl generally visited with friends. Amélie reached for the valise, bending to one side as she carried it. It hit against her right thigh with each slow step down the stairs. She telephoned for a hack to take her to the Arcade depot.

She had no thought beyond the simple act of leaving Bud, of leaving Los Angeles. She had no destination, no plan. She was reacting as if escaping a holocaust, purely by instinct. She was in the same mental haze as when, years ago, she had left with Mademoiselle Koestler.

She waited for the cab on the windswept front veranda, a heavily pregnant woman with a white, bewildered face.

· 7 ·

Three days later, Saturday, Bud arrived home from Santa Paula on the 7:45, the early morning train. He stepped out into the Arcade depot with his tie missing, his collar gone, his suit rumpled and stained. Pale, hard stubble showed on his face. He could smell vomit and stale liquor on himself. As he left the depot he inhaled deeply. To the east, the rising sun blazed orange on a peak of the San Bernardinos, and he had to look carefully to make sure it wasn't a brushfire.

He didn't hail a cab, he didn't take the trolley. He walked along Fifth Street with its big houses. During the night the wind had stilled. A hired girl whisked leaves from a front stoop. This was the long way home. Bud had taken it because, along these quiet, residential streets, he had less chance of meeting a friend. He was not concerned about his appearance. He didn't want to talk to anyone.

For three days in Santa Paula he had gone from one to the next of the saloons that crowded the flat little oil town. Each night he passed out in a different brothel. Every time he thought of the child—3 Vee's child—his mind had bumped into such pain that he groaned aloud. The swell of Amélie's stomach, recently his pride and pleasure, haunted him like a foul succubus.

He turned on Grand, slowly climbing Bunker Hill. Thank God none of his neighbors emerged from their houses. As he came to his own front path, a figure rose from one of the bentwood chairs on the veranda. It was 3 Vee. Disheveled as if he had been waiting through the night, he rested his hands on the spoolwork railing. The brothers stared at one another through thin, clear morning sunshine. A cart grumbled uphill.

"Where's Amélie?" 3 Vee asked. The words came hollow, as if his beard were a cave.

"Get the hell off my property."

"Where is she?"

Bud bounded up the veranda steps, ignoring his brother, and jerked open the front door. "Amélie? Amélie!"

Footsteps padded through the dining room from the direction of the kitchen. Liu appeared in the hallway dressed in shapeless blue pajamas.

"Where is my wife?"

"Isn't she with you?" Liu said.

"Would I be yelling if she were?"

"She left when you did."

"Like hell."

"I heard you come home on Wednesday afternoon, just before Juanita and I went down to the apartment." Liu's voice was perplexed. "When we came back to start supper, Mrs. Van Vliet was gone. There was no note. We thought she caught the Santa Paula train with you."

"If you weren't sure, why didn't you telegraph? You knew I was at the Union Oil laboratory."

"I tried to telegraph," 3 Vee said, coming inside and closing the door. "The wind had the lines down."

Bud turned on his brother. "What's this got to do with you?" he growled.

"Utah told me what happened. She's sick, Bud. She always is after she loses her temper." 3Vee's red-rimmed eyes twitched. "She's been giving me hell. What did you say to Amélie?"

"Get out!"

"Why did she run away?"

Bud lunged up the stairs and went into their bedroom. His wife, his Amélie, eight months through a difficult pregnancy, was missing. Why didn't it abort itself, he thought, viciously yanking open the armoire. The odor of her light, flowery scent hit him and he fell back. Without checking her clothes, he slammed the door shut. He went to her bureau, pulling open drawers. One fell, spilling her delicate underwear. He turned to the vanity and saw the case for the diamond jewelry that was his last anniversary gift to her. Pressing the catch, he stared stupidly into empty, grooved velvet. Her emerald engagement ring lay in one of the grooves.

3Vee stood in the doorway, grasping the jamb with both hands. "What did you do to her?" he demanded.

"You're the one, little brother. You did it to my wife. Between the two of you, you put the horns on me."

3Vee closed his eyes. "I was drunk," he said so low that his voice rumbled. "She didn't want me."

So she told me the truth, Bud thought. He picked up the ring with its small, perfect green gem, hurling it to the carpet.

Bud said, "Get out of my house, you miserable son of a bitch!"

"Not until I find out what you've done to her."

"What I've done to her? That's a funny remark coming from you. Credit where credit is due. Anything lasting *you* did. Your wife gave me a few simple questions that I repeated to my wife. Amazing, when you ask the right questions what snakes you uncover. I heard her out. Oh, believe me, for once I was patient. And when she finished, little brother, I told her I'd support your bastard." Bud's voice went thick. "I told her I'd take the blame for your kid, even though it would always be a monster to me."

"You said that to her?"

"Should I've sent you a thank-you note?" Mockery was in Bud's voice, not in his bleak eyes. "I'm sorry. I'll sit down and do that little thing right now."

"I've always loved her. You knew it. You warned me off, said she was a little girl, too young for me. And then you took her. She was so pretty, she's such a—"

"I know what she is. She's been my wife for almost seven years. A minor matter the pair of you seem to forget."

"I told you. She didn't want me. I was drunk. My God, how could you tell Amélie, of all women, that her child was a monster?"

"It's your child, that's how."

"And you honestly expected her to stay here with you? Are you that insensitive? You know she wouldn't let her child near a man who said that. She's too honorable to let a child be hurt, any child. Don't you know by now how much family means to her?"

"Our little saint of the hearthside appears to have run off without a line to her husband."

"What would you expect her to say that you hadn't said already?"

"Something along the lines of her whereabouts."

3Vee wiped a hand over his forehead. "She's looked so ill. She had that trouble. And now this. You've killed her."

"She's alive enough to take the best jewelry I ever gave her."

"That's all any woman is to you, something to buy!"

Bud glanced down at the leather jewelry case: *Mrs. Hendryk Van Vliet II.* He had spent days scouring Paris to find a gift that would suit her taste, not his. He said, "And this one, believe me, cost me plenty."

3Vee made a growl deep inside his throat. His body tensed. Above the dark beard, his skin grew mottled. He lunged at Bud.

The brothers had never fought. The difference in their ages had precluded routine fraternal tussles. The protectiveness Bud felt toward 3Vee had nipped the usual older-brother cruelty. He had shielded 3Vee. His teasing had been good-natured. He had rendered his affections carelessly and freely.

But now he had every reason for hatred.

3Vee tackled him around the waist, a constricting, bearlike hug that took the breath from him. 3Vee was almost a head taller, wider, thicker, and—though less muscular—his sinews were hardened by physical labor. The usually gentle brown eyes shone with rage.

Bud, taken by surprise, fell back against the vanity. The delicate French piece toppled, the central mirror crashed. Startled by the noise, 3Vee loosened his grasp. Moving his feet with the precision of a boxer, Bud regained his balance. A far more violent man than

3Vee, he had boxed, wrestled, and fought his way through schoolyards, oilfields, barrooms. He raised his fists, but not before 3Vee landed a blow on the gristle of his nose. Bud aimed his right fist at 3Vee's beard, his left at 3Vee's gut. 3Vee lifted both arms to catch his brother in his stranglehold. This time Bud was prepared. He ducked and feinted, his fists hammering into 3Vee's kidneys. In this room from which his wife, his love, had gone, taking her jewelry and his soul, he wanted to destroy his brother.

3Vee fought from pain and guilt. Bud fought from a loss so deep he couldn't encompass it. 3Vee clutched as if to force out breath. Bud hit as if to kill.

Delicate chairs fell. Cream Austrian shirred blinds were yanked from one window. A pane of glass shattered.

"She won't come back," 3Vee gasped. "You'll never see her again. You're as bad off as me. You'll never hold her, never hear her voice."

Bud didn't will his knee to go up, but as it did, he experienced a bitter release, for he sought the root of his misery, his brother's testicles. 3Vee grunted. His arms loosened. He bent over, cupping his hands to himself. He collapsed slowly onto the floor, a rag doll propped at the shoulders by the armoire.

There was only the sound of two men gasping.

Bud lurched into the bathroom, squatting to thrust his battered, bleeding face under the bath's swan-neck faucet. His filthy jacket was split between the shoulders. Rising, he grabbed a towel and used it gingerly, then wet it and carried it dripping into the disordered bedroom. 3Vee leaned groaning against the armoire. Bud tossed the wet towel at him.

3Vee held the wetness against his face and felt himself gradually come to life. Pain thundered through his body, and he was aware only of himself. Eyes closed, he breathed shallowly, adjusting to aching muscles. Then he heard the strangled sobs.

Bud was kneeling by the bed, weeping. 3Vee had never seen another man cry. He had never expected sobs from his driving, mocking brother.

"Bud . . . I . . . don't. Please don't."

Bud lifted his tear-stained, battered face. "Next time I'll kill you," he gasped out. "I never want to see you again. I never want to see your wife. I never want to see your child—or any children you might have with my wife."

"She loves you. Very much. She told me that."

"I'll mail a check covering your share of Paloverde Oil."

"I don't want it. Take it all. You don't have the cash."

"I don't want any connection with you. From now on, I have no partner. I have no brother. And any act that will harm you or yours, I'll do. Now get the hell out. Leave me alone." Bud rested his face on the silk coverlet of the bed he had shared with Amélie, and the terrible sobbing began again.

3 Vee shuffled, wide-legged, down the stairs. He sat in the straightback hall chair. He had never before believed his brother capable of more than familial affection and sexual drives. The young man he had known wasn't capable of love. Now, listening to the sobbing from upstairs, he saw how bitterly he had underestimated the capacity of his brother's emotions. He loves her, 3 Vee thought; he loves her with a totality that I'm incapable of. And she loves him. In a few seconds I destroyed their lives.

3 Vee pressed his fingers to his forehead. He wished he could decently regret those few seconds. But they meant more to him than the rest of his life. So instead of regret, his guilt grew to self-annihilating proportions. "My conscience hath a thousand several tongues, and every tongue brings in a several tale, and every tale condemns me for a villain." What was that? *Richard III?*

3 Vee waited for his brother to come downstairs. He needed to give comfort, as he had been given the comfort of the towel. But there was no sound from the bedroom. Bud remained upstairs. Finally, after the hall clock had chimed noon, 3 Vee stood and walked stiffly onto the porch. He paused on the veranda. Only then did he realize that neither of them had considered that the child could be Bud's.

CHAPTER 13

· I ·

Death waited for Doña Esperanza.

Dr. Widney kept repeating that rest would cure her. Hendryk talked resolutely of the summer holiday they soon would take at the Hotel del Coronado near San Diego. Yet Doña Esperanza, with her medical knowledge, understood what was happening within her own body.

Through that cool April and May she rested in the parlor, an afghan covering her poor swollen legs. She stayed in this seldom-used room rather than the sunroom where she and Hendryk normally sat because of the portrait of her father. It hung above the mantel and pictured him mounted on a white horse. Gazing up, she took in every detail of the painting: Don Vincente's dark beard, his rosy cheeks, the suit with silver and gilt braid that had cost him eight hundred acres of flatland, the amethyst ring that he had lost at euchre. She examined the portrait as if it could answer the mystery of regeneration, which is also the mystery of death.

Her "people" heard somehow what was happening to her. They came, often from a distance, always afoot, impoverished, elderly men and women, knocking at the back door. No matter what the time, no matter how bad her pain, Doña Esperanza received them. As they left, each would kiss her large, liver-spotted hand, one final salute.

Other guests came, too, the stout black-dressed ladies, her friends and kin, drinking chocolate with her, vowing in their soft Spanish voices that she was looking more fit and soon would be up and about. Every day Utah, pregnant again, brought Charley. At night, Hendryk neglected his newspapers to talk to her. Often he spoke of his arrival in Los Angeles. The wild mustard had been blooming and the flat little town had seemed to be set in vast fields of gold. "It was the place I had dreamed of, and the reality, for once, my dear, turned out better than the dream." As he said this, his pale blue eyes looked at her meaningfully, and she understood that he, who found compliments an impossibility, was saying how happy his life had been with her.

Each evening before nine-thirty their sons dropped by. It couldn't be accident, she knew, that they were never in the house at the same time, yet she never conjectured about this with Hendryk.

She longed to know of her second grandchild, Bud and Amélie's child. She understood the foolishness of mortal yearning but, oh how she wanted to know whether it was a boy or girl, whether it was dark or fair. She longed to hold it in her arms just one time. She had been told only that Amélie had gone away, and time and again she wanted to find out why. But then she would look into the face of her elder son. Lines of drink and overwork cut deep into the tanned skin and she never could bring herself to question him. Pain is harder for the strong, she thought.

One foggy evening in late May, Hendryk and Bud were eating supper. Doña Esperanza could no longer come to the table and Maria's niece, now the cook, having spread the usual side dishes, served soup followed by slices of boiled beef with a variety of vegetables.

Hendryk ate the last of his beef. Setting down his knife and fork with determined clinks, he asked, "How long will Amélie and the child remain in France?"

"What makes you say they're in France?" Bud's retort was harsh, cold.

Hendryk blinked, yet he didn't falter. "That's where you went for the birth."

Bud had left Los Angeles the day after his battle with 3 Vee. He fully expected to find his wife in France, where, once before, she had gone after leaving him. In the Merciers' Rue Saint-Lazare apartment, the Comtesse Mercier had greeted him with the cry, "What has happened to my daughter? Why is she not with you? Why are you here?" The worry in her protruding brown eyes was genuine enough to convince Bud that she was ignorant of Amélie's whereabouts.

He hired the best of French detectives, visited every Lamballe connection, wired Colmar only to learn that Mademoiselle Koestler had just died. After three days he returned to the Mercier apartment. The worry remained in the comtesse's eyes, yet from the expression on her still-pretty face, Bud sensed that she had learned something since his last visit. The cold bitch, he thought. She kept Amélie's illness from me before; she's not likely to tell me anything. He ordered the detective to redouble his efforts, then he took the first available boat home, pausing in New York long enough to hire another firm of detectives. Neither the Frenchman nor the Americans had turned up a clue. Bud continued to pay their considerable fees.

Hendryk was asking, "Is it a boy or a girl?"

Bud forked up some watermelon pickle.

"Bud?"

"As far as I'm concerned, it doesn't exist."

Hendryk drew himself up, his chins quivering. "You see how ill your mother is," he said. "She wants to know."

"Mama's never asked me."

"The child is her grandchild."

"That's for sure," Bud said, and his ugly laugh bewildered his father.

"Amélie cannot know how ill your mother is. She certainly would bring the child here, if she knew."

Bud pushed away his plate and went into the adjacent sunroom, gazing out into the wadded twilight. The girl cleared the dishes and brought in a ring of quivering flan.

"Bud," Hendryk called. "Dessert."

"I don't have the time," Bud called back. "They need me at the new drilling site."

At that Hendryk, with his loathing of the oil business, saw the root of all Bud's problems: Paloverde Oil. Until the day oil spouted from the ground, he thought, Bud and the pretty little girl were happy together, Bud got along with his brother, Bud never behaved so with me. Paloverde Oil has changed him. Hendryk knew that Bud was gambling with García abandon. Having sunk all his cash in this ephemeral craze, he was selling off his real estate, piece by piece. He was working eighteen hours a day, maybe more.

"You're my son," Hendryk said loudly, "so it's my duty to tell you this. Bud, you're consumed with this oil madness. You've quarreled with your brother and your wife has left you because of it. Are you going to let it push you away from Mama and me, too?"

Bud emerged from the sunroom. "Papa, I can't talk about her, that's all. My God, not to know if she's alive or dead!"

Bud's eyes were wet. Hendryk, searching his memory, found he couldn't remember seeing Bud in tears. Not since infancy, he thought. He put his hand on his son's sleeve. "Go on," he said gruffly. "While a man is young, he should work hard."

· 2 ·

In June, the weather turned hot. Doña Esperanza could no longer leave her high walnut marriage bed. Hendryk hung Don Vincente's portrait by its cord on the wall facing her.

The Sunday after this, 3 Vee sat with her. Doña Esperanza refused Dr. Widney's morphia. She had just taken Maria's infusion of *chia* with pounded manzanita berries and momentarily she was out of pain.

"What is it, Vincente?" she asked. "You look so sad."

"Sometimes, Mama, I wish I was a Catholic like you and Utah. What a blessed relief it must be, the confessional."

"Anything you need to say, you may tell me. Soon it will be a secret again."

He shook his head.

"It's about Amélie and the child," Doña Esperanza said.

"Did Utah say—"

"I have always known what you feel for Amélie. You've never hidden it from me. You and Bud have quarreled, and she left when no woman would."

"I—Mama, I believe the child is mine." As 3 Vee said the words, his head bent lower. Confession, rather than relieving him, made him feel yet more culpable. "They loved one another, she and Bud, and I came between them. Maybe I've killed her."

As Doña Esperanza looked at the person on this earth whom she most regretted leaving, her eyes were tender, even though they were sunken in the dark shadows of her illness. "3 Vee, you mustn't blame yourself."

"How can I help it?"

"What point is there tormenting yourself?" Doña Esperanza asked. "The past has happened, and what will be is out of your hands, and in God's. Maria and I were talking about it this morning."

"Maria?" He raised his head. "Then you know where Amélie is?"

For a moment there was a hint of Doña Esperanza's rare smile. "You don't believe that old pagan foolishness about Maria, surely?"

"I'd like to believe," he said. "I want to know where she is."

"I would give anything to see the baby just once," Doña Esperanza said.

"So would I." He paused. "Maybe it's dead."

"Vincente, don't." She reached for his hand.

"Mama, how can I be burdening you now?"

"I asked you to," she responded, taking his hand and holding it against her cheek. Her eyes closed. Maria's concoctions made her drowsy.

3 Vee, his palm against his mother's hot, dry skin, looked up at the painting of his grandfather. The horse's white body was enormous, its sticklike legs rearing at improbable angles. Don Vincente, age about thirty, held himself as if he were dancing, not mounted on a horse. Only the suit was decently executed. It was the silver-braided suit that 3 Vee had worn the night of the fandango.

I'm as big a gambler as he was, 3 Vee thought.

Bud had mailed him a check for his share of Paloverde Oil, and with this money 3 Vee was buying oil lands. Utah encouraged him—Utah, who abhorred gambling. Envy of her sister-in-law with its new sexual warp spurred her. It didn't matter that Amélie was no longer in Los Angeles; her rout wasn't enough for Utah. She wanted full victory. To Utah superiority would be decided by who had the most money. She needed to be richer than Amélie. Oil she saw as the means. "Find us a gusher," she told 3 Vee.

He did not drill again at the Los Angeles Central Field, which he had discovered; there he might run into his brother. He was ranging eastward and westward through the county, filing oil prospects under the Mineral Act. One well near the *brea* pits had come in but Utah sold it. It wasn't a gusher.

Doña Esperanza, breathing softly, relaxed her grip. Carefully 3 Vee withdrew his hand and pulled up her coverlet. He kissed her white hair and tiptoed from the room.

Maria sat outside the room on the floor, as small as a young child. Just so, as a girl, she had hunched on the *corredor* of Paloverde, waiting to be of service. She looked up at 3 Vee. All her facial bones showed under that oddly taut skin. Only her eyes seemed alive. She must be well over eighty, he thought.

He squatted next to her, inhaling the odors of herbs and olive oil. "Mama says you and she have discussed Mrs. Van Vliet—Amélie."

"Who in Los Angeles hasn't?"

"Where is she?"

There was a shiver of laughter. "What makes you think I know more than anyone else?"

He sighed. "Help me, Maria."

She gave him a long, searching look. "My job soon will be finished," she said. "Then I will die."

"Maria?"

"I cannot help you. When the time comes, you will have grief and guilt enough. You've taken from your brother. He will take from you."

"What do you mean?"

"For a life, a death," she replied cryptically.

Exasperated, 3 Vee got to his feet, glaring silently down at her.

She let her shawled head tilt forward onto her knees so that her face was hidden. "It is no blessing," she said, "my gift."

· 3 ·

One hot day in August the red-shingle house on Broadway was jammed to overflowing. Doña Esperanza was dead, and in Los Angeles, grief still remained communal. After any death all who knew the deceased came to ease their varying degrees of sorrow and to help the family through the day and night before the funeral while the coffin remained in the house. These gatherings were classless. All from the poorest acquaintance to the richest came, the women bearing foods. The Van Vliet dining table had all the leaves in and every inch of the best damask cloth was covered with glistening hams, triangular *empañadas*, potato salad, guacamole, great bowls of thin-sliced oranges, dark balls of pickled kumquats, dates from the nearby desert, fresh *buñuelos* and just-fried *churros*, angel-food cakes, devil's-food cakes, golden slabs of pound cake.

Above the smells of food drifted the scent of roses. Gardens had been shorn of roses and the plunder filled the small breakfast room where the polished wood coffin stood. Crimson roses had been woven into a blanket, white roses stood in tall vases, miniature blooms were set in liqueur glasses along the window ledges. Such profusion was routine in Los Angeles, where flowers grew effortlessly. Chairs for the chief mourners had not been set around the coffin. It was the only departure from custom.

This was the first time since their fight that Bud and 3 Vee had been together, and only once did they meet, at their mother's coffin. For a long second, they stared intently at each other, then Bud turned abruptly, staking his claim to the sunroom. 3 Vee and Utah went into the parlor where the sepia photograph of Doña Esperanza stood on the mantel below the equestrian portrait of her father. Utah, heavily pregnant, tried to control Charley Kingdon, a dark, inquisitive, active little boy, as she accepted condolences.

All that day people came, for this shy lady had been beloved. All shared the family's grief, the men who had settled here early, like Hendryk, and the newcomers. The old, dark-clad ladies stayed to weep, and so did their husbands, their children and grandchildren, for they considered themselves her kin. Franz Van Vliet, the grocer, never budged from his seat in the hall, and neither did his stout wife, who was a Californio from up north near Monterey. Oil crews of Bud's were there, and his friends.

The only group absent were those the Van Vliets called "Mama's people," for they already had said their farewells to the last born with the name García. Their grief at losing her was great. Hers was a generous heart. Hendryk summed it up. Weeping, the normally prosaic Dutchman asked, "What good does it do Los Angeles to have two railroads, trolley cars, so many tourists, electricity, and this oil industry if the great, beating Spanish heart is gone?"

The morning after the funeral, Maria was found dead in her attic room. In her hands she clasped the rabbit-hide pouch that contained her magic.

· 4 ·

One fog-shrouded December morning, 3 Vee was prospecting near San Pedro, where Hendryk had landed. Doña Esperanza's death had numbed the edges of his mind, yet he was still driven in his search for oil. It was afternoon when he came to the abrupt brown hill. He walked his horse to the summit where rocks had been mounded into a cairn, a surveyer's guide. Salt filled the air and gulls wheeled in great noisy arcs. Fog hid the sea.

Enjoying his solitude, 3 Vee took Utah's package from his saddlebag. As usual, she had given him too much food, and when he had finished what he could eat, he leaned back and threw bread to squabbling gulls. The tightness in his chest had eased. His mind browsed. He felt he was on an island, and the old legend that had given California its name came back to him: *Know that on the right hand of the Indies, there is an island called California, very close to the Terrestial Paradise. This island is inhabited by dark women who have no men among them and who live as Amazons, of great physical strength and are very couragous.* A vision of his mother when she was young—tall, stately, dark-haired—rose up in 3 Vee's mind. *Their island was the strongest and most rugged in the world with its steep cliffs and rocky shores. Their weapons were all of gold, as was the harness of the wild beasts which they tamed and rode. In all the island was no other metal. . . .*

3 Vee's head tilted as if a physical presence had intruded upon him. His armpits began to sweat. He knelt, pressing his cheek to the dry, cold earth. "It's here," he said. And at that moment, he imagined he could smell the odor branded in his memory: the rich petroleum odor of roofing *brea*. His dark eyes filled with tears.

This deserted spot near San Pedro was called Signal Hill. 3 Vee bought ten acres of it very cheaply, hired a drilling crew, and spudded in. He had never been good at giving orders. Still, he had good men and God knows it wasn't their fault when, at 2,061 feet, they lost the bit, fishing to no avail. 3 Vee bought a new bit and steel cable, which didn't stretch like Manila hemp. He moved the rig and engine and spudded in again. Again no trace of oil.

He punched five dusters in a row.

He was almost to three thousand feet on the sixth when Utah, her voice shrill, told him they had less than a hundred dollars left. She was nursing their second son, Tom, who was three months old, and 3Vee had Charley, a wiry two-year-old, on his lap, trying to keep him quiet so the baby could suck in peace. Clasping Charley more tightly, 3Vee leaned back in the chair. The weakness of relief had hit him. The money's gone, he thought. At last it's gone. Irrationally, this eased his guilt at Amélie's disappearance.

"We can't live here in Los Angeles," he said.

Utah agreed. "It's God's will we got to leave." Lately she had been interpreting her own decisions as coinciding with the deity's.

They moved north to Bakersfield, a hot, quiet agricultural town in the inland valley. Utah borrowed from her father-in-law to put a mortgage on a large square house with numerous bedrooms that she rented to a "select group of ladies and gentlemen." An often irascible landlady, she nevertheless kept her boarders with her good table and pies at every meal.

3Vee seldom shared the big upstairs bedroom.

He worked for Union Oil, prospecting. He bounced along in a spring wagon packed with current novels and books of poetry, maps, a pick, a Brunton compass, a bale of hay, a cask of grain, a ten-gallon water keg, two canvas canteens of Jamaica rum, and extra sides of bacon. The rum and bacon he shared with the Basque sheepherders he met along his way. Under mountain stars, he ate slabs cut from the great round loaves of the shepherd's bread while the shepherd fried his bacon. The Basques accepted 3Vee for the most basic reason: Spanish was their second tongue and his. They could talk to him. He made a break in their solitude. It pleased them to tell him of unusual rock formations, oil seeps and where the red grass that signified oil grew.

Away from Los Angeles with its defeats, betrayals, guilts, memories, away from his brother, 3Vee was oddly content.

·5·

Bud stood outside the Queen Anne cottage where he had once lived. Returning from that futile trip to France some eighteen months earlier, he had taken rooms on the second floor of the Hotel Nadeau at Spring and First. Since then he had never been inside the house that he had built for his wife. Liu, who had gone into the produce business, stayed on with Juanita as caretaker.

Lights blazed at every window, men's voices called out. Taking a deep breath, Bud trotted up the steps. In the dining room the auctioneer's two assistants were busy tagging furniture. Bud had been drinking heavily, and that enabled him to greet the men jovially. The parlor doors were open. Every available surface was piled with china and Amélie's trousseau linen. He picked up a pillow slip. It was embroidered with the initials *ALD*. He imagined that through the musty odor of long-unused cloth he could smell the rose-petal sachet that she had spread in her linen closet, the smell of their nights together.

By now Bud was positive she was dead. Her last words to him—*Bud, always remember this. I love you*—were never far from his mind. It was incomprehensible to him, in his welter of work-shrouded misery, that any power other than death could keep her from him. Yet he continued to pay detectives on two continents. And, for this same unfathomable reason, he had put off selling the house until now.

Bud was in that teetering state between insolvency and great wealth. His Paloverde Oil assets were worth a good-sized fortune. But he had no cash. Every dollar the company made he reinvested in mineral lands or drilling equipment. He always needed more money. He was too courageous, too vital, he had too much blunt ambition to let elusive sentimentality stand in his way. Tomorrow this house and furnishings went on the block. Yet...

Dropping the pillow case, he called to the auctioneer. "Crate the linens for me. They aren't for sale."

As he started to leave the parlor, he almost tripped over a carton of books. On top was a roll of drafting papers. He stared down curiously. What were these? He lifted the papers, unfurling them. 3 Vee's work. His brother had been gone from Los Angeles for several months, and his absence had lessened Bud's hatred a fraction. He was able to look at the drawings. They were the plans for an oil-burning locomotive. He frowned. In this room, surrounded as it were by Amélie, he couldn't concentrate.

"Don't forget," he called. "Linens and china aren't for sale."

The head auctioneer came heavily downstairs. "You said just the linens, Bud."

"Linen and china—and while we're at it, save the piano." They were possessions that had come with her at their marriage.

"That's a Bechstein. It'll fetch a lot," said the auctioneer, who got twenty percent.

"You heard me!" Bud snapped.

Thwacking the rolled papers against his palm, Bud left the house and strode downhill to the Nadeau.

The whore he had been keeping this particular week lolled in his bed. He called from the suite's sitting room, "Time to toddle along, honey."

"Ah, Bud, I'll stay on. You don't have to pay me none."

"Sugar, it's not a question of money. I'm ready to pluck the next blossom."

The girl, a blonde with a voluptuous body, rose, displaying her wares. Bud unrolled the plans on the lamplit table by the window. She came over and in full view of Spring Street put both arms around his neck, pulling his head to her abundant breasts. He held up a five-dollar bill between his fingers. "I'm busy, so get the hell out," he said, adding, "baby." Pouting, she did as she was told.

3 Vee's sketches were imaginative rather than practical. Bud, however, had worked with his brother long enough to get the gist. A nozzle would spray oil and steam into the firebox. "Steam is essential, I think," 3 Vee had written under one sketch. Bud's mouth tightened. It was just like his brother to write *essential* and then add *I think*. Bud's bitterness toward 3 Vee remained an animate part of him.

He examined the drawings closely, and from time to time he jotted down a specification, altered a line. And here lay the intrinsic difference between the minds of the two brothers. 3 Vee, who could create an idea, lost interest in it long before he brought it to term—or profit. Bud saw things as they were. He had never created a new idea; handed one, he could make it work.

Yes, he thought, pouring himself a tumbler of whiskey. Here it is, the market we need for our California crude. He drank and worked through the night, weeding out the most obviously impractical schemes. He continued to work without sleep through the following day and as the sky turned dark that night, he sprawled across the unmade bed, which still smelled of the whore and her cheap violet eau de cologne. Since I came upstairs, he thought, the bed Amélie and I shared has been auctioned off. Why didn't I let them knock down the china and linens and piano? I'll never be able to look at them again without hurting.

He got up and went back to the table, staring down at the plans. There's only one way to see if it'll work, he thought. Borrow a locomotive.

· 6 ·

Early one morning a week later, Bud clattered over the wet cobbles of Market Street in San Francisco. July rain hammered on the hack's roof. He grasped the pigskin satchel next to him. It held a fresh collar and a set of blueprints. For the last several days, Bud had stood over Professor O'Day, formerly with the Union Oil laboratory, now attached to Paloverde Oil. Alternately withholding and administering bourbon, he had watched over the professor's narrow shoulders as meticulously scaled blueprints emerged.

Wheels grated and splashed. The cab swerved and stopped. Gripping the handle of the satchel, Bud stepped into the Palm Court of the Palace Hotel. A porter took his valise as Bud whispered a question to the doorman. He whispered a reply and Bud tipped the doorman exorbitantly. He crossed the vast luxurious hotel lobby and checked in. He carried the satchel to his room himself. In the barber shop he submitted to hot towels, lather, a gliding razor, the astringency of bay rum. Back in his room, he buttoned on the fresh collar, all the time priming himself with arguments to force his way through servants, secretaries, buffers. He walked briskly down a long carpeted hallway and he knocked at Suite 407.

The door opened. The old man before him, photographed, scurrilously cartooned, was known to every Californian—Collis P. Huntington, president of the Central and Southern Pacific railroads, the man who had ruined many men, including Hendryk Van Vliet and Colonel Thaddeus Deane. Huntington's massive shoulders were noticeably bent, his neatly trimmed beard and mustache were totally white. He wore a plainly cut frock coat and a skullcap to cover his domed, hairless head. Despite his age, he remained a powerful and authoritative figure.

Bud gazed into cold, acquisitive eyes, startled that the old man had answered the door himself. He felt as if he had volunteered for the army and now had to talk his way out of facing a firing squad. I can't fail, he thought. Not now. Paloverde Oil depends on this interview. My life depends on it. "My name is Bud Van Vliet," he said. "I have plans in this satchel that'll save you millions of dollars every year."

"Do you know what time it is, young man?" Huntington said. It wasn't a question.

"Before business hours, sir. But personally I work long and hard, and I've heard you do the same."

"Then you steal in here by dawn to act as my benefactor?"

"My own first, sir. Yours second."

Huntington gave a brief bark that might have been amusement. The silk-capped head nodded, a gesture for Bud to follow him. They crossed ornately furnished reception rooms. The old man opened a velvet-covered door.

His private office differed sharply from the other rooms. A plain brass lamp above a long board table lit a strew of letters and contracts. One corner was cleared for work. Behind this space, Collis P. Huntington lowered his massive haunches into an ordinary wooden chair. He adjusted a small metal clock. "I'll give you fifteen minutes," he said. "No more."

"I'm from Los Angeles. I own a company called Paloverde Oil."

"I know of Paloverde Oil. Small. Undercapitalized. Well, you, like everybody in Los Angeles, will soon have difficulty selling your oil. Down to ten cents a barrel, isn't it?"

"Not quite that bad."

"It will be. Then how will your Paloverde Oil survive?"

"No problem, sir. Not with my plan."

"Which, I take it, is connected somehow to my railroads?"

Bud took a deep breath. "I have plans for an oil-burning locomotive."

"Oh?" Huntington remarked casually. "And does yours work?"

"I don't know of any others, sir."

The old man grudged another bark. "None have crossed my desk, and they would, they would. You're sharp, young man. I like that. Now. Let me see."

Bud opened the satchel and pulled out four blueprints. He unrolled them, pinning down the corners with the clock, a brass inkwell, paperweights. As Huntington examined each blueprint in turn, Bud heard the muffled sounds of the morning clatter of drays, cable cars, carriages from the street below.

"What's this tube?" Huntington asked.

"It's connected to the nozzle that sprays into the firebox."

The capped head nodded.

Finally the old man sighed. "There's some sense here," he said. "It'll work."

"Probably," Huntington said.

"Then you'll let Paloverde Oil install an oil burner—at our own expense, naturally—in one of your locomotives."

"I won't."

A cable car was turning on Market Street, and Bud decided he had heard wrong.

"I'm sorry?"

"You heard me correctly. No."

"May I ask why, sir?"

Collis P. Huntington leaned back in his cheap, comfortless chair. "You aren't a fool, Mr. Van Vliet. However, you're young. So you don't yet understand the nature of power. I mean the force that God alone can give a man, the force that permits him to rule over other men. Given this gift, a man must dedicate himself to it. And, in the final analysis, a man doesn't have power. Power has him."

"I never finished high school, sir, so philosophy isn't my strong point. But I've always been quick at arithmetic. In the West, oil is cheaper by far than coal, even for you. In dollars and cents, how can you turn this down?"

The old man stared at the blueprints so avidly that Bud felt a jab of relief that he had spared time to have his lawyer file for patents.

"I just explained," Huntington said, lacing his long, bony fingers. "When I was young, the Central Pacific and the Southern Pacific opened up the West. California. Now the weak and petty say I've robbed them. Yet without me—and my partners, of course— this land would be worthless. I gave, not took. For none of them had the strength to build the railroad."

"Yes, sir. And my innovation will increase your strength."

"No, Mr. Van Vliet. There you're wrong. One day San Francisco will give way to your dusty little town because you have oil. Oil *will* fuel a train. And boats and any other means of locomotion there is. Therefore those men who control oil will control the means by which this planet moves. The oil producers, not railroad men like myself, will control the world."

The old man might be avaricious, Bud realized. Yet he had vision. More important, he was able to act upon that vision. And in this moment Bud was able to grasp an elemental fact. Human advancement comes not through men of nobility, creativity, generous spirit. It comes through men like Collis P. Huntington.

The pale, hooded eyes blinked. "One may have power," Huntington continued, "but the relationship is like that of a horse carrying a man. One must never willingly relinquish the reins. Do you understand? You must hold on with every means at your disposal. And that, Mr. Van Vliet, is why I said no to you."

"Let's say another line, the Santa Fe for example, successfully uses an oil-burning locomotive, sir? What will you do?"

"Naturally I'll be forced to give way, to make the changeover." The old man slumped for a moment in his chair, then drew himself up. "But I have my obligation to power. I shall not hasten by one day its transfer from railroads to oil. Why did Amélie leave you?"

Bud, during business negotiations, had schooled himself to control his emotions. Yet Huntington's question was so unexpected, so startling, he had no reply. He heard only his own jagged intake of breath.

"Come, come. Why the surprise? Mr. Van Vliet, I know who and what you are. Or do you imagine I let every fresh-shaven, well-set-up young man into my privacy? Two servants and my secretary are in the adjacent rooms. The servants are picked for their physical strength. Had I not known your name, I would have called them. I keep watch, Mr. Van Vliet. That's another obligation to power, and one you should learn. You don't know where she is, do you?"

Bud was unable to speak. Yet the question implied that Amélie was alive. She's alive, he thought, alive! His relief was shattering.

"In exchange for information about her whereabouts," Huntington said in a cold, flat voice, "I could get you to do whatever I ask, couldn't I?"

Bud looked into greedy, blanched eyes, remembering who it was he faced. "You could bargain," he said, and cleared his throat. "You won't."

"Oh? Why not?"

"Because we're alike, you and me," Bud said. "The gift of power has us both. And you prefer me on your side. You want me owing you. When my engine works, you want me to bring it to you, not to some other line."

"She was a charming little girl. Poor Thaddeus. He so doted on her. What makes you so sure of yourself?"

"I'm right," Bud said numbly.

Huntington glanced at the clock. "Your time is up Mr. Van Vliet." He stood and watched Bud roll up the blueprints. "I have something you want, and you have something I want," he said as he led Bud through the empty reception rooms to the door. "A simple business deal."

Bud was silent. He had to restrain himself from begging, pleading. But he knew the terms of the bargain.

At the door Collis P. Huntington extended his long veined hand to point at the satchel that contained the blueprints. "When you succeed, I'll have it?"

"Yes," Bud said quietly.

"She calls herself Mrs. de Rémy. She lives in Oakland."

The door shut. Bud dropped the satchel and leaned against the wall, bending over to clutch his stomach. He was breathing in tortured gulps.

CHAPTER 14

· I ·

In early afternoon the rain stopped. Bud walked briskly along an Oakland street that paralleled the Southern Pacific tracks. A few shawled women were venturing forth, picking their way through mud. The small children clinging to them were paler than their Southern California counterparts. He had obtained the address by questioning various Oakland grocers. It was an unornamented gray-painted building that resembled a wooden crate tied with string divided into four equal flats: two apartments upstairs, two down.

Bud turned up the walk. Sodden leaves strewed the weedy front yard, and blocking the lower left porch stood a baby carriage, high on its wheels, upholstered in pink plush, sheltered by a pink silk parasol. In such drab surroundings it was as out of place as a rajah's howdah. So the child is alive, Bud thought. Pink. Then she has a daughter.

Never once had he considered the child as his. He didn't now. His mouth hardened. Moving along the unraked path, edging round the carriage, he pushed the cracked porcelain bell, then took off his hat, waiting. Across the street a freight train was rattling by.

The door opened and he looked into the face of his wife. Her lips turned pale.

In her absence, her reality had faded for Bud, and he had come to visualize her as she looked in photographs. The camera was unkind to Amélie. Her charm lay in her mobility of expression, her luminous skin, the sparkle of her eyes and the color of her hair. His first impression was that her face was more finely bred, prettier, and infinitely more vulnerable. Her hair was arranged differently in a style that he thought of as French. Her shirtwaist and skirt were beautifully cut, and she wore them with an elegance that also seemed French. She doesn't look Californian any more, Bud thought.

In her eyes, he too had changed. His face was leaner, which made the Van Vliet nose stand out more strongly. His tan, deepened by work in the oilfields, made his eyes bluer, harder. New lines furrowed his forehead, and the older facial lines around his eyes and mouth were cut far deeper. In his pearl-gray summer suit and narrow-toed boots, he looked like a successful predator. He had had a very bad eighteen months and it showed.

"Bud," she whispered.

He had planned a speech. In his confusion, he forgot it. "Hello," he said.

"How did you find me?"

"I've got detectives in Paris and New York." He realized this reply was irrelevant. "Collis P. Huntington told me."

"Mr. Huntington? How did he know?"

"There probably isn't much of anything he doesn't know," Bud said. "Amélie, why did you hide from me?"

"Bud? It really is you," she said, reassuring herself, not questioning.

The train had rattled into the distance and in the silence they heard a sleepy call. "Mama."

Bud's soft expression faded. Amélie straightened her shoulders. "You must leave now," she said.

"When can I come back?"

"You cannot. Ever."

"My God, Amélie."

"If you leave now, we can forget this. It will be easier for us."

"Not me."

"Yes. Bud, you know why I hid. Go. Please."

"Mama?"

For a moment they stared at one another as if they were suspended in time. It was one of those contests of wills when the battle is lost from lack of nerve, or embarrassment, or from hesitation or an act of simple kindness. Bud was aware of the flower scent she still wore, the chittering of birds in the eucalyptus tree, a faraway cart creaking. The warmth of her body reached out to him and he was aware of the stirring of sex. And all the time he stared into hazel eyes. "I had forgotten," Amélie said. "You always win."

"Not always, Amélie."

"Mama?" The child called again.

"She has been napping," Amélie said. "Wait in the sitting room, back there." She ran lightly down the narrow, dark hall, ducking into a door, closing it after her.

He followed, glancing into rooms. A small bedroom furnished with a painted bureau, a bookcase filled with shabby books (secondhand, he thought) and a cheap iron bed covered with a paisley shawl. He was spying on her poverty, yet he couldn't help himself. He longed to know every detail about her. He heard muffled voices through the door of the child's room. In the bathroom, a froth of undergarments lay on the floor, and he remembered that Amélie, personally so fastidious, had a casual disregard for order. The numerous times they had made love in the daytime, he piled his clothes over a chair while she let hers fall to the floor. There was a half-eaten piece of bread and a round of cheese on the kitchen table. She has no girl to help. And this, to Bud, was the final proof of her poverty. Even when the Van Vliets had been verging on bankruptcy, Doña Esperanza had never done her own work. Of the "nice" women he knew, none, ever, went without at least one hired girl.

The rooms along the hallway, all facing north, were gloomy. But the rear parlor, with uncurtained windows that faced both north and west, was cheerful: bright watercolors, some framed, others unframed; white-painted rattan furniture with colorful cushions. A bookcase, the twin of the one in the the front bedroom, held battered toys. The room, despite its simplicity, was definitely Amélie. She had never liked ornately carved furniture and dark oil paintings hanging on paneled walls.

He stepped over a rag doll and sat on a sofa draped with a shawl. He could hear her laughter and the child's voice. He was sweating when they entered the room. Amélie was a small woman, and this made the little girl in her arms seem larger. Bud had an impression of curly black hair, pink cheeks, plump stockinged feet dangling. A spasm shook him and he glanced away.

Amélie, seeing his reaction, half turned as if to protect the baby. "This is Tessa," she said.

"Tessa?"

The baby, hearing him say her name, twisted to gaze at him. Her eyes were dark, her face oval with a gentle chin. Looking at the child in his wife's arms, Bud saw his brother's face. My enemy, he thought, and barely admitted to himself that he meant not 3 Vee but this tiny girl.

She squirmed and Amélie reluctantly put her down on the linoleum floor. Tessa stood, stockinged feet apart, watching Bud. It was then that he saw that her dark eyes weren't brown. They were a black-rimmed, very intense blue, like his own. "Hi, honey," he said, leaning toward the child. "I'm Bud."

"Bah."

"Bud," Amélie corrected.

"Buh." This time the voice was determined. Buh or nothing.

Uncle Buh? he thought. His jaw tightened and he sat back on the sofa.

He turned to Amélie. "How've you been managing?" Finances were the last thing he wanted to talk about, but he wasn't ready to face either the child or conversation about the child.

"You know I took the diamond set. Well, I sold it. I teach piano."

There was pride in her voice, pride that in the cold light of this Spartan room was especially vulnerable. Yet Bud couldn't help reflecting that her shirtwaist and the flared skirt had the simplicity which years of marriage had taught him doesn't come cheap. You don't buy clothes like hers giving music lessons.

"And you," she said, "have been managing well. I read about Paloverde Oil in the newspapers."

"I've been selling stock, and that takes fiscal exaggeration." He grinned at her. "Don't let the word out, but I'm up to my tailbone in debt."

"Is that why you saw Mr. Huntington? To borrow?"

"No. I'm trying to interest him in my oil-burning locomotive." Bud's voice faded. In the presence of the child, he realized that the oil-burning locomotive wasn't his either. It, too, was 3 Vee's creation.

She was holding out her rag doll to him. Why the hell doesn't she laugh? Bud thought. 3 Vee always was a solemn little kid.

"Pretty," he said automatically, and turned back to Amélie. "Mr. Huntington seems high on oil—"

"Dodo," the child said.

"The doll is called Dodo," Amélie explained.

Tessa continued to hold out the toy. One arm was gone and the head had been crushed out of shape. "Play with Dodo?" she asked.

"Dodo is yours, sugar," he said.

"Come on, Tessa," Amélie said. "I must take her next door." Her voice was cool, dismissing.

"Next door? Why?"

"Tessa visits with Mrs. Farnesi while I give lessons."

The child pushed the doll toward him again and this time he took it. "Thanks, sugar."

Amélie was standing in the doorway. "Come on, Tessa, time to go to Mrs. Farnesi's."

"Mama, play Buh?"

"You can play next door. And have cookies to eat there, too."

"No more Buh?"

"Mrs. Farnesi would like one of your cookies."

At this the baby ran into the kitchen and Amélie followed. Again Bud heard the childish voice and Amélie's laughter. The peculiar twisting in his chest was jealousy. When they returned, Tessa wore boots and a loose red coat. She carried a cookie in each hand. "Bye-bye," she said shyly. "Buh."

Amélie took the rag doll from his hand and carried the child down the hallway. The front door opened, a draft rustled. Voices. Amélie returned alone. "I am late, Bud," she called from the bedroom. He went down the hall, watching from the door as she pinned on the small leghorn hat. He remembered watching her unpin her hair, her bare arms raised in graceful angles to her head.

"I'll walk you wherever you're going," he said.

"Bud—"

"For God's sake! Don't keep making me beg."

"I do not mean . . . All right," she sighed.

Wordless, they left the house and walked along a street perpendicular to the tracks, heading toward the bay. A few shacks stood in weedy flatland, and in the distance the sullen gray water was rimmed by the hills of San Francisco.

Finally, she turned to him. "It is impossible, Bud," she said.

"What is?"

"You want to keep seeing me."

"What's wrong with that?"

"You will tear me apart, and that is all you will accomplish."

"What are you talking about?"

"All the time you were thinking of ... well, what we once were to one another."

"All right. Yes. I want you back."

"And that is how you will tear me apart."

"Amélie, explain it to me."

"You could not even look at her," Amélie said in a low, miserable voice. "It hurt you even to look at her."

"I'm just not used to babies. I need time, that's all."

"You have never lied to me. Tessa looks so like ... 3 Vee. And Doña Esperanza." She reached her gloved hand as if to touch him, but hesitated. "Bud, I read about your mother. I am so very sorry."

"It was best. She suffered a lot," he said gruffly.

They walked in silence a few more steps, then Amélie said, "She looks like 3 Vee, but she has a lot of you. Her eyes. She is fearless and generous, like you. But there, now I am doing it. Searching for clues in her. I never did before. But since you came, I have. She is a conundrum, a mystery. As if it matters. Tessa is Tessa. And I love her." She spoke fiercely.

"You're remembering what I said that last time. Sweetheart, you know how hurt I was. I didn't mean any of those things."

"From the way you just acted with Tessa, I would say you meant every word." Her tone remained fierce.

His anger, too, flared. "I'm a man! I've spent over a year in oil-fields. You'll have to pardon me. I'm not much at playing with babies. I'm not up on the etiquette of rag dolls." He took a breath. "Sweetheart, I've spent the time in hell."

"It has been difficult ... terrible, for me, too."

"Then you still care?"

A boy skidded his bicycle near them. The wheels, large and small, sprayed mud, and Amélie moved closer to the rank, wet wild oats.

"Why do you think I have been hiding from you? Bud, I was terrified I would weaken. Now I have seen you with her, there is no danger. I cannot let her live with you."

"You've given me all of ten minutes with her," Bud said. "All right. I admit it. She reminds me of 3 Vee. Why shouldn't she? He's her uncle."

"You do not believe that," Amélie said, and her voice was implacable.

"I'm willing to try to like her."

"Tessa is not a puppy!" she said with passionate hauteur. "She does not have to earn your affection."

"Don't be so touchy. I said it wrong. Just let me get used to her."

"How?"

It was on the tip of his tongue to say that she and the child should come back to Los Angeles to live with him. Instead, he lied prudently. "I'm up here financing the locomotive. Whenever I'm free I'll take the ferry over. Maybe sometimes I can tend the baby while you go to work. How does that sound?"

"As if you are being very, very clever."

He felt that irritation that she, alone of women, could rouse in him. "And you're being so brilliant? Playing hide-and-seek in a slum? Or do you believe that poverty's good for her soul?"

"Anything is better than the way you avoided looking at her. You never once could bring yourself to use her name."

They had reached a new subdivision. The houses were tall and narrow, with identical cheap gimcrackery on identical porches. She started to turn into a shell-lined path. Her slender neck was stiff, her chin was raised. She looked haughty as she always did when near tears. Bud's anger melted. He reached for her hand, detaining her.

"The way I feel about . . . Tessa, you're right. There hasn't been a day when it doesn't eat at me, make me sick with myself. And at the same time I've been searching for you. I have nightmares . . . you're in a coffin. Oh my God, sweetheart, I meant it when I said I've been in hell."

"I see it in your face," she said, her voice shaking. "But Tessa is very gentle, so very open. Maybe it is because she sees so few people, maybe she was born like that. She exposes herself completely. I cannot let her be hurt. That will come inevitably, but not through me."

"I won't hurt her. You know me that much, Amélie."

"Can you come for her feeding tonight?" she said after a long pause. "Or would tomorrow be better?"

"Both," he said, forgetting his lie of business involvement.

"Five tonight, then," Amélie said. Again her voice shook. She was risking what meant most to her: her child.

"Thank you," he said, lifting the hand he held, unbuttoning the glove and rubbing his thumb on the delicately webbed veins of her wrist. A breeze stirred the topaz hair. He gazed at her, his mouth trembling. Her lips parted and her eyes grew moist.

She pulled away and ran down the path to the house.

· 2 ·

That week he remained in the Palace Hotel, each morning catching the 10:05 ferry for Oakland, returning on the 6:20. Amélie, tactful, never asked him how he was able to spend so much time away from his business. He always arrived with a present for the child: a bisque doll with jointed limbs and blue eyes that opened and closed, a wicker doll carriage that resembled her own, a painted cradle which, the smiling saleslady informed him, was sturdy enough to hold an infant. The child ignored the expensive new toys. She used the wrapping paper to make lumpy little bundles, pretend-gifts for him.

He stayed with her when Amélie was giving a music lesson. After a time, even when Amélie was at home she willingly left her mother to go off in her carriage with him. Sometimes she demanded to walk, and when he set her down, she would run away from him with a few uncertain steps, then turn with a smile that showed a gap between her two front teeth. When she returned, she put her hand trustingly in his, as if they had shared a unique adventure.

Bud was aware of how much hung on his relationship with the baby. He had trained his reason to dominate his emotions. Yet now he found his emotions intractable. *I'll always see it as a monster.* And even as he held her hand, that's how he did see Tessa. Bud had been almost eight when his brother was born, and his recollection of 3 Vee's infancy was clear. Tessa's oval face, the tangle of dark curls were the same as 3 Vee's. 3 Vee's milk teeth had gapped, too. Each time he looked at her, he saw his brother.

Besides, he was jealous. That Amélie had left him, that she chose to remain in this meager, lonely life, proved her devotion to the child. His tenderness for Amélie increased each day, and the child was his rival. Discovering Amélie had only two cups, two soup bowls, two dinner dishes, he could barely restrain himself from going into the Emporium and buying her a hundred-piece set of Havilland. The awkward way she peeled a potato brought an ache to his chest. He yearned to fill the leaky oak icebox with out-of-season fruits and lobsters. He resented all the work the child caused her and he wanted—oh, how he wanted—to hire a nursemaid.

Cool, wary, Amélie watched him with Tessa. Then, on Thursday evening, as she said goodbye to Bud at the door, the nightgowned child in her arms, she said, "Bud, stay for dinner tomorrow?"

· 3 ·

There was no table in the parlor. They ate sitting on the sofa. Oyster soup, asparagus salad, tiny green peas with Chateaubriand. He was very aware that the meal had strained her resources. He had brought a bottle of champagne and they drank from gold-rimmed wineglasses borrowed from Mrs. Farnesi. Amélie wore a shirtwaist he hadn't seen before. It was chiffon, floating at the arms and clinging on stays around her slender throat.

Peas scattered as they cut their steak. They laughed. They toasted with champagne and laughed again. For the first time she was the old Amélie.

When she went for coffee, he sat on the floor. "It's more comfortable, believe me," he explained, leaning back on his elbow.

She handed him down both cups, then sat next to him.

"We used to have picnics on the ground," he said. "Remember? When we met at Paloverde." Paloverde, he thought. So many memories ruined by one ugly moment.

"Perhaps I should have given you an orange," she said. "I am not much of a cook."

"You didn't burn a thing," he said. "Where did you get the pretty shirtwaist? Who gave it to you?"

"Oh, one of the numerous admirers you surely have noticed lurking about."

"Who?"

"My mother sent it for my birthday."

"She wouldn't tell me where you were."

"I know. I asked her not to."

"How many have there been?"

"Birthdays?"

"Admirers."

"Hundreds," she said.

"None?"

"Ah, so you consider me unpopular." She leaned over to kiss him lightly.

He moved the coffee cup and shifted forward to return her kiss. As their champagne-scented mouths touched, he took her face between his hands. "Sweetheart," he whispered, stretching on the floor, pulling her small body next to his. Her fingertips traced his cheeks, his neck, and he was aware of the movements of her lashes, of her breath, of the infinite sweetness of her touch.

"I have never wanted anyone else," she whispered.

"Truly?"

"Truly."

"Me either. It's only been right with you."

"I missed you so very much."

"Ah, sweetheart..." Aching tenderness, far greater than he had experienced with her before, overcame him and he couldn't speak. He held her palm to his heart. Against the back of his hand he could feel, through the softness of her breast, the pounding of her heart. The abundance of long-denied love pressed on him. Yet he wanted to cancel out the ugly words he had thrown at her, he wanted to prove to her that he treasured her more than any culmination. He kissed her eyelids, her forehead.

"Mama." It was Tessa's voice from behind the closed door of her room.

Amélie tensed. "Bud," she murmured.

He didn't release her. "She'll go back to sleep."

"I must see what it is."

"Mama..." This time it was a cry.

Amélie pulled away, standing.

Bereft of the bubble of love that had warmed him, Bud was a grown man lying on a linoleum floor in an unheated, shabby room. "Don't you ever let her cry it out?"

"She hardly ever cries."

"No wonder. You spoil her at every turn."

Amélie didn't reply. As she stepped away the curved train of her suit skirt tipped the coffee cup. She didn't notice. He jerked away, but not before warm liquid seeped into his jacket.

He heard her ask, "What is it, Tessa? A bad dream?"

The baby's sobs gradually subsided and then he heard the creak of the rocking chair and Amélie's voice, soothing, telling a story about a princess called Tessa who had a bad dream. It went on interminably. She's punishing me, Bud thought. He went into the bathroom to sponge the dark stain from his jacket.

He was in the rattan chair looking moodily at the dark window when she returned.

"Bud," she said, "it is late."

"Nine-thirty."

"I am tired."

"I said she's spoiled; is that a crime?"

"I do not consider that she is."

"What do you call it? She gets her own way at every turn."

"She is only a baby. She very rarely cries. She is so brave, so gentle. She trusts you completely, and she has from the first minute. Or have you been so busy charming me through her that you have never noticed her at all?"

That hit close enough to the truth to grate. Bud's eyes narrowed. "I've spent the week playing nursemaid."

"She has given you her heart."

"And what about your heart?" he said angrily.

Amélie clenched her fingers until the knuckles shone white. "I may not go to her when you are in the house," she said, and her voice was very quiet. "Is that what you mean?"

Before this moment neither of them had alluded to that ruinous afternoon when the Santa Ana had hurled its fury at Los Angeles.

He took a few breaths to regain his temper. "Amélie, a few minutes ago wasn't it clear to you that I'm crazy for you?"

"I am sorry," she said. "I did not intend that to happen. It was unfair to you."

"Unfair? It was the happiest moment of my life. Tell me you weren't happy, too."

She turned so he couldn't see her face. "Bud, try to understand. You judge Tessa all the time. Nothing about her pleases you. Oh, you try to hide it, but it is there. Even if she were not precious to me, I could never take my own happiness at her expense. That would be despicable."

"Are you telling me that we're over and done with?"

She turned and he saw that her face was set. "Unless you can honestly tell me that your emotions toward Tessa have changed, yes."

Bud glared at her, his face flushed with anger. He grabbed his hat, strode the length of the hallway and let himself out.

It wasn't until he was wrapped in the cold, salty air of the bay, the ferry paddles splashing in dark water, that he realized no sane man gets in a fury if a baby needs comfort at night. And he knew with a kind of weariness that Amélie was right. Nothing about the child pleased him. Nothing. She symbolized loss, betrayal.

He didn't think of divorce, yet—as he leaned against the rail—his arms were clutched around himself, hands gripping at biceps like a man in the throes of mourning.

·4·

She stood in the lighted doorway long after she saw him disappear into the moonless July night. From the sound of his rapid footsteps, she was positive he hadn't turned to look at her.

Shivering, she closed the door and went into the parlor, bending stiffly to pick up the cups. One, overturned, pointed a finger of drying coffee on the linoleum floor. She returned from the kitchen with a dishcloth and wiped it up. She carried the borrowed wineglasses back to the kitchen, setting them on the table to wash in the morning when, less distraught, she hoped she wouldn't break them.

Amélie found no exhilaration in earning her own keep, nor was she fool enough to find poverty ennobling. Still she was surprised at how little her straitened circumstances had mattered to her. It was not material comfort she missed, it was Bud. She had missed him in a way that had made her wonder if she could survive their separation.

Yet under the circumstances she had no choice. Sitting at the kitchen table, she remembered when Dr. Marsh, after that endless torture, had finally placed her daughter in her arms. The baby's red face was askew from the birth struggle and there were forceps indentations below her wet, dark hair. "We managed it," Amélie had said, a note of triumph in a voice dulled by exhaustion. *We* meant her bleeding self and this small, new disowned scrap of life, her daughter. I love her, she had thought, and therefore we will both survive.

Can expressing love harm a child?

Sighing, Amélie stood and returned to the parlor to shake the pillows, erasing the signs of their bodies. There was nothing she could do to erase those few minutes that they had stretched out together on the floor. Her body refused to forget the pleasure, her mind refused to forget the sweetness.

She heard a sound from Tessa's room.

The baby was standing in her crib, crying. Amélie picked her up and felt the wet diaper. "It is all right, darling. You had an accident, that is all."

"I hurt, Mama."

"Where?"

Tessa clutched the ruffle at the neck of her nightgown. Amélie touched her lips to the rounded forehead. The heat was more than would be caused by tears. She changed the child and wrapped her in a patchwork quilt, a gift of old Mrs. Farnesi. Sitting in the rocking chair, she held Tessa in her arms until she quieted and fell asleep.

·5·

As Bud entered his room at the Palace Hotel, he saw a yellow telegram that had been slipped under the door. He opened it.

HAVE LOCATED A FOUR FOUR OH LOCOMOTIVE STOP O'DAY

Bud's habit of escaping into work took over. He went back down to the lobby and wrote out two Western Union forms. Amélie's read: *Must return to Los Angeles. Will write. Bud.* The other told Professor O'Day to meet him the following evening at the depot.

·6·

Professor O'Day, who was seldom completely sober, told Bud the story. The locomotive, out of commission in a San Bernardino roundhouse, belonged to a small line. The general manager earned a minimal salary and kept an expensive mistress. "It's all arranged.

Hand over the lucre and the locomotive's yours," Professor O'Day said in his drink-slurred voice.

Bud was on the early train to San Bernardino. The town lay sixty miles to the east of Los Angeles, on the edge of the Mohave Desert. Even this early in the morning, the summer heat was fierce. Most passengers, however, kept their windows closed, preferring to stifle rather than to choke on coarse particles from the unwatered roadbed. Bud's window was open. Cinder-laden dust grimed his face, a hot wind disordered his thinning hair. The pigskin satchel containing the blueprints was at his feet.

To the north, the San Bernardino range swept up seven thousand feet, and as the sun rose, the color of its ridges lightened from black to pinkish brown. Arroyos scarred the flatland, and these shallow, sandy riverbeds—some a half mile broad—were dotted with huge boulders. It seemed unbelievable that enough water could ever race through this desert to carry such massive rocks. At intervals, the train passed irrigated land, citrus groves, and large vineyards where pruned vines surrounded tree-shaded houses—oases shimmering in the dry heat like a mirage.

In San Bernardino he went directly to the railyard where the money-hungry general manager had his office. The man's swollen torso resembled a watermelon. Bud explained who he was, the stout man pocketed bills, then led him from his office into a vast, dim roundhouse.

A flat roof trapped the heat. It must have been well over 130 degrees. The wood walls trembled as a locomotive roared, spurting a cloud of steam. Another burst and then another in a deafening roar. They moved across black-cindered earth, stepping over the glint of rails, circling the locomotives and cars housed there for repairs. Forges blazed, casting an orange glow upon sweating, black-smeared workers. The scene was a dark vision of hell.

The 4-4-0 General had been shunted into a corner. Bud took off his jacket and began to examine the locomotive. Undeniably it was a 4-4-0. He could tell by the wheel arrangement: two pairs of small pilot wheels in front and two pairs of large, driving wheels in back. (The 0 signified that there were no small traveling wheels under the cab.) However, The General was at least thirty years old. Under its rust, the boiler was cracked. The flues were dented and one had been broken off. It could never travel from this roundhouse with coal, much less oil.

Bud ran a hand over his sweat-drenched forehead. Part of him rebelled at the rotten bargain he had made, and another part exulted at the challenge. The harder it is, he thought, the less time I'll have to think of Amélie and her child.

Resting a foot on the battered cowcatcher, he said, "For starters, I'll need a boilermaker and a machinist."

"There's nobody free to help," the general manager said.

"Then you're reneging on our agreement?"

"My men don't know how to convert a locomotive to petroleum."

"Nobody does." Bud smiled, yet his voice was hard as he inquired, "Should I make my request to the owners of the company?"

"No, no. I'll find you suitable men."

Bud climbed into a nearby passenger car, took off all his clothes except his calf-length silk-and-linen drawers, and put on the faded coveralls that he had packed in his satchel. When he returned to The General, a wiry, hairless little man was fanning himself with a denim cap.

"Mr. Van Vliet?"

"Bud."

"Horace. Machinist."

Bud unrolled his plans on the black dirt, and the two squatted. "The way I see it," Bud said, "the first thing to do is build a scale model of a boiler and do our figuring on the bench."

Horace, chewing a wad of tobacco, nodded his head in agreement. They moved to a forge. In its dark square, Bud built a kindling fire, dropping in dampened bits of coke. He had learned smithing at fifteen as a tool-dresser in the Newhall oilfield. Corners of coke began to glow. Horace, without being told, plied the bellows.

Working a forge was backbreaking, yet Bud welcomed the hard and exacting labor of building the scale model. Stopping only long enough to eat, he spent two straight days over the forge until finally, pulling off an old leather smithy's apron, he rubbed at the small of his back and walked groggily toward the passenger car where he had left his clothes. Beyond dusty windows the blackness was lit by forges and the yellow cast of kerosene lanterns. He curled on a seat, pressing his soot-blackened cheek to the plush. He was conscious of the burns on his hands, of the odor of Hall's Liniment.

He fell asleep almost instantly . . .

The child sat on the linoleum floor. Near her was a fine, large doll, which she ignored. In her clumsy, childish way, she was intent on making a package from the paper that was piled about her. "I bought you the doll," he said, "so why won't you play with it?" The tiny girl, intent on her wrapping, did not look up. Frustrated, he was consumed by the impotent self-pity one feels in such dreams. He argued with the child, who seemed to be a full-scale adversary. Finally, she got to her feet, toddling over to him with her package. Normally there was nothing in her odd-shaped bundles. Bud saw that she had put something in this one. "Buh?" she said, back to a child's size. "Oh, you damn little bastard!" he cried. "I don't want to play your baby games!" She gave him that trusting, gap-tooth smile, continuing to hold out the gift. He hit the lumpy wrapping angrily. An object fell from the paper. And he saw that it was a living, beating heart. From a great distance he heard a voice say, "She has given you her heart." And when he looked at her, the little girl lay on the floor at his feet. Dead. Her lips were parted with pleading trust, her small, limp hand was curled up defenselessly.

He awoke with a wrenching sob.

His eyes were wet. The sweat on his body was cold. He wiped a hand over his eyes. The air was filled with the nighttime racket of the roundhouse. He couldn't sleep. A crazy nightmare, he told himself. I didn't hurt her. She's perfectly all right.

His mind went burrowing after memories of Tessa: the trustful way during Amélie's absences that she had permitted him to help her, the way she sat on his lap as his inexperienced hand pulled a comb through her soft black curls. While he had read the *Tribune*, she sat on the couch beside him with a tattered magazine, imitating him, pretending to read. There was a tranquility about the hours he and Tessa had spent together.

Bud realized he was thinking only of Tessa, not of 3 Vee. What transmutation, he wondered, had taken place during his nightmare that he could now see the child without seeing his brother? Bud shifted his cramped position. She *does* like me, he thought. And soon he fell back to sleep.

After that, working at the forge he often had a momentary vision of the small hands that held out her pretend gifts to him. As hot metal hissed in water, he heard her childish voice pronounce his name. *Bub.* Penciling a correction on his plans, he saw that sharing smile. *She has given you her heart.*

Bud rarely left a task unfinished. After five days he and Horace hadn't completed the scaled-down fire tubes; they still had to forge the all-important nozzle that would spray oil and steam. Yet Bud knew he had to go back to Oakland. He didn't explore the guilty fears that had attacked him during the nightmare. I want to be with her again, he thought. And let it go at that.

Stopping in Los Angeles, he found Professor O'Day reasonably sober. He ordered him to take the train up to San Bernardino to inspect the modifications and keep on with the work. "Stay away from the booze," he said. "I'll be back in three or four days."

· 7 ·

A yellow light shone on Amélie's porch.

As Bud turned in at the path, a man emerged. White-bearded, stout in his frock coat, he carried a physician's bag. "Doctor?" Bud asked. Fear tingled in his brain.

The other man tipped his hat.

Bud asked, "Is somebody ill?"

"I'm Dr. Aurelius Marsh," the man said in a clipped voice. "And you?"

"Bud Van Vliet. Who's sick?"

"Tessa."

"Tessa? What's wrong?" Bud asked, not recognizing that his alarm was equal to what he would have felt had the reply been Amélie.

"Mrs. de Rémy has her hands full," Dr. Marsh said. "She won't be able to answer your ring. So we have a few minutes." He cleared his throat deliberately. "May I ask your relationship?"

"I'm her husband."

"Husband?"

"Her name's Mrs. Van Vliet."

Dr. Marsh's eyes opened with a quick, sharp glance that was more than professional. And in the dim light from the porch, Bud saw that he was younger than he had first appeared. His beard and hair were prematurely white. He doesn't want to believe me, Bud thought. He's interested in her. "What's our relationship got to do with your professional services?" he asked coldly.

"A good deal." Dr. Marsh shifted the bag in his hand. "I'm about to betray a professional confidence, so please bear with me. Before Tessa was born, I needed the address of Mrs. de Rémy's nearest kin. You understand why?"

Bud nodded.

"She gave me the name of her mother. I wasn't surprised. I'm used to the sad subterfuges—wedding rings, married names, a husband who has died. You did say your first name was Bud?"

"Yes."

"You were the one she called for during the delivery."

Bud stared at the yellow porch light. A circling moth cast intermittent shadows.

"She came to me only three weeks before the child was born. Her condition, in layman's terms, was close to mental collapse. The first two visits I didn't examine her. Her composure was so fragile that I sought only to reassure her. The third time I saw her I came here. The place was icy cold, furnished only with a bed. Every doctor has lost a patient who simply no longer cares to live. When I confronted Mrs. de Rémy with this fact I saw an immediate change in her. She told me in no uncertain terms she had no intention of dying. *She* was the only person who could look after this child. The baby was hers alone. Unmarried mothers often feel that way. And when she gave me Comtesse Mercier's name and address, I thought, so she's in society. That must make it worse, poor girl. She is a very small woman, and it was a very difficult breech delivery. Mrs. de Rémy was in great pain. I feared both for her life and the life of the child. I did what I could for her, but it was her determination, her willpower that enabled them both to survive. She is a most unusual lady."

"What's *your* relationship to her?" Bud said.

"Given half a chance, it wouldn't be purely professional, I assure you. I would like to ask Mrs. de Rémy to marry me."

"It doesn't matter to you, her child?"

"Not in the slightest. As a matter of fact, I would be delighted to adopt Tessa. She's a wonderful little girl. Bright. Trusting. With a sort of, well, it can only be called gentleness. I could make a good home for them both. Oh, not what Mrs. de Rémy is worthy of, but far better than this." He smiled at Bud, as if asking for his aid in this enterprise.

"Whether you call her Mrs. Van Vliet or not," Bud said abruptly, "that's her name. She's got a husband. Me."

The doctor took a step backward, examining Bud. "Obviously," he said, "I was wrong in my assumption. In such a princely neighborhood your wife stands out. There must be a reason why she came here to have her baby in secret. I'll be absolutely frank, Mr. Van Vliet. I suspect that Tessa's not your child."

Bud felt a flush of anger rise to his face. He clenched his fists.

"I should not have spoken to you of my feelings for your wife," Dr. Marsh said. "But now I am speaking to you as a doctor, not as a man. Your wife is utterly devoted to Tessa. She loves the child without any reservations. What are *your* feelings for Tessa, Mr. Van Vliet? Frankly, if there's a chip on your shoulder about her, you had better turn around and walk away. She doesn't need anyone with doubts around her now. She needs all the help she can get."

Bud's earlier fear, never quite absent, grew. He reached for the doctor's lapel. "What's wrong?"

"Diphtheria."

Diphtheria, the scourge of parents; diphtheria, the stalker of young children. Diphtheria the killer. The longest-lived of Bud's three sisters had strangled to death of diphtheria when she was five. Bud had been seven.

He ran up the path to the flat, taking the steps in a bound, rapping urgently. The door opened and closed quickly behind him. Dr. Marsh stared a moment longer at the yellow light on the bleak, empty porch. His shoulders were bowed as he went to his buggy.

· 8 ·

Amélie wore a soiled apron. Her hair was tied back, accentuating the sharp, fine bones of her cheeks and jaw. Anxiety and fatigue were implicit in the rigidity of her spine.

"I saw Dr. Marsh," Bud said. "He told me." She nodded. Without questioning his sudden reappearance, she edged around the elaborate carriage that blocked the hallway. Bud followed her. In Tessa's room a croup kettle curled up vinegar-odored steam. A cloth safety-pinned around the lampshade dimmed the light.

Tessa lay in her crib, breathing in little gasps. Her eyes were closed and he would have thought her asleep if it weren't for the hand pulling restlessly at flannel wrapped around her throat. He bent over the rail. "Hello, Tessa," he said quietly.

Her eyes opened, eyes glazed with fever, blue eyes rimmed with black, the eyes he saw in the mirror. "It's me," he said. "Bud. I'm home." He pushed back her soft, damp hair, black like her Californio ancestors, black like the long-dead Yang Na maidservant.

Tessa, he thought, Tessa. Why had he been so positive she wasn't his child? Why had he circled so endlessly about the fact she couldn't be his? What had been wrong with him? Why? His mind struggled with an alien abstraction. Had he needed a living symbol of his betrayal on which to vent his misery? Had this baby, signifying the defiling and loss of love, been the visible creature to hate? How like Mama she is. Why not? She's mine, he thought fiercely. Mine.

Her eyes remained open, looking up at him. His knuckles touched her smooth, hot cheek, and she grasped his finger, yawning. He could see grayish-white patches in her throat and he knew the membrane was already beginning to form.

"She was practically asleep," Amélie whispered. "Dr. Marsh swabs her throat. It makes her cry and gag. She is worn out." As Amélie spoke, she moved around the room, gathering strewn linen and bits of clothing.

After she left, Bud remained at the crib. Tessa's nose was pinched, her cheeks as crimson as live coals. She pulled at the neck bandage.

"Will it feel better if you sit on my lap?" Bud asked.

She nodded.

He wrapped her in the quilt and held her in the rocking chair. "Better?" he asked. She cuddled closer. The heat of her body penetrated his body. He could feel her wracked breathing.

He was only seven, yet he remembered it very clearly. He had stood at the foot of the stairs listening to awful, strangling gasps. His father and the doctor had pushed by him, rushing up the stairs to his sister's room. *The membrane. Hurry. She's strangling.*

After a few minutes the sounds stopped. The doctor had cut into her windpipe to permit her to breathe. And then Bud heard another terrible, low sound, his mother's cry of mourning.

He rested a cheek on Tessa's soft, moist black curls. Amélie, returning to get a water-filled enamel bowl, paused to look at her husband and her child. Bud, his mouth dry with fear for Tessa, was hardly aware of her presence. When the child's painful breathing lengthened into sleep, he carefully laid her in the crib, putting her battered rag doll under the covers next to her. He went out, leaving the door open.

On the stove in the kitchen, a large pot bubbled and steamed with the antiseptic odor of carbolic. Amélie was dropping in soiled clothes. She heard him but didn't turn. She stirred the clothing with a wooden paddle. He came up behind her and began to knead her tensed shoulder muscles.

"She's asleep," he said.

"Yes."

"I wish she were in Los Angeles."

"Why?"

"I don't know. It's always best to be sick where you belong." My sister died, he thought. "Magic," he said.

"If there were such magic, I would sell my soul to get her there. It is so awful to watch the illness and not be able to stop it, or to help her. Bud, I am afraid, so afraid."

"I won't let her die," he said.

She turned, embracing him with a drowner's strength, her arms tight around his waist, her mouth raised in a kiss that was desperate, explicit. He moved a knee between her skirt, her hands went down to his buttocks, pressing him closer. He lifted her, this small, proud woman he loved, carrying her to her room.

He fell with her across the narrow bed. Cheap iron springs squealed. With swift, trembling fingers, they pushed aside clothing and she arched her body in a frenzy as if she were being carried toward him on the crest of a great wave.

Amélie's love had never faltered. She was torn by terror and anguish. Yet if she had not witnessed Bud's change toward Tessa, she would never have permitted him to remain in the child's room, never invited him wordlessly into her own bed. But once she had perceived the difference in her husband, she had no room for coyness, no wish to hear reconciliatory speeches. Understanding how great his betrayal had been, she had never blamed him for his bitterness.

His obvious feeling for Tessa negated all the misery of the past. Her fingers dug into the knotted muscles of his back. This was Bud, her rock, her shield, her comfort. From him came her strength, her help. He was her handsome brown man, her stubborn Dutch *cholo*, her sweet ruthless Bud, the unfathomable reason she hadn't been able to go to Paris to have her child. He was her love. And as he filled her, she dissolved into a turbulent pool, gasping his name over and over as the ripples shook her.

He sprawled on top of her, his mouth sobbing against her cheek.

After a few minutes she shifted as if to get up. He gripped her shoulders. "She's all right," he said. "Listen."

Their heads tilted. In the next room the difficult breathing came with the regularity of sleep. Amélie relaxed. Bud shifted his weight to his elbow.

"There's something I need to explain," he said.

"Bud, why? I saw you with Tessa."

"I must say it. Until now I've been so vicious about her. That business with 3 Vee, she's no part of it. Yet I blamed it all on her, as if she had ruined what was between you and me. Every time I looked at her, I saw 3 Vee. Then, when I was working on the locomotive, I began thinking about the time I'd spent with her. Nothing to do with 3 Vee. Just me and her. And the things we'd done together. You know, the walks, her quiet games. Ordinary things, yet they were very sweet. She accepted me so completely. It was if she knew we belonged together."

"From the first she wanted to be with you."

"Remember? She gave me her doll."

"Yes, Dodo."

"You said she's given me her heart."

"That, too."

"What if I tell you she has mine?"

"Darling, seeing you with her has already told me that."

"You're sure?"

Amélie was smiling. "I know you quite well." She touched his nose.

"Tessa's mine," Bud said. "She's my little girl, and as long as I live, there's only one way I'll think of her. As mine." In his voice there was the same low, embarrassed sincerity as when he had repeated his marriage vows.

"Bud, you do not have to—"

"I *do* have to. Amélie, I'm so very ashamed. The way I acted disgusts me. I'd apologize, but there's no way to apologize for such ugliness." He paused. "I would rather be dead than deny I'm her father."

Horse's hooves sounded in the quiet darkness, and they both looked toward the window.

Bud spoke again. "We'll nurse her together. I'll have my valise sent over from the hotel."

Amélie nodded.

"Thank you," he said.

"For what?"

"For not saying thank you."

"Bud, darling Bud." She kissed his hand and saw red, unhealed burns. "What happened?"

"I've been in San Bernardino, building a scale model of the locomotive."

Kissing the hand again, she said, "The hands of an oil magnate." She was smiling.

"You told me you didn't have admirers lurking about," he said. "What's Dr. Marsh?"

"An admirer."

"He wanted me to convince you to marry him."

"But you informed him that I had a husband?"

"I did. And he told me that you called out my name when you were having our Tessa."

They held one another with the old tenderness until a nasal whimper, like a cold draft, came into the bedroom. Amélie jerked.

Bud shook his head. "This is my tour," he announced, standing and straightening his clothes.

Tessa was sleeping. He went into the kitchen and fed the fire with sticks of wood. The wash began to boil more vigorously. He returned to Tessa's room and sat in the rocking chair. It creaked and the child stirred, whimpering again. Bud eased his weight cautiously forward to watch her. Tessa rubbed her flushed cheek on the pillow and was still. Her tormented little gasps were the only sound in the room. Unconsciously, Bud slowed his breathing to her rhythm as if this breath could help her.

His life had become completely entangled with the life of this little girl who looked at him so trustingly with eyes of his own deep blue, a little girl who shared with him her small pleasures and treasures. The sweat-soaked nightmare in the roundhouse had been the last time his subconscious had wished her harm. He could not forget that he had yearned to have her banished, crushed, destroyed. And now in this room that smelled of carbolic and vinegar, the memory terrified him. He looked at the baby in the stranglehold of diphtheria, thinking: Dear God, it's all my fault. I wished this on her.

And then he obliterated the thought.

A stubborn, determined man, he loved with these same two qualities. His affections were never paradoxical. He loved this small, black-haired García. By God, she *was* his daughter.

It sometimes happens that a bullet enters the brain and rests amid surrounding tissue that nature manages to heal. Such a bullet is impossible to probe, and no good surgeon tries. Thus were Bud's doubts buried, and he would never again look upon the enigma of Tessa's conception. He loved her. To bring forth from his brain his own shameful malevolence toward the child would surely kill him.

·9·

Amélie lifted Tessa from her crib and sat with her in the new straightback chair Bud had bought. The child struggled.

"No! Mama, no!" The protest was shrill, nasal.

"It will be over in a minute, Tessa."

"No! No!" All trust was gone from Tessa's eyes.

In the two days since Bud's arrival, the diphtheria had taken its most virulent course. The mucus had thickened, and now it was beginning to clog her throat and nasal passages with a false membrane the consistency of a lightly boiled egg. The fear that tormented Amélie and Bud was that the membrane would continue to grow and harden. If the disease didn't relax its hold, the membrane would reach Tessa's larynx and strangle her.

Bud, with his sleeves rolled up, stood at a table lined with medical jars and bottles. From a metal box he took a sponge-tipped stick. He unscrewed a jar labeled nitrate of silver, dipping in the tiny sponge.

Tessa, watching, squirmed yet more violently. Amélie tried to grasp her hands.

"It's procedure to tie the little hands behind the back, so." Nurse Lenze, massive in her starched blue-and-white uniform, had come to stand at the door.

Nurse Lenze had trained at the Berlin Hospital for Communicable Diseases, and under the fluted cap of that institution, her face was red and her features coarse. Despite her ferocious appearance, she was a kind woman. Amélie and Bud wished to tend the baby themselves, yet they needed someone to do the other work. Only a nurse would come into a quarantined house. Nurse Lenze bore her employers no ill will that her highly trained services were used for cooking, washing, cleaning.

"We've terrified her enough without tying her up," Bud said.

"She's a good, trusting baby," Nurse Lenze replied, her eyes moist with sadness. She had seen many such cases. None had survived.

Amélie managed to capture both of Tessa's flailing hands and held them in one of hers. She glanced up at Bud. He took his place at her side, behind Tessa's head.

"Now," he ordered.

With a spoon handle, Amélie pushed down Tessa's coated tongue. An odor of decay came from the baby's mouth. Quickly and gently Bud touched nitrate of silver to spots deep in her throat.

Tessa gagged, spewing out thick strings of phlegm. Amélie held a bowl to her mouth, then passed a damp, soothing towel over the fever-heated face. Tessa, limp, clung to her mother.

Bud and Amélie exchanged glances.

"The iodine?" Amélie murmured.

Bud sighed.

"Must we now?" she asked.

"It's been over four hours."

"Tessa," Amélie said, "you will have your ice cream right after your medicine."

"No!" Tessa was weeping again.

Nurse Lenze, at the table, used a dropper to measure tincture of iodine into a mug filled with lukewarm water. Bud picked up the mug and carried Tessa to the window. Dark clouds pebbled the afternoon. "Do you want to hear more about the princess?" he asked.

Her arms tightened around his neck.

"I know, darling," he said. "But listen about the princess. She was very sick, and the king and queen didn't want her to stay sick, so they had to give her medicine. They hated to hurt the princess because she was good and clever and beautiful and they loved her very much. But they had to do it so she could get well and go outside. And the princess understood, so she drank everything all up. That's how brave she was. And then one day . . ."

Tessa, who had stopped crying, looked expectantly at him.

"The princess was all well. And everybody in the kingdom gathered outside the palace, cheering because they knew how brave she'd been. And here's the clever part. All the dogs in the kingdom marched by, like soldiers, barking a salute as they passed because they knew the princess had drunk all her medicine."

Tessa accepted the mug. She sipped warily, then drank. The other medicines forced on her were far worse. Sulphate of quinine, bitter, hurt her throat. Salicylic acid nauseated her, causing her to retch long afterward.

Amélie took her from Bud's arms and laid her in the crib. She stripped off her nightgown and began to sponge her.

Nurse Lenze brought in a flannel stomacher soaked in eggnog. Tessa barely ate, and this nourishment was meant to penetrate her skin. By the time the child was dressed again and had eaten a few demitasse spoons of ice cream, she felt better. She wanted to get out of the crib and play. Playing was forbidden. Dr. Marsh had been adamant. Amélie and Bud held her, taking turns singing. Nurse Lenze brought in three large croup kettles and the odor of vinegar filled the room. Moisture formed on walls, dripping down the paint like acid tears.

Finally Tessa slept.

Bud and Amélie went into the parlor and Nurse Lenze brought them coffee and slices of pound cake. Bud ate hungrily. Amélie sipped creamed coffee.

Distant thunder roared beyond the Berkeley hills, which were gentler and greener than those surrounding Los Angeles. Amélie and Bud's heads leaned toward Tessa's room. There was no sound beyond her tortuous breathing. Thunder tramped closer, lightning veined the sky, and then the wind began to toss the weeds and molting eucalyptus in the yard. Rain pelted the windows.

Bud stirred uneasily. To an Angeleno unused to summer rain, the downpour seemed ominous.

Amélie gazed out the uncurtained window. Damn You, she thought, cursing a God she didn't believe in. Despite her weariness and terror, she knew her curse was irrational. Nor was she able to pray for Tessa. How could she expect favors from a God who either didn't exist or, existing, carelessly tortured His own creatures? She glanced at her husband. Bud was the one who had come here to help her. Bud, the one who never slept. Through the night hours it was he who tended Tessa, sang to her, changed her, fed and guarded her. Bud is the one I should pray to.

Yes, she thought. I will pray to Bud. And if, by some chance, she is not his, then I will offer him a pledge. From this time on, Tessa belongs to him. Nothing will make me say otherwise.

The rain had lessened and it was growing dark when the child stirred. Bud took out his watch. "It's time," he said.

"The chlorate?"

Sighing, he nodded. "She's going to hate us."

"Dr. Marsh says it is the only way to stop the membrane from forming."

"Sometimes I wonder if he knows what the hell he's talking about."

"I do, too. Bud, it is our only hope. If the membrane spreads— if..."

Tessa struggled while Amélie held her mouth open. Bud, using a rubber tube, blew chlorate of potassium into her throat. The small body arched in protest. When he finished, Tessa collapsed, gagging feebly, crying in her misery.

Bud and Amélie didn't speak. Both had seen that in a few hours the membrane had whitened. It was growing harder.

· IO ·

The cloth-draped lamp threw elongated shadows. It was the predawn hush, when crickets and frogs are silent, when human resistance and energy are at their lowest ebb and death stalks.

Bud and Amélie watched Tessa sleep. Her small chest heaved. Her breath came in fetid, coughing gasps. She stirred, pulling at the poultice around her throat. Her eyes opened in fear. Amélie picked her up, undid the flannel and began to walk with her, stroking the heaving back. Bud went to the kitchen where Nurse Lenze always kept a pot of water boiling on the stove. He returned with another croup kettle and took the child.

Suddenly her body stiffened. A paroxysm shook her. Her neck arched. Her eyes rolled back until only the whites were visible. Her arms flailed like broken wings.

Bud and Amélie glanced briefly at one another. No discussion was necessary. This was the final phase. This was what had killed his younger sister. The membrane in Tessa's throat had closed.

Amélie ran into the parlor where Nurse Lenze, fully dressed, lay on a new cot. Amélie shook the woman awake.

"Nurse, nurse!"

The nurse jerked instantly to sitting position. "It's happened?"

"Yes. Get Dr. Marsh. Hurry!"

Quicker than seemed possible for one of her bulk, the nurse had stamped into her boots, pulled on her uniform cape, and slipped out into the darkness.

When Amélie returned to the child's room, Bud was sitting with Tessa on his lap, his mouth pressed to hers. He was trying to suck the membrane from her throat.

Amélie pulled the towel from the lamp.

"Bud! She has gone blue!"

Bud raised his head from the struggling, gasping child.

"Dr. Marsh cannot possibly be here in less than fifteen minutes. Bud, oh my God! In fifteen minutes she will be dead. Bud?"

He understood her unspoken question. Diphtheria's last desperate gamble: cutting into the child's windpipe. As they stared at one another, the harsh gurgling in Tessa's chest isolated them from past and future. There was only this one moment of decision. My sister died, he thought. Yet none survive without the gamble. "Get my razor," he said quietly.

She ran into the bathroom while Bud carried Tessa into the kitchen and put her down on the scrubbed table. He had difficulty holding the convulsing child. She had the slippery strength of a fish thrown onto land. She, too, had been torn from her element. Unable to take in air, she was drowning in her own lung fluids.

Amélie extended his razor box.

"Take one," he ordered. "Hold the blade under boiling water."

She went to the stove and lifted the lid on the kettle of boiling water. Steam burst out. Thrusting the razor into the water, she didn't flinch or appear to notice that steam was turning her hand crimson.

"Enough," Bud commanded.

She shook the blade free of water.

He closed his eyes. Unlike Amélie, he believed in God, not the ornate Catholic God at the Plaza church where his mother had worshiped, but Hendryk's unpretentious, businesslike Episcopal God. No ritual prayers for Bud. He made a simple request that God give him concentration, skill, strength. His mouth drew into a line, a muscle jumped at his temple. Opening his eyes, he looked into the bewildered terror of Tessa's face.

Amélie gave him the razor. He took it by the ivory handle and stared down at the swollen arch of Tessa's neck. Keep a steady hand, he thought, remembering the times he'd skinned animals when hunting. He felt the narrow cylinder of her windpipe with his fingers. "Press up her chin," he said. "Hold her still."

He brought down the blade. His hand was absolutely sure. Then, holding the incision open with his fingers, he quickly inserted a bit of dark rubber tubing.

Dr. Marsh, his coat buttoned across his belly, the worn flannel of his nightshirt hanging below black broadcloth, stood at the kitchen table examining Tessa. The baby lay inert, eyes closed. She was immobilized by post-convulsive stupor.

"You should give up the oil business, Bud, and become a surgeon. I couldn't have done a better job myself."

Bud and Dr. Marsh had met several times over the last few days. And Bud had come to admire the man's professional competence. Yet at this moment he could take no pleasure in the compliment.

"Will she be all right, then?" Amélie asked.

"She's alive and breathing," Dr. Marsh said. Nurse Lenze and I will take over. Bud, go have yourself a drink."

"I don't need one," Bud said. His tension was beginning to ease. He felt light-headed and pleased with himself.

"Then go put some liniment on your wife's hand. And close the door after you."

Bud found a jar of cocoa butter and went into the parlor. Handing Amélie the jar, he said, "We'll get her home as soon as possible."

Amélie nodded.

"We did it. She's going to be all right," he said.

Amélie, lips white, said nothing. She was still gazing into the dark void of death. Bud was positive he had just saved Tessa's life. In his cockiness, he was irritated by Amélie's doubts, her continuing anguish.

"She's going to be fine," he said. "Put that on your hand."

"I cannot open it," she said, handing him the jar. She was shaking.

He unscrewed the lid and smeared the thick ointment on her scalded hand. Amélie spread her fingers carefully. Only now did she begin to feel the pain.

"Come on, Amélie, it's over and she's—" He stopped in midsentence.

His stomach clenched in a spasm. Gasping aloud, he ran into the bathroom and sat there streaming. A child has a very small throat. He had no medical knowledge. None. I could have killed her, he thought.

Shivering, sweating, his intestines voiding, he leaned against the wall, too weak to sit up.

· I I ·

Six months later, on a crisp, clear February morning in 1895, a crowd waited outside the Arcadia depot. The entrances were draped in red, white, and blue bunting, flags whipped in the breeze, and people were waiting, watching expectantly.

Los Angeles was taking its routine delight in a fiesta of progress.

Inside the depot, a uniformed brass band stood in ragged formation. Trestle tables had been set with glasses and champagne. The three rows of seats arranged along a platform bordering the railroad tracks were filled. Hendryk, among the first to arrive, sat in the center of the front row, stout and dignified in his frock coat and silk hat, beaming with stern, paternal pride whenever a friend leaned over to congratulate him.

The little girl perched at his side handed him a large toy dog. Shyly, she said, "Here, Grampa."

"Thank you, Tessa."

"*De nada*," the child replied.

It was a phrase she had learned from Bud, but Hendryk believed that his granddaughter could speak Spanish. He gazed fondly at the child. How like her grandmother she is, he thought. What a shame Mrs. Van Vliet never saw her. If only these modern young couples could properly manage their lives, as we managed ours. Well, at least Bud has them here now. If he would come back to the business and settle down. If only he would return to his senses. Hendryk steadfastly refused to notice that his wish was a direct contradiction of his pleasure at Bud's success with Paloverde Oil.

Tessa sat very still. The narrow scar on her throat was fading to invisibility. Unlike other mothers who dressed their daughters only in pastels, Amélie selected the vivid shades becoming to her child. Tessa wore a crimson bonnet and coat that accentuated her black curls and rosy cheeks.

Hendryk's maimed hand stroked her plush dog. He was thinking of Tessa and Amélie's absence. Neither Bud nor Amélie had explained it to him—or to anyone else. At first Angelenos had been wildly curious. Then, typically, the town had lost interest, formulating its own myth: Amélie had gone home to France to bear her first child in the family castle.

Bud and Amélie moved to greet a newcomer. A hush fell over the crowd. For this depot, and hundreds of others across the land, all painted the same drab mustard, in effect belonged to this one old man. "Great God!" whispered Chaw Di Franco to his wife, Lucetta. "It's Collis P. Huntington!"

The assemblage of Bud's friends, old and new, in and out of the oil business, his gringo-diluted Californio kin, the grocery Van Vliets, all turned covertly to watch their host and hostess lead Collis P. Huntington to a front-row seat.

Hendryk's buttery face wobbled as he stood. The Dutchman's staunch belief in democracy was battling with awe. Collis P. Huntington. His old enemy, the great power who had nearly destroyed him, a railroad baron more powerful than most kings! Hendryk had never thought he would meet the man. And here he was, Bud's guest, chatting affably with his son. At Bud's introduction, Hendryk thrust out his right hand. "Welcome to Los Angeles, Mr. Huntington," he said, the words clipping out with a more pronounced accent.

"Mr. Van Vliet," said Collis P. Huntington. "A big day for your Los Angeles, and for your son."

A faraway sound roused the crowd. There were cries of "Here she comes!" The band conductor raised his baton, and brasses blared "She'll Be Coming 'Round the Mountain."

Everyone, including the railroad magnate, watched the tracks glittering beyond the depot. The platform quaked as a locomotive roared into view. Palm fronds and branches of citrus blossoms decorated the cab and cowcatcher. Flags whipped at the smokestack. Across the boiler was painted *PALOVERDE OIL—123*.

There were no passenger cars. Bud wanted to be positive that oil could safely fuel a train. His first set of plans, drawn from 3Vee's original conception, had been discarded. The scale model had been modified and modified again. Three months of work and the rusty old locomotive had puffed out of San Bernardino, after a scant couple of miles limping to a stop. The railroad men had loaded her with coal to get her back. Bud and his mechanics had tested more burners. This, the successful one, used a flat nozzle that sprayed oil over a wide area.

The locomotive, its greenery aquiver, shuddered to a final halt in the depot. The engineer raised his cap, and the spectators cheered the first train ever successfully powered by petroleum.

Bud had lifted Tessa to his shoulders so she could see over the crowd. Her hands clasped his forehead, her plump, black-stockinged legs hung down over his chest as Bud's friends gathered around offering congratulations. Afraid that the child might lose her balance, Nurse Lenze approached.

"I want to be with you, Daddy," Tessa whispered in Bud's ear. Her voice was soft and low-pitched for a child. Bud swung her down, holding her in his arms. "I want to be with you too, Tessa. Come on, let's say hello to the engineer."

The child stared apprehensively at the still-smoking behemoth. "No," she whispered.

"You don't want to come with me?"

She clung to him. "Yes," she said louder.

Clasping the little girl to his chest, Bud climbed up easily into the cab. The engineer showed Tessa the controls. Bud put her hands on a lever, holding his own over hers.

"I'm driving the train," she said proudly.

"You sure are," Bud said.

At the sight of Bud holding his child up to the mammoth locomotive's controls, his friends and kin, drinking his champagne, smiled and waved. Collis P. Huntington, however, was a man of Spartan coldness. He didn't smile. It was impolitic of Bud not to have first shown his triumph to his guest of honor. Amélie knew of the bargain Bud had struck with Huntington. Sensing his displeasure, she said, "There you see my husband with his true love."

Looking at the young woman he had first known as a charming little girl, Huntington said, "You mean, the child?"

"Tessa had diphtheria," Amélie explained. "It has left her with recurrent fevers."

"That is very sad."

"Not really. We believed she would die. He saved her from strangling by cutting into her windpipe. How many fathers would have the strength to perform such an operation?"

"Very few."

"The worst after-effect of the disease is invisible, I am afraid. Our daughter, before, was an open and fearless child. Now she has become shy. Bud took her into the cab to show her there is nothing to be afraid of. We are trying to erase the memory of fear."

"Your father, without any excuse, would have done the same with you," Huntington said. His smile was warm. Colonel Deane might have been the dearest friend of his youth. The Deane Letters might never have revealed his chicanery to the world. Amélie was startled by his words, but she decided that yet one more of the attributes of power must be the ability to forget a grudge.

"Come, Amélie. Let us see how your strong and determined Mr. Van Vliet has married his oil industry to my railroad." And taking her arm, he led her to the locomotive that Tessa was pretending to drive.

BOOK 3
The Movies: 1917

*Later people said the movies
came to Los Angeles to escape
the Edison Trust. It wasn't
true. Biograph, Selig, Kalem,
Essanay belonged to the Trust.
We came for the sun. We had
no interior lighting then.
And here the sunshine was
reliable four hundred days a
year.*

JACOPO RIMINI
(Autobiography of Jacopo Rimini)

Paloverde had become Greenwood.

On the ledge where the Van Vliets's secret forebears had given thanks for the earth's fertility, on the site of the razed hacienda, now stood one of Southern California's great houses. Its architecture proved that while Bud might play down his ancestors, calling them unsuccessful cattle farmers, at heart he remained a García. Greenwood, the first of the Mission Revival style, was an exuberant version of Paloverde. The red tiles of the vast roof were a hundred years old and had been imported from Tampico, Mexico. The exterior stucco, rough-scored to resemble adobe, was painted blazing white. Unlike the original, however, the house had windows facing outward. Those on the second floor were fronted with charmingly irregular verandas that overlooked the terraced gardens, a swimming pool, tennis courts, the dark mysterious cypresses, the sycamore and copper beeches where wren tits nested.

Like Paloverde, Los Angeles had been transformed.

More than 450,000 people lived within its limits. The city's thriving port berthed ships, including Paloverde Oil tankers, that carried supplies through the recently opened Panama Canal to a Europe ravaged by war. The city entertained itself with fourteen musical clubs, eight German lieder societies (which would soon vanish), and more than a hundred halls that projected the jumpy new motion pictures. Henry Huntington's big Red Cars, the finest electrical railway system in the world, webbed through sweet-odored citrus groves and flat beanfields, connecting the suburban small towns to the monolithic blocks of downtown. The sprawl was a necessity. Each Southern Californian wished his own place with his own garden where his transplanted geraniums and his children could run wild. Lush maroon bougainvillea vines prettified even the meanest shacks.

Like all terrestrial paradises, the city was a trifle insular. The war was a remote reality. The Van Vliets, Bud, Amélie, and their only daughter, Tessa, were doing what they could for their relatives in France. 3Vee and Utah, who still lived in the Bakersfield boarding house, had three sons of military age, and already the oldest, Charley Kingdon, had enlisted with the *Légion d'Étrangers*. The fraternal quarrel still continued, so this was unknown at Greenwood.

Tessa had grown up at Greenwood, and sometimes when the wind swept the flanks of the hills, she thought she could hear a whisper telling her that this was García territory. This inaudible voice, rather than frightening her, gave her a sense of belonging. She did not know that there were other whispers, other ghosts, that lingered in this place.

CHAPTER 15

· I ·

The Wilcox place, about seven miles west of Los Angeles, had been wooded with toyon, a red-berried bush that resembled holly to Wilcox, a Kansas prohibitionist. Long before the subdividers came, the toyon had been cut to make way for crops and citrus groves, but the name the Kansan had given his ranch stuck.

Hollywood.

Hollywood attracted sedate teetotalers. The place was dry—the Hollywood Hotel didn't even have a liquor license. Then, upon righteous Hollywood a blight descended. Glove salesmen, out-of-work vaudevillians, actors who had hit bottom, furriers, clothiers, cowboys, junkmen, actresses (at that time a local euphemism for prostitutes) raced up and down quiet streets in their tin lizzies followed by cranking cameras strapped to other automobiles. Whooping and shooting guns, they raced horses across peaceful umber hills, they set up their cameras at Henry Huntington's Red Car stops, they trampled on housewives' geraniums.

The locals fought. Landlords nailed up signs: NO DOGS OR ACTORS. Shops refused credit. The nickelodeon people were shunned by everyone. But then Blondeau's Tavern failed and one group of invaders took it over as a "studio." It proved to be a beachhead. Other "producers" rented nearby barns, the ragtag infiltrated poorer rooming houses. Most of the suburb remained aloof, but by then its name was *hors de combat*.

Hollywood no longer signified a geographic entity. It had become the accepted term for moviemaking no matter where in Los Angeles it took place. Hollywood meant an industry as crudely alluring as the face of sin—and as profitable. Less than a decade in Southern California, the movies by 1917 had become the area's major industry.

· 2 ·

On the first Tuesday in May of that year, Tessa Van Vliet drove to the end of a row of dusty cars that lined a street just south of Hollywood Boulevard, halting in the shade cast by orange trees. She wanted to protect the Mercer's Pantasote top from afternoon sun.

Carefully tucking a thick manila envelope under her arm, she picked her way over dusty ruts and ridges. Her red pongee silk suit had a peplum flaring over a hobble skirt that exposed four inches of narrow black-stockinged ankle. Her slender feet were shod in hand-made kid. Though tall, she had Amélie's delicate bone structure. Otherwise, with her oval face and black hair, she was a García—except, of course, for the color of her eyes. They were dark blue.

She came to a fenced-off barn. At an improvised gate, a man with sleeves rolled up to show sun-reddened arms looked at her. "Well?" he demanded.

"I'm Tessa Van Vliet," she murmured.

"Nobody gets in here."

"I'm expected." Her low, soft voice hesitated. "At least I think I am."

"Are you or aren't you?"

"Tessa Van Vliet." She forced her voice louder. "Didn't Mr. Rimini say anything about me?"

"Van Vliet?" The man consulted a clipboard. "Yeah." Without apology, he opened the gate.

Inside the barn, Tessa gazed around.

This was a movie studio. The major part of the barn roof had been removed and replaced by a Venetian-blind arrangement of muslin strips. Ortho film was too slow to shoot interiors, yet too much sun meant overexposure. These cloth diffusers solved the problem. Scenes—a castle wall, a bedchamber, gardens—were painted on canvas backdrops, and in front of them stood minimal props, a bed, a tree. Two actors in ill-fitting thirteenth-century attire, their faces sweating into white paint, lugged Cooper-Hewitt floor lights. A man in a turned-around cap squinted into a Bell & Howell camera. A plump, costumed actress, peering at a mirror nailed to the barn wall, painted a dark mouth onto her white make-up.

Tessa smiled. These were the actors and sets for a one-reeler that ran twelve minutes. She had written the story.

The cameraman turned to stare at her. Hastily, Tessa crossed to a row of cubicles on the far side of the barn. Here floorboards were bleached lighter, a memory of horse urine. The stalls had been boarded off into offices. She knocked at a plywood door.

"Who is it?" a man's voice shouted.

"It's Tessa Van Vliet, Mr. Rimini."

"What?"

She called out her name.

"Oh. Tessa. Come in, come in."

Behind a kitchen table that doubled as a desk sat a man in knee boots and a tweed jacket too tight across his barrel chest. Under thick, brownish hair in need of trimming, his kind, humorous face had the full-blooded health of a prosperous butcher. In New York he had been just that, a butcher. Jake Rynzberg. He wasn't ashamed of his name. His new business, however, sold illusion. Jacopo Rimini had a better ring to it. His films (one- and two-reelers) began impressively with A RIMINI PRODUCTION.

The partition around his office reached up only nine feet. A hammering from the barn rang loudly. Rimini held out a hand for Tessa's envelope.

"It needs more work," she said.

"That's for you to think, me to say." His eyes, the color of creamed coffee, twinkled.

She surrendered the envelope. He ruffled pages, scanning. Finally he said, "The bit where he helps her on with her shoe, that's good. I need it next week, so get it into shooting order."

He held out the treatment. Tessa didn't take it.

"You're worrying about the price?" he asked.

"Price?"

"Last time you didn't worry, so we'll make it the same."

"Mr. Rimini—"

"Five dollars extra," he interrupted. "Buy yourself a new string of beads."

Tessa had undone her suit jacket. She wore her pearls—her parents' twenty-first birthday gift. It never entered Rimini's mind that the long rope could be cultured, much less real. Pearls that size and luster were worth a fortune. And Tessa's name meant nothing to him. Los Angeles and Hollywood had the symbiotic relationship of fleas to a dog. The fleas, the movie folk, played out their vendettas and dramas unaware of their host; Los Angeles went about its normal business, occasionally scratching. While it was true that Bud hired men to keep the Van Vliet name out of newspapers and magazines, the more knowledgeable Angelenos were aware that Van Vliet was to Paloverde Oil what Rockefeller was to Standard. Hollywood—newcomers absorbed in themselves—didn't know that another name stood behind the PALOVERDE OIL signs on tile-roofed service stations.

Rimini glanced across the table at the hesitant young woman. He was thinking: she writes the kind of property that Griffith and De Mille pay real money for. What if she turns out to be more of a pusher than she looks?

"Five dollars extra, and not another cent—that means ten dollars." At this he smiled.

"It's not worth any more than the last story," she said.

Bewildered, he looked at her. "So?"

Tessa swallowed, and the narrow pale scar on her throat was visible above her creamy silk blouse. "I heard you're going to make a feature-length movie," she blurted.

He drew a sharp breath. "You're a spy," he said roughly. In the movie business secrecy was everything. Whoever got a story idea to the exhibitors first, sold it. He planned a full-length movie, his first, about Samson and Delilah. "Who told you I'm making a feature?" he demanded.

"A friend. Mr. Rimini, I have a story. It's good . . . I think."

"*If* I make a feature, I'll hire an author, not a writer. Somebody with a Broadway play." He pushed the treatment toward her. A dismissal.

Though shyly hesitant, Tessa at times could show the Van Vliet determination. She clutched the gold chain of her purse and didn't move. In the barn hammering rang louder.

"Well?" Rimini muttered. "So what's the idea?"

"An aviator in France—"

Interrupting, he held up a hand. "Stop right there. Keep on with these nice little stories. Chivalry's what they buy tickets to see."

"But—"

"War movies, they lose money. Even if I was making a war movie, I'd never do it." His lapse, as usual, was intentional, a consolatory bit of humor.

"Mr. Rimini," Tessa said in a rush of words. "Aviation *is* chivalry. You know everybody thinks of aviators as heroes. Now they're battling in the sky, and their aeroplanes are like shining armor. I want to show the parallel. You know, like Mr. Griffith and Mr. De Mille do in their movies. The historical episode shown with the modern. A knight in the Third Crusade, and my aviator."

At the names of his successful rivals, Rimini's round, twinkling eyes had narrowed into lines of shrewdness. "Not bad," he said. "I'll talk to my author."

"But this is *my* story," she said. "I'll write it out, and you can look."

"No money," he said. "But I'll look."

"Thank you," she said.

"Now. I'm wasting sunlight." He picked up a megaphone, preceding her into the barn, shouting into the megaphone, "Stop the hammering! Turn on the damn arc lights! Where's Joe? What's that son of a bitch actor doing on my time?"

Rimini ignored Tessa. But as he shouted, he was thinking about her. The war movie idea didn't really interest him. But how had she known about the feature? He had enough saved in the Security Bank on Spring Street to make a feature. Who had told her?

· 3 ·

Lya Bell had told her. The two young women had arranged to meet at the Hollywood Hotel so Tessa could report on Rimini's reaction. As Tessa drove along Hollywood Boulevard, she was in a euphoric fantasy. He's going to look at *The Aviator*, she thought, leaping in her mind from Rimini's purchase of her story to the completed film. She did not consider her own success. Tessa lacked that kind of ambition. Her exhilaration was a return to a childhood game, a game she had not wanted to play. Yet she knew as soon as she stopped playing, she would be thrust back into a world in which she felt inadequate.

Diphtheria had bequeathed Tessa bouts of fever that mystified doctors. They looked in her throat and ears; they drew blood from her arm. They could find no clue. In her darkened sickroom she invented her own world. On her white silk counterpane realms flourished, and in these imaginary lands generosity and kindness and nobility were the rule.

She had been educated by governesses and tutors. She had not learned the Machiavellian ways of a girls' school nor acquired the thick skin essential to the art of making friends. Yet she was wise enough to recognize her childhood as uniquely happy. She had her stories. She had her parents. With Bud, especially, her blue eyes took on a transparent sheen. As a little girl her greatest pleasure had been to perform some small task for him, handing him his rolled newspaper or carefully lighting a safety match for his cigar.

As she grew older, the fevers came less often. Yet she remained at home, close to her parents. And it was because Bud so obviously smiled on Paul Schott that Tessa became engaged. Paul Schott, a large-boned, brisk young executive in Paloverde Oil's acquisitions department, was attractive to women. And because, much as she tried, Tessa couldn't love him, she felt yet another part missing in herself. After six months of indecision, she had returned his square-cut diamond. Thwarted, Paul Schott proceeded to tell her that she was fatally dull, and it was Paloverde Oil he wanted, not her. The words squirmed out of his bitter mouth. She pitied him for trading his ambitions for life with a fatally dull woman. But she was horrified with herself—oh, she despised herself! How could she have been willing to settle, gratuitously, for a man she didn't love?

She had never gone to movies. But now she began haunting the dark new theaters. *Birth of a Nation. Judith of Bethulia. Squaw Man. Romance of the Redwood. Joan of Arc.* The flickering screen engrossed her. One day she had seen in *Motion Picture Herald* that producers needed story ideas. The jump from fantasy to actually creating story lines came easily to her, and she had approached Jacopo Rimini. Her family friends looked down on the film industry as a bastard, a mingling of carnival and peep show. But Amélie and Bud, happy that Tessa finally was recovering from Paul Schott, encouraged her writing.

Tessa bumped across trolley lines, steering around a big Red Car that was taking on a passenger. Here at Vine Street, Hollywood started, and the boulevard became a straggle of small houses, vacant lots, a cafeteria, the Japanese store, a café shaped like a hot dog, a library, a gift shop, a grocery. Where Hollywood Boulevard crossed Highland, all four corners had been built on, and on the northwest corner, behind shade trees and a tall pole that fluttered the Bear Flag and Old Glory, sprawled the Hollywood Hotel.

New York producers and directors stayed at the Hollywood Hotel, and these luminaries drew the moths—hopeful actors and actresses. Those unable to afford the hotel rates lived in cheap rooms nearby, strolling over to display themselves. A group of these handsome young people was gathered at one end of the veranda.

As Tessa parked her car under a pepper tree, Lya Bell moved from the group. She waved. At first glance, Lya Bell was extremely pretty, with a striking resemblance to Mary Pickford that was deliberately enhanced by a similar arrangement of soft yellow ringlets.

Lya called, "Tessa! Yoo-hoo, Tessa." Her voice was shrill, with a North Carolina accent.

Tessa, smiling, hurried up the veranda steps.

Lya grasped her hand, as if hauling her aboard. "Come over here. Quick! I'm just dying to hear what-all happened."

Tea dancing was starting, a regular afternoon attraction at the hotel. Through open windows came a gramophone's tinny rendition of "Rose of No Man's Land," and the group at the end of the veranda moved inside. Tessa and Lya sank into recently vacated wicker chairs.

"I asked him," Tessa said.

"You didn't!"

Tessa nodded. "I waited until after he'd accepted the treatment, then I asked. He wanted to know how I'd heard he was making a feature—"

"You didn't tell him!" Lya cried, alarmed.

"Of course not. He was angry, but when I convinced him I wasn't a spy, he listened. Lya, I never thought I'd be able to get out the words."

"Oh honey. You! I declare, you're so innocent you probably let him know you were dying."

"All I know is he agreed to look at a treatment. Not to count on anything, but he'd look." Tessa's excitement faded. "He said he doesn't like aviation stories because they're about war."

"War movies don't make money." Lya's small mouth pulled forward in a knowing manner. "What you should have done is tell him that Mr. Lasky or Mr. Zukor had asked you to write an aviation story."

"I never thought of that. But I did think he'd be more interested if I made it into one of those films with ancient and modern episodes."

"Like Cecil B. De Mille does. That was clever. I bet he does film it. Tessa, you know the farm girl in the story. Don't you see her as a little blond thing?"

"Exactly."

"Good."

"But she needs more scenes," Tessa said.

"I'll insist you write all my scripts when I'm a star."

They were laughing at themselves. Yet in the humor there was a communion of hopes. And when they fell silent, Tessa's eyes were shining and Lya's head moved in time with the music. Under soft blond ringlets, her green earrings swung.

Lya Bell, born Leah Belinda Sloper, daughter of a Raleigh postal clerk, had a child's body, flat-chested and hipless, slightly too small for her head. Her features were dainty, her large gray eyes wide-set. Her girlish prettiness camouflaged driving ambition. Her mind had few facets and these were welded into her desire to be a movie star. To get a part in a Jacopo Rimini one-reel comedy, she had made love to him sitting on his lap in the horse-odored office. Rimini discovered, as others had, that the movie camera was cruel to Lya Bell. It bleached out her eyes, and her jerky repertory of pouts, glances, smiles made her look like a pecking chicken. Rimini didn't intend to cast her again. Still, he enjoyed her amatory skills. So he had hinted about the feature film. She had passed on the information to Tessa without a hope of personal gain. For Lya gave as the indolent do, easily. Other than her ambition, the emotions behind her sweet face were sluggish.

Tessa and Lya always met at the Hollywood Hotel. Tessa drove the Mercer and real silk hosiery clung to her slender ankles, so Lya knew her friend was well off. She had no idea of Tessa's wealth. Had she known, it wouldn't have mattered. Lya didn't envy money—unless it was money accompanied by movie fame.

The record changed.

"Tessa, hon," Lya said. "Look over there. Isn't that Billie Bitzer?"

Tessa glanced at a short man entering the lobby. "Who?"

"Billie Bitzer is D. W. Griffith's cameraman." Lya rose, fluffing her hair. "Let's see if I can make him notice me." She winked and disappeared with tiny steps into the lobby.

Tessa sat back in the wicker chair thinking about *The Aviator*. Whatever her reasons for writing, she was sincere about it. She knew nothing of flying or war, but she had spent the summers of 1912 and 1913 visiting her grandmother in France. Her aviator was a French ace, tall, with sleek black hair and deep-set brooding eyes.

"Do we know one another?" asked the tall young man with sleek black hair and deep-set dark eyes.

·4·

Three empty wicker chairs separated them.

He wore shabby gray flannels and his left leg was thrust out, resting on a wicker stool. His pose was not relaxed. The tension about him was alarming. Yet because he was a young man, the tension was attractive. The tautly fleshed face was as pale as a convalescent's. His black eyebrows were raised questioningly at her.

She flushed, realizing that she had been seeing him as her aviator. "I ... I don't think so ..."

"The way you were looking at me, I figured we were old friends," he said. His smile mocked her.

"I was staring. I'm sorry ... rude."

"Not rude," he said. "An invitation."

He used both hands to lower his left leg. He rose and came toward her, the limp emphasizing his vitality. He sat with angry care in the chair Lya had vacated.

"You look like ..." Tessa hesitated. "Well, someone I'm inventing."

"Let's see. You're a writer. And the baby blonde is an actress."

"How did you know?"

"Gypsy blood." Again that mocking smile flickered on the sharply handsome face. "And some eavesdropping."

"Oh."

"Your eyes are blue, not brown. Black hair, blue eyes. A shame color doesn't show on film. You could be a movie star, too."

Tessa knew he was teasing, but she could never respond to that kind of banter. "I'm not pretty enough," she said, her voice low with embarrassment. "Anyway, I'm too tall."

He eyed the slender length of her hobbled crimson skirt. "Why not walk on your knees?"

The record in the lounge had stuck, and voices rose as the needle was changed and the gramophone cranked.

"I'm no good at it," Tessa murmured.

He was rubbing his thigh. He looked up. "What?"

"You said something clever," she explained. "I don't know what to say back."

"It wasn't clever."

His fingers continued to dig into his thigh. She wondered about the limp. It obviously annoyed as well as hurt him. The injury must be new. Was it the reason for his pallor? How had he been hurt?

"Ever sell your stories?" he asked.

"Two. They're both one-reelers. One's being made and the other's finished."

"What are they about?"

"Richard Coeur de Lion . . . well, the first one's more about Saladin."

"Am I Crusader or infidel?"

"You aren't . . . anything. Yes you are."

"Why do you keep correcting yourself? Are you a nervous type?"

With those she knew well—her family, the servants—Tessa was calmly unself-conscious. Strangers made her hesitant, indecisive. And this man, with his faintly sarcastic smile, was far too attractive. He did make her nervous. Heat rose to her face. She said with forced vivacity, "You're an aviator."

He gave a coughing laugh, an unpleasant sound. Her blush deepened.

"*You,*" he said, "are the one with gypsy blood."

"What?"

"I used to fly."

She leaned toward him, her elbows resting on the wicker of the chair arm. "What's flying like? It must be exciting! Don't you feel you're soaring like a bird? When you loop the loop, do you get sick—I mean like seasickness? What makes the aeroplane go up and down? Stay up there? I don't even know the mechanics. Where did you learn—"

"Forget I said that!"

"Please. I need to know. The story's important to me, and I don't know anything."

"Then why the hell are you writing about aviation?" His voice, without a trace of humor, lashed out. His jawline was hard.

She sat deep in the chair. Through the window came music from a cracked record.

> There's a long (click) *long trail awinding* (click)
> *Into the land* (click) *of my dreams*
> *Where* (click) *the nightingales are* (click) *singing* . . .

Of course, Tessa thought. That's how he was injured. Her hands shook, and she clenched them in her lap. "I'm sorry," she said. "So sorry."

> (Click) . . .*moon beams* . . . (click)

"They need extras over at Universal," said Lya's high little voice. She was resting a hand on Tessa's chair.

"Was it Billie Bitzer?" asked the dark young man.

"Why, hello, Mister Man," Lya said, tilting her head with a smile. "No, but it was clever of you, spotting how much they're alike." Her voice turned earnest. "Tessa, if I'm all the way out there in an hour, I've got a job. It's dress extra." Lya, who owned three glittery evening gowns and a white-rabbit cape, qualified as a dress extra. "Be a doll?"

"Of course," Tessa said, on her feet. Suddenly she blurted to the dark young man, "I'll be here tomorrow."

He rose stiff-legged. Polite. Yet not replying.

As the girls went toward the Mercer, Lya inquired, "Anyone?" *Anyone* meant was he in movies.

"No."

"How all did he know about Billie Bitzer then?"

"He was eavesdropping on us."

"Honey, it's no crime. Men do that to girls." Lya paused, musing. "He *could* be somebody. He's got a kind of magnetism, doesn't he? Dark, like Fairbanks."

Tessa, stooping to crank the motor, glanced at the long, shady veranda. The man was gone. "I don't even know his name." Her sigh was drowned by the noise of the motor. "What on earth made me say I'd see him tomorrow?"

"Tomorrow," Lya said. "Let's pray they'll still be shooting tomorrow."

"He won't be here," Tessa said. "Well, I won't, either."

· 5 ·

The following afternoon around two, Tessa pulled up in front of the Hollywood Hotel. Her hands, in kid driving gloves, clasped the wheel, loosened, tightened again. She sat rigid, watching a woman and her little girl emerge from the bank across the street.

"Hello," he said.

Startled, she turned. He wore the same shabby flannels and cardigan as yesterday. The sweater was unbuttoned.

"Hello," she said, surprised at the sharp pounding of her heart.

He leaned his arms on the rolled-down window. "That temper of mine," he said. "Let me explain about it. My mother set about whipping it out of me. Her arm wasn't strong enough for her task. Ergo, *she's* the one who ought to apologize. But she lives in Bakersfield, so I'll have to do it for her. On my mother's behalf—certainly not mine—I'm sorry." He smiled.

"I'm sorry, too," she said. "I shouldn't have asked you so many thoughtless questions."

"Your blond friend hasn't been here today. To my knowledge, anyway."

"She's over in the San Fernando Valley. They're shooting a ballroom scene at Universal Studio." Tessa drew a breath. "The reason I'm here is because I told you I would be."

He patted the Mercer's hood. "Another fascinating bit of information about me. Though born in Los Angeles, my parents took me away when I was but a babe. I've been in town three days and all I've seen is this hotel. I'm a native son in need of a guide."

"I can show you the ostrich farm. Or would you rather see the Pacific?"

"Your answering skills are improving. Half and half. Ostriches are an abomination, a flightless bird. But I'd enjoy seeing the beaches." He circled the car, limping. He winced as he climbed in and sat beside her.

She made a U turn, driving around the Red Car stop. He glanced at the hotel. "You don't belong there," he said. "After three days in town, I'm an expert on the Hollywood species. He—or she—has an innate habit of looking around constantly in order not to miss a trick. The voice must be raised—or lowered to a resonant whisper. That's to signal one's importance. Even before my eavesdropping stint, I could tell you were traveling with the wrong pack."

"How?"

"You have," he said, "a quiet innocence."

"Stupidity, you mean. I should never have asked you about flying."

"It seems to me we decided to keep our mouths the hell shut about that! If you're here for background about aviation, you've got the wrong boy!" His voice cracked with anger.

To Tessa's horror, she began to weep. The tears came without warning.

"Pull over," he said quietly.

She turned right on Highland, swinging over to park in the first block south of Hollywood Boulevard. Here the streetcar lines had spawned a new subdivision of unsold lots. Tessa's tears halted as abruptly as they had started. She kept her handkerchief over her averted face.

"Better?" he asked.

Staring at the empty lots, she nodded.

"You aren't," he said. "I'll talk until you're in condition to drive."

She blew her nose. "It's all right," she said.

"Don't you want to hear my story?" he asked. "I'll bare my soul." His expression changed and as he fingered back his hair, deep lines formed across his pale forehead. "I left home when I was sixteen. I hung around flying fields. I did stunts, aerobatics. I earned my keep by building aeroplanes. You might say flying was my life." He leaned back, gingerly rubbing his left thigh. "There's a kind of music from wires and struts. A wonderful freedom up there. Happiness. I would turn off the engine and hang between heaven and earth. When you're up there, you own everything.

The world, trees, bushes, grass, houses, buildings, ocean belong to you. People salute you because they know you're their ruler. The joy, the joy's so intense you know why you were born." He paused. "Most of the time it's not that damn apparent, is it? As you might have noticed, I loved flying. I even loved it on cold mornings. And greater love hath no man. The air gets colder as you climb. Your hands and feet get frostbite, no matter how many layers you put under your flying togs."

Tessa had turned to watch him. The mockery was gone from his face.

"In 1914 I went over there to join the *Légion d'Étrangers*, not because I adored the French, but because I wanted to fly. We had a couple of rattly Nieuports—much in demand, those Nieuports. They told me I was too tall to be a pilot, but I proved myself by flying rings around the others. So I went on missions." He cocked his hand as though working a machine gun. "I helped coax old Vanderbilt into giving money, and after that we were called the Lafayette Escadrille. Wartime flying's a thing apart. I could never get used to shooting some poor bastard because he flew a Fokker. But if I didn't shoot him, he'd get me. That brings up the matter of danger. When you need to change rounds in a Smith, you have to half stand and hold the stick between your thighs, which makes you a sure target. The others said I had no nerves. I had the nerves all right, but I kept them under control. I loved flying." He took a deep breath.

A horse and surrey clipped by. They watched, and as it turned on Hollywood Boulevard he began speaking again.

"Well, all good things come to an end. They end a little faster in wartime. I was shot down. It seemed to take forever, the fall of that burning aeroplane. I could smell meat cooking—except it wasn't meat, it was my leg. They said it was a miracle I lived. Frankly, a bad miracle. I'm not exactly happy I did live. I'm afraid, you see. I'm afraid to go back up."

"You'll get over it."

"No," he said. "If my speech made me sound heroic, forget it. I loved flying, and now it terrifies me."

"How long has it been?"

"Three months, but it's not a matter of time. I don't even look up if I hear an engine. I just begin to shake and it's all I can do not to start screaming. I'm a lapsed Catholic, but not lapsed enough to kill myself. Maybe I will kill myself."

"No," she said.

"Why? Let the body join the spirit, I say. And as for eternal hellfire, if there is such a thing, I've been there already."

She reached out and took his hand.

"I never told this to anyone," he said harshly, but he didn't remove his hand. "So do me a favor, don't keep mentioning it."

"I won't."

"She called you Tessa. Now we're better acquainted, shouldn't I know your last name?"

"Van Vliet," she said.

He looked bewildered. "When did I tell you that?" he asked.

"What's your name?"

"You just said it. Van Vliet."

They stared at one another. And spontaneously, at the same moment, they began laughing.

"Of all the girls in the city," he said, his hand still gripping hers, "of all the girls to spill my guts to. My long-lost cousin." He pulled the gloved hand to his cheek before releasing it.

"What's your name?"

"Kingdon. Also Van Vliet." He chuckled, leaning against the car door, gazing at her. "But where are your hooves and horns?"

"Is that what they say about us?"

"Mother does. What do your parents say about us?"

"Nothing."

"Nothing?"

"I wouldn't have known you existed. Except Grandpa Hendryk—"

"A fat old man with a Dutch accent?"

She nodded, smiling.

"He had three missing fingers," Kingdon said. "I couldn't keep from staring. Fascinated. And frightened."

"When I was little I thought of it as his elephant hand."

"It *did* look like tusks," Kingdon said. "He visited right after LeRoy—that's my youngest brother—was born. He gave me horehound drops and informed me that God had blessed the city of Los Angeles, making it His favored spot on earth."

"Grandpa Hendryk was a Booster," she said. "He lived with us until. . . ."

"He's dead? When?"

"The year the war broke out. Nineteen-fourteen." She paused. "He told me that I looked like my cousin—"

"Not to keep interrupting, but that had to be me. Tom and LeRoy are blond Dutchies."

"We do look a little alike," she said shyly. "3Vee, that's your father, isn't it?"

"Impoverished younger brother, yes."

"I asked Grandpa what cousin. He said it was not for him to tell me. I was delighted to discover I had a cousin—it's lonely being an only child. I couldn't wait. I was, oh, about four. I ran into my parents' sitting room. When I blurted out questions, my father got up and went into their bedroom. Mother took me on her lap, explaining that I was a big girl, and it was right for me to know I had cousins and an uncle and aunt, but I shouldn't talk about them ever, especially not in front of Daddy. Daddy had fought with his brother, and he, Daddy, had been very hurt. I had visions of some brutal giant pounding him with his fists."

"My father," Kingdon said, "never punched anyone in his life. Believe me, if he had, it would've been me. I was a wild kid. Or Mother. She has her moments, Mother, when she's a total bitch."

Tessa felt herself redden. She had never heard anyone talk like that about a parent.

"It was difficult for *me* to believe," she said. "My father's strong. He plays polo, he hunts. At that time as far as I was concerned, he was invincible and immortal." She paused. "I've never really gotten over that feeling. I suppose I have what's known as a father complex."

"All right. You kept silent at home. But the name Van Vliet isn't exactly unknown in Los Angeles. I gather the breakup wasn't amicable. There must've been a lot of talk. Didn't anyone in school mention our close-knit clan?"

"I didn't go to school."

"That's understandable. Why would you? The heiress of the golden West."

"I was sick a lot." She touched the almost imperceptible scar at the base of her throat. "Kingdon, how terrible it must've been for you in the hospital."

"Since you persist in bringing the matter up," he said, his voice lowering with intent to wound, "a hospital is a fine and fitting place to amputate your life."

She didn't glance away even momentarily. His biting sarcasm no longer disturbed her. She understood it. But it was more than understanding. Their being cousins had brought Kingdon into the small circle of people with whom she was one. In the past few minutes she had bestowed upon him that trust which can bridge the separation of skins.

A Ford chattered by. Kingdon, fishing in his cardigan pocket, brought out a pack of Sweet Caporals, opening it, offering her one.

"I don't smoke," she said.

"Mind?"

She shook her head.

"You have a fine, soothing way, Cousin Tessa," he said, inhaling, blowing a smoke ring. "Weren't you going to show me the Pacific? My father assured me that most of the beaches of Southern California were once part of our ancestral holdings."

"The old cattle farmers owned a narrow bit of sand, which was useless because it wasn't connected to the rest of the ranch. That's what *my* father told me."

She smiled. He smiled back, then he got out to crank the starter.

·6·

It was almost dark when she dropped him off a block east of the Hollywood Hotel. Here he rented a room in one of the small apartments surrounding a "court." In this case the court was merely a wide path edged with bougainvillea, hibiscus, and passion flowers that, since it was dusk, had opened to display creamy, magnificently marked blossoms.

Kingdon's nose and forehead were pink with sun. They had been in Venice, the local resort version of the original. She had adjusted to his limp as they ambled past domed and minareted amusement parlors and crossed the arching bridges over shallow, saline-odored canals. As they walked, he had told her about the aces—Nungesser and Guynemer, French pilots, Boelke and Richthofen, the Germans. Occasionally she sat on a bench, putting on small, wire-rimmed glasses to pencil notes. He had rested, telling himself she had stopped because she needed to write down information, not because of his crippled leg, telling himself he was giving her background for her flick, not spilling his despair.

Mrs. Codee's apartment, 2B, was dark; an elderly widow, she ate dinner with her daughter. He used his key, moving through the overfurnished little parlor into his narrow bedroom. He didn't pull the string of the dangling light bulb. The dim cell of a room had only one sign of his occupancy: the cigar box on the chest. He opened the wooden box, his mouth twisting as he peered inside. A jumble of ribbons and metal. Captain Kingdon Van Vliet, having downed eleven German fighters, had earned most of the available French decorations. Each reminded him of another man's agony and of his own irrevocable defeat. Angrily, he flipped down the lid. *Why do I keep these?*

He wasn't sure why, but he surmised it had to do with his kinship to the dead of the Lafayette Escadrille. *I'm one of them,* he thought.

Springs squeaked as he sat on the narrow bed. He used both hands to raise up his left leg. The agony radiating through his body showed in his sunburned face. Settling the pillow under his knee, he lay back, hands under his neck, staring out at the purplish dusk.

Tessa, he thought. *Tessa. She'll be here at ten-thirty tomorrow morning. I'm glad she's my cousin.*

The thought was raw. Uncomplicated. With her he need not agonize over his lack of desire. He was a Catholic. Lapsed, he told others, but Utah's punishments had carved him with guilt, and therefore the more he lapsed, the more he was entrapped. The teachings of the Church held him. Tessa's cousinly flesh was proscribed to him. Thus it was all right that he didn't want her. Yet in almost four months he hadn't wanted any woman. Not since he had plunged between burning canvas wings, his thigh roasting, a senseless voice screaming *HailMaryfullofgrace* over and over, had he wanted a woman. He was no longer afflicted by the fleshly urges and needs that had plagued him since puberty.

Well, Ma, he thought, *no need for you to worry about that any more.*

He hadn't seen his mother, his father, his brothers in eight years. He had written home infrequently. Two weeks earlier, when they had released him from the military hospital in Maryland, he had thought vaguely of returning to Bakersfield. Yet he found himself in Los Angeles. *Why? What difference does it make where I am?* He had tossed with insomniac pain at night. He sleepwalked through his days. Without flying he was a dead, dark, despairing soul.

He took out his Sweet Caporals. Mrs. Codee had said no smoking. She was a Catholic and a landlady like his mother. He lit a cigarette.

Here, he thought, lies the great aviator and lover.

He blew out a stream of smoke. I wonder if there was anatomical damage that the doctors neglected to mention. "Captain Van Vliet, the leg will heal, more or less. However, we regret to inform you of an, uh, injury of a personal nature. You're a complete eunuch."

A muscle twitched under Kingdon's eye. I'm too nervy to be a complete eunuch, he thought. I'm only a eunuch where it counts. Which makes it fine that the brunette with the fine, firm breasts turns out to be, of all women, my cousin. Otherwise known as the virgin heiress to Paloverde Oil. I can look and not touch.

Is she still a virgin? Purely academic curiosity. Still, if I can't tell the ones who do from the ones who don't at thirty paces, I certainly have lost it. Yes. A eunuch. Tessa? I don't like thinking about her this way.

He squinted through wispy smoke. The final rays of the setting sun blazed. Red sky at dusk, clear sky at dawn. Tomorrow will be clear. Good flying weather. Good? As far as I'm concerned, tomorrow could rain frogs. Oh God, God, why didn't you let me die up there, where I belong?

He ground out his cigarette on the floor. Clasping the agony of his thigh, he rolled over, pressing his face full into the mattress as if he were willing himself to suffocation.

· 7 ·

Certainly Utah alone hadn't been responsible for his discordant nature. Without her, he could easily have felt a sinner, for like many sensitive people raised in the Church, he demanded an impossible perfection of himself. But undeniably it was Utah who had furnished his sense of unworthiness.

Charley Kingdon had been a wild, active child. His deep-set, almost-black eyes sparkled with amber rays of mischief. At the Bakersfield parochial school, he stood out for his predilection toward trouble. He climbed the playground elms, jumping from the branches—twice he broke bones. He ran too recklessly, laughed too vitally. He attracted classmates to his spirited rowdiness. Oddly enough, the sisters found themselves smiling on this difficult pupil. "All boy" was the verbal character analysis these good, simple women permitted themselves. Privately, each noted Charley Van Vliet's obvious striving to be good enough to serve God; his very imperfections denoted the largeness of soul that is a prerequisite for sainthood.

Utah's religion was punitive. She saw her oldest son's behavior as personal retribution. He was conceived in sin, she thought, and whenever Charley Kingdon climbed on her ample lap, snuggling his face to her breasts, she wanted to cuddle him. Yet inevitably she felt that he had already been damned enough by her transgression. I ain't got the right to encourage him. "Get down, Charley Kingdon," she would say. "You're too big to be climbing all over me."

She punished him with her hairbrush until he was six. Then one wilting July afternoon, she was in the backyard picking fruit for the supper pies. She heard childish giggles coming from the shadows behind the unused carriage house. The laughter was soft yet excited. A premonitory chill of sweat ran down her spine. Clutching ripe plums in her apron, she circled trees. She had become obese, and her footsteps were audible. The children were too involved to hear. "Charley Kingdon, what're you doin' back there?" she called. She turned the corner. Her mouth formed a horrified circle. She let loose her apron, and plums dropped around her rigid body.

Her son and a little girl sat facing one another. Their lower garments were pushed away. It was that old, poignantly innocent sexual game of you-show-me-yours-I'll-show-you-mine. Utah's horror bubbled over. It was what she had always feared, the sign of her own concupiscence in the flesh of her son. Shrieking his name, she swooped. She never did identify the little girl, who ran off in terror adjusting her bloomers. Utah poised over Charley Kingdon. His eyes riveted to his mother's bloated red fury, he stood, buttoning his knickers.

Utah grabbed his thin arm and dragged him across the yard and up the wooden steps to the kitchen. The stove was hot, ready for the supper pies. She shoved his arm against cast iron, holding it there. "This here's a sample of what comes from sinful ways!" she cried. "Flames everlasting is where you belong!"

For a long moment he kept from crying out. With a child's bravery, he accepted his mother's verdict. He deserved this agony. Only when he could no longer bear the intensity of his pain did he begin to weep. Utah, sobbing, for once clutched him in her arms for comfort.

After that Kingdon went through a repentant religious phase that truly never passed. In his mind he was falling further and further from grace. A darkness weighted him down. His heroes became those men in winged bicycles who managed for a few minutes to escape the earth. As the years passed his dreams of flight mingled with the compelling desires of adolescence. He left Bakersfield at sixteen. Since then he hadn't been in a church. He found himself worthy only when he flew between fragile canvas wings.

·8·

Tessa told him that her parents were back east, where H. Van Vliet II was floating bonds to expand Paloverde Oil. Evidently, Kingdon thought, his uncle wished to own the world and was raising cash for the purchase.

Each morning promptly at ten-thirty, Tessa came by for him. With a picnic hamper in the back seat, they ranged the network of interconnecting towns. They penetrated the dusty shade of groves in the San Fernando Valley from Van Nuys to Lankershim. They explored the beach towns of Santa Monica, Ocean Park, Redondo Beach, and went back to Venice. They drove east to Mission San Gabriel and listened to the music of old bells set in adobe-brick walls. They braved the traffic and bustle of Spring Street so she could point out where their grandfather had once presided over Van Vliet's Hardware. The Van Vliet Block had been torn down for Paloverde Oil's main headquarters, a vast, modern ten-story monolith—as high as it was believed safe for buildings to rise in this earthquake-prone area. They parked the car and walked by shops on Broadway where the Van Vliets's red-shingled house and the Deane mansion had once stood side by side.

He refused her invitation to come to Greenwood, the site of Paloverde. She didn't question his refusal.

Even though they had spent almost ten days together, Tessa had not neglected her work. As they said goodbye one afternoon in front of the court, she drew an envelope from her purse. "I've finished the treatment for *The Aviator*," she said. Her tone was embarrassed.

"Want me to check it?" Kingdon's face was tanned and his limp less pronounced as he walked down the flower-bordered path to his apartment, the envelope in his hand.

He read it that evening. It was a romanticized version of air warfare. Even so, if Tessa had left out the episodes with the noble crusader, *The Aviator* would have been bearable. The next day when they met Kingdon told her so.

"I had to say I'd put that in before Mr. Rimini would agree to look at my treatment," she said.

She confessed in such low-voiced, blushing confusion that he understood how shameful a betrayal it had been to her.

A gentle, unworldly girl, my cousin.

·9·

Kingdon, Lya, and Tessa sat on the running board of the Mercer watching as five cowboys rode uphill to hide behind a false-fronted church. Dust settled. Rimini, a stocky figure in boots and pith helmet, raised a pistol and fired. The men burst into view, yelling and shooting their way toward the truck with the camera mounted on it. Rimini was directing the cowboy serial himself. Tessa, finding him absent from his barn-studio, had come to this arid patch of land hoping to learn what he thought of *The Aviator*. Kingdon was here because he had fallen into the habit of spending his days with his cousin. Lya, wearing her new yellow crepe de chine, had come along to show herself off to Rimini.

The riders dismounted. Sweating and dusty, they took turns drinking from an *olla*, paying no attention as Rimini shouted, "Blanks cost good money! So don't waste 'em! Now let's get on with the next scene. I'm not paying you to lie around all day!" The group remounted and trotted toward bushes near the false church.

Tessa went over to Rimini.

"Mr. Rimini, have you had a chance to read it?"

"A good story line," he replied.

"Thank you." She smiled. "Then I'll do a shooting version?"

He dug his boot into the dry earth, raising a cloud of dust. "Yesterday a rattler was right here. Fat, brown with yellow, and rattles on his tail. A lot of 'em, like a corncob."

"It's the season," Tessa replied. "They don't bother you unless you disturb them. Mr. Rimini?"

"Do me a favor. Even if they don't bother you, they bother me. Wear boots if you come out here again." He paused. "I promised I'd look. I looked."

"Should I—"

"You wasted enough time already."

"But . . ." Her forehead crinkled. "You said you liked it."

"My like don't mean the same as the exhibitors' like. They won't buy a war film. Now go home. Write me a historical. Use the crusader if you want to. Pay your rent."

"I'll do it for nothing. Mr. Rimini . . ."

But he was walking away toward the camera truck, glancing nervously down at the ground looking for snakes. Tessa followed. She watched as the two cameramen moved aside to let him look into the viewfinder. Ostentatiously, Rimini ignored her.

Tessa waited. She couldn't give up. Kingdon and *The Aviator* had become inextricably linked to her. The ten typewritten pages of her treatment had become as important to her as an arm, a leg, her heart.

Lya had picked her way over stubbly foxtails. Resting her gloved hand delicately on the hot metal fender of the camera truck, she said, "Hello there, Mr. Rimini. It looks to be such a wonderful movie. So action-packed. My, my." It was her Southern belle role.

Rimini glanced up from camera. "Lya. You. Do me a favor. Tell your friend here she should listen to sense."

"Everybody listens to you, Mr. Rimini," said Lya, fluttering her lashes at him.

Tessa, Lya, and Kingdon drove off to the sound of the cowboys shooting more rounds of Rimini's expensive blanks. They were silent until they were standing at the counter of a shack in the Cahuenga Pass. ALL THE ORANGE JUICE YOU CAN DRINK, FIVE CENTS.

"You handled it wrong," Lya pronounced. She set her glass on oilcloth and glanced at the shirtsleeved proprietor, signaling that she wanted a refill.

"I agree," Kingdon said. "Tessa should've pushed him to the ground and held him down, arguing until he agreed to make her flick."

"Don't be ridiculous," Lya said impatiently. "Don't you know in this business nobody talks. The screen's silent."

"I'll remember," Kingdon said.

"You have to dramatize." Lya struck a provocative pose. "When I interviewed for the Babylonian sequence of *Intolerance*, I wore a black wig, a gauzy blouse, and bangles and necklaces. I got the part."

"Should Tessa have staged the Battle of the Marne?"

Lya's flat, pretty face had become shrewdly intent. "Only the parts of the battle she needed. Let's see. An aviator's shot down behind enemy lines. He crashes through buildings?" She glanced at Tessa. Tessa nodded. "Now personally, I think it's right gripping. Will the pilot live or die? The audience'll be on the edge of their seats. But Rimini, he can't see that, and for one little reason. He's never seen an aeroplane crash."

"I thought the key word in Hollywood was 'visualize,'" Kingdon said.

"Cornmeal mush," Lya said. "Rimini never visualized anything he didn't see first."

"He never saw real cowboys shooting," Kingdon pointed out.

The proprietor set out a fresh tumbler of orange juice for Lya. "A world of difference," she said, sipping greedily. "He's seen *movies* about cowboys."

"So all we have to do is show Rimini the Battle of the Marne. Or will several dogfights be enough?"

"Not a dogfight. The crash!" Lya said excitedly. "We have the church. We can get the cameramen to go along with us. Then all *you* have to do is find a stunt pilot to crash into the church—or is that all very expensive?"

"There's a war on, or haven't you heard?" Kingdon's face was taut with that self-wounding anger. "Every aeroplane is being used for training. And every stunt pilot is teaching in the Army Air Corps. Is that news to you?"

"All I know, Mister Man, is that in Hollywood nobody gets anyplace doing what's possible." Lya's little mouth was set in a firm line.

Tessa saw her determination and admired it. Lya's not fatally dull, she thought.

<h2 style="text-align:center">· 10 ·</h2>

By now Kingdon was driving the Mercer. He and Tessa dropped Lya off at her hillside boarding house, then drove three blocks west to Cherokee, to the court.

Braking, he said, "Absolute genius."

Tessa blinked. "Lya's idea, you mean?"

"What else?"

"The aeroplane?"

"You've been a million miles away. You're still a million miles away."

"You said it was impossible."

"Me? I simply pointed out that this year pilots and aeroplanes are busy." Kingdon fished for his cigarettes with a shaking hand. Lya's suggestion that he become involved—find an aeroplane and stunt pilot—had prodded his deepest wound. "Devious little type, isn't she?"

"She's my friend. She's trying to help."

"What's that got to do with her being devious?" He struck a match. It didn't light. "So long as you understand it is impossible."

"Kingdon ..." She hesitated, took a deep breath. "Kingdon, my parents will be home tomorrow."

The match flared, went out. "Nice for them," he said.

"Have dinner with us on Friday."

He took the unlit cigarette from his mouth. "Alas. I'm otherwise engaged."

"Please?"

"You have my regrets."

"But why?"

"I don't have the necessary olive branch to wear between my teeth."

"I want you to meet them. It's important to me." Her voice trembled.

No serpent's-tooth child, Tessa. She was genuinely devoted to her parents, and for this reason Kingdon had avoided mention of them. But that did not mean his loathing of H. Van Vliet II had in any way lessened. His mother had bequeathed him an inbred hatred of his uncle—and of himself. Both hatreds clutched him so he could barely breathe.

"Then the great man knows of me?" he asked.

"He will."

"Not yet, though?"

"I didn't write to them about you. I wanted to wait until they were home."

"And immediately following your announcement, I'm to knock on the gate, calling out, 'Here's your long-lost nephew.' Or would it be more fitting for me to drop to my knees—or what's left of my knees—and crawl into their illustrious presence?"

"I just want you to have dinner with two very nice people."

"Sweet, lovely people."

"They are."

He dug his fingers into his thigh, glad of pain. "Listen, Cousin, get this firmly into your mind. I do not want to meet your lovely parents. I—do—not—want—them—to—know—about—me."

"But why? How can my knowing you be a secret from them?"

"Quite simply. Keep your mouth closed."

"You'd like them, Kingdon."

"You believe that? You honestly believe I'd like your father?" Managing to light his cigarette, he took a long, furious drag. "My father's son could *like* your father? Listen, my father made a bloody ass of himself. He dug for oil right in Los Angeles. He dug by hand. He moved earth with a pick, a shovel, two buckets, and gallons of sweat. He's not an insensitive man. Imagine how delighted he must have been to welcome the people who came to laugh at him! A man digging for oil by hand! And just as he hit big, your father stepped in. They named their company—my father's blood—Paloverde Oil. Recognize it? And incidentally, I didn't hear this story from my father. I read it in old newspapers. Your father, Cousin, got his billion-dollar company the easiest way. By stealing it from his brother!"

"My father never stole anything in his life."

"No? Well, here's another story. It wasn't just Paloverde Oil. I'm sure you're familiar with the oil-powered locomotives that the great man proclaims his? Those babies were my father's idea. My father drew up the original plans. Patented, of course, by your father!"

Tessa drew a ragged breath. He thought she was going to cry as she had the other time he had showed rage with her. Instead, she turned on him, her blue eyes almost black. "I didn't know your father had the idea, but I *do* know about the locomotive. The original plans couldn't have been workable. They were modified and modified, and when the engine finally crawled out of the round-house, it had to be fueled with coal to get back. There were months of work and testing. My father spent every penny he had and borrowed money on top of that. He worked in the machine shop himself, and still things went wrong. He often laughs about it."

"I'm sure he does," Kingdon said. "It's got a humorous side, making a fortune from a rotten set of plans."

"My father gives; he doesn't take," she said in a level voice. "He supported his whole family when he was fifteen. Any relation or friend who needs help comes to him. Him. And he doesn't just hand over money. That's easy. He does everything he can. He helps people he doesn't know—anybody descended from an Indian who worked on Paloverde. He looked after Grandpa Hendryk when he was dying; he nursed him through the nights because Grandpa Hendryk was dazed and frightened. He cried at the funeral. Your family wasn't there. He saved my life when I had diphtheria." She touched her neck, and Kingdon saw what he hadn't before noticed. The tiny, almost invisible scar. "Why would he have stepped out of character to steal from his younger brother?"

"Damned if I know. Obviously the papers got it wrong. The story should have been about the Second Coming! I don't know anything about any of this, Tessa, including why you want to take your impoverished, lame cousin home!"

She shrank back toward the car door as if his words were physical blows. "Kingdon, don't . . ."

His preconditioned loathing for his uncle still raced. "Why?" he demanded. "Have you inherited your side's sanctity? Or do you take pleasure giving alms? Or were you making contact with some idiot ready to fry himself doing a crazy stunt so you can get your story made? Is that your interest in needy cripples?"

Her lips had gone white. "You must know how I feel," she murmured. "Please . . . don't say any more."

"No worry about that! There's not going to be another chance." He opened the car door. "It's been one colossal blunder. The minute I found out who you were, I should have stayed the hell away!"

Limping up the path, he turned. "I'd appreciate it if you'd do the same!" He fumbled with Mrs. Codee's lock, opened the door, and slammed it viciously behind him.

CHAPTER 16

· I ·

By six the next morning, Kingdon was in the double seat of a Red Car, his left shoe planted on the wooden floor strips in a way that tensed his thigh muscles painfully. At that hour there weren't many people waiting at the trolley stops: Sherman, Beverly Hills—where to the north the Beverly Hills Hotel floated, exotic and pink, above the beanfields—Sawtelle, Santa Monica, Venice. It was around six-thirty when he slowly crossed the Venice Air Field, the dew that clung to weeds staining his flannels a darker gray.

In front of the hangar, with its barnstyle roof, two aeroplanes were tethered. One, at least eight years old, resembled a winged tricycle. The other was a Jenny in what looked to be prime condition. As Kingdon surveyed the Jenny, his face contorted into that odd, sardonic smile worn by corpses.

A tall man emerged from the hangar adjusting the straps of his overalls. Kingdon recognized him. "Tex Argyle," he shouted.

The man looked up, recognition turning to a smile. "Kingdon Van Vliet. What the hell are you doing here in California? Heard you were over in France. Didn't you make captain in the Lafayette Escadrille?"

"I did," Kingdon said.

Tex asked no further questions. Both men belonged to a closed brotherhood, aviators, who alone understood their own bravery and cowardice. However, Tex silently noted Kingdon's limp and his awkward stance.

"What's the story?" Kingdon nodded at the Jenny. "I heard the Army had requisitioned everything that flies."

"She crashed in Orange County. Bought her for junk and put her back together. I do exhibitions to bring rubes to the Venice Pier."

"Ever do stunts for movie people?"

"Never been asked."

"Would you?"

"Depends on who asked me," Tex replied, showing crooked teeth in a grin.

· 2 ·

Kingdon was back in Hollywood by ten. He waited, as usual, on the cement steps leading to the court. He picked up a fallen bougainvillea leaf, squinting at the sun through papery, veined purple. Like the stained-glass window in church, he thought. He looked at his watch continually, and when it said five of eleven, he went back inside to ask Mrs. Codee if he could use a telephone. She needed two, as did everyone. The city had rival telephone lines, the Home and the Sunset. The Van Vliets were on the Sunset line.

An English voice answered, "Greenwood."

"Miss Van Vliet, please."

"Who shall I say is calling, sir?"

Kingdon pressed down on the instrument, cutting the connection. Breathing deeply, he made the call again.

Again the English voice answered.

"Miss Van Vliet, please. It's, uh, Captain Kingdon."

"Please hold the wire, Captain."

Kingdon waited.

"Hello, Kingdon?"

Her voice surprised him. It had a quality, soft yet husky, that he had never noticed.

"Me, incognito," he said.

"I didn't think ... I thought ..."

"You're doing it again. Contradicting yourself." He paused. "This morning you must've dropped by before I got back."

"I didn't come. You said—"

"Let me finish. You must've missed me while I was out at the

Venice Flying Field. I have a friend there, Tex Argyle. Tex owns a Jenny—that's a Curtiss J—ND, a good aeroplane. Maybe, just maybe, Tex'll do that stunt for us. I'm not sure what it'll cost. We didn't go into that. If money's a problem, can you borrow from the butler?"

"It's all right, then?"

"I told Tex we'd be back today," he said.

"Thank you," she said, and her voice was almost inaudible.

· 3 ·

The fragility of the aeroplane appalled her: narrow spruce struts with taut wires attached by buckles, paired canvas wings shivering in the light sea breeze. How could a man trust this to carry him into the sky? And dare to battle in it? What a fool I was, she thought, comparing aviators to knights. Armor is metal. This is cloth. There is nothing here to stop a bullet. And Kingdon feels a coward!

Kingdon hooked a finger to a wire, pulling. "I worked a few months in Curtiss's factory in Hammonds Point—that's New York," he said. "My job was testing the tension of these interplane wires." He curved his palm along the smooth camber of the propeller, then fingered the sooty streak left by exhaust. "Aeroplanes run on castor oil and gasoline," he said. "Did you know that? Sometimes in France it got so cold that we had to heat the castor oil before injecting it." His eyes glittered. He spoke more rapidly than usual.

Tex ambled over.

"Tex," Kingdon said. "Tessa."

"Hello, Tex," she said, extending her hand.

The lanky man raised his hand to show a blackened palm. "Grease," he said. "Well, what d'you think of her?"

"The Jenny?" she asked. "I don't know. I've never been this close to an aeroplane before."

"Then you ain't known Kingdon long."

"No."

"Never seen him fly?"

She shook her head.

Tex turned to Kingdon. "Want to take her up and show your girl?"

"I'm only his cousin," Tessa said quickly.

"Still a pretty girl," Tex replied. "Kingdon?"

Wind rushed along the Jenny's doped, varnished wings. A rabbit flashed across the field. Sunlight caught the lines and angles of Kingdon's face.

Tessa murmured, "Kingdon, don't."

"He ain't going to ruin his looks," Tex said, grinning. "Just plume himself a bit."

"Where are your togs?" Kingdon asked, his voice metallic.

"The office," Tex replied.

"No!" Tessa said sharply.

"Don't tell me no," he muttered. "Tessa, don't." His expression was a naked mingling of fear and hope.

She reached out to touch his arm. "Kingdon?"

"I have to try," he said quietly.

"No need to worry, Tessa. He's the best damn pilot around."

"Be careful," she whispered.

Kingdon was already limping toward the hangar.

· 4 ·

In the office cubbyhole he could hear his own rasping breath. A vein at one temple stood out, throbbing, as he pulled on Tex's worn flight jacket. The leather was fleece-lined, yet under the matted wool goosebumps rose on his flesh.

He removed his gold signet ring, carefully setting it on the dusty desk. From a pocket he dragged ivory beads that he always carried, the never-used rosary that he longed to use. What's the matter with me? he thought. Why am I always tearing at myself like an animal trapped by metal teeth? Allowing God's trap to close on me, then endlessly gnawing at my own flesh attempting to free myself. Unable to bear existence on this earth and unable to rise into the sky. Not living, yet fearing the deed of suicide. The beads fell with a clatter to the desk. Seeing a pencil stub, he reached in the top drawer and found a pad.

For Tessa, he wrote. He stopped, gazing at the printed name, thinking how she had looked yesterday, pale, shaken, huddled in the car seat, all but telling him she loved him. If I were alive, I'd love her. Good luck I'm impotent, he thought with a bleak smile. It lifts the burden of incest from the Catholic branch of the embattled family Van Vliet. The Episcopal side knoweth not guilt. *This being good-bye, I can apologize about yesterday, and thank you for—* He stopped and ripped the sheet from the pad, tearing the paper into shreds like a man destroying a bad will.

He picked up the ring and rosary and shoved them into his pocket. Lifting Tex's goggles and leather flying helmet from a hook, he left the hangar and walked out onto the field.

The Jenny's motor warmed up with machine-gun coughs. The propeller whirred. Two mechanics stood out of the windstream, watching Kingdon limp toward them. Out of habit, he walked around the aeroplane, a meaningless ritual of inspection. Terror blinded him. He could feel the Jenny shivering like a frightened bird.

He put his right shoe on the metal foothold. Supporting his weight with his arms to favor his left leg, he swung awkwardly into the cockpit, lowering himself into the wicker, strapping himself with broad leather bands. *The German struggled against the straps while the Fokker plummeted to earth trailing blackness.* Kingdon checked the controls. Rudder, elevator, ailerons. His heart was pumping as wildly as the engine. Did I live? he wondered. Or did I die and the German survive? Or are we both under the damp earth of Fère-en-Tardenois?

The engine deafened him. Twelve hundred, he thought. Stick back. Throttle.

His eyes blank with remembered dread, he taxied. Bumping. Jolting. Hopping over rough earth. There was a line of eucalyptus standing at the end of the field. Kingdon's gloved hands wrapped tighter on the stick. If he plunged into those trees, he would end the scream that had begun halfway round the earth. His mind swam with the thought. Peace eternal...rest in Peace...*pax vobiscum*...go forth, oh Christian soul. Yet both feet were steady as he worked the rudder, and his hands had a life of their own, pulling, pulling.

The rough bouncing ended. As he entered the air, his muscles loosened and he battled the sudden pressure on his bowels. The moment passed. He climbed above the trees, pushing at the pedals, turning, banking. On the field below they were looking up at him, waving. Then he was over the Venice boardwalk and hands were shading eyes raised up toward him. Painted minarets caught the sun. He rose higher. Below him stretched the vast bay: clusters of beach towns strung on glinting trolley lines, the ruffled white edges of the surf.

He let out a deep, shuddering sigh. The terror was less. And so was his savage despair. Always, the freedom of flight had eased him.

He turned to circle the flying field, and his shaking stopped. He decided to show her an Immelman. He climbed straight up, but as he began the downward dive, his terror returned. Again his sphincter muscle threatened to loosen. He pulled out and flew level. The freedom is conditional, he thought. Will I ever forget the smell of burning flesh, that endless screaming prayer? He pointed the nose of the plane down a little and shut off the engine, gliding. Wind sang in the wires and struts. Kingdon smiled. Something, he thought, is better than nothing. At least I have this. Maybe later, I'll regain more. Looking down, he saw the crimson dot that was Tessa's hat.

He made a perfect three-point landing.

She came running to the Jenny. As he climbed out, she said, "I was terrified."

He pushed up his goggles. "A mere nothing to what I used to do," he said.

"I don't want to see what you used to do, then."

He smiled. As they walked toward the hangar, he put his arm lightly over her shoulder. He heard friendly laughter, a remark about the Lafayette Escadrille getting all the girls.

"While I've got you dazzled," he said, "is the time to mention I'm sorry about yesterday."

"I should've realized, well, how you would feel about my father."

"It isn't possible for me to meet him. Not yet. Maybe later. Probably later." They had reached the hangar and his arm dropped from her shoulder. "I'll tell you when I'm ready, all right?"

"Yes," she agreed, adding shyly, "Kingdon, you were splendid up there."

· 5 ·

The United States had been in the war since April, and by now everyone in Los Angeles was affected. There weren't yet many Americans in France, but each day at the Southern Pacific and Santa Fe stations young draftees formed sad little lines on their way to training camps. Older men joined the National Guard, drilling in vacant warehouses three evenings a week. And every other Sunday they turned purple as they sweated under a hot sun in field drill and lay on their full bellies for machine-gun practice. Women stopped serving their families sugar. They wore muslin Red Cross uniforms as they rolled bandages or knitted the woolen caps that prevented those new steel helmets from freezing to the head. Being so close to the border gave an exhilarating sense of danger to the normally peacebound city. Who knew when a Hun horde might swoop north from Tijuana? And to ferret out the enemy lurking within, the Department of Justice gave out white cards so that volunteer agents might spy on their neighbors.

The war preoccupied everybody, and at last Los Angeles began to see Hollywood in a rosy light. Mary Pickford, Douglas Fairbanks, and Charlie Chaplin were selling more Liberty Bonds than anyone. Yet Jacopo Rimini was right. As screen material, the war was a flop. Maybe people wanted to forget the horrors facing their young men. Only a fool would hope to make money with a film like *The Aviator*. Rimini had scheduled a biblical to follow the cowboy serial.

This was the final day of shooting. A hard sun beat onto summer-browned Santa Monicas, and tiny brown lizards scuttled, their mobility all that made them visible. Insects whirred in chaparral. The morning changed from warm to hot.

A couple of tin lizzies chugged up the rutted path and halted. The reporters had arrived for a wrap-up lunch. Rimini went forward to greet them. He invited them to the shade of a truck, where he tapped a keg of beer, then he led them to the makeshift canvas tent that served as a dressing room for two crinolined women and the rangy actor who was his star.

Tessa and Lya watched from the shady side of the Mercer. Lya's wide-brimmed straw hat disguised the glitter in her pale eyes. Tessa kept glancing anxiously at the ridge behind the false-fronted church.

"I wish Tex was doing it," she said.

"You keep saying that, hon. Kingdon *told* you he wanted to. And he said there was nothing to it, just making a few loop-the-loops and landing in that level spot there." She pointed at a meadow below the church.

"He's only flown twice since he was hurt."

"He's a pilot. Besides, maybe Rimini'll hire him to do the stunts—or even play the aviator. That's what you've got to remember. He could get into movies as a pilot."

Tessa shuddered.

More beer was being served from the keg.

A faraway droning sound came.

Lya grasped Tessa's hand. "This is what counts, right now," she said. "And you know something? I reckon it's going to work. So stop your fretting." She moved to the truck. A cameraman glanced down at her, nodding.

The droning grew louder.

"Hey," one of the reporters called. "Aeroplane."

Aeroplanes were a rarity. Everyone looked up, sheltering their eyes.

The Jenny came out of the north, from the direction of the San Fernando Valley, soaring swiftly over the hills as if shaking off pursuers. Above the church it banked, looping and circling in a series of aerobatics that wove patterns in the clear, acid-blue sky.

"An exhibition pilot," a cowboy remarked.

"Exhibition, nothing. He's a fighter, I can tell you that much." The fat reporter held up his hand to shield his eyes, watching as he talked. "I was over at the Front last month, and this man's seen action, a lot of it."

The Jenny rose high, rolling, abruptly streaking downward. Tessa gave a terrified cry. Everyone stared in morbid fascination as the aeroplane tore earthward, faster, faster. The engine snarl was the only sound. The pilot's head, showing above the bathtublike nacelle, seemed to blur.

An audible gasp rose. The aeroplane was diving straight at the scaffolded church steeple.

"Oh Christ!"

"He's done for!"

Suddenly the motor was cut and the Jenny tore into the steeple with a splintering crash. Wood scattered like toothpicks.

Tessa, skirts raised to her knees, was running, stumbling, righting herself, stumbling again toward the ruined church and the gliding aeroplane. The still photographer, his camera slung on its tripod over his shoulder, followed her. The Bell & Howell movie camera whirred loudly as the assistant cameraman cranked.

The Jenny glided to a perfect landing. On the left wing a small patch of canvas was torn. That was the only damage. Kingdon climbed out of the cockpit. He was very white. He was smiling.

Tessa threw her arms around him, asking incoherently if he were all right, if he were hurt, was he hurt?

"What's all the fuss?" he asked.

"What happened?" She kissed his mouth. "How did you pull out? You should've let Tex—"

"Tessa, everything was planned, and went according to plan. What did you think a barnstormer does? Take off, fly level for ten feet, then land?"

"You're shaking."

"That," he said, "is normal."

"I was so terrified I thought I'd die."

"Exactly how I felt. But, Tessa, I did it. I did it!" This time he kissed her. His kiss was not sexual, and neither had hers been. Both kisses, born of terror and closeness, were like those of warriors in ancient times—the kisses of victory.

After an initial spasm of real terror, Rimini was quick to realize that it had been a stunt. He made sure that the camera had captured the scene and then began to run toward the plane. Lya was right behind him. In her high, breathless Southern voice she was telling him that the pilot was a member of the Lafayette Escadrille, a real ace and a war hero. He had been buzzing her and Tessa.

"What's his name?" Rimini asked as he ran.

"Kingdon," Lya gasped. Then thinking that Van Vliet was wrong for marquees and too difficult to say, she invented a name as she sped over stubbled hilly ground. "Kingdon Vance."

"Kingdon what?"

"Captain Kingdon Vay-ance" she repeated. "And he really is a hero."

Rimini slowed, then stopped, watching Kingdon and Tessa move across the sloping meadow, a handsome, tall couple. He was limping. An aviator, Rimini thought. Yes.

The reporters were milling around them.

"Who the hell is that?" one asked.

"That's Miss Tessa Van Vliet," Rimini answered. "Of Rimini Productions. My best author. She's written a story for me. *The Aviator*. It's about the Lafayette Escadrille. Well, just between us, it's about her sweetheart. That's him, there. Captain Kingdon Vance."

"Will he star?"

"If I can get him. An aviator like that's not easy to tie down."

<h1 style="text-align:center">·6·</h1>

The story broke in the evening papers with a grainy photograph of Tessa and Kingdon embracing.

LAFAYETTE ESCADRILLE ACE'S SWEETHEART WRITES
HIS TRUE STORY FOR FILMS

Miss Tessa Van Vliet has written the exploits of her sweetheart for a film entitled *The Aviator*, which will be produced by Rimini Productions this September.

Captain Vance is credited with downing 32 Huns. He said *The Aviator* is a fine, honest depiction of a flyer's life. It is possible, said Mr. Jacopo Rimini of Rimini Productions, that Captain Vance will star in the feature-length epic.

Bud made a habit of buying his evening papers from the newsboys on Spring Street outside the Paloverde Oil Building's main entrance, and now the *Herald* and the *Evening News* lay open on his lap as José chauffeured the Bentley amid the automobiles, trucks, horsedrawn wagons and occasional buggy that crowded downtown Los Angeles.

Bud's hair was gone except for the neatly trimmed fringe that circled his tanned skull. His flesh retained its brown health, his blue eyes were alert, his body as muscular and compact as ever. The look of youth was gone, replaced by an aura of success. Bud, however, never stopped to consider that he was different from the fifteen-year-old boy who had run his father's hardware store and worked a tour in the Newhall oilfield to keep the family from bankruptcy. In a way, he was that same boy. He had that old bone-crumbling need to win new territory, and this imperative meant that he must constantly be enlarging Paloverde Oil. It was no longer a matter of simply drilling—though he had leases throughout California, Texas, Oklahoma, and Mexico. There were Paloverde Oil's three huge refineries, the chain of local service stations, the harbor facilities in San Pedro as well as the fleet of tankers, the offices in every major city, the lobbyists in Sacramento and Washington, D.C. War had increased the need for fuel oil. His gambles had paid off. Again he was juggling finances in the hope of competing on an even level with Standard Oil and Royal Dutch Shell.

Bud remained one of the most popular men in Los Angeles. Friendship meant much to him. And he remained deeply in love with his wife, which was unusual among his friends. But at this moment, he was thinking of his other love, his forefinger drumming on the grainy news photograph. My daughter, he thought. *My Tessa.*

Bud couldn't let himself remember that he had once considered Tessa 3 Vee's child. As he had razed Paloverde, so he had obliterated his doubts of her paternity.

He occasionally remembered that Tessa's first year and a half of life had not been spent with him. But that he attributed to a quarrel. He and Amélie had always fought. They still fought, and that fight had come at a bad time for them both. He had neglected her for Paloverde Oil, or some such. She had been pregnant and emotional. She had left him, but he had forgotten what the fight was about. All memory of his original aversion to the dark-haired little girl was gone. He had saved her life. He loved her as much as he loved Amélie.

I'll kill whoever let this slide into the papers, he thought. Paloverde Oil had a newfangled department, six men and two female secretaries, with PUBLIC RELATIONS painted on the glass door. They're paid to show Paloverde Oil in a favorable light and to keep the name Van Vliet out of the newspapers, dammit! The back of his neck tensed as he examined the picture of his tall, dark daughter embracing a dark, taller young aviator.

Kingdon Vance, he thought, his mouth drawing tight. Charley Kingdon Van Vliet—it has to be him, doesn't it?

He was rubbing the painful knots in back of his neck as the Bentley turned into Greenwood, rolling smoothly over crushed gravel. The late afternoon sun cast the gardens in shadow and washed gold on the tips of the towering cypresses. Bud was too preoccupied to notice. He looked up from the newspapers on his lap only when the car stopped and he realized that he was home.

Greenwood had fifty-five rooms and required twenty indoor servants, eight full-time gardeners and the staff of the garage. Bud enjoyed all the trappings—the house, the gardens, the swimming pool, the tennis courts—though he wasn't sure why. It was nothing more, really, than an up-to-date version of the Garcías' old rancho. The entry hall was a two-story patio, with tubs of flowering bushes that gave the comfortable armchairs a charmingly rustic incongruity. Tiled steps led to the second-story hallway from which opened the private rooms of the family. A series of skylights admitted sun and air. Styles might change, but Amélie had insisted on as much light as possible.

Bud stood for a moment in the patio, the newspapers folded under his arm. If they were dining alone, Amélie met him there with his drink. Otherwise, the tray was upstairs in their sitting room, so they could talk while she bathed and her maid helped her dress. Then Bud remembered that tonight they were going out, so his drink would be upstairs. He needed the drink. He climbed the stairs, yet instead of going to his own rooms he turned in the opposite direction.

He knocked at Tessa's door. Getting no answer, he opened the door and looked inside. "Tessa?"

She wasn't there. The curtains were drawn against the strong western late-afternoon light, and the gloom held a memory of scent, not the light flower of Amélie's preference, but a softer, more mysterious perfume.

Tessa had furnished her rooms with pieces brought from the Lamballe place near Le Havre, heavy country French fruitwood so old that it was cracked and dotted with wormholes. Bud found it tacky, yet he had humored his daughter's preference. Her bed was carved with apples and pomegranates, the drop-leaf table next to it was covered with picture frames. Bud examined them. His parents. His father holding Tessa on his lap. Madame Deane in her prime, and one of her as the widowed Comtesse Mercier. The old bitch still looks good, he thought. Various Lamballes. None of the aviator, whoever's son he was.

Bud moved into her study. Here, the curtains were open and sunlight blazed on the books that lined three walls. A long table was piled with papers and at one end stood a new Remington. Books were strewn over a deep leather couch.

Moving a dictionary, Bud sat with the newspapers on his lap, looking around. A large number of books always depressed him, and Tessa's, in particular, upset him. Why was any daughter of his involved in reading? He didn't admit the memory that 3 Vee had been an avid reader. Well, he thought, Amélie has always liked to read, and she once said that Tessa didn't read with her mind but with her sexual organs. It was a curious remark and Bud had never probed into what his wife meant. He was old-fashioned enough not to want to think of his daughter as having sexual organs. He doubted if other men thought of her that way. Tessa was a good-looking girl. But other than Paul Schott, she had never had a serious boyfriend. Men crowded around girls who gave off that imperceptible, slightly randy aura of sex.

Bud was glad his daughter wasn't like that. When Tessa was a little girl she had looked at him as if he glittered, and even now she sometimes glanced at him that same way. But she never played him for gifts, as his friends said their daughters did. She never wheedled for a roadster, a diamond pin, a party. Now, for the first time, her lack of acquisitiveness and her tranquil, dreamy way seemed a flaw to Bud. She's hard to understand, he thought.

He heard someone enter the next room. Curtain rings slid on brass rods. "Tessa," he called.

She came to the door. With her royal-blue-and-cream-striped summer dress, her hatless black hair rumpled, her sun-flushed cheeks, she had a wild yet shy happiness about her. Her waist was narrow, her breasts full, and Bud realized with a little shock running through his aching neck that she was more than good-looking. She is a beautiful woman, he thought, frowning.

"Daddy, what's wrong?"

He asked at random, "Why did you open the curtains?"

"I hate them closed. It reminds me of lying in bed. Doctors taking blood through little rubber tubes."

"Is it that bad?"

"Not really," she said half-heartedly. "Yes. I'm glad it doesn't happen so often now. I hate them peering under microscopes at my blood. It's as if they're looking for some concrete reason why I'm being punished."

"Diphtheria," he said. "That was the punishment."

"I know it doesn't make sense," she said. "Often feelings don't. Aren't you going out tonight? What are you doing in here? Shouldn't you be getting dressed?"

"I wanted to talk to you."

She came into the study and sat on the ottoman at his feet.

"Who's Kingdon Vance?" he asked.

She tilted her head, momentarily bewildered, then she smiled, that slow, hesitant smile. She looked even more disturbingly beautiful. "I forgot. Vance is the name Lya made up. Kingdon Van Vliet."

Bud could feel the old weakness sweep through him. The pain at the base of his skull worsened. He didn't realize it, but he was gazing at Tessa with cold rage. "That's what I figured," he said. "He was Charley when I knew him."

"Daddy, you haven't seen him since he was a baby," she said, and her words sounded reproachful.

"No," he said. "I haven't."

"Why do you look so angry, then?"

"You took me by surprise, Tessa. Seeing him, keeping it secret, not telling us. Me! I've been home two weeks and you never once told me."

"Kingdon asked me not to."

"He contacted you in private?"

"No." She leaned toward him earnestly. "Lya and I were at the Hollywood Hotel. He and I started talking. We didn't know who we were. I mean, it came as a shock when we found out we were related. I was writing *The Aviator*, and you know how little I know about flying. Kingdon's been flying for years. He was in the Lafayette Escadrille."

"So I read in the paper." Bud handed her the *Herald*.

She took it, and as she read her sunburned face turned pinker. "I never dreamed they'd print that. We were hugging one another because the stunt was over," she whispered. "Oh, Daddy, I am sorry. I know how you and mother hate having our name in the paper."

"What I hate is having you sneak around behind my back!"

"Please don't be angry," she said, reaching out her hand to him. "I wasn't hiding him from you. It was for him. Daddy, he crashed, and his leg was very badly injured. He's hurt inside, too. And today was the first time he could force himself to really fly again. He's a sensitive person, and I think he's always been hurt inside. He wasn't ready to come here and meet you. That's why I didn't say anything."

"And, like the papers say, you're sweethearts?"

"No, of course not. He's not interested in me that way. His father's your brother."

"He stopped being my brother years ago." Bud's neck twinged

sharply. He got up and began pacing. "Why's he afraid to see me? What's wrong with him? I'm his uncle, aren't I? Or is he courting a very rich young girl secretly?"

"Please stop it," Tessa said quietly. "He's drowning, and I'm his lifeline. If he weren't a Catholic, he might kill himself."

"Very devout to abstain." The sarcastic, battering tone he had never used with her came into his voice.

Tessa was looking at him with a curious expression. He turned away from her and saw a swallow perched on the window ledge. He rapped loudly and the bird flew off. Bud watched it soar over the gardens, leaving his property. When he turned back he saw Tessa was crying. She rarely wept, and certainly never because of him. It's because of 3 Vee's flyer, Bud thought. He went to her, putting his arms around her.

"He did this crazy stunt, Daddy. I was positive he was trying to kill himself. I don't know what's wrong with him. I just know he hurts."

"You should stop seeing him," Bud said.

She pulled away from him, wiping her eyes. "I don't truly understand what happened between you and your brother," she said quietly. "But whatever it was, there's no reason for Kingdon and me not to be friends."

The suppressed, unthinkable memory ached in Bud's head. "Tessa, I'm not going to order you to stay away from him. You know exactly how I feel, and I leave it up to you." His voice hardened. "If he doesn't want to come to my house, fine. That makes two of us. I don't want him here. Is that clear? I don't want him in my house."

·7·

Amélie had just dismissed her maid. Her topaz hair, touched now with gray, had been waved prettily around a face that time had treated well. Fragile and erect in her creamy formal gown with its tracery of bugle beads, she wasn't too different from the old Amélie.

"I heard you come in a half hour ago," she said.

Bud stared at her. How could she not know? It was in all the papers. But of course the answer was very simple. Amélie scanned the morning *Los Angeles Times* for war news—a Lamballe was a brevet general, two younger cousins lay under marble crosses. Other than that, she never read newspapers, a holdover, she admitted, from the Deane Trial.

"Bud," she said, pouring him a Scotch. "What is wrong?"

"I've been with Tessa." He flung the newspapers on the table. "Behold. Kingdon Vance, war hero, flying ace. We knew him as Charley Kingdon Van Vliet!"

Amélie stared down, her face draining of color.

Bud said, "3 Vee's boy is hanging around Tessa! That's what's wrong!"

"Hanging around?" Amélie's clear voice came in a little gasp. 3 Vee's son? Her daughter? Though doctors had reassured both her and Bud that they were capable of having other children, the years of relentless infertility had done nothing to assuage Amélie's doubts. She had vowed never to think of Tessa as 3 Vee's child. Yet vows have no meaning at such moments. The memory of a dark, rocking carriage impinged as she picked up the paper and began to read. "He is kissing her," she said.

Bud gulped his drink. "Something to do with the stunt being finished. It's nothing."

"But it says they are sweethearts."

"No! She gave me a lot of business about his being wounded, hurt. She's helping him and that's that."

"You are positive?"

Bud downed the remainder of his drink. "3 Vee's boy sneaking around my girl! Isn't that enough?"

"Bud, we must tell her."

"What?"

"About herself."

"She knows every damned thing!"

"I mean—"

"She knows I hate his father's guts!"

Bud's face was red with anger, his mouth was stretched with pain. And Amélie realized how deep his long-ago pledge went. Utterly loyal to Tessa, he would do anything rather than question whether she was his. *Can* he question it? Amélie asked herself.

"You are sure there is nothing between them?"

"I told you already. Nothing! She's got some bee he needs her help, that's all."

I must tell Tessa, Amélie thought, her hand tensing on her skirt.

"How could she go sneaking behind my back?" Bud sat, his hands on his knees, his head pulled into his shoulders like a wounded animal. His eyes were baffled. "We've always been open with her, and she's told us everything. Amélie, I lost my temper with her. I never did that before. She began to cry. Amélie, I made her cry." His own eyes were wet.

And Amélie knew she could not go to Tessa. How could she expose the doubts that Bud had banished with such pain? How could she reopen so grave a wound? I will not do it, she thought. I will never do it unless I have to.

Bud made an incoherent sound of misery.

"Darling, darling," she said. She fell to her knees in front of him, taking his face in her hands, forcing him to look at her. Bud pulled her into his arms and they clasped at one another, kissing hungrily, desperately. They went into their bedroom and fell on the bed with an urgency that was meant to annihilate a past that filled her memory, a past that Bud would not, could not, remember.

CHAPTER 17

· I ·

Rimini, the ex-butcher, had learned his new trade by mimicry. He had a small but authentic talent for transposing scenes of De Mille, Griffith, Sennett into something uniquely his own. Pushed for time, he didn't bother to transpose. He would copy the action of an entire sequence.

Hiring Kingdon Vance—Captain Kingdon Vance—had been like tossing a coin. Heads was the enormous publicity potential of a genuine Lafayette Escadrille ace, tails was Kingdon's ignorance of acting and the fact that no war film yet had paid for itself. Rimini had enough money for one feature. He viewed the film of Kingdon's crash into the church over and over again. And every time he got that same feeling of fear and fascination.

He signed Kingdon. He got hold of Fairbanks's films and summoned Kingdon to his home, setting up a screen in his long, narrow dining room. Beyond the swinging door, Mrs. Rimini and her black maid kept up a continuous rattle of pots and conversation, a noise barely audible over the whir of the projector.

The Lamb. His Picture in the Papers. Double Trouble. Kingdon watched them, his leg outstretched, an unlit cigarette dangling between his lips. Rimini refused to let him smoke where there was celluloid film. The odd bluish light outlined Kingdon's taut, handsome face.

"See the way he lifts an eyebrow to show his interest in the girl," Rimini said.

"I thought he was showing her he's a pansy."

"What if they do think he's a pansy? To them he's all man."

"That's contradictory."

"Don't worry what it is. Just copy it." Rimini's voice was louder. "Here. Watch how well he moves his body."

Fairbanks leaped from a window, landing gracefully on both feet as he mouthed a silent challenge. "He does have something," Kingdon said.

"He has a lot of somethings."

Tessa was writing the shooting script of *The Aviator*—minus the Crusader. At Rimini's orders, most of Kingdon's scenes involved him taking off, doing aerobatics, landing, or sitting in the cockpit. A minimum of acting would be required.

Rimini invited both Tessa and Lya to the screenings. Tessa he asked because he noticed she had a soothing influence on Kingdon. Lya's invitation had nothing to do with her sexual skill or the fact that she would have a bit in *The Aviator*. Very simply, Rimini respected her dedication. Lya's passion for film extended to every nuance, and with apostolic fervor she pointed out bits of business to Kingdon. The four of them, Lya, Tessa, Rimini, and Kingdon, sat on rosewood dining chairs shipped from the Bronx, and Lya's high, rushing Southern voice would say, "Watch now. This turn, it's very slow." Or, during *Good Bad Man:* "See how clever he is about winning. If he gloated, the audience would hate him. But that grin—I reckon they love him, don't you?"

One evening when Tessa was driving Lya home, she asked, "Won't people notice Kingdon's mimicking Douglas Fairbanks?"

"It's the best way for him to learn," Lya answered. "He won't come across the same at all. He's wilder, more intense, know what I mean? Besides, he's a pilot. That's how they'll think of him. A pilot."

"He's as handsome as Douglas Fairbanks," Tessa said shyly.

"He is, isn't he? Why didn't I notice before? He'll have one million fan clubs."

"Just from being in *The Aviator?*"

"You are a babe in the woods, aren't you? Hon, movie stars aren't born, they're promoted. You saw how that eentsy bit of publicity we did worked? Well, Rimini's got big plans."

"Kingdon won't like being promoted."

"Now you're being right silly. Everybody dreams of being a movie star."

"Not Kingdon," Tessa said firmly.

When her script was finished, Rimini rushed into production. The first day's shooting was scheduled for the barn-studio. Lya stood at a mirror showing Kingdon how to pat on white greasepaint, then outline his eyes with kohl.

"Jesus!" he said. "Makeup!"

"The camera needs big contrasts," she replied.

"What a way to earn a living!"

"Mister Man, you don't need to pretend, not with me. You're excited."

"I am about the reconditioned Spad I'll be flying. But, Lya, looking like a whiffy clown doesn't exactly thrill me."

At the end of that day's shooting she said, "You're not half bad."

"I owe everything to Douglas Fairbanks."

"Wipe off your makeup. We take the same trolley home. Did you know my room has an outside door?"

"The trolley's fine," he said. "But this acting's hard work."

"Oh? Sweet on your cousin?"

"Let's leave Tessa out of it!"

"My, my," Lya said. "Aren't you a big, rough man?"

"Just bushed."

"She's very rich, isn't she?"

"I told you to—"

"Tessa's my dearest friend," Lya said sweetly.

· 2 ·

After several days at the studio, Rimini scheduled the flying sequences. Tex flew his Jenny with German crosses painted on wings and fusilage, Kingdon a renovated Spad blazoned with concentric circles. Above the peaceful Santa Monicas they looped and dove, firing round after round of blanks at one another. The Spad's propeller stuck and Kingdon—in the air—climbed out to give the blade a push. The camera caught it.

Tessa missed the second day of outdoor shooting. That evening Kingdon used Mrs. Codee's Sunset line telephone.

The English butler said, "Miss Van Vliet is unavailable."

"Would you tell her it's Kingdon Van Vliet." The hell with hiding from butlers and rich uncles, he thought. I'm a movie star.

After a pause, the man replied, "She's confined to her bed, Mr. Van Vliet."

The following morning was foggy. The crew and cast, including eight extras wearing spiked German helmets, loitered around the grounded aeroplanes. Rimini kept staring up at the gray blanket. Finally, at three that afternoon, with reluctance, he dismissed everyone.

Kingdon had become friendly with the jovial cameraman, Max, and asked if he could borrow his car.

He drove to the Hollywood Souvenir and Book Shop, then wound east toward Los Angeles. Groves and fields dwindled; he followed trolley tracks through vacant land. To his left the Santa Monicas loomed, dark and mysterious. He came to a row of lush green syringa. Behind the tall, clipped hedge, the hillside fulminated, an oasis of greenery.

Kingdon stopped Max's car, wondering what he was doing at his uncle's house. What drew him here? Tessa, of course. But why hadn't he waited out her illness? She had told him that the bouts of fever rarely lasted more than a few days. Besides, after that one time she had never again suggested he visit. Why not? Was she really ill? Or had she decided not to see him? Had she told the butler to lie to him? Had she ever uttered one dishonest word? Why was he asking all these questions?

He started up the gravel drive. He passed a vine-covered gatehouse, but there were no gates. He came to a fork with the sign SERVICE ENTRANCE. He didn't take it. He wound up through hills covered with carefully tended flower beds and groves of pruned trees in which birds sang. Beyond a terraced garden he glimpsed a huge swimming pool with two diving boards. Private pools were a rare sight in Los Angeles. You normally either battled the surf or paid to use one of the seawater plunges at the beach resorts. Kingdon was impressed.

The drive turned, revealing the house, and he was even more impressed. He did not know that Greenwood had been modeled after Paloverde. To him it resembled the San Gabriel Mission, only far larger and without the bells.

Kingdon slammed the car door in the misty hush. He tugged the intricate wrought-iron chain of a bell. A butler opened the door. The English one? How many butlers do they have? Kingdon pushed the unwrapped book of poetry at him.

"For Miss Van Vliet."

"Who shall I say—"

"The delivery man." Famous movie star reverts to impoverished nephew.

After the servant closed the glass-and-iron door, Kingdon stood there for several moments, gulping raggedly as if he were up where the air is thinner. Slowly he limped down the broad flight of steps. Reaching the car, he glanced up.

She stood in one of the center windows.

Her loose nightgown, of some white material that might have been silk, had no sleeves, and her slender arms were bared. Her dark hair was loose, surrounding her face and falling below her shoulders. He couldn't see her properly. In the shadows of the deep veranda, behind panes of shimmering glass, she was a myth, an enigma. He raised his hand, a salute of recognition. She held up the book, then clasped it between her breasts. The gesture compelled him, touching a part of him that he thought was dead.

He forgot the house, the lavish grounds, the hatred of his uncle. He stared up at the shadowed woman. I was sick with pain, twisted by deformities of the soul, and she soothed me. She is the only person I've ever met uncontaminated by evil. She is truly good, and that's the mystery surrounding her. I should have written that in the book; it's flowery enough. His inward sarcasm didn't alter his feelings. I love her, he thought. And he was stricken with a surge of passion that was fierce, devouring, alive as nothing he had ever experienced on this earth or above it. His emotions were turbulent, stirring every part of his body.

No! She's my cousin, he thought, trying to repel himself out of desire. It's the nightgown, it's her breasts. It's not having wanted or had a woman in so long. She's my cousin! Yet none of this he truly felt. He loved her, and he could no more suppress his love than stop breathing.

She moved from the window.

As Kingdon started the car, he was sweating, shivering, inwardly cursing himself. Temptation in the well-pruned wilderness, he thought. The defender of the true faith battling with the physical reality of desire. Yes, Mother, he thought. Your fears were justified. Of all the women in the world, I had to seek out the daughter of your enemies, my own cousin. You didn't wield that hairbrush hard enough.

I love her, he thought. The missing half of me, the gentle, tranquil half. Tessa. She loves me. I love her. And yet he understood the impossibility of it. The impediments weren't this huge mansion, her fortune, their parents' just or unjust hatred. The problem was his own intransigent heart. He would never be able to forget his guilts. She would always be forbidden. Unclean. Wrong.

It's not fair to her.

I'll forget these few minutes, he thought as he sped down the gravel drive and swerved back onto the empty dust of Hollywood Boulevard.

I'll forget.

But how?

· 3 ·

He went to Lya's hillside rooming house. It was almost five. Descending the slanting path he had seen her take, he rapped at the door he had seen her use.

Lya opened it a slit. She wore a kimono with a bronze dragon spouting fire. Her yellow hair was twined around strips of newspaper to curl it, and the flat, pretty face shone with a gloss of cold cream.

"Why, Kingdon, honey," she said. "I was just getting ready for supper."

"That's what I had in mind."

"Oh?"

"The Alexandria," he said. The Alexandria Hotel at Fifth and Spring drew the important Hollywood crowd.

"It'll do you and me a world of good to be seen there," she said.

"First, however . . ."

He gave the door a sharp push and she fell back.

"The landlady's a tiger," Lya hissed. "Come on in, quick."

He closed the door, looking around. Crepe myrtle shadowed the crowded room. Three glittery formal gowns hung outside the closet door. Dolls, the kind given as amusement-park prizes, sat on a low boudoir chair. Opposite the Murphy bed, which was conveniently down, hung Woolworth-framed photographs of Pearl White, William S. Hart, Douglas Fairbanks, Lillian Gish, Wallace Reid, Charlie Chaplin, Fatty Arbuckle and—of course—Mary Pickford. Directly in front of these, standing on a tripod, was a motion-picture camera. Kingdon wondered where she had gotten it.

"Pushing your way in." She hugged the kimono around her thin body. "The very idea!"

"Your very idea. You invited me."

"I don't remember doing any such thing."

"The day shooting started. Before that you hadn't seen me. Noticed me, that is."

Lya's rosebud mouth formed a smile. "Getting near a camera brings a person into focus," she said.

Much as Kingdon disliked her admission, he found in it a comradeship. He and Lya shared the common language of those whose lives are dedicated to a single goal. She lived by the distortion of a hand-cranked camera. His existence was centered between doped canvas wings.

"You look wild. Rough," she said, her pointed tongue licking her lips. She glanced down. "And ready."

As he reached for her, she stepped back and pulled the curtains. In the dim light she faced him, untying the sash, slipping off the kimono, standing unmoving. Her body, nude, appeared straighter, leaner, smaller-breasted and more narrow-hipped. Her waist had very little indentation. The paper curlers made her head larger. Staring at her, Kingdon knew how very much he yearned to feel his cousin's tall, slender body pressed against the length of his, to be warmed by the warmth of her woman's breasts. I need this, he told himself. Lya's willing. Who am I betraying? Love, he thought. He stripped hastily down to his underwear. The angry scar-map that stretched all the way up his left thigh shamed him.

Lya was naked on the Murphy bed. His body shaking with impersonal lust, he lowered himself onto her, and as he did, he realized the fronts of her evening gowns, the photographs of movie stars, the dolls faced them. An audience.

He shut his eyes and thrust into her lean complaisance. Her shallow gray eyes searched through the gloom. Her body arched and writhed, an orgiastic pantomime for the glimmering lens.

· 4 ·

The fog lasted three days. Rimini, frantic at the additional costs, rampaged across stubbled hills, barking through his megaphone at the hidden sun.

At the end of the week it finally emerged. Tessa, too, showed up. Her fits of illness embarrassed her, and she blushed as she thanked Kingdon for his phone call, his visit, and the book of poetry. After that she came every day, parking under a live oak, ready to make any changes that Rimini requested, watching the shooting. Kingdon avoided being alone with her. And every night he went to Lya's room to act out his side of a lie in front of an empty camera.

One night Lya presented him with a copy of *Motion Picture World*. It featured an article about him. He was also beginning to be mentioned in gossip columns, invariably referred to as Captain-Kingdon-Vance-wounded-hero-of-the-Lafayette-Escadrille. Lya's name was often linked with his. When Kingdon asked if she were behind the stories, she admitted it.

"A friend of mine is a publicist at Lasky Studio."

"Your list of friends is enviable," he said. "Tell the man I don't want him dirtying up the Escadrille."

"It's all true, isn't it?"

"That's why I don't want it used. *The Aviator*'s the lie."

"Honey baby, you're being plain stupid. How-all do you think stars are born?"

"By being whores," he said bitterly.

She rolled over on the Murphy bed. She was naked, he wore his underwear. Having once glimpsed the full extent of his wound, she was adamant about not seeing it again. Hollywood, her Avalon, her Isle of the Blest, was a place of two-dimensional perfection where the scars could be washed away. His inerasable wound nauseated her.

She raised up on her elbow, looking seriously at him. "You're at a crucial time. You can be the biggest there is." She spoke without envy or greed.

"Lya," he sighed. "It's just not what I have in mind."

"A movie star can have whatever he wants. Money, aeroplanes, women."

"The moon, too?"

"I'm serious. Listen, you're a very complicated man and that's why you come across so well. But being complicated stops you from knowing what it is you want—well, maybe you know, but you don't go out and get it. You fight yourself every step of the way."

That night he came to a decision. Lya was right. He was his own worst enemy. The wounds outside and in hurt too much. For once in his life he was going to stop fighting and behave in a simple, straightforward way. He was going to have what he really wanted. He lay awake thinking of Tessa.

On September 25, the last scene was shot on the barn-stage. Kingdon sent out for a keg of beer. The cameraman, Max, fished out a bottle. Jokes and toasts rang through the crowd. Girlfriends and wives appeared. Mismatched couples disappeared. At one point everyone linked arms, singing "Auld Lang Syne."

It was after dark when Kingdon walked Tessa to her car. A moonless night, the scent of the nearby orange grove was overpowering. The sound of dry earth underfoot was intensified by the velvet darkness. A cool damp had slipped in from the Pacific.

"So much for *The Aviator*," he said.

She sighed.

"Are you sorry it's over?" he asked.

"Yes."

They were at the Mercer. He took her arm. "So am I. Remember when I met you at the Hollywood Hotel? I was one of the walking dead. Numbed. As if I'd been given enough ether to kill me, but my brain wasn't quite dead. I couldn't think or feel. I shook in my shoes whenever I heard an aeroplane. And here I am, doing stunts. Tessa, are you wondering why I'm unhappy *The Aviator*'s finished?"

"Yes."

He put both hands on her shoulders. He could see the outline of her face but not her expression. He felt the trembling warmth of her breath, he smelled her perfume, which was deep and mysterious. "It's because I have to make a little speech."

"Don't say anything . . ."

"How else will you know what's in my mind?" he asked.

"I love you."

"You already told me."

"When?"

"You think it all the time," he said. "You stood in the window touching my book to your heart."

"I . . . Kingdon . . ." She reached for his hand on her shoulder, briefly, lightly pressing it between her breasts. There was a tentative awkwardness in the gesture, still it roused him far more than Lya's practiced wiles.

He bent to kiss the silk over her soft breasts, and she held his head to her, murmuring his name. He moved his hands over her body, feeling the slender curves tremble under his touch. He had a peculiar sense of having done this before, of inevitability.

"Home is where the heart is." His whisper was muffled by her breasts. "This is my home."

He raised his head to kiss her cool eyelids and her eyelashes fluttered against his lips. He kissed her mouth, bracing both his legs on either side of hers so their bodies could be yet closer. This kiss, or so it seemed to him, put them outside time and reality, and he no longer had to consider the implications of the future. He parted her lips, touching her tongue with his own, barely moving away to whisper, "Sunday?"

"What?"

"I said I'd tell you when I was ready to meet them." He touched her earlobe, which was soft. "Sunday dinner. The hour an honorably intentioned suitor comes to call."

"We're going to the cottage," she murmured.

"Where's that?"

"Sunset Boulevard almost to the beach. The cutoff has a big sycamore with our name carved on it."

"Van Vliet?"

"Yes."

"I'll try to remember that one." He kissed her again. "You didn't persist in your invitation. Why?"

"He doesn't like you. My father."

"There he has the advantage. He can remember me. I can't remember him. Still, I'm sure I won't like him."

"Kingdon?"

"Oh, don't worry. Since my Douglas Fairbanks lessons, I'm able to put on an act. Love, I'll win him."

She raised her mouth to his. Kissing her, he traced her breasts with his hands. He trembled.

Her mouth still on his, she murmured, "The car?"

At first he didn't understand her. Comprehending, he surged with an emotion more devouring than he had experienced standing on the steps at Greenwood. He pulled her closer.

Suddenly they heard voices. People emerging from Rimini's barn. Reality.

"You never have," he whispered. "I'm willing to wait—not really willing . . . . My God, you've got me doing it."

"Darling?"

"Love, love, the back seat of a Mercer with movie folk strolling by isn't how I intend to introduce you to the vale of earthly delights."

Aching, longing, yearning, he pushed her away.

· 5 ·

The Van Vliets' cottage lay an hour of driving from Green-wood, in a canyon approximately two miles from the Pacific. The main hall was connected by a long grape arbor to individual sleeping quarters; each cabin had a screened porch overlooking the polo field. Bud found polo less exciting than the rodeos of his youth. But the bankers and others he did business with enjoyed playing, and sometimes he even let them win. A financially rewarding sacrifice. He, Chaw Di Franco, Chaw's twin boys, Tim and Jonathan, who were in Paloverde Oil's legal department, and Hovis Gold (through Doña Esperanza a third cousin to Bud) generally practiced here every Saturday and Sunday. But following this weekend, Bud and Amélie were scheduled to leave for Washington, D.C., and no guests had been invited. Anyone who dropped in, of course, would be expected to stay and enjoy a barbecue.

No matter how many guests were at the cottage, Bud and Tessa got up at dawn, just the two of them, saddling their own horses for a prebreakfast ride. They wore old clothes. Today Bud had on faded denims and a wool shirt fraying at the cuffs. She wore the broadcloth split riding skirt and white pullover she had owned since she was sixteen. They rode through the canyon. An underground stream watered taproots of oak and sumac. The birds hadn't yet outsung their morning joy.

Tessa's lips were curved in a smile as she absently patted her horse's neck. She was wrapped in a dream. Kingdon had roused in her a side of love she hadn't known existed. Paul Schott's kisses had been chaste, as befitted her father's employee, and her few other beaux, shy as herself, had hardly dared to touch her. Her mother had never spoken of carnal love. Her private education and inherent reticence had protected her further. She knew only slightly more of matters sexual than had Amélie at fifteen when she rode into a tumbledown rancho with Bud Van Vliet. Now, Tessa was wrapped around her secret core, her flesh alive, expectant.

"You're quiet this morning," Bud said.

Tessa clenched her reins. "Kingdon's visiting tomorrow." The words rushed out.

Bud, in his surprise, tensed. His Morgan stallion broke into a trot. At the bottom of a leaf-covered slope he halted, waiting for Tessa. "Your mother mentioned that he stopped at Greenwood when you had the fever."

"Then it's all right?" Tessa asked, hopeful.

"What do you mean, all right?"

"That he's having lunch. Daddy, you said he wasn't to come to the house."

Bud shrugged. "Doesn't matter either way to me. This trip east. I have to work."

Tessa's hope faded. Her expression of misery combined with what Amélie called the Van Vliet look—a stubborn tightening of the jaw.

"It's important to me," she said in a low voice.

"I brought up a pile of papers. You saw."

Neither spoke as they splashed through a rivulet. Maidenhair fern grew in the shade of a drooping live oak.

Bud sighed. "Tessa, you know I'd welcome anyone else. Anyone."

"Is your hatred so deep?" she asked, unable to look at Bud, watching a startled bird rise from the ferns.

Bud's face was as unhappy as hers. Then he remembered. Amélie had warned him that rejection might push Tessa toward her cousin.

"I guess," he said, forcing joviality into his voice, "if the mountain's finally decided to come have lunch with Mahomet, the least Mahomet can do is take off a couple hours."

Before this, Tessa and Bud had never battled. His inability to surrender was unknown to her. She gave him a long, happy smile.

"There's a certain interest," he said, "if you must know, in meeting my nephew."

"Thank you," she murmured.

"*De nada*," he replied.

Had Amélie been there, she would have understood his intent. And under normal circumstances she would have stopped him. But these weren't normal circumstances.

They rode back to the cottage and had a large breakfast together. Amélie did not join them. She always slept late and had her breakfast in bed. Finishing his second cup of coffee, Bud announced abruptly, "Need to get a move on. I have to go into town—there's some leases I forgot in the office safe."

"I'll drive with you, Daddy."

"No. Better not. I have to talk to some people before I face the Washington government boys, and who knows how long it'll take. Thanks, though." Smiling, he kissed her.

·6·

Bud parked the Stutz outside the cheaply constructed bungalow court. His cheeks were hot. He loathed himself for what he was about to do. He wished he knew more about his opponent.

Paloverde Oil had investigators who checked future employees, certified the validity of mineral leases and made sure, financially, of its customers. It would have been easy for Bud to have initiated a dossier on Charley. He had asked for his address, no more. He shrank from having his daughter's friend—his own kin—raked over. I was a sentimental fool, he thought as he walked up the path bordered by bushes quivering with huge yellow hibiscus.

At apartment 2B, he pressed the porcelain button and waited. He rang again and waited. Shaking his head, he turned and started back to his car.

"Sir," a masculine voice called. "Mrs. Codee's not in, but if you'd like to leave a message . . ." A young man stood at the open screen door. Tieless, his soft-collared shirt open, his sleeves rolled up to show strong forearms, he held a towel. "Sorry I didn't hear you before. I was shaving."

There had been newspaper photographs, yet Bud wouldn't have needed them. The deep-set brown eyes, the oval face, the thick black hair, even the arched nose. Yes.

Peering across the sunlit court at his nephew, Bud was shaken by a wild conflict of emotions. He couldn't reply. Always he had felt a protective urge toward those in his family, and for Bud they included descendants of his mother's "people." And always he had the strength to be compassionate toward the young. Yet looking into this face, 3 Vee's face, that locked-away secret stirred. And Bud, battling the forbidden memory of loss, his irrevocable, unbearable loss, peered at his brother's son, thinking, a Garcia.

Kingdon was squinting at him. "You're not here to see Mrs. Codee," he said. "Uncle?"

Bud cleared his throat. "Yes. Bud Van Vliet. You're Charley."

"Kingdon."

"I wanted to see you, Kingdon."

"You're jumping the gun, sir. Or didn't Tessa tell you I'm visiting tomorrow?"

Bud took a step toward his nephew. "Talking'll be easier today."

"Easier?" Kingdon's fingers tightened on the door, as if he were ready to close it. "To warn me off Tessa, you mean?"

Bud inhaled, forcing his mind to unclench and his body to relax. "We, your aunt and I, have been hoping you'd visit. We're your family. And as for Tessa, you're her cousin. It pleases me you're friends."

"Funny. Tessa thinks you don't like me."

"Do we have to stand here, a door between us?" Bud said. "Come on, Charley. Kingdon. Buy you a drink."

"At ten-thirty?"

"I thought actors were a thirsty breed."

"I'm a pilot."

"How about a cup of coffee, then?" Bud smiled. It was that old, brutally charming smile.

Kingdon hesitated, then held the door open. "Come on in. Mrs. Codee's away."

"Mrs. Who?"

"I rent her second bedroom. She won't mind if we use the living room."

Bud had the impression of clutter, of innumerable mementos of cheap tourism, photographs of vivid blue skies and bluer bays, satin pillows embossed with resort names, plaster bric-a-brac. He doesn't even have a place to himself, Bud thought, and this made the boy yet more vulnerable. Again he examined Kingdon. There was less of a resemblance to 3Vee than he had originally thought. His nephew had a tension that 3Vee lacked, a curled wire inside him, a tautness of muscle. He's wilder than 3Vee ever dreamed of being, this one. *Has he taken her already?* The thought repulsed Bud and his expression hardened.

"You were right about that drink, sir. We need one. I have some bourbon. All right with you?"

"Fine."

As Kingdon went down the short hall, Bud noted the effort to walk easily. His leg hurts all the time, Tessa had said. And he's hurt inside. Still, Bud thought, he doesn't want pity. He felt a surge of affection. But his bewildering revulsion remained, and his purpose for coming here did not waver. Yet at the same time, he ordered himself: Go easy on the boy.

Kingdon returned wearing a striped tie and carrying two tumblers and a pint bottle of something called Mountaineer's Joy.

"How's 3Vee—your father?"

"Haven't seen him in almost eight years. I guess he's the same old cormorant."

"Cormorant?"

"A fishing bird that the Chinese domesticate. They tie a silk string around the cormorant's neck. The bird does what nature compels it to. It dives for fish, but the string prevents it from swallowing the catch, so it returns and disgorges the fish for the owner. My father discovers oil, but he can't afford his own rig, so he brings his findings to Union Oil. He's never going to be more than a cormorant. A failure. He knows it. My mother lets him know it. Isn't that what you wanted to hear?"

Bud shook his head. "No, not of anyone. Especially not of 3Vee.

People tell me I'm a difficult opponent, Kingdon, but nobody to my knowledge ever called me vindictive. He's my kid brother..." Bud was speaking with difficulty. "I... well, that's what I used to call him. Kid."

Kingdon, silent, poured them each a drink. He handed a glass to Bud, and Bud set it on the table amid Mrs. Codee's souvenirs.

"Sir, can we start over? I told Tessa I'd make you like me. So far I haven't been very ingratiating."

At Tessa's name, Bud stirred uneasily. His affection for the boy had increased even as he was thinking: How can I have him near her? "I'd like to be friends," he lied. "They tell me aeroplanes will be a major consumer of petroleum some day. I don't believe a word of it." He chuckled. "But then I didn't believe the horse would be replaced by the internal combustion engine. Gasoline was a waste product then. So I'm in need of an aviator to teach me the new ropes."

Kingdon didn't reply. He was looking at Bud as if he were trying to learn a new language by lip reading. Someone in the court slammed a door; a faraway child shouted.

After a long pause, Bud said hoarsely, "I'm not going at this right, either. Kingdon, she's my only child. I love her very much. I don't really know her. She doesn't have the normal handles people have. Not a hint of greed, envy, pride. She's completely without vanity. Who can understand a person like that? What I'm trying to say is she's true innocent."

Kingdon drank and said nothing.

"Whereas you—oh, hell, Kingdon. I've been where you are. You're an actor, a flyer. Good-looking. If there's pretty women for the taking, only a fool or a eunuch resists. For all I know you have someone else right now."

A nerve jumped in Kingdon's eyebrow, then his face was utterly still.

Bud went on. "Tessa was right. Before I met you, I didn't like you. I wanted to hate you. And now I find I have an affection for you. Do they still use the term 'ties of the blood'? I feel that tie with you. A kinship. Did you know we're part Indian? No. How could you? I've only told my wife—and now you. It didn't mean a damn to Amélie, but to me—we Californios are so damn proud of being all Spain. I'm saying this to avoid the point."

"The point being I should get in my gasoline-burning aeroplane and fly off?"

"She's good, Kingdon. I don't know why. She just is. Yes. I'm asking you to leave her alone. There. My cards are on the table."

"I'm not picking up my hand."

"The deeper she's entangled, the harder it'll be for her."

"Let's see. Isn't the next step, Uncle, for you to attempt to buy me off?"

"You're not the cynical bastard you're pretending to be."

"Did you ever consider I love her?"

"That," Bud said, "is my ace."

Kingdon gulped down the remainder of his drink. "Then I don't understand the game. How will my loving Tessa keep me away from her?"

"You're a Catholic." It was Bud's turn to wait, watchful.

"Ex-Catholic," Kingdon muttered.

"Then you've never considered the relationship a barrier?"

"Why should I?" Kingdon asked. "The Church has no holds on me."

"That so?"

"None."

There was silence in the room. Then Bud spoke again. "You'll notice that I'm not mentioning any arguments between 3 Vee and me, and I don't insult you by mentioning the money involved here. I question only your religion—your ex-religion. I asked, Kingdon, how you feel about having your cousin as your wife?"

"Tessa's not a Catholic."

"I know she isn't. And I suppose consanguinity"—Bud said the word carefully—"doesn't matter to her."

"You're making much of the Church's influence on me, Uncle."

"I know your mother. I know Utah. Even when you were a baby, she was beating sin and guilt into you. It's there, Kingdon, and deep. The more you try to escape, the harder you're entangled."

"Saying things, Uncle, doesn't make them true."

"I'm asking whether you're being fair to Tessa—and yourself." Bud paused. "No. All I'm asking is whether you're being just to her. Kingdon, she loves you without any reservations. But what about you? Are you coming to her with the open decency she deserves? Or are you covering up every hidden guilt because you need her?"

Kingdon moved to the false mantel cluttered with Mrs. Codee's souvenirs. The white linen of his shirt was taut across his shoulders; muscles quivered, then were still.

Bud's revulsion turned inward. He sank back in his chair. Having asked his obviously wounded nephew to probe his deepest motivations, he found himself unable to so much as ask himself the simple question: Why am *I* doing this? Still there was no profit in examining motives at the point of victory.

"If I'm wrong about you, come to the cottage tomorrow at noon," he said. "It's all the answer I need."

Kingdon didn't reply.

After a minute Bud said quietly, "I better be getting along."

"Goodbye, Uncle," Kingdon said. He did not offer his hand.

Bud picked up his hat and closed the door quietly behind him. He drove three blocks, then parked. Sweat drenched him. His saliva tasted bitter. He crossed his arms on the steering wheel, burying his face in his arms. The weakness of failure overpowered him. But why? He had won, hadn't he?

· 7 ·

The next morning, after they rode and ate breakfast, Tessa took a long, steaming bath scented with lavender salts. At the cottage she never put up her hair. She tied it back with a crimson ribbon that matched the roses on her Liberty print dress. Sitting on the screened porch of the living room, she held a book but watched the drive from the main road where the stableboys were walking the polo ponies.

Kingdon hadn't arrived by one. Lunchtime. The Stewarts had dropped by. Bud held off serving the steaks until almost two. Tessa didn't eat. After the Stewarts drove off in their Rolls-Royce, Amélie retired with Kathryn, her maid, to list clothing she would need on the trip to Washington. Bud spread mineral leases and maps on the big library table. Tessa returned to sit on the porch, her hands clasped over her bare, cold arms. All pretense at reading gone, she stared down the drive.

A car raised dust. Tessa stood. It was only the closed motor truck that belonged to the cottage. Bud came out of the house and rested his booted foot on the running board. The driver handed him a stack of newspapers. He stared at one and then walked slowly back to the screened porch. Mute, he gave Tessa a copy of the *Evening Clarion*. She looked down at the headlines.

CAPTAIN KINGDON VANCE ELOPES WITH LYA BELL.
LAFAYETTE ESCADRILLE ACE FLIES ACTRESS
SWEETHEART TO MEXICO TO WED HER.

The aviator and his lovely blonde bride met while he was starring in *The Aviator*, a Rimini Production.

"I'm the happiest and proudest man alive," declared war hero Captain Kingdon Vance this morning in Tijuana, Mexico, after his marriage.

Tessa didn't read further. Carefully, she refolded the paper, setting it on the bentwood chair. She gazed out at the polo field, which was covered with evening shadows. Scars of hoofprints showed black.

"Tessa, honey, come here," Bud said, holding out his arms. The misery on his face was real. Tessa, however, remained expressionless. The blow hadn't sunk in. Turning away from him, she moved under the grape arbor to her cabin.

That night Bud was unable to sleep. Pulling on his bathrobe, he went outside to smoke. He heard the crickets, an owl, and a peculiar, rhythmic throbbing. He walked slowly to Tessa's cabin, his cigar a red moving dot in the night.

The sound was Tessa's strangled sobs, the sound of irreconcilable grief. Bud shivered. On the surface he had committed a vast cruelty. His brain told him he had had no right to interfere. And certainly once he had met and liked 3Vee's pilot, what had been the point of using the boy's wounds and guilts to throw him off balance? What difference did it make to *him* that they were cousins? They came of good stock. *How could I have done this to my Tessa?* he asked himself. Yet his heart denied self-macerating reason. He listened to Tessa's adult grief with the same emotions of that long-ago night when he had cut her throat that she might breathe. He stood at her door, weak and shaking at what he had done, yet triumphant. *I've saved my Tessa.*

He knocked. "Tessa," he said. "Let me help you."

She had stopped crying when she opened the door. Still dressed in the crumpled Liberty print, nose and eyes red, cheeks pale, she went to wash her face. As Bud listened to the slow splashing, he knew he could not pose as her comforter. He couldn't continue bestowing the Judas kiss.

When she emerged from the bathroom, he said, "Saturday morning I visited him."

She looked at him with raw eyes. "What for?"

"To remind him you were cousins."

Tessa went to stare out a window. A dim moon whitened the polo field. She said nothing.

"Tessa, there must have been something between them, him and Lya Bell, before this."

She nodded. "I'm going away," she said.

"Where?"

"France."

"You can't."

"I'm going," she said.

"Do you hate me?"

"You had no right," she said, her hands tightening on the window sill. "No right at all."

Again reason told him to weep, to grieve. Yet that wan baffling gratitude persisted. I've saved her, he thought.

CHAPTER 18

· I ·

Tessa's pen halted. She raised her head and looked out of the window over the gardens. Her abstraction changed to a bewildered shame. Unbelievable, she thought. Did I ever take this, my home, for granted? Three years of working in the Rouen orphanage had widened her perspective to include guilt. Even small things, like biting into a crisp green apple or drying her hands on a thick towel, could flay her. Who am I to deserve comfort? Why me? Who suffers that I might have this? In her new view of life, she understood that renunciation of possessions isn't of necessity saintly virtue; stripping oneself to the lowest human denominator also divests one of the hair shirt of guilt.

Three years to the month had passed since the September night she had wept away her innocence. Not only Tessa, but the world had altered far more than this brief span implied.

The Great War had carved a temporal chasm. All that had existed on the far side appeared uncorrupted—or antiquated. Automobiles, no longer nervous contraptions beset by mysterious internal ailments, toys of the rich, had become installment-purchased necessities speeding on changeable tires across widening networks of Southern California roads. Movies had come into their own, and even in the remotest jungles and deserts people were aware of a town called Hollywood. Prohibition had become a law of the land.

And there was a creature called the new woman. Long skirts and petticoats, corsets and envelope chemises had been discarded for weightless silk underwear and narrow dresses that bared the knees. Rouged lips held cigarettes that were lit in public. The new woman proved her daring modernity by bobbing her hair.

Tessa had bobbed. She and Agnes, the other American volunteer at l'Orphelinat de Rouen, had used blunt institutional scissors on one another. It was not an act of rebellion; war produces an over-abundance of orphans and there wasn't time to bother with long hair. Tessa's slender neck rose like a stem to the glossy black petals that swung to her earlobes. She wore a red crepe frock with a pleated skirt that showed the new flesh-colored stockings. Yet she hadn't become boyishly modern, and neither had she aged or hardened. She had the look of a woman acquainted with the vocabulary of sorrow. Her eyes, however, weren't mournful. When they weren't red-streaked from writing too long, they shone serenely.

A discreet tap. "It's time, Miss Tessa," said a woman's voice burred with a Scottish accent.

"Oh, Kathryn, come on in."

Her mother's thin, freckled maid opened the door, moving through the study and bedroom to turn on the bathroom faucets.

Tessa raised her arms over head, wearily arching her back before she assembled the sheaf of papers on the study table, a chapter of her novel, as yet untitled, about l'Orphelinat de Rouen. Her first writing since *The Aviator*, and very different. The novel was no escape; she wasn't inventing stories. Her experience had been very real. She agonized in her fear of misrepresenting the too-silent toddlers, the lethargic-eyed infants, the vicious children, the maimed ones, the vermin-infested newcomers—humanity's rejects all.

Kathryn called over running water, "Is it out tonight?"

"Yes. To the Ambassador."

"That huge new hotel out on Wilshire Boulevard?"

"Yes."

"What's happened to people nowadays, wasting good money in hotels when they can eat better at home?" Kathryn emerged from the dressing room holding up two long formal gowns, a crimson peau de soie and a midnight-blue chiffon.

"The blue, please. I'd rather stay home."

"You're not tired?" asked Kathryn, her mouth thinning with concern.

Two months ago Tessa had arrived home with one of her fevers, alarmingly thin, coughing. The fever had passed, she had gained back some weight, the cough was gone. Her parents and the staff of Greenwood remained preoccupied with her health.

"Not at all," Tessa replied with forced cheer. She would have preferred going to bed early, just as she would have preferred drawing her own bath and choosing her own dress, but as the latter would have hurt the little Scotswoman, so the former would have worried her parents. As an unmarried woman nears thirty, she owes it to her family to accept every masculine invitation. Tonight she was to be with the euphoniously named head of Paloverde Oil's service station division. Hollis Horace.

Kathryn departed, leaving on the bed a small silken pile of underwear and the deep-blue dress with its skirt outspread toward the matching silk shoes below.

Tessa began undressing. She told herself her parents were right. She herself didn't want to go through life vicariously. I want my own children, I want a husband. I want again to feel the living heat of passion . . . she ordered herself not to think of Kingdon. It was impossible.

Lying in the hot, scented bathwater, she berated herself for a lack of versatility in love. I've got too much Van Vliet stubbornness, she told herself. To love only a wild and complicated cousin is suspect because so do fifty million other women. Captain Kingdon Vance, The Aviator, The Daredevil, America's Beloved! Get it through your stupid head that you're crying for the moon. You can't have him. All right. He kissed you. One velvet-black night you and he trembled for a few moments. Since then he married your friend and has become a devoted husband. You've read of the Flying Sweethearts in two languages, French and English. Now be realistic. Accept what's available.

Buoyed with good intentions, her pearls knotted below her bosom, her bias-cut chiffon floating, she descended the stairs. Hollis Horace, a large and well-stuffed man, shook her hand carefully. The Paloverde Oil men who invited her out treated her as if she were a rare porcelain object that Bud had entrusted them to carry. Hollis Horace had taken her out four times. He appeared reasonably fond of her—or maybe he preferred a woman who was as boring as he. What was the phrase that Paul Schott had used? Fatally dull.

Hollis Horace was driving a brand-new closed Chrysler Six. She rarely noticed outward trappings, but she told herself that she must try to pay attention to such things. "It's a good-looking car," she said.

Hollis Horace, beaming as if she had paid him a profound personal compliment, opened the door for her. "The fellow who sold it to me invited us for cocktails. If it's all right with you?"

Cocktails were against the law, which accounted for Hollis Horace's anxious tone. Tessa's brief hesitation came from her old shyness. Large groups of strangers terrified her. Possibly another time she would have made an excuse. Tonight, the exemplary Tessa said, "It sounds like fun."

· 2 ·

Kingdon arrived at the Chrysler dealer's party already drunk. Not staggering drunk, blind drunk, pugnacious drunk, or obnoxious drunk—although he could be those. But tonight he had a pleasant buzz, for he was celebrating the end of shooting. Since finishing *The Aviator* he had made sixteen films, and as he gestured and posed for the camera, it was himself he betrayed, for he invariably acted the role of a pilot. Except when he was in the sky, too distant for the camera to ferret out, he loathed Captain Kingdon Vance, movie star. As the door of the brightly lit house opened, Kingdon was thinking *Flick's wrapped up and I can sleep late tomorrow* with the same sense of release he had experienced as a boy when school ended for summer vacation.

Lya gave a high little laugh and let the butler take her new, full-length white ermine cape. Lya, the distaff side of what fan magazines called the Flying Sweethearts. She had pursued her own career with absolute devotion but little reward. Her few credits were the roles Kingdon got her in his films, and Rimini grudged even those. The camera remained as cruel to her as ever, a cruelty Lya refused to believe in. As Kingdon's wife, she had the respect and material rewards of his stardom, and though he told her truthfully that she had earned them, she ached for the thing itself. Her discouragement was hidden by powder and Tangee lipstick.

Lya had transformed herself from Mary Pickford sweetness into a jazz baby, with eyelashes mascaraed into points, yellow hair shingled and marcelled. She had dieted until her face was angular and her body yet more boyish. She slumped fashionably so that spoonsize hollows formed under her collarbones, and her nipples barely marked the gold lamé dress that fell straight as a tube to her sharp knees.

She put a ringed hand on Kingdon's sleeve. "Honey, you take care of yourself, hear," she said. "One drinkee, no more." She started toward the terrace.

"Where're you headed?" Kingdon asked.

"Circulating," she said.

"Oh? Who's here?"

"You know as much as me. We just walked in the door, remember?"

"True. But you never circulate unless there's a reason."

Her arched, penciled brows drew together. "You should talk! Let a girl notice you and there you are, twitching right after her. I can't even keep track any more!" Lya's jealousy flared in a form that was meaningless to her. She had no envy of his women, only his career. Then she was smiling. "Archer," she cried. "You really know how to entertain. This party's got style."

Their host, the Chrysler dealer, descended on them, his large, strong teeth bared in a smile. Nobody ever preceded Archer with a Mr., and Kingdon couldn't remember hearing him called a first name. Archer sells automobiles, Kingdon thought, so it's not him Lya's after. One thing about my wife. She's faithful to Hollywood.

Lya's infidelity no longer wounded him. As she had said, he also took advantage of this particular aspect of his career. His husbandly concern was more generous. His strongest tie with Lya from the beginning had been their peculiar comradeship. She cared about movies in the same all-consuming manner that he cared about aviation. She never dissimulated about her striving. In this respect he was tender to her. He pitied and helped her. He did all he could for her marginal career. He tried to stop her from making a fool of herself.

She and Archer moved toward the terrace. Kingdon went into the sunken living room. Though he had learned to control his limp, the pain was constant; twinges shot through his thigh as he descended the four steps. He got a highball. Archer had a good bootlegger; the Scotch was genuine. A black man was playing the piano, and Kingdon leaned against it.

The guests glanced at him, nudging. He disliked this part of fame, but he had become accustomed to the puffing flashbulbs, the eyes always on him. Another drink—or was it two—and he didn't much notice the stares of newcomers.

St. Louis woman with all her diamond rings . . .

In the entry a heavy-set man was helping a tall, slender girl take off a velvet cape. The deep blue of her chiffon dress was quieter than the glitter and beads of the other women, and for a moment Kingdon stared, not quite believing it was she. He had trouble catching his breath.

· 3 ·

Tessa took the first step into the living room before she let herself glance at the crowd. She saw Kingdon. She went white, immediately afterward turning crimson. The flush faded, leaving small, pale marks at either side of her mouth. He was watching her from the piano.

Drags that man around by her apron strings . . .

A strand of hair lay on his forehead. Fingering it back, he moved toward her.
"Tessa."
She swallowed. "Kingdon," she murmured.
"Long, long time no see."
She continued staring at him until a small cough at her side reminded her of the amenities. "Kingdon, this is Hollis Horace. Hollis, Kingdon Vance."
Hollis's forehead squeezed into lines as he recognized Kingdon. "Captain Vance," he said.
Kingdon shook hands, then turned back to Tessa.
"How's the oil magnate?" he inquired. His expression was one she remembered. Angry, hurt.

"Fine."

"The dress matches your eyes," Kingdon said. "I hear he's drilling up half of Mexico."

"Tessa?" asked the solicitous voice at her side. "Would you care to leave?"

"Kingdon's my cousin."

"Cousin?"

"The living proof that blood doesn't always tell," Kingdon retorted. "Tessa's side of the family is virtuous, intelligent, and successful. As opposed to my side. Ask Uncle Bud—I presume you've had the pleasure? No. Let me guess. You work for him."

The tone was as baiting as the words, and Tessa saw that Kingdon's bitterness toward her father had increased. Her own anger at his interference had faded so long ago that now it seemed improbable. "Hollis *is* with Paloverde Oil," she said. All at once her voice choked and her eyes grew wet.

Kingdon's nastily knowing expression wavered into chagrin, and through her blur she saw what she should have noticed earlier. He was quite drunk.

"Let's us go someplace private," he said. "Time us blood relations caught up."

Hollis Horace protested, "Tessa—"

But Kingdon had taken her arm, which was bare and cold, guiding her swiftly across the hall into a study. He closed the door. They were alone in the small, oak-paneled room.

She sat in a tapestry chair, opening her gold mesh bag, fumbling through it for a handkerchief. He perched on the desk, fingering the telephone. There was only one; the Sunset and Home lines had merged into Southern California Telephone.

She blew her nose.

"Better?" he asked quietly.

"Better."

"I didn't mean to dive in on you like that," he said, holding up his glass. "Too much."

"You never used to drink."

"That was before I was known as the Daredevil. I didn't have my dashing image to uphold."

"Where's Lya?" she asked.

"Interesting question."

"Isn't she at the party?"

"Oh, certainly. By all means. She's at the party. At this moment she's doubtless having an intimate celebration with some film personage. Upstairs."

Tessa looked down at her evening purse. "I . . . read that you're very happy."

"In Hollywood," he said, "we're artists and therefore entitled to our own happiness and morality. After the first ten times, I shared her happiness—I can't be surprising you about Lya?"

"I . . . yes."

Kingdon played with his glass. "About that Sunday, should I apologize?"

She clenched the handkerchief. "No."

"Did my uncle mention he'd dropped by Saturday?"

"Yes."

"How did you feel about it?"

"Sorry for myself. Furious at him." She looked down at her purse. "Afterward, I realized I'd made too much . . . well, of everything. I . . . I had assumed you meant . . . well, I assumed."

"You overconfident heiresses always assume too much. I *did* mean. I meant more than you."

"I doubt that," she said.

His right shoe swung against the desk, thumping lightly. "You read about me. I haven't had the same advantage. The name Van Vliet, female gender, never appears in print, not even in the society pages."

"After that Sunday, I went to France. I was a volunteer nurse at l'Orphinelat de Rouen. The Rouen orphanage."

"Rouen. Let me see. That's where Joan of Arc was burned."

"Yes."

"Were you seeking canonization?"

"No. I knew how petty it was, being there because I couldn't bear Los Angeles." As she spoke she remembered the three-year-old girl who had her legs shot off and who used her calloused palms to push her little cart, the blind infants born of syphilitic mothers, the ragged scarecrow of a boy who stationed himself outside the orphanage, his hand extended. He was poorer even than the inmates. She saved her bread for this boy until she realized it was within her power to help him. She had cabled her father. Until then she had written only to her mother; this was the first time since her arrival she had communicated with Bud. The money she asked for was her own. However, transferring funds in wartime was problematic. Money had arrived the following day, a feat that must have involved Washington. After that she had written often, he sent whatever the children needed, and soon all bitterness had faded. "The orphanage was a hell, yet I had a passport to come and go."

"Was? What happened to the place?"

"My father made an endowment."

"And now the parentless mites are Paloverde heirs and heiresses. A heartwarming ending. Will you go back?"

"No. It makes me, well . . . it's as if I'm taking advantage."

"Don't take my remark about Saint Joan to heart. You don't have to defend yourself."

"To myself I do," she replied. "I distrust charity. To me altruism is always suspect. And two months ago, on the day I realized that my father's money had done so much for the orphanage, and I'd done so little, I left."

"You've always underestimated yourself."

"I don't want to talk about it," she sighed.

He shifted on the desk. "Do you still write?"

"I've started again," she said, adding in a low voice, "I've seen most of your films."

"That," he said, "is hardly anything to boast about."

"You're good."

"Tessa, you don't discuss your time in the orphanage. And one of the three hundred and fifty-seven reasons I drink is because my career delights me. So shut up!"

"Do you think I'm such a mouse that you can frighten me with that tone?" she asked.

"Trying," he admitted, raising an eyebrow, smiling. "Not that I'm against the sordid crassness of money. Remember our drives together with the well-filled picnic baskets from Greenwood?"

"Of course."

"Well, other than a quart of milk and some soda crackers in the evening, that was all I ate. My funds were about to give out, and if you and Lya hadn't thrown me into Rimini's clutches, I'd either have had to move into the Sawtelle Old Soldiers' home or gotten a job."

"I never thought . . ." She looked at him. "Kingdon, what a fool I was in those days."

"You still are," he said. "The good are always fools. I pointed out that detail so you'll realize I didn't give you up lightly. You were against my religion, and not only that, there was a matter of pride. Seeing your father reminded me that you lived in a palace, whereas I—"

He was interrupted by the door opening. Hollis Horace held her wrap over his meaty arm. "Tessa, our dinner reservation is for eight."

"Oh. Hollis. Yes." She stood. "Kingdon, will you tell Lya I'm sorry I missed her."

Kingdon pushed off the desk. "Lya," he said, "will be sorry she missed you."

Tessa was glad he didn't suggest they meet again. There was no question of a threesome. No more Lya, Kingdon, Tessa. The days of innocence were gone. There would be just two of them. And her background, every decency she believed in, urged her not to meet a married man, a man married to her old friend. And yet how could she find the strength to refuse? Hollis helped her on with the cape. Its cold satin lining chilled her arms. She glanced into Kingdon's dark, brooding eyes and knew that this was the last time she would see Hollis Horace.

· 4 ·

Kingdon was hunched behind the desk when the door opened. It was Lya.

"So here's where you're hiding," she said, coming in. "We've been searching high and low."

She was followed by a tall man with a body so narrow he appeared to have been drawn through a reed. His face was an intelligent wedge.

"Kingdon, do you know David Manley Fulton?"

Kingdon never had met David Manley Fulton, but he knew who he was. An Englishman who directed epic dramas more intellectual than De Mille's, but along the same line.

"I've never had the pleasure."

"Captain Vance," Fulton said, extending a long thin hand. A star sapphire glinted on his middle finger.

Normally when Lya introduced him to a male in the industry, Kingdon felt a scraping like a fingernail inside his head. She's sleeping with him, he would think. But this time he was taken up with thoughts of Tessa. And besides, as he took the attenuated hand, he decided: a queer. "I'm pleased to meet you, Mr. Fulton. I admire your work."

"No more than I admire yours, Captain Vance," Fulton replied in an Oxford accent that might have been fraudulent. "One hears you were with the Lafayette Escadrille."

"Just after it was formed, I let myself be downed."

"But you did fly in France?"

"With the Légion d'Étrangers," Kingdon said. "Rimini's publicity has built him a studio and me a career, but between us, don't believe a word you hear."

"Mrs. Vance has been telling me of you."

"A wife's hardly impartial, either."

"Kingdon makes a big virtue out of modesty, Mr. Fulton," Lya said. "He always has. But it's true. He was a real ace."

"Short A," Kingdon said.

David Manley Fulton chuckled. "Good show, anyway. I plan to do a film about the chivalry of aviators. The last Knights of the Round Table, so to speak."

"Crusaders," Kingdon said, thinking of Tessa. He wanted to get away from David Manley Fulton. There was a disturbing facet to his narrow elegance, the clipped tones, the heavy-lidded eyes. Come to think of it, there was a disturbing element to his films, an understructure of decadence.

"Would you be interested?" Fulton asked.

"In helping you research?"

"Kingdon!" Lya cried. "In being in his film."

"Lya!" Kingdon mimicked. "You were present when I signed my contract. And so were attorneys on both sides. It's legal and binding. Rimini Productions pays for our bacon, booze, and bunny skins."

"If one were to discuss with Mr. Rimini about borrowing you . . . ?" Fulton paused delicately.

One could take a long, flying you-know-what, Kingdon thought. His shrug revealed the thought.

"Well, I must be off," the Englishman said abruptly. Lya waved coquettishly.

"That must've been quite a conversation," Kingdon said.

"Oh, he's a sissy, and I didn't know what-all to say, so I talked about you and the war."

"I'll bet he ate it up," Kingdon said, reaching for his drink. "Lya, why don't we go away for a few days?"

"You've forgotten," she reproached. "Tomorrow Mr. Horthy gets in."

Lya had hired Padraic Horthy, the eminent New York drama coach, ostensibly for both of them, in actuality for herself. It was a huge extravagance, but then neither of them was frugal. She was paying Horthy's fare and considerable salary in the hope that he could turn the trick for her.

Kingdon finished his now-watered drink. "Tex wants to sell Zephyr Field. I'm thinking of buying."

"Why?"

"My pleasure."

"When would you find time to run it?"

"Instead of acting," he said.

She turned on him, her sharp face crinkling with annoyance. She couldn't comprehend that movies didn't fully involve everyone. She thought of Kingdon's flying as part of his screen persona, no more. "Quit your teasing!" she snapped.

It was the same angered reproach his mother had used, and he immediately realized the foolishness of his idea. The accouterments of stardom—tailormade tuxedos, ermine capes, the best drama coaches, bootleggers, and girls—are impossible to walk away from. He held up his empty glass. "I'm returning to the party," he said.

Lya went with him. He didn't mention Tessa. He didn't intend to see her again, and even if he had, Lya wouldn't have cared. So why didn't he mention her?

· 5 ·

Padraic Horthy was a large, sloping old man topped by a halo of curly white hair. Lya had refurnished the guest cottage for him. Each morning at ten he circled the swimming pool on his rope-soled slippers and entered Eagle's Roost, as Kingdon and Lya had named their house. The drama coach stayed until six, filling the library with cigarette smoke and his deep actor's voice, going over scenes from plays with Lya. Sometimes they reversed roles, Padraic Horthy playing a dying coquette while Lya acted her lover. Or they invented gibberish instead of words. Or they played the scene infinitely slowly. It was customary for studios to hire musicians to get actors into various moods and Padraic Horthy often played a gramophone record throbbing with sentiment. He enjoyed good living, yet he was no charlatan. He worked Lya until anxiety snapped at her like electric sparks on a cat.

Her high little Southern voice raced. She ate quickly, slept badly. She and Kingdon had never shared the same room. Now she made it clear she didn't want him even to come near her. She told him that sex drained one, and she was remaining celibate for the time being.

Alternately he pitied her and was embarrassed by her. He tried not to compare her to Tessa.

He was drinking more heavily than usual when his next picture started. The story of a barnstormer who cures people's troubles by taking them up for flights, it grated on an already raw nerve. He drank more. Some mornings when the makeup man worked on him, Kingdon would glance in the mirror and hardly recognize his own face.

The film ended in early December, and on his first free day, he stayed in bed reading the paper, smoking, a bottle on the table next to him. Lya's heels tapped along the hall.

She knocked.

"Enter," Kingdon said.

She took in the messy bed, the papers, the bottle. "You should stop," she said.

"Why?"

"I mean it, hon. Don't go at it so heavy."

"Why?"

"Oh, Kingdon! You know why."

"I don't."

"It shows in the close-ups."

He gave a laugh.

"It's for your own good."

He laughed again. "The funny part," he said, "is you really believe my close-ups are my good point."

"Of course they are. All the reviews say so." She paused. "What all are you going to do when you get up?"

"I thought I'd try the new plane," he said. "Lya, come along?"

"Mr. Horthy's waiting," she said. "Kingdon, have coffee before you leave the house, hear."

Her heels tapped downstairs. He lay back on the pillows, lighting another cigarette. Holding the cigarette in his mouth, he reached for the telephone, holding the tall instrument on his chest.

His call was answered by the English butler. The Van Vliets hold on to their servants, he thought, as opposed to the Vances, who have a monthly turnover. Class tells.

"Miss Van Vliet," he said.

"Whom may I say is calling, sir?"

Kingdon thought of a number of evasions, subterfuges, roles. "Kingdon Vance," he said.

In less than a minute another instrument was picked up. "Kingdon?" the low soft voice asked.

"Me. I'll be at Zephyr Field in an hour."

"No," she said.

"It's just west of La Brea Tar Pits."

"I said that too quickly. Kingdon . . . no . . . I mean . . . I don't want to meet you."

In the numerous scenes he had imagined of his asking to meet her someplace, she had never refused. So much for creative fantasy. He closed his eyes and hung up the receiver, pressing down hard. I didn't mean to do that, he thought. I didn't call her. Abruptly he set the instrument back on the bedside table and went into his huge black marble movie-star bathroom to take a shower. He hated that bathroom.

·6·

La Brea Tar Pits is a redundancy. *Brea* means tar.

On the vast Los Angeles basin halfway between the river and the sea, pools of odorous gum had trapped emperor mammoths, saber-tooth cats, condors, giant ground sloths, dire wolves, and other Pleistocene creatures, leaving their fossilized bones as a treasure trove for scholars. The pools contain asphalt, a residue of petroleum, and a bristle of derricks now surrounded them. Near the southern limit of these derricks, where unpaved Wilshire Boulevard crossed unpaved Fairfax Avenue, three flying fields met. One belonged to film director Cecil B. De Mille, another to Sidney Chaplin, brother of Charlie Chaplin, the comic. There was a large sign above a frame shack on the third field:

ZEPHYR FIELD
Tex Argyle, Proprietor

Tessa waited in front of the shack. She had removed her felt cloche and wind tugged her bobbed, shiny black hair.

Kingdon parked behind her new Pierce Arrow.

"Why did you refuse?" he asked.

She gestured awkwardly. "Oh ... you know ..."

"I do? Frankly, you surprised hell out of me."

"Lya and you are married."

"That relationship is as intact as it was an hour ago," he said. "Why are you here?"

"I made up my mind not to see you."

"That's funny. I decided the exact same thing." He dropped his cigarette, stubbing it out with his heel. "Think this conversation would make sense to an impartial eavesdropper?"

"No," she said, "but I don't see anyone listening."

He smiled. "Come on."

He was careful not to take her arm, though the field was rough. In front of the hangar a mechanic warmed up a new Curtiss Oriole. Kingdon surveyed it with critical pleasure.

"Your aeroplane?" Tessa said over the engine's roar.

"We're in a new age," Kingdon said, "and it's true the British in their nicety of language have kept the *aero*, but we sloppy Americans call this a plane. Remember that. A plane. I just got her. She's custom-built." He pointed. "See? The fuselage is covered with plywood. Far sleeker than my Canuck or my old Jenny. Aren't you impressed? Aren't three planes quite a deal for an old-time soda-cracker eater? Want to take a spin?"

The questions were fired at her in quick succession. She simply nodded.

Tex earned his living flying in Kingdon Vance movies. Zephyr Field barely broke even, with most revenue coming from sightseers and passengers. The spare togs for these customers were stored in the hangar. Tessa put on a padded coat and a leather flight coat. Kingdon handed her a leather helmet, goggles and padded gloves. When she was dressed, he puffed out his cheeks. "Fatty," he said. They went out to the plane and he showed her where to put her narrow shoes so that she wouldn't tear the Oriole's wing. He followed her. The mechanic spun the propeller, then removed the wheel chocks. Kingdon opened the throttle and they were climbing.

To the east lay the city, surrounded by a patchwork of greenery: dark citrus groves, silvery olive orchards, beanfields and truck farms. Roads webbed to lush-gardened towns and suburbs: Hollywood, Sawtelle, La Ballona, Beverly Hills (with its great oval speedway), Santa Monica, Redondo Beach. Northward, the Cahuenga Pass wound into the Santa Monica Mountains, place names that mingled Californio, Indian, and American. Probably because Tessa sat in front of him, Kingdon found himself wondering about the boundaries of Paloverde. He rarely thought of Paloverde, for his uncle had expropriated the rancho's house and name.

"Paloverde," Tessa shouted. The wind-distorted word shocked him. How did she know his thoughts? She made a sweeping gesture that included the city, farms, and vacant chaparral along the mountain chain. The movement of her glove formed an animal with its muzzle pointing toward the Pacific. A gust of wind immobilized the Oriole, and Kingdon felt he owned the land beneath him, the vast animal of land that a king on the other side of the earth had granted a long-dead García.

"We should've held on," he shouted. The slipstream surely carried away his voice, yet she nodded in agreement. He could see his helmeted reflection bob in the goggles above her full, gentle mouth.

It'll be easy to keep it like this, he thought. Cousinly. Platonic.

They flew together for the next several mornings. He didn't touch her, not even when he showed her how to work the stick and pedals. His Canuck had dual controls, and aloft he let her take over. The plane dipped and the ground shot up at them. After that, they agreed she was a natural-born passenger.

On Friday morning, he said, "Let's fly down to San Diego for lunch."

She hesitated.

"I owe you," he said. "This time I'll provide the food."

CHAPTER 19

· I ·

With the tailwind, they covered the hundred twenty miles to San Diego in less than two hours. There, the obvious place to lunch was Hotel del Coronado. The mechanic was honored to lend Captain Kingdon Vance his Model T. They rattled onto the ferry. A stiff breeze whitened the caps of choppy blue waves, gulls swooped in blue sky. Kingdon's and Tessa's very black hair whipped against their faces, catching on their smiling mouths.

It was December and the exuberant white wedding cake of a resort hotel was crowded with Easterners and Midwesterners escaping winter. As Kingdon opened the Model T's door for Tessa, croquet players looked up, people on wide verandas leaned forward, children nudged one another, and old ladies jerked gray heads in his direction. *Why the hell didn't I remember to bring something to change into? Captain Kingdon Vance, movie star in full regalia, salutes you. How Lya would love it!*

Tessa stiffened and her walk became clumsy.

The hotel was American plan—meals included—and Kingdon had telephoned from the flying field to make sure they would have a table. In the lobby the manager waited for them.

"Captain Vance," he said, "it's a privilege to welcome you and your friend to Hotel del—"

Kingdon interrupted, "I want a private dining room."

"A private room, sir?" The manager's voice trailed into disappointment. *Hide this free, ambulatory attraction?*

351

"Where we can lunch by ourselves," Kingdon said, glaring round the sunlit lobby. Men in white flannel and women in summer dresses glanced away.

"A private dining room," the manager repeated, accentuating *private*.

"As opposed to a public one."

"There's no room reserved for you," the manager said. "Every room is occupied."

"You expect me to believe that?" Kingdon was carrying a large paper sack, and he glanced down as if it might contain a Lewis gun.

"Captain Vance, may I speak to you privately?" said the manager, drawing Kingdon a few steps from Tessa. "The young lady isn't your wife."

Kingdon glanced at Tessa, alone, in her flight jacket obviously attached to him, exposed to curiosity. "By George," he said. "You're right. Not my wife."

"It's, uh, illegal for me to give you a room."

"Listen," Kingdon said loudly, "and listen good. I had no idea your place was filled with peeping Toms, otherwise I would never have brought a *lady* here. But we're here. We're hungry. So move your fat ass and get us what I asked for. A *dining* room."

The manager backed away. "Yes, Captain. If you'll wait a minute, Captain."

Kingdon returned to Tessa. She was crimson. "Pretend like Great-grandpa owned this bit of land, too," he said. "Head up. Otherwise I'll tell him who your father is."

She managed an unhappy smile.

Within five minutes they were following the manager to a large sitting room banked with windows that overlooked the bay. Triangular sails floated across blue water.

"I trust these facilities will be satisfactory, Captain." The man took his revenge by glancing at Tessa, then at the open door to an adjoining bedroom.

Kingdon put down his paper bag and reached swiftly for the manager's lapels. Tessa's voice stopped him. "Thank you for the flowers," she said softly. "They're lovely."

The manager backed out the door saying, "Compliments of Hotel del Coronado."

Kingdon turned on Tessa. "What flowers?"

She pointed to a vase of tall red roses.

Drawing a long, jagged breath, he said, "Next time, try not to forget your damn picnic basket."

It was meant to be funny. Neither of them smiled.

· 2 ·

The bag contained two bottles of champagne that he'd had the foresight to put in the cockpit. Corks exploded from warm, over-jounced wine.

He gulped down a bathroom tumbler full. The manager had roused ideas Kingdon preferred to leave dormant. Platonic, he thought over and over. Yet each entry of a waiter wheeling a cart annoyed him. Her silence annoyed him. As he poured himself the last of the second bottle of champagne, he remarked, "You haven't said a word in fifteen minutes."

"Neither have you."

"That dirty-minded bastard. Why did you stop me from strangling him? It would've been justifiable homicide."

"We ought to lock the door."

He looked sharply at her. Crimson, she gripped the handle of her coffee cup.

"Wonderful," he said. "In one day you've learned to think like a hotel pimp."

"He was horrible. But right. I've thought about it all week." Her voice, always low-pitched, was barely audible. "All week... you've been so careful not to come near me. Kingdon, why?"

The answer, which he wasn't ready to give her, was circular. From the beginning he had loved her, yet he hadn't fought his love until he saw her, shimmering and indistinct, in her bedroom window. Before that, his wartime impotence had mitigated love. But since that cloudy afternoon, his disastrously chaotic dogma had torn at him. He burned for flesh that was forbidden. If I didn't constantly remember her trembling under my touch, he thought, there would have been casual touches, maybe a cousinly kiss on the cheek. Possibly I would have shown my successful self to my dear uncle, or taken her to Eagle's Roost. My God, what's so wrong with simple action? I want her. Why can't I just take her?

That answer completed the circle. He knew without asking that she was still a virgin. And he knew that if he, a married man, took her, it could only be a dishonorable act toward her, his love.

"You said, well, that you'd had other girls."

"A multitude. I'm married."

"I know," she said, looking up at him, her eyes miserable. "Lya's why I didn't want to see you."

"She'd bless the bed we lie on. Tessa, I'm married to her for life. She's a Catholic. We were married in the Church. But other than that, it's a loose arrangement." He paused. "Someday you'll get married."

She shook her head. "No."

"Don't be silly. You owe it to Paloverde Oil."

"There's something wrong with me. Otherwise I'd have married years ago. There've been men, as you said, happy to have Paloverde Oil. Some maybe even liked me."

"You'll have to do something about that boastfulness."

"I wanted a family, I wanted children, the things other women have, and I could have had them. But I couldn't marry any of those men. It went deeper than not loving them. I was uncomfortable with them." She looked directly at him. "I can talk to you, argue with you, not get upset when you're angry. Why? It shouldn't be like that. You're far more complex than others, better-looking, dashing—"

"Oh, indubitably dashing."

"—so you should inhibit me the most. But you don't. It's exactly the opposite for me and you. I'm drawn to you because you *are* family. Growing up the way I did, alone, makes it difficult for me to be with outsiders. I'm only really at ease with my family. You're part of me." She pushed back her chair, standing. "If it's not you, it won't be anyone."

"I want to make a clever retort," he said. "I can't think of one. Tessa?"

As he kissed her, her arms circled his waist, tight. Trying to rebuke himself, he wondered how he had come to this, a hotel manager's smirk. Yet he could feel no ugliness, only gratitude that for once in his life the body he clutched wasn't anonymous. He heard a child shriek somewhere outside.

Her palms pressed above and below his waist, her breath was champagne and coffee, her tall, slender-boned body trembled. He cupped her breast and felt the savage pounding of her heart.

A searing wildness overtook him. "Wait!" he ordered harshly, as if she intended to leave. He went to the door and turned the key.

In the bedroom a window was open, and the sea-damp white curtains belled inward.

She yanked back the covers, and they fell together onto the bed. He wanted to undress her slowly, but he found himself fumbling with her blouse buttons, her skirt, the scraps of silk underwear. He wanted to take off all his clothes to feel her breasts against his naked skin. Instead, he tore off only his trousers, leaving on his shorts. Not modesty. It wasn't only Lya who recoiled from his scar. All women flinched from his mutilated thigh.

With a rough groan, he moved onto her. He encountered the barrier, but he wasn't thinking any more as he thrust into the long-needed haven of her body. She came up to meet him, uttering a small cry, her hands pressing him closer, and he lost control, moving deeply, without technique. He coupled with artless speed as if Tessa were the first woman he had ever known, coming with a series of gasps.

He clung to her, feeling his heart slow, his sweat dry against her naked body. His face was buried in the curve of her neck, and he began to stroke her hair, wishing it were still long.

Outside the open window the same child still shrieked. He got up to close the window, pulling down the blinds, and in the dimness turned. She lay with her hands at her sides, one knee slightly lifted, apparently not embarrassed by his scrutiny. But when his gaze fell on the sheet, she noted what he saw, the blood. She turned away from him, pulling the upper sheet over the stain.

"That should give them something to talk about," he said. "Don't be embarrassed. It must be a good sign because I've never seen it before."

She watched him unknot his tie, unbutton his shirt, pull off his undershirt. He sat on the edge of the bed to take off his lisle socks, his garters.

His body was perfectly formed, tall, long-legged, wide in the shoulder, narrow of hip and waist. Slowly, his left side away from her, he took off his shorts. The scar curled about his left hip, circling his thigh. Slick, hairless, lumpy, the angry red of a boiled crab.

He stretched out next to her on the bed. Very lightly her fingertips moved over the scar tissue, feeling the hardness and depth. It was incredible to Kingdon that anyone could touch his mutilation that way, with love. How could she accept this ruined part of him with love? She lifted, bending to kiss his hip, then lay back down.

"Does it hurt?" she asked.

"After you kissed and made better?" he said. "It makes me feel self-conscious."

"My kissing it?"

"No. The scar. Yes, it hurts, deep in the muscle." He saw a small brown mole between her breasts. "A funny place to hide a beauty mark," he said, gently rubbing his shaved cheeks on her breasts until he had marked the whiteness. He kissed the mole. "Mine?" he asked.

"Always."

He lay holding her, his mouth on hers, breathing the same air. Her hands explored the smooth muscles of his shoulders, his back. "I have something that belongs to you, love," he said in her ear.

This time he took her sweetly, lingeringly. He'd had women educated in eroticism, yet never had he found this same contentment.

"I'll have to find a place for us to meet," he said.

"No."

"What do you mean, no? This manager wasn't unique of his breed. There's no way for me to sneak women into hotels. Tessa, haven't you noticed? You have yourself a famous movie aviator."

"I'm going to get a house."

"Move away from your parents?"

"They're used to it. I was in France for three years." She kissed him under his chin. "Kingdon, I'm not going to tell them about us."

"Once bitten," he said with a trace of sarcasm.

"My father and you don't mix," she said. "I don't like keeping secrets, but . . ."

"You're not getting a house," he said. "You've read in newspapers and fan magazines of my ecstatic marriage. Don't you know that marital bliss doesn't come without effort? It's in my contract that Lya and I be seen here, there, and everywhere that Rimini's publicists consider necessary. Right now I'm between pictures, so there's time. Normally it's up at five-thirty, and home at six to learn my lines and/or attend parties with my loyal spouse. I won't have you hanging around for my crumbs."

"It's my life," she said firmly.

He tapped two knuckles against her head. "A genuine hard Van Vliet skull." They both laughed because it was a family joke.

"I'll work on my novel. See my mother and father. My usual routine." She touched his cheek. "Stop feeling guilty."

"How do I go about doing that?"

"Think how happy I am."

"You're a funny girl," he said. "Shy, quiet. Yet the most serene, tranquil person I've ever met." He kissed the beauty mark between her breasts. "What's wrong with you? Why do you just lie here? Why don't you do what I tell you? Hurry up and find us a place!"

· 3 ·

Bud was dead set against Tessa buying the house. Having inherited money from Hendryk, she had no reason to seek his advice. Yet she did. "Please take a look, Daddy," she said. The invitation meant she loved him, didn't want to hurt him, and had forgotten that terrible night at the cottage. His objections therefore remained unvoiced as she drove him westward on Sunset Boulevard, the narrow, unpaved street winding along the foothills. She, too, was quiet. His daughter's silence, as always, relaxed him and he forgot his anger.

They came to Beverly Hills. The six incorporated miles had a thousand inhabitants, most of them rich movie folk. The hills to the north of Sunset, once part of Paloverde, spilled green terraces; now and then Bud caught a glimpse of a red-tiled roof, sunlight on a tall window. Here were the homes of Charlie Chaplin. Tom Mix. Harold Lloyd. Pickfair, the home of Mary Pickford and Douglas Fairbanks. Lya Bell and Kingdon Vance's Eagle's Roost. Briefly Bud wondered if Tessa had ever seen it.

To the south lay ranches and thin, pale December rows of barley and beans. At the Beverly Hills Hotel, with its bungalows and semitropical gardens, the fields had been interrupted for a new subdivision with five converging, tree-lined streets. Tessa turned south on Beverly Drive. Most of the lots had for-sale signs, but a couple of houses had been built.

She parked at a tile-roofed little bungalow. "Here we are," she said.

"It's small."

"Big enough for me."

"There's not another house on the block."

"Writers like quiet," she said, reddening, looking very pretty and very stubborn.

They strolled through empty, paint-odored rooms. The dining room and living room were connected by an archway. There was a narrow hall with two bedrooms separated by a bathroom. In the kitchen, she pointed outside. "The servant's room and laundry are there, behind the garage." She led him down steps into a crazy-paved slate-floored den. "And here's where I'll work."

"I've always known you'd fly the coop," he said gloomily. "But I figured it'd be after a wedding."

"I'll be home to dinner as often as you are."

"Tessa, I'm just not clever where you and your mother are concerned. I've tried, but it never works." He glanced around the den with its gray slate floor. "You shouldn't be living alone in a shack like this!" he burst out.

"Daddy, I was gone three years."

"For God's sake, marry one of those men hanging around. I'll build you a proper home, a place you can raise your family. Tessa, you're our only child. Give us some grandchildren."

She sighed. "I'm just not the marrying type."

"What type are you? The last thing you are is one of these modern 'career women'!" He couldn't control the loudness of his voice. "You love children."

She turned her head, but not before he had seen her grief, the same reaction as to a physical blow. He wondered, did this decision not to marry have anything to do with that wild, vulnerable boy, 3 Vee's pilot? I'm being ridiculous, he thought. Before she met him she was engaged, and that didn't work out. Charley's over and done with. She's forgotten. Yet, unwilling, he remembered his own two times in hell: There had been no forgetting Amélie.

"Come on," he said, putting his arm around his daughter's slim waist. "Show me the plumbing. A man's meant to inspect the plumbing in a new house."

He banged on copper pipes and peered under the water heater.

· 4 ·

Kingdon was a different man in her house. At first this frightened him. It was as if a stranger had been inside him, waiting to come into existence. It wasn't the takeover that he feared but the disappearance of the new personality. This Kingdon never felt impelled to utter barbed cruelties, never needed more than one drink, never was attacked by demons prodding him with pitchforks of guilt. Only during rare flights in a plane had he approximated the calm he felt in her house.

Tessa hadn't altered.

Even on the days he was around, she continued to have her twice-weekly lunches with her mother, her dinners at Greenwood. He would be learning his part in the back garden and she would go into the den, closing the narrow stained-glass door behind her. He would hear the typewriter.

He never slept there, yet her casual way proved it was his home.

Certain things about her took him by surprise. A shy woman, he expected her to be embarrassed by nakedness, hers or his, but she wasn't. She enjoyed cooking and wasn't very good at it. She rarely glanced at the newspapers. She bought every kind of book and left the ones she was currently reading open, spine up, around the house. Order and neatness meant little to her. She often sat, her eyes fixed on some indeterminate spot, engrossed in her thoughts for long periods of time.

To Kingdon, the most surprising thing was that she accepted their happiness.

One night after dinner when Lupe, the deaf Mexican maid, had gone to her room behind the garage, Kingdon asked, "Then you're used to happiness?"

Tessa, who was reading *The Man of Property*, looked up. "It's never been like this for me," she said.

"So we're two formerly miserable people."

She took off her glasses, thoughtfully tapping them against her book. "When I was a child," she said, "I didn't see much of other children, and when I was with them they had a glamour that made my private little games and stories seem stupid, contemptible. With the others I was very shy and awkward. But my parents loved me and accepted me." She leaned forward. "Kingdon, at the orphanage I noticed something. During the influenza epidemic, it wasn't a rule that a healthy, well-fed child would survive. Often it would die and a far weaker one would live. After a while I understood that the survivors had one thing in common. At one time a parent—someone—had loved that child utterly. That person might be dead, but the love remained like, well, like a smallpox inoculation. Love is what shielded the children. I'd survived a tracheotomy, and to survive diphtheria at that stage is unusual. I lived. And my childhood was happy. For the same reason. My parents loved me."

"There you're ahead of me," he said. "Dad wasn't around much. Mother was Mother. She has a keenly developed knowledge of good and evil, and let me tell you I was a real challenge: Her oldest son, one of those demons that needs a cross held up or else everything turns black and withers."

Tessa moved to the couch and sat beside him. He buried his face in her breasts.

"Aren't you afraid?" he asked, his voice muffled.

She rested her cheek against his black hair. "The only person you ever hurt is yourself."

The night wrapped around them, crickets chirping in barley fields, a coyote howling in the expensive hillside to the north, a freight train whistling down the Southern Pacific tracks.

· 5 ·

After a month he gave himself dispensation to spend one night a week at the house. Lya, used to his absence, never questioned him—as he never questioned her.

She continued her lessons with Padraic Horthy. The drama coach had been supplemented by a White Russian dancing master who supposedly had taught ballet to the late czar's late daughters.

They were on the way to a première at the Million Dollar Theater.

"A ballet flick in the works?" Kingdon asked.

"You never can tell, honey," she said, her high voice filled with purposeful mystery.

"Anything I can do?" Kingdon asked.

The custom Lancia with its radiator cap in the shape of an airplane slowed smoothly. The fingers of light outside the theater reflected on Lya's pale eyes.

"Anybody I can talk to?" he added as the car stopped.

"You're a dollbaby," she said. "There's nothing and nobody."

And, pulling her sable wrap round her thin body, she let the chauffeur help her from the car. The crowd roared. *Captain Vance. Kingdon. Kingdon. The Sweethearts. Lya and Kingdon.* Lya linked her arm in his and he raised his free hand to the waiting fans. Never before had Lya turned down an offer of assistance. Later, his wife's refusal would haunt Kingdon. He should have known then that there was something very wrong.

·6·

In April, Rimini Productions shot a film about an American pilot fighting with Pancho Villa. Cast and crew went on location in Tijuana. Kingdon missed Tessa more than he imagined possible.

On the fifth morning there, he stared into the mirror and the face was a stranger's: long, angular, with dark, bewildering hollows where the eyes should be. Rationalizing that he hadn't interrupted shooting for months (he meant he hadn't been drunk since the December morning Tessa had met him at Zephyr Field), he took off in one of the company's planes.

He arrived at the house around one. Throwing open the front door, he shouted, "Tessa?"

There was no reply. After Lupe straightened the house, she retired to her quarters behind the garage; deaf, the servant ignored telephone calls and the doorbell. Kingdon roamed through silent, cool rooms. It must be one of the days Tessa lunched with her mother. He rarely went into the den, but it was there that he could feel her presence most strongly. He descended the four narrow steps to wait on the leather couch. A sheet of paper lay on one of the arms. Page 324. She never showed him any of her novel, so it was with a sense of spying that he read:

> the seven children in Anna's charge, the most unlovable
> was her favorite. A foul-tempered waif with lusterless
> brown hair and an oddly coquettish name, Mimi. Mimi

was four, and from her defiant mouth came curses that Anna, at twenty-five, had never heard. The seven children slept in the wide corridor. A linen hospital screen separated Anna from her charges, but for once she didn't mind the lack of privacy. Almost every night she would waken to find Mimi standing mute next to her cot. She would change wet nightclothes and though it was strictly against orphanage rules, she would take the child in with her, curling around the pitifully thin body until the child was warmed and drowsy. The simple contact brought Anna profound happiness. She would think of Rupert, pretending this was their child. You're mine and his, Anna would think, and I love you because

There was no period, just the dangling sentence.

Kingdon reread the page, his face broodingly thoughtful. Then he went to the long table she used as a desk and picked up a pile of folders. Chapter One, Chapter Two, all the way up to Chapter Sixteen.

He was still reading when he heard the door open.

She must have recognized Tex's car, which Kingdon had borrowed when he arrived at Zephyr Field. The lanky pilot was the only person they had ever invited here.

"Tex?" she called.

"Me." Kingdon said.

She came to the narrow stained-glass door. Her plum-colored helmet of a hat, the Vionnet jersey dress, the pearls, made her seem unapproachable. She looked down at him and the stack of folders. After a long pause, she said, "I thought you were still in Tijuana."

"Meant to be," he said. "I took off and flew in."

"We lunched at the club. Would you like something?"

"No, thank you." He held up a folder. "Chapter Twelve."

She flushed.

"Angry at me for reading?"

She didn't reply.

"It's good. Very. I was surprised, if you want to know—after *The Aviator*. This comes from a different place." He paused. "Anna's you?"

"In a way," she murmured.

"How does it end? Will she have the baby?"

Tessa bit her lip. "Yes."

"Then you're pregnant?"

"I...I'm not sure. I'm late."

He realized he was drenched with sweat. "We agreed it was up to you to make sure this didn't happen. You got a pessary." His voice lashed out. "You did it on purpose!"

"That's not true."

He took a deep breath for control. "The studio has a place for when an actress gets in trouble."

"I'm not in trouble."

"What else is being late?"

"I'm not in trouble," she repeated stubbornly.

She intends to have it, he thought. Horror took over. Sweat chilled his body. No. I won't let it happen. No. Never. She'll have to stop it.

"I know you aren't going to leave Lya," she murmured.

"That's the first sensible remark this afternoon. Now. We'll put things right."

"Please, Kingdon...don't...."

"Don't what?" He reached for a pencil and a piece of paper. Scrawling, he said, "Dr. Kenneth Green, Green Sanitarium, Arcadia. Telephone two three two." Lead snapped loudly. "He's good. Safe. Lya's used him."

"Isn't an operation against what you believe in?" Tessa's voice was so low, the drumming in his ears so heavy that he barely heard her.

"I don't believe in anything except this." He pressed the sheet of paper on the table.

"I can't..."

"Cousin, there's nothing to it. I'll drive you and foot the bills. All you have to do, Cousin, is make the appointment." His gratuitous cruelty increased his horror.

"No," she whispered.

"What other choice is there? When you've got it arranged, I'll come by. Call me when it's set."

The anguish on her face was such that he couldn't go near her. So instead of passing her on the steps, he went out the door to the garden and ran around the house to the car. He roared along the quiet street, swerving by the Beverly Hills Hotel and up the winding, hilly road. Revulsion against himself and the situation burned into him like the flames of his Nieuport over Fère-en-Tardenois. He remembered his mother burning him when she had found him behind the carriage house. He remembered her whipping him when she discovered he had been going to a whore. God, God, what a clever bastard You are, giving me my cousin to love so that the fruits of our love must inevitably be obscene to me. He hated himself, God, and Tessa in that order. "I won't go near her," he said aloud, "not until she tells me she's got an appointment with Green."

He slammed the fender of Tex's car into the retaining wall of Eagle's Roost. Searching through the liquor cabinet, he found three bottles of sickeningly sweet Cuban rum and was unconscious on the massage table in his black-marble bathroom when Lya found him.

·7·

By the time Rimini arrived, he was in the living room, wearing an initialed bathrobe, his hands trembling on a coffee cup. Rimini planted his stocky legs on the Oriental rug in front of him.

"I'll roll it out on a line, Kingdon. There's been plenty of films you've held up. So it's not just the money, keeping the crew playing Mexican poker while you take joyrides and tie one on. It's more than that. It's the Eastern bankers. They live in New York, where it's colder. They hear about the drinking and the fights you get into. They don't understand. They're cold, so they shiver."

"Kingdon's films've always made money, and you know it." Lya, loyal movie wife.

"I told you, Lya, it's not me. It's those cold New York bankers. They've made me a long-distance call. Want to know what they said? Olive Thomas."

Olive Thomas had been a movie star with everything. Twenty years old, no more; beauty, fame, a happy marriage to Mary Pickford's kid brother, Jack. Everything. Last September, Olive Thomas, in her youth, beauty, happiness had killed herself for want of heroin. The suicide splattered over every newspaper, and the country waited in hopeful horror for another celluloid god or goddess to expose the blood of humanity. In the meantime, they avoided Olive Thomas's movies.

Rimini looked from Kingdon to Lya. "So Selznick had to alter his motto from 'Selznick Pictures Create Happy Homes' to 'Dope Fiends Create Ruined Studios.'" He spoke archly, as if this were one of his witticisms.

Lya managed a bright smile. "Mr. Rimini, Kingdon's no dope fiend."

"That's no reason to cheer. Drinking's just as against the law."

Kingdon, who hadn't said a word since Rimini had arrived, stared into his coffee cup, thinking of Tessa's face.

Rimini strode up and down, barking out his commandments. "No more fights. No racing around cracking up fancy cars that everybody recognizes. Lya, you pardon the expression, no girls—at least in public. No joyrides on Rimini Productions' Mexican time."

"There's only three more days in Tijuana," said Lya.

"Stay away from the bootleg," Rimini said to Kingdon. "Stay away from everything except the camera."

Tex flew him back to location the following day. Clouds hung over the dirty little town, and instead of three days they stayed seven. Kingdon didn't hear from Tessa. Every night, under a crucified plaster Jesus, he lay on his bed drinking (legal here) until he passed out. He hadn't been on a bender for so long that he had forgotten the nauseated hangover depression, forgotten his hands trembling on the stick while his brain juggled with the thought of letting a dive continue a fraction too long.

In seven days he disobeyed every one of Rimini's commandments.

· 8 ·

To go to the house he never used his custom Lancia with the airplane radiator cap, or the white Rolls-Royce. He traveled incognito, in the Chevrolet 2-Passenger Utility Coupé he had bought for the servants' use. He sat in this car looking through the plate-glass Ternstedt-regulated window. It was late afternoon and a twilit gloom hung over the isolated bungalow. He had been back in Los

Angeles a full week, which meant it had been two weeks since he had seen Tessa. Rimini had given a publicity bash for the new flick, so she knew he was back. She hadn't gotten in touch with him. He had expected her to, had hoped she would. If prayer had been permitted him, he would have prayed to hear her low, gentle voice saying *It's arranged.*

He realized she stood at the open front door. He wondered how long she had been there. They looked at one another for a moment. Then he got out of the Chevrolet and limped stiffly up the path. Not until he put his hand on the low iron patio gate did either of them speak.

"I haven't telephoned your doctor," she said.

The dark shadows below her eyes, her diminished color told him what he didn't want to know.

"So it's certain," he said.

"It *was* an accident, but I'm not sorry." The muscles under her cheeks tightened with the effort of not permitting tears.

"I am. Sorry," he said.

He closed the gate behind him. They faced one another, two tall, dark-haired, handsome people with similar expressions of misery.

"Kingdon, don't make me go to him. Please don't. You can . . . but please don't."

He didn't promise anything. He kissed her, then they went through the living room to the bedroom. He undid her blouse, pulled down her silk brassière straps. Her breasts were fuller and the nipples—usually a light pink—were the color of pale toast. He pressed a kiss to the small mole, careful not to hurt her.

She cradled his head. "I've been terrified you wouldn't come back."

"I couldn't stay away. Ah, love, love."

Afterward, they twined together on the bed, he stroking her shoulders, she kissing his fingers in turn.

"Now," he said, "I won't push you. I'm going to reason with you."

She released his hand. He held her fingers.

"It's not just my personal Eumenides," he said. "Think what you'll do to a child. No father. Illegitimate. Think of yourself. You don't have a husband. You're no ordinary ribbon clerk—"

"I'll go to France," she interrupted.

"Returning in approximately nine months with an infant. I doubt if even dear Uncle Bud could keep that item of news out of the papers."

"Mother went to Oakland and had me."

"She did? Alone?"

"Yes."

"Why?"

"They've never explained. My father came up. That's when he saved my life. They returned with me, and everybody in Los Angeles forgot that Mother had been gone."

"Communications are better now."

"I'll tell people I adopted a child from the orphanage. Something. It doesn't matter. My parents will accept the child."

"What makes you so sure?"

"They will," she said too loudly. "They're all I care about. Them. And you. Kingdon, darling, is it so ugly to you, our child?"

Never had he permitted himself to think of it as his child. She has a minor growth that needs surgical excision before it's too late, he had thought. *Our child?* Dusk washed its final rays through the window, touching the bed with a rufous purple. An involuntary shudder passed through his body.

"It's impossible enough for me to accept this." He ran his hand lightly, caressingly, along her naked hip. "Tessa, I won't push you. But I won't lie, either. I've been drunk for two solid weeks. Yes. It's ugly to me."

She sighed.

"And frankly, I don't accept the premise that your parents will welcome your little stranger, either." He paused. "Remember? Your father's enthusiasm was slightly less than if you'd invited Jack the Ripper home. What happens when they discover it's by me?"

"I don't know," she said unhappily.

"This isn't a butcher, love. I wouldn't hurt you, ever. Good Dr. Green works cleanly, and his operation's a reverse tonsillectomy, no more. Or so I hear."

"You said you wouldn't push me."

"Did I really say that?"

"Kingdon, please don't . . . please?"

"I just want you to realize what you want to do is against reason and decency."

"Having a baby by the only man I can ever love?"

"Your married cousin."

Finally she began to weep. He kissed her tear-wet face. I won't push her, he thought. I don't need to. It seemed inevitable to Kingdon that she would come around to reason—and if reason failed, she would comprehend his full, admittedly irrational abhorrence for the child. In the darkening room he held her, comforted her, and knew he was more strictly bound to her than ever.

· 9 ·

The following morning around ten, he returned to Eagle's Roost. As he slammed the front door, Lya emerged from the library.

"Kingdon," she said. "I must talk to you."

"Go ahead," he replied. "Shoot."

Closing the door behind her, she gripped the heavy brass knob. "It'll take a while. It's important," she said. "We'll have to wait until I've finished with Mr. Horthy."

"I'll restrain myself," he said.

Her thin face tensed. "I won't be long," she said. "Wait in my room."

He didn't argue. Slowly he climbed the stairs, thinking how typical this was of Lya. She, obviously anxious, was finishing her lesson rather than break for their talk. Poor Lya, he thought, poor driven Lya. He wished he could give her whatever the ingredient was that made his shadow, and not hers, live on the screen.

Her room was filled with the scent of lilies. She used the flower as a signature. Lilies were arranged stiffly in cut-glass vases; they were embroidered on the vanity runner, on the tiny silk pillows heaped on the chaise, on the emerald-satin coverlet of the big bed he had never shared. Since they had moved here, she always came to his room—and she hadn't done that for six months.

Fifteen minutes later he heard her heels click up the circular staircase. She entered the room, pausing a fraction of a minute at the doorway. She had renewed her cupid's-bow lipstick. Shutting the door, she went to the vanity, leaning on one hand, her back to the triple mirror, her shoulders hunched, her chest flattened, a pose made famous by *Vanity Fair* models.

However staged the scene, there was true anxiety in her pale gray eyes.

"Kingdon, we've always had a dignified marriage," she said. "We've never had wild scenes. We've always kept our dignity."

She looked expectantly at him. She wanted him to ignore the early months of their marriage, when he had lashed out in bewildered pain at her constant destruction of the trust he had tried to build. She wanted to see only his disinterested companionship of the past years. All right, he thought. We'll play the scene her way.

He said nothing.

She went on. "You've had your flying. I've accepted that it's always meant everything to you—oh, honey man, you needn't deny it. I've never grudged you your flying."

He began to wonder what she had in mind. And he went cold. She knows about Tessa, he thought.

She was waiting for a reply, and so he said, "You're a brick."

"And you've respected my career. You've helped me whichever way you could, and I appreciate it." Her voice raced. "And you'll keep on helping me, I know, now I've got this marvelous chance."

He felt himself relax. "Lya, that's wonderful. Where? How? What is it?"

"David Manley Fulton's making a film about Pavlova."

"So that's why the ballet." He smiled, his happiness for her real.

Her face remained serious. "Working with Mr. Horthy has made me see what-all's wrong with my career. I haven't put my whole self into it." She moved to a window and held back a brocade drapery, staring pensively at the view of the terraced garden and pool. "Kingdon, it hurts me to even think this way, but we're close enough, honey, so I can tell you the truth. Marriage has drained me. I need more time. I've thought and thought, and there's only one answer. A divorce."

"A divorce?" he echoed.

"I know we're married in the Church," she said, sighing. "But I've been talking to people. You know what Father McAdoo told me? If neither party wanted children, the marriage isn't a true marriage."

A muscle jumped at his eyebrow. He was thinking of Tessa.

"Oh, poor Kingdon! Don't look like that. But it's the honest truth, isn't it? Neither of us wanted a family."

"The subject never came up."

"That's just it! Neither of us were even interested enough to mention children. It's nothing personal, Kingdon. You do see that, don't you? I wouldn't hurt you for the world. But I have to make this film free of heart and mind." She paused. "And you, well, maybe this all's the best for you, too. You've been drinking again. You need to clean up that problem, and I haven't been able to help you. Maybe away from me you'll have time to work on it."

"*The Dying Swan,* is that the title?"

"How did you know?"

"Occult powers," Kingdon said. "Go in peace, Lya. Practice your fouettés and arabesques."

"Honey, I knew you'd understand! David Manley Fulton wants to start right soon. I've been fretting about getting you a place."

She was fiddling with the stiff corded tie of the maroon drapery, and he thought of soft cotton curtains, strewn books, cool vines, the infinitely soothing quiet. "Fret no more," he said. "Tessa's got a house."

"Tessa?" It was Lya's turn for surprise. "Your cousin?"

"She lives in one of those new little bungalows on the south side of the hotel."

"You've been seeing her?"

"Sometimes," he said. "I drop by."

"Oh, I'm sure you do." There was a dangerous glint in her pale eyes.

"Lya, it's been rotten. We've kept it under the rug, but it's been rotten, you and me."

"Thank you, Captain Vance!"

"Don't start throwing things. I'm the one at fault."

"Does her father know? Her mother? The Grand Duke and Duchess of Los Angeles aren't going to be excited about *you.*"

"Look, I've given you dispensation," he said, starting toward the door.

"Oh, how rich! You and that dumb cow, your cousin. I didn't even know she had privates, she's so aloof and mighty. Maybe she doesn't. Maybe that's the attraction. With her you don't have to pretend to be the great lover who flies down from the sky!"

Lya's vulgarity always sought to castrate. But why was she angry? He had given her what she wanted.

He reached for the doorknob.

"That's right! Go suck on her udders."

"Shut up!" he shouted. "Leave her out of this!"

"Why? Kingdon, honey, you and her, in the Church it's incest."

Kingdon slapped her cheek. She raised her hand to her face. "This'll cost you," she hissed. "Oh, how you'll pay for this!"

"You can have it all," he said thickly. "I never wanted any of it!"

· I O ·

By the time he had packed his pigskin valises, he had calmed down. He decided to ask her what he could do to help facilitate the infinitely slow workings of the Church.

He paused outside her door, his hand poised to knock. He heard her shrill little voice, the words inaudible, the tone cooing. She must be talking to a man, he thought. He wondered, idly, who he was. Somebody to help her career. It isn't David Manley Fulton, he thought. Women don't interest him. But that leaves any director, any producer, any actor more influential than I. His anger had melted. He could never stay angry long. Lya, the incorruptible, in her lily-embroidered scanties, attempting to woo success. The door muffled a seductive ripple of laughter. I hope she really has the part, Kingdon thought.

He went downstairs to get the new manservant to help carry the valises to the Chevrolet.

CHAPTER 20

Kingdon got out of bed and she, not fully awake, glimpsing him through almost closed eyelids, focusing blurrily, saw only the colors of him, the tousle of black hair, the tanned arms and neck, the broad white shoulders and narrow back, the crimson scar. He pulled on his blue bathrobe and went barefoot from the room. She rolled onto his side of the bed, inhaling the odors that were him.

Her Indian ancestress, along with shining black hair, had bequeathed Tessa the ability to float in time. She didn't nudge or prod events. Aware of this difference in herself, this lack of an inner clock, she was vulnerable to the anxious rush of those around her. Yet she had the ability to enjoy happiness.

She lay, her cheek pressed into his pillow, thinking about his arrival five days earlier, after only a couple of hours' absence. Carrying his valises from the car, he had announced cheerfully, "I've been thrown out." He had reported Lya's conversation without embellishment, and Tessa hadn't questioned his intentions. He was here. She was happy.

Even his insistence, both silent and verbal, that she stop the baby hadn't marred her content. I'll wait until it's too late for the operation, she thought drowsily, and then he'll accept it, too. It had been an accident—that hateful thing must've leaked. Yet she didn't intend to give in, even though she understood and felt his pain. All her life she had wanted a child, and now the season was here. I'm going to have a baby, she thought, floating in the smells of him.

Her mind shifted to the child. She thought a lot about it. Unlike most pregnant women, she didn't see through a placental haze. The child was vivid to her. It would be tall, lean, black-haired, stubborn; it would excel in the things she did badly, quick clever things with its arms and legs, throwing balls, kicking them. After three years working in an orphanage, she had no sentimentality about children. Her child would have its share of innocent selfishness. She visualized it, feet apart, defying Kingdon. Curled on her side, she fell back to sleep.

"Tessa?"

He was holding a tray. She pushed herself up to a sitting position as he set it down. On the newspaper was a yellow hibiscus. He put it in her hair, twisting the stem behind her ear. Critical, he said, "Your hair's too short." He handed her a steaming cup of coffee and, careful not to jar her, sat on the bed, swinging his legs up, resting his shoulders against the headboard. They sipped.

"There were two quail and a deer in back," he said. "The deer was eating your honeysuckle vine and the quail were enjoying your grass seed."

"They're welcome," she answered. "Is it nice out?"

"Overcast."

"Good," she replied. He was scheduled to shoot retakes today. "Then you'll stay home."

"In May mornings are generally like this. It'll clear up."

"Sometimes it stays cloudy."

"'Here is a young couple who are all talked out, reduced to discussing the weather. Is there anything that could brighten their evenings?'" he said, quoting the advertisement for Dr. Eliot's Five-Foot Shelf of Books, leering at her.

She laughed and at that moment the telephone rang. They stared at the instrument, which was on her side of the bed.

"That," Kingdon said, "is the assistant director reminding me I'm on call. Ignore it."

Tessa, putting down her cup, answered.

"Tessa? It's me. Lya. I need to talk to Kingdon." The voice rose. "Now!"

"Hello, Lya." Tessa had turned crimson. "Wait a moment." She lifted the telephone to the middle of the bed.

"Yes?" Kingdon said.

"I have to see you!"

"Where's the fire?" he asked.

"Oh, Kingdon, please, it's desperate!"

"I'll be right over," he said.

"I'm not at the house. Let me come there? Please?"

Kingdon glanced at Tessa. Lya's terrified voice had been clearly audible to her. She nodded.

"The six hundred block of Beverly Drive," he said. "There's only one house, and that's it."

After he hung up, he was silent for a minute. "I should've known—the past few days have been too good." Pulling off his robe, he went into the bathroom to shower.

· 2 ·

For Hollywood, work was long, strenuous, profitable. The suddenly rich gamboled, and sometimes their erotic hanky-panky, their addiction to alcohol, cocaine, or opium reached beyond the walls of their Mediterranean mansions. Olive Thomas, whom Rimini had mentioned, was the most public tragedy. In the past few years, however, many incipient tabloid headlines had been squelched, for Hollywood and Los Angeles, ignoring the rules of geography to remain physically aloof, shared a yen for secrecy. The virtuous who boycotted scandal-brushed movie stars were the same people who came as tourists. A cash crop. Who knew what might stop their coming? Leaders of both communities formed an uneasy alliance to keep Hollywood's face clean.

Lya, driving Eagle Roost's other Chevrolet instead of her white Rolls-Royce, pulled deep into the driveway so even this anonymous automobile was hidden. She wore a heavily veiled hat, a long, matronly black coat.

Tessa opened the back door for her old friend. Lya ducked inside.

"Hello, Lya," Tessa said awkwardly. In her life she never of her own volition had acted shamefully. Greeting Lya in this house where she and Kingdon lived together made her blush and sent quivers into her stomach.

Lya, pulling off her veiled hat, stared blankly, then nodded in recognition. "Where's Kingdon?" she demanded.

"We're having breakfast." At this admission of intimacy, she turned redder. She took Lya's coat and hat. "We're eating. Please . . . will you join us?"

In the bay-windowed breakfast room, three places were set. Lya sank down, taking a gold case from her purse, tapping out a cigarette with shaky fingers. Kingdon held out his lighter for her.

Tessa remained standing. "I'll let you two talk," she murmured.

"No, honey," Lya cried. "You stay. I need every mite of help I can get." The hard prettiness of her face cracked.

"What's the matter?" Kingdon asked.

Lupe shuffled in with orange-scented muffins. Lya watched the old Mexican woman leave, waiting until the swinging door had shut.

"Lupe's almost completely deaf," Tessa said. "From the kitchen she can't hear a word."

"You're positive?" Lya demanded.

Tessa nodded.

"Lya, what is it?" Kingdon, accustomed to Lya's dramatics, knew her terror was real.

Lya, jabbing out her cigarette, held her thin hands over her face, sobbing. After a moment, Tessa bent over the chair, folding her arms around the heaving shoulders to comfort her. After a series of spasms, Lya calmed herself.

"It's David," she said in a high, child's voice.

"David Manley Fulton?" Kingdon asked.

"Yes. David."

"What's he doing?" Kingdon's voice held anger. "Backing away from *The Dying Swan?*"

"He can't." Lya's eyes glazed. "He's dead."

"Dead," Tessa whispered.

"David Manley Fulton is dead?" Kingdon asked. "How?"

"Shot."

"Suicide?" Kingdon asked.

"I don't know," Lya said. "Murdered."

"I thought you didn't know," Kingdon said.

"He is. Murdered," Lya said.

Tessa curved a consoling hand on Lya's shoulder.

"Why isn't it in the paper?" Kingdon asked.

"Nobody knows yet."

Kingdon looked sharply at his wife. "Who told you?"

Lya's shallow gasping was the only sound in the breakfast room.

"Lya?" Kingdon asked.

"I've seen him." She shuddered. "He was lying across the bed. Just lying there, his eyes wide open. I was so terrified I just about died myself. I didn't know what to do. I didn't know! It was so horrible. That's when I telephoned you."

"Why me? Why not the police?" Kingdon paused. "What were you doing there?"

Lya buried her face in her hands again.

"Kingdon," Tessa murmured. "Give her time."

"There's no time!" Lya cried. Mascara smeared her cheeks. "None at all. Remember the other morning when I asked for the divorce?"

"To devote yourself to the arts," Kingdon said.

"Not only that. I was going to be married."

"To Fulton?" Kingdon's voice was filled with disbelief.

"Yes. David."

"But everyone knows that he's—"

"That's the whole thing, the whole problem. He is and he isn't. He likes men and women both—oh, you know what-all I mean. Last winter he hired a young male secretary and this person needed money, so he threatened to expose David. There wasn't just that one affair. David had told him of others. Sometimes they did it with other people around. They did." Her voice raced, incoherent. "You know how terrified everybody is of scandal. David Manley Fulton's one of our most talented directors, but that wouldn't have mattered. A story of that kind, he reckoned, would ruin him. To counteract it, he was going to marry me."

"Proving his own devotion to the arts," Kingdon said, "as well as yours."

Lya ignored his bitterness. "David said as his wife he'd make me the biggest there is."

"What about the logistics?" Kingdon asked. "We're married, you and me. All right. We were going to avoid children, and possibly that's valid grounds for annulment. Still, we both know what's involved in getting an annulment. Years. And you're a practicing Catholic."

"We weren't going to wait for the Church. I wasn't going to confess or take communion," she said, her eyes cast down. "We were going to Mexico tomorrow. Down there I'd get a quickie civil divorce. And we'd be married. That would prove the secretary person was lying."

"How?"

"You know your reputation. The lover. The papers would say David Manley Fulton had taken me from you."

"Neat little plot," Kingdon said.

Lya, shrugging, held up her palms, an admission of her culpability. The gesture touched Kingdon. He had every reason to hate and despise her, yet he could never hate her for being openly what she was—always he found her honesty purifying.

"The houseboy doesn't come until late, and I went over around dawn to arrange the last details. And there he was. On the bed. His eyes staring." Lya's voice shrilled.

Tessa soothed, "You're safe now."

"No! I'm not!"

"A neighbor spotted you?" Kingdon asked.

"I always park in the alley and sneak in the back door dressed like a cleaning lady."

"The movie syndrome," Kingdon said. "Where's the problem, then?"

"Some things that belong to me are in his place."

"What kind of things? Guns?"

"Kingdon," Tessa reproached.

"I told you!" Lya cried. "He was dead when I got there!"

"Calm down, Lya, calm down. I shouldn't have said that. Nobody here's out to hang you. What does he have of yours?"

"A diary, and some personal items. You—please, Kingdon, you have to get them for me!"

"That'll interest the police, me visiting to pick up your diary."

"Nobody knows yet," Lya said. "The houseboy doesn't arrive till around ten, maybe later."

"What personal items?"

"I left some underwear. David liked women's underwear."

"Sweet yet virile," Kingdon said, thinking of Lya's crepe de chine scanties, flimsy bandeaux, each embroidered with a single white lily. "My God, Lya, you little fool."

"If the police find my things, I'll never get another part in my entire life."

He was about to say that losing a nonexistent career was hardly her greatest problem. He didn't let himself make the remark.

I can't go, he thought. Not now. He remembered the unalloyed content of the past five days. Tessa. He took a muffin, breaking it apart. He avoided looking at the wild eyes that gazed out from smudged mascara. Lya. Expecting him to say yes. He had never refused to help her. Maybe out of guilt for marrying her when he had loved Tessa, maybe out of his profound empathy for her poor, driven soul, always he had helped her. She had come to rely on him.

"I'll be ruined," she whimpered.

"If it weren't for me," Tessa asked him quietly, "would you go?"

"There is you," Kingdon said.

Again Lya began to sob, rocking back and forth. The jerking of her spare body held an emotional blackmail. Tessa looked steadily at him.

Finally he pushed back his chair. "Where does the great lover keep your scanties?" he inquired.

· 3 ·

As Kingdon drove on the unpaved stretch of Wilshire Boulevard toward Los Angeles, he remembered Lya's remark about parking in the alley and decided to go in the back door, too. The square bungalow seemed empty. He got out of the Chevrolet, reaching in his pocket for the key Lya had given him.

He was climbing up the wooden steps when the back door opened and a uniformed policeman emerged.

A shock went through Kingdon. The policeman appeared as surprised as he was. "What do you want?" the policeman demanded.

"I was dropping in on Mr. Fulton," Kingdon replied, managing a smile.

The policeman's long, freckled face set momentarily, then a grin of recognition formed. "Say, you're Captain Vance, aren't you?"

"Guilty," Kingdon said.

"Your movies are swell. The wife'n me see them all."

"Thank you," Kingdon said. "Is something wrong here?"

"Come in, Captain. I'm sure the lieutenant would like to talk to you."

"You could be wrong, you know. Maybe he's not a fan." Kingdon's banter rang false to himself.

The policeman's freckled face once again was businesslike. He held open the screen door. "Come in," he said again. He left Kingdon waiting in the kitchen.

Nauseated as if he had been drinking, Kingdon was assaulted by questions. Had Lya known the police were here? If she knew, what was her purpose in sending him? Her agony of terror was real—but had it been caused by the act of murder? Had Lya murdered David Manley Fulton? No, he thought, rubbing his left thigh. No. The British director was her road to the Big Career. But what if he had backed out of the ballet movie? Or had decided on another wife to star in it? Had Lya really sent him to retrieve her possessions—or had she dispatched him here as her blood substitute? He remembered the thin, pretty face cracking with horror. There was no depth to Lya. She was her surfaces. She told the truth, he decided. She arrived, found her part-time heterosexual dead, went into shock, and came to me, who had always bailed her out. Yes, he thought. Murder's beyond her emotional range. She could no more kill Fulton than sing high C.

Hearing voices, he assumed an actor's position of repose, leaning against the sink.

A short, very erect police officer with a thin brown mustache came in. Extending a hand, he said, "Captain Vance, I'm Lieutenant Dupree. And I can't tell you how much I enjoy your movies. I'm an aviation nut—have been since nineteen-ten, when I went to that airmeet at Dominguez Hills. Your stunts paralyze me. You do them yourself, don't you?" The smile ingratiated.

"Yes. Lieutenant, what's wrong here?"

"Is Mr. Fulton a close friend?"

"Hollywood's one big, jolly family," Kingdon said. "To be honest, I'm here to discuss a part. What the hell's the matter?"

The mustached face was grave. "Will you come with me, please, Captain Vance?"

He led Kingdon through the dining room and down the hall to a bedroom. The walls were paneled with black silk, the squat armchairs and round ottoman were upholstered in black. A black velvet quilt covered the bed.

Amid blackness, white drew the eye.

On the bed stretched a long, thin body in a white satin robe. A streak of red marked the chest. A white towel covered the face. One arm was outflung, the hand dangling, and on the middle finger, a sapphire ring.

A shuffling noise distracted Kingdon. At the dresser a policeman flipped through a sheaf of large photographs. All were brightly lit, and all were of naked women in a drearily similar pose, kneeling at the black silk ottoman, their faces turned to be clearly visible to the camera. Even from where he stood, Kingdon recognized, or thought he recognized, several actresses he knew. Was Lya in the stack? His nausea worsened. The pictures were dropped into a manila envelope.

"Captain Vance, can you identify the body?" Lieutenant Dupree asked.

Kingdon rubbed his eyes. "I hope not," he said.

Lieutenant Dupree pulled away the towel.

The intelligent, wedge-shape face gazed up. Already the flesh had fallen back, and the nose was a huge, jutting axe. In France, Kingdon had seen a great many dead soldiers, battered, hacked, bloody, mutilated. None of those violently dead corpses seemed quite as dead as this Englishman lying calmly on his black velvet spread. The odor of feces was strong. Death's final indignity, the loosening of sphincter control. Kingdon looked down into sightless eyes, thinking: *Go forth from this earth, O Christian soul.* He could find no animosity toward this Englishman who, alive, had sought to use his reputation as a coverup for a personal sexual purgatory.

"Is this David Manley Fulton?" Lieutenant Dupree asked.

"It is," Kingdon replied, turning away. "Shot?"

"Twice, through the chest. Robbery's not the motive." He paused, as if waiting for Kingdon to speak. Kingdon was silent. The lieutenant went on, "The ring's worth a lot."

"I suppose so."

"Why are you here?"

Kingdon frowned, bewildered in the face of death that the question mattered.

"Was it to do with your wife?"

"I told you. To discuss a part."

Lieutenant Dupree said, "Ted." And the policeman who had been going through the photographs left the room, closing the door after him. The lieutenant said, "Your wife's Lya Bell."

It was a statement, but Kingdon replied, "Yes."

"Then I better tell you. Her name's on the back of compromising photographs."

The man's sympathy was dangerous.

Kingdon's reflexes jerked to life. Adrenaline flooded his body. Once, when he was a boy, he had heard that metallic rattle and seen the yellow-marked snake coil back ready to strike. He had been told that one should freeze. He hadn't frozen. Without thought, instinctively, he grabbed the rattlesnake below the head and above the rattles, and with one hurling motion he had broken the thick body. That violence, or so it seemed to Kingdon, held the primitive core of honesty.

Grapple the truth, he told himself. "Lya's often carried away by her career," he said, sitting in an armchair. "She hoped Mr. Fulton would use her in his next movie. I suppose you know, Lieutenant, that a certain amount of Hollywood business is transacted in the bedroom. Anyway, Lya confessed that she'd been indiscreet, and Mr. Fulton had some of her things. I came here to discuss getting them back for her."

"Were you here earlier?"

"No. And I had no reason to kill him."

"You just gave me one, Captain Vance."

"If that were reason for me to kill, a great many other men in Hollywood would be dead." Kingdon paused. "It's not all one-sided. She accepts my flings, I accept hers. We accept one another." I don't, Kingdon thought suddenly. I have *never* accepted. Always I've yearned for serenity and trust.

Lieutenant Dupree rubbed his small mustache. "We figure that Mr. Fulton died between three and seven this morning. Where were you?"

Asleep, Kingdon thought, watching a deer and quail feed, putting a hibiscus in very black hair. He said nothing. His silence was in part for the usual reason that he wanted to protect Tessa. And in part because he didn't want her to be connected even in his own mind with the sad, lewd women in the flashlit photographs.

"I wasn't here."

"Do you have anyone to vouch for you?"

Kingdon took out his cigarettes.

"Do you know where your wife was?"

Kingdon's hand clenched the gold case. "My God. Lya didn't kill him. She weighs ninety pounds."

"Captain Vance, I could show you ninety-pound mothers who killed two-hundred-and-twenty-pound sons, frail little girls who axed hulking husbands. It's the passion of the murder, not the size."

"He was going to help her career. Lya had every reason to want him alive and in the best of health."

"Were you alone last night?" the lieutenant asked, waiting. "Well?" he asked.

"I've met Fulton once in my life. At a car dealer's house last September. I haven't seen him since."

"Let me put it to you on the square, Captain. Our being here is an accident. The Filipino houseboy came in early and called us. I'm positive you had nothing to do with—" He glanced at the corpse. "And I'd give a month's salary if you hadn't come up those back steps. But you're here. And I have to question you. Captain Vance, I admire you, and I'm not the only one. You're not just a movie star, you're a great pilot, a war hero. And me, I'm no brilliant detective like in *Collier's*. If I handle this wrong, everybody in the country'll be shouting for my tail. My greatest pleasure would be letting you out of this house. Just give me a handle. Somebody you were with. A girl. It'll be confidential."

Kingdon stared down at his hands. The veins were ropy with tension.

A rap sounded on the door. The lieutenant opened it, a policeman whispered, the lieutenant turned to Kingdon. "Excuse me a minute," he said.

The door closed. Kingdon didn't move. He realized the room had an odd muffled quality, as if there were wadding under the black silk paneling, as if David Manley Fulton wanted darkness and privacy.

He might have thought that Lieutenant Dupree purposefully had left him alone in this soundless room to contemplate the corpse, a ploy to wring a confession. But the idea was too theatrically calculated to have come from the sweating, anxious bantam cock of a police officer.

Kingdon stared at David Manley Fulton's dangling, bony hand. The sapphire glowed. Buffed nails glinted. A trace of pink powder remained on the thumb. Useless, a manicurist clipping and polishing nails that would turn blue and cease to grow. Gazing at the corpse, Kingdon experienced that same awareness as when his hand trembled on the stick during a dive. It was the awareness of how near life is to death. Shuddering, he buried his face in his hands.

· 4 ·

The door opened. Lieutenant Dupree said, "You can leave now, Captain Vance."

Kingdon looked up, numb. "What? No more questioning?"

"That's no longer necessary," said the lieutenant.

Several policemen were gathered in the corridor. They stopped talking as Lieutenant Dupree preceded Kingdon into the entry hall.

Tessa stood there, her eyes shadowed by a plain, wide-brimmed felt hat, her gloved hand holding closed a sable-trimmed coat that he had never seen. The opulent fur combined with her gentle expression to convey an aura of great and inherited wealth, of a family with vast influence.

"Miss Van Vliet." Lieutenant Dupree's voice was humbly solicitous. "You better go out back. Let Captain Vance drive you home. I'll send a man with your car."

As Kingdon opened the door of the high little Chevrolet coupé, he was blazing with anger, not because she had rescued him, but because she was her father's daughter. He remembered his uncle's long-ago interference and he ached to accuse Bud of meddling again. But he knew that Amélie and Bud were sailing the Mediterranean in a friend's boat. So he contented himself with "My uncle owns the Los Angeles police? Is that why I'm free?"

"They wanted to know where you were last night. I told them."

He let out the clutch too fast and the car jerked into motion. "I could've told them," he snapped.

"We're cousins," she said. "I explained to the little one with the mustache that sometimes you stayed with me."

They both looked back toward the gray bungalow they had just left. A crowd was gathered on the front lawn, and a pair of men that Kingdon recognized as reporters were talking to the policeman stationed on the porch.

"Behold," Kingdon said. "The vultures."

"What happened?"

"The houseboy came in early. The police were there to greet me."

"I worried something like that had happened. I drove Lya back to Eagle's Roost, then went home to wait for you. When you didn't come, I began to worry if . . . well, if Lya had told the truth. Does that sound terrible?"

"The same idea occurred to me." He reached over to touch her gloved hand. "I didn't want the vultures near you, love."

Silent, they drove west to Beverly Hills and Eagle's Roost.

In the entry court, a chauffeur leaned against a limousine. Rimini strode on the low terrace. As Kingdon braked to a stop, Rimini descended the steps.

"Tessa," he said, "if you'd stuck with Rimini Productions, you'd be in a better car than a Chevrolet." He used his heavily joking tone. He hadn't seen her in the four years since *The Aviator*. He had learned, however, with amused embarrassment that she was sole heiress to Paloverde Oil—and he had told her to pay her rent with her earnings! Buy new beads! He opened the car door courteously.

"What are you doing here?" Kingdon demanded.

"I've got a friend in the police department," Rimini replied. "Thirty minutes ago he telephoned in that Fulton had been shot and you were being held for questioning at his house." He turned to Tessa. "And you got him released by saying he'd been with you? He's your cousin?"

"He is," Tessa said. "And he did spend the night at my house." She swallowed.

Rimini's broad, shrewd features drew into lines that were at once believing and disbelieving.

Kingdon held out his hand. "Meet Charley Kingdon Van Vliet," he said. "Tessa, I'll have Mike drive you home."

Rimini tucked his butcher's hand under Tessa's arm. "I'll do the honors. What I've got to say is a few minutes worth, that's all." And he led Tessa toward the arched, Gothic doorway.

Lya, in fresh makeup and a maribou-trimmed peach-satin robe, lay on the living-room sofa where morning sunlight could filter through a window to touch her blond hair. Pertly contrite, she greeted them. Her terror was gone, erased as if by a magic potion—or a drug.

Rimini seated himself in the nail-studded oak chair that flanked the huge fireplace.

"I'll circle directly to the point," he said. "You. Kingdon, the point is you."

"Me? I'm cleared."

Rimini ignored the remark. "We won't talk about movies. You always said movies aren't important to you. There's no Tom, Dick, or Harry who doesn't care about being a movie star, but I'll accept what you say as true. A Kingdon's different. All right. You don't care about movies. What's important to you is aviation. Well, what about flying?"

"It's the one thing I'm good at," Kingdon said quietly.

"The best," Rimini agreed. "I always get the best. But let's look at this square. You let money slip through your fingers like water. So you don't have the cash to be a gentleman pilot?"

"No, I don't," Kingdon replied.

"I'm extravagant," Lya said.

"As a couple we don't rate as frugal," Kingdon said.

"You spend all you make?" Rimini asked.

"Pretty much," Kingdon said. "Yes."

"Then, Kingdon, you don't have a choice. If you want to stay in the movies, or if you want to be a pilot, it's the same thing. Trust." He paused meaningfully. "Nobody lets themselves go up with a pilot they don't trust. If they don't trust you, you can't get a job flying. Of course now I hear you've got rich relations—"

Kingdon jumped to his feet.

"Sit down, sit down. I'm not trying to hurt you. The way I see it, you're involved." He raised a thick, silencing hand. "Don't get me wrong. I know all about Fulton and what he likes—liked. You aren't involved personally. It's Lya here." He turned to the woman with whom in a barn-studio he had shared a few meaningless sexual encounters. "Lya's explained about her and David Manley Fulton. What she didn't say, I've painted in. Lya, you'll catch the mud. But the important thing for both of you is that Kingdon be where he belongs. At your side."

After a pause, Kingdon said, "That's where I'll be."

"Easy to say now," Rimini replied.

"It's a promise," Kingdon said.

Rimini stood. His high polished boots were a holdover from his early films, when he had worked in snake-infested hills; nowadays he seldom left his new high-walled studio on Gower Street, at the eastern edge of Hollywood.

"Good," he said, pacing. "Good. Lya's not under contract, but from the beginning, when you eloped, she's gone along with Rimini Productions publicity."

"The Flying Sweethearts," Kingdon said bitterly, "take a flying bow."

"That sweethearts business is going to help you both. And you need it. The Olive Thomas mess blew like the *Titanic* going down. One poor, hopped-up young actress kills herself and every woman's club and church is outraged. They're watching Hollywood with tigers' eyes, ready to pounce on the next one. And this is it. David Manley Fulton's it!"

"I met him once, for five minutes," Kingdon said.

"What does that matter? My friend in the police department told me they've discovered enough juice in that one house to kill a hundred careers. Lya posed for private French postcards, along with Mabel Leonard, Lillian White, and—"

"She's in with a good crowd," Kingdon interrupted, not looking at Tessa.

"Is there anything else I should know?" Rimini asked.

"She also left her diary and a few unmentionables immortalized by a lily," Kingdon replied.

Rimini glanced at Lya. She nodded.

The broad face grew heavy, as if the flesh were being pulled downward. "Then she's in enough hot water to drown. And so are you. They'll be listening with big eyes, the reporters. You won't have any privacy at all. None."

"Privacy?" Kingdon said. "I gave that up for Lent."

"You haven't seen anything. Now the newspaper boys'll stand over you when you sleep. They'll follow you to the bathroom. And God help you if you're out of line. Drink, or be seen with a girl, and every tabloid in the country'll headline the news. The readers'll forget you're a war hero, a flying ace. What they'll remember is that you aren't standing by your wife in her hour of need. Marriage means a lot to them out there. Kingdon, you gotta live clean. No breaking the Eighteenth Amendment. No girls. No nothing but a forgiving smile."

"That's how I save Rimini Productions?"

"That's how you save yourself." Rimini sat down, gazing at the toes of his boots. "The legal department," he said, "advised me to cut you loose. Forget the profits on the Vance picture you got in the can, they said. Forget Kingdon Vance. Put him on suspension and don't make any more pictures with him until this blows over. I said you and me went back to the beginning, I said you're still working for Rimini Productions. So this advice is from an old friend who's also your boss."

"I'm sorry," Kingdon muttered.

"Kingdon, take it from me. Unless you play this careful, you'll be ruined. And . . ." He paused. "Lya's going to be stoned to death." He knew Kingdon well enough to understand that this threat held more weight for him.

"My first nonflying role," Kingdon said, rubbing his thigh. "Noble cuckold."

Lya smiled at him. "Thank you, hon. I'll make it up to you."

Rimini was glancing at the clock. "In a few minutes Eddie Stone'll be here." Eddie Stone was head of publicity for Rimini Productions. "Who knows when the reporters'll start?" He turned to Tessa. "Girlie, ever ride in a chauffeur-driven limousine? Now's your big chance." His jocular tone held respect.

"I never knew his name wasn't Vance," he said when they were sitting in the plush upholstered back seat. "To be honest, when I first met you the name Van Vliet meant nothing to me."

Tessa looked out the window. "Kingdon's father and mine are brothers."

"There's more than that between you. I saw you look at him, him look at you."

"You wanted me to hear what you said to Kingdon?"

"You always were a nice girl, a sweet, innocent girl, and you haven't changed," Rimini said. "Yes, I wanted you to hear."

Her face was drained, tired.

"I can't tell you what to do. I'm not big enough to tell Paloverde Oil what to do. Tessa, he shouldn't be seen with a handsome young female cousin. But a man's expected to visit his rich uncle. Can you move into your father's house?"

"Is it . . . necessary?"

"Kingdon's my friend, the wild berserker. This is going to be only impossible for him. The papers'll have a field day for months with him, the hypocrite so-and-so's. They believe in marriage—when it's somebody else's ball and chain. He's got to stand by the little bitch. If he doesn't, he's finished." He paused, staring into her eyes. "It's necessary."

"Thank you . . ." she murmured.

When they reached her house, the chauffeur opened the car door for her. Rimini watched her walk slowly down the path.

· 5 ·

Tessa went directly into the back garden, which faced east. Clutching her coat around her, raising up her face as if seeking the sun's warmth, she stood absolutely immobile. A glossy black crow from the surrounding fields landed on the grass. It strutted toward her before flapping heavily into the air, giving its death-warning cry. *Caw caw caw.* She gazed after the bird until it disappeared. Haze softened nearby hills and the sky was a thin, tender blue. The early-morning clouds had burned off as Kingdon had said they would. The sleep-odored warmth of their bed lay in a foreign dimension; she might have shared that bed with him on another continent, she thought.

She recalled his face as Rimini had laid down the law. Kingdon's twitching nerves had been as visible to her as if his skin were transparent. Rimini's threats of ruin hadn't swayed him. He promised to help Lya, she thought, because he's utterly decent. He covers his decency with biting wit, but he always behaves with honor. His compassion is balanced by self-criticism. He's a torn, sarcastic man, and he always ends up doing the right thing. He'll stand by her.

She was not jealous.

Tessa's insecurities, which were many, did not extend to love. She knew when she was loved. And certainly Kingdon never tried to hide what he felt. He had battled his love for her but never concealed it, or his need of her.

A sweet sad whistle came from the Southern Pacific tracks. A breeze rattled through vines, ruffling the thick sable of her collar.

How can I leave him?

How can I go to France? *This is going to be only impossible for him.* Yet . . . I can't stay here.

She pulled her coat tighter around her, shivering. She was thinking of the black-haired child, their child, so real to her in its small tempers and willfulness. She imagined it racing around the garden, arms outstretched, the way very small children run, wild and recklessly free in the physical joy of being alive.

Tessa took a step as if pursuing the child, her slender heels sinking into the deep, damp grass.

Kingdon, she thought.

Her face twisted. She moved swiftly to the house, going into the den. Opening a drawer, she retrieved a paper with Kingdon's angular penciled scrawl.

·6·

As soon as she hung up the telephone, she packed a few nightclothes and toilet articles. Still wearing her felt hat and fur-trimmed coat, she drove east for fifteen miles, avoiding downtown, passing through wealthy Pasadena, moving into the blue shadow of the San Gabriels. Get it over with, get it over with, she thought in a mindless litany.

The Green Sanitarium, once the winter hideaway of a copper baron, was surrounded by high walls topped with glittering broken glass. In the fanciful grounds patients strolled talking movie deals. The sanitarium catered to Hollywood: actors and actresses in the throes of nervous breakdowns, alcoholism, morphine addiction, stars both married and single who didn't desire children. Abortions were Dr. Green's speciality. His office, once the copper baron's library, was lined with dark medical books, and behind his desk hung a row of framed diplomas. Dr. Green stood to greet her, a smile on his round face.

"Well, Miss Van Vliet," he said. "I can't tell you what a relief it is to meet someone not called Smith."

He was trying to set her at ease. She managed to return his smile.

"You'll be here three days. We encourage patients to have visitors," he said.

Even if her parents weren't sailing in the Mediterranean, she would never have told them she was here. And as for Kingdon, certainly she couldn't let him come, not after Rimini's speech. "There's . . . nobody."

Dr. Green gave her a glance of spontaneous sympathy before picking up his pen and taking her medical history. A nurse led her along a paneled hall into a white-painted examining room in which a sterilizer bubbled. Tessa put on a cold, starched white gown. Dr.

Green came in and washed his hands. Rolling on gloves, he examined her internally. Afterward, a nurse tied rubber above Tessa's left elbow for a blood sample. The blood rising dark through the syringe thrust Tessa back into twilit childhood when doctors had searched fruitlessly for the cause of her sporadic illnesses.

She asked, "Why are you doing that?"

Dr. Green replied for his nurse. "It's routine with any surgery. Have you heard of blood types? That's what we're going to do. Type your blood. It's a relatively new procedure. And especially interesting to me. You see, I studied at the University of Vienna, and my pathology professor was Karl Landsteiner. Probably that name means nothing to you, but he's the man who made the discovery that all human blood falls into one of four types." Dr. Green spoke quietly, continuing to soothe her. "And if a patient needs a transfusion, his body can accept only blood of the same type as his own. It has to do with interagglutination. Nowadays when we run into any difficulty, we can give the patient a transfusion of the correct type."

The nurse unsnapped the rubber. "Upsy-daisy," she said, helping Tessa sit on the edge of the leather examining table.

"This is a very minor operation, of course," Dr. Green said. "It's most unlikely you'll need blood. But if you do, your sample will have been typed. You see, you're absolutely safe." The pitted face was lined with reassurance.

Under the starched gown Tessa's body was ice. Stop being so sympathetic, she thought. Get it over with, get it over with, get it over with.

At seven the following morning, in a brightly lit operating room, she lay on a high table. Dr. Green, wearing a surgical mask and cap, bent over her. "Don't worry about a thing," he said. His operating nurse placed an ether cone over Tessa's face. Before she drifted into unconsciousness, odd questions came to her. Why had her mother gone to Oakland to have her? What were those four blood types? Who had written:

> *Come away, O human child!*
> *To the waters and the wild*
> *With a faery, hand in hand,*
> *For the world's more full of weeping than you can understand.*

Why did Mother leave . . . Blood types . . .

When she regained consciousness in the big corner bedroom where she had slept the preceding night, she heard a strange yet familiar clicking. Her eyes focused and she saw a gray-haired nurse knitting. Her body pressed heavily into the mattress. She felt as if someone had drained her carefully typed blood. The poem, she remembered, was "The Stolen Child" by William Butler Yeats. It was in the book that Kingdon gave me, and I learned the poetry by heart.

The nurse, seeing Tessa awake, put down her knitting and came to the bed. She had hair on her long upper lip and a sweet smile. "How do you feel?" she asked.

Tessa lied, saying she was fine.

Afternoon shadows slowly filled the room. The nurse left and returned a moment later with a tray. The odors of chicken broth and toast nauseated Tessa. She turned away. The sky darkened, curtains were drawn, lights lit.

The nurse took Tessa's pulse and temperature. She said nothing, but Tessa knew from the pains in her head and the darting jabs in her stomach that she had a fever. The nurse hurried out. Tessa rested her cheek on the pillow, longing to cry, unable to cry.

I never imagined it would feel this empty, she thought.

· 7 ·

"Tessa."

She swam out of her fevered sleep. For a moment she was disoriented, then she remembered she had had the operation two days ago and had slept in this room three nights.

Kingdon gripped the footboard of the bed.

"What are you doing here?" she asked. Her illness flattened her voice.

"You were having a nightmare."

"Yes. How did you know?"

"You began twitching and moaning."

"How long have you been here?"

"A half hour." He moved a chair to sit by the bed.

"You shouldn't have come."

"Dr. Green encourages visitors."

"Mr. Rimini—"

"Pays me but doesn't own me," he said. "For three days the press has had the house under siege. I've telephoned your place on the hour. No answer. Finally tonight, the coast cleared. I went over. Lupe said you'd gone away." He held out a yellow envelope. "This was stuck in the front door. You and your handicapped help. Lupe never heard my calls or the Western Union boy."

"Who's it from?"

"I haven't opened it."

"Would you?" she asked.

He slit the windowed envelope, holding the telegram up to the dim light, reading, "BE HOME MAY TWENTY-FOUR STOP LOVE YOU STOP MOTHER AND DADDY. You told them about this?" His tone was baffled.

She shook her throbbing head. "No."

"Why didn't you tell me?"

"You shouldn't be here."

"Tessa, your voice is flat and faraway."

"I have one of my fevers."

"Dr. Green got out of his bed to discuss your fever. In his opinion it's connected to the operation, but not in a physical sense. He used long German words—he thinks he's one of those new psychiatry boys."

"He studied in Vienna. But it was to do with blood."

"He must have taken a few classes on the subconscious. He believes you're ill because you're hurting inside. My fault."

"It's not you."

"Like hell," he said quietly. "While Lya and Rimini were talking about Fulton, I was too ashamed to look at you. It's all despicable and sad, and me, I'm part of it. The corroboration of Mother's doctrine. A Kingdon is drawn inevitably to evil and equally inevitably blights the good."

"It's me," she said. "Kingdon, I hate myself."

"There's no profit in that. Ask me. I know."

"The nightmare, I've had the same one over and over. A child is dying in the orphanage, and I'm with it in the corridor where we slept. It's night. I'm frantic. Sponging down the child, spooning medicine into its mouth. But it's slipping away, and however frantically I work there's nothing I can do. Nothing. It dies. I'm sobbing and wringing my hands. You see how tender-hearted I am?

In Rouen I did weep for the dying children, and then paid for tombstones and wept some more. Home in Los Angeles, St. Tessa of the French War Orphans buys herself an abortion and doesn't weep." The bitterness, so foreign to her, came out in a whispered monotone.

"I should've known you'd feel like this, love," he said, tenderly pushing back her fever-dampened hair. "No woman who volunteers to work three years in an orphanage would take a Dr. Green special lightly." He drew a breath. "Lya was caught four times— none my fault, she admitted—but I drove her here, and she asked for champagne afterward, to celebrate, she said."

"This *was* your baby."

"You had a curettement," he said quickly.

"I killed a baby. Ours."

"That's being dramatic,"

"Our baby," she repeated, "and I killed it."

Women's footsteps sounded in the hall, and then there was silence. The dim night light threw deep shadows on Kingdon's face as he thought of the opposing dogmas of his former religion. Which was the greater sin, the expulsion of an unborn fetus or having an illegitimate child by his cousin? Weeks ago he had decided that abortion was the lesser sin.

He bent his head toward the pillow. "A baby is wrong for us, love. All those dead Catholic Garcías who owned Los Angeles say it's wrong. Can't you hear the voices? They're ringing with the church bells. Tessa, I'm crazy and sick inside for you." He put his arms around her. "Love, it's my fault. I'm the one who needed you to come here."

"Everything's so awful. Hollow and empty."

"I'm glad you did it," he said. He was crying.

He pressed his wet cheek against her fevered one, and neither of them spoke. A nurse opened the door. When they didn't move, she tiptoed away, leaving them in the darkened room.

·8·

The car wound up through the well-tended gardens. As the enormous, tile-roofed house came into view, Bud smiled. "There's no place like home," he said.

"Be it ever so humble," Amélie added wryly.

Bud frowned. "I don't like Tessa's not coming to the station."

"José explained she is getting over a fever," Amélie said. He was the chauffeur, grandson of old Juan, the Van Vliet coachman. "Stop being impatient. You will see her in one more minute."

"Think it's got anything to do with this mess about Kingdon's wife?"

Bud had asked her this question in various guises on the journey back to Los Angeles. As soon as they had heard of the David Manley Fulton murder case, and Kingdon's connection to it, they decided to come home. Getting from Cannes to Los Angeles in twelve days was not easy, and Bud had accomplished it by using anger, his good-natured smile, and every prestigious connection necessary.

As Rimini had predicted, the case was selling innumerable papers. Besides the suspense of an unknown murderer, there was the surrounding juice. Naturally the photographs couldn't be reproduced, but tabloids hinted at the positions that actresses (among them Phyllis Leonard, Lillian Paige, Nicole Wayne, and Lya Bell) had assumed for a noncommercial camera, just as they made insinuations about David Manley Fulton's "unnatural vices." Police had discovered women's lingerie worn by the director. Locked in a drawer were other filmy articles, some of which could be identified by initialing or by a single embroidered lily. It was pointed out to those readers who might be ignorant of the fact that "the lily is the trademark of Lya Bell, wife of famed movie aviator Captain Kingdon Vance."

On the train west, five days in their private car, the Van Vliets sent out for newspapers at every stop. They had read all about Lya Bell's scanties, and of the husband who was standing by her. Forests were denuded that the populace might read of one Englishman's death.

"Tessa gets fevers," Amélie said, firm.

"She hasn't had any since she got back from France."

"Stop worrying. There she is."

Tessa, wearing a short-sleeved blue linen dress, waited at the door. Bud, chuckling, leaned forward, opening the car door before the Rolls came to a halt. He trotted up the broad steps, opening his arms.

"Daddy," Tessa cried, hugging him.

"I missed you," he said gruffly, kissing her cheek.

"I missed you."

They hugged and kissed again.

"Staying the night?" he asked.

"I . . . Daddy, I'm renting my house . . . moving back here."

"For sure?"

She nodded.

"Wonderful!" he said, hugging her once more.

Amélie, by nature more astringent than Bud, greeted her daughter with affection and only one embrace: small, fragile Amélie kissing tall, dark Tessa, then holding her daughter's hands, backing off. The two women examined one another. They were closer by far than most mothers and daughters, and pleasure shone in hazel eyes and blue. Amélie's finely marked brow raised in a question. "How are you?" she asked.

"Today the temperature's gone," Tessa replied with an unaccountable blush.

At that moment the Daimler, driven by José's assistant (also descended from "Mama's people"), drove up with Kathryn, Amélie's thin Scottish maid. Other servants came out of the house, helping to unload baggage, welcoming home their employers.

As the Van Vliets reached the glassed-in entry, Tessa said, "I have a guest."

And a tall, masculine figure rose from one of the chairs that surrounded the fountain in the center of the skylit patio.

"Welcome home, Uncle Bud, welcome home, Aunt Amélie," Kingdon said as he came toward them.

·9·

"So you are Kingdon," Amélie said, her heart slowing, dizziness washing over her, sensations resembling the terror she had experienced in a carriage not far from this spot. How like 3 Vee he is, she thought. The past is inescapable. Her fingers dug into Bud's sleeve. "I know you from your films."

Bud, with his arm around Tessa's waist, introduced his nephew to his wife. They shook hands.

Bud said, "Kingdon, well, we're both sorry about this mess. If there's anything we can do to help your wife or you, let us know."

"That's what we wanted to discuss with you," Tessa replied.

"For sure," Bud said. "Later, though. Mother's worn out. Maybe in a couple of nights Kingdon can come to supper and we'll discuss it. How does that sound?"

"As if I were five years old," Tessa replied.

Bud looked at her in surprise.

"It won't take long," she said, meeting his gaze.

"I am not tired," Amélie said. "We can have tea and talk. Tessa, will you order while I take off my hat and coat?" Lines showed in the sparely fleshed face, but her voice was clear.

In their rooms, Bud demanded, "What was the point of that? I need to find out what's been kept out of the papers. I want to find out who killed this Hollywood pervert—if I can. What's he doing here, anyway, Kingdon? Getting at me through Tessa? I've got to figure it out."

"I do not choose to deal with our daughter as though she were a Paloverde Oil acquisition."

"Get down off that high horse. You think I do? Hell, she's more important to me than anything about Paloverde Oil, and you know it! He's been at her once before. I need to think this out in advance."

"Think quickly, then," Amélie advised.

As she washed her hands, she splashed her blouse, and had to change. Her fingers fumbled nervously with the tiny crystal buttons. When she emerged from her dressing room, Bud was on the telephone.

"You will be downstairs soon?" she asked.

He nodded.

Outside she paused, looking over the balustrade into the vast patio below. Kingdon sat on a loveseat, Tessa on a low chair. Not talking, too far from one another to touch, they reminded her of mourners after a funeral. But why? The scandal? Yes. That's it, the scandal. I remember how it is to have the hounds baying after you.

Kingdon spoke, Tessa tilted her head, and he nodded. The fine, pale hairs on Amélie's neck rose in that ancient, prehuman signal of danger. Their silent way of communication made her realize that they were more than friends, more than cousins. Their mysterious grief was a shared thing. Are they lovers? No! They cannot be! I will not have it. Never! She remembered her vow never to speak of the past—unless it was necessary. I cannot keep it secret another day, she thought. However much it destroys me and them, I must speak. Silence is wrong. Cruelly wrong. Immoral.

She could not ignore her code of honor, and as she descended the broad staircase, her delicate features assumed a remote and aristocratic pride.

Bud joined them a few moments later. They drank tea, nibbled fresh-baked delicacies, and the fountain splashed. Bud sat in what to an outsider might appear genial relaxation; Kingdon ate a thin slice of walnut cake with an actor's assumption of ease. Tessa was more than normally quiet. Amélie therefore felt obligated to relate stories of their Mediterranean cruise. The others appeared oblivious that her body—behind the Georgian silver tea service—was frozen erect.

"And there we were, climbing up through this lovely garden. Madame Renoir still owns it. She showed us all of his things. Somehow the painting we bought is very personal." She stopped, then said, "Tessa, more tea?"

"Thank you, Mother, no." Tessa set down her cup, glancing at Kingdon.

Again the chill passed through Amélie's body.

"The reporters," Tessa said, "they're always at Eagle's Roost. Kingdon...needs a place to get away. He...wants to visit us here."

Bud turned to Kingdon. "Your wife will drop by, too?"

"The spotlight doesn't disturb her. Besides, she'll have her hands full. My parents are arriving tomorrow."

"They are?" Bud said.

"Rimini Productions feels a gathering of Lya's near and dear will soften the hardest heart."

"I see," Bud said.

"It's no hardship on any of us. They've come down often. Mother and Lya are fond of one another. I'm starting a picture, so I won't come around that much."

"It's not anything to do with that old business, you and Tessa?" Bud asked.

"Nothing, sir," Kingdon replied without expression.

Amélie gripped her hands in her lap. "Kingdon," she said, her clear voice belying her agitation, "it would be best if you visited other friends."

Tessa looked up in surprise. "Mother?"

"You don't care for mud-splattering, is that it, Aunt Amélie? I promise to make no large-scale entrances. I just need a quiet place once in a while."

"Where you can see Tessa?" she asked.

"He just said it's nothing like that," Bud put in quickly. His Mediterranean tan had gone sallow. "He's got a wife. He wants to come to the house to relax."

"Bud, you surely cannot encourage—"

"Encourage what?" Bud demanded. "Can't my own nephew come to my house?"

"Bud, we must tell them. Otherwise how can we live? Dealing with them so unfairly. They have to know."

Bud was looking at her in genuine bewilderment. "Know what?"

She began, "3 Vee—"

"That old feud!" Bud burst out. "I'm sick and tired of it! I want to see my brother again! Now stop making something out of nothing!"

He got up and stood over her. Silver tea things rattled as his hand came down heavily on the table. The hand was brown, freckled, thin-skinned, shiny, veined as prominently as a leaf. Why, Amélie thought, that is an old man's hand. She looked up and saw that the flesh under Bud's chin was slack, his jawline no longer firm. When had he aged? Where had he gone, that bright-haired, tanned, very beautiful young man who had led her into a dusty *sala?*

He was gazing into her eyes with a baffled pleading. Bud, who never had begged off a fight; Bud, who had battled and beaten death on death's own ground.

He does not understand that he is pleading, she thought. He does not remember the ambiguities.

The clarity and delicacy of Amélie's thought processes had never permitted her to ignore the uncertainties of the past. Bud, however, had a stubborn, binary mind. For him there could be only two possibilities. Either a matter was true or it was false. The same lack of shading that had built Paloverde Oil had also enabled Bud first to deny Tessa completely, then to accept her with his whole heart.

Amélie remembered that night in Oakland, and Bud's low, sincere voice swearing that Tessa was his. Never once since had he hinted at her questionable paternity, never had he so much as given Tessa a veiled glance, never had he hesitated in his lavish outpouring of love. When he had learned of Kingdon, it had been his enmity of 3 Vee that had been the hindrance. When he had admitted going to Kingdon to break up their relationship, the impediment in his conscious mind, Amélie knew, was Kingdon's Catholicism. She had long ago realized that Bud, with Van Vliet determination, had overwhelmed the past. Yet now, for the first time, looking into his haunted eyes, she understood that to expose the past would shatter him. To force him to look on the old uncertainties would destroy him.

She glanced toward her serene-faced daughter and the tautly vulnerable young man, 3 Vee's pilot.

Her decision should have been clear-cut.

Amélie's self-honesty was such that she didn't for a single heartbeat delude herself that Kingdon sought privacy from reporters. His refuge here was Tessa's quiet voice and fine-boned body. How can I keep quiet? Decency and morality demand I tell them. Now.

A hush lay on the sunlit room, and she scarcely breathed as she looked again at her husband's veined and mortal hand. Her conscience was downed with shameful speed.

"I never realized how you felt," she said. "Of course Kingdon is welcome here. After all, is this not Paloverde, where he belongs?" She drew a sharp breath. "I shall invite 3 Vee and Utah to dinner. Tom and LeRoy, too."

"That's a fine idea," Bud said, and his voice trembled. It took Amélie a second to remember that he had used these same words and tone of shaken gratitude when Doña Esperanza invited a terrified fifteen-year-old girl to tea. Today is a day for the past, she thought wearily.

"Do you think your family will accept?" she asked Kingdon.

"Dad, certainly. And the boys." He glanced at his uncle. "I believe you know my brothers, sir." Bud nodded. "So Mother'll be here. After all, she can show off three sons, and you've only got this one female offspring."

Kingdon's irony could not have been phrased worse. Amélie shivered. Gripping the edge of the tea table, she got to her feet. "If you will write down the addresses for me, Kingdon, I will send notes tomorrow." She looked up at her husband. "Bud, you were right. I am exhausted from the trip."

The two men stood as she went swiftly up the broad staircase, a fragile, middle-aged woman averting her head as if in shame.

CHAPTER 21

· I ·

On the Saturday night following Bud and Amélie's return to Greenwood, electric flambeaux lit the front terrace in expectation of guests. For the first time in almost three decades the Van Vliet brothers would be together.

Invitations—written by Amélie, not her secretary—had been mailed to Utah and 3 Vee, Lya and Kingdon, Tom and Bette Van Vliet, LeRoy Van Vliet and his fiancée, Mary Lu Prentice. Kingdon's younger brothers both lived in Los Angeles. Tom was with a law firm, LeRoy had just entered an accounting office. Bud, having looked up his nephews, had invited them often to lunch with him at the California Club, a sign of favor that had given the young men a good deal of cachet with their superiors.

All the invitations had been accepted. This afternoon, however, Lya had been taken to the Hall of Justice for interrogation and Kingdon, naturally, had gone with her. At four-thirty he had telephoned to say that it was questionable if they could be at the gathering.

At formal parties the Van Vliets received in their blue-and-white drawing room, surrounded by Amélie's collection of modern French art. The new Renoir was already hung. Tonight being a family affair, they waited in the chairs placed casually among the tubbed trees around the patio fountain.

Tessa's cheeks were red. In the three weeks since she had left the sanitarium, her fever would drop to normal, then return in varying intensities; when it was low-grade, as now, she kept it from her parents. The temperature made her skin sensitive, and the small pressure of her pearls hurt the back of her neck. She sat absolutely still. Her malaise was increased by anxiety. She hadn't seen Kingdon since the day of her parents' return. But she had taken his call this afternoon, and his voice had mingled anger and desolation. Absorbed, she didn't notice her parents' quiet.

Normally it was during this predinner drink that Bud and Amélie told one another of the day's happenings, discussing the news, Paloverde Oil, friends, upcoming trips for business or pleasure. But tonight, Amélie sat gazing into a tub of hyacinths, her soft, full mouth set. Bud's fresh-shaven cheeks were drawn in and his fingernail tapped impatiently on his glass.

Tires rounded gravel curves. The tension in the still air of the patio increased. Sinclair, the English butler, moved to the glassed entry.

Two young couples entered. LeRoy and Tom were short, sandy-haired, with the tilted Van Vliet nose, intuitively mediocre young men. Bud hurried to the glass vestibule to greet his nephews and be introduced to their two young women. The animated one with a short frizz of very red hair was Bette Van Vliet. Mary Lu Prentice, dowdier and quieter, had bare, plump arms. The four warily surrendered coats, gloves, hats to Sinclair, responding to Bud's genial remarks, darting awed looks around the airy recesses of the huge indoor patio.

Tessa, shy herself, was overly sensitive to their momentary awkwardness. As Bud genially herded his guests toward the fountain, she came forward to welcome them. It was Amélie, however, who had the gift of setting strangers at ease. Smiling, she greeted each by name, adding a friendly remark. She requested, too, that they call her Aunt Amélie.

Bette Van Vliet, Tom's wife, who considered herself modernly daring, came from a good Cincinnati family. (Who were these oil multimillionaires anyway but parvenu Angelenos?) Bette tossed her bright frizz of hair, asking, "Aunt Amélie? Is that respectful enough?"

At this impertinent sally the other three sucked in their breath.

Amélie's clear, pretty laughter sounded. "It is, Bette, if you make a deep curtsey as you say it."

Bud and Tessa laughed, and their guests followed suit, relaxing visibly.

"Will you join us in breaking the Eighteenth Amendment?" Bud asked.

As Sinclair passed sherry, tires were again heard rolling over gravel.

This time Bud was on his feet, moving swiftly. Before the butler could get near the vestibule, he had flung open the front door.

· 2 ·

Utah had grown vastly stout. Her black fur cape was open, displaying a massive, tightly corseted body encased in purple satin that blazed with machine-sewn mauve sequins. Ropes of beads rested on her enormous bosom, and her thick, round legs were planted far apart to support her weight. A bellicose stance. Her cheeks sagged and the flesh under her chin hung without indentation to her thickened neck. Her complexion remained high, and she had the wrinklefree skin of the obese.

3 Vee's beard was completely white, and the thick black hair on his head was salted with white streaks. His many years outdoors had furrowed his skin. His cheap, dark suit (the others wore dinner jackets) wrinkled badly across his stooping shoulders. His eyes, however, remained the same—dark, softly shining as if lit by an unquenchable interior light.

He looked many years older than Bud.

Over the threshold the brothers surveyed one another in a kind of wonderment that sought beyond the erosions of time.

"Kid," Bud said hoarsely. "Kid."

He started to reach for 3 Vee's hand, then raised both hands to his brother. They clutched one another's biceps, pulling close. Each was swept by the universe of boyhood, the dreamy dark younger brother, the assertive, protectively teasing older one who had dwelled in a red-shingled house on the outskirts of a hot little town, the thousands of suppers shared under hissing gaslight, the tall, gracious Californio lady, the stubborn little Dutchman—all this was in a brief hug. When they pulled apart their eyes were moist.

Bud cleared his throat. "You've got a white beard, kid."

"And you're bald."

"We're old, 3 Vee. How did it happen?" Bud blinked, then moved to kiss Utah's cheek. "Utah. You're looking tip-top. Still a fine figure

403

of a woman. And you've done yourself proud, with those sons of yours."

She could barely form a brief smile of mollified pleasure. This house was far grander than she had imagined. A palace! "Tom, he's got a law degree. And LeRoy's an accountant. They graduated the college in Berkeley."

"That's more than the rest of us." Bud grinned.

She bridled. "3 Vee went to Harvard."

"That he did." Bud feinted a fist at his brother's stomach. "Remember? You came home wearing gloves on the hottest day of the year."

"You teased them off me."

Bud glanced through the door down the lighted gravel drive. A white Rolls-Royce was being backed toward the garages. "Did Kingdon and Lya get back?"

The flesh under Utah's chin bobbled as her mouth pulled into a closed circle.

"They're still downtown with the lawyers," 3 Vee said. "Kingdon just telephoned. Lya's exhausted, he said, but he'll come by if he gets home early enough."

"He's doing well," Bud said. "Holding up his head in a difficult situation."

"He made his own bed," Utah said.

Tessa had crossed the patio. Bud put his right arm around her shoulders, pulling her close. "This is my Tessa," he said. "Tessa, meet your Uncle 3 Vee and Aunt Utah."

"Uncle 3 Vee," she murmured, leaning forward to kiss him.

His body froze. His facial muscles tightened.

"Aunt Utah," she said. This time she hesitated. Utah's swollen face jerked away.

The back of Tessa's neck, where the pearls cut, was cold. She hadn't expected Kingdon's parents to shower her with affection, not after the long feud, but she realized now that she had counted on their acceptance. Kingdon spoke with disappointment of his father, and with amused irony of his mother's fanaticism, yet Tessa —alone—was aware of how much he craved their approval. Her uncle's brown eyes flickered, then he turned away. Her aunt's longer examination was mutilating. Tessa knew that her presence had ruined the warmth of reunion, and in her fevered anxiety she wondered if 3 Vee and Utah had divined the abortion. She knew it was illogical, yet she thought: their grandchild.

She moved closer to her father's warmth, and his fingers tightened on her shoulder as he said in a hospitable tone, "Let Sinclair take your things."

Utah handed over her Persian-lamb cape, Kingdon and Lya's Christmas gift. 3 Vee extended his shabby, soft hat.

The others had risen, and Amélie welcomed her guests. In her magnificently simple dinner gown, she held herself with an air of ease and dignity that belied the worry she felt. She told herself that there was no reason to fear that Utah would say anything. It never entered her mind that 3 Vee would speak out. Yet she was shamed, deeply, that she herself had compromised honor by remaining silent. When the flurry of greetings ended, she said, "I am becoming acquainted with your delightful family. Of course we already know Kingdon."

Bette Van Vliet, with her wide-eyed expression of daring, inquired, "Don't you think Kingdon's divine, Aunt Amélie?" And, receiving amused assent, Bette continued, "How did you meet our famous aviator?"

"Tessa knew him years ago," Amélie replied.

"Before he and Lya were married?" Bette asked Tessa.

"Yes. Lya and I were friends. I wrote scenarios for one-reelers, and she acted in them..." Tessa's hesitant reply faded. Utah's round eyes were on her.

"Career girls!" Utah snorted. "A career ain't natural for a woman." She refused sherry.

Bette took another glass. "I think careers are divine for women. Making tons of money, just like a man!"

They moved into the paneled dining room, which was lit by massive French silver candelabra. Porcelain place cards, silver shepherdesses holding hand-printed menus, and an epergne dripping huge black grapes decorated the table. Sinclair and Pedro at each course poured an appropriate French wine, not bootlegged but from the cellar, into one of the six crystal glasses that stood at each setting. Tessa began several times to address her uncle or her aunt. 3 Vee kept his eyes averted. Utah managed to take in everything and keep Tessa under surveillance. Each time Tessa thought to speak, Utah's strident voice would address Bette or Mary Lu.

Finally, as they ate roast beef, Utah turned to Tessa. "On the way over I got to figuring. Ain't you close to thirty?"

"She's twenty-eight," Bud said. Utah, the female guest of honor, sat on his right.

"Bette there's twenty-two, and Mary Lu's twenty. You better quit being so choosy, or you'll end up an old maid," Utah said archly, leaning toward Tessa.

"Blame me," Bud said, his voice genial, his eyes cold. "Every young man who appears on the property, I call out the dogs. Isn't that right, Tessa?"

Tessa managed a smile. Her head ached fiercely. It was no longer illness or the too-obvious dislike of Kingdon's parents. During the disastrous meal she had become positive that something terrible had happened to Kingdon. Maybe he has been arrested, she thought. She pressed her icy hands to her knees.

The dessert, pyramided cream puffs glazed with caramel, a *croquembouche*, was brought in, and while Sinclair deftly carved it, the front doorbell chimed. It was Kingdon.

He apologized to Amélie, proceeding around the table, kissing his mother's cheek, shaking hands with the men, smiling at the women. When he came to Tessa, his smile faded briefly. He had changed to dinner clothes, yet still looked rumpled. In spite of his evident weariness, a current entered the dining room with him, and everyone listened as he, with muted sarcasm, joked about the cameras and crowds. He was making an effort, and when Kingdon made an effort, his physical presence was compelling. The momentary relief that had swept over Tessa faded. Why is he trying so hard? she wondered. What went wrong? Her head throbbed.

She realized that Amélie had spoken to her. "Mother?"

"Bette was asking whether you belong to the Junior League?"

She belonged, Tessa murmured, but she wasn't active. And after that she couldn't look at Kingdon, for Utah kept staring at her.

Amélie was standing. "Utah, Bette, Mary Lu, Tessa. Let us have our coffee in the drawing room."

· 3 ·

After the door closed on the women, Bud gestured for the servants to leave. The five Van Vliet men gathered at one end of the table around the decanters. Bud opened the humidor, offering cigars.

"What happened downtown?" Bud asked Kingdon.

"The usual," Kingdon replied. "We were covered with shit, then sent home."

At Kingdon's profanity, Tom and LeRoy's freckled faces reddened. In their embarrassment, the brothers were as alike as twins. Recent arrivals in Los Angeles, they shared the city's opinion that Hollywood was a cancerous growth and that movie people were either sexually depraved, scum, or charlatans. They weren't quite sure how to classify Kingdon. In Bakersfield they had stayed away from their older brother and the wildness invariably surrounding him; now they desired to remain aloof from his involvement with the David Manley Fulton case. They had never mentioned it, not even to one another, but each was profoundly relieved that Kingdon didn't use the family name. Yet despite their priggishness, they were decent young men, and had offered their brother any aid they could give.

3 Vee took a cigar. "What do you mean, Kingdon?" he asked.

"Lya kept a diary. The police just uncovered it at Fulton's place. I haven't heard too much about it—the police don't give out their hard-won evidence gratis—however, at this point let me nominate my wife for the Pulitzer Prize for Fiction. I suppose it's the oldest lie in the world for a woman to tell her lover he's wonderful. Oh, that miserable pervert must have quivered when he read that he was 'The master of rapturous nights'! Unfortunately Lya doesn't let it go at joys of the flesh. She writes of the great beyond. She would rather be dead than separated from the master. And in the final entry, dated May 2, she writes, and I think I have this correct, 'I cannot bear the thought that David may alter our plans. David, my darling, my dearest! I love him so much! My life would be a desert without him. Better we were both in that bourne from whence nobody returneth!'" Kingdon had raised his voice to falsetto. Now he lowered it to his normal timbre. "Hell. She's a damn rotten writer and a little fool. She kept the diary just for Fulton to see. But the police think the words are writ in blood."

Bud set down his brandy snifter. "Will she be charged?"

"The lawyers think with the diary there's evidence enough so she might be."

Tom, the new attorney, nodded. "Sounds bad," he said.

"I'm sorry," 3 Vee said helplessly.

Bud poured Kingdon another brandy. "Who's her lawyer? Could you get Darrow?"

"I've managed to convince Julius Redpath."

"Redpath. Yes. He's as good as Darrow. Not as flamboyant, though."

"Flamboyance," Kingdon said, "is something this case needs no more of."

"How're you on cash?" Bud asked.

"Uncle, you're related to a famous—"

"Don't get the itch, Charley," Bud interrupted. "I know Redpath's fees."

"I'm not much on taking help, Uncle," Kingdon said. "Sorry. Rimini's loaning me what I need."

"Redpath's never lost a client yet," Bud said. "Besides, there's others as badly implicated. He'll make enough of *that* to keep Lya in the clear."

"Did she kill him?" 3 Vee asked.

At this question his brother and three sons turned on him in surprise. The matter of guilt and innocence had no part in this discussion.

Bud grinned. "Ah, kid, you haven't changed. What's the difference? We'll get her out of this mess."

And Kingdon said, "She didn't. Dad, you know Lya. She's not capable of murder."

"Everyone is," 3 Vee said quietly. He glanced questioningly at Bud. "Toilet?" he asked.

"Second door to your left," Bud replied.

·4·

As 3 Vee emerged from the bathroom he saw Tessa starting up the stairs. Hearing him, she turned, her chin raised so that she seemed to be looking down her rather long, delicate nose at him. After a marked hesitation, she came slowly down the stairs, the high heels of her silk slippers clicking. 3 Vee watched her.

He had been in a tumult long before entering Greenwood. The house itself would have been bad enough. The lavish grounds had been shadowy in the night, but flambeaux had illuminated the familiar ledge between the hills. Paloverde, he had whispered aloud. Paloverde. Bud had copied the white adobe walls, the roof of red tiles. The second story was wrong, of course, as were the exterior windows—yet these, with their narrow balconies and hanging flower pots, undeniably added charm. Then he had seen Bud, the arousal of fraternal love. And Amélie. As he grasped her hand, his breath caught in his throat. The years of vivid dreams had faded into nothing when compared to the reality of her. He loved her still.

The business with Kingdon had wrenched him further. 3 Vee had taken a leave of absence from his job (he still surveyed for Union Oil) to bolster his son and daughter-in-law. He had accomplished nothing. Typical, he thought. This evening it was Bud who had taken charge, making every practical suggestion, even to an offer of money.

Most of all, though, 3 Vee had been shaken by this cool, handsome young woman who hadn't bothered to hide her ennui from her poor relations. My daughter, he thought. Never once in all these years had he considered that Amélie's child might not be his.

For some reason he had expected her to be lively and small like Amélie. He had been shocked by her García look. All evening he had glanced at her covertly, for he didn't care to rouse Utah's never-dormant jealous anger. Now, as Tessa walked toward him, for the first time he was free to examine her. The glossy black hair cut into a stylish bob, the self-assured oval face, the long, slim legs whose outlines showed through the carmine silk skirt of her dinner gown. Under his scrutiny she slowed, touching her knotted rope of pearls, and he found a petty satisfaction that he had caused this stuck-up young woman a momentary awkwardness.

She halted at the bottom of the stairs, resting one slim, ringless hand on the banister. "Uncle," she murmured in her soft voice.

"Well, Tessa," he said, forming an avuncular smile. "So I interrupted your escape."

"Escape?"

"You've found an excuse to leave the party, haven't you?"

"I was going up for an aspirin."

"Do poor relations give you a headache?" he asked, forcing humor into his tone.

She gave him a long, distant glance.

"I won't keep you, then," he said.

She didn't move.

After a silence, he said, "I suppose you've been told you resemble your paternal grandmother?"

"Yes. Grandpa Hendryk told me . . . often . . ." Her voice receded into the breathy whisper that, 3 Vee supposed, all these rich, modern girls considered smart. "I have photographs . . . you look like her, too . . ."

"A García."

She nodded. Her eyes were a very dark blue, like Bud's. Yet Bud's eyes were genial—or hard. Tessa's eyes, to 3 Vee, had mysterious depths. He told himself it was a trick of her facial structure.

Muted feminine laughter came from one side of the patio, muffled masculine conversation from the other. 3 Vee folded his arms across his chest, feeling foolish because he was unable to talk to this elegant stranger, his daughter.

Tessa said, "Uncle, what happened?"

"Where?"

"Downtown?" she asked, and he was positive the tremble in her question was avid curiosity.

"Another day, another scandal in the lives of the Kingdon Vances," he said, and grew hot. Though Kingdon waxed humorous about his cruelly ridiculous position in the headlines, 3 Vee disliked joking about serious matters.

"Scandal?"

"Lya kept a diary. The police just found it in David Manley Fulton's house."

Her eyes glazed. She moved toward a chair and gripped the back tightly. After a moment she sat down.

"Tessa, are you all right?"

"The headache . . . it's a fever. I had diphtheria and sometimes I get fevers. This one's lasted so very long." Her head was averted.

He sat next to her.

He was beginning to understand that her pauses and hesitations and silences came from shyness. She lived, as he did, inside herself. Emerging to meet strangers was as hard for her as for him—maybe harder. She had confessed to illness. And 3 Vee, being 3 Vee, imagined he had spoken more brutally than he had, and that it was this cruelty that had brought her to the edge of tears. Shame caught him by the throat, and he yearned to apologize to this secret child of his, to hold and comfort her. Yet, at the same time he wished that the similarities between them were fewer. Wouldn't it have been easier had Tessa been, as he had imagined, like Amélie? Or a Van Vliet, blonde and assertive, with the family nose?

After a minute, he said, very gently, "Kingdon's spoken a little about you. He said you're writing a novel. What's it about?"

"France..." She drew a long shaky breath. "I don't know if it'll make sense to anyone."

"But it does to you?"

She nodded.

"France? A novel about your mother's family?"

She shook her head. "An orphanage where I worked in Rouen."

"How long?"

"Three years..."

"During the war?"

"Yes. And after." She paused. "Uncle, it's difficult for me to talk about."

"I didn't mean to push you."

"It's me. I'm not good at talking. That's why I write."

I want to know her, 3Vee thought suddenly. Yet how was this possible? Let him show the least interest in her and Utah would dredge up the whole story. Water splashed quietly in the fountain.

"One day would you like to drive down to San Pedro?" 3Vee asked.

She looked questioningly at him.

"It's killing two birds with one stone. I'd like to know you better. And there's this land I own on Signal Hill. Have you ever been there?"

She nodded. "Yes. On one side there's a view of the harbor and the ocean, and on the other a flat basin all the way to the mountains. It's like an island on the land." She had recovered her composure. Clasping her long, slender fingers, she leaned toward him, unself-conscious. "Daddy drilled there a long time ago. I was little, and Paloverde Oil wasn't so big. He used to take me with him to the sites." She raised her shoulders. "Dusters. On Signal Hill, only dusters. He sold the leases."

"Bud's smart. I drilled dusters before he did. But I never did sell my land—because of what you said. I would sit on the surveyor's cairn."

"I used to climb on it."

"The place made me feel I was part of that old legend about California being an island on the right hand of the Indies."

"With brave, strong Amazons who tamed griffins."

"Very close to the terrestrial paradise," he said, and the smile forming in his white beard was a shy, youthful smile. "Well, Tessa, now you know why Bud's the success and I'm the failure."

She stared with bewilderment at him. He saw that the usual pigeonholing of success and failure was beyond her. And with one of his characteristic leaps, 3Vee realized why he had misunderstood her. Tessa was utterly good. And true goodness, more rare than beauty or talent or great intellect, is so unique that it is routinely mistaken for some other quality—stupidity, weakness, bravery, aloofness.

"I'll telephone you before I go," he said. "Honey, you're sick. Why don't you lie down?"

She shook her head and touched his sleeve. "Uncle, I'm glad we're friends," she said.

She moved up the staircase slowly, lifting her arm to wave to him when she reached the top, then disappearing around the balustraded corridor. 3Vee stared up until he heard a door open and close. His turbulence was soothed, and he thought: Being with her is like resting in a quiet glade. Smiling a little at his poetic fancy, he returned to the dining room, where they were still talking about Lya's diary.

· 5 ·

DID LYA MURDER DAVID?
*Suppression of Evidence in the David
Manley Fulton Slaying*

We at the *Herald American* believe there has been a massive concealment of evidence in the David Manley Fulton murder. This newspaper serves the public, and the public has been denied its right to know the truth. The prominence of movie people involved in this case has made the Los Angeles Police Department afraid of the truth. The truth has become a "hot potato." The First Amendment of the Constitution of the United States has been denied.

We at the *Herald American* promise to restore Freedom of the Press. In accordance with this pledge, we are printing the diary of Lya Bell, wife of Lafayette Escadrille hero Captain Kingdon Vance. Miss Bell's diary was found by the police in the home of the murdered English film director, David Manley Fulton.

How different David is once he sets down his glasses. Oh, what a **** he is. It is so thrilling and beautiful to be in his bed. Oh, how I love to **** all the rapturous night long. His powers of recuperation are amazing. I had never imagined there could be a man like David.

Poor Kingdon. I do not blame him.

How can I blame him? But oh how I hate the War for cheating us, for making our marriage a hollow shell. How cruelly the War has cheated us both. Kingdon's problem with **** is not his fault. And I love him like a brother.

The bitter joke is that the world sees David as quite ordinary and Kingdon as a man more virile than other men, a ****!

Evidence in the David Manley Fulton case, including further entries in Miss Bell's diary, will be printed without fear.

The *Herald American* chain never explained how it came to have Los Angeles Police Department evidence. Each day that month another entry of Lya Bell's diary was printed. Circulation doubled for the chain and boomed in the newspapers that reprinted diary excerpts in late editions.

·6·

The day after the first excerpt, Rimini Productions had to take on extra help to handle the deluge of letters. Kingdon's mail was overwhelmingly sympathetic. And feminine. They wrote—the young women, the middle-aged women, the old women, devout or freethinking women, city women and farm women—women wrote offering Kingdon their sacred love, and women suggested he try profane love with another (generally the writer) in order to effect a cure. Women sent him nourishing recipes and women mailed small packages containing phials or paper spills of medicine. Most women, though, simply wanted to encourage him by telling him they enjoyed his movies. They requested autographed pictures, and secretaries signed Kingdon's name to thousands of the official studio photograph of him, goggled and helmeted, standing by the wing of his Jenny.

At Rimini Studio, reporters lounged outside the stage where *Above the Clouds* was being filmed. Between takes, Kingdon cracked jokes with them. Both Rimini and Julius Redpath, Lya's attorney, had begged him not to call the diary's bluff. Julius Redpath stated that Lya was walking in a swamp, and proof she was a fraud would suck her under. Rimini repeated that people who bought movie tickets believed a man should stand by his wife—whatever.

Neither his boss nor the expensive lawyer kept Kingdon silent. He never spoke out because of more complicated reasons. Lya knew of his bleak, womenless months after he was downed, and from this she had concocted a diary for the world to read. She had wanted stardom that much! She admitted it, and said she deserved to have her plan backfire. Kingdon remained silent because the warped and broken places inside himself empathized with his wife.

With a sardonic look, as if some joke made him laugh inwardly, he parried questions from the reporters about his war wound. Leaving them, he would return to his dressing room to gulp down bootleg.

·7·

On the Friday after the Van Vliet reunion, Kingdon didn't eat lunch at the studio. He told the director, an angry, nervously talented newcomer, that he was taking off. Then, hiding under a blanket on the floor of Tex Argyle's touring car, he escaped the reporters. Tex drove him to Greenwood.

Bud was in his offices at the Paloverde Oil building on Spring Street, Amélie at a concert of the Los Angeles Philharmonic, which she had helped found two years earlier. Tessa was writing when the maid, giggling with excitement, told her Captain Vance was here. And Kingdon, who had followed the girl upstairs, said, "I'll take over." He walked into the study and closed the door.

From across the room, he and Tessa stared at one another like the survivors of an accident. They hadn't made love since the day Lya had appeared, her pretty, shallow face cracking with fear, at the house in Beverly Hills. Too much lay between their last union: the abortion and Tessa's illness, his public humiliation.

"It's not exactly easy, is it?" he asked. "Maybe we've forgotten the raptures of—" He made clicking sounds to simulate asterisks.

"We don't have to," she murmured.

"What? You believe everything you read in the newspapers?"

"Oh, Kingdon."

"Listen, want to know how I traveled here? Greater love hath no man than to crouch on the floorboards of a car all the way." He was prowling around the study.

"I've been thinking," she said. "The house, it hasn't been rented yet, and I could move—"

"You want to be part of the excitement?"

"Living there would be easier."

He had picked up a paper from the disorder on her desk, and he read, "'Anna stretched out time.' What sort of sentence is that? How do you go about stretching time?"

"Kingdon, I want to move back into the house."

"Why?" he said. "So I'll have one more thing to hate myself for?" His eyes were too bright, and a muscle jumped in his angry face.

Tessa moved to him, taking his hand, leading him into her bedroom, closing the door. She locked the other door to the hall, returning to press his hand. "This place is apart," she said. "In here it's just us."

"How did you arrange that?"

"We can do whatever we want. And this is what I want to do," she said, kissing him.

They stretched on the bed, and when it finally ended, he lay smiling at her as she gazed musingly at sunshine streaming through the windows.

"Tessa?"

"Mmm?"

"Look at me."

She turned.

"Was it all right?" he asked.

She lowered her lashes. "Nice."

"It seemed that something different happened," he said, kissing her earlobe. "For you, that is."

"Mmmn."

"Well?"

She touched his face.

"Tessa, you're not answering."

"I'm embarrassed."

"About what?"

"That . . . well . . . that you knew it had never happened for me before."

"Love, I've always been grateful you didn't pretend."

"I didn't know how."

He laughed. "Would you have?"

"No. And I've always enjoyed everything we did. So let's not talk about it . . . please."

"Tessa, I know this place is apart, and it's just us, with no allusions to the outer world, and so on. But I have to say I've always considered you a pretty damn good—" He made the clicking, asterisk sounds.

They laughed. The sunlight had reached beyond the carved bed when they finally got up.

They sat on the terrace in back of the house, having a drink, not talking. Doves raised soft throaty calls, bees buzzed in camellia bushes. Idly they watched a very tall man in a straw boater climb the hilly lawn, moving in and out of the shadows of huge sycamore trees.

"Who's that?" Kingdon asked.

"I'm not sure," she replied, squinting into the sun. "Maybe one of the gardeners."

The lanky man puffed closer.

"It's not one of the gardeners," she said. "He wouldn't be—"

"No, he wouldn't," Kingdon said. He could see the tall man clearly now, and though he didn't know the man's name, he recognized him. A reporter.

The reporter took off his hat, placing a wing-tip shoe on the bottom step of the terrace.

"Captain Vance," he said.

Kingdon was on his feet. "What the hell are you doing here?"

"Toby Mellon, *Herald American*," the man said, turning to

Tessa. "Miss Van Vliet?" His deep voice seemed to emerge from his concave stomach.

Tessa nodded.

"Have you and Captain Vance been friends long?"

Kingdon moved in front of Tessa. His fists were clenched. "She's not part of any of this," he said. "So get the hell away from here."

"Miss Van Vliet, how do you feel about Captain Vance's injury? Our feminine readership would be interested in a woman's—"

Kingdon knew the rules. Rudeness to the press was a felony, and hitting a reporter was a crime punishable by professional death. He drove his fist into the waiting gut. The man shambled backward, his arms flailing as he tried to keep his equilibrium. He slapped down into a sitting position. His straw hat rolled, stopping in a bed of flowers. Kingdon was shaking off Tessa's restraining hand.

"What's happening out here?" Bud asked from the French window behind them.

Kingdon and Tessa were startled. They hadn't realized he was home.

The reporter reached for his hat, saying, "You're H. Van Vliet, aren't you?"

"My friends don't call me H.," Bud said, grinning. "And since only friends come here to Greenwood, you better call me Bud, like everybody else does." He moved down the terrace steps, holding out his hand to help the tall reporter to his feet. "And you're?"

"Toby Mellon. With the *Herald American.*"

Kingdon muttered an obscenity.

"Charley," Bud reproved mildly, raising his eyebrows.

"How long have you and Captain Vance been friends?" Toby Mellon said. "Or are you friends, sir—uh, Bud?"

"I told you. Everybody who comes here is a friend." Bud's teeth flashed in that old charming smile. "Still, Charley—I never *can* get myself used to the Kingdon—isn't exactly my friend."

"Then he *is* Miss Van Vliet's friend?"

"I don't know about you, Toby," Bud drawled, "but I was born right here in Los Angeles, and well, we're pretty hospitable folk . . ." Bud elaborated on the neighborliness of Los Angeles, and each time the reporter tried to interrupt he was silenced by a jovial torrent of words that lasted until Kingdon sat down. Then Bud asked, "Now what was I saying before you wanted to know all about our old

Californio customs? Oh yes. Charley—I mean Kingdon. Well, as I told you, around here, people always leave out the welcome mat for a friend. But family, well, family belongs."

"Family?"

Bud gave a look of ingenuous surprise. "Toby, didn't you say you were a reporter?"

"Yes, but—"

"I thought you boys knew everything about everybody. Sure, family. Kingdon's my nephew."

"That's not common knowledge."

"Common knowledge? What's that? Everybody *I* know is aware that Charley's my brother 3Vee's boy. Now, Toby, are you a keeper of the law? Or will you join the Van Vliet family for a drink?"

Kingdon, watching, saw it was overdone so cleverly that only an idiot would ask further questions. Anyone of normal intelligence would accept Bud's act as multimillionaire playing just plain folks. He had another drink, resenting his uncle, wishing Tessa's idea of moving back to her house were feasible. He needed her so much. But he couldn't protect her. Only good old Uncle Bud could do that. Despite what Toby Mellon's chain prints, I'm not a capon, he thought, so why am I sitting here filled with humility? Has she ever hidden that she needs me as much as I need her?

Tessa was intent on the conversation between her father and the reporter. He stared at the back of her neck until she turned.

He mouthed, forming words as distinctly as for the camera: Marry me?

We're cousins.

That doesn't matter any more.

Are you sure?

God has given me His personal assurance.

You'll feel guilty.

Stop quibbling. Yes or no.

Yes. When?

"As soon," he said in a low voice, "as this is finished. Before I'm out of hock to Rimini."

Toby Mellon's head twisted to them. "What's that?" he asked.

"One of our quaint Californio family jokes," Kingdon replied.

That night Toby Mellon wrote his best story, which he titled: AT GREENWOOD WITH CAPTAIN KINGDON VANCE AND HIS OIL TYCOON

UNCLE, H. (BUD) VAN VLIET II. He expected his byline on the front page of the morning edition.

The story never ran.

Bud had made a telephone call. After that, reporters who came to Greenwood were served coffee and entertained by Amélie's secretary. If Bud personally knew the owner of the man's newspaper, he would make an immediate telephone call. Otherwise a Paloverde Oil vice-president would place substantial advertising with the paper, and sometime during the transaction, it would be made clear that Mr. Van Vliet had an aversion to seeing his wife's or daughter's name in print. Indeed, he preferred having his patronym kept out of the newspapers entirely.

CHAPTER 22

· I ·

On a drab June afternoon, 3 Vee perched on the stone cairn atop Signal Hill. The manmade harbor below was the murky gray of an elephant's hide and the windows of expensive homes, built to take advantage of the view, had the flattened, watery look of eyes afflicted by cataracts. It had rained all morning, and mottled clouds threatened more rain.

From the brow of the hill, 3 Vee watched the Shell drilling site. A boiler puffed steam and five burly men in helmets and overalls worked the derrick. One of the men held up a bottle questioningly. 3 Vee shook his head. The men of Shell's rotary crew were his friends.

He was here, almost every day, watching them. His hopes drew him. If Shell hit oil, his land would be worth a fortune. But it was more than that. He needed to escape from the maroon brick pile of Eagle's Roost. His daughter-in-law Lya reminded him of a small, sharp-faced vixen trapped in a cage. The investigation of the David Manley Fulton death was nearing a Grand Jury hearing, and the papers printed a constant stream of bizarre evidence about the director's male and female relationships. Each day the police received ten or so voluntary confessions that all proved false. Lya went over each bit of news endlessly. To 3 Vee, her shrill chatter was a cry of pain. He had watched Padraic Horthy coach her, and he tended to agree with Kingdon: Murder was out of Lya's emotional range. He pitied Lya and disliked her.

Kingdon accompanied her when she met with the attorneys and detectives; he went with her to parties and premières; he faced the public at close range when he took her tea-dancing at the Alexandria Hotel.

They never shared a bedroom.

This, too, 3Vee pondered. Kingdon had been involved with girls ever since he was a wild fourteen-year-old rebel in Bakersfield, and if hints from Rimini (and others) were true, he had continued his exploits during his marriage. 3Vee had observed no evidence of womanizing. If he doesn't sleep with his wife, 3Vee thought, if ... Can Lya's diary be true?

Kingdon moved jauntily through his days. Yet the few times 3Vee had chanced upon his son unawares, he had seen desolation on the lean, handsome face. Once, just before dawn, from his son's room had come muffled sounds that 3Vee decided were sobbing. Tactfully he questioned Kingdon about insomnia. Kingdon, laughing, replied, "I snore. That's not for publication. Dad, leave me this one last privacy."

Utah, alone of the household, was happy. She reveled in servants, her new dresses, the large diamond brooch in the shape of an airplane that Kingdon had given her on her birthday. The current chauffeur drove her to mass at St. Catherine's. She and Lya entertained Father McAdoo. "Father McAdoo, he treats me like a real somebody," Utah announced.

Two of the crew were lifting casing, a steel cylinder like a tremendous long stovepipe. Stopping, grinning, they looked down the hill. Then, over the racket of chains and gears, 3Vee heard their appreciative whistles.

Tessa was picking her way up the muddy path. At the whistles, her narrow brown shoes moved more swiftly around puddles. Fifty feet from him, she lifted a gloved hand, an uncertain greeting.

3Vee had never fulfilled his promise to telephone her.

Twice he had received a message that she had called him. He hadn't returned her calls. He had yearned to see her, yet he had concluded, sadly, that a friendship between them, however tentative, could lead only to trouble. Neither his brother nor Amélie, 3Vee was positive, wished him to play fond uncle. And as for Utah. Well, Utah.

Utah said Tessa was a snob, stuck-up, a typical useless rich woman, an old maid, conceited, cold. Since 3Vee had started out with several of these false impressions, he could hardly blame Utah for her observations. It was not at Tessa, though, that his wife was directing her spite, it was at him. A warning. Hands off, Utah was telling him. Lya never mentioned her old friend, and Kingdon, too, kept silent about Tessa—as he did about everything concerning his visits to Greenwood.

Tessa moved slowly uphill to him.

He was standing. "Tessa," he said. "It's good to see you."

"I thought maybe...I hoped you wouldn't mind if...I came here..." That original hesitancy had returned.

"I've wanted to see you," he said.

She looked at him gravely.

"It's true. But..." He floundered, glancing down at the drilling platform. A roustabout raised a hand, making a circle with his thumb and forefinger. "Well, you can see this is no place to bring a pretty girl. But I'm glad you're here. Sit down, Tessa, sit down."

He stretched his handkerchief on a dry stone. She sat, he rested a mud-caked boot on a rock, and they watched the crew working.

"They're still clean," she said. "They must've just changed tours." She pronounced it correctly. Towers.

"They did."

"And they haven't hit good oil showings yet," she said. "Once they come to oil sand, they'll worry about blocking it off with rotary mud, so they'll stop using the rotary drill and bring in cable tools and a cable-tool crew."

"Spoken like a real pro." 3 Vee grinned at her.

"I wanted to show you I'm no dilettante. Uncle, my father says you know more about oil than any college-trained geologist."

"Bud said that?"

"Yes. He said you had more than knowledge, you had a feel, like an artist has, a kind of sixth sense of what's under the ground."

"That doesn't sound like Bud. It's too mystic."

"He doesn't generally talk about the unknown," she said, "but he's aware it exists. Where's your land, Uncle?"

"There." He pointed to a vacant area between the Shell site and a luxurious Mission Revival house.

"Why did you drill?"

"I had it worked out that Signal Hill was part of an oil-bearing anticline, a very large structure. That means at an early stage most of the surrounding oil migrated here."

"Your land is tremendously valuable."

"I'm not sure any more that oil's here."

She glanced down at the Shell rig. "Others think it is."

"Me. Bud. Union Oil, and now Shell. As you said, they've all been dusters. Probably that's a dry well, too."

"Would you try again?"

"The only money we have is from selling the boarding house, and luckily your Aunt Utah's clever enough to hold the family pursestrings."

"But would you?"

He gave her his rueful little smile. "Call me a mulish Van Vliet. Yes, I would."

She swallowed sharply. "Yesterday I got an advance on my novel."

He turned to her, his bearded face glowing. "Tessa! How wonderful! I'm proud of you, very. It must be a fine book."

"It's not finished ... but they sent me a check. Not a big one ... " Her grip tightened on the strap of her black alligator purse. "Not much money."

"*You* don't have to worry about that. The main thing is you'll have a book published."

"Is ... well, is fifteen hundred dollars enough ... " She hesitated, then blurted out, "To drill?"

He blinked, taken by surprise. "You want me to have your money?"

She nodded.

"But why? Tessa, why? You hardly know me. I haven't been kind to you."

"Uncle," she murmured, "it's terrible to be born to do something and to be prevented from doing it."

She spoke with such anger and sadness that he understood. Tessa had been thwarted in whatever part of life it was that held meaning for her, and as a prisoner releases a caged bird, so she yearned to free another. Unable to speak, he gripped her hand.

"Uncle?"

The sadness of her expression reminded him of those noises in the night, Kingdon's "snores."

He gripped her hand tighter. "I'm too touched for words, honey, that's all. Nobody ever did anything like this for me, ever."

"Then it's enough?"

It wasn't, but it was a start. "Tessa, I'll take your gift on one condition," he said. "Kingdon needs money—"

"Kingdon?" She formed the name softly.

"You're shocked because he's a movie star? He needs money. He's not careful, neither is Lya, and the case is costing a fortune. He's borrowing from Mr. Rimini. So I'll take your check and try one more time. That is, if you don't object to my making him a partner."

She leaned forward to brush a kiss on his beard. "Uncle, you're a very nice man."

"Afflicted with parental guilts, that's all," he said. "Honey, *you're* the only truly nice person I've ever met."

A stick lay on the cairn, and she used it to scrape mud from her shoe. "Will Kingdon take anything, even from you?" she asked, blushing.

She cares for him, 3 Vee thought. A country full of women cared for Kingdon, swarms of women yearned after his manufactured shadow, and that Tessa belonged to this mass lowered her in 3 Vee's eyes. Well, he thought, at least she's acquainted with the dashing aviator, so she's entitled to her crush. Oddly, 3 Vee, for all his perception, never considered that there was anything between Kingdon and Tessa. They're too different, he thought.

"I'll figure out a way to convince him," 3 Vee replied.

Tessa opened her purse, taking out a folded check. "Do I write something on the back? Or the front?"

He laughed, remembering thirty years earlier, when he had taken financial backing. Bud had known every nuance. Tessa didn't know how to endorse a check. "The back: sign your name and under that write 'Pay to the order of Vincent Van Vliet,'" he said.

She took out a gold fountain pen and endorsed the check. Her eyes shone with pleasure. "This time," she said, "you're going to hit oil."

At dinner that night 3 Vee told Utah, Lya, and Kingdon that a friend had staked him. Utah's throat reddened dangerously. 3 Vee remarked to Kingdon that he wanted to pay room and board, and when Kingdon demurred, 3 Vee said, "Well, in that case, you'll be my partner, for whatever it's worth."

"Nothing!" Utah burst out. "And if paying board to your own flesh ain't the stupidest thing I ever heard! You think we're back in Bakersfield, in the rooming house?"

"Thank you, Dad," Kingdon said quietly. He raised his glass, in which was bourbon, not wine. "Good luck."

3Vee used Tessa's publishing advance to buy lumber for his derrick and to establish credit at Herron Company, on Los Angeles Street, so he could order drilling supplies.

· 2 ·

Kingdon's decision to marry Tessa was more a manifestation of an old fact than a new idea. For a long time he had known that their close kinship was less important to him than being with her, and this knowledge was a cloud. Now he felt two reactions to their secret engagement. He had an ease, a relaxation about their changed status that enabled him to accept the childish subterfuges necessary to their being alone. And he was more than ever conscious that a price would be exacted from him.

The price was Lya. She was relying on him more and more. Constantly she asked his opinion of newspaper items. She wanted to know what to wear for police questioning, and how she should treat Julius Redpath, her attorney.

In her hour of travail, Lya had turned to religion. She had always gone through the outward forms. Confession. Communion. Now, she seemed to believe she could erase her hectic, troubled present by increasing her allegiance to the Church. She, with Utah, went aggressively to Mass, and the two spent hours talking of lapsed souls and the sins of birth control, Darwinism, and secular education. Utah gestured pugnaciously, Lya dramatically. Kingdon wondered that he had ever considered it strange that Lya had remained a practicing Catholic. Of course she had never lapsed. The color of ritual and dogma fulfilled her yearning for the theatrical.

He would have worried about the divorce—except Lya had promised to reward him for standing by her. And what other reward was there?

One evening, after his parents had gone to bed, he and Lya sat smoking in the library, going over a newspaper revelation of David Manley Fulton's use of drugs.

"When the mess is cleaned up finally," he said with assumed casualness, "do you want Eagle's Roost?"

She looked up from the *Examiner*, her pale eyes guarded. "What-all do you mean?"

"Will you keep on living here?"

"We took so much trouble. The pool, the Spanish paneling, the marble from Italy, the furniture. I reckon it's our home."

"Not mine."

"If you want to move, hon, I'll fix us another place."

"You know what I'm talking about. It doesn't interest me, our kind of marriage."

Again Lya chose to misinterpret him. "Any time you want," she replied, smiling. "And any way."

"You promised me a divorce."

"Never," she said flatly. "How could I, hon? We're married in the Church."

"That's not valid. Remember? When you wanted to be a Dying Swan, you said we weren't truly married."

"How could I let poor David talk me into that?" she sighed. "My punishment is just."

All at once Kingdon jumped up. He hadn't meant to move. He heard himself shout. "Your punishment? What about mine? Trapped in this parody!"

"Kingdon, what are you shouting about?"

"I'm not shouting!" he shouted.

"Hush. You'll wake up Mother and Dad. You're talking crazy. A divorce? Why? Have I ever said one word about you going all the time to see your cousin—"

"Mention her name and I'll kill you!" he yelled, the tendons in his neck standing out.

He slammed from the library. His vision blurred with rage. He pounded up the stairs, halting at the top. "Bitch, bitch!" he muttered. "*I'll* have to get the divorce."

Yes, that's it. No shortage of evidence. I could get an annulment—or would half a hundred local ladies step forward to refute Lya's diary? I can see the headlines: CAPTAIN VANCE NO GELDING, AVER MOVIE ACTRESSES.

If I get the divorce, he thought, Lya will drag Tessa into it. Tessa in this filth? Can Uncle Bud, in all his glory, keep her out of the papers? VANCE–VAN VLIET ROMANCE: EUNUCH WOOS HEIRESS.

How much of this tearing can we bear? What will we, Tessa and I, feel for one another when it's over? What will she feel for me? He went into his bedroom and poured himself a drink. At the window he gazed up at the sky where he belonged. He thought of tenderness, love, calm, and the five days in his life when he had possessed them. He thought of the Beverly Hills bungalow. Five days. Will it ever happen again for me? Cold, disinterested stars looked down on his misery.

· 3 ·

To form the Grand Jury each local judge submitted a name and from these nominations a lottery was drawn. To be one of the twenty men on the Grand Jury was an honor. It was not surprising, therefore, that Bud Van Vliet had many friends among the chosen. Indeed, this year his oldest and best friend, Chaw Di Franco, was a member.

The Grand Jury met to hear evidence surrounding the firing of two .38-caliber bullets into the narrow chest of David Manley Fulton. As was the law, each witness gave his testimony alone, without legal counsel.

"In there all by myself?" Lya repeated. "I'll be too terrified to open my mouth."

"What? After Padraic Horthy's coaching?" Kingdon replied. "Come on, Lya, you can handle it."

"Never," she said, shivering.

They were in the white Rolls-Royce, the window closed between them and the new chauffeur as he drove them to the Los Angeles Hall of Justice. Kingdon's rage of three nights earlier had melted. How could he be angry at this meager, shaking woman?

The brim of Lya's black cloche reached her penciled brows and her black jersey collar reached her chin. The stark costume, meant to be discreetly inconspicuous, emphasized the anxiety blazing from her white face.

"I'm testifying, too," Kingdon said. "What's to it? We'll answer a few of the questions we've answered a thousand times already, and without flashbulbs and reporters. It's not a court of law. It's a group of men sifting facts. That's what a Grand Jury is."

"You don't under*stand*," she wailed. "They're my enemies. It'll be just me and them."

"Your friends will be waiting in the corridor. Me. Julius Redpath. Rimini. Eddie Stone and his publicity boys. My uncle will be there."

"I can't!"

"Pretend it's your big chance. The role of Southern belle in distress. Flutter your mascara."

"There's twenty of them!"

"Believe me, after you see the mob outside, you'll find it a bloody relief to be in such a small group."

Smiling into the terrified eyes, he hid his own qualms. Kingdon, too, dreaded the questioning, for questions directed at him were insinuations, hints, prying about his wound, his virility, his worth as a man.

"Can't you come with me?"

"You know I can't." He paused. "Lya, this is as private as the confessional."

They had reached Wilshire Boulevard and the great combed brown oval of dirt that was the Speedway. As they turned east, the limousine skidded. Lya gave a shriek. He reached for her hand, and she clutched at his fingers with a strength that made him wince.

Lya's terror baffled him. True, under the harassment and constant observation, she had become dependent, an incessant chatterer. Yet after the morning when she had come to Tessa's house, she never once had been out of control. At times she appeared to have sublimated the drive for movie stardom in her real-life role. She gave tearfully magnificent performances to police and press.

"Will you stand by me?"

"My God, Lya, haven't I showed everyplace at your side wearing my loyal and hopefully masculine smile? So help me, I would go into the hearing with you. But . . . they . . . will . . . not . . . let . . . me. It . . . is . . . against . . . the . . . law." He separated his words lightly. "All right. You slept with Fulton and kept a diary about it. So what? Other ladies have been as indiscreet as you. They have as many reasons to hate the poor skinny bastard. There's no reason, I repeat, no reason for the Grand Jury to indict you for the murder."

As he said *murder*, Lya glanced at the sliding window that separated them from the chauffeur. Calvin, was that his name? Calvin (or whoever) had been with them three days. Servants were known to sell their stories. I can see it now, Kingdon thought: THE MAN WHO WENT EVERYPLACE WITH LYA BELL.

Lya was taking small, gulping breaths.

"I did," she said.

Kingdon stared at her. Her red-painted mouth curved around that odd gulping.

"You what?"

She didn't reply.

A hurtful cold was radiating from his scar tissue. "Have I got this right?" he asked. "I just said there's no reason for the Grand Jury to indict you for murder. And you said, 'I did'?"

Again she didn't reply.

Kingdon's fingers probed the aching chill of his thigh. Never once had he seriously considered that Lya had killed David Manley Fulton. Why? She didn't have it in her to hate or love another human being, but what did that prove? Human hate and love aren't the only barometer. She screws in front of a movie camera, he thought. Passions surge through her thin body. If she were a man, I'd have figured right off she did it. Men kill for ambition. Caesar was ambitious, and so's Lya Bell. What a fool I am. Fool? My God, I'm the world's number-one sucker.

"You killed that pervert bastard," he said hoarsely, "and then you sent me off to his house to pick up your scanties and lies."

She made no sign that she had heard him. The soft panting went on. Once, during the war, a Spad had glided down near the airfield where he was stationed. The Spad, an easily handleable aircraft, could be landed by a wounded pilot. So when nobody climbed out, he had run over to the plane. The two aviators were dead. The faithful Spad had returned to earth without a guiding intelligence.

Staring at Lya, Kingdon had the same eerie prickling as when he had discovered the two dead men strapped into the cockpits. She's dead, he thought. Yet the mechanical functions continue.

His rage lessened. "How?" he asked.

"You know he was shot," she replied tonelessly.

"You've never handled a gun. You don't own one."

"Mr. Horthy and I've worked on murder scenes. David had a pearl-handled revolver that he kept in his room." Her voice was uninflected, drained of the Southern accent.

"He was your great white hope."

"When I went there that morning, David told me the secretary person had changed his mind. He wasn't going to make a scandal. David said that made me unnecessary. I asked about the Pavlova movie, and he laughed. David laughed. He said I wasn't a dying swan. He said he'd seen chickens jerk about like I did. He said maybe he'd make a movie called *The Dying Chicken*, a comedy, and star me. He was cruel, so cruel. He stretched out on the bed, laughing. I don't remember picking up the gun, or firing it. But there I was, standing over him. There was a cloud of smoke. The smoke surprised me. It smells like sulfur. It was hanging right there in the room when I telephoned you."

"They never found the gun."

"On the way to Tessa's I stopped at the La Brea tarpits and threw it in."

A murder weapon rests amid the skeletons of mammoths and dire wolves, he thought.

"Kingdon, you have to help me. You *must*."

"What should I do? Resurrect him?"

"I'll be in there alone, without one friendly face. If anybody pushes me, I know what'll happen. The whole story'll come pouring out of me."

For a brief flicker of time, Kingdon saw this as a perfect solution—the electric chair is less problematical than a divorce. Then he sighed, ashamed of himself. He understood what Lya was saying. He remembered that quaking, mindless terror as he had walked around Tex's Jenny. If Tessa hadn't been there, gazing at him with too obvious love, he could never have gone up. Fear would have devoured him, destroyed him.

"Your uncle, he knows everybody. He can fix—"

"Not this, he can't. He can't fix murder."

"The men on the Grand Jury are all big and important. He must know a lot of them. He can ask them not to push on me."

"Suborn a jury, that's the expression."

"I'll go away afterward. I'll get a divorce. I'll do whatever you tell me." Her bright cupid's-bow mouth wobbled in her pallor.

"Calm down," he said. "We aren't on a set."

"If your uncle would speak to one of those men—if I had just a single friend in there, it would mean the world."

"Lya, you know me. Rotten at asking favors. Always bollix it up. Come on. Do you honestly see me getting Hendryk Van Vliet the Second to fix—"

"Not fix, Kingdon. Just ask a friend of his to be a friend of mine, and keep the other men from pushing on me. Hon, hon, I'm so afraid."

Kingdon stared out the window.

"I give you my sacred word," Lya said. "I'll get a divorce, quietly, without a fuss."

Kingdon turned to her. "All right," he said, and his voice was expressionless. "I'll see what I can do."

·4·

The wide, impressive steps of the ten-story courthouse were jammed with pushing, shoving women and men. Kingdon's fans. Sheriff's men surrounded the white car, moving in a phalanx up the steps.

Bud, looking down from a window at the end of a fifth-floor corridor, decided the scene was like a newsreel, which it soon would be, for Pathé cameras were cranking. The crowd surged. Only Kingdon's and Lya's hats were visible.

Bud glanced over to where Main and Spring met, remembering the old brick courthouse. Angelenos had come to the unornamented building to stare at the tall, handsome French widow and the proud, fragile girl. My Amélie, Bud thought, his fingers rapping on the dusty window ledge. In those days we had no motion pictures, no cars, no airplanes, no oil. Los Angeles was a small town, and we couldn't have assembled a mob like this. So much for progress.

An arm flailed out, jostling Kingdon's hat.

Bud frowned. He had two opposing emotions for his nephew. On one hand, he was genuinely fond of Kingdon, proud of his courage, pleased with the way he stood beside that wife of his, never letting her down. On the other hand, Kingdon's friendship with Tessa infuriated him. Nowadays Tessa accepted no invitations—unless it was with her parents. If an escort for her were arranged, she would make an excuse. "I have a chapter to finish." Bud had pointed out that Kingdon was a married man, and she, blushing, had replied that she, like the rest of the world, was aware of that fact. Sarcasm was very unlike Tessa. The delicate matter of Kingdon's disability Bud couldn't broach. It was old-fashioned of him, yet he had never caught up with the new fad of the sexes talking frankly about the carnal act. Only with Amélie, and this long after they had explored every subtlety, every inch, of one another's bodies, had he been able to speak without embarrassment. He had asked Amélie to explain the meaning of Kingdon's wound to their daughter. Amélie had gone very pale, and he hadn't been able to push her.

Kingdon and Lya had disappeared through the door below. The press was kept in the marble-floored entry. Sheriff's men guarded the staircases and elevators, preventing reporters and thrill-seekers from coming upstairs. Bud moved to the iron-grilled elevator shafts and greeted a uniformed attendant.

"Big day, Mr. Van Vliet."

"For sure," Bud said.

"I'm a great fan of Captain Vance's. Jeez! Imagine a wife who tells the world what happens in your bed?"

An elevator door slid open. Kingdon and Lya emerged, followed by Rimini and Julius Redpath with his two associates.

Rimini stood near Kingdon, and Kingdon kept his hand on Lya's arm. Julius Redpath, who wore a shabby, Boston-cut suit and an air of legal earnestness, moved forward to greet Bud respectfully.

Kingdon said, "Lya, first go in the little girl's room to fix your face and straighten your hat."

She gave him a mute, pleading look.

"After that we'll talk to Uncle Bud," he said, glancing at his uncle. "Alone, sir?"

"For sure, Kingdon," Bud replied. He was in a mood of deep affection for his nephew.

· 5 ·

The conference room managed to smell and look dusty without evidence of dust. Around a long fumed-oak table were arranged eight sturdily uncomfortable chairs. Lya, her face repowdered, her hat on straight, sat at the end of the table, her fingers clenching her envelope purse.

Bud and Kingdon stood near her. Kingdon's ease was assumed. His uncle's presence in the courthouse—an accessory of a kind to the messy scandal—was generous in the extreme, and for Kingdon this increased the difficulty of asking a further boon.

"Lya's upset," he said in a tight voice. "She's never been questioned without counsel."

"Nothing to it." Bud smiled down at Lya. "Just repeat what you've already told the police."

"Lya can't get it through her head that this is a group of good citizens trying to figure out what the hell's going on," Kingdon said. "A group of men even as you and I."

"A couple of them play polo with me," Bud said, for once careless, falling into the trap. "And Chaw—Chauncey—Di Franco, Lya, he's my oldest friend. We wet our diapers together. God, the stories I could tell about me and old Chaw. Well, he's calmed down, and so have I. But he's still the nicest man you'd ever want to meet." Bud put both palms on the table, leaning down to say earnestly, "Lya, you don't have to worry. The fellows in there aren't impressed by the crap—pardon me—by the garbage in the newspapers. This is a group who think for themselves. Chaw and I were born right over there." Bud glanced out the window in the direction of Main Street. "Think of it this way. The Grand Jury's going to get you out of this mess."

Lya's pointed tongue darted over her lipstick.

"Uncle," Kingdon said, "since you've known Mr. Di Franco so long, and you're such good friends, I know Lya would feel better if you would speak to him. Then she'd know she has a friend, too."

Bud's expression hardened. With the years his face had thinned to the longer García contours, making the nose more dominant. At times like this it was apparent that the habit of power sat easily upon him. He was intensely generous—but he never permitted himself to be used.

"Kingdon," he said, his voice remaining friendly, "I took off from a meeting with Secretary of the Interior Fall. We were discussing my leasing oil-reserve lands. Very rich oil reserves. Shouldn't that prove to Lya that she has a friend here? Me?"

A muscle jumped at Kingdon's temple. He was touched that his uncle, who kept his name and doings private, was at their gossip-tarred sides in the Hall of Justice, showing support in public; he had intended saying so. Yet his uncle was also Tessa's father, the man who once had sent him from Tessa. He heard himself say, "You're here, Uncle, to show Tessa your altruism."

"I'd be here if nobody, including my daughter, knew about it! You're my nephew, Kingdon, and that's why I'm here. It's also why I'm not repeating this conversation to the District Attorney!" His anger, out in the open now, was direct and honest.

Kingdon drew a breath. "I'm sorry, sir."

"You believe me?"

Kingdon rubbed his thigh. Again he wanted to thank his uncle, yet the words were impossible. "You want me to beg your pardon again? Or should I get on my knees and clean your shoes with penitential tears?"

"Please, Mr. Van Vliet," Lya said in a shrill, breathy voice. "I can't go in there with them all hating me. I just know each one of them'll jump on my every word."

She clutched her hands together convulsively. Kingdon sat next to her, moving her hands apart, gently placing them on the table. "It's all right, Lya," he said. "I'll be a good boy. I won't let you down."

Rising, he took his uncle's arm, drawing him to a window. "She's ready to break," he said in a low voice. "She ought to be with a doctor, not the Grand Jury."

"Explain that to Julius Redpath, Kingdon. He'll get her a delay."

"What's the difference when she testifies?" Kingdon was whispering. "Lya's right. They do loathe her. She gets letters that drip venom. My God, you wouldn't believe the hatred! It squirms on the paper."

"These men are no ignorant hatemongers. They're a Grand Jury."

"The twenty men across the hall are more exalted than the rest? They don't look down on us Hollywood riffraff? Uncle, they'll enjoy tearing her apart."

A softness, a memory of that proud young girl, flickered on Bud's expression, then was gone. "They're only sifting through the evidence. They'll ask her the identical questions she's answered for the police."

"She had Redpath at her side then."

"She's an actress. Tell her to cry. That'll soften them."

"She needs one friendly face. Otherwise she'll blurt out the wrong things."

"Kingdon, how can she get in any deeper?"

"By telling the truth," Kingdon said quietly.

Sunlight slanted through the dusty window, casting shadows in the deep inverted wrinkles of Bud's raised, questioning brows. Finally he asked, "She did it?"

"And has been duly punished," Kingdon replied.

"How long have you known?"

"She told me on the way here." Kingdon paused. "We have this agreement. She'll give me a divorce if I can get you to speak to a friend, any friend, on the Grand Jury."

"Ethical questions aside, Kingdon, you've made a rotten bargain. You can get a divorce any time you want."

"You're right. And I would have asked you regardless. Lya has always roused an element in me, well, not exactly sympathy, but close to it. Whatever she does, criminal or immoral, I can always feel a tickle of the same feather, and know that even if I'm not guilty, I could be."

"That sort of reasoning is beyond me."

"The point is, then, my wife's already gone through her hell. She's taken the punishment meted out by a malevolent God. I refuse to be party to His further cruelties."

"You don't have to protect her."

"I do."

"Why?"

"I just tried to explain."

"Did she protect you? She couldn't even keep your most personal secret..." Bud's voice faded.

Kingdon was staring at him, anguish narrowing his brown eyes.

Bud felt his face grow hot, yet he stared back. Get it out in the open, he thought, and didn't lower his gaze. "In France you had enough rotten luck for a lifetime," he said.

Kingdon looked away, pressing his forehead to the dirty glass. Bud remembered the arsenic taste of defeat of four years earlier, when he had successfully warned his nephew away from his daughter. Then he had wanted to put his arm around the taut shoulders. Now he did.

"Oh, hell, Kingdon," he said. "Chaw's done worse things in his life than not lean on a witness."

Kingdon nodded, his forehead still on the window pane.

Bud crossed the impersonal conference room and pulled out the chair next to Lya. Sitting, he said, "Lya, Kingdon's been telling me how nervous you are. You're my nephew's wife, you're my Tessa's friend. Besides, you're a very pretty woman, and I've always had a weakness for pretty women." He smiled. "I can't have you nervous. So this is what I'll do. Those friends I mentioned before, I'll have a talk with them. Especially old Chaw. And when you go into the Grand Jury room, you'll know people are with you."

"You'll do that? You truly will?"

"My friends are your friends."

She gave a high little laugh. "You're just plain wonderful."

Kingdon was limping noticeably when he came to the table. "Thank you, Uncle."

"*De nada.*"

"It's not nothing," Kingdon replied. "I know what it is. Other men in your position use their power like this all the time, but you don't." Still shaken by his uncle's belief in Lya's diary, Kingdon spoke with harsh, rapid honesty. "What I threw at you a couple of minutes ago isn't true. You're here because you're a decent, magnanimous man."

Voices were loud in the corridor. The Grand Jury was taking a breather. Bud picked up his derby, moving with his graceful ease from the conference room, and Kingdon glimpsed him shaking hands with a portly, white-haired man. The door closed.

Lya took out her flat silver compact, wiping the mirror, renewing the bright red on her upper lip, pressing the narrow bow on the lower lip. Again Kingdon's flesh tingled with that eerie sense of a mechanical creature going through its mechanical functions. By every rule in the book, he thought, I should be able to hate her. She has not only made me an accessory to murder and a worldwide laughing stock, but through her Tessa went alone to Green Sanitarium. He still rebelled at the thought of Tessa bearing his child—yet he had wanted to be with her, to comfort her for the loss that had belonged to them both. But watching Lya now, as she wet her thumb and forefinger to rewind her spit curls, all he could feel was a mangling pity. No wonder my reasoning is beyond Uncle Bud, he thought. It's beyond me, too.

The corridor had quieted. A khaki-uniformed sheriff opened the door. They both stood.

"Mrs. Vance?" the sheriff asked.

"I'm ready," Lya said.

"Good luck," Kingdon said.

She threw back her head, raising her eyes in a expression of bravery that Padraic Horthy had taught her. "I reckon I have nothing to fear," she said.

·6·

The Grand Jury investigation reached no conclusion. The gathering of leading citizens found insufficient evidence to indict any person or persons for the murder of David Manley Fulton.

Hollywood's private jury found otherwise.

The spectacularly unsolved case would be followed in September by the Fatty Arbuckle scandal. He was charged with the murder of a movie actress, Virginia Rappe, and headlines ranged from ARBUCKLE HOLLYWOOD ORGY to UNNATURAL HOLLYWOOD RAPE to HOLLYWOOD RAPIST DANCES WHILE VICTIM DIES.

The box office fell steadily. Natural enemies like Marcus Loew, William Fox, Adolph Zukor, Carl Laemmle, and Jacopo Rimini banded together in an uneasy armistice, forming the Motion Picture Producers and Distributors of America. To head it, they hired Will Hays. He had taken cash gifts from businessmen who wished him to use his political influence to nudge the handsome, easygoing Warren G. Harding into the White House. The studio heads didn't care about the political and financial ethics of Mr. Hays. Important to them was the vigorous battle that he, as Postmaster General, had waged against smut in the mails.

Will Hays vowed that movies would become as "pure as the mind of a child, that clean and virgin thing"; and to carry out his oath, the Hays Office viewed every foot of film with an eye to editing out exposed bosoms and hints of the reproductive process. Hays himself composed a morals clause that henceforth would be inserted into each studio contract. He gave producers a list of 117 scandal-prone actors and actresses. These men and women, secretly and eternally, were banished from the movie screen. This list was called the Doom Book.

Kingdon Vance's name wasn't in it.

Lya Bell's was.

Lya heard about the inclusion and it was more devastating to her than a Grand Jury indictment would have been. Though she had come to Hollywood with no talent, the wrong mannerisms, eyes too pale, she had never accepted these flaws. To her, life meant strips of celluloid moving through a projector. She had studied, planned, maneuvered, groomed herself, gone to bed with anyone who could help her to be included on this film—life. The Doom Book cut her off from her one meaning of reality, from her existence.

·7·

Several months before the much-consulted, never-mentioned Doom Book came into existence, an event took place that had far more impact on the city.

3 Vee, wearing his helmet, his sleeves rolled up to show the black hair of his arms, squatted on the top step of his rig on Signal Hill watching the Shell site. During a routine water-shut-off test, the Shell crew had found seventy feet of oil standing in the bore hole. The news traveled. Shell had to build a high link fence to keep sightseers off the derrick floor. Visitors crowded to this fence, their cars parked every which way.

These dusty automobiles made 3 Vee smile, for he was remembering Bud's fears that Los Angeles crude, with its high proportion of that waste product, gasoline, would become a glut on the market. Sure, Bud had said, the gasoline-fueled buggy would be practical—at some point in the twenty-fourth century.

3 Vee got to his feet, stretching. On his platform was a pile of ground-up dirt. He stared at it. Machinery clanked with a life of its own. The sun was overhead. 3 Vee picked up a shovel, grasping the

smooth, sun-heated handle firmly in both calloused palms. Slowly he dipped the shovel in the ground-up dirt. His bearded face sober, he eased the dirt into a tall can filled with water. The water rippled and almost immediately a shining film rose to the top.

The tool dresser, wiping his forehead, came over to look. He let out a whoop. "Oil traces!" he shouted.

The omens were good.

Fifteen minutes later, a long, deep rumble came from within the earth, the sound rising to a keening, whistling rush.

3 Vee knew the sound. So did the other three men on the day tour. Spilling from the platform, they galloped around an expanse of fenced green garden, racing uphill through the dry foxtails.

A black geyser rose over Shell's crown block, a gusher shooting one hundred fourteen feet in the air. The Shell crew danced, embracing in the fluming black shower, their shouts of exultation drowned by the gusher's roar. Behind the fence, spectators yelled to one another, strangers bound together by the excited awe of being present at a historic moment.

3 Vee's fists clenched and unclenched. His own crew crowded around him.

"Hot damn, 3 Vee! You're about to be the biggest millionaire in the whole damn city of Los Angeles!"

"Ten acres of that! Jesus Christ, ten acres of *that!*"

3 Vee moved away from the crowd, walking deliberately to the little café at the bottom of the hill. The place was deserted. The owner, a former merchant marine, and his customers were rejoicing with the crowd. From his trouser pocket 3 Vee took a piece of paper. The edges had bent sharply, and, grubby with his fingerprints, the number was barely readable.

Tessa had recently installed a private phone in her study. When he heard her voice, he asked, "Do you remember a verse that goes like this? 'The desire of the moth for the star, Of the night for the morrow, The devotion to something afar From the sphere of our sorrow'?"

"Shelley?" she asked.

"That's right. It's easier to enjoy the things you want from afar, Tessa."

"Not for me," she said. "I've always wanted my stars nearby. Does that sound snug and womanly?"

"You've thought about it, then."

"A lot."

"So have I. For me, accomplishing what I set out to do is an intimation of my own mortality."

"Uncle, are you saying your well came in?"

"No. Shell's got a gusher. I'll be next."

"Oh, Uncle . . ."

"Who else would be foolish enough to recite poetry to his benefactor?"

There was silence on the other end.

"Tessa? Are you there?"

"I'm crying . . . Uncle, I'm so very happy for you . . ."

"However gloomy I act, you should know this. It was the dearest, kindest, nicest thing anyone did for me. Ever."

After 3 Vee hung up, he laid out a nickel for the call. He didn't telephone anyone else. He stood with his hands on the crumb-strewn counter. On the day the first Los Angeles well came in, he—drenched with black crude—had raced a mile to town. He was remembering the hush in Van Vliet's Hardware, he was remembering plump Hendryk, erect and proud in his frock coat. He remembered a young and golden Bud laughing with joy. He remembered Amélie's hazel eyes fixed on him in surprise, then fear and slowly—oh so slowly—in forgiveness. He remembered his brother's wife, a fragile and lovely girl who, unknown to him then, was with child.

On September 10 his well came in. By then Signal Hill was fevered with endless caravans of Mack trucks, Morelands, Whites. Rig hatchets rang night and day. Keen-faced oil-company representatives offered huge sums for oil and gas leases. Men who had never been near an oilfield got jobs, and whores had already set up a cluster of tents. Each girl waited outside her tent, ironing the same shirt over and over until some roustabout went inside, pulling down the flaps. Wells caught fire and oil companies battled the flames with steam from boilers, with mud, with hundred-pound charges of dynamite.

On noisy Signal Hill, where he had dreamed of a mythical island, on Signal Hill, site of his most stubborn defeat, 3 Vee became a millionaire.

·8·

One hot October morning, the new Chinese chauffeur drove Lya and Kingdon around the clattering roar of Signal Hill to Los Angeles Harbor. Reporters waited at Pier 22, where the *Sultana* was docked. Kingdon and Lya posed on deck.

"Miss Bell, what takes you to Paris?"

"A movie offer," Lya replied.

"Who's producing?"

"I'll tell you—if I decide to take the part." She made her Southern-belle smile. "It's way more challenging than anything I've ever done."

"Captain Vance, are you going?"

"I'm a working man, alas."

"You just finished your last—"

"And next week I start another flying turkey called *Winners of the Blue Beyond*."

A female reporter chirped, "But a cruise through the Panama Canal would make a perfect second honeymoon."

"So they tell me," Kingdon replied.

"Then everything's still blissful?"

"We're the same old lovebirds," Kingdon said. "And now if you'll excuse us?"

The couple escaped.

Lya's stateroom was decorated with five huge baskets of lilies. None had cards. Kingdon had sent them all.

"If you need anything, wire me," he said.

"Thanks, hon."

"You have the name of the man in Acapulco?" he asked, taking a bottle of champagne out of one of the flower baskets.

"Señor Antoya," she said, going into the bathroom for glasses.

The cork popped, Kingdon poured. "Bon voyage," he said.

"Hon, don't you worry a bit about Señor Antoya."

"It's you I worry about," he said, drinking. "Lya, if you need anything, we've always been friends, remember that."

"You already gave me more than I asked for," she said. "Why're you doing all this for me?"

"Damned if I know."

"You're difficult to understand," she said. "That's why you come across so well."

"If you need anything, Lya, feel free."

"I'm going to find a lot of work in France," she said brightly, mechanically.

"It'll be a cinch," he lied, knowing there was nowhere on earth that she would be permitted to act in front of a camera.

"I reckon they won't pay any never-mind to that Doom Book," she said. "They're mad for Americans."

Was she aware that her punishment was a life sentence? He hoped not. He kissed her cheek. "Take care, Lya," he said.

"Mister Man, you're more likely to get into trouble than me."

CHAPTER 23

· I ·

One foggy night in November, eucalyptus logs blazed in every downstairs fireplace of Eagle's Roost.

The biggest fire, set in the living room, warmed Utah as she went through her last-minute survey. The room's heavily scaled furnishings suited her far better than they had Lya. Utah rearranged an ashtray, then opened a nut dish, putting an almond between her teeth. At the crunch she gave a nod. In her boardinghouse she had prided herself on fresh food. Glancing with disapproval at the leggy cabinet with open doors that showed a surplus of illegal bottles, she turned to a gilt-framed mirror.

Tilting her head, she examined herself. The diamond airplane that Charley Kingdon had given her for her birthday glittered on the jet-embroidered expanse of her left breast, and in the fold where her neck joined her body lay a diamond necklace. Her hand reached to touch flesh-warmed stones so she could see her new sapphire ring and the cuff of diamonds and sapphires. 3 Vee had said that this elaborate jewelry was inappropriate for a family dinner, and any other time that he ventured an opinion in the matter of taste or manners, she deferred to him. Tonight, however, Bud, Amélie, and Tessa were invited. This wasn't a family dinner. This was a triumph. Utah didn't intend for the spoils of her long-awaited victory to languish in the safe that Lya had installed in the dressing-room floor.

Heavy footsteps descended the stairs.

3 Vee appeared. Hands on her hips, surveying her husband, Utah repressed her smile of pleasure. A grand-looking man, she thought. Anybody could see right off he came from a high-toned family.

"Your tie ain't straight," she said.

He came toward her, working his finger under the wing collar of his boiled shirt.

"You got to get used to dress clothes," she said, adjusting his tie.

In Utah's mind, 3 Vee, for all his white beard and gray hair, remained a boy. She worried about his far-reaching mental processes still, and was more protective of him than of her sons. She licked a finger and pressed down his unruly eyebrow. "That's better," she said. "3 Vee, this is your big night." She went to the liquor cabinet, poured a thimbleful of Scotch, and handed it to him.

"Why, Utah," he said, surprised. "Thank you."

"Only for tonight," she said, and sat in an intricately carved chair. "The one thing that won't look right to *them* is Lya's being in Paris. Charley Kingdon stood by her. She should stand by him. He should make her!" Utah popped another salted almond into her mouth, struggling between annoyance and pleasure in the occasion. Pleasure won. "We got three fine sons—why, Charley Kingdon's even famous. And now you're just as rich as Bud."

3 Vee gazed into the burning logs.

"Stop looking so broody. Say something."

"Bud's very glad for me," he said.

"Him? Hah! Now he's not the grand nabob of the family!"

"He can buy and sell me a hundred times over," 3 Vee said. "It's not in me to hold onto a fortune."

"Always talking yourself down! It's no wonder that he's shoved ahead of you."

3 Vee downed his minuscule drink. "Utah, it's me who always struggled to catch up with him. He always protected me—at least until..." 3 Vee went to the long-legged cabinet.

"You already had your drink," Utah warned.

"You said it's my night." He poured himself two fingers of Scotch. "Utah, Bud's never been petty. It's taken me a long time to realize this. He's the real García, not me. He nursed Papa. Any of our kin who need help go to Bud. He took care of Mama's people, and he still hires the ones who're left, or sends them money. He's built hospitals in Los Angeles, given money to the university, planned the parks—"

444

"He wants to be king of the mountain!" Utah interrupted.

"He's a builder, a doer, and the city's indebted to him."

"And what about the oil? Who discovered oil for this town?" That indisputable fact dispelled Utah's rancor. She smiled at her husband. "Did Charley Kingdon get back?"

Kingdon, between films, had spent the day flying.

"About an hour ago."

She glanced up at the black-enamel clock. "Quarter of eight, almost. They'll be here any minute. Better fetch him."

Obedient, 3 Vee rose, but at that moment an upstairs door slammed shut. Kingdon, whistling, trotted downstairs. A strand of black hair fell on his forehead, and he was smiling.

Charley Kingdon was Utah's least-understood, wildest, most independent son, and he raised in her memories of her old sin. Yet her maternal instincts were strong. His obvious happiness pleased her. "Don't you look like you had a good day!"

"Keen eye there, Mother," Kingdon replied, laughing.

3 Vee examined his favorite son. This entire year Kingdon hadn't been happy. So why now? Maybe he's going to accept the oil money and buy a flying field, give up the movies. 3 Vee knew Kingdon's discomfort about acting. Yet Kingdon, refusing his share of the profit from 3 Vee's strike, was making two extra films a year to repay what he had borrowed from Jacopo Rimini for Lya's defense.

3 Vee asked, "Did you tell Mr. Rimini you've decided to take it easier?"

"I told him. He doesn't believe it." Kingdon stood in front of the fire. "Mother, Dad, there's something special."

"Tonight," Utah reminded sharply, "is your Pa's night."

"Kingdon's my partner."

"A very silent one," Kingdon said. "This isn't business."

"What's it about?" Utah demanded.

"When everybody's here, I'll explain. But I'm very happy about it. So will you promise to understand?"

"It ain't possible to make a promise about something you don't know!" she snapped.

Kingdon ignored his mother's anger. "When I got home I looked in the dining room. Mother, that's some banquet you're planning."

"Charley Kingdon, you tell me what's so important you can't let you own pa have his big night?"

The doorbell rang.

Tom and Bette had come in their Ford with LeRoy and Mary Lu, who had been married in June. There was a burst of greetings.

3 Vee surveyed his sons, one tall, taut, dark, the others short and sandy-freckled, his two little daughters-in-law in their dinner gowns. "Utah, aren't we lucky?" he asked, resting his hand on her shoulder.

Her round face beaming, she shared his pleasure until she glanced at the clock. Her mouth drew into a tight circle. "They're late," she said.

"Ten minutes isn't exactly no-show," Kingdon said.

And Bette, with a pert toss of her curly red bob, added, "We're early. Or isn't everyone here aware that no party begins until the lord and lady of Greenwood arrive?"

They heard an automobile on the drive, and Kingdon ran out to the foggy courtyard. Amélie and Bud had never been to Eagle's Roost. Kingdon opened the back door of the Daimler, saying, "Welcome." He handed Amélie out carefully, shook hands with Bud. He took Tessa's arm and led them into the house.

"Some place you have here," Bud said, looking around the entrance hall.

Kingdon waved at the suit of armor. "Movie-star Gothic," he said. "I'm trying to sell it to my father, but his taste's too good."

The new manservant took the coats, then Kingdon escorted Bud, Amélie, and Tessa down the steps to the living room.

When 3 Vee's first well came in, Bud had driven to Signal Hill to offer his congratulations. Paloverde Oil had leases there now, and the brothers bought one another cups of coffee in the drab little café at the bottom of the hill.

"It's a big night, kid," Bud said. "The Van Vliet clan rides high."

Amélie hadn't seen Utah or 3 Vee since the night at Greenwood. "Utah, how proud you must be," she said, then moved to grasp 3 Vee's large and calloused hand. He reddened. "3 Vee, we are so happy for you. If only Doña Esperanza and Papa Hendryk could be here tonight."

The manservant bore in a silver bucket showing the swathed necks of two champagne bottles. A recently hired maid followed with a silver tray clinking with wide-bowled glasses.

"We're making the toast at supper," Utah hissed to Kingdon.

"Remember our discussion," Kingdon said. "This is part of it."

Utah flashed him a look of anger. Bud and Amélie turned to him, as did his brothers and sisters-in-law, and everyone watched, silent, as the corks popped and bubbling wine was poured. The glasses were handed around.

Kingdon went to Tessa, taking her glass. "You don't get to drink this," he said, putting his free arm around her waist.

They stood near the fireplace, and the flickering eucalyptus flames softened the harsher light of electricity. Kingdon's dark hair shone as he bent toward her; her face was raised toward his in profile. They gazed at one another, he smiling, she not, their expressions as dreamy as if they were alone.

Kingdon lifted his glass. "To the bride. To my wife." His voice went low. "My love."

The servants' departing footsteps had faded. The warm room was absolutely still. Into this silence rang a sharp cry as Amélie's glass fell, shattering on parquet. Spilled champagne darkened the beige of her dinner dress, spreading downward. She didn't move.

Tom spoke first. "Aunt Amélie, here," he said, pressing his linen napkin into her trembling hand.

LeRoy bent to pick up the shards of crystal.

Tom, the lawyer, turned to Kingdon. "You're already married."

"I've been a free man for several weeks. Lya got a divorce when her boat docked in Acapulco. A very fine *avocat* down there, Tom, a Señor Antoya."

Bette Van Vliet said, "Congratulations, you two!"

And Mary Lu Van Vliet added, "It's wonderful."

The room was silent again. The odor of spilled champagne seemed heavier.

Utah's lips were quivering as if she desired to speak, but no sound came from her mouth. Her massive bosom heaved. Amélie raised one small hand to her unlined throat, where a pulse beat visibly. 3 Vee's expression mingled surprise and horror. Bud gazed at Tessa as if she had raised a gun against him.

Tessa's face was wiped of joy. "Daddy?" she murmured.

Bud turned slowly from her.

"You cannot be married." 3 Vee's voice was ragged, as if he had a sore throat.

"We flew to Yuma this morning," Kingdon said.

"Sin!" Utah burst out.

Amélie winced.

"Mother," Tessa asked, "what is it?"

"Impossible," Amélie whispered.

"You must have...guessed what we...felt," Tessa said hesitantly. "Cousins marry."

And Kingdon, his grip tightening on Tessa's waist, said to Utah, "Lya had it from Father McAdoo that our marriage, hers and mine, was invalid. And as for Tessa and my being cousins—Mother, you've heard of dispensations?"

"Have it undone," 3 Vee said.

Amélie stared from Tessa to Kingdon, fear in her hazel eyes.

Tom took her arm. "Here, Aunt Amélie," he said, leading her, unresistant, to the nearest sofa.

"Sin," Utah repeated hoarsely.

Kingdon looked at his mother bitterly. "I'm delighted," he said, "that everybody shares our happiness."

"Tessa," Bud said, not looking at her. "Don't you understand? This can't be a normal marriage."

Kingdon saw his father staring at him. "Oh Jesus, Dad, even you? Is that what the four of you want? Signed affidavits from previously requited ladies, a note from—"

"No," Amélie interrupted from the sofa. Her expression of alarm remained, but her voice again was clear. "You've been Tessa's lover for a long time."

"Well," Bette said brightly, "I think this is more thrilling than one of Kingdon's movies." The remark and a toss of her red hair went unnoticed.

"It was monstrous of me to have let it continue," Amélie said to Kingdon. "You cannot think of dispensations. There must be an annulment. There is *reason* for annulment."

Bud had turned the jaundiced white of tallow. He went to where his wife sat, curving both hands on the arm of the sofa, bending over her. "Sweetheart, I've been thinking. We have a son-in-law we know and like. Tessa loves him. And—well, he's fine with me."

Amélie gazed up into his unmanned pallor. "Bud, are you all right?"

"Please. It's not so terrible, is it, for them to be cousins?"

Momentarily his eyes shone with pinpoints of light. His lips tensed with pain. And then the light was gone. "Why are you making such a fuss?"

A log in the fireplace burned in half, falling. 3 Vee jumped. "Bud, you can't mean that."

"If the marriage is all right with me, who are you to object?" Bud snapped.

And 3 Vee, with a burst of perception, saw that his brother, by some unimaginable effort, had obliterated all memory of the past. He glanced at Amélie.

Her lips formed the words: I will explain to them later.

Utah saw nothing. Her body seemed to swell, a great bejeweled, glittering bulk. The emotions coursing through her were too violent to catalogue. Rage and anger. A retroactive sexual jealousy. Utah hadn't joined with her husband for many years, yet that carnal envy of her sister-in-law remained. Her inferiorities bloated her. To them, she thought, I'm still a nobody. She was filled with loathing for Tessa. Maternal failure dragged at her. Her every effort had failed. She had punished Charley Kingdon's boyhood fruitlessly; his instinct for the forbidden, which she believed had come to him from his unsanctified begetting, had won out.

Her torrential emotions drenched her in sweat. "You ain't cousins!" she shouted.

Bud's shoulders sagged under his dinner jacket.

Amélie stood, taking his arm. "Utah," she said coldly, "take your spite out on me, not them."

3 Vee said to his wife, "For the love of God, Utah, the children will be hurt enough. Let it be told decently."

Utah's face was a gleaming red. "How can it be said decent? It's too late."

Bud sat heavily on the sofa. He was rubbing his chest.

Tessa moved from Kingdon's encircling arm. "Daddy?" she asked in her soft, low voice.

"What the hell's got into everybody?" Kingdon asked. "I've finally married the girl I've always loved, who's always loved me, and it's like Kaiser Bill's marched on Los Angeles. Isn't one of you human enough to give your blessings?" He turned to Utah. "Mother, we'll get the dispensation. I promise you I'll re-enter the Church and we'll get the dispensation. Will that make it right?"

Make it right? The words sank into Utah's consciousness like iron into a pond. Every word he said, this man with the dark and tormented face, proved her ancient sin.

"Don't ask me the questions!" she shouted. "Talk to your fancy mother-in-law. Ask her why her husband shunted her out of town to have her princess! Ask your pa why his brother hates him. *I* ain't the one with answers!"

"I think I've got indigestion," Bud said.

This homely remark broke the tension for Bette and Mary Lu. They tittered. Their husbands glared at them. The girls were silent.

Bud's fingers went under his jacket, massaging his rib cage. His face was creased with bewilderment.

"What is it?" Tessa asked. "Does it hurt, Daddy?"

"Your daddy's fine!" Utah was shrieking now. "You're just not talking to him! That there's your uncle! 3 Vee's your daddy!"

Amélie rose to stand between her husband and Utah, as if to protect Bud from malevolence.

"Ain't one of you got a grain of fear?" Sweat dripped down Utah's face. "Or are you Van Vliets so high and mighty that God's holy word don't mean a thing to you?"

"God doesn't condone inhumanity either." 3 Vee sighed. "Couldn't you have waited?"

"Amélie," Bud said, "I can't catch my breath. We better get home."

"Sir," Kingdon said, "would you like to lie down and rest?"

"A doctor—" Amélie said.

"No!" Bud snapped. "I'll be fine at home."

He arched his chest, trying to breathe.

Amélie glanced urgently at Kingdon. He ran into the hall, shouting for the manservant to get Mr. Van Vliet's chauffeur to bring the car around. Bud got to his feet, moving stiffly as if he had been bedridden. Amélie cupped both palms under his right arm, Tessa gripped his left hand, and slowly they crossed the room.

Near the step up to the entry, Utah clutched Tessa's shoulder, halting her. "Maybe sin don't matter to them, or to you! But it does to Charley Kingdon! I raised him decent. Sin matters to him. This is no marriage. It's a blasphemy!"

Tessa wrenched free, following Bud and Amélie. Kingdon

helped his aunt on with her fur cloak. He handed Bud his hat and draped his topcoat around his uncle's shoulders. Tessa clasped her wrap, not putting it on.

The Daimler had drawn up. As they went outside, Bud inhaled several breaths of damp, foggy air. "That's better," he said.

Kingdon asked, "Tessa, should I come with you, or follow in my car?"

"With me," she replied.

"I'm better," Bud said, taking another deep breath. "Don't let my rotten belly ruin 3Vee's party."

"Credit where credit is due," Kingdon said. "I ruined it."

"Well, you two take your own car." Bud sounded almost jaunty. "You'll be right back."

· 2 ·

As the sound of the first car receded down the driveway, 3Vee turned to Utah. "You ghoul," he said. "You unspeakable ghoul."

He left the room, his footsteps heavy on the stairs.

Utah listened, overwhelmed by that sick nausea which invariably came after she lost her temper. She looked dully from the champagne bottles to the shattered crystal on the parquet floor. Her two younger sons and her daughters-in-law averted their eyes from her. Utah's desolation was so great that she whimpered. Yet why, she wondered, should *she* experience self-hatred? It was the others, wasn't it, who had sinned?

The manservant came to the entry. "Madame, dinner is served," he announced.

Utah turned to him with mindless surprise.

· 3 ·

Bud stood in Greenwood's downstairs bathroom. The relief he had taken in fresh air was gone, and fullness again pressed inside his chest. He had sent Amélie—protesting that she must telephone Dr. Wallview—downstairs to the pantry to fix him baking soda in warm water.

Unlike most men of his age, Bud was in extremely good health. The worst infirmity he suffered was indigestion, which—he told himself—was what ailed him now. He undid his top trouser button, seeking relief from the pressure. Nothing happened. He could taste the salted almond he had eaten at Kingdon's.

Suddenly, clearly, he saw Utah, her thick body swelling up like a desert toad in the rain. He heard her buzz-saw voice. He couldn't remember the words, yet a sense of annihilation dragged at him. The victories of a lifetime, Paloverde Oil, his fortune, his philanthropies, this house which was Paloverde, respect, affection, meant nothing. Why? What had Utah been shouting about?

The greasy salt of the almond remained in his mouth. Annoyance pierced him. Where the hell is Amélie? he thought. Why is she taking her time when she knows I've got my indigestion? He rested his hands on one of the pink-marble washbowls, realizing his palms were drenched. Sweat wilted his boiled collar. Once I get that soda, he thought, I'll feel better.

Utah had been yelling about the old argument, the one before Amélie left for Oakland. I can't for the life of me remember what we quarreled about, he thought. She stood in the parlor window looking proud and very ill. What the hell would I argue about when she was in the last stages of her pregnancy? His wet hands clasped on marble. The baby, he thought. Yes, it was something about the baby. Oh God.

Tessa . . .

It was then that the blow struck between his shoulder blades.

The pain was so vital, intense, and unrelenting that it filled the world. Yet his senses remained sharp. He saw his hands gripping the sink, the veins puffed like blue worms. He could smell his own aftershave, taste that damn almond. The pain pressed him down. He was aware of the slow sag of his body, as if his muscles were melting and his bones were turning to water. Yes, that ancient feeling of defeat was upon him. Tessa, he thought again, and he was collapsing, a boneless slug, on the tile floor.

The movement took a long time, the hardness rising slowly to meet the back of his head. He felt no blanking of consciousness. He lay gazing up at the rough pink of unpolished marble, the undersides of two washbowls. Pipes snaked into the wall. He tried to call out. No sound came. Pain sat on his body from his shoulders to his groin. Pain, a solid presence.

"Bud?" Amélie's voice, from a distance. "Bud?"

He tried to answer. A crinkling sound was pressed from his lungs. The vibrations of her light footsteps faded.

Another sound grew, a whirring that he recognized as tires on gravel. Car doors slammed and the front door of the house opened and closed. He heard the sharp click of a woman's heels and a faintly uneven masculine step that grew closer, then halted at the bathroom.

"Oh Jesus," a man's voice whispered.

"Daddy . . ." the woman murmured, her voice barely audible. She bent down. Black hair framed a white oval. It looks like Mama, Bud thought. Yes, it's Mama. She'll fix the hurt. She's good at curing people. He tried to explain about the pain pressing on him, but no words came. She seemed to understand. She was undoing his tie and collar stud, undoing another button of his trousers.

The man's footsteps pounded. "Amélie. *Amélie!*"

Then another woman was bending over him. She had slightly tilted hazel eyes, and he knew right away who she was. The little girl next door. Colonel Deane's daughter. But what was she doing here? The edges of his consciousness blurred.

"Bud," she was saying, her cheek touching his. The scent of flowers came through the pain, and he realized he wanted her. Mustn't, he thought. She's only fifteen. She's a tiny thing, aggravating, yet she touches me in a way none of the others do, so tenderly.

"Bud, Bud, darling. Listen to me. You cannot go. You cannot leave me."

Leave her? Why would he do that? This odd, foreign little girl was touching his face lovingly, and the solid mountain of hurt on top of him seemed lighter.

"Amélie Deane." He heard his low, agonized whisper. "You have very pretty hair."

And the pain clamped down. He vomited over her.

An hour later, Kingdon and Tessa sat in Tessa's study. The door was open. They could see across brightly lit emptiness, beyond a balustraded corridor, the closed oak door of the master bedroom. In there three doctors and two nurses were working over Bud. Amélie was either with them or in her dressing room.

Kingdon held Tessa's hand. His thumb rubbed the platinum band he had placed on her finger in compliance with an order drawled by the Yuma justice of the peace. He knew he should say something comforting. His uncle even now might be dead, or breathing with that hoarse rattle that precedes death. Yet even out of his huge love for Tessa, he couldn't summon a single drop of sympathy. *3Vee's your daddy*. The words kept resounding through Kingdon's mind, and he couldn't concentrate on anything else. His being cried out that the curved hatred of his mother's lips had formed a lie, but he knew from the reaction of the other three that she had touched near the truth.

He heard a sound from the master bedroom, a rumble that he identified as furniture being moved. Tessa stood. He continued to clasp her hand. The rumbling ceased. He drew her back onto the leather couch. Reassurances are in order, he told himself. He was mortally ashamed that he couldn't join in her anxiety. Yet how could he think of any matter beyond *3Vee's your daddy?* Classical lines, he thought, doubtless translated from Greek tragedy.

The door of the master bedroom opened. He tensed. It was the brightly lit room that roused him to vicarious fear. In the French hospital ward, they had kept a darkening screen around his bed until he was out of danger. You knew someone had died when lights shone on an empty bed. Without thinking, he clasped Tessa's hand more tightly.

Amélie shut the door behind her and came quickly around the corridor to Tessa's study. Wearing a white silk robe, her unbobbed hair escaping in tendrils from tortoiseshell combs, she looked more fragile and vulnerable than he had ever seen her. She crumbled onto the couch as if every vertebra in her regally erect spine had given way.

In that moment Kingdon was as positive as he had ever been of anything that his uncle was dead.

Tessa leaned momentarily against him. "Mother?" she said.

"They have him in an oxygen tent," Amélie said.

"The pain?" Tessa asked.

"Even with their drugs, it is so intense that we cannot understand it as pain."

"But he's alive," Tessa said, a statement of faith.

"Dr. Levin, the heart man, does not offer much hope beyond that fact."

"It's the only important one," Tessa said. Tears filled her eyes as she reached both arms around her mother. For a minute Amélie let herself be comforted, then she pulled away. Her eyes were dry.

Tessa rang for something to eat, and a maid wearing a lumpy bathrobe, crying, carried up a tea tray set with a plate of thin-sliced lemon cake. Tessa poured, and they sipped tea and ate the cake in silence.

Amélie set down her cup. "It is time," she said. "I must tell you."

Though Kingdon had felt the power of Amélie's social charm, he had never liked her. His mother's hatred had been implanted before memory, congenitally. On his own observation, he thought his aunt a cool customer. But now his old antipathy was overcome by admiration. How many women, he asked himself, can peel the skin of truth while death hovers?

"Mother," Tessa said, "you don't have to. Not tonight."

"I have compromised until tonight. Because I feared this, what has happened to Bud, I put it off. The telling has been put off dishonorably long."

3 *Vee's your daddy.* Kingdon wondered if that elegant, classical phrase could have been voiced soon enough?

They sat side by side on the leather couch with its view of the closed bedroom door. Tessa was in the middle. Kingdon leaned forward, his arms on his thighs, so that Amélie, unimpeded, could tell him secrets that he had no desire to learn.

"Los Angeles," Amélie said. "The important thing you must realize is that this story revolves about Los Angeles. A dusty hamlet at the edge of nowhere. When it rained, pigs rooted in the mud of Main Street. *I* lived half the year in Paris. You can imagine what a cultured semi-Parisienne like *me* felt for this place." Her voice,

wryly unsentimental, explained her closeness to her father, and the
Colonel's bewildering problems with his former friend, Collis P.
Huntington, and the Southern Pacific Railroad. "That summer I
was fourteen. 3Vee was seventeen. Ah, Kingdon, he was such a
foolish, sweet boy, caught up in the loneliness of being sensitive and
creative in a raw Western town." She told of the Colonel's suicide
and Madame Deane's decision to sue the Southern Pacific. "That
meant we must stay on." She told of the scandal and her own increasing need to avenge her father. "I began to see myself as Electra.
I wanted to inter his memory with dignity. The way to do that, or
so it seemed to me, was to put the railroad in as bad a light as Papa.
There were some letters—"

"The Deane Letters?" Kingdon asked.

"Yes," Amélie replied.

"Strange. I never associated you with them."

"They were sent by Mr. Huntington to my father. I needed
someone to help me in my plan. A man. 3Vee was at Harvard. Anyway, he was a boy. At my father's funeral, Bud had been the only
one to step forward and offer his condolences. He, obviously, was a
man. I coerced him into helping me." She drew a sharp breath. "We
began meeting here—at Paloverde."

"And you fell in love," Tessa said.

Amélie shook her head. "Not at first. Bud was not like 3Vee. He
was completely at home in Los Angeles. How could I care for a native of this awful desert island? Yet he was everything I admired.
Strong. Generous. And, like my papa, a little ruthless. Besides, he
was a very beautiful young man." She shrugged, gazing at the
closed bedroom door. "I promised to marry him because I thought
to do otherwise would be dishonorable. I did not realize I loved him
until my mother sent me back to France."

"Mother, you don't have to—"

"I do," Amélie said. "He kept his part of the bargain and had the
letters presented at the trial. I returned to Los Angeles to marry
him."

She drew another breath, shivering slightly. "3Vee was not at
our wedding. He had run away from home. No one knew why.
Bud and I had been married seven years when he came back with
Utah. Paloverde was our weekend place and we gave them a party
here. 3Vee drank far too much and wandered away from the
patio. I knew he was unhappy. I followed to calm him."

She drew herself up, her spine once again erect. "He was drunk enough to confess that he cared for me, that he had always cared. He said he had seen me and Bud—well, together—at Paloverde, and that was why he had run away." She clutched her hands in her lap. "What happened next was so out of character that I could not believe it. He was drunk, miserable. He terrified me at first, but then I fought. It was over in a minute." She turned to look at Tessa. "Not long after, I realized I was pregnant." She sighed.

"One minute out of a lifetime. If the universe were just, that minute would be erased."

"It's not a well-run spot, our universe," Kingdon said, his sarcasm hiding torment. Trying to dredge up his old affection for his father, he discovered only hatred.

"He has paid for it with a lifetime of guilt," Amélie said.

"A cheap enough price," Kingdon said.

Amélie ignored his bitterness. "They are brothers," she said. "The inherited signs and likenesses would be the same. I would give anything to offer proof either way."

"Did you have other pregnancies?" Kingdon asked.

"We saw doctors. Here. New York. London. Paris. Each assured us more children were possible. But no, I was never pregnant. Before or since."

"Has Uncle Bud ever fathered another child?"

"Once. He was very young. Rose, her name was Rose. He wanted to marry her. She insisted on an abortion. He felt as if he were paying to kill his own child." Amélie, staring at Kingdon, didn't see Tessa's wince of pain. "The girl died. Rose. It was terrible for him."

"Why did you leave Los Angeles?" Kingdon despised his interrogative voice, yet he couldn't silence it.

"When I was in my eighth month, Bud found out what had happened. He had always wanted a child. And he felt he had been betrayed again. He did not believe that I had been forced. He said—Tessa, darling, forgive me—he said he would never accept the child. My child."

The delicate skin around Amélie's eyes and lips had a bluish cast, as if she had been bruised. "I left him. I cared enough for you to run away and not tell him where I had gone. After a year and a half he found us. You were ill and he saved your life." She spoke too quickly. "Since then he has loved you completely. At first I thought he never mentioned the past out of loyalty. But then I realized it lies buried in his brain like a mine in no-man's land." Her knuckles whitened as her hand clenched. "Ready to explode and kill him."

"Father used to spin tales of Paloverde," Kingdon said, "ancestral home to all of us. That's one story we never heard." His face was dark with the brooding expression that the camera occasionally caught.

"I meant to tell you the day we arrived home from Europe. I knew then that you were in love. Not to speak was dishonorable in the extreme. I hoped it would end. Kingdon, you *were* married. Bud had managed to forget the past. I was terrified that forcing him to face old memories would be too dangerous." Her voice shook. "It is killing him."

Tessa covered her mother's small, clenched fist with her own slender hand. "Don't say that, Mother."

"Now you know why the marriage must be annulled," Amélie said.

It was Kingdon who replied. "No. I cannot do that."

"But—did I not make it clear?"

"Very."

"Then what choice do you have?"

"Aunt Amélie." He drew a sharp breath. "I'm not sure of myself at all. I have none of your assurance that there's a natural code of honor, none of my mother's belief that she and the Deity concur. I'm not your stubborn Van Vliet hardhead. I tickle every question with a million feathers of doubt. Only in this matter do I suspend questioning. I can't afford questions. I love my *cousin*, I'm married to my *cousin*. For the rest of my life I'll stay married to my *cousin*. Tessa?" he asked.

Just then the door of the master bedroom opened. The three of them stood, watching a gray-haired, heavy-set man come toward them. They remained silent until he entered the book-lined study. Then Amélie said thickly, "He is gone."

"No, Mrs. Van Vliet, no. He's still alive." The doctor's voice was too emphatic to be reassuring. He nodded at Tessa and Kingdon. "I'm Dr. Levin," he said. "An oxygen tent sometimes frightens the patient, and we thought that seeing you, Mrs. Van Vliet, would soothe Mr. Van Vliet. He's conscious."

"Is . . . is his pain as . . . bad?" Tessa asked.

"Very much so, I'm afraid."

Amélie took a step toward the door.

"Only for a minute," the doctor cautioned. "One minute, no more."

"Mother?" Tessa asked.

"Of course. Come with me," Amélie replied.

Dr. Levin barred the door, speaking to Amélie. "Mrs. Van Vliet, I don't think you understand. This could well be the last time he *is* conscious."

"We shall take thirty seconds each," she said peremptorily.

The doctor stepped aside.

Kingdon watched them walk swiftly down the corridor. Amélie's white silk robe floated around her. Even in his misery he grasped that his aunt was committing a vast generosity. She had confessed to a passionate and lasting love for her husband, and this possibly was her final minute with him. To share it, Kingdon thought, to share it? As the two disappeared into the master bedroom he leaned against the door jamb of the study.

"You're Kingdon Vance, aren't you?" Dr. Levin asked.

"Van Vliet," Kingdon replied.

· 5 ·

Every lamp was lit, and a Tiffany shade bled stained-glass colors onto the two doctors whispering over a chart. A nurse sat by the bed.

A frame-type oxygen tent covered the head of the bed. Morphine slackened the muscles of Bud's face, yet as the mica window didn't hide him, so the drug didn't mask his pain. His mouth twisted constantly.

As Amélie leaned toward him, his eyes opened. He blinked in recognition. "I love you, darling," she said. He blinked again. She touched her lips with two fingers and pressed them to the mica window. She moved aside.

Tessa stood next to him. "Daddy," she said.

His lips opened and closed twice.

Dr. Levin came in, glancing at them. They left the bedside and went to the sitting room. Amélie closed the door and, leaning an arm against the paneled wall, gasped out tearing sobs. With exquisite delicacy, Tessa let her cry. Finally Amélie took a handkerchief from her robe pocket and blew her nose. Tessa put an arm around her mother's shoulders, leading her to a loveseat, cradling her head.

"Oh God!" Amélie said. "He is such a strong man. To see him like that. How I hate that woman! To have him go like this."

"He's not dying. Mother, it was very dear of you to let me share. Do you think...it upset him, seeing me?"

"Of course not."

"I didn't think so either. But, well, what did he say?"

"'Mama.' He must have thought you were Doña Esperanza." Amélie blew her nose again. "Kingdon is very distraught. You had better go back to him."

"I can't leave you alone."

"Darling, Bud is the only one who can help me."

Tessa reached for her small, icy hand. "Before, to me you always called him Father. Why not now?"

Amélie sat upright. Her face twisted into a network of wrinkles as she battled further tears.

"Mother, Uncle 3 Vee was miserably unhappy one night," Tessa said. "That's all."

"I never have lied to myself."

"I am not lying either. I just know Daddy is my father."

"Be reasonable. Tessa, there's no way for you to be positive."

"Instinct. I always go on instinct."

Amélie sighed but said nothing.

"I know what you're thinking," Tessa said. "That I need to believe for my own purpose. But that's not it."

"I should have told you sooner. I sacrificed you."

"You went away to have me.... Mother, that was very brave. I, well, I couldn't have done it."

Amélie gave her a sharp glance with tear-reddened eyes. "Tessa, when we got home from that cruise, that was it? You had stopped a baby?"

Tessa bent her head miserably. "To have it...I'd have had to leave Kingdon for months. I've wanted a baby so much...but it was at the start of the mess with Lya. I couldn't bear not to be with him then."

"A child? Tessa, I should have told you years ago!"

"There's no point for you to feel guilty."

"Tessa, you cannot even consider—"

"The Lamballes marry their cousins, Mother. Why can't the—"

She was interrupted by voices from the bedroom. Her head jerked. Amélie moved toward the door, straining to hear the muffled words. "Go to Kingdon," she sighed. "I cannot argue the finer moral points, not tonight. Go to him."

·6·

Kingdon's dinner jacket and black tie were thrown on the turned-down bed, and he was in her bathroom, dashing water on his face. He glanced up, his face streaming. "How is he?"

"I know he's going to be all right."

"He probably will," Kingdon said, pulling a towel from the rack. "I'm the only Van Vliet who doesn't hold on like a bulldog. When the final bugle blows for me, I'll go on the run."

Tessa chose a robe from her closet and threw it over a chair. She started unbuttoning the back of her dinner gown. If I can get out of this dress, she thought, the evening will be over.

Tessa had been honest with Amélie. She *was* positive that Bud was her father. If her mother was uncertain, she was not, and her conviction sprang from the mysterious place where she lived much of her time. She attributed her intuitive powers—and these encompassed her writing—to the ancestry Bud had confessed to her, the people who had once roamed the vast, mustard-covered plain. Her hesitations, which were many, came when she faced the arbitrary rules of civilization. Her considerable intelligence played small part in her decisions. She remained stubbornly faithful to instinct.

Kingdon dropped the towel and emerged from the bathroom. "Why, of all the women in the world, did dear old Dad have to pick your mother to rape?"

"She said he'd always cared for her."

"Hardly the cultivated way to show affection. Personally, I've never seen Dad as the caveman type. Still, what does a eunuch like me know of such matters?"

He's in pain, she thought, and I can't help him, not tonight. She remembered Bud's tormented mouth and his white, slackened face. Raising her arms, she continued to unbutton the soft crepe de chine of her dinner dress.

"The mystery of the Van Vliet feud solved," Kingdon said. "Uncle Bud's anger was just. When he found out, do you imagine he challenged Dad to a Californio-style duel, pistols at fifty paces? Or do you think they battled it out with fists? Dad's far larger, but Uncle Bud's wrath was righteous, so his strength was as the strength of ten. Besides, he looks stronger."

"Uncle 3Vee is not my father."

"So you weren't listening," Kingdon said.

"Mother told us it happened once. That doesn't mean anything."

"No? Your mother seems to lack your certainty. And Uncle Bud appears to have had a doubt or two in the days when he permitted himself doubts. Or wouldn't you say packing off a woman in her eighth month shows a certain lack of—shall we call it trust?" He gave a brief laugh. "Once I was rummaging around in the attic. I came across an old box with a wedding license dated less than six months before I was born. I asked Mother about it. She took the whip to me, doubtless punishing me for the sins of the father. Dad, virile pursuer of women. He certainly doesn't look the part, does he? That apologetic little smile—I figured him for a noodle. Well, tonight I revise my official portrait."

"Hating him won't help anything."

"Tessa, you're misinterpreting filial admiration."

The buttons undone, she let the dress fall to the floor, stepping out of it. "You're only wounding yourself," she said.

"For my part, I see this as a discussion of the subject that's captured worldwide interest. The Van Vliet masculinity."

"He's struggling to breathe. Every breath is agony. Kingdon, he *is* my father."

"How've you had time to consult with the gypsies?"

"I can't explain. I'm just sure."

"Mystic bonds, you mean? Ties of the blood?" He nodded. "They exist. Yes. Obviously. Otherwise why did I move across the Hollywood Hotel veranda to you? Of all the girls in Los Angeles? There's proof positive they exist, ties of the blood."

In her long crimson satin slip she turned to him. "Kingdon, I

know how much you hurt. But I can't help you tonight. All I
can think of is him, lying there as if a giant foot were crushing him."

"Again you're right. What's the point of discussion? In Hawaii
the old kings and queens were always full brother and sister.
Pharaohs likewise married their sisters, but I'm not going to bring
up that old bunk. Why go into the fact that morals are a matter of
time and geography? Let's leave it that we're married, and we're
going to stay married, my sister, my love."

"Kingdon, you're tired. Go to bed."

He grasped her shoulders. "Yes, bed," he said.

I can't, she thought wearily. How can I, when I'm out of my
mind with worry? To make love while Daddy's in there struggling
to breathe would be obscene. Her elbows tensed at her side. "Not
now," she murmured.

"What? And you without a single doubt?"

"It's not that."

"Oh? Sheer coincidence that tonight you give me my first turn-
down?"

"His face, Kingdon, it's the color of death. He's drugged, and
nothing shows except the pain."

"Whose face?"

"Oh, stop it, please stop it."

"Whose?" he demanded again.

"My father. Your uncle."

He squinted at her. He had drunk nothing all day, yet his red-
rimmed eyes made him appear drunk. Finally he asked, "I don't
repel you?"

"I love you."

"And me you. That's not the question."

"It's nothing to do with our making love. Kingdon, I . . . well, I've
always been too close to him. Please, please don't push me, not tonight."

"This is the dark after the wedding feast."

He shoved down her straps. Crimson satin tore. His arms hard
around her waist and shoulders, he bent her backward, kissing her,
his lips parting hers. Then he groaned, biting kisses into her neck,
forcing her toward the bed. They fell on the coverlet, he sprawling
on top of her. He was as urgent as he had been that first time in the
Hotel del Coronado. She clutched his head against her breasts.

Horrified at herself, she tried to recapture her father's slack, tormented face, but the image was remote, and unwillingly she responded to Kingdon's wild haste. He took her hand, briefly pressing it to the thick flesh of his scar, whispering, "I'm aware that flames burn. Already I've been in hell. Love, love, have you any idea what you mean to me?"

"Kingdon...I love you so much....Always and forever... Now, please, now!"

"Don't shut me out again," he said as he pressed into her.

"Never..." Light was bursting through her body, and the word was a tremulous coital cry.

· 7 ·

Just before dawn, the skylights of the patio turned the mottled black of long-tarnished silver. Tessa, wearing a plaid skirt and a mismatching print blouse, had come downstairs to get her mother some coffee. The front doorbell rang. Expecting another doctor, a nurse, more hospital equipment, she answered. 3 Vee, who hadn't changed from his new evening clothes, stood at the door clasping his shabby hat. Seeing her, his expression altered from supplication to alarm.

"Why're you up?" he demanded. "Where's Kingdon?"

She gave him a look of bewilderment. It was as if an earthquake had shaken Los Angeles, toppling houses and stores, cracking the pavements, and he hadn't felt it.

"My father's had a heart attack," she said.

3 Vee's footsteps echoed heavily in the shadows of the patio. He sank into an armchair. Water trickled in the fountain. Finally he asked, "A bad one?"

Tessa believed that Bud would survive, yet to keep repeating that seemed to her a Victorian euphemism. She said, "The doctors aren't hopeful." Then her voice broke. "Uncle, he's in terrible pain, but he's going to be all right."

3 Vee was looking up the broad staircase. "Indestructible. That's how I've always thought of him, too. Invulnerable." He turned to Tessa, his brown eyes oddly luminous. He began to speak in a soft hush. "All my life he's been there. The older brother, the successful

older brother against whom all my accomplishments are measured. My yardstick. You're not competitive, Tessa, so I doubt if you can understand what I'm trying to say. This has nothing to do with Bud, only how I feel about him. As a boy everybody liked him, and I told myself in a cultural vacuum like Los Angeles of course he'd be popular. I dreamed of conquering my schoolyard enemies. It was Bud who protected me. He did well in school—without effort. I told myself Harvard would prove my superior mental powers." 3 Vee sighed. "I've always measured myself against him. Even the years we weren't together he was in the corners of my mind. At each of my failures, God help me, I'd think, 'At least Bud's not here to see.' " 3 Vee shook his head. "My entire life's been spent standing against a wall marked with Bud's accomplishments. How could I not have known he was dying?"

"He's alive," Tessa said. "Uncle, Mother explained . . . you and her."

3 Vee jerked upright. "That's why I came. Is Kingdon here?"

"He's upstairs sleeping."

"Thank God. I waited up for him. When he didn't come home, I worried. He drives as fast as he flies his plane. It's a foggy night. He drinks too much. And after the way Utah said—"

"He's fine," she interrupted. "He's going to stay at Greenwood."

"Live here?"

"Until Daddy's better." She paused. "Then we'll move to our own place."

3 Vee stared at her. His brows, though age-thickened, had remained black. The incongruity between dark, bushy brows and his trimmed white beard gave his expression an Old Testament fierceness. Tessa, sitting on an ottoman near him, smoothed her skirt.

Finally 3 Vee asked, "Amélie told you that before you were born, I was, well, I was with her?"

"Once," Tessa replied.

"Honey, it was nine months before."

"I know."

"She told Kingdon, too?"

"Both of us."

"It must have been difficult enough for him to marry you as his cousin. Now this." 3 Vee's voice constricted. "I don't know what to say or do. To have Kingdon and you punished instead of me!"

"Uncle, it's all right. He . . . still . . . cares for me." She went crimson, making her hesitations explicit, and 3 Vee realized that when she had said Kingdon was upstairs sleeping, she meant in her bed. He flushed, too.

"It's not so shocking," she said. "We're married. And we *are* just cousins."

"Kingdon believes that?"

She again smoothed her skirt. "He's not positive," she said miserably.

"In the end he'll believe what Utah said. And it'll destroy him."

As he spoke, 3 Vee clenched his fists, torn by the memory of Kingdon's bleak face as his son had pleaded with Utah about the Vatican dispensation. The elopement no longer surprised 3 Vee—he had compared Lya's shrill ambition with Tessa's serene ways and understood his son's choice—but positive that Tessa was his daughter, he was both shocked and terrified.

It was fear of Kingdon's reactions to Utah's incontestable revelation that had sent him into the foggy night searching for his son. And it was this same fear that demanded he argue the couple out of their marriage. This will tear Kingdon to pieces, he thought. Openly confronting the sad family secret went against 3 Vee's reticence, but he sat in the patio weighted down with parental guilt, telling himself that it was up to him to extricate his son from certain destruction. They can't stay together, he thought.

Kingdon's biting wit was a barrier that 3 Vee had never been able to penetrate. He looked into Tessa's unguarded oval face. She's so gentle, he thought. I can convince her.

She looked up. "Uncle, she shouted it out as if she wanted to hurt him."

"You have to understand Utah." Though 3 Vee had told Utah she was a ghoul, his mind always sidestepped casting blame—except on himself. "For Utah there's a punitive God who chases sinners up and down the length of eternity. She believes that Kingdon was born in sin, and she's always seen it as her duty to save him from perdition. She feels she's the appointed guardian of his immortal soul. He doesn't need her. He's probably the most deeply religious man I've ever known. The more he flees from the Church, the deeper he's bound to it. Does that sound contradictory?"

"I've always understood that."

"Then you know what it did to him when he heard the truth tonight?"

"It's not the truth," Tessa said. Her soft voice was determined.

For the first time 3 Vee saw in her the Van Vliet stubbornness, but he didn't yet realize that he would have a harder struggle with her than with Kingdon. Rather, he was weighted down with a huge sadness for her. Poor girl, he thought, she can't let herself believe.

He was quiet for a few moments, then the prodding of his guilts and his love for Kingdon made him speak again. "I'm not talking lies or truth, honey. I'm explaining why Kingdon will believe you aren't cousins."

"If only there were some way to prove who I am."

"As far as I'm concerned, if nobody had told Kingdon, I would have kept on pretending Bud's your father," 3 Vee said, his face wearing a look of mournful embarrassment.

"He is," Tessa said wearily. She looked up to the right of the staircase as if she could see Bud. "It's so horrible. To think he's been hiding inside himself all these years, never able to look on part of his life because he was loyal to me." She sniffed back a sob. "He's in an oxygen tent. He didn't even know me."

Not covering her face, she began to weep.

At her tears, 3 Vee yearned to cease his hammering. It was his natural aversion to confrontations that forced him on. I'm always afraid to speak out, he told himself. It's just like me to drift into the cowardly cover of silence. He shifted his bulk in the armchair. "Believe me, the last thing I want to do is interfere between you and Bud."

"My father," she corrected.

"Kingdon doesn't believe that," 3 Vee said gently. "Tessa, you can't stay together."

"The story's terrible for him," she admitted. Crying forced her voice into breathiness. "He's filled with doubts."

"Of course he is."

"But he told Mother he wouldn't leave me. He told me never, never to reject him—not that I could. Uncle, we cannot separate."

"I've wronged you both terribly." 3 Vee leaned forward in his chair. "Maybe that's why I can't give up."

She glanced up, this time to the left, and 3 Vee knew she was looking toward her own door, behind which Kingdon slept. "There's no point in discussion."

"Tessa—"

"He loves me, he wants me, and until that's over, I'm incapable of leaving him."

"What about his doubts?"

"They'll gnaw him whether we're together or apart. You know that," she said, making no attempt to check her tears.

Looking into her wet blue eyes, 3 Vee had a curious sense that the tears were part of her, a stigmata. She's as determined as Papa and Bud, he thought in surprise.

She wiped away her tears with her fingers. "Do you have a handkerchief?" she asked.

He fished in his pocket and she took the crumpled linen, blowing her nose. The ordinary sound made her weeping real. And he wondered how he had been able to argue with her, tonight, when her world had exploded in her face.

"This isn't the time," he said. "I didn't mean to make it harder. I'm a frightened man desperate to set things right. How you must hate me."

She shook her head. "Uncle, you're holding onto your guilts as if they're special. We're all guilty. Why be harder on yourself than anyone?"

"Because I'm guiltier."

"You aren't. You loved Mother, that's all."

This truth, seen from the point of her goodness, shamed him more than any denunciation. He sighed. "We'll talk about it later." He got to his feet. "Your mother won't want me around now. Neither will Kingdon. I'd like to know about..." He hesitated before saying, "Your father."

"Every few hours I'll telephone," she said.

She walked with him to the entry. Outside, remnants of fog shrouded the dawn. 3 Vee shivered. He glanced up at the brightly lit windows of the second story. Mist lapped over the balconies, pressing against glass panes. 3 Vee's chill increased and he hunched his shoulders as he moved down the broad flight of steps. Bud, he thought. Kingdon. He couldn't tell which name roused greater fear.

From his car seat, he glanced back. Tessa remained at the open door, her arms clasped over her bosom. In the haze, with a nimbus of light behind her, she resembled a tall, serene angel guarding Paloverde against all evil, including him and death.

·8·

Bud lay behind an enormous window. Pain had him pinned down, yet innumerable times, or so it seemed to him, he had attempted to release himself from the nightmare window and had failed. Beyond that glass, a voice shrieked. He couldn't make out the muffled words, but he knew they were evil. Once, distant and ghostly, Amélie had tried to shield him from the malign sounds. And once his mother had come for the same purpose.

Now again he could hear the shrieking. But what was the voice saying? He knew the words were poisonous. He shouldn't try to hear. Yet when had he been able to ignore a challenge? It was necessary for him to break the glass and listen to those words—even if it killed him.

Mustering all of his strength, he raised his right hand slightly, but the cost of the movement was enormous. He rested, gasping, then, with a lunge, pushed. His fingers met a surface as warm and smooth as an oil slick. At his touch, shapes wrinkled, converging on him. One side of his prison lifted.

"Mr. Van Vliet," said a bespectacled man. "I'm Dr. Levin. Dr. Wallview called me in. Please don't be alarmed by the oxygen tent. It's here to make you comfortable, that's all."

"Can't hear." The difficulty of forming words overwhelmed Bud.

"Don't try to speak. The blurriness of your senses is nothing for you to worry about. It's caused by opiates. You need to rest."

"Heart?"

"Yes," the doctor replied. "Blink if you're in less pain."

Bud blinked.

An anxious oval swam into view. The woman he had seen earlier wasn't his mother; his mother had been dead for decades. This was Tessa. His efforts at speech had wearied him unbelievably, yet he opened his mouth to ask his daughter to sit with him.

"Mr. Van Vliet," the doctor said, "please try to relax. The only cure is complete rest."

Bud gazed up at Tessa, his lips not moving.

"Would it help if I'm with you?" she asked.

He blinked.

"Then I'll stay here," she said, and the firmness of her low-pitched voice soothed him. She won't let any doctor banish her, he thought, not my Tessa.

He told himself he mustn't fight their drugs. He had had a heart attack. But he was alive, and by God he was going to stay alive. Rest, he told himself. The diffused shape that was Tessa touched the mica window reassuringly.

Bud closed his eyes. The dangerous voice no longer cried in the distance. It was a phenomenon, he decided, caused by the drugs. Everything's all right, he thought. My daughter's with me.

He slept.

CHAPTER 24

· I ·

At Greenwood voices were lowered, runners silenced the tile floors, oxygen tanks were moved cautiously, no one was permitted to drive up to the front of the house.

Among the hundreds of telegrams were messages from President and Mrs. Harding, from Secretary of the Interior Fall, from Mrs. Woodrow Wilson, from eleven senators. Senator Hiram Johnson personally delivered a crate of oranges. John D. Rockefeller, though a business rival and notoriously frugal, sent a silver paperweight shaped like an oil derrick. Mr. and Mrs. William Randolph Hearst took tea with Amélie. Henry Huntington visited with his wife, who was the widow of his uncle, Collis P. Huntington. Flowers and books arrived from friends, cards came from everyone in Los Angeles whose life, however remotely, had touched Bud's. Paloverde Oil employees sent presents, and a drilling crew from Signal Hill delivered a new metal helmet. Greenwood servants pooled together to buy him an upholstered wrought-iron chaise for his veranda. His García kin baked him cookies and persimmon cakes, and his Van Vliet cousins sent him a framed collection of the currently popular line drawings of the California missions. Pottery jars of homemade cactus jelly arrived from those ancients the family still designated "Mama's people."

At Christmas another flood of gifts deluged Greenwood. By then Bud was sitting up in bed, propped with pillows. Amélie and Tessa took turns opening his presents. Against doctor's orders, Bud in-

sisted on scrawling a personal line of thanks for every gift. He
wasn't what Dr. Levin characterized an easy convalescent.

The nature of Bud's heart attack made Amélie cautious about
any announcement of the marriage. She—with Kingdon and Tessa
—decided to let it remain secret. Greenwood's corps of servants
told no one. The medical staff accepted Kingdon's presence as that
of a devoted nephew, but Hollywood so bedazzled everyone that
doctors as well as nurses watched hopefully for a glimpse of the
famous movie aviator. They didn't see much of him.

· 2 ·

Kingdon was drinking heavily.

He finished one film, started another. The eye of the camera
seemed more intrusive than ever to him, so he kept a flask in his
leather flight coat. Each evening he would spend a few quiet
minutes in the sickroom, and there his uncle and aunt's obvious affection for one another made him reconsider the modern theory
that love doesn't survive marriage. It's going to be worse for us, he
would think despairingly. Time's no escape. He would excuse himself and go downstairs, heading for the hard liquor locked in the
butler's pantry.

He also drank whenever he thought about returning to the
Church and managing a papal dispensation to marry his cousin.
Was she? The question tore at him. As though it mattered! He was
incapable of leaving her. Ridden by Utah's dour and unrelenting
God, he condemned himself as the lowest of sinners.

The drinking numbed him very little. Flying offered at best a
mild lessening of interior tension. Only when he and Tessa were
joined could he forget the ambiguities.

One Tuesday afternoon in early January when the clouds were
too thick for the camera, Kingdon and Tessa walked to a remote
corner of the gardens, he balancing a glass on top of a silver cocktail
shaker, she carrying a notepad clipped with a fountain pen. He
poured himself a large drink, setting the shaker on the marble ped-
estal of a statue. She sat on the grass, dreamily jotting herself a note
for the revision of her novel.

"This is the first time you've written since Uncle's attack," Kingdon said.

"I didn't realize it, but you're right. He is looking better, isn't he?"

"Like new." Kingdon sat next to her, his left leg stretched out. "When did you say dear old Dad was dropping over?"

"Three-thirty."

"Now's your chance," he said. "Tell me I ought to see him."

"He's so terribly ashamed."

"Christ, I wonder why." Kingdon drained his glass and reached for the shaker.

"He loves you."

"And loving much, should be forgiven much?"

"What good does avoiding him do?"

"Has he told you again to give me my walking papers?"

"Sort of . . . not really."

"Tessa, you're not being clear."

"He brings it up. I don't listen. Kingdon, he's so sad."

"This afternoon, do me a big favor. Tell him to quit mailing me the oil checks. For room and board the amount's too much. For atonement, not enough."

"You're his partner."

"And if he inquires what to do with the money, tell him he can shove it up his goddam ass!"

"Kingdon, don't!" she cried. The shrillness of her voice upset her, and she said, "I'm sorry."

He put an arm around her shoulder. "No, *I'm* sorry. These honeymoon spats," he said. "Tessa, thinking what I am?"

"Yes."

"It's on our minds a lot."

"These honeymoons," she said.

"We weren't a tenth so active before."

She bent her forehead to her raised knees. Kingdon spoke the truth. Passion besotted them. She thought of it constantly, was ready for him always. Sometimes they didn't wait to get to the bed. They made love in the bath, on the study couch amid scattered papers, in the greenhouse surrounded by pink and red azaleas blossoming for the interior patio. She had been slow to learn fulfillment, and at first it had come as a softly mysterious stirring. Since their wedding night, she had been swept into a continuous torrent of climaxes.

473

"I . . . I've gotten better."

"So've I. The act's taken over. It's like a rosebush pruned to produce one single huge blossom."

"That's a bad metaphor," she said. "I love you as much."

"And me you. Before, I even had a sense of sin—"

"Don't."

"Let me finish. I want you so often because you're mine, yet forbidden."

"Oh, Kingdon."

"Love, don't look so sad. Think of the bright side. With me there's no chance of infidelity. I'll never get the itch for another woman. Why should I? Who needs to prowl when there's this delicious sense of evil in my own home?"

"You don't need to feel—"

"Yes. Damn it! I do!" He hurled the glass at the statue, and Tessa jumped as it shattered. "Why? Go ask Dad. You're the only truly good thing in my life, ever, and he's dirtied it."

"We aren't dirty."

"For me we are," Kingdon said. "Love, love, for me we are."

· 3 ·

Through the open window of her sitting room, Amélie heard a sharp crack, like glass breaking. She glanced down into the garden. Kingdon was burying his face in Tessa's shoulder. The shared intimacy of grief. Quickly, Amélie looked away, into the cloud-drabbed sky. She held a book in her lap. She had been trying to read, but her concentration had snapped. She continued to gaze into the gray-purple sky.

Her erect back didn't touch the spooled rungs of her chair, yet there was a suggestion of a curve to her spine, as if a weight were pressing on her shoulders. "He is drinking," she whispered aloud. "He is forever drinking." Some nights she would glance down into the patio to see Kingdon hunched over a cocktail tray, and later she would hear Tessa helping him upstairs. "I am to blame," Amélie whispered.

As soon as Bud's oxygen tent had been removed, her sense of honor had impelled her to have a "talk" with her son-in-law as well as Tessa. Tessa had reiterated her conviction that Bud was her father. During the interview with Kingdon, his dark García features had been set in cynical amusement, and therefore Amélie had been doubly horrified when he began to weep. Men do not weep, she had thought helplessly until, remembering that she had held him as a baby, she put her arms around him. After Bud, Kingdon's slender frame seemed shockingly defenseless. Controlling his shudders, he had pulled away. "I like you, Aunt Amélie, know that?" he said. "And I love your daughter. We're inseparable and indivisible and she assures me that our union's holy. So let's leave it at that." His sarcasm, his tears, had affected Amélie to the point that she could not oppose him again.

One of the guest rooms had been fixed up as an office for Bud, and from down the corridor came the rumble of masculine voices. Amélie felt completely alone. She was trapped in the same wretchedness as she had been that hot summer preceding her father's suicide. Then, she had been a child, condemned to watch a man's disintegration through the bars of a child's inadequacy, unable to help. She glanced into the gardens. Kingdon and Tessa, holding hands, were moving down to the pool house. There was nothing unhappy about them now, yet a conviction of disaster swept over Amélie. I must do something, she thought. But what?

She was still lost in her thoughts when Tessa's footsteps sounded on the stairs. Amélie opened her door. "Tessa, dear. Do you have a minute?"

When her daughter entered the room, her dark blue eyes were suffused with light, an expression of remote dreaminess. Amélie didn't know how to begin.

Finally she asked, "Do you think it will rain?"

"The sky's gotten very black," Tessa replied.

Amélie placed her slender shoes side by side as if her feet weren't in them. "I do not feel I know Kingdon very well," she said. "But he is gallant in just the right offhand way. And very complex. Tessa, did he always drink so much?"

The happiness in Tessa's eyes dimmed. "When I first met him, I don't think he drank at all. Still, after he went into movies, Mr. Rimini said he had a problem. He did . . . I know that. But with me, he never took more than one cocktail. Or some wine."

"So this is unusual, then?"

"I've been so worried, Mother." Her soft voice was raw with misery. "I don't know how to handle it. Nagging's wrong, and so's locking the liquor cabinet. Anyway, they wouldn't work. I keep hoping he'll get over it."

"Over it? Hope? Tessa, surely you understand why he drinks."

"After he was wounded he wanted to fly, but he couldn't go near a plane. He conquered that."

"It is not the same."

"He felt trapped on the ground."

"Tessa, there are so many other considerations involved here. He was raised a Catholic—"

"Mother, don't," Tessa interrupted in a dogged whisper. "Please, it's no use. Don't waste yourself trying. Kingdon and I have been through it all. It's impossible for us to separate." Her face was very white.

"Am I making it worse for you, darling? I do not mean to. I do not know why the sins of the parents should be visited on their children. But when they are, the parents react badly."

"He really did want to return to the Church. Getting a dispensation meant a lot to him."

Amélie looked out over the gardens. "Where is he now?"

"In the garage, getting his car. He's driving over to Zephyr Field."

Alarm sharpened Amélie's features. "He is not going up in this weather, surely?"

"No. Just visiting Tex. He doesn't like being in the house when Uncle visits. None of this is Uncle's fault, and Kingdon knows it, so he thinks he's wicked, wanting to blame him."

"A villain *would* make this easier," Amélie agreed. "Alas, there are none."

"Mother, it's not important to me, but it is to Kingdon. Have you heard of a way to prove paternity?"

"No," Amélie said, her clear voice shaking, "and maybe you are better off without it. Proof might be far worse."

"How can you believe that?" Tessa whispered. "Why should that one time be so important to everyone?"

"Because it is," Amélie replied. And fear, like a dream of smothering, closed over her. She loved her daughter with a fierceness that seemed too large for her fragile, aristocratic body. Before Tessa was born, she had been ready to make any sacrifice for her. She was ready now. But no sacrifice was demanded. She could only gaze into her daughter's unhappy blue eyes—Bud's dark blue eyes—and feel the unreasoning vertigo of panic.

Tessa held out her arms, embracing her.

After she left, Amélie tried to still her fears by returning to the pages of her book. Maybe it would be best if there were some way to prove . . .

· 4 ·

A half hour earlier at Eagle's Roost, Utah had been setting out mahjongg racks. The chauffeur had been dispatched to pick up the other players, three women she had met at St. Catherine's.

3 Vee opened the study door. "I'm going to see Bud," he told her. His quiet courtesy reminded her, inevitably, of her own vulgar loudness.

"You ain't been to Signal Hill in a week. You think them oil wells can drill themselves?" She tried to keep her accusations low-voiced.

"The foreman knows his business."

"3 Vee, you're a dreamer. You only go as far as the starting line. Then you lose interest. It's all going down the drain again."

"You didn't marry a businessman, Utah."

"I seen it happen before."

"Don't wait dinner for me."

Utah's temper snapped. "You'll lose a fortune while you're chewing the fat with your fancy relations!"

He said nothing.

Utah's face crumpled and she looked like a great fat baby about to cry. "They hate me," she whimpered. "And so do you."

"I don't," he said. "Utah, I'm late."

She followed him into the entrance hall, handing him the derby she had given him for Christmas.

He took his old shabby hat. "It looks like rain," he said. "That's brand-new."

"At least let me drive down to the field and see you ain't being robbed blind." She knew bookkeeping from her boardinghouse days.

"You're having guests."

"I'll get the chauffeur to take me after the mah-jongg."

"It's not necessary."

"You hate me for telling Charley Kingdon the truth!"

3 Vee closed the front door.

Utah sank into a hall chair. Carved oak shuddered under her weight. She turned the new derby in her hands, sighing. She was shamed and saddened that she had lost her temper that night, yet she never regretted crying out the truth. She remained bitterly positive that 3 Vee had given Bud and Amélie the one thing in the world they couldn't have, a child.

What had she done wrong? Charley Kingdon would have found out soon enough, she thought, setting the new derby on her lap, crossing her thick arms, which were cuffed in stone-marten fur. Why was she being punished so cruelly for losing her temper? Charley Kingdon hadn't given up Tessa. Instead, he refused to talk to either of his parents and had gone to live with "them." For this 3 Vee blamed and shunned her.

He refused her every offer to help run his business. It was the same old story. Having proved his point that there was oil under Signal Hill, he had no interest in production. He was a rotten boss, around very little. Utah was certain he was being robbed. She loved her husband. She was proud of him as a gentleman. But above all she ached for him to be the victor in his ancient sibling warfare.

She heaved her weight out of the hall chair. The derby fell from her lap and rolled across the parquet floor. She left it for the servants to pick up. There were four of them in the house, yet it always seemed empty. She went into the study and closed the door. All I did was shout it out instead of whispering it ladylike, she thought. Why does he hate me? Why don't he at least let me look after the wells? Why am I always alone?

The mah-jongg set was old, the salesman had told her, and valuable. The room was dark with the approach of rain and she couldn't properly see the ivory oblongs. Picking one up, she held it close to her eyes as if the graceful Oriental calligraphy might answer some of her questions.

· 5 ·

Ballooning clouds obscured the dusk, and at nightfall the rain started abruptly, slashing hills and flatland, drumming hollow on roofs, drenching the parched chaparral. Expensive bulb flowers, early tulips and daffodils bred for gentler climates, were flattened. It was the first of the winter rains, and adobe earth, baked to hard recalcitrance, was unable to soak it up. Within an hour, an inch or so of water lay on the ground while any street that followed the path of an arroyo had become a racing river.

Kingdon paid no attention to the weather. He was at the Vernon Country Club because 3 Vee was visiting Greenwood. The club, a speakeasy, attracted movie people, and half a dozen stunt pilots, including Tex, crowded around the corner table talking aviation. Kingdon repeatedly stood the group to expensive, reasonably safe illegal booze.

Around eleven he got unsteadily to his feet.

"Want me to drive you home?" Tex asked.

"Why?"

"Seems like a good idea," Tex said.

"I can manage alone," Kingdon said. He was drunk. He often drove when he was drunk. The wiper slapped from the top of the windshield, and between strokes headlights showed a dark, watery landscape that to his bleary eyes seemed to belong to another planet. Rain thumped on the Lancia's metal roof.

He was in a new subdivision near Western Avenue when the car began skidding. His reflexes, though blunted by alcohol, were trained by long years of flying. Without thinking, he turned into the skid, not braking. The tires continued to slide and under his gloveless palms he felt the wheel slip. He saw the tree trunk, solid and unavoidable. Instinctively he threw up a hand to protect his eyes. Metal crumpled. He heard his left wrist snap. Icicles hit his face. Everything slowed. Rain seemed to float through branches, descending in a series of visible drops. And in that somnambulistic moment, his brain roamed free, unshackled.

How easy it would be, he thought, if I were dead.

He thought of suicide often, and more than once his hands had trembled on the stick. As he spiraled toward the fields of Fère-en-Tar-denois in a flaming Nieuport, his voice had screamed in anguished prayer. But it wasn't the fear of pain that stopped him now. Nor the fear of death. To him the act of self-destruction was not only sin. It was cowardice.

But what if death came as an accident?

One simple accident, he thought. An accident could put an end to the years of useless battles within myself, the misery I cause others, the sadness I bring to Tessa's face. An accident isn't cowardice.

He moved back to consciousness. His left wrist hurt with a sharp tingling and his right eye throbbed. The car door was opening. A man holding a slicker over his head stared at Kingdon.

"Thank God you're alive. What a crash! The car's shot to hell, and I figured the worst. Hey—it's Captain Vance, isn't it?"

The man insisted on driving Kingdon home. Tessa sent for Dr. Wallview, who bandaged his facial cuts and ordered a beefsteak for the eye. He taped and splinted Kingdon's left wrist, saying, "A clean fracture."

The following morning Kingdon slept late. When he woke, Tessa was in her study on the telephone. Groaning, he got out of bed. The splinted tape around his wrist prevented him from showering. He examined himself in the mirror. The white bandages on his forehead made his swollen eye look like a lump of coal. His face was the color of library paste. His hand shook too much to risk shaving. What a beaut you are, he told himself as he brushed his teeth.

Tessa was in the bedroom, staring out a window. It was raining lightly.

"I've been in worse accidents," he said, getting back in bed.

She turned. She was, he saw, as pale as he. "It wasn't an accident," she said, her voice trembling.

"Right, right. Famous movie pilot purposefully wrecks custom-built car during heavy rain. You saw me last night. I was polluted."

"Why?"

"Why what?"

"Why are you drunk so much?"

"It's illegal, why else?"

"If . . . if it hurts you so much, being married to me, I . . . They're right." Her voice grew firm. "Kingdon, we shouldn't be married."

He squinted at her with his good eye. "Love, I'm hung over. I'm in no shape to discuss impossibilities. You and me, we were separated for three years. The experiment failed. How many times have we gone over this?"

"You're drinking to cover the pain."

"Stop talking *de profundis*, Tessa. You're stuck with a part-time problem drinker, that's all." He rubbed his aching temple. "What did you say to my boss?"

"That you skidded in the rain."

"The truth. To which he replied?"

"Not to worry. Your close-ups are finished, and they'll use Tex in the rest of the flight sequences." She paused. "He asked me to keep you away from liquor."

"See? No need for your writer's imagination. Why look for complicated explanations? It's your fault. From here on in, keep me away from rotgut and I won't crash into trees on rainy nights."

"It really was an accident?"

"Yes," he replied honestly. "And another thing," he said. "I've paid back Rimini all I borrowed. So he's no longer my boss."

"You're through with movies?" she asked.

"As soon as this one's in the can, I'll be off salary. I don't ever want to act again. You'll be married to a poor but honest aviator."

She smiled.

"That's better," he said. "Now listen and listen carefully. I ran into a tree. That's all. You are not to read meanings into my actions. I accept you at face value. You accept me the same way. Do you understand?"

Her eyes seemed to pierce through his head to the back of his skull, and he had a feeling that she understood him better than he understood himself. "Yes," she said softly. "It was an accident."

He lowered himself down to the pillow. "Next time I pour myself a second, remind me of this hangover."

She kissed his forehead lightly. "Better?"

"Better."

She rang for coffee.

Kingdon, knowing he loved her irrevocably, thought of those few heartbeats during the crash when he had been free. He thought of the simplicity of death.

·6·

Greenwood, like Paloverde before it, had been unfenced from the smooth thighs of chaparral above and the valley below, but as Los Angeles sprawled west, nearby houses sprang up and the children who played in sandy vacant lots were lured by the mysteries hidden behind tall trees and shadowy green thickets. The juvenile trespassers had pleased Bud and amused Amélie—until one almost drowned in the swimming pool. Reluctantly, they had walled off their grounds.

The gates were closed when 3 Vee drew up. He left his Maxwell to ring the bell that summoned the old man from the gatehouse. It was two days after Kingdon's accident, an event 3 Vee hadn't yet heard about. He was here as arranged, to visit Bud. His hand was near the electric button when he saw Amélie hurrying down a syringa-lined footpath. Since the fandango she had been alone with him only once—and that against her will—on the morning when a hot Santa Ana wind had blown their lives to tatters. He was surprised when she waved. She was coming to meet him! As he watched her, he felt he was spying through a green tunnel of time at the little girl next door, his friend, his love.

"Amélie," he said, taking off his hat.

"I need to talk to you." She opened one of the gates. "If you leave your car, we can go up to the house together."

He parked properly and they started up the gravel drive. It was a sunny afternoon. Two gardeners were clipping browned camellia blossoms, and Amélie was clearly waiting to pass them before she spoke.

3 Vee wondered what she wanted to say. He was certain that he was in hot water of some kind, yet he took pleasure in being with Amélie, not looking at her but breathing in her flower perfume, moving a few inches nearer to her so he could imagine a faint warmth emanating from her. He had difficulty adjusting to the fact that the top of her hatless head didn't reach his shoulder. How could she loom so large in his mind?

"It is Kingdon," she said finally.

His fears and guilts, pushing away every other emotion, coagulated in his stomach. "What's wrong?"

"Two nights ago, during the storm, his car hit a tree."

"Why didn't someone call me?" 3 Vee's voice was harsh. "How badly is he hurt?"

"A fractured wrist. A black eye. Physical damage—"

"Physical damage?" 3 Vee interrupted. "What do you mean? Is he in a coma?"

"No, no. Nothing like that. But he is lucky to be alive. He was drinking, it was raining hard. He drinks so much, 3 Vee. He drives too fast."

"He's always been a daredevil."

"It is not only the recklessness and the alcohol. He is so unhappy," Amélie said. She paused. "The summer before my father died, it was as if Papa were being stretched on the rack. There was a tension about him as if his muscles and nerves were too tight. I actually could hear his misery. Everything about him was pitched too high."

An expression of fear crossed 3 Vee's bearded face. "You're saying that you think Kingdon wants to kill himself?"

"I am saying that this—this *thing* is too strong for any of us. Oh, in the abstract, I can accept the situation. In reality I am horrified. So are you. And Utah more so. Bud . . . well, Bud." She sighed. "As for Kingdon, he is tormented in a manner I cannot truly comprehend."

"When he was young he had a sort of impetuous drive to try everything, as if he wanted to get it out of the way. I figured he would end up a priest." 3 Vee looked down at the small woman at his side. "You know me. Good at perceiving the inner workings of people, unable to act on the knowledge. I knew immediately how disastrous this would be for him, and I've wanted to talk to him about it. To help him. But how? He won't even stay in the house when I'm here."

"I have noticed. 3 Vee, I am sorry."

"And Tessa. Tessa. The night of Bud's heart attack, I tried to convince her the marriage should end before it began. She refused. And every time I bring it up, she's difficult. I don't mean hard. Tessa can't be hard. But she's adamant. Either she says nothing or she asks why they shouldn't be married. They're cousins, she says. Cousins! She flatly refuses to admit that Bud's not her father."

"What makes you positive that he is not?"

Here the drive bent around a live oak that spread dense, spoon-shape leaves of darkest green to form pools of black shade. In this darkness, Amélie's face was a chiaroscuro egg, pale and blank. Her mind, he knew, worked with clear symmetry. She was as logical as the music of Mozart. 3 Vee, consumed by paternal tumult, accepted her question as rhetoric. Amélie surely believed as he did, that Tessa was his.

The red-tile rooftops of the house appeared above them. Amélie turned from the gravel drive onto a narrow footpath shaded by lemon trees. She did not speak again until they came to a bench at

the side of the path. Amélie sat on the smooth, white marble. 3 Vee stood before her, his hands clasped behind his back. "Other than fictional strawberry birthmarks," she said, "is there no way to prove paternity?"

3 Vee, certain now that Amélie agreed with him, replied, "You're right. We've got to convince her she's not Bud's child; then she'll understand how impossible this is for Kingdon." He picked a lemon blossom, twisting the small waxy whiteness between his thumb and forefinger. The sweet fragrance was intensified. "I read something a year or two ago about work that's being done in serological genetics. By Landsteiner, a pathology professor in Vienna." It was the sort of pleasurably useless information that he cherished, and accordingly had filed away in his mind.

"Karl Landsteiner? The man who discovered that people have different types of blood."

"So you have heard of him."

"A little. His discovery made transfusions possible for the war wounded."

"He's in this country now, at the Rockefeller Institute."

"3 Vee, tell me about his work on proving fatherhood."

"Let's see if I can explain it. There are four blood types, and Landsteiner believes that they are governed by the Mendelian laws of heredity. A blood type that is in neither the mother nor the father cannot appear in the child. Therefore you can say a man isn't the father. But you cannot establish that he *is*." 3 Vee knew he wasn't doing a good job of explanation, so he added, "It's too technical. I need to write it down to show you."

She had been watching him intently. Now, briefly, her mouth curled in a smile and her eyes danced with that old, almost malicious gleam of intelligence. "If the blood types of the mother and child are known, they can figure out the blood-group property the father *cannot* possess, is that it?"

"I'd forgotten how quick you are. Yes, that's it. I've never heard whether Landsteiner proved his theory."

"Then we will pay Dr. Landsteiner to prove it."

With this remark, 3 Vee recalled that she was an extremely wealthy woman who could endow knowledge. But as always when theory must hatch into fact, he grew uncertain. "As I remember," he said, "paternity can be proved in only about fifty percent of the

cases. And even then—Amélie, what if Tessa refuses to believe I'm her father?"

Amélie's mouth grew tight. "We shall only tell her if the answer is Bud."

3Vee stared at her aghast. What was she saying? Could she have any doubt that they were linked through Tessa? "You . . . you mean you want them to stay together?" he said.

"They refuse to separate. What do my wants matter?"

"Then there's no point in Landsteiner's work for us, is there?"

She didn't seem to hear the question, or at any rate she ignored it. "Tessa has been ill so often. Her blood has been examined carefully. Dr. Wallview surely has the type on record. We need not tell her what we are doing. From what you say, we will need her type, mine, yours, and Dr. Landsteiner."

3Vee gazed up at the red-tile roof, barely visible through the trees. A puff of white cloud hung over Paloverde—he never thought of it as Greenwood. What Amélie wanted them to do would remedy nothing, and if the young couple ever discovered the tests (assuming tests could be done) the results would be cruelty for Tessa, crucifixion for his son.

"No," he said.

"No?"

"We won't talk to Landsteiner. Amélie, you care for Kingdon, too. However terrible this is for him, at least he has doubts. Doubt is inverted hope. It's something for him to hold onto."

"Are you so positive she is yours?"

"Of course I am."

"Why?"

"For one thing, Bud can't—"

"Bud can! Bud has!"

He wondered how and when, but didn't dare ask. He paced a few steps. "It was an unproven paper, no more," he equivocated.

Amélie looked up at him. Her hazel eyes were not cold but baffled. "I don't understand you," she said.

"Kingdon, I can't destroy him."

"This is *for* him. Unless they are cousins, he will never know."

"What if he finds out?"

"It is you who does not wish to find out," she said in a whisper. Now her eyes were cold.

A chill passed along his bowed shoulders.

"Before Papa shot himself, I asked you what a note was. You could not tell me. Do you know now?"

"Of course," he muttered.

"We have a note outstanding, 3 Vee, you and I."

Her face had lost expression, and sunlight showed the mortal softening of cheek and jawline. 3 Vee stared into that proud face and knew unquestioningly that he was going to hear the words he had dreaded hearing for almost thirty years.

She held a small, clenched hand to her collar. "I despise myself for calling that note, but I must." She lowered her hand as if by tremendous effort. "3 Vee, you took me against my will. It was terrifying, degrading. It ruined something that was very precious between me and Bud. You cast doubts on a child I had wanted with all my heart." Her eyelashes went down, and then she was again looking up at him with those awful, implacable eyes. "You separated me from Bud. You caused us both the worst kind of pain. I do not want to dwell on the wrongs, but that time was far from easy. I have kept silent when I should have spoken. And when Utah spoke and Bud had a heart attack—my God! I thought we had killed him. I thought he was dead."

"Amélie," he said brokenly, "do you think I haven't reproached myself a million times?"

"Then you must do as I say."

"If Kingdon finds out the results of the tests, I will have destroyed him."

"Or saved him," she said. "Do you not wish to save him?"

"Tessa's your only child. Isn't that proof enough?"

"You owe me, 3 Vee. *You owe me.*"

She rose from the bench and again directed their steps toward the house, resting her hand on his arm. At her touch the self-hatred alternately chilling and burning 3 Vee was further confused by a stab of physical pleasure. She was watching him with that proud, frozen expression she assumed at her most vulnerable moments. This was Amélie, Amélie, who for a few minutes out of a lifetime had been his. Her fingers pressed through his sleeve.

"You have always envied what belongs to Bud," she said. "Everything he has and is, you wanted and still want. His friends, his ability, his body. This house. Me. You cannot bear to think that my daughter is his too."

He stared down at her, a large, stoop-shouldered, white-bearded man with glowing, hurt brown eyes gazing into a fragile face that was lined with human knowledge.

"That is the truth," she said.

He did not reply. He saw only one drowning truth. Love to him was not an impersonal word. Love to him was names spoken in various tones, and the name he heard most clearly was Amélie. Amélie, Amélie, he thought. Amélie.

He would surrender not because of her bitterly honest reproaches and accusations but because she meant more to him than anyone in his life.

Yet his desire to protect Kingdon remained as strong. "I'll try to get in touch with Landsteiner," he said, and then had to turn away so she wouldn't see his tears.

Her hand fell from his arm and she said quietly, "I never meant to throw the past at you, 3 Vee. But we are at cross-purposes. Kingdon is so unhappy, and I believe there is a chance." She hesitated. "Tessa should have known years ago. I charge myself with that constantly."

He nodded.

"You will get Dr. Landsteiner out here?"

He nodded again.

He heard her through a reverie. He was questioning the way that Amélie had managed to hold onto her funny, proud girlhood code of honor; he was questioning the mysterious laws of chance that had joined his life to hers. *The face of all the world is changed, I think, Since first I heard the footsteps of thy soul.* . . . I must stop thinking in Victorian poetry.

He was unable to speak until they turned the final curve. Here, for the first time, the house was clearly visible. Looking up at the blazing whiteness, he said, "Amélie, you're right. I have always envied Bud his ability, his success, his friends. Paloverde. He has nothing to do with what I feel for you, though. Before he so much as looked your way, I loved you. I always have, and I still do."

·7·

Early the next morning, 3 Vee drove to his office, which was the converted study of a bungalow on Signal Hill. He closed the French windows, muffling the racket, bracing himself for the call to the Rockefeller Institute. The call was like discharging a thunder-bolt. When an Angeleno telephoned New York it was always on a matter of gravest portent. Even the city's prime movers, men like Rimini and Bud, usually sent telegrams. It wasn't the cost. Who could take lightly the miracle of talking to someone on the far side of the continent?

Sitting at the battered table that served as a desk, 3Vee unlaced his working boots, then on a used envelope he scribbled: *Get Land-steiner out here.*

It was a promise to Amélie that had been made at a turbulent emotional peak. Now he was faced with the reality of keeping it.

Gripping the candlestick telephone, he lifted the receiver. The operator came on and he asked her for the long-distance operator. She put him through to the telephone building at 435 Olive Street. The long-distance operator got him a trunk line. The wires buzzed mysteriously and suddenly he heard a faraway voice. New York! The long-distance operator there connected him to the Manhattan operator, who got him the switchboard at the Rockefeller Institute. The incantation of disembodied voices was a rite of progress, and during the fifteen minutes it took for the call to go through, 3Vee's uncertainty wavered into exaltation.

Karl Landsteiner was a remote, questioning Austrian accent. 3Vee's anxiety jolted back. Clearing his throat, he gave his name, mumbling that a "friend" was interested in the doctor's work on the establishment of paternity by serological means.

"This postulation is not accepted by the medical profession." Dr. Landsteiner's reply was tainted with irritation.

"I read the paper you published." 3Vee wiped his damp forehead. "Could you elaborate a little?"

Dr. Landsteiner elaborated at length, his voice growing tenta-tively warmer as he explained that the blood typing was done with red cells. A suspension was made with a two-percent saline solution. "But, *ach*, why be clinical? It is all Mendel. You under-stand Mendel, yes? That which is not in either parent cannot be transmitted to the child."

"I understand," 3Vee said, wiggling his toes in his loosened boots.

"So. When the child has a blood type neither in his mother nor the alleged father, then we must agree with the man that he is not the culprit. If, for example, both parents belong to the A group, they cannot produce a child with B-type blood. Or if a mother belongs to the B-type and the child to the A, the father cannot be an O or an AB. You cannot establish paternity. You can prove only who is not the father. So. It is only in about half the cases we can prove anything. Mr. Van Vliet, how can I help your friend?"

3 Vee stared at his own injunction: *Get Landsteiner out here*. Faced with the moment, he asked himself why. He believed, with obsessive conviction, that he had fathered Tessa and that proving this could possibly boomerang into tragedy. He thought, briefly, of Amélie's touch on his arm.

"Would it alter the tests if the, uh, alleged fathers are brothers?"

"Somewhat," Dr. Landsteiner replied. "But in the beginning I say to you, and you must say it to your friend, serological genetics is not yet accepted."

"You believe in it, though?"

"From hundreds of tested cases."

3 Vee made a small humming in his throat. He longed to excuse himself and hang up. But again he thought of Amélie, those proud and haunted hazel eyes. He said into the telephone, "My friend needs to be, well, certain about a child."

"That is not easy. Only a few know how to evaluate the findings."

"He is rich. I—he will compensate you, a very large grant, if you come out here to Los Angeles."

"Los Angeles?" Warmth left the doctor's voice and there was only annoyance. "My work here is the particularity of blood. Antigen differences. This is important."

"The grant could be helpful in your work," 3 Vee said, half hoping the doctor would refuse.

After a buzzing pause, Dr. Landsteiner said, "An assistant, possibly, can take the time. In April."

"This is the beginning of January. Can't you make it sooner?"

"The end of March, then." Compromise traveled three thousand miles of cable.

"That will be fine," 3 Vee said.

He hung up, crumpling the envelope into the wastebasket, leaning forward to hold his head, which suddenly began to ache. Bud, he thought. In his place, Bud—using whatever means necessary—would have had the world-famed doctor on the next train to California.

CHAPTER 25

"'Rimini Productions,'" Tessa read, "'announces that Kingdon Vance will star in *The Valiant*, a tale of heroism in the embattled air above the Western Front. Captain Vance— '"

"—will play his obligatory role of the doomed aviator," Kingdon put in.

It was the middle of February and his left wrist was no longer taped. They sat in Tessa's study. She held up the newspaper to show him the story.

"Angry I didn't tell you?" he asked.

"Yes."

"Angry I'm making another flick?"

"That too."

"One more and I'm in good financial shape."

"You were happy, you said, to be leaving Rimini."

"Tessa, I need more money. Or rather, Tex and I do. There's the enclosed Fokker passenger plane I told you about. And the new hangar."

"My father would lend—"

"I know that," he interrupted. "But you know me. A dark, despairing, difficult man who won't borrow from his father-in-law." He formed an actor's grimace.

She smiled.

"I'm forgiven, then?"

"Yes."

"Then why are we arguing?"

She didn't want him to make another movie and she should have argued her point. She didn't. Kingdon, possessed of sharp wit, could be a cruel opponent, but that wasn't why she held back. Always she had understood that his irony came from a profound sense of unworthiness and it was therefore obvious to her that had she chosen to use her softness, her hesitancy, her Van Vliet stubbornness, she could have vanquished him. The burden of his insecurities weighed on her. Rather than insist he bow out of *The Valiant*, she put down the *Los Angeles Times*. "So we can make up," she said, kissing him.

Before shooting began, Rimini Productions gave out a press release. Lya Bell, deciding to start a new career in Europe, had obtained a divorce from Captain Kingdon Vance. There was little reaction. The public was now completely occupied with the Fatty Arbuckle rape-murder trial in San Francisco Superior Court.

Kingdon wrote to Lya in Paris. She never replied. He knew she was alive, but he had no illusions about her well-being. The Doom Book had been circulated around the world, she was everywhere banished from the brilliantly lit movie stages, and for her this was a more cruel punishment than death. He continued to send her letters, using the mail as one might try a medium to contact the dead.

The studio made no announcement of Kingdon's remarriage. It was still secret. The family was waiting for Bud's complete recovery.

The camera plane flew slightly below Kingdon's left wing. He didn't look toward it, and the machine-gun rush of his own engine drowned out its sound. He felt alone as he eased the stick back, climbing.

As always his thoughts were liberated by flight: I'm a man who has walked all my life along a narrow, windowless, doorless corridor and suddenly has noticed that certain of the panels are, in fact, doors. The doors occur at random intervals. To the eye they are no different from the paneling. One must allow oneself to touch the panel, exerting pressure. If there's a catch mechanism, the door will swing open on the freedom that is accidental death.

Why has this knowledge brought me salvationary joy?

Tessa.

Up here I feel no sense of sin. I remember her goodness, her absolute lack of malice. The tranquil frown as she reads. The thread of white scar at the base of her throat, the warm consolation of her breasts and the flat little mole between them, her serenity.

Why on solid earth are we, she and I, evil?

Look no further than those classic words quoted by Mother: 3 *Vee's your daddy.*

Those words form the barrier between good and evil, between a dispensation for marriage and incestuous lust. I will touch the panels and if by chance one is a door, I will pass through it.

Kingdon wasn't contemplating suicide. He didn't consider he was playing Russian roulette. He had merely decided to press his courage to the limits—and if he failed, the door would open on death. As he flew, the air rushing around him, he wondered how long he would continue to exist on this whirling, tormented planet.

· 2 ·

The Valiant had started filming on March second. Shooting had been under way almost two weeks when Kingdon got Rimini's summons. Late that afternoon, Kingdon and the director sat in a projection room viewing the rushes—the unedited, spliced-together film shot the preceding day. Kingdon knew what the summons meant. He emerged from darkness, blinking in the glare of a naked bulb, pausing to light a cigarette in an onyx holder before shoving open the plywood door. Stages had become high-walled to accommodate the more and more elaborate sets. He was in a deep stucco canyon. Shooting done, crowds hurried toward the Gower Street exit. Performers still wore white makeup, and in the dusk their faces shone like doomed moths. Kingdon, moving in the opposite direction, raised his arm to salute those he knew, thinking: What a long way Rimini Productions has come.

Rimini had planned his office to intimidate. Kingdon, crossing the series of Persian rugs stretching to a massive ten-foot desk, noted that the dim light furthered the admonitory effect by casting shadows into corners. He wondered if he would have been so casual had he not known Rimini when his office was a stall with floor-boards bleached by horse urine.

Rimini switched on the desk light, illuminating the annoyance on his heavy features. "Sit," he ordered.

Kingdon remained standing, pressing his fingertips on the glasslike polish of the desk. "What's up?"

"You know damn well what's up! The usual. I just looked at your stunt plan! You've thought up some harebrained maneuvers, but never one like this!"

"Crazy but good, eh?"

"No," Rimini said. "En oh."

"I can spell."

"It's too dangerous. We'll use a double."

"I always do my own stunts."

"Not at night you don't!"

"That," Kingdon pointed out, "is because we've never shot at night before. It's a new idea."

"Remember to forget it! And that's an order!" Rimini's voice was loud. Always choleric, he had learned the efficacy of displaying anger. Hollywood respected anger as a dramatization of success. Only those at the top could afford anger.

"Why're you getting apoplectic? It's a simple enough stunt."

"Simple!" Rimini extracted graph paper from a drawer, unrolling it on his desk, moving his stubby forefinger along dotted lines identified with small planes as a flight path. "You call this simple? You go up and down twice and then you pull out just above the barn!"

"I've done most of it before," Kingdon said.

"You never looped back for a second dive and—"

"The writers, your writers, thought up some impossible mechanical defect." Kingdon ground out his cigarette in Rimini's ashtray and removed the butt from its holder. "I always dive into some building or other."

"Not like this." Rimini's thick finger followed a corkscrew line on the diagram. On either side of the twisting line were drawings of arc lights. At a spot penciled *150 ft.*, the line leveled to parallel the ground. "Not through arcs."

"It's a night battle," Kingdon said patiently.

"I told you. No night shooting."

493

"An airplane moving from light into darkness is an electrifying effect, Rimini."

"You want to be electrocuted, do it on your own time. This stunt's too dangerous even for daylight!"

"Tex and I worked a week planning it."

Rimini pressed his butcher's thumb on the graph paper. "Kingdon, we go back a long way." The anger had left his voice, and he spoke with difficulty. His rage over the stunt didn't come from a desire to protect that most valuable of properties, a star. He argued for friendship's sake. Kingdon had made him a fortune and given him an ulcer, yet despite these two facts he had forgiven him, and considered him a friend. "Listen to me for once. You just broke a wrist. You aren't in shape."

"The wrist's mended. And I'm in tip-top shape. Or haven't you heard? I'm on the wagon."

Since the accident, since he had skidded into the realization that he wasn't trapped in life, Kingdon's joyless drinking had ceased. He could face the tormenting doubts of loving Tessa without alcohol. He was in pain, yet now the pain was bearable because he understood that in his infinite mercy, God, the giver of life, could also bestow premature death.

"I heard," Rimini said.

"I do my own stunts," Kingdon said. "My contract says so."

"Forget the damn fine print. You work for me." Rimini pounded his clenched fist into the plan. "This is out! Out!"

"Fine, if that's what you want."

At this abrupt surrender, Rimini's eyes narrowed. He examined Kingdon's face. "Oh?"

"What do I need a plane for? I'll flit down to earth on my own power."

"So that's it." Rimini's voice was openly gruff with affection. "Tomorrow Eddie Stone'll start leaking out that Lya's diary was a fraud. I never should've made you protect that little—"

"You didn't make me do anything," Kingdon said. "And tell Eddie to leak in the latrine. Lya doesn't need any more trouble. Just leave her alone."

"You're one of the few decent men I know," Rimini said, coming around the desk. "That impotence business, it's forgotten anyway. Everybody's watching Fatty Arbuckle. The poor dumb bastard is accused of shoving a bottle up a party girl. Now he's the one they watch. Quit worrying about your balls. Do some nice, easy stunt."

"Any suggestions?"

"Wing walking."

Climbing out of the cockpit to walk on the wings while the plane was airborne never failed to elicit gasps from an audience. Stunt pilots considered wing walking a desultory excuse for getting paid.

"Good idea, there," Kingdon said. "A shame the script doesn't call for wing walking. The climax of *The Valiant* is a dogfight."

"The climax is whatever and however I say it is!"

"We shoot this tomorrow night."

"*I* run Rimini Productions!"

"And my contract gives me the freedom to plan the aviation sequences."

"Kingdon, we argue over the stunts every movie. But this—"

"If you want to break the contract, it's all right with me," Kingdon interrupted. "I walk out. It's my last flick. I don't give a damn if nobody in Hollywood will hire me. But you, you're stuck with half of a very expensive undertaking. Without me, you can't finish. How'll you explain that to the Eastern banking boys?"

Rimini's heavy neck turned crimson. He glowered, a bull with the pics in. Like every studio, Rimini Productions operated on credit, and Rimini's greatest fear was endangering his credit. The day he appeared a doubtful risk to the bankers he would be out of Hollywood and back in his butcher shop.

He tried one last pyrotechnic display of anger. "What a way to live! Killing yourself to prove you're no flit."

A Riminism. Kingdon smiled. "I knew you'd see it my way," he said. In the amble that disguised his limp, he moved across the Persian rugs. At the door he halted. "Rimini, you're right about one thing."

"What's that?" Rimini growled.

"We *are* friends."

As he closed the door, Kingdon caught a glimpse of the older man scowling down at the plans, his close-cropped graying head bent over the vast expanse of his desk.

Kingdon said good night to the pair of secretaries. In the corridor, alone, he limped heavily. True friendship isn't a lesser version of love; being a friend puts more demands on honesty. Kingdon's jaw was set. He was realizing the infinite number of guilts involved in testing just one panel to see if it was a door.

· 3 ·

That morning, Landsteiner's young assistant had arrived in Los Angeles on the Santa Fe Limited.

3 Vee had arranged an immediate appointment, and at four that afternoon Amélie was waiting for her brother-in-law at the Pig 'n' Whistle. The hour that downtown shoppers foraged, the long café was crowded with matrons devouring parfaits, vividly iced cakes, and triangles of cinnamon toast. Amélie, alone at a small round table, sipped tea and examined the frieze of capering piglets. As 3 Vee walked toward the table, he saw her as the masterpiece of a great artist set down among cartoons, human and otherwise.

Amélie's confrontation in the gardens of Greenwood had made the heavy awkwardness go out of 3 Vee. Her honesty, devastating as it had been, as well as his own declaration of love, had cleaned an obfuscatory window between them as far as he was concerned. She was his brother's wife, he himself was married; he was too old for flirtatious nonsense—and besides, this surely wasn't the time for it. Yet sitting opposite her, he found himself lacing his fingers and beaming as he complimented her cloche hat, her trim Chanel suit. What he really meant was that the creamy beiges set off her luminous skin.

When their waitress had set down his metal teapot, he said, "You don't belong here. You should be in the Café de la Paix."

"Paris? I was born in San Francisco."

"You're not bumptious enough to be a Californian."

"Try a few more compliments," she said, smiling. "It will sound as if we have chosen the Pig 'n' Whistle for an assignation."

At this their smiles faded and they looked down at the tea things, silent.

"What," 3 Vee asked in a whisper, "if it had been me who found you and Tessa in Oakland? Would you believe *I* was her father if I'd saved her life?"

Amélie's voice was grave. "I told you. From the beginning I have never been sure. I still am not sure." She added dryly, "But then, poor me, I am only a Van Vliet by marriage."

3 Vee stared at her in surprise. "You mean I'm being stubborn?"

She smiled briefly, then, her expression again sober, she glanced at her small Tiffany lapel watch. "Quarter past. We had better leave."

"We've got fifteen minutes still, and the office is only across the street. Sixth floor."

"How long will the test take?"

"The doctor will draw blood from us, that's all. Landsteiner's assistant does everything else."

"When will he have the results?"

"Tomorrow or the next day." He drew a ridged fingernail down the hot teapot. "Amélie, nothing will be altered. But if we tell Tessa, maybe she'll—"

Amélie held up a silencing palm. "And you ask if you are stubborn?" Her lips were set in an earnest line. "We will stay with my plan."

"But—"

"3 Vee, have you ever made a bargain with fate? Have you ever told yourself the die is cast and whatever shows up, so be it? I believe genetic laws do govern us. I will accept whatever Landsteiner's man tells us."

"Me, too."

"Wrong, 3 Vee. You are wrong. You need Tessa to bind us, you and me. And through her, you will inherit Paloverde. You paid a lot of money to get this man out here, but you will never be able to accept it if he says she is not yours."

Four twittering women sat down at the next table.

Leaning toward him, Amélie spoke in a clear whisper. "We will keep quiet if she is not Bud's. We will not tell Bud. We will not tell Tessa or Kingdon. Only you and I will know. And with that knowledge, 3 Vee, my entire life will have been a sham."

He drew back in his chair. "Amélie, please don't."

"I am judging myself, not you. Nothing can alter what I feel for you or Tessa or Bud. This concerns only me." The color had drained from her face. "Bud has given me everything. Love, happiness. If Tessa is his child, I will have repaid him. I will have given him the future. If not, I have been useless to him."

Amélie, with her tempered-steel delicacy, used a measure more exacting than most to weigh her own worth. 3 Vee, understanding this, said quietly, "He's been blessed."

"Again you are wrong." There was no bitterness in her voice, only sympathy. "You are a very dear man, 3 Vee. Sweet and kind. But you are not practical. You never come to grips with reality. A child is the one concrete victory we win over time. Oh, how Bud hates to lose. If she is not his, he has lost the final battle." Her voice trembled. "And I will have caused his loss."

Bud's loss was 3 Vee's gain. So positive was he of Tessa that, despite his sorrow for Amélie's grief and his own guilts, he had a split second of fraternal triumph. He buried it by counting out change for the tip.

Amélie gathered her purse and gloves. "Funny, is it not, how many motives one can uncover?" Her slender shoulders went up in a Gallic shrug. "I started this, or so I thought, only to help Kingdon."

· 4 ·

The following morning had a kind of sharp clarity that makes tourists decide to come back and settle in Los Angeles. The glass doors were open and Bud was breakfasting on the terrace overlooking the gardens, disobeying Dr. Levin's orders that he remain in bed until ten. His body without convalescent flaccidity, his yellow cable-knit cardigan intensifying the tan he had acquired on the balcony of his bedroom, he looked rested. And younger than before his heart attack. The table was set for four—custom, not usage. Amélie slept late, taking her light breakfast in bed. Tessa, now that she was married, ate in her study at the same early hour as Kingdon.

Bud glanced up in surprise when he saw Kingdon step onto the terrace. "I figured you'd left hours ago."

"Late call today, Uncle. We're shooting tonight."

"Sit down, then," Bud said, and when Kingdon had taken his place, he pointed to the covered silver dishes with deep bottoms that held boiling water. "Kidneys there. Shirred eggs. Ham slices.

And the toast rack's keeping the toast cold. Jam. Coffee. If there's anything else you'd like—eggs boiled or scrambled—I'll holler."

"This is fine, sir." Kingdon opened the dish of kidneys and served himself.

Bud reached over to pour his nephew some coffee. "You and Tessa want to move out," he said.

Kingdon looked at him.

"Wondering how I know? Well, it's simple. You've never talked alone with me. That means you've got something on your mind. I'm right, aren't I?"

After a fractional hesitation, Kingdon nodded.

"Now I've got you, a captive audience, I'm going to talk first."

"Go ahead, Uncle. I'll eat my breakfast and ignore you."

They both chuckled.

"First of all," Bud said, "it's very decent of you, staying here this long."

Kingdon glanced back at the house, then down at the magnificent gardens. "Not exactly a hardship."

"On your honeymoon? Kingdon, I'm not that ancient." He took a few fresh orange slices on a small plate. "I didn't want you for a son-in-law, you know that. I always liked you, though. You've got a lot of courage—I don't mean the obvious kind, flying. I mean the way you kept your mouth shut and protected Lya. God knows it would have been easy to dump her. And it was rotten of me to have believed, well, what she wrote about you."

"You don't have to say this."

"There," Bud said, sitting back. "I've apologized."

The apology meant little to Kingdon. His uncle's expression, however, uneasily sincere, moved him intolerably. "I'm spooked, too, Uncle," he said. "Here I am, in the embarrassing position of liking my own father-in-law."

"Kingdon, that's good." After a moment's silence, Bud pointed toward the gardens. "See that tree? There, in the circle."

The circle was planted with cacti. The tree, the only one, stood perhaps ten feet high, and the bark of its slender trunk was a vivid green.

"Know what it is?" Bud asked.

Kingdon shook his head.

"It's a paloverde. Green wood *en español*. They're almost unknown in the Los Angeles area. One was here, on this ledge, and that's why the old don called his place after it."

"I never knew that."

"The paloverde belongs in the desert. It's learned the same tricks as the cactus in order to survive. A paloverde doesn't waste moisture producing leaves. It stores sunshine in the bark. That's what makes it bright green. In wet times, though, a paloverde seems to remember it's a tree, and so puts out a few tiny leaves. But as the earth dries out, they drop off. Naturally, since the old cattle farmer chose the name for his rancho, the paloverde's always been significant to me." Bud looked directly at him. "The Garcías weren't a fruitful group. Our connections all come from my great-grandfather's sister. Still, we're a healthy bunch, Kingdon. And the Van Vliets have nothing puling about them, either."

Kingdon slowly put down his fork. The rich animal flavor of kidney dissolved in his mouth. His uncle was talking about children. But how can he, of all men, suggest children? Can he, like Tessa, have some inner recognition, an intuitive certainty? If so, what gave him the heart attack? Bud's eyes gazed at him with candor. The mystery lay buried.

"Uncle, as you say, the paloverde's not big on leaves."

"Don't get your back up, Kingdon. You know how Tessa is about children. For sure she'll want at least one."

Kingdon drank his coffee.

"Tessa tells me you won't be working for Rimini much longer," Bud said.

"This is my last flick. I'm buying into Zephyr Field with Tex Argyle."

"Is it a good living?"

"Sightseers, mail, passengers; Tex'll keep on with the stunts, and so on and so forth. It's an okay flying field. No, not a good living."

"Have you boys thought of manufacturing airplanes? The Loughead brothers"—Bud pronounced the name correctly, Lockheed—"have a nice little factory. And Glen Curtiss is doing well building airplanes, too. Of course he's moved back East, but he's a local boy."

"You *have* done your homework."

"To be blunt, I'd rather you were interested in oil."

"Me? Uncle, I'm no businessman."

"If Paloverde Oil made planes, you'd be sharp. Very."

"Know something? You're right."

"Besides, you're in oil, even if you don't take 3 Vee's checks."

"He told you about that?"

"Only once. He takes it very hard, you not talking to him." Bud paused. "One feud per family is enough."

"I was going to call him. If you see him before I do, tell him I'll be in touch."

"Good, good," Bud said, smiling. "Kingdon, I always think of your father as a kid I have to buffer for. When he's here and we're weeping nostalgic tears into our beer, I find myself worrying he's not down at Signal Hill, worrying he's screwing up. He's damn brilliant about ideas, your father, but rotten at day-to-day operations. He doesn't even know how many barrels he's pumping, or who buys his crude. He's liable to lose everything."

"He'd like that, my Dad. He prefers the dream to the reality. Once he loses it all, he can start over." Kingdon picked up his fork, asking casually, "You'll remember to tell him I'll call?"

"For sure I'll remember."

"Now what about the house?" Kingdon asked.

"House?"

"I agreed we're moving. Isn't offering us a house your next move?"

"You and Tessa have a house. In the Beverly Hills beanfields."

"How do you know about that?"

"I'm not as stupid as I appear," Bud said. "Now. Why did you come down this morning?"

Kingdon's face was blank. "I figured you wouldn't let her move back to the beanfields without a fight. Uncle, you're a formidable man."

"I'm just a hick-town boy," Bud said, chuckling. "Besides, Amélie's always stopped me short when I tried controlling Tessa's life. Still, I could tell your wife to start packing."

"That I can manage on my own."

They smiled at one another. Kingdon pushed his chair back and got up. Bud half rose. "I'm glad we had a chance to talk," he said.

"So am I," Kingdon replied, and though he had agreed to nothing, and said very little, he had accomplished what he had set out to do. He had made his peace with his uncle and absolved his father. As he went inside a curious calm filled him, as if he had taken an opiate.

<h1 style="text-align:center">· 5 ·</h1>

Tessa was as he had left her, curled on her side in bed. But she was awake now, and as he quietly shut the door, she said, "Morning."

"To you, too," he said, sitting on the bed.

"You've been eating kidneys."

"Shared your father's breakfast."

She noticed that he said "your father" rather than "Uncle" but didn't remark on it. Instead she asked, "What did you talk about?"

"I told him it's time we had our own place—don't look so worried, love. I did it gently. At least I think I did. He didn't have another heart attack."

"What else?"

"Oh, nothing. He offered me Paloverde Oil. I turned him down. Then he offered to buy me an airplane factory. He's done a pretty thorough job of investigation."

"Did you turn that down, too?"

"I thought I'd discuss it with Tex tomorrow."

She sat up, taking his hand. "I've been wanting to tell you..." Her usually serene face was touched with worry.

"Tell me what, love?"

"Tonight," she murmured.

"Tonight? When you've bitched my curiosity? Is that fair?" He pushed a seed of sleep from the corner of her eye.

"We'll have more time."

"I'll be home around ten."

"So late? Are you going somewhere?"

"No. There's a night stunt." And to stop further conversation, he bent to kiss her lips. She smelled of morning and that faint and mysterious musky scent that he had attributed to perfume, but now realized was natural to her. "Make me supper?"

Whenever he came home late, she would prepare an omelette aux champignons or one of the other dishes she had learned in Rouen and they would eat at the big, scrubbed deal table in the kitchen. Her culinary skill wasn't a patch on Amélie's stout French chef, yet

Kingdon's favorite meals at Greenwood were those Tessa prepared in the shadowy kitchen.

"Something special," she promised.

"And large. You know how ravenous stunts make me."

Pushing to his feet, he had to fight the gravitational tug of her body. She was all he had ever known of comfort, acceptance, unquestioning generosity—the only truly good person he had ever known. He loved her with an intense physical passion that in no way lessened these attributes.

·6·

At eleven that morning, Amélie was in her dressing room, surveying a long row of evening gowns and the racks of dainty, narrow shoes made of satin, crepe, brocade, and silver kid. When she heard the telephone ring, her mouth tasted acid. She stood erect and rigid until Kathryn came to say, "Will you take the telephone, Mrs. Van Vliet? It's Mr. 3 Vee."

Amélie experienced a swirl of dizziness, very like the precursor of her old fainting spells. She had been poised for this moment since yesterday when the beetle-browed young doctor had used a syringe to draw a blood sample from the crook of her elbow. Yet now she found herself bewilderingly unprepared. The line of silk gowns blurred.

"Mrs. Van Vliet, are you all right?"

"Tell Mr. Van Vliet I will speak to him," Amélie said in a faraway voice.

And she walked, as stiffly as if she were bruised from a bad fall, to her escritoire, sitting, gripping the silver telephone a minute before she was able to say, "Yes?"

"He just called me," 3 Vee said, and was silent.

"Go on."

"He's talked to Landsteiner in New York. None of this has been proved."

"So you have told me thirty times." Her dry tone surprised her.

"Tessa has B-type blood." Again his voice trailed.

"That I told you myself," she said.

"You're an A," he said quickly. "I'm an O."

The letters swirled around her, and the vertigo increased. She could make no sense of his words.

"Amélie?"

"Yes."

"As far as this blood typing goes, I'm excluded."

"Then Bud is her father."

"The method's not proved. They need statistics and . . ."

His voice rambled on, explaining why paternity tests remained theoretical. Amélie had expected this response from him—if the answer were Bud. Gulping at air as if she were on a high mountain peak where the atmosphere is thin, she held the telephone away from her ear.

She had won her toss with fate.

To her 3 Vee's reservations were as irrelevant as the rest of the past. She was ridding herself of the question mark imprinted here at Paloverde almost thirty years earlier. Having long ago forgiven 3 Vee, no bitterness tore at her. And her lack of rancor enabled her to exorcise the years of misery, the betrayals, the secret she had borne inside herself like a dormant plague virus; she was able to say farewell to her own lapse in integrity, to all her ineluctable losses. It was Amélie's strength and weakness to worship reason as others do a god. The laws that governed heredity were reason. She had decided in advance, as 3 Vee could not, that the dice she used were not loaded but honest.

She interrupted him. "Tessa has always known the truth. I must tell Kingdon as soon as he comes home."

· 7 ·

In the cubicle of an office at Zephyr Field, Kingdon pulled on the fur-lined boots he had used in France. He hadn't needed them in Los Angeles sunshine. But tonight was cold, and the air temperature would drop three degrees with each thousand feet he climbed. He wore long johns under his flying trousers and a heavy fisherman's sweater. He shrugged into his leather jacket and reached for his goggles and helmet. He walked out onto the field. The hangar lights showed a dim row of autos. The crew had lined them up on both sides of the field and would switch on their headlights to form a path for his takeoff and landing.

The morning's curious calm remained with him.

He wasn't afraid.

The normal fear that precedes any stunt he now saw as a useless trinket he had saved in the attic without reason. He had gone beyond fear that rainy night when he had decided to test the panels in the corridor of his existence.

On various parts of the field cameras had been set up. Passing one, he saw that it was covered with a small quilt. Like a horse, he thought grinning. The cameraman was blowing visible breath on his hands. "Good luck, Kingdon," he called.

"Take care of that camera," Kingdon replied. "You won't get any retakes on this one."

The cameraman's laughter fading behind him, he circled an arc light, an octupuslike creature with a great blinded eye and thick cables for tentacles. Most of the crew waited around the tethered plane. Rimini, wearing a topcoat, strode up and down. Seeing Kingdon, he marched toward him, holding out his hand. Kingdon shook its cold thickness.

"The flight plan looked better to me," Rimini said, letting Kingdon know he should abandon yesterday's doubts.

"A winner," Kingdon replied.

"Thank God you're quitting pictures. Nail-chewing don't agree with my ulcer."

"You'll get soft and fat."

Rimini said, "Kingdon, bring her down easy."

"I'll fake a little."

"That's the ticket."

And Tex came up. Always laconic, he said, "See you later."

"See you," Kingdon replied, shaking hands.

This friendship too went deep, and the handshake engendered pain. Yet Tex flew, so there was no need for averting of eyes. Fly long enough, they both knew, and fate catches up with you.

Kingdon pulled on his helmet and goggles, and somebody handed him fur-lined gloves as he circled the Nieuport. Reconditioned, it had a Curtiss OX-5 90-horsepower engine. He placed his right boot on the wing and grabbed a strut to haul himself up. Awkwardly swinging his stiff leg into the narrow cockpit, bracing both hands on the padded rim, he lowered his body into the familiar odors of dope, gasoline, and castor oil. He fastened the webbed belt before he settled down to make his check. He kicked the rudder bar left, then right, looking over his shoulder to see the rudder move. Odd, he thought, to be doing this in the dark. He checked the stick forward and back, then sideways. It moved easily. The elevators and ailerons responded properly. The connecting cables produced satisfying squeaks.

"Ready," he called.

Tex stepped up to the propeller and placed both hands on the upper edge of the wooden blade. Kingdon turned on the fuel switch, and Tex pulled the propeller around a couple of times, sending fuel through the hollow crankshaft and into the cylinders.

Tex shouted, "Contact!"

Kingdon flipped the ignition switch to *on*.

"Contact!" he roared.

Tex put his full weight on the propeller. The Nieuport jerked to life, barking, vibrating, belching white smoke. Car headlights straggled on, forming a path across rough yellow weeds. The engine assumed its hornet whine, the mechanics let go of the lower wings, ducking away, and Tex, Rimini, and the others turned their backs to the moving plane to avoid the flying dirt and gravel. Kingdon bumped along in the path of light. He kept the stick slightly forward until the tail lifted. As he picked up speed, he eased back on the stick.

And then he was free, climbing in the vast night, heading toward the glittering lines and sprinkles that were Los Angeles. Below his left wing was the smaller patch of brightness that was Hollywood. With the night he experienced more strongly than ever before the wonder that, for him, dwelt in the sky. He was hung in a celestial web between the stars, an earthly primate given wings, able to question matters pertaining to both heaven and earth. He wondered what it was that pursued him, and what it was that he fled. Do I flee God? he wondered. Do I believe in God? Or have I projected my own torn and divisive nature and called it a god? That's the atheist's creed. But why, if I am not certain whether I believe in God, am I so positive of sin and evil?

Mother held my hand on the burning stove (how old was I—five or six?) and as I screamed she told me that to continue in my sinful ways meant I would burn in flames everlasting. An ungrammatical woman using phrases like *continue in sinful ways* and *flames everlasting* impresses a terrified boy. I screamed prayers as I fell burning over Fère-en-Tardenois, so maybe I do believe. Strange, thinking of fire in this cold.

With altitude, the air had chilled, piercing his lungs, penetrating his fur-lined boots and gloves.

Up here, I cannot see the earth that once the Garcías ruled, the ground on which my father and uncle fought, loved, lusted, and almost tore apart one slight, proud lady.

Tessa, he thought. Tessa believes with certainty that she is daughter to Hendryk Van Vliet Number Two. "He *is* my father," she persists. Why then should I be positive that she is my sweet sister? Is it my certainty that I am unworthy, that I will always continue in my sinful ways? Well, maybe tonight will put the fix on that.

He banked, turning back toward Zephyr Field. The arcs were on now, golden spears of light thrust into the darkness; pulling back the stick, he nosed above them. Hovering. On impulse, he switched off the motor and was enveloped in a stillness like, he imagined, the blessed cloak of God. He crossed himself. I'm some atheist, he thought. He used his teeth to pull off his gloves. He needed his hands bare for the exacting delicacy that was his pilot's skill. He intended to give the stunt due respect. In his mind there had never been any doubt that he would do less than his utmost. In every daredevil there is a reason and a need to confront his own courage on the battleground of his life, and Kingdon was no exception. He squinted behind his goggles, mentally going over each detail of the flight plan.

He turned on the noisy engine.

Easing the stick forward, he started into the dive. Wind tore by him. Again he thought of Tessa. This morning his uncle had spoken of the paloverde tree that in the land of little rain stores sunshine in its green bark and rarely puts out leaves, not too subtly equating the tree with the love that Kingdon bore Tessa. As Kingdon passed the first blaze of light, he suddenly knew what it was that Tessa had wanted to tell him, and why she had timorously put it off. Another arc blinded him, and wind penetrated his goggles so his eyes watered. That's it, he thought. A child. He should have been repulsed, far more so than the first time, yet his chest swelled out with the pressure of exaltation. A baby, he thought. A baby!

Lights flashed by him, disappearing into the slipstream. He saw the fourth arc where the plan called for him to pull out of the dive. His palms tensed on the control, attempting to ease it back.

The stick fought him. The stick refused to move. It had locked! His hands jerked and yanked. The pull of the earth had transformed the fragile plane into a trajectory.

Kingdon knew then that he wasn't touching a panel but a door. He was about to be free and he didn't want freedom. He wanted to remain part of the lives tangling below, he wanted to nose himself into the future and watch Tessa grow big with their child. Tessa, he thought. She knew that morning after the accident that I never meant to kill myself. She has always understood me better than I do myself. He braced his boots on the rudder bar, yanking with all his strength. With frenzied power he kept trying to pull out of the dive. Love, love, love, help me.

I'll never be with her again.

A wing tore from the hurtling Nieuport, and he plunged, spinning. Wind rushed at him, a hurricane bursting the capillaries of his skin, flattening the flesh of his face until it looked rubbery, severing muscles, pressing goggles to break the small bones of his nose. His sweating hands continued to tug at the inexorable control. His body slipped forward, and as the webbed belt tore into his abdomen a globe of pain, greater than any he imagined, filled the cockpit. Tessa, I hurt.

The city reached up, surrounding him, engulfing him, and at the last instant before he crashed, he thought: Oh, Father, accept Thy humble child.

CHAPTER 26

· I ·

Royalty does not receive such a funeral.

It was solemnized in the months that followed on every continent. For twelve minutes, one reel's worth, a memorial film jumped and flickered to the accompaniment (by order of Rimini Productions) of a piano or organ rendition of Siegfried's Funeral March from Wagner's *Die Götterdämmerung*.

On the day of the funeral crowds lined the newly laid-out streets from St. Catherine's, where the requiem mass was said, to the burial site at the Hollywood Memorial Park Cemetery. Rimini couldn't have staged this cortège had Kingdon not been a García, a Van Vliet, a member of the Lafayette Escadrille as well as a scandal-touched yet deeply admired figure. A decent and brave man.

Leading the cortège, on horseback, came members of the First Families, the silver of their bridles and costumes glinting in the sharp cold sunlight. Then, the unadorned, horse-drawn caisson that carried the flag-blanketed coffin. As the caisson passed, onlookers threw flowers, most of which were crushed into the fresh horse manure by the more than five hundred cars that followed. Immediately after the coffin, a black limousine carried the bereaved parents. 3 Vee stared straight ahead while Utah, heavily veiled, shuddered with sobs. The next car, another of the undertaker's limousines, was shared by Tom and Bette with LeRoy and Mary

Lu facing them on jump seats. As they crossed Sunset Boulevard, Bette and Mary Lu switched seats because driving backward nauseated Mary Lu.

Greenwood's black Daimler followed with Tessa in the back seat alone. As she and her parents had moved slowly down the front steps of the house, Bud had paled. He wasn't yet meant to leave Greenwood. Doctors' orders. "I'm fine," Bud had said, sitting heavily on a step. Amélie had sent José running to telephone Dr. Levin. Torn, she had stayed home despite Bud's hoarse insistence that she go with Tessa.

The newspapers had learned of Kingdon's remarriage at the same time they heard of his death. The Hollywood press corps, resentful of the silence imposed on them by Paloverde Oil, had found their revenge in this unquenchable story. Kingdon and Lya long had been "America's Flying Sweethearts," so there was no difficulty slanting stories to prove that Tessa was a husband-snatcher, a rich and worthless relation horning in on the gallant aviator's fame. Here and there a knowing fan would point out the slow-moving Daimler. "That's her!" and those nearby would shrill insults.

After the Daimler came the chauffeured automobiles of the grocery Van Vliets, who knew Kingdon only on the screen, García kin, who were acquainted with him the same way, a very few old family friends who rated as kin, and then Mr. and Mrs. Jacopo Rimini. Following them, the Cadillac of Governor Stephens, down from Sacramento because he was a friend of Bud's, the current staff of Eagle's Roost, the far more numerous servants of Greenwood, among them descendants of "Mama's people," the mayor and three members of the County Board of Supervisors. A military band played a muffled drumroll, and the Hollywood VFW post marched slowly behind.

The cars directly after the veterans drew excited shouts, for they bore the famous: Theda Bara, Vilma Banky, Mary Pickford weeping on her Douglas Fairbanks's shoulder; Rudolph Valentino, who was to take Kingdon's place as the screen's brooding lover; Elinor Glyn, the popular novelist who had written two scenarios for Kingdon. Richard Barthelmess. Mabel Normand at the wheel of her Hispano-Suiza. Will Rogers. The Gish sisters.

The stars' exotic automobiles were followed by humble, brass-nosed, black Model T's; Rimini Productions had closed for the day, as had the Spring Street headquarters of Paloverde Oil. The Rimini people mourned Kingdon, for though he had been difficult at times, he had been a soft touch, and never had blamed anyone for his own shortcomings, a rarity among Hollywood stars. The Paloverde Oil workers and 3Vee's night drilling crews were at the funeral because there is glory in a connection, however remote, with a hero.

As the caisson approached the cemetery, a squadron of planes banked down in formation, dropping roses. The pilots were Glen Martin, Jack Northrop, Allan Loughead, Donald Douglas, Cecil B. De Mille, and Captain Eddie Rickenbacker.

Burial had been announced as private, but there was no way to keep press and public out of Hollywood Memorial Park Cemetery. At the iron gates a young woman ran toward the caisson, and a hatless mechanic rescued her from the hooves of the horses. Police hired by Rimini held back the crowd from the gravel drive to the Court of the Apostles. The people jammed among the new onyx and marble statuary weren't all curiosity-seekers or fans. Many studio workers and airplane mechanics lacked a car and therefore weren't able to be part of the cortège. Liking Kingdon, they had traveled on the Los Angeles network of trolleys to bid him farewell.

· 2 ·

Utah was handed from the limousine by the undertaker. The crowd stared respectfully at the massive grieving figure, draped in black from her veiled hat to her thick, round ankles; they pulled back, forming a path as she and 3Vee, flanked by their sons and daughters-in-law, moved toward the open grave.

José, Greenwood's head chauffeur, helped Tessa from the Daimler. The crowd surged angrily. Reporters pressed forward. Photographers called out, "This way, Mrs. Vance." Tessa turned her tear-ravaged face, bewildered.

Jacopo Rimini battled through the press people to reach her, and as he shoved he reverted to Jake Rynzberg, forgetting the good publicity he had courted so assiduously, putting his arm around her, saying far too loudly, "Just don't look at the sons of bitches, Tessa."

Her eyes, raw with grief, stared at him as if she didn't understand the language he spoke. She turned to where the others waited. It was natural for her to be with them; even if she hadn't been married to Kingdon, they were her uncle and aunt, her cousins.

Utah lifted her veil. Her face, red with weeping, pulled into a series of concentric circles about her open mouth; she resembled one of those great round masks used in ancient Greek drama to show a deity casting imprecations. Tessa shrank back to the foot of the grave, standing apart from her uncle and aunt. Other relatives, pausing momentarily, not wishing to take sides, stood opposite 3 Vee and Utah: a peculiarly divided family grouping that was mentioned in the late editions. Bishop Cantwell waited at graveside.

"Mrs. Vance," called a photographer, moving toward Tessa. Flash powder exploded. "I'll kill you," Rimini growled at the man. A woman shouted, "Home-wrecker!" Another woman jostled Tessa.

3 Vee tensed, ready to go to her. Utah's veil was still lifted and she stared at him. She had wept and prayed with Father McAdoo for the two days and three nights since Kingdon's death. Her prayers were in the form of requests that God be lenient with the unconfessed sinner. Yet the grief in her eyes was real. She had lost the son who was her pride and sorrow; she was laying her second child in the uncaring earth. She was in a frenzy similar to her rages. She is capable of anything, 3 Vee thought, even once again of crying out her accusations. He didn't dare move from her side.

Bishop Cantwell began to speak, the Latin words thin in the outdoors, carried away by the breeze. Tessa's body shook and tears streamed unchecked down her face. Photographers, oblivious to the rites and Rimini's glares, aimed their cameras at her. Spectators gazed, whispered.

She, of all women, 3 Vee thought, shy and uncomfortable with strangers, must be horrified by being the center of this barbarian exhibition. He knew that in her grief she was also worrying about Bud. He gazed openly at her, wishing to impart his sympathy.

And then he remembered another funeral: unbearable sun blazing on a dusty little town, himself sweating into a new woollen suit, gazing at a proud, young girl, trying to convey his sympathy. It was Bud, he thought, Bud who took the few steps, Bud who lifted his hat from that shining cap of hair and said the right words.

A plane flown by Tex dipped low over the cemetery, dropping a single rose. An Army trumpeter stepped forward and the brassy, mournful notes of "Taps" rose in the clear air.

Tessa turned, her streaming eyes meeting 3Vee's. She had none of the prideful stoicism that so long ago had supported her mother. She's softer, gentler, 3Vee thought. The eyes fixed on him were bewildered, as if she didn't understand what was happening. She came to me, he thought, she gave me her affection, she gave me money that I might be whole, she tried to make peace between Kingdon and me. And in return, what have I done for her? Given her doubts about Bud, doubts that killed the young man she loved, my son.

He looked steadily at the tall, grieving woman, and something sadder than sorrow, harsher than self-accusation overwhelmed him, and he felt himself dwindling to that boy he had been forty years earlier, propelled backward in time to face his own ghost, that sadly sweating, cowardly boy. How could he fail Amélie's daughter in the same way that he had failed Amélie?

"Excuse me, son," he whispered to LeRoy, who stood at his left.

Utah gripped 3Vee's hand. "You ain't going to her," she whispered.

"She's alone."

"You belong here, with me."

"Utah, she's got nobody."

"I need you," Utah replied, the folds of her neck quivering with sadness.

"I'll be back," he said.

Aware of the thousand curious, probing eyes, feeling more exposed than he had ever been, 3Vee edged around the grave, reaching Tessa as the last trumpet notes echoed. The pallbearers began to lower the coffin in brown earth. He put his arm around her fine-boned shoulder and she buried her face in his jacket. They held one another, weeping. And for some unfathomable reason, he wanted their shared bereavement to proclaim what he feared Utah might shout. He wanted everybody to know that he was Tessa's father.

The flag had been folded and there was a moment of hesitation as to which woman should receive it. A soldier stepped smartly up to Tessa, saluting, handing her the bright triangle of cloth.

3 Vee, unable to abandon Tessa to her paroxysm of tears, aching to make sure his brother was all right, rode back in the Daimler with her to Greenwood. Her sobbing quieted and she smoothed the folded flag on her lap. "He loved the sky," she said at last. "It's wrong for him to be in the earth. I can't believe he is. At the funeral I kept thinking he was flying one of the planes."

"He was so vital and alive. Tessa, I never really understood him. There were so many layers to him."

"He was good, that's all. He couldn't believe that anyone could be untamed and at the same time good. He always acted decently and then figured out tortuous reasons for his behavior."

"You're right, yes. I can't imagine any other man standing by Lya."

"He still writes—" Tessa caught herself. "He wrote to her."

"I blame myself for not being a better father to him."

"He wouldn't want you to feel that, Uncle," she said. "He was going to get in touch with you."

Bud had already told 3 Vee of his son's conciliatory intentions. It brought him no comfort, for he saw it as the final proof that his son never really intended to pull out of the dive.

"Uncle, he flew stunts," Tessa said, as if she had read his thoughts. "He wasn't trying to kill himself."

He turned his head away.

They were circling the edge of the Los Angeles City Oil Field, 3 Vee's long-ago discovery. A few derricks still pumped amid the houses.

"Daddy never should have tried to come today," Tessa said, her voice worried.

"He'll be fine."

She rolled down a window. The cold air shivered the white violets in the car vase. Abruptly she began to cry.

"Bud's tough," 3 Vee reassured.

"It's Kingdon . . . How can I leave him . . . buried . . . ?"

He drew her close again. "If it's any consolation, the cemetery once was Paloverde land. Honey, he belongs."

She was still weeping softly when the old man opened the gates of Greenwood. The car climbed up the gravel drive. Suddenly, between the flanks of hills, white stucco blazed, and 3 Vee drew a sharp breath. Paloverde, Paloverde, he thought, and it seemed right for them to be returning to the nucleus of their family universe. Paloverde, home of the Garcías, site of love and loss for Bud and himself, and for Kingdon, too. Paloverde, once center of a vast expanse of man-high mustard and now home to half a million people. Paloverde, the tumbledown ruin where he had watched his golden brother feed an orange to a luminous, unattainable girl. Paloverde, where in a few drunken minutes he had forever altered the future. Paloverde, which he once had considered his, yet which by every right including deed and primogeniture belonged to his brother, who was stronger and more generous than he, and who, unlike most people, had learned the trick of love. Paloverde.

As José opened the car door in front of the house, Amélie stepped briefly onto a balcony, raising her hand to Tessa.

"He's all right," Tessa said.

In the bright, sky-lit patio, she pulled off her simple black felt hat. Her hair was pressed close to her head. Her eyes were puffed, and her face drawn.

"Uncle, before we go up, I must ask you—"

"What, honey?"

Her grief turned to embarrassment. "I've never believed the . . . thing . . . But Kingdon believed it. And Daddy, well, Daddy can't admit anything. Mother's not sure."

So Amélie hasn't told her, he thought. "You want to know if I believe I'm your father?"

She nodded.

He loosened his tie, giving himself time. Why is she asking now? Kingdon's dead, so how can it matter? Yet if it doesn't matter, why can't I reassure her? Sweat broke out on his forehead.

"Uncle?" Her dark, blue eyes were enlarged by tears.

In that crowded tearoom, Amélie had said, *You need Tessa to bind us, you and me. And through her, you will inherit Paloverde . . . you will never be able to accept it if the tests show she is not yours.* Amélie is right. I cannot accept it.

"Why ask now?" The question came with difficulty.

"It's important to me. Very."

A peculiar brightness glittered in his eyes and his muscles grew taut. This is the moment. Now. If I can renounce my claim on Amélie and Paloverde, I can give Tessa something at last. She wants my blessing. His dark brows drew together. Slowly, reluctantly, his right hand inched up. His shoulders quivered with the effort. He touched her hair.

"Bud's your father," he said. "Your mother will explain it properly." The words seemed to tremble like a benediction. "You're Bud's."

She nodded.

"You've always been sure," he said. "Why is my opinion important?"

She turned crimson. "I was going to tell Kingdon the night he crashed. But I was afraid . . . even before we heard *that* story. I was afraid that he didn't believe there ought to be . . . that we oughtn't to . . ."

"Are you telling me there'll be a baby?"

She lowered her head. "I've wanted one so much, Uncle. But now, I couldn't have gone ahead, I don't think I could, if you hadn't said . . ."

Briefly the futile, horrible weight of grief was lifted from him and an unexpected joy spread through his body. He couldn't control his smile.

"Honey, that's wonderful."

"You *are* glad?"

"Very."

"You kept trying to separate us," she said.

"The stubborn streak," he said, kissing her forehead. "I'm very, very happy."

She sighed, and her breath was warm on his neck. "Thank you, Uncle."

"It has been a terrible day, yet miraculous, too," he said a little shyly.

She picked up the folded flag and, his arm around her waist, they went slowly up the broad staircase to the room where her parents waited.

The laws governing change work fast in Los Angeles, and though there was an inheritor to Paloverde's wealth, the house itself would not, could not, endure, for the city of which it was a part flowed relentlessly over its grounds, the hills, the rich and fertile ledge. Yet it sometimes happens on spring mornings that amid the green landscape of terraced hillside houses, a breeze stirs, prickling the skin. And if you stand on the once-sacred plateau, if your ears truly listen, you will hear voices chanting thanks for the vast golden haze below.